A DRAGON OF A DIFFERENT COLOR

RACHEL AARON

ISBN: 1974466795
ISBN-13: 9781974466795

PROLOGUE

One thousand years ago.

The immortals were dying.

Algonquin lay at the very bottom of her lakes, tendrils of water frantically probing the silt for the source of the terrible emptiness creeping through her. It was a desperate search, and a futile one, because Algonquin knew the problem couldn't be here. This was the realm of the physical. Problems on this side were simple, mechanical, but the death growing inside her wasn't linked to her fish or her water or the land that had been her shore for millennia. It came from the other side, from the swells of power that rolled through the world only spirits knew like waves through the sea. So much magic, it had no end. And yet, somehow, it was ending.

With a frustrated cry, Algonquin left her shores and sank, flowing down the chasm that was her vessel in the deep magic, the place where spirits were born. It was not a journey she made often, or happily. As a Spirit of the Land, she belonged to the land, to the physical forces of sun and wind and rain. This dark hole below the magic was nothing but her shadow, the vessel that shaped the magic that rose to become the Spirit of the Great Lakes. But she'd loved this place too, once, before the Mortal Spirits had come. Before they'd grown so strong. But the magical side of the world was theirs now. Even Algonquin, who fought them every chance she got, never came here without fear. Whatever was happening now, though, it couldn't be solved from the sunlit side, so she steeled herself and went deep, plunging through the dark recess of the vessel that gave her shape and life into the realm beyond it. The terrifying chaos mortals called the Sea of Magic.

Or what was left of it.

For the first time ever, Algonquin rose from the gouge her lakes had dug into the magical landscape eons ago to find nothing. No pounding magic, no swells, no waves. Even the Mortal Spirits were gone without a trace, leaving the floor of the Sea of Magic empty as a desert.

Considering how long she'd fought them, that might have been a blessing, but as much as she hated the human monsters, nothing could still the terror of finding a barren plane where a sea should have been. She was pulling herself out of her vessel to try and discover what had happened, where all the magic had gone, when she saw it.

Across the empty plane that had been the Sea of Magic, a mountain now rose from the ground where no mountain had been before. It was straight and round like a post, but unlike every spirit vessel Algonquin had ever seen, it went up, not down, soaring so high, she couldn't see its peak. She could feel it, though. Somewhere up there, beyond her reach from the floor of the now bone-dry desert, mortals were working magic. Not normal mortals, and not normal magic. These were the most dangerous of their kind, the traitors who called themselves Merlins. Together with their horrible gods, they were working what little magic remained, gathering and bending it into something it should never be. Something hard and dry.

Something she couldn't touch.

"No!" she yelled. "*Stop!*"

But her voice made no sound. There was no magic left here to carry it. No life, no power. Just the horrible emptiness beating down on her like the summer sun in a drought, and as it scorched her, Algonquin's own magic began to evaporate.

"No," she said again, grabbing at her water as it vanished. "*No!* I don't want to die!"

But there was no stopping it. Somehow, the humans had stopped the flow of magic. Stopped the sea itself. With no more power flowing in, what was left was rapidly shrinking, leaving her floundering in a smaller and smaller puddle.

Leaving her to die.

"No," she sobbed, but her voice was tiny now. Time passed differently on this side. In the real world, the growing emptiness had been alarming but measured, a problem to be dealt with. On this side, it was panic. Her magic vanished out from under her, leaving her tiny and weak at the bottom of her vessel. By the time she realized just how things were, she couldn't do anything. She couldn't yell, couldn't stand. Couldn't do anything except watch herself vanish.

Watch herself die.

No! She was the land, part of the Earth itself. She could not die! If she vanished, who would protect her fish? Who would push back the dragons and hold the human tide at bay? She couldn't die. Wouldn't. She'd do anything to stop this, anything.

"Please!" the last of her cried in the dark. "Someone, anyone, help me!"

I don't want to vanish!

Her last plea was nothing but a thought. The disappearing magic had taken everything else with it, even her voice. She was an empty cavern now. A ghost, and even that was fading fast. Desperate, she prayed for help. Prayed to the dark, promised it anything if it would only keep her from vanishing. Keep the deathless from death. Then, just as the last of her was collapsing into dreamless sleep, something whispered back.

Anything?

The voice was one she'd never heard before. It wasn't even properly a voice. It was more like a shift in the dark, and it came from far, far away. But it *was* an answer, the only one she had, and so Algonquin reached out to it with the last of her magic, promising it anything if only it would save them. Save *her*.

Her cry was a single drop of water. A plea so weak, even she barely heard it. The answer, though, was crystal clear.

I come.

The promise slipped like smoke through the emptiness, but Algonquin was no longer there to hear it. She was gone, an empty vessel forced into a deathlike nothingness that mortals ten centuries later would arrogantly call sleep. But though she couldn't answer, the promise was made, and far away, beyond the walls of the planes, something turned in the emptiness between worlds and began to move.

CHAPTER ONE

Brohomir, Great Seer of the Heartstrikers, (now) eldest child of Bethesda the Heartstriker, consort to a Nameless End, and Tetris World Champion for thirty-three years running sat at the end of a sunny box canyon deep in the New Mexico Badlands, playing with his baby dragon.

"Good, gooooood," he said as he grabbed another terrified rat out of the burlap sack beside him. "Watch closely. This one's going to go high."

The little feathered dragon snapped her needle-sharp teeth at him, her golden eyes locked on the rat as Bob reeled back like he was going to toss the animal high into the clear blue sky. Then, right before he let fly, he turned and dropped the rat on the ground beside him instead.

The little dragon wasn't fooled for a second. The rodent barely hit the sand before she was on it, devouring it in a single, violent bite.

"*Very* good," Bob said proudly, patting her head.

The hatchling licked her chops and darted back into position. Bob was reaching for the next rat when a long black shadow fell over him.

"Dramatic as ever, I see," he said, tucking the wiggling rodent back into the bag as he turned to squint up at the tall figure silhouetted against the bright desert sun.

"You're one to talk about drama," the Black Reach replied as he stepped into the canyon.

Bob smiled politely and opened his arms to the little dragoness, but she just snorted and turned away, skittering down the canyon to hunt the lizards that sheltered in its dirt walls instead.

"So," Bob said, turning back to the elder seer. "How did you get here so quickly? Express boat from China? Or have you finally gotten over your irrational fear of letting humans fly you?"

"Neither," the Black Reach said, watching the hatchling hunt. "I didn't have to rush because I never left in the first place. I knew I'd have to come right back after the incident in your mother's throne room, so I decided to stay and see a bit of the country. I haven't been to these lands since before the Europeans invaded."

"I hope you didn't cut your vacation short on *my* account," Bob said. "We need the tourism income. This coup of Julius's is costing our clan a fortune."

The Black Reach nodded, but he wasn't looking at Bob. His eyes were still locked on the young dragoness crouching at the end of the canyon, her tail twitching back and forth like a cat's as she waited for the lizard she was stalking to make its move. "You know I can't leave her with you."

"I know no such thing," Bob said. "She's a Heartstriker."

"She's a seer," the Black Reach said angrily. "And so are you. I cannot permit one clan to control both of the forces that shape our race's future." He turned back to Bob with a stern scowl. "Give her to me."

Bob smiled sweetly. "No."

The Black Reach's old eyes narrowed in his too-young human face, but Bob just turned and whistled. The little dragon's head shot up at the sound, and she whirled around, leaping into Bob's arms with enough force to make him stumble backward. "Good girl," he said proudly, hugging her close as he grinned at the Black Reach. "You see? She loves me. How could I possibly give her away?"

The oldest seer looked disgusted. "She's not a pet."

"She's not," Bob agreed. "But she's *so* clever. Watch this." He grinned down at the dragon in his arms. "Go on, darling. Show him what I taught you."

The little dragon growled deep in her throat, and then she was gone, her dark feathered body vanishing like smoke. When the haze cleared, Bob was holding a human child. A tiny, delicately boned toddler with fine, perfectly straight black hair and predatory golden eyes that absolutely did *not* belong on a mortal face.

"You see?" Bob said, delighted. "She's gifted. Even Amelia couldn't hold a human shape straight out of the egg, but she picked it up on the first try."

"All the more reason not to leave her with you," the Black Reach said. "Be reasonable, Brohomir. She has her whole life in front of her. If you truly cared for her future, you would not risk it by dragging her into your doomed plans."

"But that's exactly why I need her," Bob argued, clutching the girl closer. "She's my ace. My winning move."

"Then she is useless," the seer said. "We both know how this game ends. The only thing I can't see is why you're still playing it."

"I'd think that'd be obvious," Bob said with a shrug. "We've both seen the future, but unlike you, I don't like mine. Hence: plots."

"The last thing *you* need is more plots," the Black Reach snapped. "This isn't my fault. I'm not forcing you to act. You can always choose to turn back, abandon your plans, and be spared."

"Oh," Bob said, grinning wide. "I get it now. This is my official warning, isn't it?" He laughed in delight. "I'm flattered you came in person! Estella only got a phone call."

"Estella wasn't being half so reckless."

"Yes, well, she always did lack vision," Bob agreed. "But tell me honestly, Mr. Death of Seers. In the ten centuries you've been working this gig, has that line ever worked? Did any seer ever hear your warning, say 'you know, he's right,' and abandon their plans?"

"No," the Black Reach said bitterly. "But that doesn't mean I get to stop. This is not my 'gig.' It's my reason for being. I am Dragon Sees Eternity. Like my brother, Dragon Sees the Beginning, I was created by your ancestors for a single purpose: to ensure that the mistakes of the past that destroyed our home and doomed all dragons to be refugees on this plane are *never* repeated. That is my sacred duty, the task for which I exist. But though I can never be lenient in my responsibilities, I *can* be merciful. I reach out to every seer the moment I see them starting down a forbidden path and offer them my knowledge. I gave each of them the opportunity the dragons who created me never had: a chance to turn back, to choose another way and avoid destruction. That is the gift I give to every seer, and now, I'm giving it to you."

"Again, I'm flattered," Bob said. "But—"

"No," he growled. "No buts. Stop trying to be clever for a moment, Brohomir, and *listen*. You are embarking down a future that has only one outcome, and it is the one I cannot allow. We've had many good conversations over your short life. I would even go so far as to call you my friend. So *as* your friend, I'm begging you, don't do this. Don't make me kill you."

Bob sighed, looking down at the rocky, reddish dirt between them. "It's not every day one receives a heartfelt plea from one of the two great dragon constructs," he said at last. "I'm touched, I really am, but I'm afraid my plans remain unchanged."

"Why?" the Black Reach demanded, his deep voice shaking with frustration. "You know you are doomed. We've both seen it, so why do you persist?"

"Because seeing the future isn't the same as understanding it," Bob said, raising his head to smile at the pigeon who fluttered down from the clear blue sky to perch on his fingers. "You're the one who taught me that a seer's greatest weakness is his own expectations. We grow so used to seeing everything before it happens, we forget that we can still be surprised. That events which appear unquestionable from one angle can look entirely different from another."

"Is that your strategy?" The Black Reach sneered. "Hide in my blind spot? Even though I've known every possible turn of your life since before you were born?"

Bob shrugged. "What other hope do I have? As you just said, you've been plotting all of this since before I was born. I can't compete with that level of knowledge and planning. But the fact that we're having this conversation proves there's at least one angle you haven't seen yet, and so long as that's true, I have hope."

He leaned down to press a kiss to his pigeon's feathered head, and the Black Reach turned away in disgust. "Sometimes I wonder if you really have gone mad," he muttered. "But I've said my piece. You can see the death that's coming as well as I. If that's not enough to scare you into changing course, there's nothing more I can do."

"But you'll still try."

"Of course I'll try," the construct said. "Until it becomes past, the future is never set." He gave Bob a sad smile. "You're not the only one who can hope."

Bob smiled back. "Does this mean you've given up on taking my darling away?" he asked, hugging the little dragon-turned-human in the crook of his arm. "Since time is so short and all?"

"I shouldn't," the Black Reach said. "It's not good practice, but..." He trailed off, studying the little dragon, who watched him curiously in return. "I don't foresee any lasting harm to her under your care," he said with a shrug. "You may keep her until the end. We both know it won't be very long."

"Your kindness is appreciated," Bob said warmly. "Thank you."

"If you want to thank me, then listen," the Black Reach said angrily, glaring at Bob one last time before he turned and walked away. "I will see you two more times before the end. Let us hope you make better use of those chances than you did this one."

"I always strive to improve!" Bob called after him, but the cheerfulness rang hollow even in his own ears.

The ancient construct was already gone in any case, his tall body vanishing into the glaring light of the desert beyond the mouth of the sheltered canyon. Bob was still squinting at the place where he'd been when something shot through the blue sky above him. Something very large, moving very fast.

Bob dove for cover, clutching the golden-eyed child to his chest as he rolled them into the shelter of the canyon seconds before the shadow of the hunting dragoness passed over them.

"That's our cue," he whispered when the danger had passed, staring warily through the canyon at the sliver of blue sky above. "Come along, love. This desert's about to get *very* crowded, which means it's time for us to go."

The little girl snapped her teeth and pointed angrily at the bag of rats lying abandoned on the ground.

"Later," he promised, climbing out of the canyon's lee. "Or Bob's not your uncle."

He'd been waiting ages to make that joke. Unfortunately, it went right over the little dragon's head, leaving her staring in confusion as he carried her down the hidden path out the back of the canyon and up the slope into the copse of dry sagebrush behind it.

"Here, right?" he asked his pigeon, who'd flown ahead.

The bird cooed, fluttering up to perch in the thorny, twisted branches where another bird was already waiting. A huge black one with sharp, intelligent eyes that watched the pigeon as though she were the end of the world.

"I can't believe I let you talk me into this," Raven croaked, taking a large step down the branch away from the pigeon. "I know playing with fire is a dragon's first instinct, but this is pushing it. Even for you."

"Ah," Bob said, setting the little girl back down on her feet. "But if you didn't also think it was worth the risk, you wouldn't be here, would you?"

"*I* didn't have a choice," Raven snapped. "Algonquin's got us all by the tail feathers. Next to that, even your madness seems sane."

He paused, looking at Bob like he expected the dragon to argue, but the seer just smiled. "Is everything ready, then?"

"Ready as can be, given the circumstances." The bird tilted his head at Bob. "You?"

The seer pulled out his brick of a phone—an identical replacement to the ancient blue Nokia he'd sunk into a rice paddy in China, except that this one had slightly fewer scratches—and angled the green-tinted screen down so Raven could see the flashing message icon through the sun's glare. He had over a hundred texts pending, mostly from Chelsie, but the newest was the one that mattered.

Unfortunately—and probably spitefully, given the source—the text was in Mandarin Chinese. Not Bob's strongest language considering he hadn't used it in over six centuries. He studied the pixelated characters for several seconds before giving up and turning the phone to Raven.

The bird gave him a horrified look. "Really?"

"You're famous for speaking every language," Bob said with a shrug. "Make yourself useful."

He thrust the phone at the spirit again, and Raven shook his head wearily, hopping down from the branch to perch on the dragon's shoulder where he had a better view.

"'We're coming.'"

Bob blinked. "Is that all?"

"There's another bit promising death to you and all your clan, but that's the general gist," Raven reported.

"Marvelous," Bob said, slipping the phone back into his pocket. "Then yes. I'm ready."

Raven looked more worried than ever. "You're playing with a lot of lives, Heartstriker. Are you certain this is going to work?"

"The future is never certain," Brohomir said honestly. "But I've been setting up this domino chain for nearly my entire life, so I'm *pretty* sure. On the upside, though, if I'm not right, we'll *all* be dead, and I won't have to listen to you say 'I told you so.'"

The bird tilted his head, and for a brief moment, Bob felt what it was like to have every raven in the world staring at you at once. "This is no time for jokes, seer," the Spirit of Ravens rumbled. "I'm taking a big gamble trusting you."

"We're all gambling," Bob assured him. "But that's all we can do. The future is a moving target. You can make all the careful plans you want, but nothing is ever certain until the moment actually comes. Even then, the whole world can turn on a heartbeat. That said, if you follow my instructions to the letter—to the *letter*, mind—we stand a very decent chance of achieving the age-old dream of having our cake and eating it, too."

Raven blinked his beady black eyes. "You are a very strange sort of dragon."

"Nonsense," Bob said. "I'm just a dragon, as greedy and ruthless and results-oriented as any other. But that's why you can trust me. All of this is to my benefit even more than it is to yours, which is as close to Scout's honor as my kind gets. And speaking of results, you've got your marching orders, which means it's time to fly away home. I know you true immortals have a flexible relationship with time, but the rest of us are on a schedule."

Raven shot another dark look at Bob's pigeon. "None of us has much time if you mess this up."

"Then let's make sure I *don't* by keeping our timetable," the seer said, tapping the bare spot on his wrist where his watch would be if he'd been wearing one. "Hop hop, blackbird."

With a final roll of his black eyes, Raven spread his wings and flew away, vanishing between one flap and the next. When he was gone, Bob looked back down at the little dragon, who'd spent the entire conversation rolling in the dirt at his feet. "Shall we be off, too?"

As usual, the girl didn't even seem to hear the question, but her head shot right up a second later when the sound of a car engine broke the desert quiet. She scrambled up into the tree as the noise got louder, changing back into a dragon so she could snake through the tangled branches to get a better look at the SUV full of mortal tourists that had just pulled over at the trailhead down the hill.

"Right on time," Bob said cheerfully, holding out his hand to his pigeon. When he had her comfortably nestled on his shoulder again, Bob started down the hill. "Come, love," he called. "It's time for you to learn the joys of grand theft auto."

The dragoness scurried down the tree, kicking her feet in the loose dirt as she ran after him down the desert hill toward the unsuspecting humans and the car that would soon be theirs.

• • •

At that same moment, Julius Heartstriker, youngest son of Bethesda the Heartstriker and founder of the newly formed Heartstriker Council, was still trapped in the most frustrating meeting of his life.

"For the *last time*," he growled, glaring at his mother across their new three-sided Council table. "We will not vote to unseal your dragon until you vow—*vow*, in *blood*—that you will never try to undermine this Council again."

"And for the *last time*, I'll vow to do no such thing," Bethesda said with a toss of her glossy black hair. "Future rebellion is my right as a dragon. What sort of deposed clan head doesn't try to take back her power?"

"None," Ian said quietly, his newly brown eyes gleaming with barely restrained violence. "Which is why deposed clan heads are usually rendered head*less*. But Julius showed you mercy, and you took it. Don't cry now because it's time to pay." He stabbed his finger down on the pledge sitting on the table in front of her. "Sign it. Or you'll never fly again."

That was harsher than Julius would have gone, but he didn't say a word. It'd been two hours since they'd freed Chelsie and the Fs and moved on to the unsealing of Bethesda, and his willingness to tolerate his mother's antics was long gone. He'd never expected her to meekly accept her fate—he wasn't sure Bethesda the Heartstriker knew what 'meek' meant—but he hadn't thought it would take *fifteen drafts* to find a version of "promise you won't try to undermine the new system again and you can have your dragon back" that she would sign.

"We've been more than fair," Ian reminded her. "But it's over. The Heartstriker Council is here to stay, and if you want to stay on it as anything more than *this*"—he pointed at her sealed human body—"you'll stop being stubborn."

The Heartstriker gave him an ugly look. "This is extortion."

"Then you should be used to it," Ian said, growling deep in his throat. "Sign it, Mother."

Bethesda's face grew sullen, and then she reached out to grab the paper off the table. "*Fine*," she snarled, stabbing her razor-sharp nail into the pad of her thumb. "You want to cement the doom of this clan? On your heads be it."

She stabbed the bleeding wound down on the paper, sealing the deal with her blood. When it was done, magic bit down sharp as her teeth, making them all gasp. Still, it was over, and Julius couldn't help letting out a sigh of relief as he took the signed vow back from her. "Thank you."

"Enjoy it while it lasts," she snarled, licking the blood off her finger. "It doesn't matter what you make me sign—this enterprise is doomed. Dragon clans are ruled by fear and fire, not councils. If I can't rebel, someone else will, and when the inevitable finally comes, the last thing you'll hear is me saying 'I told you so.' Right before I bite off your heads."

Technically, that was exactly the sort of threat she was no longer supposed to be making, but Julius was too sick of arguing to care. He just signed his name at the bottom of the bloody contract with a normal ink pen as fast as he could before passing it to Ian, who did the same. When all three of their names were signed, magic bit down again. The Council's magic this time, not Bethesda's. As powerful as clan magic was, it couldn't force a dragon to act against her own self-interest. Only blood oaths could enforce behavior, which was why they'd had to go through all of this. Now that her blood and their names were on the same contract, though, they were bound together. Bethesda was now forbidden from undermining the Council's authority by her own fire, which meant they could *finally* move on.

"Now that's finished," Ian said, waving the bloody contract to dry it before placing it in his leather dossier, "I motion to unseal Bethesda the Heartstriker. All in favor?"

They all raised their hands.

"Motion passes," Ian said, glaring at their mother as she shot out of her chair. "I trust future Council decisions won't be this obnoxious."

"That depends on you," Bethesda said flippantly. "All of this voting and talking was your idea, not mine. Now, if we're *quite* finished, get this cursed thing off me. You wouldn't believe the ache this seal is putting on my poor wings."

Seeing how she'd happily left him like that for a month and a half, Julius had little sympathy. But as fitting as it would have been to let her suffer, a promise was a promise. "Let's go get Amelia."

Bethesda cringed at the mention of her eldest daughter's name. "Isn't there someone else?"

Julius shrugged. "Not unless you want to owe Svena another favor. The seal Amelia put on you is too complicated for anyone else."

"Assuming Amelia's sober enough to manage it," Ian added, glancing at his watch. "It *is* nearly five o'clock."

"It's always five o'clock for the Planeswalker," Bethesda said bitterly. "But if there's one thing Amelia's always been good at, it's magic under the influence. So long as she's not passed out, we should be fine."

The truth of that made Julius wince. It was on his list to stage an intervention for his oldest sister soon. Right now, though, Amelia's high-functioning alcoholism was the least of his worries. "I just hope she's feeling well enough to manage it. Last time I saw her, she didn't look so good."

Not since Marci had died and taken half of Amelia's fire with her.

"That's nothing," Bethesda said flippantly. "I cut Amelia in half when she was just a little older than you. It was supposed to serve as an example to the rest of her clutch, but she ruined it by surviving. Anyway, if she could live through that, she can live through anything. I'm more worried about her 'accidentally' sealing something else, the spiteful little snake."

At this point, Julius wouldn't mind if Amelia 'accidentally' turned their mother into a toad. Again, though, done was done, so he stood up and grudgingly motioned for Bethesda to lead the way.

"I can't believe we have to go and find her ourselves," she complained as they walked out of the throne room. "How dare Frieda and the others abandon their positions! Now nothing works."

"I'm sure we'll survive without the Fs," Julius said. "We need to learn to run things for ourselves, and they deserve to fly free. All of them."

He glanced pointedly at Chelsie's Fang, which was still lying untouched on the balcony where she'd dropped it when she'd gone for their mother's throat, but Bethesda was too busy rolling her eyes to notice.

"You say that *now*," she growled as she yanked open the plain wooden doors that had been quickly installed to temporarily replace the ornate ones Bob had broken when he'd smashed his way into the throne room. "But when there's no breakfast tomorrow, you'll be singing a different—"

She stopped short. The throne room doors opened into the Hall of Heads, the long tunnel that served as both a display gallery for the taxidermy heads of Bethesda's enemies and a lobby for the golden elevator that connected the Heartstriker's peak to the rest of the mountain, including Amelia's rooms one floor down. But though they were still a good fifty feet away, the elevator doors at the hallway's opposite end were already rolling open to reveal an extremely nervous-looking Katya.

They must have spotted each other at the same moment, because the moment the white dragoness's eyes met his, her expression changed to one of relief. "There you are!" she cried, running toward them. "I've been looking everywhere! I tried asking, but there was no one working the concierge desk. No one working anywhere, actually."

Bethesda shot her youngest son an "I told you so" look, which he pointedly ignored. "I'm sorry you had trouble," he said, stepping forward to greet his friend. "What can we do for—"

"Is it Svena?" Ian interrupted, pushing his way forward. "Is she ready to clutch?"

Katya's nervous look returned. "Actually, she finished clutching just a few minutes ago."

Which meant Ian was now a father. "Congratulat—"

"So why am I finding out *now*?" Ian said angrily. "She promised she wouldn't lay without me there."

"She did," Katya admitted, dropping her eyes. "But that was before."

"Before what?"

The youngest daughter of the Three Sisters sighed. Then, like a soldier facing a firing line, she drew herself to her full height. "Council of the Heartstrikers," she said formally, her blue eyes looking at them each in turn. "Svena the White Witch, Queen of the Frozen Sea, has commanded me to inform you that all treaties, agreements, and other friendly relations between our two clans are hereby dissolved. Furthermore, effective immediately, Ian Heartstriker is removed from his position as consort and banished from our clan. He is also banned from contact with Svena's offspring, all of whom shall now be raised as members of our clan regardless of gender."

The room was silent when she finished. Finally, in the scariest voice Julius had ever heard, Ian said, "What?"

"She doesn't want to see you anymore," Katya explained.

"I understood that much," Ian snarled. "But that's not her decision to make. Those are *my* children. She can't keep them from me!"

"Forget the whelps!" Bethesda cried, shoving past him. "What about the defense of my mountain? Svena's supposed to be protecting us from Algonquin. That's the only reason I let you ice snakes in here in the first place!"

"Then maybe you should have considered that before you let your seer betray her," Katya snapped.

That statement left Bethesda looking absolutely bewildered, and for once, Julius was right there with her. "What are you talking about?" he asked, squeezing between Ian and his mother so he could speak to Katya directly rather than through the taller dragons. "How did *Bob* betray Svena?"

"You mean you don't know?"

"Obviously not," Ian growled. "We've been trapped in a meeting all afternoon." He grabbed her shoulders. "What happened, Katya?"

Julius fully expected Katya to bite his hands off for grabbing her like that, but whatever had happened between Bob and Svena must have been a special kind of bad, because Katya just looked sad. "I was hoping you could tell me," she said. "Two hours ago, Brohomir killed Amelia the Planeswalker."

Her words hit Julius like a punch. "Bob...killed Amelia?" When she nodded, his fists clenched. "*Impossible.*"

"That's what I thought, too," Katya said. "But Svena saw it with her own eyes. She teleported into Amelia's room just as Brohomir finished turning her to ash."

"But that can't be true," Julius argued. "Bob would *never* hurt Amelia. She's his favorite sister. There's no way he'd—"

"Well, he did," Katya said angrily. "And now *my* sister is furious. Svena's always considered the Planeswalker her only true rival. By murdering her, Brohomir has stolen her victory. That's more than an insult between clans. It's personal, and Svena's taking it very badly."

Obviously. "Can't you talk her down?"

"You think I didn't try?" Katya said with an angry puff of smoke. "Our clan's barely recovered from losing Estella and our mothers. The last thing we need is to break faith and make enemies with the biggest clan in the world. Svena *knows* this, but she won't listen. I've never seen her this angry." She shook her head. "You're lucky she didn't bring your mountain down on top of you the moment she saw Brohomir do it."

"*Did* she actually see him do it?"

Katya shot him a furious look, and Julius hurried to explain. "I'm not saying Svena's lying, but Bob's a seer. He often does things that look terrible on the surface but turn out to be fine once you realize what's actually going on. Maybe he was just—"

"This isn't the sort of thing you can mistake," Katya snapped. "If you want proof, go to Amelia's room and see for yourself."

She said that like a challenge, and Julius was upset enough to take it, marching around Katya and into the elevator behind her. The rest of the dragons followed right on his heels, cramming into the gold-plated box as Julius repeatedly mashed the button for the floor Amelia shared with Bob.

• • •

"I take no joy in saying this," Katya whispered. "But I told you so."

Julius didn't say a word. He was too busy staring at the pile of gray-white ash that had once been Amelia the Planeswalker.

"Must've been some fight," Bethesda said, poking at the puddles of water that covered the stone floor with the toe of her stiletto. "Svena launched enough ice to sink a battleship." She eyed Katya suspiciously. "Are you certain your sister didn't kill Amelia herself?"

"If she had, she wouldn't blame a seer," Katya replied angrily. "She'd come and tell you herself."

"And she'd probably be throwing a party instead of a fit," Julius added.

"I don't think Svena would ever take Amelia's death well," Ian said. "Not even if she was the one who caused it. That stated…" He knelt beside the divan where Amelia's pile of ash was sinking into the cushions. "Svena didn't do this."

"How can you be sure?" Julius asked.

Ian shot him a scathing look. "Use your nose. Amelia's magic is everywhere in this room, but it's all old. The newest I can smell is twelve hours stale at least, certainly nothing from this afternoon. Whoever killed her, Amelia didn't fight back, and Svena has invested far too much in this rivalry to accept such a cheap victory."

Julius didn't need Katya's nod to know his brother was right. Svena was a cruel, ruthless dragon, and proud of it, but she had her own kind of honor. She would never stoop to killing her rival while Amelia was lying helpless. Even her wintry scent was concentrated in the middle of the room, a dozen feet away from the divan that had been the Planeswalker's deathbed. Bob's scent, on the other hand, was everywhere. Including all over Amelia's ashes.

That was the most damning evidence of all. Even Julius couldn't deny that the only way Bob's scent could have gotten on those ashes was if he'd had his hands in them. Even if he'd discovered Amelia's remains after the fact, Bob had undeniably been here, and since nothing surprised a seer, that meant he'd known. He might not have done it, but he'd known Amelia was going to die today, *and* he'd let Svena see him. Whatever the truth actually was, he'd deliberately let the Daughters of the Three Sisters assume he was guilty, and now they were all in deep trouble.

"Why?" Julius asked the ashes. "Why would he do this?"

"Who knows?" Katya said bitterly. "But for what it's worth, I'm sorry this happened. For both our clans." She put a sympathetic hand on his shoulder. "I know what it's like to have your seer turn on you."

Julius appreciated the sentiment, but he didn't think that was it. Estella had been psychotic, but Bob was...well, *Bob*. He was flighty and ridiculous and impossible to understand, but no matter how bad things looked, he always came through in the end.

Except when he was telling Julius not to free Chelsie.

"There has to be something else going on here," Julius said, scrubbing his hands through his hair. "Something we're not seeing. Some plot or scheme or—"

"Of *course* it's a plot," Bethesda said. "That's all Brohomir does. But whatever he's working on this time, we've got a real problem. I signed your little extortion note, but Amelia and Svena are the only dragon mages in the world good enough to remove my seal. Now one's dead and the other's on the warpath, how am I getting my dragon back?"

"*That's* what you're worried about?" Julius yelled at her. "The *seal?* Your daughter is..."

He couldn't even say it. He'd thought he'd hit rock bottom after Marci's death, but in a horrible way, that had been comforting. Terrible as he'd felt, at least he'd known things couldn't get worse, but he was wrong. Not only had he lost Marci, he'd lost Amelia, too, the only dragon he could have remembered her with. He'd lost his sister. He'd lost his *friend,* and unless he was willing to call his own nose a liar, Bob was the cause. Whether he'd killed her himself or just let it happen, his brother had clearly had a hand in this, which meant Julius had lost him, too.

"Why?" he whispered again. "Why would Bob betray us?"

Bethesda snorted. "Welcome to my life."

Julius couldn't remember ever hating his mother as much as he did right now. But when he turned to tell her that her commentary was not appreciated, he found Bethesda standing right beside him.

"As delighted as I am to see you getting a taste of your own medicine, there's more at stake here than your hurt feelings," she said. "I don't know what spurred Bob to throw us under the bus today, but he did a very good job. With Amelia dead and Svena hating us because of it, we've lost both of our defenses against Algonquin's magic. If she attacks the mountain now, we're sitting ducks."

Julius hadn't even considered that angle. "Do you think she will?"

His mother shrugged. "I'm surprised she hasn't already. We might have dropped a bit on her priority list since your ill-timed coup has left us too weak to pose a real threat to whatever she's doing in the DFZ, but we're still the world's biggest dragon clan, and the one on her doorstep. Trust me, that hammer is going to fall, and it's not the only one. Heartstriker has many enemies. No one's made a serious try for us in centuries thanks to our size and the fact that we're relatively isolated here in the Americas, but recent events have changed that calculus. Mark my words, when news spreads that Chelsie's quit, Amelia's dead, Bob's gone rogue, *and* I'm sealed, there will be no safety anywhere. We'll be up to our necks in dragons hungry to take a bite out of our territory. Algonquin won't need to lift a watery finger. All she has to do is bide her time, and the other clans will do us in for her."

"It can't be that bad," Julius argued. "We're down, sure, but we still have Conrad, Justin, and a hundred other Heartstrikers. If we call everyone back to the mountain—"

"We'd just be giving Algonquin a bigger target," Ian cut in. "And that's assuming our family would answer the call."

"They did before."

"Yes, when *Bethesda* called," Ian said, glancing pointedly at their mother, who looked sickeningly smug. "I'm confident the Council is the right path for Heartstriker's long-term stability, but we're not there yet. Anyway, even Mother would have a hard time getting Heartstrikers to return to the mountain again under these conditions. In case you haven't noticed, everyone's run home to secure their own territories."

Julius had noticed. It was hard *not* to notice when a mountain built for hundreds of dragons was suddenly empty. "So we'll explain the situation and ask them to come back."

"No dragon with an ounce of self-interest is going to leave their home territory undefended while things are this uncertain," Ian argued. "And since you freed Chelsie, we have no way to make them."

"That's a *good* thing," Julius said. "We shouldn't rely on fear to get our way."

"A lovely sentiment that doesn't help us now."

"Why is this even a thing?" Julius demanded, frustrated. "Algonquin declared war on *all* the clans. We should be banding together against her, not fighting amongst ourselves."

"Don't be stupid," Bethesda snapped. "This is the *best* time to fight. Algonquin's a force to be reckoned with, but we're the dragons of the Americas! The only clan that comes close to Heartstriker in numbers or territory is the Golden Empire, and no one's crazy enough to go after China. Two weeks ago, I'd have said the same about us, but between your backstabbing and Algonquin's wave hanging over our heads, we're bleeding inside and out. We've always been a tasty target, but now we're a badly wounded one as well, and no dragon anywhere can pass up wounded prey."

The way she said that made Julius wince. He'd never heard his mother sound so grim before. But tempting as it was to dismiss all the doom and gloom as typical Bethesda hyperbole, he didn't think she was exaggerating this time. "What should we do?"

"What *can* we do?" she said, sinking down on the end of the velvet divan beside her eldest daughter's ashes. "It's over. I'd already accepted that Brohomir had betrayed *me*, but with this blow, he's cut the rest of the clan off at the knees as well. We can't rally, can't fight, can't defend ourselves. At this point, the only option we have left is to cut our losses and go somewhere safe to rebuild."

He stared at her in horror. "You mean leave Heartstriker Mountain?"

"We can't stay," she said, waving her hand around at the empty room. "Amelia's magic was our primary defense, but every ward she set vanished with her death. *I'm* in her room, for fire's sake. That alone is proof that security has been utterly compromised."

Julius couldn't argue there, but…"This is our *home!*" he cried. "We can't abandon it."

Bethesda shot him her dirtiest look yet. "Yes, well, maybe you should have thought of that before you ruined everything."

He'd thought he was immune to his mother's insults by this point, but that one hit too close. He might not have personally sealed his mother's dragon or killed Amelia, but Heartstriker's weakness was undeniably Julius's fault. Even if it hadn't been, he was one of the clan heads now. It was his responsibility to keep them all safe, and he was racking his brain for how to do that when Ian suddenly spoke up.

"We are not abandoning anything," the tall dragon growled. "I don't care how many enemies are against us, I did *not* claw my way to the top of two clans to lose both in one day." He glared at Julius and Bethesda. "You two do whatever it takes to protect us in the short term. I'm going to bring back Svena." He turned his glare on Katya. "Take me to your sister."

The white dragoness bared her teeth at him. "First of all, you're not at the top of our clan anymore, so you don't get to give me orders. Second, you do *not* want to be around Svena right now.

She's fresh off the loss of Amelia and the trauma of laying eggs. She'll eat you alive."

Ian bared his teeth as well. "Take me to her, Last Born."

For a terrifying moment, Julius was certain there was going to be blood, but then Katya sighed. "Your funeral."

Ian turned on his heel, marching down the empty hallway that had once been packed with Amelia's magical traps. With a shake of her head, Katya followed, reaching out to Julius as she walked past. "I'm sorry things turned out this way."

"Me, too," he said. "More than I can say."

That last part was painfully true. There were no words to describe the pointless tragedy playing out around him. Looking down at the pile of ash that had once been his laughing, audacious, brilliant sister, Julius felt like there was nothing left. Death had taken it all— Marci, Amelia, Ian and Svena, even Bob—leaving him with nothing but his selfish mother, a broken clan, and a mountain he couldn't defend.

His only comfort was the knowledge that there had to be something he wasn't seeing. Some greater end Bob was working toward that would make everything turn out okay. There was just no other reason why his brother would throw away everything he'd been working toward. So long as he believed Bob wasn't actually insane, there *had* to be a method to this madness, and Julius was going to make the seer tell him what that was if it was the last thing he did.

First, though, he had to take care of his sister.

Since they tended to die in spectacular violence, dragons didn't usually have funerals. Most blew away in the winds of their defeat, but if their ashes could be collected, the task was traditionally entrusted to someone close to the deceased: a mate, an heir, even a favored mortal. But other than Marci, who was also dead, Amelia didn't have a favored mortal, and the only mate she'd ever mentioned was the Concept of Mountains, whom Julius had no idea how to contact. Any other time, he would have saved the honor for Bob, but that was out of the question now for obvious reasons, and since he'd never trust Bethesda with his sister dead or alive, Julius had no choice but to do the job himself.

At least there was no shortage of appropriate vessels. In true Amelia fashion, there were liquor bottles scattered all over her room, including a very expensive-looking whiskey cask lying on the floor right next to the divan where she'd died. There were even a few drops left at the bottom, but Julius didn't dare pour them out. He actually felt spirits were quite appropriate, and the scent of alcohol was a welcome break from the constant smell of death as he carefully tapped Amelia's ashes into the bottle.

When he'd collected her as best he could, he replaced the stopper and straightened up, cradling the bottle in his arms like a sacred object while his mother watched in disgust.

"What was the point of that?" she asked, brushing the last of the ash off the couch with her hand so she could sit. "Her soul's already burned out. All you've got there is her physical dust."

"It was still her," Julius said stubbornly. "Amelia deserves better than to be left here."

Bethesda clearly thought that logic was beyond stupid. For once, though, she held her tongue. Good thing, too, because Julius was done with this conversation. He'd had enough of his mother to last five lifetimes, so he left her to her disgust, clutching Amelia's ashes to his chest as he walked out of Amelia's lair and down the hall toward the cavern that took up the other half of this floor of the hollowed-out mountain.

Bob's room.

• • •

Julius had no idea what he expected to find. A clue, perhaps. Maybe some sort of message that would explain why Bob had done what it was now impossible to deny he'd done. When Julius finally jimmied the seer's door open, though, all he found was junk.

Bob's cave was a hoarded mess. Though technically the same size as Amelia's, the dragon-sized cave felt tiny and cramped, mostly because it was packed floor to ceiling with every sort of clutter imaginable. Priceless paintings were piled on top of old washing machines. Heaps of golden coins lay scattered next to broken bird-cages and boxes of vintage auto parts. His closet was stuffed with chess sets—every one of which was open and missing the same piece, the white king—while his bathroom was crammed with taxi-dermy birds, including a stuffed dodo Julius was positive had been stolen from a museum.

What all of this useless junk was actually *for*, he couldn't begin to fathom, but after an hour of sorting through the piles, Julius was starting to seriously question his conviction of his brother's san-ity. The only good thing he could say about Bob's hoard was that at least it was reasonably clean. There was some dust, but nothing worse than he'd had in his own room. Though, of course, his room hadn't been stacked to the ceiling.

By the time Julius's search made it back around to the hall door, he was past ready to give up. If Bob did have a record of his plans, it wasn't here. The best he'd found were the seer's ever-present sticky notes, which covered the hoard like confetti. But though the notes were numerous, trying to make sense of the nonsense Bob had written on them was almost worse than finding nothing at all. Even when his own name appeared—which happened with disturbing frequency—it was never in a useful context. It was always things like "Sic Julius on Wrecking Ball" or "Confirm Julius footwear RE: icy conditions."

Even when a note did seem relevant, there was no way to know *when* it was supposed to happen. The colorful notes were stuck to seemingly random objects all over the cave, with no organization or clues as to when they'd been written. Multiple times, he'd found notes that looked centuries old with text that referenced something recent, like the one he'd found on the ceiling above the bathtub with a reminder for a concert that had taken place two weeks ago. But it was just as common to find apparently brand-new notes with detailed plans for things that had happened decades ago.

He supposed the confusion made sense if you believed what Bob said about seers living in the future as much as the present, but that didn't help Julius's situation right now. In the end, the only thing he found that *was* remotely useful was a pile of moving boxes containing what had once been the contents of his room.

That was the only good surprise today. Six weeks ago, Bob had claimed he'd sold all of Julius's stuff to buy Justin a ticket to the DFZ. But while all the boxes were sealed and postmarked to be mailed to an auction warehouse, nothing had actually been sent off yet. This meant Julius was able to reclaim his belongings, including his replica Frostmourn. He also found his clothes, his books, his computer, even his bedsheets. It was *all* here, and yet, weirdly, none of it felt like his.

It was hard to describe. Bethesda had only kicked him out a month and a half ago. That wasn't even enough time for his stuff to stop smelling like him, and yet all of it felt like it had belonged to another life. The dragon who'd touched and treasured these things had never been to the DFZ. He'd never stood up for himself or said no to his family. Had never met Marci. In other words, he wasn't Julius, and aside from trading out the stiff suit Fredrick had loaned him for his favorite pair of jeans, a comfy T-shirt, and his second-best pair of high tops, he ended up putting everything else back, sealing it all neatly back in its boxes before walking over to collapse in the worn recliner at the center of the cave's lone bit of open floor.

The chair must have been where Bob spent most of his time when he was here, because it smelled more like him than anything else in the room. Julius breathed in the familiar scent as he dug out his phone, waving his hand through the projected cloud of the AR interface to bring up his archive.

Modern phones didn't normally keep a local call record. Things like that were usually left to the cloud. For once, though, Julius's paranoia had served him well. Despite going through three phones and multiple networks over the last two months, he'd meticulously downloaded and backed up all of his correspondence since leaving home, including the cryptic texts and calls he'd received from the Unknown Caller, Bob's not-so-secret identity. He'd intended to read through all of the seer's messages in the hopes of finding something that might explain today's tragic events, but the moment Julius tapped the archives icon, he got distracted by a much bigger folder in his archives. The one where he kept all his messages from Marci.

Just reading her name brought the pain back with a vengeance. Upsetting and annoying as the Council meeting and discovering Amelia's ashes had been, at least they'd provided a distraction. Now, though, the distraction was gone, leaving him staring at the automatically generated transcript of Marci's last call during her plane ride to the DFZ. The one where she'd told him she'd be back soon, and almost said something else.

His vision started to blur. The thin black phone slipped from his fingers, falling into his lap beside the bottle of Amelia's ashes as he frantically pressed his palms to his eyes. Not now. He couldn't afford to fall apart again, not when the clan he'd fought so hard to change was on the verge of collapse. This Council had been his idea. He'd promised his family a better future when he'd over-thrown Bethesda. He couldn't back out on that now. Somehow, some way, he had to make this work. *Had* to, or what was all their suffering for?

He was still telling himself that, working up the courage to pick up his phone again and make another try at reading Bob's messages, when a cold hand landed on his shoulder.

Julius jumped up with a yelp, almost knocking the recliner backward as he leaped to his feet and spun around to find Chelsie standing right behind him.

"*Don't do that!*"

"Sorry," she said, looking uncharacteristically sheepish. "I made a noise."

"Would it kill you to say something?" Julius gasped, clutching his pounding chest as he sank back down into the chair. "What are you even doing here? You're supposed to be free."

Instead of answering, Chelsie turned to grab a folding chair out of the pile of junk in the corner, shaking it open and setting it down in front of him. "I couldn't leave yet," she said as she sat down. "When I jumped off that balcony, I left something behind."

Julius frowned. "You mean your sword?" If that was her problem, it was an easy fix. Chelsie's Fang was still lying right where she'd dropped it, on the balcony upstairs. But his sister was shaking her head.

"I'm never touching that thing again. Even if I wanted to, I don't think it would let me. All the Fangs of the Heartstriker serve a purpose. For mine, the Defender's Blade, that's the defense of the clan. With the exception of you and the Fs, though, I can't think of a single Heartstriker I'd lift a finger to save if they were dying in front of me, so I don't think the Defender's Fang will be welcoming me back anytime soon."

"Glad to know I'm in the 'wouldn't let die' category," Julius said with a nervous smile. "But if you're not talking about your Fang, then what—"

"My egg," Chelsie growled, her green eyes flashing dangerously in the dark. "It was in my room this morning, and now it's gone. Normally, I'd blame Bethesda, but this was one secret I did manage to keep from Mother. You, Fredrick, and Bob were the only ones who knew."

"I didn't take it," Julius said frantically. "I'd never—"

"I know," she said. "Fredrick wouldn't either. Even if he would touch it without my permission, he hasn't had a chance. He's been out flying with his brothers and sisters from the moment you broke Bethesda's seal and set them free."

Even with all the tragedies, that was enough to make Julius smile. Good for Fredrick. He and the other Fs deserved some joy after everything they'd been through. But if Fredrick hadn't touched Chelsie's egg, and Julius hadn't either, that left only one suspect. "You think *Bob* took your egg?"

"There's no one else," Chelsie said bitterly. "And it wouldn't be the worst thing he's done today."

Julius dropped his eyes as the crushing sadness came back with a vengeance. "You've heard about Amelia."

Chelsie nodded, and Julius took a deep breath. "Do you...do you know why? You knew Bob better than most. Can you explain what could have motivated him to do something like this? I thought Amelia was his favorite sister."

"She was more than that," Chelsie said, leaning back on the chair as she searched for the words. "Amelia's looked out for Bob since the very beginning. He was the runt of his clutch, just like you. Before his visions started, Bethesda had already written him off. She would have eaten him if Amelia hadn't gotten there first. She stole Bob and ran away, which was the only reason he lived long enough to discover he was a seer. Bethesda welcomed him back with open arms after that, but for the first few decades of his life, Amelia raised him."

"That only makes everything even sadder," he said. "You make it sound like she was practically a mother to him."

"She was in every way that mattered," Chelsie said with a shrug. "She was the one who raised and protected him. She even taught him magic. He wields the Mage's Fang, never forget. That sword should have been Amelia's, but Bethesda never trusted her enough to let her get near the Quetzalcoatl's skull. She trusted Bob, though. Despite his loyalty to the Planeswalker, Bethesda would never let a seer slip through her claws. From the moment she realized he was the real deal, she's followed his advice to the letter. I think the only reason she accepted your coup with such grace was because she knew Bob was behind it."

If the violence of the last week was Bethesda accepting him with "grace," Julius couldn't imagine the alternative. Still, what Chelsie said helped to explain Bethesda's uncharacteristic despondence when she'd realized Bob had betrayed the clan. Their mother was many things, most of them terrible, but she wasn't a quitter. The Heartstriker was as famous for her dauntless tenacity as she was for her egg laying, which was why her sudden willingness to just give up and run had seemed so odd. Now, though, Julius understood. It wasn't facing seemingly insurmountable odds that had Bethesda down—it was the fact that she was having to do it without her seer.

"Do you think he's really betrayed us?"

Chelsie frowned, thinking the question over. "No," she said at last. "But only because the word 'betrayal' implies that he was on our side to begin with, and the only side Bob's ever been on is his own. There's no tragedy that strikes this clan that Bob didn't see coming and work to his advantage. He knew what would happen to me before I'd even left for China, and I'm sure he foresaw your mortal's death well before Mother kicked you out. A *good* brother, one who actually cared about his clan, would have warned us when he saw these disasters coming. *You* would have warned us, but Bob didn't. He didn't lift a finger to save us, because Bob isn't nice or good. He's a dragon, and dragons look out for themselves."

Julius closed his eyes. He wanted to deny it all—especially the part about Marci—but it was hard to argue when Bob had taken every opportunity to tell Julius the exact same thing. He'd always said that Julius was all the nice Heartstriker had, and now that the truth of that smacked them all in the face, Julius had to wonder why he'd been foolish enough to let himself think otherwise.

Even so.

"I still can't believe he killed Amelia," he said stubbornly. "Even if he really is a terrible, selfish dragon, it just doesn't make any sense. Why would he invest so much in helping me change our clan if he was going to turn around and bring it all crashing down the same day we finally get the Heartstriker Council together?"

"I agree," Chelsie said. "It doesn't make sense, but that's the problem: seers *don't*. They don't follow normal logic. All their plans are based on observations the rest of us won't see for decades. There's probably something coming that will make Amelia's death look like a brilliant move in hindsight, but until that actually happens, we have to accept that we can't know."

"So that's it?" Julius said angrily. "You want me to just *accept* that bad things happen and do nothing?"

"I never said 'do nothing,'" she snapped. "Why do you think I'm here? Just because I've accepted that I may never understand *why* Bob took my egg doesn't mean I'm going to let him keep it!"

The way she said that made him more nervous than ever. "You don't think he'd hurt it, do you?"

"I've learned never to put anything past the Seer of the Heartstrikers," Chelsie growled. "He knows I'll protect that egg at all costs, which means so long as he has it, he has me by the throat."

He hadn't considered that angle, but as soon as Chelsie pointed it out, Julius's mind flashed back to the confrontation in the elevator when Bob had ordered him not to free Chelsie. He'd done it anyway, of course, but he hadn't considered the fact that that apparent failure might have been in Bob's plan, too. After all, Bob saw *everything*. He might not have known for sure if Julius was going to refuse, but so long as it was a possibility, he would have had a backup plan. Something that would make sure Chelsie stayed under his control no matter what Julius did. Something she couldn't walk away from.

"Oh no," he whispered, putting his head in his hands. "No, no, no. He took it hostage."

"He did," Chelsie said, her eyes angry. "I'm sorry, Julius. I wish we were as good as you want us to be, but the truth is Bob's not so different from Mother. Just like her, he can be charismatic and charming when it suits him, but when it comes to getting what he wants, he's as ruthless as any other dragon. Including me, which is why I'm here."

Julius looked at her in confusion. "What?"

"You're his linchpin," she said, staring at him like a predator in the dark. "I don't know why, but all of his recent plots have revolved around you. I'm betting this latest one does, too, which is why, until my egg is safely back in my possession, I'm not letting you out of my sight."

He stared at her in horror. "You can't *possibly* think I'm going to keep being Bob's tool after this."

"Your intentions are none of my concern," she said, standing up. "But you *are* his tool, and that makes you mine as well, because for all their knowledge of the future, seers aren't gods. The only way they make things happen is by manipulating others, and since all of Bob's strings seem to run through you, that makes you his weakness. Tell him off all you like, but sooner or later, he's going to appear and shove you in a direction. When that happens, I'll be there. I will *find* him, and I will take my egg back by whatever means necessary."

The way she said that sent chills down Julius's spine. He'd never seen his sister so deadly, and that was saying something. Julius wasn't sure what had been the final straw—threatening her egg or taking away her hard-won freedom before she'd even tasted it—but Bob had clearly crossed a line, and Chelsie was going to make him pay for it in blood.

"You're not going to kill him, are you?"

"Not unless he makes me," Chelsie said coldly. "But I'm done being a pawn on his board. He and Bethesda have had me by the throat for almost my entire life. Now, thanks to you, I'm free, and as a free dragon, I will not tolerate the things I love being put in danger ever again."

Every word she spoke sent Julius sinking deeper into his chair. And here he'd thought this day couldn't get any worse. As angry as he was at Bob for all of this, though, he didn't want his brother to *die*. Especially not by Chelsie. There'd been too much death already, too many tragedies. The whole point of making a Council in the first place was so family wouldn't kill family anymore. That said, though, now was not the time to put himself in Chelsie's way. She had every right to be angry over this, and as much as he wanted to talk her away from the violence he could feel radiating off her like heat, the instincts that had kept Julius alive through many bouts of dragon fury told him his best bet was to just let it go. So that was what he did, lowering his head meekly before his sister.

As always, the submissive play worked like a charm. The moment it was clear he wasn't going to fight about it, Chelsie's fury blew over, leaving her...not calm, exactly, but no longer on the edge of blood-shed, which was good enough. "Glad to know we have an understanding," she said stiffly, sitting down again.

"You're my sister," Julius replied with a sincere smile. "I'll always help you any way I can. That said, I promise I'll call the moment Bob contacts me, so you don't have to stay here and keep watch. I appreciate your company, but you're free now. You should be off enjoying that, not babysitting me."

It might have been his imagination, but for a moment there, Chelsie actually looked touched. The soft emotion vanished as soon as he spotted it, though, leaving only the usual hard, ruthless dragon glaring down at him as she shook her head. "I can't. Not until my egg is safe. I appreciate the offer, though, which reminds me. I have a present for you."

He blinked in confusion, but Chelsie was already navigating her way back through the maze of Bob's hoarded room to the door. "It's not much," she said as she reached down to grab something off the floor of the hallway outside. "Just something I picked up to thank you for sticking it out and setting me free even after I told you not to and...well, everything really."

Her voice was flawlessly casual, but the words still made Julius's chest swell. "Thank you" wasn't something that came easily to any dragon's lips, especially one as proud and prickly as Chelsie. He was struggling to think up a reply that his jaded sister wouldn't brush off as a mere platitude when Chelsie turned around to reveal the battered canvas shoulder bag she was holding in her hands. A very *familiar* canvas shoulder bag.

Marci's bag.

"Where did you get that?"

"In the DFZ," Chelsie said, walking back to him. "I went back there the morning after we ran. I'd hoped to retrieve her body, but Reclamation Land was seething like a kicked-over anthill. In the end, this was all I could grab. I was planning to use it as leverage to make you get out of bed, but you managed that on your own. I thought about not giving it to you at all after that. I wasn't sure if it would be too painful, but I knew I'd want it if I was in your position, so..."

She trailed off with a shrug, holding out the bag. After almost a minute of staring, Julius took it with shaking hands, closing his eyes as his fingers slid over the familiar beige canvas stained burgundy at the bottom where blood had seeped in. Marci's blood, filled with Marci's scent.

After that, all attempts at decorum vanished. He clutched the bag to his chest with a sob, curling himself around it into a ball in Bob's battered armchair. He was so lost, he didn't even notice Chelsie moving closer until her hand landed on his back.

"I buried her," she said quietly. "I couldn't do much, just a shallow grave. I know that's cold comfort, but at least you can rest knowing she's not lying out in the open."

His sister was right. It *wasn't* a comfort. "Marci deserved better."

"She did," Chelsie agreed. "They always do, but...this is how mortals end, Julius. No matter what we do, how hard we try, they always die. All we can do is remember them, and I thought if you had something physical to hold on to, it would help."

Julius didn't see how this pain could ever be helped, but he wasn't about to let the bag go. "Thank you," he whispered, curling himself tighter.

She pressed her palm down against his back. Then, like the shade she was named for, Chelsie was gone, leaving him alone. This time, though, Julius was glad of it. Awful as it was not to have something to distract him from the pain, he needed to be alone with the bag that smelled of Marci. Needed to be where no one could see him, and he didn't have to be anything but empty.

That was where he stayed, curled up in Bob's abandoned armchair in their soon-to-be-abandoned mountain, holding tight to the memory of a person who was never coming back.

CHAPTER TWO

"So let me make sure I've got this right," Marci said slowly. "I'm dead."

"Correct," her father said.

"That's what I was afraid of," she muttered, tilting her head back to look up at the endless dark.

She had no idea how long they'd been here. It felt as if she'd been crying forever, but eventually the tears had dried up. Now she and her dad were just standing next to each other in the infinite blackness, which, while not uncomfortable, definitely wasn't where Marci wanted to be.

"So where are we, exactly?" she asked, arching her neck all around as she tried to find an edge or marker, something that would prove they weren't actually standing in an endless void. "Is this some kind of limbo or—"

Hell was her next guess, because she absolutely refused to believe this cold, dark nothing was heaven, but her father beat her to the punch. "We are inside your death."

She turned back to him. "And what does that mean? You say 'my death' like it's a place. Is death another dimension or something?"

Aldo Novalli laughed. "I have no idea. Theoretical magic was your area of expertise, *carina*. This old man only knows what he's seen."

That answer was so like her dad, Marci couldn't help laughing with him, though hers was more the nervous, "we're screwed" sort. "If I'm the expert, we're in trouble, because I can't see a thing."

"That's only because you haven't opened your eyes yet," Aldo said encouragingly. "Try again."

That didn't make any sense. If her eyes were closed, how was she seeing her father? But waking up inside your death was the sort of experience that demanded an open mind, so Marci swallowed all her reasons why this couldn't possibly be and just gave it a shot, blinking her eyes rapidly in an attempt to open what should already be open.

The effect was immediate.

"Wow," she whispered, stumbling backward.

Marci wasn't sure what had happened, but at some point during all her blinking, the formless void had rolled back like a curtain to reveal a weirdly familiar scene. She was standing on the gravel drive-way leading up to the three-story house hidden beneath the Skyway on-ramps where she and Julius had lived in the DFZ. Even as she stared in wonder, Marci knew this couldn't be their *real* house. For one thing, the porch and front door were still intact, not chopped in two by Conrad's sword, and second, she was *dead*. But that didn't stop the house from feeling real. More than real, like a picture that had been digitally enhanced to look even more beautiful than real life, and as she stared at it, Marci realized why.

This wasn't their house. It was her memory of it. The rosy recol-lection of their home as she'd loved it best, right down to her dad's freshly repaired car parked in its usual spot out front. Likewise, the spiral of cement on-ramps overhead was empty and quiet, some-thing that had *never* happened in the actual DFZ, where cars were always racing from the Underground to the Skyways at all hours. Here, though, everything was still. No sirens or headlights flashing through cracks or flickering orange street lamps humming in the dark. No sound or movement at all. Just the house standing quietly in the cement shelter of the tangled overpasses, its windows lit up cheerily to welcome her home.

"Okay," Marci said at last, turning back to her dad. "Did I make all of this up just now, or was it always here?"

Her father frowned, giving her question serious consideration, as he always did. "I think it's a bit of both," he said at last. "This is your death, Marci. Everything that remains of your twenty-five years—your knowledge, your memories, the people whose lives you impacted—is collected here. Even I am only here as part of your memory."

"But what does that mean specifically?" Marci asked. "Like, are you *you*, or am I talking to a figment of my imagination?"

"I think I'm me," Aldo Novalli said with a shrug. "I remember your mother and my childhood and the day you were born. But I also remember things I couldn't have known. Things you experienced after my death, including how you were living in sin with that dragon boy."

"I was *not* living in sin!" Marci cried. She wasn't sure what was more embarrassing: that her father apparently had her memories, or that she was telling him the truth. She really hadn't had a relationship like that with Julius, which was a freaking tragedy. She would have lived in a lot more sin if she'd known she was going to *die.*

That thought made her want to cry all over again, so Marci shoved it aside. She'd wasted enough time on that already, and she couldn't let herself forget she was here on a mission: to find Ghost and figure out how to do whatever it was she needed to do to become a Merlin. That was why she'd taken her spirit's hand and let him pull her into death in the first place. Not so she could hang around weeping over lost opportunities like an *actual* ghost. But as she was telling herself to get it together, Marci noticed something was off.

Okay, a *lot* of things were off, but this one struck her as particularly odd. So far in her experience with the afterlife—or whatever this was—things had looked mostly the same as they had when she was alive. The black void had been new, but once she'd managed to open her eyes, everything else she'd seen—the house, her car, the gravel on the ground, her dad—had all looked as good or better than she'd remembered. She was even wearing the same white T-shirt she'd had on when she'd died, though thankfully without the hole Emily Jackson had shot through it. But happy as Marci was that her chest was no longer a terrifying, bloody mess, it *was* glowing faintly, which struck her as important.

"Do you see this?"

Aldo frowned. "See what?"

"I'll take that as a no," Marci said, pressing her palm over the light. The faint glow was no brighter than a candle, nothing like the roar of power she remembered, but it *was* in the right place...

Fighting hard not to get her hopes up, Marci gave her chest a push, bearing down not just with her palm, but with her magic, the mental hand she used to grab power for her spells. Sure enough, the faint light flickered when she poked it, so Marci closed her eyes and relaxed, but not with her muscles. The tension she was trying to undo was inside of her: the knot of internal magic she'd wound together on the balcony when Svena had forced the supernova that was Amelia's magic into her own.

At the time, the frantic origami folding had been an act of self-defense to keep Amelia's fire from consuming her. Now, picking it apart again felt like trying to unravel a limp, knotted thread. It was such slow going, the folded magic so cold and lifeless, Marci worried she was wasting her time. Then, just when she was certain she was unraveling an empty cage, the tangle gave way, and something beautiful and burning slipped out of her chest to land in Marci's palm.

When Svena had first divided Amelia's fire into her, it had felt like swallowing the sun. By contrast, the magic flickering in her hand now looked like a dying match, but it *wasn't* Marci's. The magic changed as she watched, the tiny flames dancing and shifting in her palm until she was no longer holding a fire. She was holding a dragon. A miniature feathered serpent no longer than her hand with scarlet feathers that glowed like banked coals.

"*Now* do you see it?" she asked, holding the dragon out to her father.

Aldo Novalli nodded, eyes wide. "What *is* it?"

Before Marci could state the obvious, the little dragon stirred, shaking itself like a dog before looking up with beautiful, amber-colored eyes.

"Did we make it?"

The question made Marci jump. For all that it had come out of her chest, the tiny creature in her hand was so unlike the powerful, rollicking dragoness she'd known, she hadn't actually made the connection in her head. Now, though, the familiar brash, confident voice snapped everything into place. "Amelia?"

"In the flesh," the little fire serpent said proudly, looking down at herself. "Or not, as the case may be. But either way, it's me! And from the looks of things, I've successfully hitched a ride into the mortal afterlife." She grinned, revealing a wall of sharp, white, tiny teeth. "Let's see Svena do *that*."

If Marci had had any doubts left that this was, in fact, Amelia, that line would have cleared them. But while her identity was no longer in question, Marci had plenty of others. "What are you doing here?" she cried. "I'm dead!"

"Actually, we're both dead," Amelia said authoritatively. "That was the plan. I put my fire in you, and when you die, I stow away inside your soul to the place that lies beyond death."

"The place beyond death?" Marci repeated, brows collapsing into a scowl. "Wait, so you knew I was going to die?"

The little red dragon gave her a sideways look. "You *are* a mortal. No spoilers, but—"

"I meant die *soon*," Marci snapped.

"Oh, well, that was less certain," the dragon admitted. "But my brother is a seer, so I might have had an insider tip. But don't be angry! I'm here to help you."

Marci didn't buy that for a moment. "You died to help me?" she said skeptically, and then her face fell as she realized what that meant. "Wait, when you say you're dead, too, do you mean *dead* dead?"

"As a doornail," Amelia assured her. "I'm ash on the other side." She flapped her tiny fiery wings. "This is the last of me."

Marci gaped at her. "*Why?*"

"Because I saw a chance to do what no one else could," the dragon said proudly. "Even Bob can't see what happens here, so

36

the details were a bit fuzzy, but all our best guesses said that you still had a good chance of becoming the first Merlin even after you died. You've actually already done the hardest part, which was getting here. All that's left now is to clinch the deal, and if there's anyone who can clinch a deal, it's you."

"Thanks for the vote of confidence," Marci said. "But how does my becoming Merlin help you? You're still dead."

"Ah, but I'm also still burning." Amelia turned to point at her glowing ember plumage. "Remember when I told you that so long as even a bit of her fire was still going, a dragon could live on? Well, you're seeing theory in action. I might be only a fraction of what I was before, but so long as I burn, the core of Amelia the Planeswalker, Greatest Dragon Mage of All Time, lives on. More importantly, I'm living *here*, on the other side, where no dragon has gone before. And speaking of..." She swiveled her head to look over the house, the car, and the silent shell of on-ramps that caged them in. "Swanky digs. Are all mortal deaths this enormous?"

"No," Aldo Novalli said quietly. "No, they are not."

Amelia jolted at his voice, almost falling out of Marci's fingers. "Who's *that?*" she cried, scrambling up Marci's arm.

"He's my father," Marci said, unsure why the dragon was only noticing him now. "Dad, Amelia the Planeswalker. Amelia, this is my dad, Aldo Novalli."

Aldo gave her his famously charming smile, but Amelia was still staring at him as though he were an impossibility. "How did your dad end up inside *your* death?"

"It's a long story," Aldo said. "But the short version is that I died, was forgotten, and was then restored to my daughter to help her find her way."

That sounded unnecessarily cryptic to Marci, but Amelia looked like he'd just explained the secrets of the universe. "I get it now," she said, nodding appreciatively. "That clever cat."

"Well, I wish you'd explain it to me," Marci said, exasperated. "Because I have no idea what's going on."

"It's very simple," Amelia said quickly. "We're in your death, right? Right. And do you know where your death is?"

Marci shook her head. "My dad said it was the impression left by life, but he didn't have a location."

"He wouldn't," Amelia said. "Modern mortals don't have a clue when it comes to death, though he was right about the impression thing. This place"—she waved her claw at the house, the gravel driveway, and the dirt lot beyond—"is a crater formed by the impact of your life. It's literally your mark on the world, sort of like the giant grooves dug by humanity's collective fears and hopes that become Mortal Spirits, but on a one-person scale. Following so far?"

Marci nodded, looking around at the wall of on-ramps, which she now saw that, unlike the real version in the DFZ, had no tunnel leading out. "I get that this is the mark made by my life," she said, turning back to Amelia. "But what did I make a mark *in*?"

"The magical landscape, of course."

"Wait," Marci said, leaning into her. "You mean there's a *literal* magical landscape? As in the place where spirits have their vessels?"

"The very same," Amelia said, nodding. "To understand what that really means, though, you first have to understand how magic enters the world."

This was what she'd been waiting for her whole life. "Tell me."

Amelia smiled and rose up on her hind legs, pressing her forefeet flat together. "Like most other magically awakened planes, this realm is really two halves sandwiched together: a physical world, and a magical one. The classic example is two sides of a coin, but I find it easier to imagine a plane as a sheet of paper: two distinct faces, but still one whole. A wrinkle on one side—say a mountain—causes an equal but opposite formation on the other—a Spirit of the Land. Following?"

Marci nodded rapidly. What Amelia was explaining was similar to several already popular theories, but none of those could explain…

"How are humans magical?" she asked. "If there are two sides, then we definitely live in the physical one. So where does our magic come from?"

"The same place all magic does," the dragon explained. "Here. Just because you think of yourself as living on one side doesn't mean you don't touch the other. Remember, they're not actually separate places. We're talking about two halves of a whole. As a native species of this plane, humans, just like every other magical creature, exist in both halves simultaneously, meaning you have a physical self, your body, and a magical self—"

"The soul," Marci finished excitedly.

Amelia frowned. "I've never liked that terminology because it implies one lives inside the other. A more accurate description would be that you have *two* bodies—physical and magical—that overlap, inhabiting the same space in different dimensions. But sure, you can call it a soul if it makes you feel better."

"Of *course* I'm going to call it that," Marci said, eyes gleaming. "You're talking about proving the existence of life beyond our physical bodies! Do you know how big that's going to be?"

"Huge," Amelia agreed, giving her a skeptical look. "But I don't understand why you're so excited. You're bonded to a spirit of the dead who summons armies of ghosts. How much more proof of the soul did you need?"

"Those could still have been echoes," Marci said. "Every paper I've read claims that 'ghosts' are nothing but the aftershocks people leave in the ambient magic when they die. Even with the Empty Wind, I had nothing to actually disprove that since the dead he brought back weren't exactly chatty. They had goals but no personalities or proof of independent thought, so it was still plausible that he was reacting to the echoes of the emotions those people left in the magic when they died rather than the actual individual souls. But this is different."

She put her hand on her stomach where Emily's shot had gone through. "I *know* I died, but I'm still me. I'm here and thinking and talking to you. If I can just figure out how to get proof of this back to the physical side, this could change everything we know about death and our own mortality!" Which would get her a Nobel Prize for *sure*.

"No doubt," Amelia said. "If you can get back, this will blow the lid off everything, but you're still thinking too small."

Marci gaped at her. "How is changing the concept of human mortality *small?*"

"Because you've always known it," the dragon said with a shrug. "There's a reason the soul is a concept in every culture. The idea of physical-life-only is a modern fallacy caused by the magical drought. Now that the magic's back, it was only a matter of time before someone rediscovered what was common knowledge for the vast majority of humanity's existence. Personally, I'm *way* more interested in your death specifically." She looked back up at the cavern of on-ramps. "I mean, this place is *huge.*"

"Is it?" Marci asked, because next to the stories of endless fields and the other mythical landscapes that were supposed to exist in the afterlife, she'd thought her little house was pretty modest.

"Totally," the dragon said. "Not that I've ever been to this side before, of course, but I was under the impression that unless you were the sort of person whose life left a huge impact—heroes, great rulers, beloved artists, feared dictators, that kind of thing—mortal deaths were pretty cramped. No offense, but I was expecting something much smaller. I mean, you're not famous, and you died relatively young, so where did all this space come from?"

Marci had no idea. Her father, however, was smiling. "It's because she is well remembered."

"Obviously," Amelia said. "But remembered by *whom?*"

Again, Marci had no clue. She'd cut off contact with all her old friends when she'd fled Nevada to protect them from Bixby. Even after he'd died, she'd been too busy to reach out. Most of them didn't even know that she was in the DFZ, much less dead. The UN team knew, but they were only two people and a raven spirit. That left the dragons, but other than Amelia, the only dragon who knew her as anything other than "that mortal" was…

"Julius."

Amelia grinned. "And now you know why your death is so interesting to me. It goes without saying that Julius took your loss very badly, but what's remarkable here isn't that he loved you enough to carve you out a good death—'cause let's be honest: if any Heartstriker was going to fall hard for his too-competent mortal, it'd be him—it's the fact that he's a *dragon*. And as we all know, dragons aren't part of this world. We're refugees. Non-natives, as Algonquin would say. We can inhabit the physical half of this plane because physicality is common across almost all worlds, but magically, we're incompatible. That's why we kept functioning during the drought that shut down the spirits and every other magical creature. We worked on an entirely different system, one where we created our own magic. That's also why I had to hitch a ride here inside of you. As a non-native species, I didn't share this part of your plane, so I needed an inside mage."

"You mean to be inside a mage," Marci said. "But if all that's true, then how would Julius's remembering me shape my death? If dragons can't touch this side, how did this happen?"

"I have no idea!" Amelia said excitedly, flapping her little wings. "Everything I know says that Julius's memories shouldn't do squat for you here, and yet they clearly matter. There's just no other explanation for why your death is so huge since no one else remembers you. This place has to be his doing, and that raises powerful possibilities."

Amelia said this as though it were the best possible thing that could ever be, and from a magical-theory standpoint, Marci supposed that was true. If Julius was the one behind this, then they were standing inside the smoking gun that proved dragons were capable of manipulating the native magic of this world in at least one way. But while finding evidence of the impossible was one of the most thrilling events in any discipline, Marci was having a hard time matching Amelia's excitement about the metaphysical manifestation of Julius's sadness over her death. It was one thing to hope the guy you loved liked you back, but to find out the truth like *this*, when everything they could have had was already lost, was too tragic to contemplate.

"I have to get back."

"Oh, absolutely," Amelia agreed, scrambling back down Marci's arm. "As delighted as I am to finally find proof for the theory I've been working on for centuries, we didn't come here to sit around enjoying the view. You're going to be Merlin, and I'm coming with you, so tap your cat's envoy, and let's go!"

"Amelia!" Marci hissed. "Don't talk about my dad that way!"

"Why not?" she said, glancing at Aldo, who'd sat through all the theory talk in uncharacteristic silence. "That's what you're here for, right? Ghost is the Spirit of the Forgotten Dead, and since we've just established Marci is most definitely *not* forgotten, that puts her outside his normal reach. But all the spirit/Merlin pairs I've heard of started with some kind of sacrifice, and—forgive me if I'm jumping to conclusions here—a dead father fits the Empty Wind's bill pretty solidly. My guess is the memory of dear old Dad was the price of admission for your initial bond. Now that death's forced you apart, the Empty Wind's coughed him up again to act as a guide. That means guiding us is his job, and there's no insult in asking a man to do his job."

"The insult is that you're treating my dad like he's a single-use item!" Marci snapped, glaring at the little dragon before turning back to her father. "Sorry, Daddy."

"It's all right," Aldo said. "She's not wrong. I was sent here by the Empty Wind specifically so I could guide you back to him. I should be doing exactly what the little dragon says. But for all his power, the Forgotten Dead can't see us here, and before I go back into his service, I wanted to do my job as your father and make sure you knew you had a choice."

"Choice?" Marci stared at him. "What choice? Stay dead?"

"Yes," he said quietly, reaching out to brush her bangs away from her eyes. "You've had a hard run of things since I left you, *carina*, and I'm sorry for that. A father is supposed to protect his child, not make her life more difficult."

"You didn't do anything," Marci said, shaking her head. "Bixby wouldn't have come after me if I'd just left the Kosmolabe in Nevada, and all the stuff after with the seers and Ghost and helping Julius was entirely my decision."

"I know," he said. "You've always been ambitious. This is hardly the first time you've bitten off more than you can chew, but killing yourself over doctoral coursework is a far cry from *actually* getting killed."

She rolled her eyes. "Dad—"

"No," he said sternly, grabbing her hands. "They killed you, *carina*. All these spirits and dragons and monsters, they ask too much. Of both of us."

Marci looked down guiltily. "I'm sorry. I shouldn't have forgotten you, but it was the only way to beat Vann Jeger and save Julius and—"

"I know," Aldo said. "I have your memories, don't forget. I know why you made the choices you did, and I'm not angry about being forgotten. You did what you had to do, and the living *should* come before the dead. That's why I want you to consider your choices carefully now, because there's much she isn't telling you."

He looked pointedly at Amelia, who bristled. "You make it sound like I'm trying to con her."

"Are you?" Marci asked.

Amelia looked appalled. "Of course not! He just wants you to stay dead so he can stay here with you instead of going back to the Empty Wind."

Marci's eyes went wide, but when she looked at her father, he didn't deny it.

"I don't think it's shocking that I'd rather stay in this warm, peaceful place with my daughter than go back to the empty cold of a death god," Aldo said. "But this is about Marci, not me. I'm her father. I care about her in life and death, which is more than I can say for you." His eyes narrowed. "You were happy to let her die if it got you what you wanted."

"I didn't '*let her die*,'" Amelia said angrily. "It was a calculated risk!"

"That you didn't tell her about."

"Only because telling her would have ruined everything!" the dragon cried. "If I'd warned her what was coming, that knowledge could have changed her decisions and ruined years of Bob's plans. I couldn't take that risk, and I knew it would be fine. Marci understands better than most dragons that greatness doesn't come easy or cheap. That's why I bet it all on her in the first place." She looked up at Marci. "Right?"

Marci sighed. She was flattered Amelia thought so highly of her, but…"I'd rather not have died," she said honestly. "Not if there was another way."

"There wasn't," Amelia said, digging her tiny claws into Marci's skin. "All Merlins get to this side through their spirits, and you're bound to the spirit of the Forgotten Dead. Death was *always* your ticket. All Bob and I did was nudge things around a bit to make sure you died at the right time and in the right way so that I could come with you."

"You used her," Aldo said angrily.

"She used me back!" Amelia cried, puffing out her chest. "Why do you think I'm so tiny, huh? Marci sucked me down to embers before she died, but did I complain? No! I let her take whatever she needed, because that's what friendship's all about: using and being used in return."

Aldo Novalli opened his mouth to argue, but Marci got there first. "*Enough*," she said, putting up her hands. "I appreciate you sticking up for me, Daddy, but what's done is done. Amelia's right. I did use her, and while I definitely would have appreciated a heads up about what was coming, I wouldn't have chosen differently at the end. I still would have died, so now that that's settled, I'd like to focus on *not* being dead anymore rather than arguing over whose fault it is."

"But that's what I'm trying to tell you," Aldo said desperately. "You came into this thinking you could just walk out again, but that's not how it is. This is *death*, the mortal end. It isn't something you can casually come back from."

A cold knot began to form in Marci's chest. "But there has to be a way," she said. "Why would I die to become a Merlin if there was *no way back?*"

Her father sighed. "I don't know as much about planar meta-physics as your friend there, but I've flown with the Empty Wind for a long time now, and—"

"Come on, dude, really?" Amelia interrupted. "She only forgot you a week ago."

"A week can be a very long time in a place where time doesn't mean much," Aldo answered, keeping his eyes stubbornly on Marci. "I know you came here thinking death was a doorway. Others led you to believe that, and maybe for them it is, but we're not spirits, *carina*. We're mortals, and for us, it's never that simple."

"But it *is* possible," Marci said, fists clenching. "I stopped fight-ing for my life because Ghost told me dying was the path to becom-ing a Merlin. Are you saying he lied?"

"No, no," Aldo said, shaking his head. "He was absolutely right. It *is* the only way for you, but it's not an easy path."

"I never expected it to be!"

"I know," he said, clutching her hands. "You've never shied away from hard tasks, but I don't think you comprehend the difference in degree here." He looked up with a sigh. "I think the best way is just to show you. Come with me."

He turned and walked into the house. Equal parts nervous and curious, Marci followed, climbing the stairs to the porch with Amelia clinging to her shoulder.

Now that she knew whose memories had built it, stepping through the door of the house she'd shared with Julius hurt more than Marci expected. It didn't seem possible that she could feel so strongly about a place where she'd spent such a small part of her life, but for the weeks she'd lived here with Julius, this building had been home. *Their* home, together. But just as she was thinking she wouldn't have traded her time here for the world, Marci real-ized she had. Julius had been right there when she died, yelling at her to stay, to hold on. But she hadn't. She'd let go of him to fol-low Ghost into death, thinking it was only temporary. Thinking she could come back. Now, following her father up the creaking stairs, Marci began to wonder if she'd made a terrible mistake.

When they climbed to the third floor, she figured they were headed for her casting workshop in the attic, but her father didn't turn at the final landing. Instead, he opened the window, sliding up the glass pane and popping the rusted screen so he could crawl out onto the slanted roof. He really had to crawl, too. This was the tallest part of the old house, the sharp-slanted gables that ran directly beneath the blackened cement bottoms of the on-ramps. Nervously, Marci crawled after him, clinging to the crumbling asphalt shingles to keep from sliding off. When she was stable enough to look up, she raised her head to ask her dad why he'd brought her up, only to discover there was no need. The truth was right in front of her.

"Wow," she whispered.

In the real world, the spiraling ramps above their house met up to form the final merge lane onto the Skyways. Here, though, the ramps forming the roof simply vanished, leaving a circle of darkness at the peak of the cavern that rippled like water.

"What *is* that?" Marci asked, scooting carefully along the steep roof until she was crouching at the edge, as close to the circle as she could get.

"What lies beyond," her father said, sitting down beside her. "Remember how Amelia said your death was a hollow carved into the magical landscape?" He pointed at the darkness. "That's its mouth. The place where your hollow meets the rest."

Marci's eyes went wide. "You mean that black stuff is the magical plane?"

"We're already on the magical plane," Amelia said, leaning out on Marci's shoulder to get a better view of the undulating darkness over their heads. "Remember, your death is just a scratch in the magical landscape. What you see there is the rest of it. The view from the ground, as it were."

Marci's eyes went wider still. "Hold up a second," she said slowly. "You're telling me that black watery stuff is magic? Like, *the* magic, the literal manasphere, the place where Tectonic Magic happens and all ambient magic rises from, the Sea of Magic?"

"Yes," Amelia said, giving her a funny look. "Didn't I make that clear earlier?"

She had, but hearing you were inside the magical landscape where spirits had their vessels and all magic originated was a far cry from seeing it with your own eyes. And not just seeing. This close, Marci could *feel* the power radiating down from the upside-down pool. The black substance might have looked like water, but it was humming with power like a high-voltage wire, absolutely nothing like the soft, hazy ambient magic she'd worked with back when she was alive. This was the real stuff: the pure, unfiltered, untamed, concentrated magic that filled spirits and brought them to life.

"This is incredible!" she cried, shooting to her feet. "All that talk about magic acting like water wasn't just a metaphor. It's real. It's *right there!*" She bounced on the balls of her feet. "Can I touch it?"

"Only if you want to lose a hand," her father said, reaching up to pull her back down. "This is what I wanted to show you, *carina*. We're safe here, but what's outside isn't our world. The Empty Wind released me so I could guide you back to him, but to do that, you'll have to leave the shelter of your death."

"So?" Marci said. "Why would I want to sit around here?"

"Because you *can* sit around," he said desperately, placing her hand on the roof beneath them. "Your Julius has given you a great gift. Thanks to his memories, your death is large and comfortable, and because he's a dragon, it will probably remain that way for a very long time. If you wanted, you could stay here for centuries in peace and safety. That is a treasure, Marcivale. Others are not nearly so lucky."

She didn't need the way his voice dipped at the end to know what he meant. "You're talking about your own death, aren't you?"

Aldo dropped his eyes with a sigh. "Bixby was a thorough man," he said, dragging a hand through his graying hair. "When he killed someone, he made sure they wouldn't be missed, and I was no exception. When I woke up after…after what happened in the desert, my death was no deeper than the ditch they left me in, and as time passed, even that began to shrink."

"What do you mean 'shrink'?"

"Exactly what you imagine," he said sadly, looking up at the circle where the magic pooled like tar. "Our deaths are nothing more than scratches, the tiny nicks our lives leave on a much greater world. Some are bigger than others, but all of us are forgotten in the end, and with no living memory to keep our deaths open, they eventually wash away."

"Wash away?" she repeated, voice shaking. "As in vanish?"

He nodded. "I know you didn't come here intending to remain, but I don't want you to throw away a treasure like this without knowing its value first. When I died, I had nothing. A scratch in the ground, and even that was closing as I was forgotten by everyone but you. I was on the edge of being forced out altogether when the Empty Wind appeared. He told me you'd sent him, which was good, because given his face, I never would have—"

"Wait, *face?*" Marci said. "Ghost has a *face?*"

"A horrible one," her father said with a shudder. "But what else could he have? He's the embodiment of humanity's greatest fear."

She scowled. "He's not that bad. There's worse things than death."

"There are," he agreed. "And the Empty Wind is one of them. To die is terrifying, but as you've seen for yourself, it doesn't mean all is lost. If we are remembered, some part of us will always remain. To be forgotten, though, to have all proof of your life vanish from the Earth, like you never were at all..." He shook his head. "That is the end, Marcivale. That is oblivion, death beyond death."

"You make him sound like a villain," Marci said stubbornly. "He's not evil!"

"I never said he was," Aldo replied. "I'm just telling you what he *is*. It's a definition, not a judgment, though for most people, I imagine that's a moot point. The proof of our insignificance is never welcome, which means the Empty Wind isn't, either. That's why he hides his face. He doesn't want you to be afraid of him."

"I wouldn't be afraid," Marci said stubbornly. "I've never feared Ghost." It was a big part of why he'd trusted her, but her father just kept shaking his head.

"You would," he said stubbornly. "You wouldn't want to, but if you saw him as the dead do, you would be afraid. Not because you're not brave—you're the bravest person I know—but immortal or mortal, no one wants to be forgotten."

Marci still wasn't convinced. "If he's so scary, why did you go with him? Was it only because of me?"

"That helped," Aldo said. "But to be honest, I took his offer because I had no choice. By the time he came to me, your memories were the only thing holding my death together. I was on my back in a shallow grave, face to face with *that*." He glanced at the undulating darkness with fear in his eyes, but Marci didn't understand.

"It's just magic," she said. "Potent stuff, sure, but we're mages. This is what we do."

"It's what we *did*," he said. "When we had physical bodies to shield us. We don't have that luxury here, and as you can feel for yourself, that is *not* the same magic we worked."

"I can tell it's more dangerous," she agreed. "But I've tapped straight into dragons. I'm sure I can handle whatever that is."

"No, you can't," he said, frustrated. "I keep telling you, we're sheltered here. What we're looking at is just a glimpse, a pinprick in the floor of the Sea of Magic. All the magic in the world—the stuff that poured in the night of the return and whatever extra that's come in since—is sitting directly on top of us. Even if you still had your living physical body to help shield you, the power up there could tear you to pieces. As you are now, a naked soul, just touching it would be enough to burn you away completely."

"Then how do I get out?" she asked. "You said I'd have to leave my death to go back to Ghost, but how is that possible if touching that stuff can kill me? You know, *again*."

"It's not," her father said. "Not if you're alone. If you're going to leave this place, you need a spirit's help. This is their realm. They're sentient magic, which means they can move freely through the flows. If you belong to one, he can protect you, but while the Empty Wind acknowledges you as his master, he can't claim you because you are remembered. That puts you outside of his domain, which means not only can he not protect you from the magic, he can't even find you."

Ghost had said something similar when she'd first arrived, but Marci didn't understand. "Can't he just come to my death?"

"Your death is a tiny speck at the bottom of a black, endless sea," Aldo reminded her. "Even if he knew exactly where to go, there's a good chance you could be burned to nothing just from passing through that hole to reach him. I know you're determined, Marci, but there's a difference between a hard path and an impossible one, and I fear you've been led down the latter."

"It can't be impossible," Marci said stubbornly. "If nothing else, the fact that Amelia's here proves that I have a solid chance. She'd never stake her life on an impossible bet."

"Absolutely not," Amelia agreed. "I don't do long odds on something this important. I'll have you know Bob gave us a solid fifty-fifty."

Marci almost choked. "Fifty-fifty? As in fifty percent chance of death?"

"You're already dead," Amelia reminded her. "But why are you upset? Those are great odds."

"Not when it comes to my life!" Marci cried. "That's a coin flip!"

"Exactly," the dragon said. "You have a heads-or-tails shot at something that should, as your father just pointed out, be *impossible*. That's pretty miraculous, I think."

Marci dropped her head with a groan. That was not the answer she'd been hoping for when she'd appealed to Amelia. In the end, though, she supposed it didn't change anything.

"I appreciate you telling me the truth," she told her father. "I understand escape is not guaranteed, but what alternative do I have? Sit around in here forever?"

Aldo smiled. "Would that be so bad?"

"Yes," she said, appalled this was even a question. "Death is *not* an option."

"Why not?" he asked. "You said yourself there are worse things than death, and your death is far better than most. I've never met your Julius, but going by your memories, he doesn't seem like the type who'd forget. Even if he finds someone else to love, he'll treasure your memory all his life. His *dragon* life. Given the fuzzy nature of time on this side, that means you could stay here in safety effectively forever. Best of all, you'll have company. Normally, humans are as alone in their deaths as they were in their own heads, but Ghost broke the rules when he sent me here, and you brought Amelia. You have safety, company, and an entire world to remake as you see fit. I know it's not what you died for, but your death is a paradise by all standards, and paradise isn't something to be casually thrown away."

There was a deep truth to those words. From the moment she'd first opened her eyes, Marci had never thought of this place as anything but temporary, another trap to wiggle out of. Now, though, she looked down from the roof and actually let herself imagine what it might be like to live here. Amelia would balk, of course, but her father would be happy. Even when they'd gotten on each other's last nerves, she and her dad had always been a good team. They could be one again, working together in her attic workshop. She had tons of experiments to finish, far less dangerous ones than the journey that had brought her here. With enough time, she might even be able to teach her father proper methodology. Mostly importantly, though, they'd be together, and her father wouldn't have to go back to the Empty Wind.

That was the real barb. Marci firmly believed her spirit was not evil, but her dad's description of Ghost's reality wasn't exactly rosy. Now that she understood it, Marci could see why Aldo was so insistent that she not give up this place. After what he'd been through, it probably did seem like paradise to him, and she wasn't sure if she could live with herself if she took that away.

Unless…

"Speaking hypothetically," she said slowly. "If I left, could you stay? Keep things up for me here?"

Aldo sighed. "I wish I could. But this is *your* death, Marcivale. You're the reason all of this exists. Without you to live in them, your dragon's memories are just memories."

So much for that. "I suppose leaving and coming back is also out of the question?"

"That's my understanding," he said uncomfortably. "Again, I'm not an authority. I only know what you know and what I've learned from watching the Empty Wind do his job. From what I've observed, though, mortals only seem to get one life and, therefore, one death."

"So in other words, no second chances."

"Death is notoriously hard to cheat," Amelia said. "But that doesn't mean you can't do it."

"I know," Marci said, looking up at the hole again. "But Julius was always the one who found all the loopholes. I'm just..." *Dead,* she finished to herself. Dead and trapped between her dad and a hard place. But as she was getting nice and depressed about that, something her father had said came back to bother her.

"You said you were inside the Empty Wind as he did his job," she said, looking at him. "What job was that specifically?"

"Finding and rescuing the Forgotten Dead," Aldo replied without missing a beat. "When a person is forgotten by everyone, they become part of the Empty Wind's domain, which means he can hear their voices and come to them. If they're lucky, he finds them before their death fills in completely and they're torn apart by the magic. That's why he's a wind. He has to be fast."

"That can't be right," Marci said. "If everyone gets forgotten, that means the Empty Wind is basically all of death. Are there no other options?"

Aldo shook his head. "None that I know of."

"But that's crazy," she said. "Ghost is only one spirit, and he only rose a month and a half ago. What happened to human souls before that?"

Her father shrugged helplessly, but when Marci looked at Amelia, the little dragoness was deep in thought. "That's a very good question," she said at last. "The last time I studied mortal death was before the disappearance of magic. I never made it to this side, obviously, but I knew several death gods."

Marci's jaw dropped. "You knew *gods*?"

"That's what we called Mortal Spirits back then," Amelia explained. "Anyway, I didn't know the Empty Wind specifically back then, but—no surprise considering how obsessed mortals have always been with the subject—there were tons of death-related spirits who flitted around the Sea of Magic, plucking human souls out of their deaths and carrying them off to wherever was appropriate. I was actually trying to seduce one to get more information when the drought hit and all the spirits vanished. So, since I couldn't get information and didn't have to worry about mortality myself, I abandoned the subject and turned all my attention to planar travel. Mostly so I could get out of this newly magicless dump. But now that you bring it up, I wonder. What *did* happen to human souls during the drought?"

"I'm more amazed that the afterlife was apparently governed by Mortal Spirits," Marci said. "Mortal Spirits are the ones we create, so you basically just told me that humanity makes our own gods."

"Pretty much," Amelia said. "But just because you thought them up doesn't make them any less godly, or terrifying. Humans have always created their own monsters. Excluding dragons, of course. We're imports."

Marci nodded, head spinning. This was a lot to take in, but it made her more determined than ever to get out of here. She was teetering on the edge of so many secrets. All she had to do was reach a little further, find out just a little more, and everything would snap together. It must have been clear on her face, too, because her father sighed.

"You're going to leave."

It wasn't a question, but Marci nodded anyway. "I'm sorry, Daddy, but I didn't die to stay safe and not know. There's so much we lost during the drought, so much knowledge that humanity needs if we're going to survive, and I think I might be on the edge of figuring it out. Algonquin herself said the magic didn't vanish a thousand years ago for no reason. She thinks the Merlins had a hand in it. I don't know if that's right, but if the return of Mortal Spirits means bringing back the gods who save the souls of the dead—that's a *big deal.* Well worth risking what's left of my death. Besides, I can't stay here knowing that I'm living in a house built on Julius's mourning. I don't want him to love me when I'm dead. I want him to love me when I'm there to enjoy it. I want my *life* back, and if risking my soul is what it takes, then I'm ready. I know what I want. I've always known. The only thing holding me back is what happens to you."

She hadn't meant for that to sound quite so accusatory, but to her enormous relief, her father looked pleased rather than offended. "We always did look out for each other, didn't we, *carina?*"

"Of course," she said, reaching down to squeeze his hand. "You're my dad."

"And you're my baby girl," he whispered, squeezing back. "That's why I had to try. I knew you wouldn't want to stay. You've always charged ahead, but I had to try to keep you safe. If you are determined to see this through, though, I have no right to stop you. Your life stopped being mine to dictate years ago, just like my life is not your responsibility."

"Of course it is," she said angrily. "You're my father, and you're being sheltered by *my* death. If I leave and all of this collapses, what happens to you?"

Aldo looked deeply offended. "I might be a dead man, but I'm still a grown one. Of course I'd love to stay with you in this paradise, but what kind of father trades his daughter's happiness for his own? And it's not as though you're casting me out into oblivion. I always have somewhere to go. I'm forgotten, after all."

"No, you're not!" Marci cried. "I remember you again. I should never have forgotten you in the first place!"

"You did what you had to do, *carina,*" Aldo said. "And if you're serious about leaving, you're going to have to do it again."

Marci stared at him. "What?"

"Like the dragon said, I was sent here by the Empty Wind to be your guide," he explained patiently. "If I'm to do my job, I have to return to him. He can't find you on his own, but if you let me go, I will be his again, and the Empty Wind can always find what's his.

The only reason I haven't gone already was because I wanted to be sure you weren't being pushed into a decision without knowing your options. When I saw your memories, I worried the dragons were using you, but I should have known better." He chuckled. "You've always done exactly as you pleased. Nothing, not death nor dragons nor spirits, can change that. What chance did I have?"

He smiled at her, but Marci shook her head stubbornly. "I can't just forget you again. You're my father. You raised me, taught me magic. When Mom left, you were the one who stayed. The one who loved me." Her voice began to shake. "I already lost you twice. I can't lose you again."

"You already have," he said, reaching up to brush her cheek. "I'm dead, Marci. I had my life. Even better, I had you."

"And I forgot you!" she cried, disgusted with herself all over again, but her father was shaking his head.

"You gave me up," he said. "There's a difference. I'm not here because you forgot me, but because you held my memory so dear, it was strong enough to bind a god. And make no mistake, that's what you did. I lived inside the Empty Wind. I saw his anger firsthand, the horror he could have easily become, but you never let him. You dug in your heels and held him to the nobler parts of his purpose. You kept him sane, kept him safe, which was why he was able to let me go. He's never released a soul in his care before, but he would do far worse to get you back. The forgotten dead are constantly screaming at him, begging him to wreak their vengeance and right their wrongs. But as loud as they are, your voice is stronger. Dead or alive, you are his Merlin, the voice of his reason. You're the one who helps him be more than just a mindless slave to the fears and emotions that created him, and as much as I would love to stay here forever with you, he needs you more than I do."

Marci looked away. She remembered perfectly well what had happened with the dead in Algonquin's Reclamation Land, how she'd pulled Ghost back from the brink, but it was still embarrassing to hear all of that stuff from her dad. Much as it made her cringe, though, he was right. Ghost could be every bit as aloof as the cat he pretended to be, but when things got bad, she was the one he clung to. After Emily had shot her, he'd begged harder than Julius for Marci not to leave him alone. Ultimately, that was why she'd taken his hand. Not just because he saw the path to becoming a Merlin, but because as much as she'd wanted to stay with Julius, she knew her dragon could go on without her. Ghost couldn't. He was her spirit, her responsibility, and no matter the odds, Marci had to get back to him.

"Okay," she whispered, lifting her eyes at last. "What do I have to do?"

Aldo looked down at their tangled hands. "Let me go."

Marci gritted her teeth. Even when he told her to, unclamping her hands from his felt like a betrayal of everything she cared about: her family, her childhood, her old dreams. Her father was such a huge part of her life before the DFZ, Marci didn't know how things would make sense without him. But as she stared at her fingers, trying to work up the courage to unlock them, Aldo leaned forward to rest his forehead against hers.

"It's all right, *carina*," he whispered. "Even if you don't remember me, I'll always remember you. In a life of foolishness and failure, you were the one thing I got right. You are my darling now and forever, and I will never stop being proud of you."

Marci closed her eyes with a sigh. "You're not making this easier."

"You never did the easy thing," he said with a laugh. "But it's time to let go." He leaned down to kiss her cheek. "Goodbye, Marcivale."

She couldn't answer. All her goodbyes came out as sobs as she opened her hands at last.

The moment her fingers went slack, the warmth of her father's hand was replaced by bitter cold that cut like a knife. When she looked down to see why, though, all she found was a thread.

It was thin as spider's silk, glowing against her skin like blue-white moonlight. She was leaning closer to inspect it further when drops of warm water began dripping on her palm around it. Tears, she realized belatedly. Her tears, from her eyes, which made no sense at all. Marci didn't remember crying, but her eyes were wet and puffy, and her chest hurt as if she'd been heaving. Clearly, something had happened, but she couldn't remember what. All she knew was that she'd lost something, something very important, but before Marci could figure out what it was, the freezing thread across her palm began to twitch.

"What does that mean?" Amelia asked, skittering down Marci's arm to get a better look.

"I don't know," Marci said, wiping her eyes before reaching down to lift the thread away from her aching hand. It really was terrifyingly cold. Cold as the grave. As cold as—

Her whole body jerked. Even stranger, Amelia's did the same, the little dragon jumping like a startled lizard before scrambling back up Marci's arm to the shelter of her short hair behind her ear.

"Did you feel that?!"

Marci nodded, craning her head in all directions. Since she'd first woken up in her death, she and Amelia had been the only things that had moved. Now, though, a wind was picking up, blowing the dust off the gravel drive in the otherwise perfect stillness.

"Hoo boy," Amelia said, hooking her tail tight around the back of Marci's neck. "So what happens now?"

"How should *I* know?" Marci said, pushing up to her feet. "You're the expert!"

"An expert in *theory*," the tiny dragon corrected her. "I've never been dead in practice."

Marci rolled her eyes, but criticizing her friend's recklessness would have to wait. In the brief time they'd been talking, the wind had gone from a breeze to a hurricane. On the ground, dust was being swept up into cyclones, and the lights inside the house were swaying wildly where they'd left the door open. Even the parked car was starting to slide sideways, blown across the gravel drive inch by inch. How many inches, though, Marci couldn't see because she was now flat on her stomach, clinging to the asphalt roofing for dear life. But when she looked to make sure Amelia hadn't been blown away, the little red dragon was staring at the ceiling, her amber eyes wide.

At the peak of the cavern, in the middle of the terrifying black hole that led to the outside, a hand was reaching down. At least, it *looked* like a hand. It was hard to tell since it hadn't yet broken through the obsidian surface. Instead, the magic had stretched like rubber, leaving whatever it was grasping desperately through a wall of wetly shimmering black. That would have been terrifying enough on its own, but the whole thing was made a million times worse by the fact that it was all happening directly above Marci's head, the grasping hand following her unerringly no matter which way she moved. She was wondering if she should make a break for the house's storm cellar when she saw something glittering in the center of the blackness. A thread, she realized with a start, glowing in the dark like moonlight directly in the middle of the hand's grasping palm.

And just like that, Marci knew what to do.

"Hold on tight," she told the dragon on her shoulder as she dropped into a crouch. "I'm going to jump."

"Jump?" Amelia said, her voice panicked as she looked back and forth between the grasping hand above their heads and the three-story drop below. "No, no, no. Jumping off a roof is a *very* bad idea when you don't have wings."

No argument there, but the way the hole was positioned, there was no chance Marci could reach the grasping hand with just her legs. It was just too far, the roof too steep. She had to jump to make it, and the wind encouraged her, blasting up the side of the house in front of her. If she jumped, Marci was sure it would carry her up, and since the gale was already starting to lift the roof off the house, she saw no reason to hesitate. It was jump or be tossed, so Marci grabbed the burning-cold thread in her hand and went for it, leaping off the roof just as the nails gave way.

The moment her feet left the ground, she saw Amelia's point. It might have looked close, but the hand reaching through the darkness must have been much bigger than she'd realized, because now that she was moving toward it, Marci could see that hole she was jumping toward was actually several feet farther up than she'd realized, which meant she was now sailing out over nothing. But just as Marci was wondering if it was possible to die inside of your own death, the wind blowing up the side of the house caught her like a net, blasting her straight up toward the hand reaching down.

The second she was in range, Marci reached out to grab one of the giant fingers. And immediately regretted it.

When she touched the blackness, magic like nothing she'd ever felt exploded through her. It reminded her of the first time she'd pulled off Julius, only a million times more. That had felt like plugging into the sun. This was being caught in a supernova. The shock was so great, she couldn't make herself let go, not even when her hand began to dissolve in front of her eyes, her fingers vanishing like shadows in sunlight. She was still staring in horror when the giant hand clenched down, grabbing her body like a closing trap.

At this point, Marci was certain she was going to die. Again. The intense magic was all around her, dissolving her body like sugar in water. But then, just when she was sure she was dust, a shock of cold washed away everything else as the hand yanked her through the hole into darkness, and then into a freezing embrace.

"I've got you."

The voice was so loud and relieved, she barely recognized it, but the cold that followed the words felt like home.

"I've got you," Ghost said again, hugging her so tight, all the dissolved bits came back together. "I found you, Marci."

"I knew you would," she whispered back, opening her eyes against the freezing wind as she raised her head to look up at her spirit...

And saw his face.

CHAPTER THREE

Julius woke with a start.

He was still in Bob's chair, curled in a ball around Marci's bag. He didn't smell any threat, but his heart was pounding in his chest. That usually happened after a bad dream, but he didn't remember having one. He was writing it off as stress, pulling up his blanket again to go back to sleep, when he remembered he hadn't *had* a blanket when he'd fallen asleep. He was groggily trying to make sense of how one had magically appeared on top of him when he heard the soft clink of china directly beside his ear.

This time, Julius jumped out of the chair completely. He landed on his feet in a crouch with Marci's bag under one arm, Amelia's ashes in the other, and both hands raised to defend himself from whatever was in the room with him. When he looked frantically for the threat, though, all he saw was a familiar tall dragon in an impeccably neat black suit attempting to fit a large breakfast tray onto Bob's crowded desk.

"Good morning, sir," Fredrick said without looking up from the loaded tray he was balancing on the table's corner. "Did you sleep well?"

Julius stared at him blankly for a good thirty seconds, and then he collapsed back into the chair. "Don't *do* that," he gasped, clutching his chest, which his poor heart was currently trying to pound its way through. "What are you doing here?"

"Serving you breakfast," the F said as he finally got the tray steady. "Or attempting to. With all the trouble in the mountain and no Fs around to check attendance, hardly any of the human staff showed up for work this morning. The kitchen was entirely abandoned, so I had to make do with whatever I could find. I'm not quite as good a chef as my sister, but I think I managed."

From the glorious spread of toast, jam, eggs, and other breakfast items, Julius thought Fredrick had done a lot better than merely "managed," but that wasn't what he was concerned about.

"I don't mean the food," he snapped, pushing himself up again. "What are *you* doing *here*? You're supposed to be free!"

"I *am* free," Fredrick said sharply. "That's why I'm here."

Before Julius could ask what he meant by that, the dragon dropped gracefully to his knees. His hands hit the floor next, and then Fredrick bowed down, lowering his head until his short hair brushed the stone at Julius's feet.

"Great Julius," he said solemnly. "My siblings and I owe you more than we can ever repay. You fought for my clutch's freedom against the will of Brohomir and the Heartstriker herself. Because of you, we have flown free as dragons for the first time in our lives. But as joyful as I am at this, I cannot be at ease knowing how much my siblings and I owe to you. Therefore, as the eldest, I swear on my fire and my life to serve you faithfully until our clutch's debt is repaid."

He bowed lower when he finished, pressing his forehead flush against the floor before rising smoothly back to his feet. He'd already turned to the breakfast tray to start arranging a plate by the time Julius found his voice again.

"Are you kidding me?"

"I assure you, I am not," Fredrick said, picking up a white porcelain mug. "Tea or coffee? You never mentioned which you prefer to be served, so I brought both."

"Neither," Julius snapped. "And I don't want you to serve me! The whole reason I did this was so you could be free to live your own life!"

"I *am* living my own life," the F said angrily, turning to glare down at him. "That's why I'm here. Because *I* know that *I* can't live under this debt."

"But there's no debt. You don't owe me—"

"You freed us from six hundred years of slavery under Bethesda," Fredrick said, staring at him in horror. "What would you have me do? Run away and ignore what we owe?"

"*Yes!*" Julius yelled at him. "Go! Run! Fly away! Enjoy being a free dragon. *That's* what I freed you for, so you could finally escape this place. If you want to repay me, go do *that*."

By the time he finished, Fredrick looked dangerously insulted. "With all due respect, sir, your estimation of debts is a joke. The whole clan knows you let Bethesda off practically for free. But while softhearted leniency is your right as clan head, I am not so lacking in pride that I will accept it for myself or my siblings. That's why I swore on my own fire rather than offering you a life debt. I knew you would refuse it, that you would attempt to be *nice*. But this is not a matter of kindness, Great Julius. My clutch might be at the bottom of Heartstriker, but we have always had our honor. I will not allow you to make a mockery of that now with your misplaced pity."

Julius sighed so hard it hurt. "That's not what I—"

"You gave me freedom," Fredrick said over him. "But I've been a servant my entire life. It's all I know how to be. The difference is that now, thanks to you, my service is *mine* to give, and I choose to give it to you. If you don't wish me to serve you in this way, I'll find another, but I *will* repay our debt to my satisfaction, and you have no right to stop me."

He was growling deep in his throat by the time he finished, and his eyes—which looked an even brighter green than usual this morning for some reason—had narrowed to deadly slits. It was the same look Julius's other siblings got when they were threatening to eat him, only much worse, because now that he was unsealed, Julius could feel for the first time just how *big* a dragon Fredrick was.

Not that that was a total surprise—F was pretty high up the Heartstriker alphabet—but the reveal was still way more than he'd been prepared for, and the fact that Fredrick's human form was so much taller than his definitely wasn't helping. The oldest F loomed over him in every way, and as much as Julius hated the idea of debts, especially ones that involved serving, he didn't see how he was getting out of this without starting a fight he couldn't win.

Well, that wasn't entirely true. He was still wearing his Fang. But while the sword would stop Fredrick from physically attacking, it couldn't do anything to solve the real problem, which was draconic pride. Now that Fredrick had equated leniency with pity, he would fight any efforts to lessen his burden to the death. That left Julius with two options: challenge his brother, or give up and accept his service. The first was too stupid to consider, but as bad as the second made Julius feel, he had to admit it would be nice to have a dragon who was entirely on his side. And that breakfast tray did look *awfully* good.

"Okay," he said, slumping back in his chair. "I accept your service, but if you're going to work for me, I have some rules. Rule one, no bowing. You're a dragon in the new Heartstriker now, and you lower your head to no one. Rule two, no heroics." He drummed his fingers against the sword at his side. "I have this to protect me from any threat, but you can be hurt, and I'm telling you right now I won't count any unnecessary injuries against your debt."

"I would never be so cheap," Fredrick said, insulted. "But your Fang only protects you from other Heartstrikers. As your servant, I reserve the right to defend you against enemies from outside the clan."

Seeing how Julius had zero intention of getting into an altercation with outside powers, that seemed like a decent compromise. "Deal," he said with a nod. "Anything else?"

"Yes," Fredrick said, crossing his arms over his chest. "I've vowed to serve you and your interests, but in the brief time I've known you, you've displayed a near-suicidal level of disinterest in your own well-being. Therefore, since you are clearly a terrible judge of your own best interests, I will be ignoring any orders I feel are not in your actual service."

Julius had lived with dragons long enough to know that that was a dangerously open-ended agreement, but it wasn't as though he could actually tell Fredrick what to do. Whatever he said, the F was just going to do his own thing, and Julius hadn't wanted to give him orders in the first place. Either way, it wasn't worth arguing over, so he just nodded again, holding out his hand. "Welcome aboard."

The F shook his hand with a triumphant smile, dipping his head just low enough that Julius couldn't call him out for bowing before turning back to the breakfast tray. "Biscuit or toast?"

"Both," Julius said eagerly. "And tea is fine. I don't like the smell of coffee."

That was a lie. Julius loved the smell of coffee. Especially Marci's, which was the problem. Even the faint scent from the sealed carafe on Fredrick's tray was enough to trigger memories that he couldn't deal with after last night, and he turned away with a grimace. "Get rid of it, please."

Fredrick arched a curious eyebrow, but he didn't say a word. He just picked up the insulated pot and carried it out to the hall while Julius poured himself a cup of tea with lots of cream.

From there, breakfast was surprisingly pleasant. Despite Fredrick's insistence that he was a mediocre cook, his eggs and bacon were much better than anything Julius could have managed on his own. There was plenty to be had, too, which was good. Julius hadn't eaten a proper meal since the last time Fredrick had fed him after the fight with Gregory. But wrong as it felt to be served by one of the dragons he'd worked so hard to free, a guilty part of Julius was very happy Fredrick was here. After so much conflict and sorrow, it was nice to have company, and once he stopped growling at Julius about debts, the F snapped back to his usual dry, witty self. Even in the bizarre surroundings of Bob's hoarded room, it was enough to make Julius relax for the first time in ages.

At least until he heard the familiar footsteps banging down the hall.

Julius closed his eyes with a long sigh. He barely had time to put down his fork before someone started pounding on the door to Bob's room like they were trying to break it down. Fredrick didn't even have time to get over there before the door slammed open, and Justin stomped into the room.

"*There* you are," he snarled, going straight for Julius. "I was looking everywhere for…" He trailed off when he saw the tray and Fredrick, and then his eyes went wide. "No fair!" he cried. "Why do you still have an F? No one else got one!"

Fredrick stiffened, and Julius put a hand over his face. "Justin…"

"I volunteered to serve the Great Julius," Fredrick said, his scornful voice sharp enough to cut. "The rest of my clutch is free to do as they please."

"Oh, well, good thing I'm the Great Julius's knight, then," Justin said, walking eagerly over to the tray. "Are those blueberry muffins?"

He was reaching for pastries when Fredrick smacked his hand. "I serve the Great Julius *only*," he said in a deadly voice. "If you wish to eat, the kitchen is downstairs."

Justin's answer to that was to bare his teeth, and Julius leaped to intervene before something got bitten off. "You can have mine," he said, offering Justin his plate. "I can't eat all of this, and I would hate for Fredrick's work to go to waste."

"I'd rather it go to waste than to *him*," Fredrick growled as Justin took the plate. "He might be your full brother, but now that I'm free to say it, you should know that the Knight of the Heartstrikers is a spoiled, undisciplined, ungrateful—"

"That's how it is, eh?" Justin said, looking Fredrick straight in the eyes as he plucked a muffin off Julius's plate and shoved it into his mouth. "You want to show off your freedom, Freddy? I'm game. I'll take you anytime, anywhere. I win, you cook for me for a month."

For a terrifying moment, Fredrick looked like he was actually going to take that bet, but he never got the chance. Julius grabbed his Fang before the F could get a growl out, freezing both dragons in place.

"That's enough," he said firmly, glaring at both of them. "We've got plenty of enemies already. Let's not give them a head start by biting chunks out of each other."

Neither dragon looked happy about that, but eventually, they both relaxed enough for the Fang's magic to let them go. Julius held on to his sword a bit longer anyway, just to be sure. When he was certain no one was going to do anything too stupid, he turned back to Justin. "Why were you looking for me?"

"Do I need a reason?" Justin said, pausing to scrape the rest of Julius's loaded plate into his mouth, where he swallowed it all in one impressive *gulp*. "I'm your knight. My place is at your side. I would've been here sooner, but that hack of a doctor wouldn't let me out of the infirmary."

That was worrisome. True, Chelsie had eviscerated him during the fight in the treasury, but that was days ago, and this was *Justin*. He never took more than twenty-four hours to heal from anything. "Why were you still in the infirmary?"

"Nothing serious," Justin said casually, grabbing another muffin off the tray before Fredrick could stop him. "I just used up a lot of my fire smoking Vann Jeger, so I'm a bit slower on the recovery than normal."

To prove it, he pulled up his shirt, and Julius gasped. Justin's torso was covered in bandages, some of which were spotted with red. "We have to get you back to bed."

"Nothing doing," Justin said, popping the muffin into his mouth before yanking his shirt down again. "One, there's no bed to go back to. The infirmary's as empty as the rest of the mountain since the F in charge of doctoring flew the coop. And two, my place is with you. A knight stays by his clan head's side at all times. Not that you're making it easy, hiding away up here." He snorted and reached for the platter of bacon. "I should put a leash on you."

Worried as he was, Julius couldn't help but smile at that. Justin had an odd way of showing it, but it was nice to know he cared. "You should still sit down," he said, hopping up from Bob's chair. "I hurt just looking at you."

Justin rolled his eyes. "No way. I'm not a wuss like you who has to sit down every time he bleeds, and I need to be on my guard. With Conrad gone, I'm the only fighter left. If you die on my watch in an empty freaking mountain, I will *never* live it down."

That last bit was so Justin, it took Julius several seconds to realize the rest of what he'd said. "Wait, Conrad's gone? When did that happen?"

"Last night," Justin said. "I don't know what's gotten into her, but Mother's dead serious about evacuating the mountain. She sent Conrad to Washington, DC last night to help David prepare our emergency fallback position."

This was the first Julius had heard of a fallback position. "So why didn't anyone tell *me?*" he cried angrily. "Bethesda doesn't get to order an evacuation. That's a Council decision!"

"You weren't around," Justin said with a shrug. "And it's not as if there's much to evacuate. Between Chelsie's rage quit, Amelia kicking the bucket, Bob vanishing, the Fs on strike, and everyone else running off to hunker down in their own territories, Heartstriker Mountain's a ghost town. Even the human staff is playing hooky. The only reason Mother's still here is because she hasn't finished moving her treasury into the security vaults downstairs."

"Of course she is," Fredrick growled. "God forbid Bethesda put anything ahead of her gold."

"Well, she still should have called me," Julius snapped, but his heart wasn't in it. Other than pride and the fact that it was their home, there wasn't much reason to stay at Heartstriker Mountain if there was no one here to protect, and while he was angry she hadn't discussed it with him first, DC wasn't actually a bad move. They had allies there thanks to David's congressional seat, and staying in the US capital meant that any large-scale attack would be seen as an act of aggression against the United States as well as Heartstriker. Strategically speaking, they couldn't ask for a better place to lie low.

He just wished it didn't feel so much like running away.

"Hey," Justin said, lowering his voice. "I know it sucks to be driven back, but this doesn't have to be all bad. Conrad can handle Bethesda, but you're my charge, and our birthday's coming up."

Julius blinked in surprise. With everything that was happening, he'd forgotten all about his birthday until Justin mentioned it. "What does that have to do with anything?"

"Nothing," Justin said with a shrug. "But twenty-five is a milestone, and if we have to run anyway, why not go somewhere fun? I was thinking Vegas. I know you hate gambling, but the food's great, and the girls are—"

"Not Vegas."

Justin stared at him. "Why not?"

Because Marci was from Vegas. "Just not there."

His brother crossed his arms over his chest. "This is about your human, isn't it?"

When Julius didn't reply, the knight began to growl. "You can't mope about her forever, you know."

"It's only been three days," Julius reminded him.

"Yeah, well, it's not like you didn't know this was going to happen," Justin snapped back. "She's *mortal.* Death's in her definition."

Julius's jaw clenched. "Drop it, Justin."

"No," he said angrily. "This is ridiculous. You're a dragon. I'm not going to let you waste your time pining for a—"

"*I said drop it!*"

The words came out in a roar that made everyone jump, including Julius. He hadn't known he was capable of making a sound like that. At the same time, though, he had no intention of taking it back. He might not be hiding in his room anymore, but the memory of Marci's death was still an angry wound in his chest. If Justin didn't stop poking it, Julius couldn't be held responsible for his actions.

"I'm not going to Vegas," he said, more calmly now. "I'm not going *anywhere* until—"

A loud noise cut him off. All through the mountain, claxons were sounding, their high-pitched wails cutting through the stone. The emergency lights cut on a second later, filling Bob's dark cave with a red glow punctuated by bright-white flashes.

"What's that?" Julius yelled, covering his ears against the painfully loud noise.

"The panic alarm," Fredrick yelled back.

Julius paled. He'd never heard the panic alarm before. "What does it mean?"

"That there's something worth panicking about," Justin said, grabbing Julius's arm and yanking him toward the door. "We need to get to the bunker STAT."

"Shouldn't we be running?" Because if there was something a mountain full of dragons needed to panic about, a bunker didn't seem like it would do much good.

"No time," Justin said as he pulled his brother into the hall. "Fredrick?"

"On it," Fredrick said, darting past them down the flashing hall to the elevator, and then past *that* to what looked like a blank space on the wall. A space that turned out not to be blank at all when Fredrick pressed his fingers against a crack in the stone.

"Here," he said, swinging the wall open to reveal a small emergency stair leading down.

Justin grinned. "Always count on an F to know the bolt-holes," he said, shoving Julius inside. "Move."

Julius didn't wait to be told twice. He was already running down the stairs after Fredrick. Justin followed on his heels, pausing just long enough to close the secret door on the alarms blaring behind them.

• • •

They changed tunnels several times, following Fredrick through a labyrinth of secret passages that crisscrossed the normal hallways and staircases before eventually stopping at an elevator. Not a nice one, either. This was a terrifying-looking steel box on a cable at the top of an open shaft that went straight down. In all his years in the mountain, Julius had never seen anything like it. He couldn't even say where in the fortress they were after all those turns, but he didn't waste time asking questions. He just followed his brothers through the elevator's open gate, sticking close to Justin as he hit the lone red button to start the drop.

Even plummeting through the dark at nauseating speeds, it still took a solid minute of falling before the stripped-down elevator finally jerked to a stop. When the steel cage rolled open, the stone of the hallway outside wasn't even the same color as the mountain above, which Julius took as a sign that they were even deeper than the basement tunnel where Chelsie and the Fs hid their secret rooms. Deeper than he'd ever gone before, down below the roots of the mountain itself.

"This is crazy," Julius whispered as Justin herded them out. "I knew the emergency bunker was deep, but not *this* deep."

"That's because it's not," Fredrick said, moving out of the way as Justin stomped past to punch a key code into the pad beside the metal door at the end of the short tunnel. "The emergency bunker is a quarter mile above us. This is the deep bunker."

Julius gaped at him. "How many bunkers do we have?!"

"When everyone wants to kill you? Never enough," Justin said as the light above the door turned green. "In."

The heavy bolt had barely cleared the lock before Justin yanked it open, tossing the foot-thick metal security door aside as though it were made of cardboard to reveal an enormous room that looked like a cross between a natural cavern and NASA Mission Control.

Unlike every other room in Heartstriker Mountain, which had been hollowed out of the stone to suit the needs of the mountain's draconic masters, this one seemed to be a natural formation. It had gently curving walls, water running down one corner, and stalactites hanging from the ceiling high overhead. There'd been stalagmites on the ground as well at one point, but they'd all been shaved off to create a floor for the massive array of computer consoles and spellwork control circles. Human ones, oddly enough.

"Why are we using human magic for our wards?" Julius asked as Justin herded them inside.

"Because Bethesda doesn't trust any of us to do it," Fredrick explained, looking around at the empty chairs. "Though where the mages who're supposed to be operating them are right now is anyone's guess."

That didn't sound good. "Should we call someone?"

"No time," Justin said, marching over to one of the larger consoles. "We'll just have to get by without—"

He cut off as the steel door behind them swung open again, and Bethesda herself swept into the room. The alarm must have woken her, because she was wearing a floor length, blood-red, see-through lace negligee. Her hair was brushed out perfectly, though, so it might have just been a dress. With his mother, it was hard to tell.

"I should have known I wouldn't be lucky enough to get here first," she grumbled when she saw Julius. "I was hoping to lock you out." She turned her glare to Justin. "Why are you always so fast?"

"Because I do my job," Justin said, poking at the machine in front of him. "How does this thing work again?"

"Oh, let me," Bethesda snapped, hiking up her lacy skirt as she hurried across the cave to take Justin's place in front of the central command console. "Fredrick," she said as she placed her hands on the controls. "I have no idea why you're still skulking about, but if you don't want to die, I suggest you take the drones."

Given that he was already in front of the console with the name of a major drone manufacturer printed across the front, it looked as though Fredrick was already doing just that. He stopped the moment Bethesda gave him an order, though. A move that did not go unnoticed.

"What do you think you're doing?" she growled.

"Whatever I please," Fredrick growled back, staring at her with pure, unfiltered hate. "I serve Julius now. Not you."

"You *can't* be serious."

Fredrick's reply was to just keep glaring, and Bethesda pressed a hand to her forehead. "You *are*," she groaned, closing her eyes. "What have we become?"

"Better without you," Fredrick said, giving their mother one last poisonous look before turning to Julius. "What are your orders, sir?"

Julius bit his lip. "Um, what can you do?" Because he had no idea how any of this worked. He hadn't even known they *had* a room like this until a few minutes ago.

The F turned back to the large console in front of him. It lit up the second his hands got close, throwing a complicated web of augmented reality interface options into the air above it. Fredrick plunged his fingers into the commands, and screens covering the walls flickered to life with multiple camera feeds from all over the surrounding desert.

"That works," Julius said, grinning. "Good job, Fredrick. Thank you."

"All of my clutch were taught to use the mountain's security systems," he said with a shrug. "But you're welcome, sir."

Bethesda made a disgusted sound, but she kept any actual comments to herself as she focused on the AR controls above her own console. "I'll take the perimeter. Fredrick, you focus on quadrant one. I want to know what tripped that alarm."

Only when Julius nodded did Fredrick obey, pulling up a large map of the desert surrounding Heartstriker Mountain and waving his hand over the southwestern portion. A second later, the map filled with tiny green dots that began moving in unison as all the screens on the walls flipped to show camera feeds from that part of the desert. "Drones are up."

"Good, because everything else is down," Bethesda growled, scowling into the floating interface in front of her. "I don't understand. I *just* had the sensors checked last…"

Her voice faded as she looked up at the picture that had just appeared on the biggest screen in front of them. From the high angle and the way it was weaving back and forth, the shot was clearly from a drone, but what the camera was actually showing was far harder to make out. All Julius could tell was that something was flying through the western edge of the Heartstriker's airspace. Several somethings, moving very fast, but the *way* they moved didn't make sense at all. They weren't soaring like planes or flapping like birds or even floating on the wind. They were *snaking*, weaving through the clear desert morning like eels in a tight, undulating formation.

"What is that?" Julius asked, squinting at the screen. "Some kind of water spirit?"

"Don't be stupid," Bethesda said, her face pale. "Those are dragons."

That couldn't be right. "But they have no wings," he said, pointing at the snaking shapes. "What kind of dragon doesn't have wings?"

"Chinese ones," Fredrick replied in a tight voice.

Julius's eyes went wide. Since his clan was banned from China, he'd never paid attention to the Chinese clans beyond what showed up on the mainstream news. Even now that he knew what he was looking at, the undulating shapes on the screen still didn't look like any dragons he'd seen. They were too long and compact, their sleek bodies sliding effortlessly through the morning air like silk through the sea. The longer he watched, though, the more similarities he found. They might not move how he was used to, but they had dragon heads and dragon teeth, dragon claws on their curled dragon feet. Most telling of all, though, was that they were beautiful. Breathtakingly so, in the dangerous, deadly way that only truly old and powerful dragons could be.

Even at this distance, watching through a drone camera, he could see power shimmering over the already brilliant red, green, and cobalt of their fishlike scales. Some of them even had manes, huge tufts of brightly colored fur that made them look like lions. Others had long horns that rose from their heads in smooth, arcing forks. The lack of wings let them fly in tight formation, the whole pack moving as one like a school of fish, making it impossible to tell their true numbers as they shot through the early-morning sky toward the mountain.

"They're coming right at us," Justin announced.

"Where else would they be going?" Bethesda said irritably. "We're the only things out here." She slammed her fists on the console. "I *told* you we were going to be invaded!"

"Let's not jump to conclusions," Julius said. "We don't know it's an invasion yet."

"Oh, come *on*, Julius!" she cried, whirling around. "Even you can't be this naïve. The day after I explain to you we're sitting ducks, a flock of foreign dragons charges our airspace. What do you think they're here to do? Say hello?" She cast a nervous glance up at the screen. "I'm just glad Chelsie's gone."

"Why?" he asked, suddenly suspicious. "What does she have to do with this?"

"I'd *love* to tell you," his mother replied. "Alas, you made me swear on my fire to keep that secret, so I'm afraid you'll just have to wallow in your own irony. In the meanwhile, we need to prove that a wounded clan is a far cry from a dead one. Justin?"

The knight's head popped up at his name, and Bethesda shot him a deadly smile. "Show these snakes the price of trespassing on Heartstriker land."

The words were barely out of her mouth before Justin's grin grew to match her own. "On it," he said, striding over to tap the surface of a very black, very deadly-looking console in the far corner of the room. Unlike the others, though, this was one he clearly knew how to use, tapping his fingers through the AR until the whole interface turned an ugly, angry red. "Missiles armed."

"Wait, missiles?" Julius said. "We have *missiles*?"

"Of course we have missiles," Bethesda said as the red interface appeared on her command console as well. "Whose mountain do you think this is?"

Before he could reply, she swept her hand through the tangle of menus floating in the air above her console, painting the undulating shapes of the dragons on the screen above with candy-red target icons. She was halfway through by the time Julius made it to her side.

"Mother, *stop*!" he cried frantically, grabbing her arm. "We can't just shoot down any dragon who flies over our territory!"

"Of course we can," she said, yanking out of his grip. "It's *our* territory. They'd do the same thing if we flew into Beijing."

That was probably true. Still. "We don't even know for certain why they're here yet! Shouldn't we at least fire a warning shot or—"

"And waste a surprise attack?" She rolled her eyes. "You are clearly not a wartime consigliere."

"But—"

"You can ask them about their intentions all you like once they're on the ground," she said in a patronizing voice. "For now…"

She brought her fist down on the command grid with a blood-thirsty grin, and a new set of sirens began to scream as missile launch warnings flashed on every monitor in the room. The ground above them began to rumble a second later, but as Julius braced for the inevitable roar of rockets, everything went suddenly quiet.

The triumphant smile slipped off Bethesda's face.

"What happened?" she demanded, hunching over her console. "Why aren't they launching?"

"It's aborted," Justin said, nodding at the cascade of flashing warning messages covering the missile system's AR. "Looks like a system failure."

Growling low in her throat, Bethesda shoved away from the central command console and marched over to his. Pushing Justin out of the way, she stabbed her manicured nails through the floating mesh of missile commands, grabbing the floating error messages and yanking them closer so she could read what had gone wrong. The longer she stared at them, though, the more confused she appeared.

"That's impossible," she said at last.

"What's impossible?" Julius asked, hopes rising.

"This!" she cried, flinging her hands up at the interface. "It's not a system failure. Every single missile just threw an error, and not even the same one. If they'd all failed the same way, I could see it being a hacker or a bug, but one hundred and forty-four missiles having unique fatal malfunctions at the *exact same time*? That doesn't happen! The odds would be—"

She stopped cold, green eyes going wide. "Oh no," she whispered, looking back up at the dragons on the screen. "No, no, *no*."

She started cursing after that, spewing a crescendo of profanity in an impressive number of languages. The outburst was even more shocking for Julius than the panic alarm had been, because though his mother often lost her temper, she rarely cursed. It was low class, she'd claimed, a mark of vulgarity. But she seemed to be making it up for it now, and the worst part was, Julius didn't know what had set her off. Other than getting closer, the knot of dragons looked the same now as it had before she'd tried to attack. He was staring at the beautiful shapes on the screen, trying to figure it out, when the rising sun broke over the peak of Heartstriker Mountain, lighting up something shiny and golden hidden at the center of the pack.

"What's that?" he said, squinting at the lovely spark of gold that was blinding even through the cameras.

"The end of the road," his mother said bitterly, finally switching back to English. "*That*, my dear idiot son, is the Qilin. The Golden Emperor, which is only appropriate, because we are *imperially* screwed."

He stared at the screen in wonder. "But I thought the Golden Emperor never left China?"

"He doesn't," Bethesda snarled. "Which is why I'm *upset*. Though at least this explains what happened to my missiles."

"What does his being here have to do with our missiles failing?"

His mother looked at him like he was insane. "Did you sleep through *all* your dragon politics classes?"

"I went to class!" Julius cried. Sometimes. When he wasn't hiding to escape being the rest of J-clutch's punching bag or spell practice dummy, or both. "But we didn't exactly spend much time on China since our entire family is banned from setting foot in the country."

Bethesda closed her eyes. "For the love of—*Fine.*" She marched to the front of the bunker, stiletto heels clicking furiously on the stone as she stopped under the wall of monitors and reached up to tap her nail on the one showing a close-up of the knot of dragons.

"You see all these colored dragons?" she said in her most patronizing voice. "These are members of the Twenty Sacred Clans, the original dragon clans of China who were conquered thousands of years ago by the first Golden Emperor. I thought initially they were all we were dealing with. You know, a normal invasion force composed of soldiers and shock troops. Alas, it seems we're not that lucky, because they brought their boss."

She rose up on her tiptoes to point at the gleam of gold hidden inside the dragon's tight formation. "Now do you understand? This isn't some errant thuggery to take advantage of our weakness. That's the *Golden Emperor*, the Qilin, Greatest Dragon of China, the Luck Dragon, Living Embodiment of All Good Fortune, the—"

"I've heard his titles," Julius interrupted. "And I see how him being here is bad, but—"

"Clearly, you *don't* see," Bethesda snapped. "Because if you did, you'd know those aren't just titles. I'm called 'The Heartstriker' because of what I've done, but the Qilin is called 'the Living Embodiment of All Good Fortune' because that's what he *is*. He's a luck dragon. *Literally*. That's how he conquered all the dragons in China without losing any of his own. That's how he conquered the modern human nation of China in less than three days after the return of magic and how he's held it for the last sixty years without a single rebellion. It's not because he's an amazing general or a brilliant tactician. It's because that's how his magic works. Anything he desires—power, empire, the wealth of nations, other dragons—his good fortune gives him, and now we're in his sights."

She said all of this as though it were indisputable fact, but Julius still couldn't wrap his head around it. "How is that possible? Is he some kind of seer?"

Bethesda scoffed. "Of course not. Seers see the future and use that knowledge to make sure events happen in their favor, but their magic can't actually change events. They can only see, not shove. The Qilin is the opposite. He can't see the future any more than we can, but his magic moves it around like clay, manipulating events blindly to ensure that he always gets what he wants. That's how you end up with every missile in our arsenal independently throwing a different error the moment I decide to shoot him out of the sky. It's all just bad luck."

"I thought you said the Qilin brought *good* luck."

"Bad luck for your enemies is good luck for you," she said. "And Heartstriker is most *definitely* the Qilin's enemy. Who do you think banished us from China?"

If he'd thought he'd get anywhere this time, Julius would have taken that opening to ask, why? What had happened to make the Qilin hate their clan so much? But he'd hit the brick wall of China too many times at this point to even waste his breath. Whatever had happened in the past would have to stay there for now. He was more concerned with surviving the next few minutes.

"We need to find out why they're here."

"What's to find out?" Bethesda asked. "They're the second-biggest clan in the world. We're the first, and we're vulnerable." She shrugged. "Seems pretty obvious to me."

"But how did they *know* we were vulnerable?" he asked. "It's not like we've put out a press release."

"Because this is the Qilin!" she cried. "He doesn't need normal things like inside knowledge to win. Whatever day he picked was bound to be the right day because that's how he works. He doesn't have to try. Everything he wants simply *happens*."

"Then we should make something happen first," Justin said, grabbing his Fang. "I say we go out there and—"

"No," Julius said. "We can't do that."

His brother's face fell into a dangerous scowl, and Julius sighed. "I'm not doubting your capabilities, Justin, but look around. There's only four of us. Three if you take out Bethesda, who's sealed. That's about a hundred short of what we'd need to fight a force that size."

"He *did* bring a lot," Fredrick agreed, still glued to his drone screens. "I've been trying to get a head count. The tight formation makes it difficult, but I estimate we're looking at fifty dragons. At least."

"Fifty?" Justin said, incredulous. "Last I heard, the entire Golden Court only had eighty-two. Did he bring every dragon in China?"

"Well, at least we know he's taking us seriously," Bethesda pointed out. "What a comfort that will be when he's putting our heads on pikes."

Julius sighed. "You're not helping, Mother."

"And you are?" she drawled, glowering at him. "If you're so confident, Julius, what would *you* suggest we do? Talk nicely?"

"Actually," he said, "that's exactly what I plan to do."

Bethesda's eyes went wide, and then she dropped her head to her hands. "I knew it," she groaned. "We're doomed."

"We are not doomed," Julius said, exasperated. "Stop being ridiculous for a moment and listen. I might not understand the Qilin's magic a hundred percent yet, but I've seen enough to guess it's not the sort of thing we can bash our way through. That said, he hasn't actually attacked us yet. If your claims about his power are true, Mother, then his luck could have just as easily caused those missiles to explode on top of us rather than simply not work. Since they *didn't*, we can assume the Qilin wants us alive, at least for now. That's something we can work with." He stared at the tight formation of dragons on the screen. "I think our best option is to go out there and see what he wants."

"He *wants* our clan," Bethesda said. "And you're telling us to give it to him!"

"What else are we going to do?" he cried. "We can't fight. Negotiation is all we have left."

"It's not a negotiation when you have no power," his mother said, but the words weren't angry this time. They were hopeless, which was almost worse. "This is going to be a surrender."

"Not if we play it right," Julius said stubbornly, pulling himself straight. "I didn't go through all the pain of standing up to you and forming a Council to give up now. We might be alone here, but our clan is still alive."

"For now," Justin said.

"Now's all that matters," he said firmly, keeping his eyes on his mother. "As I just said, if the Golden Emperor wanted us dead, we'd already be gone. Since we're not, we have to assume he wants something else. That's power if we can use it, so I say we try. I mean, what have we got to lose?"

Bethesda slumped back against her console. "I don't know if you're pathetic or accidentally brilliant," she said, shaking her head. "But I wasn't looking forward to running..."

She trailed off with a sigh, and then she pushed herself back up straight, squaring her shoulders with a flip of her glossy black hair.

"Fine," she said, looking down her nose at Julius. "You win. Let's go *talk*. If nothing else, we'll die facing our enemy."

"We'll die as Heartstrikers should," Justin said proudly, drawing his sword.

"Stop that," Julius said angrily. "No one is going to die, and you are not coming with us."

Justin went very still. "What did you say?"

The words came out in a terrifying growl, and Julius flinched back instinctively. He knew that look on his brother's face. He wasn't sure what came after it since he'd usually already surrendered by this point, but not this time.

His brother was as brave as dragons got, but he was also injured, outnumbered, and couldn't be trusted not to start a fight if his life depended on it, which it did. Things weren't looking good for any of them, but if Justin went up there, he would almost certainly die. That wasn't a risk Julius was willing to take. Not over something this stupid. Not when he'd lost so many already.

He didn't care if Justin hated him forever, he would not allow him to walk out and face what might very well be their deaths. Unfortunately, this wasn't something he could explain to his brother easily. Even if he could get Justin to admit he was too injured to fight, he'd insist on going with them anyway because he was pig-headed like that. But Justin management had been a vital J-clutch survival tactic from the moment they'd hatched, and unlike every other part of being a dragon, it was one Julius excelled at. He used that knowledge now, pulling on every bit of his experience as he looked pleadingly at his older brother and spoke the words that never failed.

"I need your help."

"Of course you do," Justin said. "Have you seen how many dragons are out there? They'll eat you alive without me."

"That's just it," Julius said. "They *will* try to eat me if you're there. Without you, though, I think we might have a chance."

Justin blinked. "Come again?"

"You're a power of the clan," he explained. "A Knight of Heartstriker. If you went out there, they'd have to fight, but Bethesda and I are different. She's sealed, and I'm a weakling. If we go out there alone, attacking us will be beneath the Qilin's dignity. That buys us a chance to talk, which is the entire point of this."

"But you're the clan head," he growled. "I'm your knight. My duty lies with you."

"Your duty is to protect the clan," Julius said. "We can't risk you, Justin. With Chelsie gone, Bob doing who knows what, and Mother and I trapped here, you and Conrad are the only two active Fangs we have left. If we go down, we need you to rally the rest of Heartstriker. *I* need you to—"

"Forget it," Justin snarled, getting in Julius's face. "You think I can't see what you're doing? I'm your brother, idiot. I know you, and if you think for one second I'm going to let you go out there alone to do your Nice Dragon nonsense without backup, you're a bigger moron than Mother says."

Julius sighed. "Justin—"

"No!" his brother yelled. "I look after you. Always have, always will. End of story."

"I don't need you to look after me."

"Too bad. I—"

"*Justin!*"

Justin blinked in surprise, and he wasn't the only one. Bethesda and Fredrick were staring at him as well, but Julius refused to back down. He was touched that his brother cared so much, but he couldn't let Justin treat him like a whelp who needed to be carried around anymore. Especially since this was the one part of being clan head he was actually confident he *could* do.

"Have some faith in me," he said. "You've seen me talk my way out of tighter spots than this. Mother and I will be fine, but without Chelsie to force them together, the rest of the clan could easily fall apart. I can't let that happen, not after everything we went through, so I'm begging you, Justin, help me do this. Don't waste yourself fighting here. Go find Conrad and David, tell them what's going on, rally the clan to fight off whatever the emperor has in store for us. *That's* what I need from you, not this." He reached out to touch the sword in Justin's hands. "If you want to be my knight, protect what I care about most. Don't let Heartstriker fall just when we've finally started to change things."

That was his last, biggest card, and it seemed to work. Justin didn't look happy, but he didn't argue, either. He just stood there, thinking while Julius sweated, until, at long last, he turned away.

"I'll take the southern emergency tunnel," he said, sheathing his Fang. "There's a canyon at the end I can use to make an unobserved take-off. As soon as I get reinforcements, I'll be back." He glared over his shoulder at Julius. "Don't you dare die."

"I won't," Julius promised. Then, before he could chicken out, he stepped forward and gave his brother a hug. "Thank you, Justin."

"Get off me," Justin growled, but it still took him a suspiciously long time to wiggle out of his brother's grasp. "Just make sure you don't screw up, okay? And don't let Fredrick save you. If I get shown up by an F, my reputation's over."

Julius nodded. "I owe you."

"Big time," Justin agreed, giving him a final scowl before he walked out the door. When it swung shut behind him, Julius turned to find his mother watching.

"That was smoothly played," she said, twisting her glossy black hair thoughtfully between her fingers. "I always forget how manipulative you can be for a supposedly nice dragon. All it took was a few well-chosen words, and the loose cannon was neatly packed up and sent off toward something actually useful. If you weren't so disgustingly emotional about it, I'd *almost* be proud."

Julius decided to ignore that, glancing at the monitors instead for a final check on the enemy's position. Sure enough, the knot of dragons was starting to separate, with some peeling off to keep watch from the sky while the rest came in for a landing. When he was certain none of the watchers were headed for the tunnel Justin was taking, Julius turned and walked toward the door. Bethesda followed him a second later. It wasn't until they were in the hallway, though, that Julius realized someone was missing.

"Fredrick?" he called, sticking his head back through the heavy door to look for the F, who was still staring spellbound at the landing Chinese dragons. "Are you coming, or do you want to stay down here? Because I don't blame you at all if—"

"No," Fredrick said, tearing himself away from the screen. "I'll stay with you, of course. Forgive me."

Julius didn't see how there was anything to forgive. He actually thought the F would fare much better down here. If nothing else, he could let the rest of the clan know if this turned out to be a terrible idea. But Fredrick was already glued back at his side, and Julius had no time to argue. The elevator Justin had taken up to the standard emergency bunkers flew back down moments after he pushed the button, ready to whisk them up to the surface for their first—and perhaps last—meeting with the Golden Emperor.

• • •

By the time they made it all the way back up to the ground floor, the desert was full of dragons.

The Chinese dragons had completely surrounded Heartstriker Mountain. Julius could actually hear claws digging into the stone over their heads as the three of them hurried through the elegant marble lobby. Thankfully, though, none of the invaders seemed to be actually trying to get *in*. They were just sitting on top of the exits, biding their time until the Heartstrikers emerged.

"Like wolves watching a rabbit den," Bethesda muttered, picking nervously at the lace of her crimson negligee-dress.

"I just hope they're only watching the obvious doors," Julius whispered back. "If they catch Justin—"

"Anyone who catches Justin deserves what they get," Bethesda said, lifting her chin. "Let's get this over with."

Julius nodded, but their mother was already gone, marching through the double row of tinted, climate-controlled glass doors and out of the fortress entirely. Motioning frantically for Fredrick to stay in the lobby, Julius ran after her, matching his mother's long stride as the two of them left the shelter of the roofed, hotel-style driveway and started down the road toward the jewel-colored dragons waiting for them where the white pavement of the mountain's stately private drive met the blacktop of the ruler-straight desert highway.

It was a lot farther than it looked. Despite living here nearly all his life, Julius had never actually gone out the front of Heartstriker Mountain on foot. Pretty as the desert could be, there was simply no point in *walking* into hundreds of miles of flat dirt and broken rocks when you could drive or fly, and his sense of distance was further skewed by the dragons they were walking toward.

He'd known the Chinese dragons were big when they'd flown in, but seeing the giant shapes on camera and approaching them on foot were two entirely different experiences. Even Bethesda was starting to look intimidated as they closed the final distance, stepping off the driveway into the shadow of two enormous crimson dragons that were both easily as long as Conrad was in his armor. They weren't quite as bulky thanks to the lack of wings, but it was still a terrifying thing to walk between. Julius was focusing on just getting through without cowering when the dragon on the right twitched his tail, and a giant wall of gleaming crimson scales landed on the road in front of them.

Both Heartstrikers stopped, then Bethesda crossed her arms over her chest and yelled something at the dragons in what Julius assumed must be very bad Chinese. Whatever she said, it made the dragon on the left scowl before replying in much more beautiful tones, his deep voice ringing through the sunny desert morning like music.

"Fantastic," his mother growled.

"What?" Julius asked breathlessly. "What did he say?"

"Nothing important. Just that the Golden Emperor hasn't landed yet." Her lips curled in a sneer. "It seems we are expected to *wait* for our own conquest."

That didn't make sense to Julius. He'd seen all the dragons fly in together. Why would the emperor suddenly not be here? "Where did he go?"

"How should I know?" Bethesda snapped. "He's probably taking a turn around the desert. You know, admiring his new property. Or he could just be making us wait to show us he's the one with the power. Either way, I do *not* appreciate it. This situation is degrading enough without being forced to stand around like peasants awaiting an audience."

Both of those were perfectly plausible explanations, though personally, Julius hoped the emperor was wasting their time as a power move. It was a jerk thing to do but still completely within the bounds of normal dragon behavior, and far preferable to the alternative. If the Golden Emperor already saw the Heartstriker lands as his, then they were wasting their time. He was turning to ask his mother if she could press the red dragons for more information when he heard a strange sound on the wind.

Far above them, something was jingling musically in the sky. It sounded like coins falling onto stone from a great height, but bigger. *Richer*, and it was getting closer by the second. When he looked up to see where the impossibly beautiful sound was coming from, though, all he got was a blinding flash of sunlight. He was still blinking the spots out of his eyes when the giant golden dragon landed almost on top of them.

Despite seeing the flashes on the cameras, it hadn't occurred to Julius until this moment that the Golden Emperor would *actually* be golden. Even now, with the truth standing directly in front of him, he knew he couldn't actually be seeing what he thought he saw. There was just no way a dragon could be made of metal and still be alive. But no matter how impossible the sight seemed, Julius had no other explanation for the unmistakable metallic gleam of pure, soft, yellow gold that shone from every overlapping scale. If it weren't for the curl of smoke drifting between his sharp white teeth, Julius would have sworn he was staring at a statue instead of an actual living dragon.

It wasn't just the gold that made him look that way, either. Every inch of the dragon's body was perfectly proportioned, making him look more like the golden ideal of a dragon than something that could actually occur in real life. Even when the Golden Emperor lowered his elegant horned head to allow his passenger—an elderly Chinese woman smothered from head to toe in brocaded black silk—to step down, the motion looked too ethereally graceful to be true. Julius was still staring at it in stunned wonder when the magnificent golden dragon vanished in a puff of smoke.

Even *that* was like watching poetry. The smoke shone white as new snow in the morning sunlight, floating over the rocky sand in perfect, billowing clouds that smelled of incense and dragon magic so strong, it burned Julius's nose. Bethesda actually took a step back when it hit her, her green eyes widening in fear as the smoke blew away to reveal the man who was now standing in the dragon's place.

He was beautiful, of course. This was nothing new since all dragons were pleasing to look at in their human guise, but what struck Julius was the *way* in which he was beautiful.

Though it was no longer golden, the Emperor's human form was every bit as supernaturally perfect as his dragon had been. Every detail—the fall of his long black hair, the perfect smoothness of his skin, the way the golden robe the attending blue dragon quickly wrapped around him hung in perfect balance from his flawless shoulders—looked as though it had been designed that way on purpose. As if he were the subject in a painting whose every nuance had been prearranged to appear at best advantage, and only after great deliberation. Nothing, not even the odd square of golden silk the blue dragon placed over the emperor's head like a veil, looked messy or out of place. It was all just…perfect. Terrifyingly so. As he watched, it was easy for Julius to believe that the Golden Emperor was the only truly real thing in the universe. A feeling that only intensified when the golden dragon turned at last to look at the two Heartstrikers who'd come out to meet him.

Or, at least, Julius assumed the emperor was looking at them. He couldn't actually see his face through the golden silk cloth that was draped over his head like a death shroud. Anyone else would have looked silly standing barefoot in the desert wearing only a hastily knotted silk robe and a cloth over his head, but Julius didn't think it was possible for this dragon to look anything other than exactly as he should. But while the emperor was clearly the center of everything, it was the old woman that spoke first. Old *dragoness*, Julius realized with a start, because while she looked frail and human, her scent was pure, sharp, angry dragon as she planted her cane on the desert road, pushing herself up to glare at Bethesda over the red dragon's guarding scales.

"Whore of the Heartstrikers."

Julius cringed. That was never a good beginning. To his amazement, though, his mother didn't explode. She just pulled herself taller, staring down her nose at the hunchbacked dragoness like the old crone was a stain on one of her designer gowns.

"Fenghuang."

He blinked in surprise. "Fenghuang" had been the name of his and Marci's favorite Chinese takeout place in the DFZ. From the logo on the menu, he'd gathered it was the Chinese word for phoenix. But while that sounded suitably auspicious to him, the surrounding dragons were acting as though Bethesda had just spat in the old dragoness's face.

The blue dragon who'd assisted the emperor with his robe in particular looked ready to explode. "Your tongue is not worthy to address the Empress Mother by her given name, Broodmare!" he yelled, snapping his teeth through a shimmer of blue magical fire.

Bethesda snapped right back at him, and Julius decided he'd better step in before something important got snapped off.

"You must be the Empress Mother," he said, placing himself between his mother and the others. "I'm Julius Heartstriker, youngest son of Bethesda and one of the three members of the new Heartstriker Council. On behalf of my clan, we welcome the Golden Emperor to Heartstriker Mountain."

The Empress Mother didn't seem to buy the welcome part for a second, but her wispy eyebrows rose at the word *council*. "So the rumors are true," she said, glancing over her shoulder at the veiled emperor, who had yet to say a word. "The Broodmare has finally been overthrown by her children."

"Actually, we're a representative body," Julius said, moving closer to his mother, who was being dangerously quiet. "Of which Bethesda the Heartstriker is an important part."

"Is she?" The Empress Mother chuckled. "I'm not surprised to hear you discovered a way to cling to power, Broodmare. You always were desperate and shameless, though I didn't think you'd sink so low as to elevate your *youngest* son. Tell me, did the older ones have too much pride to serve beside their belly-crawling mother, or has the Heartstriker clan become so weak that this whelp is the best you can muster?"

If she hadn't been sealed, Bethesda probably would have been breathing fire by the time the old dragon finished. She certainly looked ready to burn something, but all Julius could do was sigh. Even if his mother hadn't started it for a change, if he waited for the two dragonesses to stop insulting each other, they'd be here all day.

Whatever bad blood lay between the emperor's mother and his own, it was obviously too much to cross in one morning. But unlike most dragon clans, which were ruled by their matriarchs, Julius had only ever heard of the Golden *Emperor*. He didn't know why the empress was doing all the talking, but unless he was greatly mistaken, she wasn't actually the one with the power here. *That* belonged to her silent son, and since things were already going just about as badly as possible, Julius decided to take a risk, pulling himself to his full height so he could look right over the hunchbacked crone's head and address the only dragon who actually mattered.

"Why are you here?"

The Golden Emperor's veiled head turned slightly, and a shiver ran through Julius's body. With the bright sunlight beating down, he couldn't see a thing through the golden silk, but that didn't matter. He could *feel* the Qilin's eyes on his skin. He was still trying to decide if it was a good feeling or a bad one when the Empress Mother lurched forward.

"Insolent *whelp*," she snarled, her red eyes blazing with what would have been terrifying fury if she hadn't been so frail. "You presume to speak to the august Qilin?!"

"Who else am I supposed to talk to?" Julius said impatiently. "He's your clan head, isn't he? And my mother and I are both heads of Heartstriker, so that makes us equals."

"You are not equal to the dirt he walks on," she spat, pulling herself as straight as her bent back allowed. "My son is the Golden Emperor, Head of All Clans and Living Embodiment of Good Fortune. You are not worthy to look upon his face, much less pollute his ears with the noise of your presumption."

She finished with an imperial version of the disdainful glare dragons had been giving Julius all his life. The one that told him he was not only beneath their notice, but actively insulting them by daring to draw it. But while that used to be enough to send him apologizing all the way back to his room, Julius was not the dragon he'd been two months ago.

"*I* didn't enter his presence," he growled, stabbing his finger at the veiled emperor. "*He* entered *ours*. I don't even understand why you're bothering to insult us. You have to know by now that our mountain is empty. My clan has already evacuated, and you can see for yourself that Bethesda is sealed. You and your dragon army could kill us any time you choose. Since you haven't yet, I can only assume there's some other reason you're here, and it would be a much better use of everyone's time if you stopped insulting us and just *told us what that was.*"

His heart was pounding by the time he finished. Bethesda looked shocked as well, staring at him with an expression he'd never seen on her face before. At least, not when she was looking at him.

"Why, Julius," she whispered, putting a hand on his shoulder. "I'm so proud of you. That was actually draconic."

It was a sign of just how badly she'd twisted him up inside that a deep part of Julius still leaped to hear his mother finally, *finally* say she was proud. He was desperately trying to remind himself that being the kind of dragon Bethesda praised was not a good thing when the Empress Mother's lip curled in disgust.

"I see the Broodmare's unmerited arrogance breeds true," she said, turning to hobble back to her son's side. "But while you are clearly undeserving of such condescension, you are correct. The Golden Emperor in his great benevolence does not desire your deaths today."

Though he'd just said as much himself, Julius let out a silent breath of relief. "Then what *do* you want?"

The Empress Mother scowled and glanced at the Golden Emperor. When his veiled head nodded, her wrinkled face grew sourer still. But while she clearly didn't like whatever she was about to say, she spoke it clearly, her raspy voice loud and heavy with the ritualistic self-importance of someone who'd spent her whole life making imperial announcements.

"Bethesda the Heartstriker, self-styled Dragon Queen of the Americas, your incompetence has long been legendary. For centuries, we have ignored your arrogant folly since the petty dramas of barbarian lands are beneath the notice of those who live in the perfect harmony of the emperor's wisdom. However, in light of recent events, we find we can no longer afford such luxuries."

She paused there, and Julius exchanged a confused look with his mother. "I'm afraid I don't—"

"A week ago," the empress went on, as if she'd just been waiting for the chance to interrupt, "the spirit Algonquin, Lady of the Lakes, declared war on all our kind. The subsequent purge of Detroit killed countless dragons, including four of our own treasured subjects. Normally, policing this threat would fall to you since the Lady of the Lakes resides in your territory, but your failure to control her rise over the past sixty years has been so complete, so extraordinarily inept, you have left the Golden Emperor no choice but to take your burden upon himself. Therefore, from this moment forward, the Heartstriker dragon clan and all its requisite powers, treaties, and territories shall be brought into the exalted presence of the divine Qilin." She lifted her chin. "We will now accept your surrender."

The Golden Emperor nodded serenely as she finished, and the dragon in blue hurried forward to hand Julius a bound scroll he could only assume was the surrender treaty. He took it out of habit, but he didn't break the seal or try to read it, mostly because he was still trying to wrap his head around what he'd just heard.

"Let me just make sure I've got this straight," he said slowly. "You're here because of *Algonquin?*"

"Don't be fooled," Bethesda growled. "That's just their excuse. They're conquering us because they *can*. They put on imperial airs, but the Qilin and his followers are no different from the rest of us. They still want all they can get."

"Do not presume to compare the august Qilin with your own base desires, Broodmare," the empress growled. "His mercy is the only reason you are still alive."

"*Such* magnanimity. Kept alive to bow." Bethesda's lips curled in a sneer. "I think I'd rather be eaten."

"That can be arranged," the Empress Mother said coldly. "Remember, Heartstriker, this is your fault. Because of your negligence, Algonquin has progressed from a minor annoyance to a threat so large, even the Great Qilin can't ignore it any longer. But though it would be far simpler to stand back and let the Lady of the Lakes drown you and all your horrid children, the Golden Emperor in his mercy has decided to spare your lives. Your youngest idiot there already holds the key to your salvation. Sign it, and we shall have no more quarrel."

Bethesda cast a disgusted look at the surrender scroll in Julius's hands. "And if I don't?"

The old dragoness smiled. "Then we will kill you and your son and as many other Heartstrikers as it takes until we find one who is capable of reason."

"You can't just kill us until someone agrees," Julius said angrily. "That's not even how our clan works. We're not an inheritance system anymore. We—"

"You say that as though you expect me to care," the empress said over him. "But since you are a young and obviously simple dragon, allow me to explain: we don't. Your clan and its politics have never been more than worms in our eyes, utterly beneath our concern. The *only* reason the Golden Emperor has lowered himself to even enter the barren waste you call home is because the weakness, ineptitude, and failure that is Heartstriker has finally become so enormous, so all-encompassing, that it can no longer be ignored. So, you see, it doesn't matter to us what insane system you've convinced your mother to go along with. You lost your right to make decisions when you became too weak to enforce them. The only choice remaining to you, little Heartstriker, is whether you and your whore of a mother bow to your new emperor as the last heads of your clan, or as heads on the ground."

From the smile on her face, it was clear which choice the empress preferred, and Bethesda looked angry enough to oblige her. If she hadn't been sealed, she would probably have already attacked, and for once, Julius didn't think he would have stopped her. It was infuriating to feel so helpless, so cornered by these smug dragons with their unbeatable power, and the fact that the oh-so-merciful Golden Emperor hadn't deigned to speak to them himself yet only made it worse. Say what you wanted about Bethesda, at least she delivered her own threats. But to demand all of this through your *mother* while you just stood there safe behind a veil? That was arrogant even by dragon standards, and though he knew he shouldn't make any decisions until he'd at least read the surrender agreement, Julius was already positive there was nothing he'd accept from these dragons. Even if the emperor offered to let them all live, Julius would never trust the clan he'd bled for to a dragon who held them all in such obvious contempt.

Unfortunately, telling the Golden Emperor to take a hike was not an option. He might hate it a lot more now that he'd met the enemy, but everything he'd said to Justin downstairs was still true. They couldn't fight the Qilin's luck. They couldn't take his dragons. They couldn't do anything. They were weak, sitting ducks, just as Bethesda had said. But though the Heartstrikers were outmatched in every possible way, the Empress Mother *was* wrong about one thing. There was still one option left to them aside from join or die.

Stall.

"I'm afraid we have a problem, then," Julius said apologetically.

The Empress Mother glared daggers at him. "What?"

"You just gave us an ultimatum," he explained. "But I keep trying to tell you, Heartstriker doesn't work like that anymore. You can threaten us all you want, but we're only two heads of a clan that's governed by a council of *three*, and our third member is currently out of the country on business. Since it takes all three of us to make any formal decisions for our clan, I'm afraid we can't sign or bow until he returns."

"Any dragon can be made to bow," the Empress Mother growled, her red eyes narrowing. "But if you are that eager to die, I would be happy to oblige."

"I'm sure you would," Julius said quickly. "But you're still missing the point. This isn't about our individual lives. Your emperor is demanding that *Heartstriker* surrender and join him, and Heartstriker's a lot more than just us. We're two-thirds of the ruling council, but the magic that governs the clan, which used to be Bethesda's alone, is now split between all of us and only enacted by the Council, whose members are elected. That means even if you chop off our heads, the power to make magically binding decisions affecting all members of the Heartstriker clan—including surrender—won't pass to an heir who might be 'more reasonable.' It'll go back to the dragons who elected us in the first place, which is where it will *stay* until they choose new leaders. So, unless you're willing to wait while our clan elects new heads to replace the ones you chop off today, you need to back down. When Ian comes home, we'll hold a vote on your surrender, but without that vote, the only way you're getting our clan to surrender is if you chase down every single Heartstriker and force each of them to bow individually, and I don't think even the Golden Emperor has that kind of patience."

"It is *you* who tests our patience," the Empress Mother snarled. "You think I can't see what you're doing, whelp? But if you think your pathetic attempts to stall—"

"I'm not trying to hide it," Julius said with a shrug. "Obviously, I don't want to die, but that doesn't mean that everything I've said isn't true. We're no longer a one-dragon dictatorship with a single point of failure. We're a true clan now, with power shared by all, so if you want us to surrender, your choices are to defeat *all* of us—which, while I'm sure you could, would be long, bloody, and expensive even by your august standards—or wait until Ian returns, which should take about a day. Once he's back, the Council will convene to formally consider your terms. Until then, you're welcome to stay at Heartstriker Mountain as our guests."

He finished with a confident smile. On the inside, though, Julius's whole body was pounding in time with his heart. None of what he'd said was a lie, but if the rest of his family was as frightened of the Golden Emperor as Bethesda seemed to be, the empress could easily kill them and get her surrender from whomever took their place. But even if the next Council came in ready to roll over, they'd still have to wait while the Heartstrikers elected someone to actually do the rolling, and considering how much trouble the last vote had been, Julius was confident he could be a pain in the Golden Emperor's side to the very end. It was small comfort, but considering his other options had been "surrender or die," Julius was pretty happy with his play. The Empress Mother, however, looked angrier than ever.

"Do not presume to play games with me, child," she said, her gnarled hands shaking on the golden handle of her cane with barely restrained fury. "Your clan has already fallen in all but the last, most formal definition. Why should we waste time pretending to be your *guests* when we've already—"

Her voice cut off like a dropped knife. Behind her, the Qilin had inclined his head. It was a tiny gesture, not even a proper nod. Julius wasn't actually sure how the Empress Mother had noticed it considering she'd been glaring at him the whole time, but the instant her son had moved, the old dragoness had gone utterly silent, leaving the air empty for the deep voice that came next.

And what a voice it was. In magnificent accord with the rest of his perfections, the emperor's voice sounded like a temple bell mixed with the world's most well-played cello and…and every other low, beautiful sound Julius could think of. It went straight through him, making him want to immediately agree with whatever was said if only to hear that heartbreaking voice speak again. He was actually daydreaming about what it would sound like when he realized that, lost in the pure joy of hearing the emperor speak, he hadn't actually comprehended a word of it.

"What?"

"I said, 'we accept,'" the emperor repeated, his deep voice just as wondrous as before, but slightly more irritated. "I have no interest in a drawn-out conquest. Already, I tire of standing in this sand pit."

He shifted his bare feet, which were resting on the only seemingly non-rocky patch of the entire New Mexico desert, and his mother clenched her jaw. "My emperor," she said. "This is obviously a ploy to waste our time."

"So it is," he agreed, turning his cloth-draped head to look up at the mountain. "But they would not be Heartstrikers if they did not connive. Still, it matters not. Whether they fall now or tomorrow, the end will be the same. We shall accept their hospitality and wait."

The enormous dragons surrounding him growled in discontent, but Julius was fighting not to grin. "We're happy to accommodate you," he said, holding out his hand to the emperor. "Welcome to Heartstriker Mountain."

"You don't have to play host," the Golden Emperor said, ignoring the offered hand. "We will not be here long. You said your final member was out of the country on business?"

"Yes," Julius said. "In Siberia."

That sounded like something he'd made up to make his brother seem as far away as possible, but it was true. Svena's home really was in Siberia. He was trying to think how to assure the emperor of this without giving away too much of Ian's game when the Qilin shrugged.

"Nowhere is far these days," he said calmly. "Twenty-four hours should be sufficient to come back from anywhere in the world." He glanced over his shoulder at the morning sun, which was now well on its way into the sky. "I will give you until this time tomorrow."

"Oh," Julius said awkwardly, looking at his mother. "I'm not sure if he can—"

"He will arrive on time," the emperor assured him. "I will it."

He said that the same way anyone else would say "It is inevitable," and for the Qilin, Julius supposed it was. But while twenty-four hours wasn't much, it was still infinitely more time than they'd had when they'd come out here. Maybe even enough to find a way out of this mess. It was all they were getting in any case, so Julius decided it was good enough.

"One day will be fine," he said, nodding. "Thank you, and let me show you into the mountain. I'm afraid you've caught us a bit shorthanded, but I'm sure we can find you a proper—"

"There's no need for that," the emperor said idly. "I brought my own supplies."

Considering he was barefoot and wearing a robe another dragon had thrown over his naked body when they'd landed, Julius didn't see how that could possibly be true. Before he could ask what supplies he was talking about, though, the Golden Emperor turned and walked away, processing down the road toward the mountain at a serene, stately pace.

The other dragons fell into formation around him at once, surrounding their emperor in a wall of brilliantly colored scales and, surprisingly, what appeared to be genuine concern for his well-being. Julius didn't know if their protectiveness was due to some unknown vulnerability in the Qilin's luck magic or true respect for him as a leader. He was still trying to figure it out when the Qilin suddenly stopped.

Every dragon around him froze as well, but while they were watching the desert for threats, the emperor was looking up. Curious, Julius lifted his eyes as well, following the angle of the Qilin's veiled face up the front of Heartstriker Mountain to the half-moon jut of the throne room balcony at its peak, where a slender figure stood at the edge, watching the drama below.

Technically, it was too far to see for certain, but Julius knew it was Chelsie. There was no one else who skulked around Heartstriker

Mountain wearing all black. But while he wasn't surprised at all that his sister had been spying, Julius *was* surprised she'd let herself get caught.

She fixed the problem at once, vanishing into the shadows within seconds of being spotted, but the Golden Emperor didn't look away. For a full minute after Chelsie disappeared, he stood perfectly still, staring at the empty spot where she'd been. It went on so long, the dragons around him started to look nervous. The Empress Mother in particular seemed anxious, her bony fingers clutching down like claws on the golden handle of her cane. Even Julius—who had no idea what was happening—could feel the tension in the air like an invisible wire twisting around their throats. And then, just as the pressure was becoming unbearable, the Golden Emperor lowered his head. The terrible feeling vanished a second later, leaving all the dragons gasping in relief.

All except for the Qilin himself, who simply resumed his procession into the citadel of his almost-conquered enemy as though nothing had happened.

CHAPTER FOUR

Marci was frozen in the dark.

It was like the first moments after she'd died. Once again, she was trapped in nothing, stuck in infinite blackness that had no end or beginning, except now, instead of merely a voice in her head or a hand in her mind, Ghost was right in front of her, looming over her in the shadowy soldier's body of the Empty Wind. But while he looked exactly as she remembered, right down to the ancient Roman Centurion armor, his face was no longer just two glowing blue-white eyes floating in the dark of his helmet. Or, rather, the eyes were still there, watching her fearfully, but the dark behind them was no longer merely shadow.

It was nothing.

There was no other way to describe it. Marci had looked the Empty Wind in the face countless times now, and while seeing two floating eyes gleaming in the dark had never exactly been comforting, looking at him now was like staring into death itself. Not the bloody death of the body, either. *True* death. The nothing that came after all trace of your life was gone and even the dust of your bones had been broken down into its component atoms. His face was what it meant to be utterly forgotten, and the moment Marci saw it, she knew that was her future, too.

The sudden truth hit her like a dive into cold water. Being dead, she'd thought she understood what it felt like, but she hadn't known anything. Her death had been a place of warmth and love, a place where she was remembered. It had been a pause, not an end, but this was different. All their fighting, their struggles, the desperate clinging to life, *this* was what it came to: nothing. Even dragons died. Lakes silted up, and their spirits slowly vanished. The whole human race would eventually be fossils on a tiny speck of rock flinging through the infinite dark of space, and when even that was devoured by their exploding sun, this—this spirit right here in front of her—was what they'd be.

Nothing.

Cold, silent nothing, as though they'd never existed at all.

Marci was still trying to process that—assuming something like this could be processed by the mortal mind—when the Empty Wind turned away, breaking the spell. "I'm sorry," he said quietly, stepping away. "I didn't want you to see."

It took Marci a while to recover enough of her wits to speak. When she did, though, it was in awe. "Dude, that was *insane*. You're a walking existential crisis! All that 'look into the void, void looks back' Nietzsche stuff."

The spirit's see-through body stilled. "You're not afraid?"

"Oh no, I'm terrified," Marci said honestly. "I don't think anyone could go face to face with the truth of mortality and not be. But we've been together for a while now, so this wasn't totally unexpected. You don't team up with the Spirit of the Forgotten Dead without understanding that you're going to be in for some uncomfortable truths."

"But you're not afraid of *me*?"

He asked this as if it were the most important question in the world. For her part, though, Marci couldn't understand how it was a question at all.

"Of course not," she said, insulted. "Everyone's afraid of being forgotten. That's why you exist. But while I won't deny I have a normal, healthy, human fear of the concept you represent, I'm not afraid of *you*. You're my spirit, and let's not forget how we got here." She smiled at him. "It's kind of hard to be scared of someone who rescued you from death."

After all they'd been through together, she felt this should have been obvious, but Ghost still hadn't turned around. If anything, his broad back was set more squarely to her than ever. That was when Marci decided it was time to take matters into her own hands. It was hard to move when you had no sense of your body or space, but she managed to inch herself around, scooting forward bit by bit until she was kneeling in front of him.

"Ghost, look at me."

The Empty Wind obeyed, dropping his head to reveal the void of his true face once again. It was impossible not to flinch, so Marci didn't try. She just focused on his glowing eyes, glaring into them until she was positive she had the spirit's full attention.

"I know you," she said sternly. "I knew you were a face of death before I knew your real name or heard the words 'Mortal Spirit.' That's always been a little creepy, but it's never changed what you are to me. You're my cat, my spirit, my partner, and my friend. Always were, always will be. And if you think for one second that *anything* is going to change that, you haven't been paying attention."

The Empty Wind stared at her for a long time. Then, at last, his glowing eyes closed in relief. "I knew I was right to choose you."

"Like there was any doubt," Marci said, holding out her hands so he could help her up. "We're a power team, remember? Not even death can break us up."

And speaking of death...

"Where are we?" she asked as he hauled her to her feet. "Amelia said my death was at the bottom of the Sea of Magic, but I don't—" She stopped, hand shooting to her shoulder. Or where she assumed her shoulder was. "Where's Amelia?!"

"She's here."

"Where?" Marci asked, getting more alarmed by the second. "I can't see anything but you and dark."

"That's because I had to close your eyes again," the Empty Wind explained. "This isn't your world. I didn't want you to have to deal with it and me at the same time."

That was thoughtful of him, but Marci didn't have time to be coddled. She couldn't actually remember who'd taught her the trick of opening her eyes the first time, but she was already working on doing it again, blinking rapidly until, at last, the dark was replaced by something infinitely more terrifying.

If the blackness before had felt like endless nothing, this was endless *everything*. All around them, things were in motion, spinning and colliding and bouncing off each other like debris in a tornado. It was still too dark to see clearly what was happening, but just the impression of so much movement was enough to make Marci's stomach lurch. An impressive feat considering she didn't technically have a stomach anymore.

"What *is* this?" she asked, grabbing Ghost before she fell into the chaos.

"Magic!" cried an excited voice above her.

The cry made her jump, and Marci looked up just in time for Amelia to land on her head. "We made it, Marci!" she cried, sparks flying out of her mouth in her excitement as she craned her long neck in every direction. "This is the Sea of Magic! We're *inside* the primal power that drives everything magical that happens in the world!"

That would explain why everything looked so crazy. But while Marci was definitely excited about being inside something she'd previously assumed was a metaphor, she mostly felt like she was going to hurl.

"It's okay," Ghost said, pulling her tighter against the wall of his mercifully still chest. "Humans never can stand it here. Every soul I've rescued hates this part of the journey."

"Journey? You mean we're moving?" Because with all the other swirling, she couldn't tell.

"We're *flying*!" Amelia said happily, tail twitching. "Your spirit is a freaking jet! I'd always thought they'd be slow and pokey since they were so big and chained to their vessels, but this is something else."

"I don't see why you're so surprised," he said grumpily. "Serving the forgotten requires speed, and I *am* a wind."

The little dragon's eyes grew huge. "Wait, you mean literally? I thought that was just part of your name!"

"Spirits are always called what we are," the Empty Wind said authoritatively. "That's how we know our names without being told. I can't remember anything from before I woke this time, but I know I've always been the Empty Wind. The only one who's ever called me anything different is Marci, and only because I wasn't large enough to know my name when she bound me."

"You're definitely more 'wind' than 'ghost' in this place," Amelia agreed, leaning out as far as she could off Marci's shoulder. "Can you go any faster?"

"*No*," Marci said. When they both looked at her, she swallowed. "Please, I can barely take this much. I just want to get back on solid ground."

As if it were trying to prove her point for her, the churning chaos chose that moment to lurch in a brand-new nauseating direction. Marci turned back to Ghost with a groan, squeezing her eyes shut as she squashed her face into his freezing skin. "Where are we going, anyway?"

The answer rumbled through the spirit's chest. "The Gate of the Merlins."

Her eyes popped open again. "What?"

"That's a real thing?" Amelia said at the same time.

"Of course it's real," he said, looking down at Marci. "Remember when you were dying, and I told you I could see what we'd been looking for? The way to becoming a Merlin? That's where I'm taking you."

"Wait," Marci said, still confused. "It's a place?"

He nodded excitedly. "I must have flown by it hundreds of times, but I couldn't see it until your mortal body started to die. The moment you began crossing over into death, the door appeared right in front of me, like it was waiting for us."

Marci still couldn't believe it. "So you're telling me there's a *literal* Merlin Gate, and we're flying to it? Do I just walk through and get my Merlin license or something?"

"I'm sure it won't be that simple," Ghost said. "Nothing else about this has been. But that's what it looks like."

"Fits what I've heard, too," Amelia added. "The Merlins I knew in the few decades I was alive before the drought hit wouldn't tell me squat because they were miserly, secretive bastards, but the way they talked made it sound like being a Merlin was more than just *being* a Merlin. They always acted like they were a part of some kind of larger organization. If that's true, then having the gate on this side makes perfect sense. Where better to hide the Guild Hall for a secret society of mages and spirits than inside magic itself?"

"It would also explain why the gate didn't appear until you started to die," the Empty Wind added. "This is the realm of immortal spirits. You can't even move through the magic of this place without one of us to guide you, which I couldn't do until you got closer to my domain."

"Which is death," Marci finished, glancing up at the nauseating swirls of magic shimmering like the rainbow sheen of oil on whirlpools of black water all around them. "So if I touch this without your protection—"

"You'll be burned away."

"Right," she said, remembering how just the brief brush with the circle of pure, undulating magic at the top of her death had been enough to nearly dissolve her hand before Ghost had yanked her to safety. Her fingers looked all right now, thank goodness, but it wasn't an experience she was eager to repeat. "Guess I'm sticking to you, then. Not that I'd do anything else, but how are we going to deal with the gate? Do you carry me over the threshold or something?"

Her spirit shrugged. "I don't know. I've never done anything like this. But we'll find out soon enough."

He nodded ahead of them, and Marci turned to look before she remembered that any movement in this place made her ill. Sure enough, she had to fight not to hurl as the asymmetrical whirlpools filled her vision, making the whole world spin in five different directions. Awful as she felt, though, Marci didn't close her eyes. No amount of magical seasickness was going to keep her from getting her first glimpse of whatever a Merlin Gate was. She forced herself to keep looking, straining to see through the liquid chaos of the constantly moving magic.

It really was like trying to look through the deep ocean. Other than Ghost's glowing eyes and Amelia's fire, there was no light in this place. Thankfully, that didn't seem to be too much of a problem now that she'd shed the limitations of physical eyes. She couldn't do anything about the churning chaos, but eventually, her vision adapted, filtering out the waves and swirls and black-on-black motion of the magic rushing by to see what was actually changing.

Just like before, the first thing she saw was Ghost. The *real* Ghost, not the human-shaped shadow she clung to. That must have been just for her comfort, because the longer Marci looked, the more she realized that the cold calm surrounding them wasn't coming from the Sea of Magic. It was all him. She wasn't standing next to Ghost—they were *inside* him, inside the shelter of the Empty Wind's own magic as he cut through the black depths like a shark toward a much larger, darker shape Marci could now see looming in front of them.

Ghost had called it a gate, so that was the shape Marci had been expecting, but the reality looked more like a column. A huge, round, black pillar rising straight up like a post from the rolling expanse of the sea floor. It got even bigger as they flew closer, which explained why Ghost had seen it the moment it appeared. Even in a place as big, dark, and chaotic as this, something that big was hard to miss. Still, Marci didn't understand how anyone could possibly call it a gate until Ghost landed in front of it.

"Stay close," he whispered as they set down on the flat, seemingly rocky ground that formed the floor of the Sea of Magic. "The currents are strong here."

She could feel them. Now that they'd stopped moving forward, she realized that the black swirls were more than just nauseating movements. They were forces, swirling balls of magical torque that wrenched and pushed against her spirit's edges, bowing the faintly glimmering barrier of his wind inward.

"What *are* they?" Amelia asked, her voice excited as she leaned perilously close to one of the bulges. "I mean, clearly, they're disturbances in the magic, but what's causing them?"

"I don't know," the Empty Wind said, tightening his grip on Marci's shoulder. "The Sea of Magic is always restless, but it's been especially volatile since Algonquin's attempt to raise a Mortal Spirit from dragon blood in Reclamation Land failed."

"Guess she made waves in more ways than one," Marci muttered, crossing her arms over her chest to keep as far as possible from the chaotic flows of power banging on Ghost's edges. "Where now?"

The Empty Wind pointed at the column in front of them. This close, the curving surface looked more like a flat, featureless wall, its face polished smooth by the constantly battering currents. Between the dark and the swirls of magic that rolled through it like thicker shadows, it was nearly impossible to make out what Ghost was trying to show her. Eventually, though, she spotted a gap in the pillar's flat stone face.

It wasn't what Marci would have called a gate. The small, rectangular dent in the pillar's surface was neither grand nor obvious. It was no taller than she was, a hole that was cut less than an inch deep into the stone and blocked by a door that looked as if it had been stolen from a medieval kitchen: a tight-set slab of rough-hewn wooden planks held together with tar and iron banding. There was no knocker, no handle, no knob, no announcements or decorations of any sort. If it weren't for the fact that it was so clearly out of place in this world of swirling, nonphysical chaos, Marci wouldn't have thought it was special at all.

"Is that it?" Amelia asked skeptically.

"I think so," the Empty Wind said. "I've never been closer than this, but it feels right."

Marci thought it felt like a letdown. Still, if there was anything she'd learned from Ghost, it was to never judge on appearances. Especially if that appearance happened to be the only opening in the base of what was clearly an artificial, man-made structure poking out of the otherwise flat floor of the Sea of Magic.

"Guess we should give it a try," Marci said, holding out her hand to Ghost.

He took it, wrapping his freezing fingers around hers as they walked together to the pillar. When they were both standing on the threshold, Marci took a final breath of the Empty Wind's cold magic before lifting her shivering hand to knock.

And high above, hidden in the chaos, an enormous swirl of magic shaped like a raven nodded in satisfaction before nipping back into the land of the living.

• • •

Emily?

General Emily Jackson, commanding officer of the UN's Magical Disaster Response Team, and current prisoner of Algonquin, shifted her aching head.

What, no hello?

She let the silence answer for her. It was impossible to tell how much time had passed since Algonquin's Leviathan had grabbed her from the field in Reclamation Land, but she'd spent most of it underwater. She was still there now, wrapped up like a mummy in the Leviathan's smothering tentacles. Technically, that wasn't an excuse for staying silent. As a magical construct, she didn't actually need the oxygen she was hoarding in her lungs, but the air pressure helped keep the water from making its way through her sundered chest and into her brain cavity, where it could actually cause problems. She certainly wasn't going to waste it opening her mouth to talk, and it wasn't as though Raven needed a partner for his conversations.

I see how it is, the spirit grumbled. *Just take me for granted. Never mind that I'm risking my life visiting you in the heart of enemy territory. And speaking of enemies...*Wings fluttered over her mind to nudge her eyes. *Open up. I need to see what's going on.*

Emily wasn't sure if she could. Unbidden, her hands twitched, but the movement was only in her head, because she didn't have hands anymore. She didn't have arms, either, or legs. It was hard to tell how much she'd lost since she'd been trapped in the Leviathan's smothering embrace the entire time, but going by the few sensors that were still reporting, Emily was reasonably certain that she was down to just her ribcage, shoulders, and head. The rest was gone. Under Myron's direction, Algonquin's mages had picked her apart, meticulously undoing the metal ribbons of coiled spellwork that gave her life. She'd been conscious for all of it, held down by the Leviathan's implacable weight. Keeping her eyes shut was the only way she'd maintained mental stability as they picked her apart. If she opened them now...

My poor girl, Raven whispered. *You're afraid.*

Of course she was afraid. She might not be flesh and blood anymore, but Emily's mind at least was still human, and every human feared death. Being the Phoenix only made things worse. Having died before, she knew exactly how much there was to be afraid of. If she didn't look, though, Raven would have no information. No information meant no rescue, and so, since the only thing worse than dying was the fear of it being forever this time, Emily forced herself to obey, prying her eyes open.

And saw something new.

She jerked in surprise. The few other times she'd worked up the courage to open her eyes, there'd been nothing to see but black flesh and slime. The Leviathan's smothering tentacles must have relaxed a little after the last unraveling, though, because now she could see light shining down through the murky water. It *almost* looked like sunlight, but just as her hopes started to rise, a familiar voice trickled through the murk.

"Bring her up."

The Leviathan obeyed, thrusting Emily up, up, up out of the cold water and into the light, but not the sun. The light she'd seen came from a rack of halogen floodlights set up on the stone ledge of what appeared to be a rocky cavern somewhere underground. After a few seconds, Emily recognized the place from the few grainy pictures their spies had smuggled out. She was in the cave beneath

Algonquin Tower, the one Algonquin reportedly used to move things she didn't want anyone seeing between her lake and her fortress.

Considering how many times Emily had tried and failed to infiltrate this place, that should have kicked off a serious investigation, but she barely spared the cavern a glance. Her attention was stuck on the man standing beneath the rack of blinding yellow-white floodlights. The one she'd once called partner.

"Myron," she growled, letting the air out of her lungs at last. "Decided to finish me off?"

"Not yet," the mage said, reaching between the Leviathan's tentacles to check the lines of spellworked metal ribbon hanging from what was left of her chest. When he'd touched each one, he turned to the stream of clear, constantly moving water bubbling up from the stone beside him. "Ready when you are."

The water twisted as he spoke, rising up to peer into Emily's face, giving her a horrifying glimpse of her own startled reflection in the mirror-flat waterfall that was Algonquin's face.

"Excellent," the spirit said, the word burbling like a stream. "Hoist her up so they can see."

Before Emily could look to see what "they" Algonquin was talking about, the Leviathan jerked her up, shoving what was left of her body high into the air. After so long underwater, the light and movement made her feel sick. Not *actually* sick. Even before Myron and his mages had removed that part of her body, Emily hadn't had a real stomach in decades. Just like her twitching fingers, though, the need to throw up didn't vanish with the associated organs. Thankfully, it was over quickly. Seconds after it started, the Leviathan had thrust her to the top of the cavern, dangling her like a grotesque chandelier above what Emily could now see was a very large, and very strange, crowd.

I was afraid of this, Raven whispered, his eyes darting quickly behind hers. *It seems we're the last to arrive.*

Emily nodded, trying not to shudder. The cavern at the base of the Algonquin's tower was filled with monsters. They were packed in like sardines. Other than the circle of water surrounding the rock where Algonquin and Myron were standing, every inch was filled with limbs, branches, furry paws, and other things Emily didn't have names for. Even the ceiling was occupied, the stone crowded with things clinging to the arch of the roof like lichen or hanging upside down from it like bats. They were so many, so different, and so piled on top of each other, it took Emily an embarrassingly long time to realize she was looking at spirits. Hundreds of them. More than she'd seen in all her missions combined.

More than any *mortal has seen,* Raven said, his presence shifting to the front of her mind like a bird scooting to the tip of a branch. *But we always knew Algonquin had pull. What I want to know is what did she promise to lure them all here?*

Emily was wondering the same thing. Now that she'd realized what she was looking at, she actually recognized some of the spirits from Raven's reports. Particularly Wolf, who appeared as a ten-foot-long timber wolf sitting on its haunches at the front of the mob. Coyote and Eagle were similarly easy to spot, though not nearly as large. But while the animal spirits were easy to spot, others were complete unknowns. Some—like the large pile of moss crawling up the back wall—looked relatively harmless. Others—particularly the long, eel-like creature with a man's face lurking in the murky water beside the Leviathan's tentacles—seemed decidedly more danger-ous. It was impossible to get a head count when only a few of them had heads and some didn't even have definable edges, but Emily estimated there were at least three dozen spirits here that were large enough to meet the UN's definition of a national-level threat. This included Algonquin herself, who'd risen higher from the water, turning to address the crowd like a queen welcoming her court.

"Friends," she said, her watery voice colder and more inhuman than Emily had ever heard it. "I know many of you have left delicate domains to be here. Thank you all for coming so far on such short notice."

"Save your platitudes, lake water," Wolf growled. "You called, we came. Now tell us what's so important."

"I hope it's not her," the eel spirit in the water burbled, his deep voice smooth and treacherous as he turned his drowned-man's face to stare at Emily. "We've complications enough without wasting our time on Raven's wind-up toy."

Wind-up toy, indeed, Raven huffed. *He's never made anything in his life.*

"Raven is the least of our problems," Algonquin said, her water splitting into two spouts so she could face the wolf and the eel at the same time. "And I called you because we are *out* of time."

"Out of time?" rumbled one of the giant trees in the back. "Impossible. We are the land, the immortal spirits. Time is the one thing we can never run out of."

"Normally, yes," Algonquin said as her split water came back together. "But things haven't been normal for ten centuries, and if we don't act quickly, they never will be again."

She paused there, but no one seemed to have a comeback this time, and eventually, Algonquin continued. "We are at a critical juncture. As many of you already know, the first Mortal Spirit has risen, and he is not ours."

"How can that be?" Wolf growled. "We gave you our children precisely so that you could build your own Mortal Spirit before anything rose naturally. How did you get beaten? What have you been doing?"

"Exactly what I said I would," Algonquin replied. "We were actually ahead of schedule thanks to the Three Sisters and the culling of the dragons, but it is impossible to raise the magic of a specific place without spillover, and it seems I underestimated the mortal fascination with death. The combination of these two elements was a rogue Mortal Spirit of the Forgotten Dead who, sadly, could not be controlled. But though I was able to put him down again, his bound mortal and her dragon allies did a great deal of damage on their way out, spilling the dragon blood I'd gathered and destroying months of work. Now, with our reserves wasted and no dragons left in the DFZ to harvest, the window to build up the magic necessary to achieve critical mass on our chosen Mortal Spirit before another rises naturally is rapidly closing."

"Sounds like failure to me," the eel spirit said with a sneer.

"It *was* failure," Algonquin said angrily. "But at least *I* was doing something. If I'd left our survival up to all of you, we'd sit complacent as stones while the rising tide of human madness swallowed us whole. But I am not complacent. I will *never* surrender my water again, and I have already found another possible solution, as my new head mage will now explain."

That must have been Myron's cue. He stepped forward with a confident smile, nodding at the monsters as if they were just another audience at one of his conferences. "Spirits of the Land and Animals, I am Sir Myron Rollins, head of magical research and policy for the United Nations and one of the primary spellwork architects of the Phoenix Project. Or, as she is better known to many of you, Raven's Construct."

He motioned with his hand, and the Leviathan obeyed, lowering Emily until she was dangling in front of him.

"Though initiated by Raven, General Jackson here is the work of many hands," Myron continued, reaching out to trail his fingers through the exposed silver ribbons of spellwork dangling like streamers from Emily's sundered chest. "Despite no longer possessing any of her original mortal body, her soul retains the unique human ability to move magic. If she were a mage, this would mean she could pull in magic from the world around her to power her construct chassis and weapons, which, as you can see here, are all spellwork-based. However, General Jackson is *not* a mage. She cannot use her own spellwork, nor does she have conscious control over the magic required to power her body."

"Then how does she work?" the eel spirit demanded. "How does the wind-up toy move if she can't wind herself?"

Myron grinned. "The answer to that question is why we're here. Raven was a very clever bird. He chose General Jackson precisely because she was *not* a mage. A mage could have fought him for control, a very undesirable trait in a puppet. A normal human, though, wouldn't be able get in his way. She could only control the *results* of the spellwork—the weapons and the body's movements and such—not the mechanisms behind them. Think of her as the pilot in a fighter jet. She can fly the plane, but she can't do anything about the engine or the fuel that powers it."

"But we can," Algonquin said.

"Exactly," Myron agreed, grabbing one of the thin strips of spellwork-covered metal ribbon dangling from Emily's chest. "The Phoenix is a powerful and intelligent weapon, but because she is not a mage, she can't pull in the magic she needs to power her body on her own. To overcome this limitation, Raven devised a mechanism that utilizes the unique human ability to push magic *without* requiring a mage's capacity for control. By wiring his spellwork"—he held up the metal ribbon—"directly into the parts of her brain that regulate the subconscious human ability to manipulate magic, Raven gave himself the power to *push* his magic into her instead. It's just like how doctors use electrical impulses to force limbs to move even if the patient has no control over them. He simply offers up his magic, and the spellwork inside her body automatically grabs it and turns it into fuel."

"Leave it to Raven to turn himself into food for his puppet," Wolf said with a sneer. "He never had any pride."

"His lack of pride is our ticket," Myron said. "In his desire to create a foolproof puppet who wouldn't fight him magically but would still be capable of operating independently for long periods of time, Raven created something unique: a magical battery. Raven's Construct isn't just a weapon. She's a vessel capable of passively accepting magic from a donor spirit and storing it inside her spellwork, creating a stable well of power that she can access at will. That alone is huge, but what makes General Jackson *really* special isn't just that she's the only spellwork construct in existence who passively accepts magic rather than having to pull it in, it's how *much* power she can hold."

He pulled the ribbon of spellworked metal through his fingers, unraveling it down from inside Emily's chest to show them just how long it was. "Mages can pull down magic all day long, but even with the largest circles, there's only so much we can control without burning ourselves out. Spirits are different. You routinely command magic in sums that would obliterate a human mage. However, since Raven built the Phoenix with *his* magic in mind, not hers, her spell-work was designed to processes magic on a *spirit* level. We're talking about thousands of times more power than any human mage could safely handle, placed in the hands of one woman."

"I think you mean a good soldier," Emily growled. "One who's loyal to our cause. Unlike certain *traitors* I could mention."

"There's loyal, and then there's fanatical," Myron said coldly. "You were willing to shoot a potential Merlin in the back rather than risk her falling into the hands of a spirit who did not match your narrow vision of the greater human good. I'm far more practical. The world needs a Merlin, and that requires a Mortal Spirit. If Algonquin wants to raise one, that puts us on the same side."

"What part of *this* is our side?" Emily cried, fighting the Leviathan's hold. "I don't know if you've been paying attention, but Algonquin's killed more humans than all the modern dragons combined. She's *not* our ally. She's a—"

A slimy black tentacle slid over Emily's face, silencing her. Down below, Algonquin's water burbled angrily. "Ignore her," the lake spirit commanded. "She is nothing. And you." She turned her reflective face back to Myron. "We're not here for a lesson. You've said enough about how the Phoenix functions. Now tell them why she matters."

"I was getting to that," Myron said irritably, shooting a final glare at Emily as he turned to face the crowd of spirits again. "Emily Jackson isn't just a combat construct backed by the magic of one of the most active animal spirits. She's a unique creation, a spell-work machine capable of absorbing and containing magic on a spirit scale and placing it under the command of a human will. If Raven were a Mortal Spirit, General Jackson would effectively be his Merlin, and *that* is where she becomes useful to us."

"How so?" the eel asked, his drowned face sour. "Every Merlin I've met has been the master of their spirit, but the Phoenix is a puppet, and a famously loyal one at that. You might have her tied and supplicant, but Raven's still in control. He'll never allow his construct to be used against his precious humans. If you pump her full of magic, she'll just use it to turn on you the second she gets free."

"She would," Myron agreed, "*if* I left her in control. But you'll recall I said the magic that powers her is under the control of 'a human will,' not '*her* will.' Her body serves as the vessel, but again, Emily is *not* a mage. She has her hands on the controls, but she's not the one who commands her magic. That's all handled by spellwork, and that spellwork, the millions of lines of logic that determines who has mastery over the Phoenix's vast stores of power, is controlled by a single variable. A hard-coded one, but still only *one*. Change that variable, and the spells controlling all that magic shift to obey whomever we point them at."

By the time he finished, Emily was seeing red. The single-variable spellwork that determined control over her body was a known security vulnerability. One that, ironically, Myron had been brought in to *fix*. Now he was handing it to the enemy right in front of her, and that stabbed deeper than anything else could.

"You *traitor!*" she screamed, ripping her face free of the Leviathan's tentacle. "You're *dead*, Myron! Do you hear me? You're—"

She was cut off with a strangled choke as the Leviathan's tentacle snapped back with a vengeance, wrapping all the way around her jaw and down her neck. She was still fighting it when a flash of light caught her attention, and she tore her eyes away from the slimy tentacle pressed against her cheeks to see Algonquin's flat, reflective waterfall of a face hovering right in front of her.

"You have no place to call anyone traitor, little tool," the lake whispered. "It is because of you that we are in this deplorable situation to begin with. I had the human who commanded the Mortal Spirit under my full control when *you* killed her. Now we have *nothing*. Not the spirit I was building, nor Marci Novalli's, nor the dragons needed to rebuild our losses. You were the one who put our backs to this wall, and it is only fair that you should prove the solution."

"But what problem will she solve?" the eel spirit said, rising from the water at last to glare at Algonquin with wary, clouded eyes. "I see where you are going, lake water. Raven's Construct is indeed a lovely tool. A deep bucket that can hold all the magic you need to rebuild your lost Mortal Spirit *and* place it under the command of your new human stooge." He nodded at Myron, who bristled. "But a bucket is useless without something to fill it. We know what you plan to do with it, but you have yet to say where all this magic is coming from, Algonquin."

"He's right," Wolf agreed, showing his teeth. "The Mortal Spirits have always been a problem of scale. Even when the humans numbered only in the millions, the gouges their fears carved into the magical landscape were bigger than the mountains. Now there are billions of terrified mortals, and the holes they dig are bigger than ever. You know this. You asked for our children to help power the circles that funneled the magic of the entire DFZ into Reclamation Land, and you *still* needed all the dragons in your city *plus* the blood of all Three Sisters to come even close to filling a Mortal Spirit. But that blood is spilled. You have to start building that magic all over again, and while I'm sure Raven's Construct makes an excellently wide mouth, I will promise nothing until you tell us what manner of food you plan on shoving down it."

"The only kind we have left," Algonquin said sadly. "Us."

The cavern went silent. For several heartbeats, none of the spirits moved, and then the eel with the dead man's face hissed like a snake. "Have you gone *mad?*"

"Not at all," the water said, reaching out a tendril to her Leviathan. "Madness would be to ignore the doom we can all see building. I'm trying to stop it, which makes me the sanest one here."

"You are *not* sane," the eel said, taking shelter behind the rock. "No one sane would suggest killing the souls of the land to save it."

"And who is the land?" Algonquin demanded, drawing herself up. "Who speaks for us? You, bottom crawler?"

The eel hissed again and retreated to the darkness behind the rock, leaving Algonquin alone before the gathered spirits.

"I know how much I ask," she said, calmly now. "I am the spirit of Algonquin, the once-great lake that is now five. I protected and loved my water for millions of years before the first humans appeared on my shores. When they came, I welcomed them as I would any other animal, and I have paid for that choice ever since. We have *all* paid."

A murmur of agreement rose from the crowd, and Algonquin's water twisted into something like a smile. "They use us," she said. "Even before they grew plentiful enough to turn their fears into gods, they took from the land. They killed our children, burned and raped and dumped their trash into our bodies. They took our magic and forced us into sleep, and when we finally woke a thousand years later, what did they leave for us? Poison. Destruction. A whole world gleefully sacrificed to their endless greed. Just look what they did to my lakes. To my beautiful water."

Her voice was shaking by the end, and Algonquin folded, her silvery current curling into itself with a hollow, mournful sound. She wasn't alone, either. All the spirits were shaking, filling the cavern with their grief for what was lost. It was such a sad sound, even Emily's eyes started to blur. She was fighting it when Algonquin spoke again.

"We must fight back," she whispered, her water uncurling. "Humanity has done more damage in the last thousand years than anything we've seen since the mass extinctions, and that's without their gods. Now the magic is back, filling not just us, but the canyons of humanity's hate and fear. When they are full, the Mortal Spirits will return even greater than before. What do you think will become of the land then? What will become of *us*?"

No one said a word. All the spirits just pulled further into themselves, shrinking down against the wet stone as Algonquin moved in for the kill.

"We will be trampled," she whispered. "You all know how much magic it takes to form even one Mortal Spirit. That sort of power doesn't just go away. Even if every human on the planet dies of their own greed, their Mortal Spirits will remain for millions of years, just like the rest of humanity's pollution. When that happens, our beautiful world will be a wasteland, a *hell* of mad gods, and we, the immortal spirits, will have no escape. We don't even have the mercy of death to save us from what is coming. We will be forever trapped beneath the boot of monsters we cannot fight or control. *That* is our destiny. *That* is what is coming if we do not act now, while we still can."

By the time she finished, the room was so silent, Emily could hear the *drip, drip* of water sliding down the Leviathan's glistening flesh. Even Myron was holding his breath, watching Algonquin with an expression Emily couldn't read. Then, like a wave breaking, the gathered spirits lowered their heads in defeat.

"You're right," Wolf whispered. "But what can we do?"

"What we have always done," Algonquin said bitterly. "Fight to survive. I called you all here specifically because you are the spirits who have suffered the most at human hands. Some of you woke to find your children hunted to near extinction. Others have had their domains stolen entirely, the land of their roots literally mined out from under them. I know your pain, because I've lived it, too. When I woke, my water was poison and my fish were dying all around me, but I was not a helpless victim. I rose up and fought back against the cities that had hurt me, killed them as they sought to kill me. I took Detroit for myself and forged a new future, one where *I* was in control. That is what we must all do now, because we *are* the future. We are the land. We were here before words were spoken or history written. We are the living magic of this world, and we must take back control of what is ours before we lose it forever."

Her water spread as she spoke, flowing out from the puddle at her feet over the rocky ledge to embrace the spirits in a glowing tide. "We already have what we require," she said as the glowing water crept higher. "You asked how I would get enough power to fill Raven's Construct, but the answer is right in front of you. We have all the magic we need right here in this cavern to fill a Mortal Spirit, and this time, we have a secure vessel to hold it."

One of her glowing tendrils slid up the Leviathan to brush Emily's cheek. "Even the dragons can't harm Raven's Construct. It will push her to her limits, but Myron assures me her spellwork can contain the power we need long enough to spark a Mortal Spirit. Better still, by growing it inside the prison of the Phoenix's spellwork, our spirit will awaken under the control of my mage, which means we won't need to wait for it to choose a Merlin. This Mortal Spirit will be *born* into chains, and *we* will be the ones holding them."

"Don't you mean him?" Wolf said, baring his teeth at Myron, who took a wary step back. "I've always applauded your daring, Algonquin, but this is reckless even for you. Your mage has already betrayed his own kind. What makes you think he won't do the same to us?"

"Because we have what he wants most," Algonquin said sweetly, turning her mirror-smooth face toward Myron. "A chance to be Merlin. His *last* chance. It's hard to tell mortal ages, but Sir Myron here is old. There's a very good chance another Mortal Spirit will never rise again in his lifetime. Even if one did, his chance of being in the right place at the right time to claim it is next to zero. We are the only path left to his dream, which means he's ours, bought and paid for." Her water rippled in something like a smile. "Ambitious humans have always been the easiest to control."

Emily expected Myron to balk at that. Algonquin was absolutely right about his ambitions, but he was equally arrogant. *Too* arrogant to swallow such open mockery, or at least that was what she'd thought. To her amazement, though, the mage was nodding along with the spirit, smiling as if this was exactly what he wanted.

"So long as I become Merlin, nothing else matters," he assured Algonquin. "I will be the first human in a thousand years to open the Merlin Gate, and I swear to use whatever power I find there to make sure I'm also the last. You aren't the only ones who fear Mortal Spirits. I was there when Marci Novalli's pet death invaded Reclamation Land. I saw firsthand the horror and destruction powers like him are capable of, and he wasn't even fully grown. That's not something I can allow to happen again."

"It can never be allowed," Algonquin agreed. "The end of Mortal Spirits is the only way any of us survive, including humanity. Normally, their plight wouldn't concern me, but we cannot do this without them. We've always known it was Merlins who caused the drought, but we've never known *how*. Whatever they did to block the flow of magic is hidden behind the Merlin Gate, which none but a Merlin may enter. Now, though, with Myron Rollins as our inside man, we can turn their weapons to our cause. As Merlin, he can enter the gate and cap the flood of magic back to what it was right after it returned. Back when there was only enough power for *us*, and the vast hollows of the Mortal Spirits were empty. When that happens, we shall once again be the *only* spirits, and the world will be ours again, just as it was before. Is that not what we've fought for all these years?"

"But where is our victory?" whispered a spirit from the back, one of the piles of moss, who hadn't spoken before. "Even if your mage keeps his word, your plan uses us as the fuel that fills Raven's Construct and grows your Mortal Spirit. You may succeed in stopping the humans' gods, but we will still be all used up. Our vessels will be empty, and with the magic throttled to such a low level, how will we fill back up?"

"You will only be empty for a moment," Algonquin promised. "I will not insult you by pretending I ask a small thing. For this to work, I need *all* of your magic, but though the sacrifice is great, it will not be long. Once it's served its purpose, Myron's Mortal Spirit will no longer be needed, and with the chains of its Merlin to hold it down, my mage can simply give you your magic back. The return won't be a hundred percent, obviously, but there are many, many ways to get magic. Once the world is safely ours again, I will be free to pursue them for you, starting with the second-greatest threat to our future, the dragons."

Her voice grew hungry. "When this is over, I won't have to worry about the DFZ or human politics anymore. Vann Jeger and I will be free to hunt snakes to our hearts' content. When they are dead, I will drain their magic—magic *they* stole from living in our world—back into you, restoring you and raising you up above all others. So you see, my friends, I'm not asking you to degrade yourselves forever. There is no death for the deathless. This is just a short sleep, a pause compared to the full stop the Merlins sentenced us to. This time, though, when you wake, it will be into a better world. One where *we* are gods again."

All the spirits chittered excitedly. Even Emily had to admit it wasn't a bad plan. Algonquin's hatred of dragons was no secret. Now she had the perfect excuse to hunt them and no one to stand in her way. But before Algonquin could clinch the favor that was swinging her way, a new voice rang out through the cavern.

"You were never a god."

Algonquin whirled around, glaring at Emily, who was just as shocked. The words had indeed come from her mouth, but they weren't hers. The deep, croaking voice speaking through her lips was Raven's, and it was furious.

"Foolish lake," he cawed. "Can you not see beyond your own banks? These are our brothers and sisters, the souls of the earth itself! They are not fodder for your paranoid ambitions. You strut and claim that you will cut off the magic and turn everything back to the time when it was only us, but time doesn't work that way. We can *never* go back, Algonquin! The past is gone, and now you're risking our future by gambling it on powers you have never understood. We will all suffer for your hubris if you *do not stop!*"

"You're a fine one to talk of hubris, carrion feeder," Algonquin snarled, her water surging up until Emily could see the reflection of her own wide eyes inches from her face. "You sold out to the humans ages ago, spilled our secrets for all to know. You even entangled yourself with a *dragon,* and you think you have the right to speak in this place? To tell us what we will suffer? We have already suffered! For a thousand years, we were tortured while we slept, abused when we were most powerless, but now it's our turn. This time, *we* shall take the power, and *they* will be the ones to pay. All of them! We will strike down the Mortal Spirits before they can rise. Take back our magic from the humans, who damage everything they touch. Then, when it is done, we will use the dragons, who've never paid for anything, to recoup our costs. So you see, little bird, my plan risks nothing."

"But it *does*!" Raven cried. "If you do this in our name, you make the entire world our enemy!"

"It's far too late to worry about that," Algonquin said. "This world has been my enemy from the moment I woke. I am sick and tired of being filthy, of being used. I am exhausted from seeing so much destruction, and yet, when I look forward, that's all I see. More people, more dragons, more abuse, more death. If that's our future, Raven, what does sacrifice matter? What does *any* of this matter if there's nothing left to look forward to anyway?"

Raven's shock and sadness at Algonquin's words were enough to bring tears to Emily's eyes, but the anger that followed was ten times worse. "I won't let you do this," he said, his voice rising like a gale. "We are the immortal land, the eternal magic itself! If we give up hope in the future and burn the present in a futile grab for the past, there will be nothing left for *anyone*."

"There never was," Algonquin said, reaching up to wrap her water around Emily's throat. "Don't you see, foolish bird? The die's already been cast. This is our last stand. If we can't turn back this tide, we will be trapped forever in a world that's *worse* than death. A world where we are powerless, dirt for the mad gods to stomp on. I would sacrifice *everything* to avoid that, because if we lose here, if that is indeed our future, then I would rather have no future at all."

She'd entwined her water entirely around the Leviathan by the time she finished, and deep in Emily's mind, Raven began to tremble. "No," he whispered. "I won't allow it. I won't let you make this our end."

"Too bad," Algonquin said as the water she'd wrapped around Emily's neck began to trickle down her body, toward her sundered chest. "You don't get a choice. You already turned your back on us."

The water moved deeper, winding through the coils of spellwork Myron hadn't yet unwound to rest on the knot that was Emily's heart. Not her literal heart—that had gone long ago—but the start of the spell that had given her new life. It was her very first knot, wound by Raven himself around a bit of twisted metal he'd plucked from the wreckage of her family home in Old Detroit. It was the core of the deal they'd struck all those years ago, and its battered surface still bore the scratched letters of Raven's name. Letters Algonquin's water was quickly scouring away.

"Farewell, carrion crow," she said, her voice a singsong as her water wore away the last of the scratches. "And thank you for your contribution to our cause."

"No!" Raven shouted through Emily's mouth. "You can't have her! She's—"

His voice died as Algonquin scraped the last of his name away, leaving Emily alone in her head for the first time in over sixty years. She was still reeling when Algonquin's water drained out of her.

"And that's that," the spirit said as the Leviathan's tentacle uncurled, dumping Emily unceremoniously onto the stone at Myron's feet. With no arms to catch herself, she landed hard, screaming silently as her spellwork began to slide out of control. If she'd been a mage, she could have stopped it, but as Myron had said countless times, she had no such power. Without Raven, Emily Jackson wasn't the Phoenix. She was just another mortal. A dying one, her patchwork body disintegrating before her eyes. Then, just before she collapsed entirely, a new power scooped her up, folding her back together. She didn't even recognize it as Myron's Labyrinth magic until the glowing maze surrounded her completely, the neon forks forming an iridescent cage that held her in place. But while Emily was staring at her former partner's sorcery, Myron was glaring at Algonquin.

"Some warning would have been nice," he said, his chest heaving as he repositioned what was left of Emily into the center of his magic. "Did I not stress how important she was to our plan? Your tiff with Raven nearly destroyed our ticket!"

"She wasn't our ticket so long as he lived inside her," Algonquin reminded him, her watery face warping into an unflattering copy of Myron's own. "Time to keep your end of the bargain, traitor mage.

The Raven has been expunged, as promised. Now replace his name with yours and take control of his construct, and we shall see if you can live up to your boasting."

Myron scowled one last time and turned back to Emily, but while his face was as haughty as ever, his hands were shaking. "I'll do my part," he said. "But are you sure you can do yours? We only get one shot at this."

The lake spirit smiled his own smile back at him. "You'll get your magic, have no fear. As I just told Raven, this is the only victory scenario we have left. If you want your share of it, mortal, you will do exactly as we discussed."

"Of course," Myron said after a moment's hesitation. "Never thought otherwise."

The Lady of the Lakes' reflection smiled one more time, and then she let Myron's face fall away, becoming just water again as she turned back to the gathered spirits.

There were no speeches this time. No warnings. The water lurking at the cavern's edges simply welled up, flooding over the stone at the spirits' feet.

A few fled when the lake reached them. The eel spirit in particular vanished so quickly he left a bubble under the water. Most of them, though, including Wolf, Eagle, and the other animals stayed put, their heads lowered in acceptance as Algonquin's water rose higher and higher. It would have washed over Emily and Myron, too, but the Leviathan got there first, surrounding them in a protective cocoon of black tentacles.

Emily didn't waste time after that. The moment the Leviathan hid them from Algonquin, she turned on Myron, opening her mouth in a last attempt to reason with him, but it was no use. Without Raven's name to give her control, her body wouldn't obey. All she could do was gasp silently as he set her down on the wet stone at his feet.

"Stop it," he ordered, holding her still with his foot as he reached up to adjust the floodlights. "It's over, Emily. This will be a lot easier on both of us if you don't fight."

Her answer to that was to spit at him, or at least try to. She was still trying to get her mouth to work when he knelt beside her again, leaning down to whisper in her ear.

"Be still and listen," he ordered, pressing her down until she stopped twitching. "I know how this looks, but I wouldn't be doing it if it wasn't the only way. Algonquin's right. The Mortal Spirits are rising. Marci Novalli's cat was just the first, and you saw what a terror he was. The others will be worse. If we don't get control of this situation, the spirits of the land won't be the only ones in trouble. Trust me, Emily. This is for the best. I might not have come to it in the usual way, but I'll be the Merlin this world needs. I swear it."

Since she couldn't speak to tell him what a load of bull that was, Emily looked away, clenching her teeth as Myron placed his hand inside the hole Raven's absence had left in her chest.

"I'm sorry," he muttered. "Brace yourself. This will probably hurt."

She was trying to get enough control for one final rude gesture when Myron's maze of magic pulled tight, yanking every line of her spellwork with it until the world went white with pain.

CHAPTER FIVE

"I don't like this," Julius muttered. "I don't like this at all."

"Congratulations," said Bethesda, tossing back the last of her cognac as her body sank lower into the pile of gold she was using as a makeshift couch. "We've finally found something we can agree on."

Julius's answer to that was a long sigh. It had been four hours since the Golden Emperor and his court had accepted Julius's offer to stay at the mountain until Ian returned. When he'd suggested the idea, he'd assumed everyone understood this meant the Chinese dragons would be their *guests*, but the Golden Empire must have had a different definition of the word "hospitality." The moment she'd gotten inside, the Empress Mother had taken over, directing her dragons to spread out and occupy every abandoned inch of the Heartstriker's ancient fortress.

It wasn't just a draconic effort, either. The emperor hadn't been kidding when he'd said he'd brought his own things. Not ten minutes after Julius invited them in, planes full of supplies, furniture, and human servants had begun arriving, crowding the airstrip and filling the once-empty mountain to bursting again. But while the new influx had at least fixed their staffing problem—particularly in the kitchens, which were now working overtime to feed a mountain full of dragons—the Heartstrikers were not included.

While the Chinese court had made themselves at home, taking over the rooms normally reserved for upper-alphabet Heartstrikers, including, to Bethesda's great upset, the throne room and her apartments, which had now been claimed as the personal quarters of the Qilin and his mother, their "hosts" had been pushed further and further down. The guest rooms, the human staff wing, the garage—all were apparently vital to assuring the emperor's comfort. In the end, the only part of the mountain their "guests" *didn't* require were the overflow vaults in the storage sub-basement, which was how Julius found himself sitting with his mother and Fredrick on top of the piles of gold that had once been the Heartstriker's treasury.

"At least my gold is safe," Bethesda said for the thousandth time. "I stayed up all night making what was left of the staff move it down here so it would be well guarded while we were on the run. Never thought I'd be locked down here with it, of course, but at least we're together." She ran her hands lovingly over the yellow coins before refilling her drink from the only bottle from her private liquor cache Amelia hadn't polished off. "Here's to forethought."

"You should have had the forethought to check your informants," Fredrick growled, pacing the clear spot in front of the vault door as he'd been doing for the last hour. "An entire dragon clan flew across half the world to invade us, and we were still caught unawares. Gold can't fix that."

"We were invaded by the living embodiment of good fortune," Bethesda said with a shrug. "If I had his luck, no one would see me coming, either. And why are you yelling at me? Julius is clan head now, too. That makes this debacle his fault as much as mine, but I don't see you snipping at him." She finished her drink in a single gulp. "And for the record, gold helps *everything*. We might be trapped now, but Heartstriker is still a rich and powerful clan. Just you wait until Conrad, Justin, and the others are in position. We will rain down vengeance on the Golden Emperor like he's never seen! Let's see him luck his way out of *that*."

She cackled at the thought, and Julius sighed again. Part of him was terrified by her words. An open clan war was the worst of all possible outcomes. But the cynic in him saw his mother's behavior for what it was: the drunken ravings of a desperate dragon who was utterly and thoroughly trapped. They *all* were. This delay had been his idea, but Julius was all too aware that Heartstriker was already conquered in all but name. The fact that they were locked in the basement of their own fortress was just the icing on the cake.

His hope now—his *only* hope—was to find a loophole in the surrender agreement. An angle, an outside case, something the Chinese dragons hadn't considered that he could exploit to buy Heartstriker a way out of this that didn't involve giving up or starting a war. Because there *would* be a war. Julius wasn't sure about the rest of his family, but Justin would fight any foreign rule to the death. The same went for Conrad, and if the knights fought, others would join, which meant a lot of dragons he cared about would die. They could *all* die if he didn't figure out a plan to fix this, but despite having read it ten times now, the surrender agreement the emperor's aide had given them still didn't make sense to him.

"I don't like this."

"So you keep saying," his mother drawled.

"Because it keeps being true," Julius growled, smacking the scroll in his hands. "This surrender doesn't make any sense! Why are they being so nice to us?"

Bethesda choked on her cognac. "*That's* what you take issue with?" she sputtered. "They're too *nice?* I thought that was your entire shtick."

"Not when it's suspicious! The Golden Emperor has us over a barrel. He has *zero* reason to give us any concessions, but these terms read like a love letter. Listen to this."

He unraveled the scroll, sliding the elegant paper between his fingers until he reached the English translation of the Chinese text. "The introduction is exactly what you'd expect: unconditional surrender, weakness of our clan before the emperor's might, and so on. After that, though, it goes off the rails. The first 'demand'"— he lifted his fingers to make air quotes—"is that once we're conquered, Heartstriker will retain the right to self-rule and join the Golden Empire as one of its clans. We also keep control of all our territories, assets, and businesses. He's not even charging us taxes for the first hundred years."

"Really?" Bethesda scowled thoughtfully. "That doesn't sound so bad."

"It's wonderful," Julius agreed. "That's the problem. They invaded us knowing we couldn't fight back, but this surrender is written like they're afraid we'll say no. *Why?* They made it abundantly clear this morning how much they hate our clan and you personally, but there's not even a mention of you stepping down." He shook his head. "It doesn't make any sense. We're under their boot. They should be demanding heads on spikes, not giving us sweetheart deals."

"I'd demand heads on spikes," Bethesda said wistfully. "But while I'm sure the Empress Mother dreams of stuffing me for display, the Qilin's always been odd. They don't call him benevolent for nothing. With luck like his, he can afford to be."

"This goes way beyond benevolence," Julius said. "This is insanity. There's no fealty requirement, no demands for changes to our clan structure, no land grabs or tribute. Other than accepting him as our ruler and joining his empire, he's literally asking for nothing. If I'm reading this part about imperial funds distribution correctly, we might even *make* money off this deal, and that just makes no sense to me. Why bother conquering us at all if he isn't going to get anything out of it? Why is he being so *nice?*"

"If I were less depressed, the hypocrisy of hearing you say that would make my day," his mother said. "But loath as I am to admit you're right about anything, what does it matter? Like you just said, we can't turn him down. I fully intend to rally our clan and make those Chinese snakes rue the day they set foot in our desert, but unless I can do it by tomorrow morning, we're going to have to bow our heads and take his offer. If the emperor wants to be overly generous about it, why should we stop him? It'll just make our inevitable rebellion that much easier."

"Because I don't *want* to rebel," Julius said angrily. "I don't want to surrender at all, especially not if it means signing something that is so obviously a *trap.*"

"Maybe it's not," she said. "I just watched you read that contract ten times over, and it's not as though you don't know how to read between the lines. I had to sit through six hours of your legal nit-picking just yesterday, if you'll recall." She shrugged. "If you can't find the poison in that apple, maybe it's not there."

"But it *has* to be," he said, staring at the paper. "It's the only explanation that makes sense. Why would he go through all the trouble of conquering Heartstriker if he doesn't actually want to conquer Heartstriker?"

"Who cares what he wants?" Bethesda snapped, sitting up at last. "If he wants to piss away his chance to crush us, why are you fighting it? You're a clan head of Heartstriker now. You need to think about what's best for *us*." She waved her glass at the contract in his hands. "If he's going to be a fool about this, we should take full advantage. I say sign ourselves over and leverage the bastard's luck for all he's worth. It'll give Algonquin a new target if nothing else. While they're duking it out, we'll use all the space he's left us to rebuild our power so we're ready to stab him in the back as soon as the opportunity presents itself."

That was a suitably draconic plan. Julius didn't even have any particular moral compunction against betraying the dragons who'd forced them to join in the first place. But he just couldn't shake the feeling that there was something else going on here. He'd heard the cold disdain in the Qilin's magnificent voice. Dragons like that didn't conquer clans just to shower them in kindness. He was here for a reason, and if that reason wasn't actually the conquest of the Heartstriker clan, then there was still a chance Julius could find a way out of this without any bowing *or* backstabbing.

"I'm going to go talk to him," he said, standing up.

Bethesda slumped back down to her gold. "Why are you being so difficult?"

"I got it from my mother."

She rolled her eyes. "He's not going to talk to you."

"We don't know that until I try," Julius said, grabbing his Fang from the gold pile where he'd set it down and fastening the sword to his belt. "But I have to do something. I don't care how good the terms are. I didn't work this hard just to turn around and hand Heartstriker over to someone else. I stalled this for a day. I'm going to use it. It's not like we'll be any more conquered if I fail."

"Don't count on that," Bethesda warned. "As I've learned the hard way these last two weeks, things can *always* get worse. But I've also learned there's no point in trying to stop you from doing stupid things, so knock yourself out. If you need me, I'll be here plotting our revenge."

She rolled over, putting her back to him as she sprawled her human body across the gold coins the way she used to as a dragon. Julius shook his head at her one last time and turned to go, but as he reached for the door, Fredrick grabbed his arm.

"Not you too," Julius muttered.

"You misunderstand," the F said, his voice oddly quiet. "I'm not trying to keep you from seeking an audience with the Qilin. I actually think that's an excellent idea, but you can't leave yet."

"Why not?"

Fredrick cast a worried look at the metal door. "Because we have a visitor."

Julius was opening his mouth to ask who in the world would visit them *now* when the vault door of the overflow treasury swung open to reveal a very tall, very *not* Heartstriker dragon. He looked regal in a long black silk robe that looked like it had been stolen from the set of a Chinese period drama. But though his human form was clearly modeled after mortals of Han Chinese descent, he wasn't one of the Golden Emperor's dragons.

Julius knew that last bit for a fact, because he'd seen this dragon before. It was the third seer, the one who'd been with Bob the night he'd killed Estella. The Black Reach.

"Hello, Julius Heartstriker," he said, flashing him a smile that didn't touch his silvery eyes. "I was hoping we might have a word."

"Okay," Julius said, shooting a nervous look at Fredrick, who didn't look any happier. "Now?"

"Now would be best," the Black Reach said, stepping back into the hallway.

Julius stayed put. Technically, he supposed being singled out by the world's oldest and greatest seer was an honor, but that didn't change the fact that he didn't want to speak with the Black Reach, and not because he was actually Dragon Sees Eternity, the construct tasked with overseeing the future of all dragons. That actually inclined Julius to like him since his brother, Dragon Sees the Beginning, had been so helpful to him and Marci. He didn't want to talk because the Black Reach was the dragon Bob had claimed was destined to kill him, and as mad as he was at his brother right now, Julius would never want anything to do with that.

"I'm sorry," he said, backing up. "But I don't think I have time. I need to go talk to the emperor before—"

"This will only take a moment," the Black Reach promised, folding his hands behind his back. "It's about your brother."

Julius had a lot of brothers, but he didn't think the Black Reach was here to talk about Justin. "You know where Bob is?"

"I know where he will be," the seer replied. "More than that I can't say in company."

He looked pointedly at Fredrick, and Julius ground his teeth. He didn't want to play this game. Not only was this sudden visit almost certainly part of some long-running seer plot to close the trap around his brother, but he didn't have time. The day of grace he'd connived to buy them was already half over. He couldn't afford to waste more of it in the quagmire that was talking to a seer. That said, this might be his only shot at finding out where Bob was, maybe even what he was planning. After all, if anyone knew what Bob was up to, it would be the Black Reach. If that was true, though, why was he here? What information did the construct of the future need from Julius that he couldn't see for himself?

He had no idea. As always, though, trying to think his way through all the angles of seer logic did nothing but give him a splitting headache. There were simply too many variables, too much he didn't know to make the call on whether going along with this was a bad idea or a good one. But anxious as he was to get away from the seer and up to the emperor, the need to know outweighed everything else. Even knowing this was likely all part of a plot to trap his brother, Julius couldn't pass up what might be his only chance to find out what Bob was doing. So, with a deep breath, he stepped out into the hall, motioning for the Black Reach to follow him down the corridor.

• • •

The storage complex in the basement of Heartstriker Mountain was a properly draconic warren. Most of the tunnels led to vaults like the one his mother had taken over for her gold, but there were also plenty of smaller, normal rooms for spare furniture, out-of-season linens, holiday supplies, and whatever else housekeeping needed stuffed into closets. Since he didn't share his mother's love of sleeping on piles of metal, no matter how shiny, Julius had claimed one of these as his temporary room, and that was where he took the Black Reach now.

"Sorry it's so cramped," he said, moving Amelia's ashes and Marci's bag off one of the sheet-covered couches so the eldest seer could sit. "We've had some unexpected guests."

The construct arched an eyebrow at the understatement but didn't comment. He just sat down on the sofa, folding his hands in his lap like a polite guest waiting for his tea.

"So," Julius said nervously, grabbing a spare dining chair from the stack in the corner so he'd have a seat as well. "How may I help you?"

"Actually," the seer said. "I'm here because I believe I can help you."

That was enough to raise every hair on Julius's body. Nice or not, there was nothing that got a dragon's guard up like another dragon suddenly offering to help. "Why would you do that?" he asked, turning in his seat so he could bolt for the door if necessary. "You don't know me."

"But I know Brohomir very well," the Black Reach replied. "I know he has invested a great deal in you, which makes you of great interest to me." He tilted his head. "You know what I am."

It wasn't a question, but Julius answered anyway. "You're Dragon Sees Eternity, an immortal construct built by the ancient dragons from our home plane to ensure what happened there never happens again." He smiled nervously. "My friend and I had a long talk with your brother, Dragon Sees the Beginning."

The Black Reach nodded as though being outed as a magical amalgam from another plane were perfectly routine. "And do you know how I do that? How I guard against the mistakes that must never be repeated?"

Julius began to sweat. "You kill seers."

The Black Reach nodded. "It is a heavy duty, but a necessary one. If you've met my brother, you've seen your old plane, the tiny speck of wasteland that's left of it, anyway. What happened there was a tragedy, the final result of an eons-long path of greed and short-sightedness. All were complicit, but seers were the driving force. They were the ones who sold the future to buy the present, dooming all dragons in the process. The only reason you exist is because a handful of your ancestors were fast enough to get through the portal ahead of the collapse and take refuge here, on this plane." He put a hand on his chest. "I exist to make sure that never happens again."

He said this with the utmost gravity, and Julius absolutely agreed. No one who'd seen the ashen waste of the dragons' old home could ever claim what had happened there was anything but a disaster. But that still didn't explain why the Black Reach was talking to *him*.

"Because you are important to Brohomir," the seer said before he could ask. "You are the key to his plans."

"But I don't know what those are!" Julius cried. "I have no idea what he's doing or why he's doing it. I don't even know where he is!"

"That doesn't matter," the Black Reach said dismissively. "Wherever he is right now, it is certain he will come back to you."

"Oh," Julius said, not sure whether to be relieved or terrified. "Did you foresee that?"

"No," the seer said, shaking his head. "You are Brohomir's pawn, and he shrouds you well. But while I can't see your future specifically, I've always known his. That's why I'm here. I've watched your brother since before he hatched, which means I've observed his specific interest in you for a long time. It's been quite fascinating. I've seen a lot of strategies for manipulating the future over the past ten thousand years, but I've never seen a seer pin everything so completely on one point." He reached out to tap a long finger against Julius's chest. "You."

Julius swallowed.

"At this point, the word 'linchpin' is an utterly inadequate description for the role he's put you in," the Black Reach went on. "At this stage, *every* plot Brohomir spins up leads back to you in some fashion. I can see them all, every string he pulls and line he casts, and yet I still don't understand why."

"That makes two of us," Julius said, slumping in his chair. "What you're saying isn't exactly a surprise. Bob's told me a couple times now that I was his crux, though he didn't make it sound quite that important. But I still have no idea what he wants, or why he picked *me*."

"That's perfectly normal," the Black Reach assured him. "No pawn sees the whole game. But since you are so important, I feel I must warn you that your brother has turned down a dangerous path. I may not understand all his motives yet, but I have seen his future, and it is not one I can allow. If he continues on his present course, I will have no choice but to—"

"Kill him," Julius said, stomach clenching. "You're going to kill him, aren't you?"

"I am," the seer said quietly. "But before you label me the enemy, know that I am here precisely because I want to avoid that fate. Like every seer before him, Brohomir knows what he must do to preserve his life. He's known I am his death since he was younger than you, and how to avoid it. He knows perfectly well the temptations he must not touch, yet he still pursues them, and I don't know why."

He leaned forward, bracing his elbows on his knees so he could look Julius in the eyes. "That's why I've come to you. You're his pivot, the point around which all his plans revolve. I was hoping that, if you told me what he's asked you to do, it might help us both better understand his motives and prevent an unfortunate end."

He said that so earnestly, Julius almost answered before he could think about it. But as desperate as he was to save his brother, he wasn't *that* stupid.

"Why should I tell you anything?" he said suspiciously. "You just said you're going to kill him."

"Only if he makes me," the Black Reach said, his eyes sad. "I do not enjoy killing seers, Julius. I may not be a living dragon as you are, but I'm not actually made of stone. I've known every seer that's ever been born on this plane. I watched them all grow and guided them as best I could, but it's neither my purpose nor my place to dictate the future of our kind. Even when I care for a seer greatly, I can't force them to choose as I would like. I exist for one purpose: to be a check on the power of seers and ensure our future is never sold again."

"But, if that's all you do, why are you their death?" Julius asked. "Why is *every* seer's first vision you killing them if you only come out when they break your rule?"

"Because no seer can resist," the Black Reach said angrily. "You saw what Estella did just with the chains, and that was only a minor manifestation. The power to force the future is always there. Waiting. *Tempting.* It may take thousands of years, but sooner or later, *every* seer comes up against a battle they can't win with knowledge of the future alone. When that happens, they inevitably reach for the one weapon that will guarantee their victory, and I am forced to stop them."

"But why?" Julius asked again. "They've all seen their deaths, right? They *know* you're going to kill them for doing it, so why try?"

"Because every seer thinks they're special," he said, shaking his head. "They spend their entire lives knowing things others don't and using that knowledge to do the impossible. When you're that powerful, it's only a small stretch to thinking you're unstoppable. That you can do what no one else has ever done. That you can beat *me*."

"Can they?" Julius asked. "I mean, I get that you're older and better and can probably run circles around any other seer, but no one's *actually* invincible."

"I am," the Black Reach said calmly. "I know that sounds like boasting, but this is what I was created for. I was constructed by the greatest seers of our old world specifically to be a weapon against *them*. I can't be defeated, at least not by a seer."

"But can't you just tell them that? Bob's not Estella. He's not *crazy*. I'm sure if you just explained all of that to him, he'd—"

"You think I haven't tried?" the Black Reach snapped. "Do you have *any idea* how frustrating it is to watch one of the best seers ever born throw himself away? Brohomir knows *exactly* what is coming and why he shouldn't do it, but he still refuses to change, and I've reached the end of my ability to reason with him."

"I hope you're not expecting me to get through to him," Julius said. "Bob doesn't listen to me."

"But he does *talk* to you," the seer said, staring at him intently. "You're different from other dragons, Julius. I told you flat out when we started that your brother was in trouble, and you didn't even try to use that to your advantage. You didn't offer to sell him out to me or trade information for favors. You just wanted to help, to save him."

"Of *course* I wanted to save him," Julius said. "He's my brother."

"There's no 'of course' about it," the Black Reach said, leaning closer. "Do you know how long I've waited for a dragon like you? One who'd legitimately choose his brother's life over a debt with Dragon Sees Eternity? You are incredibly rare, and I believe that's why Brohomir picked you. Not just because you won't betray him, but because *I* don't want to kill you. I could end all of Brohomir's plotting right now, save his life by ending yours and all the plots he's attached to you, but I won't. I *can't*, because you're exactly the sort of peaceful, honest dragon I've always hoped would emerge one day. Under your leadership, I can foresee Heartstriker evolving to the point where you might finally be able to put a stop to the foolish clan infighting that's forever pushing seers to seek the ends I must kill them for taking. That's *power*, Julius, and I'm sure it's why Bob chose you. Where better to run your plans than through the one dragon I don't want to kill? But his cleverness is also his weakness, because by making you the center of all his plans, Bob has handed you—the only one who truly cares—the power to save his life. He's the seer, but you're the one holding all his strings. If you let them go, everything he's built will fall apart, and I won't have to do a thing."

A cold knot began to form in Julius's chest. "You want me to betray Bob."

"To save his life," the Black Reach said angrily. "Your brother is one of the best seers I've ever known, but his cleverness and audacity have led him farther down the path of self-destruction than any dragon before him. He's made a bargain with a power so deadly, I can't even tell you its name without risking the future I was created to guard. If he takes one more step, I cannot stay my hand, but you can make it so I don't have to act at all. That's not betrayal, Julius. That's saving him from himself. If you truly care for Brohomir, then help me. Disrupt his plans, foil his plots. Don't do whatever it is he's ordered you to do. Let him *fail*, and you will save his life."

He finished with a smile. Not the polite one from earlier, but a true, heartfelt smile that changed his entire face, making him look less like a deadly weapon and more like a desperate old dragon. And that was the hardest part, because Julius was now certain the Black Reach hadn't come here to manipulate him or set a trap. Whatever other games he might be playing, he believed the seer truly wanted to save Bob, and that was the problem, because Julius didn't know how.

"If that's what you need, I'm afraid I can't help you," he said apologetically. "I absolutely believe you want to save my brother.

I want to save him, too, but I can't go against his plans, because I don't know what they are."

"That doesn't matter," the Black Reach said dismissively. "You don't have to know a game to ruin it. Just don't do whatever it is he's told you to do, and the whole thing should fall apart on its own."

"But that's what I'm trying to tell you," Julius said. "Other than ordering me not to free Chelsie, which I already ignored, Bob's never told me to do anything except be myself."

The Black Reach went still, staring at Julius as though he'd started speaking an unknown language. "That's it?" he said at last. "'Be yourself'? You're sure that's all he's said?"

Julius nodded, and the old seer scowled. "That can't be it."

"I know," Julius said, not sure whether to laugh or cry at the absurdity. "But I swear that's all he's said. Believe me, if I'd known he was planning to kill Amelia, we wouldn't be having this conversation. I would have already disrupted his plots into itty-bitty pieces. But I had no idea. You and Chelsie and everyone else go on and on about how I'm Bob's chosen one, but I must be the self-operating kind, because he doesn't tell me *anything*. I don't even get crazy texts anymore." And man, he never thought he'd miss those.

The Black Reach looked down at his lap, his long fingers drumming against his legs as he thought that through. The silence lasted so long, Julius started to worry he'd gone into some kind of sleep mode or whatever constructs did when they got overloaded. Before he could decide what to do about that, though, the Black Reach rose to his feet.

"I appreciate you speaking with me," he said, inclining his head. "It's been…informative."

"Of course," Julius said automatically, hopping up as well. "But before you go, can you tell me anything? You said you knew where Bob was going to be. If you told me, maybe I could find him. Talk to him. He's a smart dragon. I'm sure I could—"

"No," the Black Reach said firmly. "Giving you his location does nothing. You're his pawn. If I move you, he'll just move you back."

He thought a moment more, and then he shook his head again. "No. At this stage, I think it's better for you to continue as you've been, though if he *does* ask you for something, keep my advice in mind."

"I will," Julius promised, biting his lip. "But it'd be a lot easier if you could give me some kind of hint about what it is he's trying to do. If you're after him, it's got to be something to do with selling the future, but why? What's he trying to make happen?"

"I can't tell you," the Black Reach said, clearly frustrated. "Not because I don't trust you, but because he hasn't done it yet. I've actually pushed the boundaries of my position a great deal just by coming to speak to you today. If I push further, I risk tipping my own hand, and that's not a chance I can take. But rest assured, I would not be here if the threat were not great. You know what's at stake now. If you're the dragon I believe you to be, you'll do everything you can to stop Brohomir before he dooms himself, which is all I can ask."

"But how will I know?" Julius asked. "I don't even understand what I'm trying to stop."

"You will," the Black Reach promised, opening the door. "When it happens, you'll know, because you'll be at the heart of it." He ducked his head to Julius one last time before stepping into the hall. "See you in Detroit."

"Wait!" Julius cried, running after him. "What happens in…"

The words died on his lips as he burst into the hall. The long, *empty* hall. Julius couldn't even smell the Black Reach anymore save for a faint hint of old ash. He searched anyway, walking all the way back to his mother's vault before he gave up. Whatever had happened, it was obvious the seer was no longer in the mountain. Defeated, Julius went back to his temporary room to try and think all of this through. He'd just settled himself down on the sheet-covered couch where the Black Reach had been sitting when he noticed Marci's bag was no longer beside it.

• • •

"I'm not saying you're wrong, sir," Fredrick said gently. "But why would the Black Reach steal your human's bag?"

"Why do seers do anything?" Julius whispered back, fists clenched in fury. "But her bag was in my room when we started, and when I came back, it was gone. No one else could have taken it."

Fredrick heaved a frustrated sigh, and honestly, Julius couldn't blame him. They were in the elevator on their way up to the mountain's peak to try and talk with the Golden Emperor. If there was ever a time Julius needed to focus, it was now, but he couldn't let this go. That bag was all he had left of Marci. "I have to get it back."

"Was there anything in her bag that the Black Reach might have wanted?"

Julius had no idea. He didn't even know what was inside it. He'd been too upset to go through Marci's things when Chelsie had handed them over last night, and there'd been no chance this morning with the invasion. Other than the blood, though, her shoulder bag hadn't looked or felt different from all the times he'd grabbed it for her back in the DFZ. The poor thing was still stuffed to the seams, despite all the times Marci had complained about never being able to find anything. He still remembered the exact tone of her voice the last time she'd sworn to get organized, or at least buy a bigger bag, trying in vain to stuff all her casting supplies into the—

He stopped, body shaking. As always, any thoughts about the past, even innocent ones, pushed him right back to the dark place he'd been before Chelsie had dragged him out. No matter how busy he kept himself, whenever he let his thoughts drift, Marci's loss was still right there, like a knife in his side. In a perverse, selfish way, he was almost glad the emperor had invaded. It gave him an emergency, something bigger to distract his attention away from the yawning emptiness. He needed that right now.

He just wished the Black Reach hadn't taken his last piece of her.

"I'm sure the bag will come back," Fredrick said, giving him an encouraging smile. "Assuming he did take it, seers don't do things without reason. But if you need some time—"

"No," Julius said firmly, pulling himself together. "Buying time was my idea. So was going to talk to the emperor. If I'm not going to make good on those, we might as well do what Mother wants and sign the surrender now."

"It doesn't have to be all one or the other," the F argued. "Ian won't be back until early tomorrow. We have time if you need it."

"I do need time, which is why I can't waste it." He closed his eyes and gave himself a shake, forcing the grief back to the corners of his mind to focus on the task ahead of them. "There," he said when he'd finished. "I'm fine. Everything will be *fine*. Let's do this."

Fredrick didn't look convinced, but he didn't push. He just moved closer to his youngest brother as the elevator rolled to a stop, the golden doors opening to reveal the hallway to the throne room at the top of Heartstriker Mountain.

Or what was left of it.

"What the—"

Fredrick recovered first, grabbing the elevator doors as he leaned over the panel to check the floor number, but there was no mistake. This *was* the top floor, it was just—

"It's empty," Julius said, stepping out into what had been Bethesda's famous Hall of Heads. *Had* been, because all the grisly trophies from their mother's bloody rise to the top were now gone. Even the clean spots from the wooden mounting plaques had been scrubbed away, leaving nothing but empty stone walls from the elevator all the way to the throne room doors.

"How did they do this?" Fredrick whispered, his eyes wide. "Some of those heads were cursed, not to mention thousands of pounds."

"I suppose anything's possible with enough manpower," Julius whispered back, keeping his eyes on the doors at the hall's end, where a pair of terrifying men in traditional Mongolian dress were standing guard at the throne room doors. *Identical* men, who didn't smell like men at all. They smelled like dragons, the same two red ones that had stopped him and his mother in the desert. The ones who were the same size as Conrad.

"Stay close," he whispered, straightening the collar of the old-fashioned, ill-fitting suit Fredrick had dug out of storage for him.

The F did better than that. He was practically walking on Julius's heels as they made their way down the now-headless hall, stopping a respectful distance from the silent guards.

"Hello," Julius said, trying to look as friendly and unintimidating as possible. Not that he could have intimidated dragons like this. "You probably remember me from this morning, but I'm Julius Heartstriker, one of the heads of the Heartstriker Council. I've come to request an audience with the Qilin."

"The Golden Emperor does not wish to see you," the guard on the left said, in perfect English. "Come back tomorrow at the appointed time of surrender."

"How do you know he doesn't wish to see me if you didn't ask?" Julius countered, smiling politely. "I promise not to take too much of his time. I just have a few questions about the surrender agreement. The sooner I get them answered, the faster we can end this awkward waiting period and come to an agreement."

Considering Heartstriker's surrender was a *when* rather than an *if*, that shouldn't have worked, but as Julius had noticed downstairs, the emperor wasn't treating it like a done deal. No dragon confident in his success would sweeten a deal that much right off the bat, and sure enough, the moment he hinted there was a chance of wrapping things up faster, the Qilin's dragons jumped on it.

While the left one kept an eye on them, the red dragon on the right pulled out his phone. Whatever message he sent, the answer must have been immediate, because a few seconds later, the twins nodded at each other, and the left dragon opened the throne room door, motioning for Julius and Fredrick to follow him inside. With a deep breath, Julius did, slipping nervously between the double doors into a throne room that, once again, looked nothing like he remembered.

Like the Hall of Heads leading up to it, the Heartstriker throne room had been stripped clean. *Everything* was gone: the three-sided council table, the Quetzalcoatl's skull, the art displays from the adjacent hallways, everything. Even the mosaics depicting the Heartstriker in all her feathered glory had been picked out of the walls tile by tile. The only thing that *hadn't* been moved was Chelsie's Fang, which was still lying on the balcony where she'd dropped it yesterday, probably because no one else could pick it up. Other than that one detail, though, Julius felt as though he were standing in a completely different mountain, but the strangest change of all was the throne.

He didn't know how they'd gotten it in here, but standing in the place where their Council table had been this morning was a massive and incredibly lifelike statue of a twisting golden dragon that served as the base for two thrones. A large one made of white jade positioned inside the dragon's open mouth, and a smaller, black jade one cradled in the crook of its tail. The whole thing was incredibly beautiful, a true work of art that absolutely did not belong here. He was still staring at it in horrified wonder when the door to what had been Bethesda's apartments flew open, and the Empress Mother hobbled into the room.

"I understand you wish to discuss your surrender," she said, cane clacking against the cracked stone of the throne room's polished floor as she made her way toward the golden dragon. By the time she reached it, the red dragon who'd let them in was already there, ready to lift the old crone off the ground and into the smaller of the two thrones. Once seated, the Empress Mother took her time getting settled, placing her cane into a crook in the golden dragon's claws that seemed tailor-made for the purpose before folding her hands in her lap. Only then, when she was comfortable and elevated above the Heartstrikers in every way, did she finally turn her red eyes on Julius.

"Speak," she commanded. "We've wasted enough time already."

Julius would have pointed out she was the one wasting time, but he couldn't say a word. He was still trying to make sense of how his world had changed so quickly.

If someone had asked him a week ago about redecorating the throne room, he'd have been all for it. He'd always hated and feared this place, which existed only to be a gaudy showcase for Bethesda's power. Now, though, standing in the emptiness left by the removed mosaics and the headless hall and the missing skull with a foreign throne sitting at the heart of Heartstriker power, it suddenly didn't matter that they were all just symbols, and his mother's symbols at that. They were still part of Heartstriker. Gaudy or not, seeing them erased like this made Julius feel more under attack than the army of dragons flying into their territory had. For the first time in his life, he wanted to lash out for his clan, to make these dragons pay for what they had done to the Heartstrikers. He was still struggling to get the unfamiliar violent urge in check when the Empress Mother rapped her knuckles against the stone of her black throne.

"Are you deaf, child?" she asked sharply. "I am doing you a great honor coming to answer your questions in person. You would be wise not to waste my generosity. Now tell me, what new groveling do you bring from your worm of a mother?"

With every arrogant word, Julius's anger flared hotter and hotter. "I'm not my mother's mouthpiece," he growled. "I'm also not a *child*. I'm a head of Heartstriker, an elected member of our Council, and *you* are sitting where our table should be."

"That thing?" The Empress Mother smiled. "I had it removed, along with everything else. This entire peak was a shrine to the violent, backward, barbaric culture that elevated a creature like Bethesda. Such an environment is no place for the golden Qilin, even temporarily, so I did what needed to be done." She arched an eyebrow at Julius. "Surely you're not here to defend your mother's taste."

"Taste has nothing to do with it," Julius said angrily. "You changed our mountain without permission!"

"We do not need your permission," she said haughtily. "Your conquest is final in all but formality. That you are free to complain about such obvious improvements is a sign of the enormous and frankly undeserved favor the emperor shows to your clan. Did you *enjoy* walking down a hall of corpses?"

Julius hadn't. If she'd asked first, Julius would have personally helped them take down the Hall of Heads. But they *hadn't* asked.

No one had. They'd just done it, and the more he thought about that, the more determined Julius became to never surrender to the Golden Emperor. It didn't matter how awful Bethesda's taste had been. Changing another clan's seat of power without bothering to seek input from the dragons whose traditions you were "improving" wasn't the action of a ruler Julius could ever call his emperor.

"Enough of this," the empress said, narrowing her eyes at what Julius realized must have been a murderously defiant expression. "I did not disrupt my rest to listen to a spoiled whelp complain. You said you had questions. Speak them or go."

"I will," Julius said, glaring back at her. "But only to the Qilin himself."

"Insects do not demand to speak to emperors."

"I'm not an insect," he said angrily. "I'm a clan head, just like your son. Until he actually conquers Heartstriker, that makes us equals, and equals speak face to face, not through a third party."

That was enough to make the empress rise from her throne, but Julius wasn't finished. "You can threaten me all you like," he snapped. "But I fought for the right to stand at the head of Heartstriker, and I will not be bullied into backing down by a toothless old dragon who thinks she has power because her son is emperor."

By the time he finished, his heart was pounding like he was in the middle of a fight. But while the anger on the empress's face was terrifying, Julius would go down fighting before he took a word of it back. Heartstriker might be on the verge of getting crushed, but until it crumbled, this was *his* clan, the family he'd fought his mother for and won. He refused to surrender that to anyone, but especially not to a dragon as haughty, insulting, and undeserving as this one.

"You certainly are your mother's son," the empress said at last, looking down her nose as though she was seriously considering roasting him on the spot. "So much pride, and so little done to deserve it. But it matters not. Demands without the power to back them up are nothing but empty words, and that's all a worm like you has left."

Julius was opening his mouth to say she was wrong. That Heartstriker was still the largest dragon clan in the world, and they would *never* bow to an emperor who demanded their obedience but did nothing to deserve their respect. Unfortunately, he didn't get the chance. Before a word could leave his lips, the Empress Mother lifted her chin, looking over Julius and Fredrick's heads at the pair of red dragons guarding the door behind them.

"The audience is over," she announced. "Take the young Heartstriker out to the edge of the desert and kill him."

Julius froze, eyes going wide. "What?"

"Did you not hear me?" the empress asked innocently. "I've decided you're going to die."

"But you—" He began to sputter. "You can't do that!"

"Of course I can," she said. "Because unlike you, I have *actual* power. I'm an empress, whereas you're barely one-third of a clan head. An *elected* third. If you die, you don't even have an heir to take up your cause. Your family will simply choose another of the Broodmare's infinite children to replace you, and while I'm sure he'll be every bit as arrogant and ridiculous, at least he'll have your death to help correct his behavior."

Her smile turned into a sharp-toothed leer as the red dragons stalked toward them. Julius swore under his breath and turned to face them, dropping a hand to his Fang. Fredrick had already moved to guard his flank, staring at the approaching red dragons with grim determination. "Sir," he said quietly. "We can't—"

"I know," Julius said, drawing his sword, not that it would do much good. His Fang only froze Heartstrikers, and while it was still a perfectly serviceable blade, Julius had never been much good with those. The Mongolian dragons certainly didn't look worried. They didn't even have weapons, and they were still advancing fearlessly, grinning at Julius and Fredrick as if taking the two of them down would be no problem at all. Which, considering their size, it probably wouldn't be.

"If you kill me, you'll have to wait even longer for your surrender," Julius warned. "Weeks, maybe months."

"A trial to be sure," the empress replied. "But one I'm willing to endure to be rid of a recalcitrant whelp bent on impeding the best stroke of luck your backward clan's ever had for the sake of his pride. I'm sure your replacement will not make the same mistake."

Julius cursed under his breath. So much for that. The red dragons were now less than ten feet away, spreading out to attack Julius and Fredrick from both sides at once. Because he was a real dragon, Fredrick instantly adjusted his position to match the new arrangement, but all Julius could focus on was how he'd just gotten them both killed. He was about to suggest they make a break for the balcony when the door in the wall behind the new throne—the one that led to what had been to Bethesda's apartments—clicked open.

The Empress Mother went still at the sound. So did the twins. For a heartbeat, no one moved. Then the empress flicked her fingers, and the twins bolted back to their guard positions by the door, leaving Julius and Fredrick standing back to back in the middle of the room as a dragon wearing blue robes came around the corner of the massive throne.

Locked in fight-or-flight, Julius's instincts focused instantly on the newcomer. But while he was obviously a member of the emperor's court, the new dragon looked legitimately baffled by the scene in front of him. By contrast, the Empress Mother had suddenly become the picture of serenity, her bloodthirsty smile evaporating as she turned to acknowledge their visitor.

"What is it, Lao?" she asked placidly. "Does my son require my attention?"

The new dragon, Lao, shook his head. "No, Empress. I was just passing through on my way to find the youngest Heartstriker."

The Empress Mother blinked in surprise, but Julius had already jumped. "That's me!" he said loudly, shoving his Fang back into its sheath. "I'm Julius Heartstriker."

"So I see," Lao said, looking him over before turning back to the empress. "Were you busy with him, Empress Mother? The Qilin wanted to ask him a question, but I'd be happy to wait if you're—"

"No!" Julius said. "We actually came up to ask for an audience with the emperor. The Empress Mother was just about to grant it when you arrived."

The old dragoness's red eyes narrowed dangerously, but when she didn't call him on the lie, Julius knew he'd just found the limit of her vaunted power.

"I'd like nothing better than to speak with the Golden Emperor," he said brightly, turning all of his attention to Lao, whom Julius's nose had just identified as the blue dragon who'd thrown the robe over the Qilin when he'd landed and handed Julius the surrender scroll. "You work for him, right?"

"I am his cousin and sorcerer," Lao said, looking nervously at the Empress Mother. But while it was clear he knew he'd interrupted something, his loyalty must have been to the emperor alone, because he didn't ask her if he should wait again. He just turned and walked back to the door that led to Bethesda's apartments in the rear half of the mountain's peak, beckoning for the Heartstrikers to follow.

Julius didn't wait to be told twice. He bolted for the exit, dragging Fredrick behind him as they fled the throne room under the Empress Mother's murderous glare.

• • •

"That was lucky," Fredrick whispered when they were safely on the other side.

"I think 'lucky' is the operative word," Julius whispered back, looking around at what had been his mother's front parlor.

Like everything else up here, the Heartstriker's private rooms had been swept absolutely clean. Unlike the empty Hall of Heads and throne room, though, these had been redecorated with potted plants, vases in a variety of styles from traditional Ming to modern art pieces, and paintings. Absolutely lovely paintings, actually.

Like the vases, the art on the walls came in a wide variety of styles with modern abstract pieces hanging next to traditional watercolor landscapes depicting gorgeously rendered dragons floating over mountains and rice paddies. The wide difference should have been jarring, but the colors, lines, and textures had been deftly arranged so that each painting balanced its neighbors. The result was perfect harmony, an effortless greater beauty that was the polar opposite of Bethesda's gaudy gold furniture and left no question as to whose rooms these were now.

"This way," Lao said. "The immaculate Qilin desires to see you immediately."

Julius followed obediently, doing his best not to trip over his feet as he gawked at the beautiful changes, which continued down the hallway that ran through the middle of his mother's suite. He was taking a mental inventory of everything that had been replaced when Lao stopped at the doorway to what had been Bethesda's sitting room, the one where she and David had been waiting for Julius the morning of their first Council meeting. When he tried to walk inside, though, the blue dragon stopped him.

"Your sword."

Julius blinked at him. "Sword?"

Lao's jaw tightened in annoyance. "However insignificant the threat may be, we cannot allow armed outsiders to enter the Golden Emperor's presence. You must hand over your weapon before I can permit you to go inside."

Julius found it odd that the Living Embodiment of Good Fortune would worry about something as mundane as a sword. But the request wasn't unreasonable, so he obediently removed his Fang, though he didn't offer it to Lao. When the blue dragon scowled, he explained, "Fangs of the Heartstriker are particular about who touches them."

He'd expected to have to say a lot more than that, but to his surprise, Lao nodded. "We've already had a run-in with the sword on the balcony," he said, leaning away from the sheathed blade in Julius's hands. "You may leave it here, along with your servant."

"Fredrick's not my servant," Julius said quickly. "He's my brother, and I'd like him to come with me if that's okay."

The Chinese dragon's eyebrows shot up. "*That's* your brother?"

Julius couldn't blame him for being surprised. The tall, stoic, elegantly scowling Fredrick looked nothing like Julius—who was short for a dragon with Bethesda's trademark sky-high cheekbones and a very undraconic habit of smiling. It also didn't help that the green of Fredrick's eyes still looked weirdly off. It hadn't been so noticeable down in the basement, but up here in the bright afternoon sunshine streaming down from the skylights that kept Bethesda's apartment hallway from feeling like a bomb shelter, they didn't even look properly green, much less Heartstriker green. They were more like the color of yellowed grass in the fall, which definitely wasn't the color they'd been when Julius had met him. He had no idea what could have caused the change, but it wasn't helping Fredrick look like a Heartstriker. Thankfully, Lao didn't know enough to realize just how strange that was.

"I suppose anything is possible in your family," he said with an elegant shrug. "The Broodmare is famous for her lack of standards, so it makes sense that her children would show a great deal of variance."

He stopped there, smiling, but Julius was too used to comments at his mother's expense to even be fazed at this point. When it was clear he wasn't going to get the rise he wanted, Lao moved on.

"You may bring your brother if you wish, but he'll have to hold his tongue. The emperor is tired from the long journey, and the burden of this invasion weighs heavily upon his mind. One Heartstriker is bad enough after the trouble you've caused. I will not allow you to aggravate things further by teaming up on him."

"Hold up," Julius said angrily. "You're upset at *us* that your emperor is stressed out from taking over *our* territory?"

"Yes," Lao said without missing a beat. "If your clan hadn't been such a failure on all fronts, he wouldn't have been forced to take such drastic measures."

"Or he could have stayed home," Julius said, exasperated. "I'm not trying to start a fight, but if you hate being here so much, you can always just leave."

"I would like nothing better," Lao said passionately. "But it is not my place to question the emperor's will. For ten thousand years, the Qilins have ruled the Chinese clans in peace, harmony, and prosperity. Like his father before him, the Golden Emperor's great good fortune has sheltered us from the constant war and strife that plagues the rest of the dragon clans. We are all blessed to dwell in his presence. If he wishes to extend that blessing to you, we trust his wisdom, but that doesn't mean we trust *you*."

He stepped closer, leaning down until his face was level with Julius's. "I don't know what you said to anger the empress," he said quietly. "But the Golden Empire's prosperity depends on the Qilin's serenity. If you upset him as you did his mother, I will throw you back to her, and I will make sure you are not rescued a second time. Do I make myself clear, Heartstriker?"

As crystal. But while Julius had no problem following Lao's threat, the larger picture was more confusing than ever. Why was everyone so concerned about upsetting the Qilin? Did something happen when he got mad? And if so, why had he risked that by invading Heartstriker? Especially with those ridiculous surrender terms? The more Julius saw of this invasion, the more convinced he became that *no one* in the Golden Empire wanted to be here, so why were they? Surely there had to be a better way of fighting Algonquin.

As always, nothing about this made sense. The more he learned about the Qilin, the less he understood. But while Julius didn't like being threatened by Lao any more than he enjoyed it from his own family, he couldn't afford to walk away. This meeting was his only chance to talk face to face with the one dragon who knew what was actually going on. Julius was willing to put up with a lot for that, so he meekly lowered his head, dropping his eyes in the ultimate display of draconic submission as he leaned over to set his Fang of the Heartstriker on the floor at Lao's feet.

"There," he said, holding up his empty hands in surrender. "Like I've said from the start, we don't want any conflict. We just want to talk."

151

Lao still looked suspicious, but Julius was being absolutely sincere. Even Fredrick played along, raising his empty hands as well. Together, it must have been enough, because the blue dragon sighed. "Remember," he growled as he opened the door. "Treat him with the utmost respect. If you say or do anything that disrupts his calm, you will pay for it."

Julius nodded, stepping eagerly into the parlor, which, like everywhere else at the top of the mountain, was totally changed.

The last time Julius had been here, the room had been a red-velvet nightmare. Now, all of the overstuffed divans, red shaded lamps, and awkward nude portraits of his mother were gone. The red-and-gold boudoir paper had been peeled off the walls as well, revealing the mountain's natural rust-colored stone, which someone had scoured to a pale rose. The floor had been scrubbed within an inch of its life as well, removing centuries of soot and dried blood. Even the tiny porthole window had been polished so clean, the glass was practically invisible, allowing the sun to transform the dark chamber into a bright, airy space that felt three times as large as before. Julius couldn't imagine how much effort it had taken to work such a miracle, but it was still nothing compared to the tall dragon in golden robes sitting in front of the unlit fireplace.

For the second time today, seeing the Golden Emperor hit Julius like a punch. It didn't seem to matter that he knew what to expect this time. It simply wasn't possible to ready yourself for something so impossibly perfect.

And perfect he was. Just sitting alone in an empty room with his face hidden by the ever-present golden veil—which was properly pinned to his hair this time rather than just being draped over his head—the Qilin looked more regal than Bethesda had in her full regalia. Admittedly, part of that was because the Qilin's overlapping robes contained more gold than Bethesda's dress, headdress, and jewelry combined.

Mostly, though, it was just him. The way the streaming sunlight struck him perfectly, illuminating the motes of dust in the air above him until they sparkled like a halo. The way his robes, which had to weigh hundreds of pounds between all the ornamentations and threads of gold, draped his body like supple silk. The way the smooth skin his folded hands looked like perfectly carved stone brought to life.

From anyone else, Julius would have suspected an illusion, some kind of trick to make the emperor appear to be more than what he was. With the Qilin, though, it just looked right, because that *was* what he was: more. He was something else, a creature who lived in perfect harmony with everything around him. Just being in his presence made Julius instinctively want to harmonize with him if only so he'd have a place in the tranquil, beautiful scene. He was still standing there gawking in dumb wonder when Lao stepped in front of him with a bow.

"Great emperor," he said, his voice humble and reverent in a way Julius had never heard from a dragon before. "I have brought the young Heartstriker, as you requested."

"Thank you, cousin," the emperor said, turning his veiled face toward Julius as he held out his hand toward one of the elegant mahogany chairs that had been set up in a semicircle in front of him. "Sit."

It was an offer, not a command, but Julius still flinched. The Qilin's voice was softer than it had been this morning, but the power behind it was no less entrancing. *Literally* entrancing, he realized with a jolt. He'd gotten a hint of it back in the desert, but now that they were together in a smaller space, he could actually feel the Qilin's magic pushing him to comply. To not make a fuss or disrupt the perfection. It wasn't as hard or sharp as normal dragon magic, but it was definitely there, and the more it leaned on him, the less Julius liked it.

"I'll stand, thank you," he said, forcing his feet to stay rooted to the floor.

It was probably his imagination, but Julius would have sworn his refusal made the Qilin uncomfortable. It was impossible to tell for sure through the veil, but his body seemed more rigid when he turned to the dragon behind Julius. "Whom have you brought with you?"

"This is my brother," Julius said proudly, reaching back to pull Fredrick forward until he and the F were standing side by side. "Fredrick."

Fredrick dipped his head in a quick bow, but while his face was calm as always, his arm was shaking against Julius's hand. Julius didn't know if that was because the F was afraid of the emperor or if he was simply not used to being pulled out of the background, but he immediately felt like a heel for causing it. He was trying to make eye contact with Fredrick to let him know it was okay to step back again when the Qilin leaned forward.

"*F*redrick?" he said, emphasizing the F. "As in Bethesda's hidden clutch?"

When Fredrick nodded, the Qilin seemed enthralled. "I'd heard rumors that the Heartstriker kept an entire clutch of her own children as servants, but I always assumed it was a story started by her enemies. Maybe even by Bethesda herself as a ploy to play up her ruthlessness. I never dreamed it would actually be true."

"It was true," Fredrick said, his voice quivering. "But not anymore." He smiled down at Julius. "My brother freed us when he came to power, and I swore a debt of loyalty to him in return."

"Which is why you're here," the emperor said, nodding as his veiled head turned back to Julius. "Now I am even more eager to speak with the new head of Heartstriker."

"I'm not really the head," Julius said quickly, drawing a dirty look from Lao, who was pouring them tea from the elegant porcelain tea set sitting on the stoop of Bethesda's freshly scoured fireplace. "I'm just one seat on the Heartstriker Council. We have three."

The emperor shrugged. "So long as you can speak for your clan, and I don't have to speak to Bethesda, it makes no difference to me. But how did you come to form a Council with your mother? When we heard she'd been overthrown, I expected to find her head on a pike."

"If things had gone differently, that probably would have been the case," Julius admitted. "But due to an unlikely series of events, Bethesda's life ended up in my hands, and I don't like killing."

The Qilin tilted his veiled head. "That's an odd statement to hear from a Heartstriker. Your clan is famous for its ruthlessness."

"I've never been very good at living up to expectations," he said proudly, accepting the teacup Lao shoved at him. "I actually used to be the lowest Heartstriker, so I knew what it was like to be under someone else's boot. When I ended up at the top, I couldn't bring myself to put another dragon in that position."

"So you spared her life."

"Not because she deserved it," Julius said quickly. "I'm not apologizing for or forgiving anything my mother has done. I don't know what happened between our clans that made you banish us from China, but I'm sure it was warranted. That said, Heartstriker isn't what it used to be. When I spared my mother and created the Council, I swore to make a better Heartstriker than the one I grew up in. One that's not based on fear, and where dragons don't have to kill to get ahead. That's what I set out to do, and I was almost there when you arrived."

"Then you should continue," the Qilin said calmly. "The terms of surrender specifically state that your clan will continue to govern itself. So long as you don't cause a problem for others, you're free to do as you like."

"Actually, that's what I wanted to talk to you about," Julius said, staring as hard as he could into the emperor's veil in the hopes that he might finally catch a glimpse of his face. "I've read your surrender terms several times now, and while they are quite generous, I'm afraid I don't understand what you're trying to achieve. Other than bringing us into your empire, it doesn't seem like you're going to change anything."

"We're not," he said, his rich voice oddly bitter. "I gave up hope for the Heartstrikers long ago. I admit you seem like an interesting exception to your family's rule, but I'm not so naïve as to believe one dragon can fundamentally alter a clan as large and bloody as yours.

I'm only here to avert a disaster, not break my empire attempting to change what cannot be changed."

"If that's how you feel, why bother conquering us at all?" Julius asked. "If you just want to fight Algonquin, we'd happily work with you as allies. There's no need to take over—"

"I hope this is not what you came to discuss," the emperor interrupted. "I granted you a temporary reprieve out of respect for your customs, but there will be no negotiation. As you said yourself, my terms are quite generous. You can have no legitimate complaints."

"I don't," Julius said. "But—"

"No," the Qilin said. "There is no 'but.' You asked for time to convene your Council. I gave it. But whether your third member arrives to vote or not, the Heartstriker clan will join my empire tomorrow morning as planned."

That was clearly meant to be the end of the discussion, but Julius couldn't leave it. "Can you at least tell me why?" he blurted out, pointedly ignoring Lao, who'd given up even the pretense of serving tea in favor of watching him like a hawk. "When dragon clans conquer each other, it's normally to claim territory or gain dominion over weaker dragons, but you're clearly not the least bit interested in any of that. You're conquering in name only, putting us in your empire, but not actually changing anything. You're not even taking tribute, and I just want to understand *why*. Why bother with all of this if you're not getting anything from it?"

"Is stopping Algonquin not reason enough?" Lao growled.

"It's a great reason," Julius said. "I just don't see what it has to do with us. Heartstriker's not capable of fighting Algonquin right now. The reason you caught us with an empty mountain is because we were getting ready to run. If you'd wanted to come into our territory and fight Algonquin, we absolutely would not have stopped you. Quite the opposite. We gladly would have helped you and been forever in your debt. You have to know that, so I don't think my confusion is out of place. If you were demanding something for our protection—tribute, territory, soldiers—that would make sense, but you're not demanding anything. We actually come out ahead in this deal, while the only thing you get is another liability to defend."

"Then why are you complaining?" Lao snapped.

"Because it's *too* good," Julius snapped back. "You dropped out of the sky in our hour of need and offered to protect us from Algonquin in return for what is basically symbolic surrender. We don't give up our right to rule or control of our territory. You're not even asking for money." He turned back to the Qilin. "I might be a terrible dragon, but even I know things that seem too good to be true usually are. Wouldn't you be suspicious if our positions were reversed?"

By the time he finished, Lao didn't look like he was going to make good on his threat to throw them back to the Empress Mother. He was already breathing smoke in preparation for cooking Julius on the spot himself. The only reason he didn't was because his imperial cousin put a hand on his sleeve.

"And this is your only objection?" the Golden Emperor said quietly. "That the agreement I've given you is 'too good to be true?'"

"That and the part where we don't like the idea of being conquered," Julius said, nodding. "I'm sure this comes as no surprise, but my mother's already planning to stab you in the back."

Lao stepped forward with a hiss. "Is that a threat?"

"I'd call it more of an eventuality," Julius said with a shrug. "You know how proud dragons are. It doesn't matter how generously you dress it up, no one welcomes being conquered. If you force us to bow, we will always be your enemies, but if you come to us as an ally, everything changes." He smiled at the emperor. "Like I said, we don't want to fight you. If your goal is to stop Algonquin, we are absolutely on your side. If you work with us instead of against us, you can still do everything you want, but at the end you'll have a grateful ally rather than a resentful vassal. That's a *way* better outcome for all involved, and I don't understand why you're not doing it. That's what makes me suspicious. You're choosing what is obviously the worst path for everyone, including you, and I can't understand *why*."

He was sweating bullets by the time he finished. On the other side of the small room, Lao was holding back by a thread, blue smoke curling dangerously from his lips, and oddly enough, that made Julius feel better. He'd wondered whether the emperor's dragons protected him out of love or fear. For Lao at least, the fuming smoke was his answer. Even the prickliest dragon didn't get that worked up without something serious on the line. The blue dragon's respect for the Golden Emperor was clearly more than just deference to his power. Lao *really* cared, and that gave Julius hope. Hope that grew infinitely larger when the Qilin spoke again.

"Lao," he said quietly. "I wish to speak with Julius Heartstriker alone."

The blue dragon whirled around, but though he looked horrified, he didn't argue with the order. He just clenched his jaw and reached for Fredrick, who yanked his arm out of the way with a growl of his own.

"It's okay, Fredrick," Julius said, glancing at the emperor before leaning in to whisper, "This could be the break we've been looking for. If he wants to talk alone, then he's going to say something he doesn't want his subjects to hear."

"Or he could kill you," the F growled back.

"He can do that at any time," Julius said, giving his brother a little shove. "Go with Lao. I'll yell if I get in trouble."

The F didn't look happy, but he nodded, allowing himself to be marched out of the room under Lao's watchful glare, leaving Julius and the Golden Emperor alone.

"Thank you for your honesty earlier," the emperor said when their footsteps had faded. "I hadn't considered how my offer would appear from your perspective. I never meant to make you doubt my sincerity."

Julius stared at him in shock. Dragons *never* said thank you to him, or admitted they were wrong. "Does this mean you're going to take me up on the alliance idea?" he asked excitedly.

"No," the emperor said, shaking his head. "I must bring Heartstriker into my empire at all costs."

Julius's soaring spirits dropped like a stone. "But—"

"But you have convinced me to show you why," the emperor continued, rising gracefully from his chair. "Come with me."

He swept out the door, leaving Julius to scramble after him. It was a chase, too. For someone who always moved as though he were walking at the head of a procession, the Golden Emperor was surprisingly fast. Julius had to jog to keep pace as the emperor strode down the hallway toward the rear of the mountain, away from the entry room where Lao and Fredrick were tensely waiting. Given the direction, Julius assumed they were headed for the treasury, but the Qilin stopped several feet short of the giant vault door that had once protected Bethesda's hoard, turning instead to the door of the only room in Bethesda's apartments Julius hadn't been inside yet. The egg-laying chamber.

Well, Julius supposed he must have been here at least once. He was Bethesda's son, after all, and even she kept her hatchlings close for at least the first week. That said, he had zero memory of the laying chamber, and he couldn't help feeling a jolt of apprehension as the Qilin opened the double doors to reveal a large, cave-like room with an enormous circular glass skylight set in the middle of the ceiling.

Since it was afternoon in the desert, this meant the entire cavern was lit up with streaming sunlight, turning the normally reddish rock of Heartstriker Mountain a beautiful rosy gold. It was so unexpectedly lovely, but Julius didn't even notice the paintings until he walked straight into one.

He might have no memory of Bethesda's laying room, but Julius was *positive* those hadn't been here before. The sunlit cave was absolutely packed with paintings. Some had been rolled into scrolls and stacked in the corners. Others were stretched out on wooden frames that had been propped up against the walls wherever there was room. Like the ones he'd seen in the entryway, the paintings were a mix of styles and mediums, though most were watercolors. Chinese landscapes featuring dragons in particular were featured in abundance, though there were also plenty of life studies, animal portraits, and dreamy, impressionistic abstracts.

All of them were breathtakingly beautiful, the work of an obvious master, but unlike the paintings hanging on the walls outside, these were unfinished. Some, particularly the rolled-up ones in the corners, didn't look as if they'd been worked on in centuries. Others showed signs of more recent attention, but only one—a large canvas as tall as Julius himself perched on an easel at the room's center—looked to be an active work in progress. Some of the paint was actually still wet, as though the artist had just stepped away for a moment.

Like most of the paintings in the room, it was a watercolor, but it wasn't a landscape. This was a portrait, a life-size depiction of a beautiful girl with long black hair. A beautiful dragon, Julius realized a second later, because though there were no obvious tells, nothing about the girl in the painting felt mortal. Maybe it was the tension in her tanned limbs beneath her simple block-printed dress, or the way her feet curled like claws into the vibrant grass. Whatever it was, she was heartbreakingly lovely. Powerful in a wild, explosive way that contrasted beautifully with the stiffly formal Chinese garden behind her.

But while she clearly didn't belong there, the dragoness appeared fascinated by her surroundings, crouching attentively beside what was clearly meant to be an ornamental fish pond once the artist finished coloring it in. The fish were already there, a beautifully rendered tangle of orange, white, and black koi. Each one was painted in painstaking detail, their little mouths nibbling at the fingertips the dragoness trailed curiously through the water above them. Magnificent as the fish were, though, what really impressed Julius was the way the artist had captured the girl's delighted smile. It was small, just a curve of her lips, but the joy of it lit up her entire face like sunshine.

That was the detail that transformed the painting from well-done portrait into breathtaking art. It was such a delight to see, Julius didn't actually recognize whose face he was looking at until he'd stared long enough to notice her eyes were green. Not just any green, either, but the same unmistakable color as his. Greener than the verdant grass under her bare feet. Heartstriker green.

Julius stumbled backward, putting several feet between himself and the picture. When he turned to ask the emperor the obvious question, though, he got another shock. While he'd been transfixed by the painting, the Qilin had removed his golden veil.

Not surprisingly, he was unsettlingly good looking. Not merely handsome like most dragons, but flawless on an entirely different level. Even the tiny quirks that gave his face character—his dark, too-straight eyebrows, the sharp line of his nose, his thin mouth— were perfect in their imperfections, an artist's ideal of an elegant Chinese prince. After everything else Julius had seen of the Qilin, that was all par for the course, but the detail he wasn't prepared for were the emperor's eyes.

Not that he'd been taking notes during the chaos of the invasion, but if anyone had asked Julius before this moment what color the emperor's eyes were, he would have guessed the same reptilian red as the Empress Mother's, but that wasn't the case at all. The Qilin's eyes were not red like his mother's or even blue like Lao's. They were golden. Not yellow like a wolf's or an owl's, but true gold. The soft, warm, glistening metallic color every dragon instinctively coveted.

Eyes like golden coins.

Chelsie's bitter words were still echoing in his memory when the Qilin sighed and turned back to the painting. Then, in a small, sad voice, he whispered, "How is she?"

CHAPTER SIX

When Marci brought her knuckles down on the plain, seemingly wooden door of the Merlin Gate, the sound that reverberated through the dark wasn't a knock. It was a gong. An enormous ringing, golden tone that shook the entire swirling sea. If she'd still had a physical body, it would have shaken her to pieces, but whatever Marci was right now—ghost, soul, or some other not-yet-named type of human leftover—at least she didn't have to worry about that. The sound passed right through her, echoing off into the endless expanse until, at last, it faded back to nothing.

And the door did not open.

"Maybe no one's home?" Amelia whispered. "It has been a thousand years."

That was a good point. "I could try opening it myself," Marci suggested, bending down to study the door more closely. "There's no handle or hinges, but if I—"

The door rattled. Marci jerked in surprise, moving closer to Ghost as the something on the other side of the heavy wood clattered, and then light shot through the darkness like a spear as the wooden slab opened inward to reveal a man silhouetted against a wall of warm, glowing light.

Oddly enough, Marci's first thought was that he looked way too young. She wasn't sure what she'd been expecting, but it had definitely been closer to Gandalf or Mad Madame Mim than the elegant twenty-something Asian man standing in the glowing doorway. He was wearing a simple white-and-black robe with an elegantly folded silk fan tucked into his sash. Other than that, though, he had nothing. No sword or weapon, not even a rope that could have served as a casting circle. Marci wasn't stupid enough to assume that meant he was defenseless, though. Even standing on the other side of the door, she could feel magic flowing off of him like water. A sensation that only grew stronger when his mouth began to move.

She frowned in confusion. The man was clearly talking, but nothing was coming out. She was wondering if there was still some kind of barrier between them when the magic rolling off the young man shifted slightly, and a voice suddenly sounded in her ears.

"Welcome," it said, "she who would be Merlin."

The words were clear with no trace of an accent, but though they were obviously said by the man in front of her, the sounds didn't match the movements of his mouth at all. They weren't coming from his mouth, either. The voice was inside her ear, as if she were listening to it through headphones, and Marci's jaw dropped.

"Is that a translation spell?"

The man raised a dubious eyebrow, but Marci was thinking too fast to care. Translation magic was one of the hottest fields in Thaumaturgical spellwork. She'd actually tried her hand at a few versions herself, but like everyone else, she'd never been able to crack the problem of how to make the translated words sound natural. Just as with its computer-based counterparts, magically translated speech lost its intonation and inflection, emerging emotionless and wooden, but not this one. Other than the short delay between when the man spoke and when the words were whispered into Marci's ear, it really did sound as though he were speaking native English, which was incredible. If she could figure out how it worked, a patent on a translation spell like this would be enough to set her up for life!

Assuming, of course, she ever got back to being alive.

That realization knocked the dollar signs out of her eyes, and Marci pulled herself back together. "Sorry," she said, standing up straight to dazzle him with her most professional smile. "I'm Marci Caroline Novalli, PhD candidate in Socratic Thaumaturgy at the University of Nevada Las Vegas and partner to the Empty Wind,

Spirit of the Forgotten Dead. I'm here to pass through the gate and join you as a Merlin."

"Humans do not come here for any other reason," the man said dryly. "But I am not a Merlin."

She blinked. "What?"

"Merlins are human," he explained. "Humans are mortal, and there is no mortal who could wait out the centuries it would take before this door opened again. Knowing this, Abe no Seimei, Onmyōji to the Emperor and head of the Last Circle of the Merlins, and his partner, Inari Okami, God of Prosperity, bound me here to serve as guardian for their greatest work and guide to any who came after."

Marci nodded slowly, eyes going wide. Abe no Seimei was a Japanese sorcerer and one of the world's most famous ancient mages. Finding out he'd also been a Merlin wasn't actually surprising, but the rest of it...

"What do you mean 'bound you?'" she asked in a rush. "Are you a spirit or—"

"Of course not," the man said, insulted. "No spirit may enter this place without a Merlin. I am a shikigami."

"What's a shikigami?"

"A crafted servant," Amelia whispered in her ear. "A spell so complicated, it develops a personality and decision-making abilities of its own."

"*They could do that?!*" Marci cried. "Because you just described magical AI, and no one's done that yet!"

Amelia shrugged. "I keep telling you, modern mages haven't even begun to scratch the surface of the magical knowledge you lost during the drought. Shikigami summoning used to be an entire school of Taoist magic, and Abe no Seimei was the grand master." She grinned at the young man. "What did he name you?"

"I am bound by the characters White, Iron, and Truth," the shikigami said politely. "But you may call me Shiro."

Amelia turned back to Marci with a *there you go* smirk. Marci grinned back maniacally, bouncing on her toes in excitement. After so long scratching at the edges of lost knowledge, she was about to walk right into the Shangri La of lost magical secrets. "Well then, Shiro," she said happily, stepping forward. "Let's get this—"

She cut off with a gasp. The moment she'd tried to cross the threshold from the dark, chaotic sea into the light, something hit her with enough force to send Marci tumbling backward. If Ghost hadn't still been holding on to her hand, she would have been blown right out into the void.

"What was that?" she cried as her spirit set her back on her feet.

"What you may not cross," Shiro replied, his voice no longer polite. "You have made it to the gate, but only those souls who are deemed worthy may enter."

"Deemed worthy by whom?" Marci demanded. "You? Do you know what I went through to get here?"

"No more than any other Merlin," he said. "But I do not make the decision. I am but a servant. The judgment of your worth lies with the Heart of the World."

"Okay," she said, crossing her arms over her chest. "What's that?"

"You will find out when you become a Merlin."

Marci felt like punching something. "I already died for this! What more do I have to do?"

"Anyone can die," Shiro said dismissively. "But becoming a Merlin is not as easy as falling into a grave. It is a privilege reserved for those whose dedication stretches beyond the boundaries of their lives. Mages are no strangers to power, but Merlins make decisions that affect *all* magic, not just their own. That much authority can only be entrusted to someone who keeps in mind the needs of all. Only a true champion of humanity may rise to claim the title of Merlin. Until you prove yourself as one such to the Heart of the World, you may not enter."

Marci supposed that was fair. Merlins were supposed to be the greatest mages in existence. That kind of power couldn't go to just anyone.

"Fine," she said, lifting her chin. "You want us to prove ourselves again? Give us your best shot. Ghost and I will ace any test you can think of."

"Undoubtedly," the shikigami said, peering into the void that was the Empty Wind's face. "You've certainly chosen a grim spirit, but you seem well bonded despite that. Ordinarily, I'd say you have a very good chance, but I'm afraid I cannot permit you to attempt the trials."

"Why not?" Marci demanded.

The shikigami's emotionless eyes slid to Amelia, who was still clinging to Marci's shoulder. "Because, as I said, Merlins are champions of humanity, and no true champion of humanity would arrive at the Merlin Gate on a predator's string."

"What?" Marci said, glancing at Amelia, who cringed. "No, no, you've got this all wrong. Amelia's not like that. She likes humans."

"Love them," Amelia said eagerly. "Seriously, I've never even eaten one."

"She's one of the good dragons," Marci said at the same time. "She sacrificed her life to help me get here."

"All the more reason to deny you," Shiro said, putting a hand on the door. "I met many dragons with my master before he died, enough to know that they never act without benefit to themselves. If a dragon gave up her immortal life to help you reach this place, she must have something very great to gain by you becoming a Merlin. Since you are clearly beholden to her, that makes you a servant of the enemy, and thus unworthy of this place."

"So you're not even going to let us try?" Marci said angrily. "Because of *Amelia?*"

"Because you belong to her, yes," he said coldly. "The Heart of the World is too important to risk exposing to a dragon's tool. If you abandon her to the magic and sever all ties, you may attempt to step through this door again. Until then, we have nothing left to discuss."

"But that's crazy!" Marci cried. "Amelia's my friend, not my puppet master. I'm not going to throw her away for a shot at getting in. What kind of cheap, backstabbing villain of a Merlin would that make me?"

"That is not my concern," Shiro replied. "You asked what you needed to do. I told you. If you will not do it, that is your decision."

"But—"

"The matter is closed," he said, stepping back. "Good luck, young lady. If you change your mind and come back without your dragon, we will talk again."

And then the door slammed shut.

Marci slammed her fists down on the boards, but there was no gong this time. Just the ineffective slap of human skin on unyielding hardwood. She pulled her hands back with a pained curse, sucking on her smarting fingers as she glared furiously at the sealed door. "Can you believe this?"

"That a dragon caused a problem?" Ghost sneered. "Yes."

Amelia sighed. "I wish I could say Shikigami-Face was just being a racist jerk, but historically speaking, he's more right that wrong. Dragons haven't exactly been good neighbors since we arrived on this plane." She shook her head, looking up at Marci with her smoldering wings tucked meekly against her body. "Thank you for not throwing me over, by the way."

Marci snorted. "Like I'd ever. You're the only one who explains anything to me, but I don't know what we're going to do." She glared at the closed door. "This is the only way in, right?"

"The only one I've seen," the Empty Wind said.

She'd thought as much. "How serious do you think he was about the no-dragon thing?"

"Pretty serious," Amelia said. "He's got the teeth to back it up, too. His master, Abe no Seimei, was one of the most powerful sorcerers in history, and he was particularly famous for his shikigami. His constructs were all no joke, but I remember Shiro specifically as being one of his big guns. I've actually encountered him once before, back when Seimei was still alive."

Marci gaped at her. "You *knew* him? Why didn't you say something?!"

"Because he was trying to slay me at the time," Amelia said with a shrug. "To be fair, I was robbing his library."

"*Amelia!*"

"What?" she cried. "I was young! I needed the books! Thankfully, I don't think he recognized me. I do look pretty different now. But I don't think we're going to be able to talk him around on this. Book theft notwithstanding, I was hardly the most dangerous dragon back when Seimei and his shikigami were active, nor the worst behaved. He comes by his prejudice honestly, is what I'm saying."

Ghost snorted. "Most do."

Amelia could only shrug at that, and Marci dragged her hands over her face with a groan. "So what do we do if we can't change his mind? Becoming a Merlin was plan A, B, and C. We can't stay out here." She threw out her hands at the chaotic black morass of magic that surrounded them.

"We're not beaten yet," Ghost said angrily. "A shikigami is neither human nor spirit. Who is worthy of being Merlin is not his to say." He turned his glowing eyes on the pillar above them. "I say we make our own way in."

"I'm not entirely against it," Marci admitted. "But I don't think force is the right answer here. Shiro's just doing his job, and that barrier of his is no joke. I barely took one step into the light, and the stupid thing hit me like a—"

She stopped, grabbing her spirit's freezing arm for balance as the stone rumbled under her feet. "What was that?"

"Not sure," the Empty Wind said, his glowing eyes darting through the dark as the swells of magic began to churn. "I've never felt anything like it before."

"We *are* deep inside the tectonic magic," Amelia said, tilting her head to listen to the rumble. "Could be a manaquake."

"Quakes don't go on this long," the Empty Wind said, his deep voice starting to sound nervous. "And it looks wrong. See?"

He pointed up, and Marci lifted her head dutifully. As always, though, she couldn't see anything in this place except the pillar, the rocky sea floor, and the swirling, nausea-inducing movement of the dark magic that surrounded them.

"Can you describe it?" she asked, looking down again before she got sick.

There was a long pause as Ghost searched for the words. "It's bulging," he said at last. "Like something's trying to push through."

"You mean like I pushed out of my death?"

"No," he said, his cold voice worried. "This comes from the outside, like a mountain growing down." He shook his head. "I can't explain."

"That's okay," Amelia said, cowering in the crook of Marci's neck. "I think we're about to find out."

Even without looking, Marci knew the dragon was right. Just like when she'd felt it pushing on Ghost's winds before, she could feel the magic expanding now, bulging like an over-inflated balloon as the chaos above them started to groan.

•••

Back in the DFZ, Myron's task was nearly complete.

He'd spent the entire morning taking Emily Jackson apart piece by piece. Under any other circumstances, the disassembly of a system as complex as Raven's Construct would have been the work of weeks, but Sir Myron had been the governing architect of the Phoenix's spellwork matrix for the last five years running. He'd taken her apart countless times before, and today, with no quality control office watching over his shoulder or deconstruction paperwork to fill out, he'd done it in record time.

The longest part had been physically pulling out the almost quarter mile of spellworked metal ribbon that controlled the regulation of her magic and arranging it back into a proper casting circle, the result of which was now sitting on the bed of a military transport truck under the watchful eyes of Algonquin's corporate mages.

Myron himself was seated in the truck's cab, squeezed uncomfortably between two armed soldiers dressed in the navy-blue body armor of Algonquin Corp's Anti-Dragon Taskforce. It wasn't the guards who made him uncomfortable, though. As the *de facto* head of magic for the UN, Myron was used to riding in armed convoys, and no mage worth the name was afraid of guns. But it was quite upsetting to sit between two fellow humans who didn't bat an eye over the fact that he had a woman's head cradled in his lap.

This was his least favorite part of working on Emily. He wasn't sure if it was security concerns or the spirit's macabre flare for the dramatic that had inspired Raven to hardwire his construct's buffer matrix to the inside of her reinforced skull, but its presence meant that no matter what they did to the rest of her, Emily's head always remained disturbingly intact. Even worse, her eyes stayed open, glaring at him accusingly. Normally, Myron liked to tie something over them to prevent this exact scenario, but there'd been no time. The moment he'd finished hauling out her spellwork and getting the metal into the right shape, Algonquin had ordered everyone into the trucks. They'd been driving ever since, pushing farther into the bowels of the DFZ Underground than he'd ever been until they reached a place so dark and deep, it didn't even show up on the GPS.

"Where are we?" Myron asked as the truck rolled to a stop.

The guard beside him grabbed the door handle with a grim look. "Old Grosse Point."

Old Grosse Point was what the maps called it, but like anyone else familiar with the thousands of films, TV shows, games, and books set in the DFZ sprawl, Myron knew the buried suburb where Algonquin's wave had first crashed down by its colloquial name: the Pit.

It looked just as it did in the movies, too. The Skyways above them held up some of the most expensive real estate in the DFZ, but down here, it was all just black. Black above, where not even a crack of daylight broke through the grime-stained underbelly of the Skyways. Black below, where the streets and houses were still covered in a foot-thick layer of silt from the flood. Even the horizon was black thanks to the cement wall Algonquin had built between this section of the Underground and her lake, cutting it off from the air and sun like the stone seal on a tomb.

The oppressive darkness was more than enough to justify calling this place a pit, but it wasn't until the guards opened the doors, breaking the truck's protective ward, that Myron realized just how fitting the name truly was. One breath of the deathly, oily, oppressive magic that filled the air here was all it took to make him feel as if he really had fallen into one of the colder, dirtier hells.

"A warning would have been appreciated," he said angrily, activating the labyrinth of spellwork woven into the lining of his coat to bring up his personal ward. "This is a class-five magical pollutant zone."

The soldier shrugged as though exposing the world's premier mage to potentially toxic ambient magic was no big deal and put on his helmet, activating his own ward with a button before offering Myron his hand. "This way, sir. Lady Algonquin is waiting for you."

Tucking Emily's head under his arm, Myron allowed the soldier to help him down the three-foot drop to the ground. The oily reek of polluted magic only got worse when he landed, his leather shoes sinking up to their laces into the slimy layer of old lake mud covering what had once been a road. Myron pried his feet free with a muttered curse, cinching his ward tight as he made his way through the muck toward his hostess.

The Lady of the Lakes was harder to spot than she should have been. This was partially because of the Pit's magic. Even with the truck's headlights at his back, Myron couldn't see more than a few feet down the ruined street before the shadows took it back, the thick magic diffusing the light like murky water. Mostly, though, it was because of the Leviathan.

Just like when he'd loomed over them in Reclamation Land, the giant monster was semitransparent, his shadowy body blending into the Pit's black miasma. The only reason Myron knew he was, in fact, looking at the Leviathan and not some trick of the dark was because the monster was holding Algonquin suspended ten feet up in the air on a pillar of black tentacles.

As always when she was forced to be around her human troops, the Lady of the Lakes was in her public form: an old Native American woman with a wise, wrinkled face and a thick braid of silver hair that went all the way down to the belt of her navy pants suit. From the way bits of her clothes kept rippling and changing, though, it was clearly a minimum effort. One that collapsed completely when she spotted Myron.

"Right on time," she said, her human face dissolving as the Leviathan lowered her to the ground. "Is it ready?"

Rather than state the obvious, Myron just pointed at the truck, where a team of Algonquin's corporate mages was levitating the silver casting circle that had once been Emily Jackson off the flatbed.

Algonquin's water rippled in happiness, and then she whipped her water down at the street between them. "Place it here."

With an irritated breath, Myron nodded, turning to walk back through the mud toward the mages to oversee the relocation.

Even with his help and the hover spell, moving the circle was hair-raising work. Since Algonquin had refused to tell him where they were going, Myron had been forced to fill the circle ahead of time, loading it up with the spirits' magic before they'd left Reclamation Land. Moving a full circle was never a good idea, but he'd thought he could get away with it thanks to Emily's enormous capacity. But while the ride over had been uneventful, now that they were at the final stage, Myron was starting to realize just how grossly he'd underestimated the amount of magic Algonquin had squeezed out of the spirits who'd sacrificed themselves to her cause. Even rearranged into a circle—a much more efficient shape than a human body—Emily's spellwork was barely able to hold all the magic Algonquin had forced it to absorb, leaving it packed like a spring-loaded snake-in-a-can. One wrong move, and the whole thing would blow up in their faces. But while that was par for the course for most of Myron's projects, it didn't make him any less anxious as he helped the corp mages float the loaded circle off the truck and down the silted road.

Finally, after what felt like years, everything was in place. Myron was on his knees, making the final adjustments, when he felt water drip onto his neck. When he looked up, Algonquin was looming over him with his own face.

"This had better work, mage," she whispered, glaring down at him with his own exacting scowl. "I'll spill dragon blood all day for the joy of it, but the sacrifices of my brothers and sisters must be honored."

"They will be," he promised, covertly wiping the water from his neck. "There's enough magic here to raise you three times over." It was more power than Myron had ever worked with before, perhaps the most magic any human had *ever* gathered in a single circle. If any of his former colleagues had been present, it would have been a circle for the history books. *His* history, specifically. The core spellwork might have been Raven's, but Myron was the one who'd arranged it into a masterpiece of magical engineering. The repurposed circle in front of them was some of the finest work he'd ever done, and the knowledge that no one but Algonquin's troops was ever likely to see it was physically painful. Though not as painful as what he had to do next.

He stood with a bracing breath, turning to glare at the lake, who was still wearing his face. "I've done my part. The control circle is complete and filled to the brim, precisely as promised. Now it's your turn, Algonquin. Tell me what Mortal Spirit we are raising to make me Merlin."

This was the question that had been plaguing him from the moment he switched sides. Algonquin had always spoken of gathering magic to raise her own Mortal Spirit, but she'd never actually said *which* spirit she was working to fill. Myron had caught a glimpse of its shape in the dragon blood when he'd been on his belly under the Leviathan during the disaster with Novalli, but not enough to determine its nature or domain or even how big it would ultimately be. He'd asked Algonquin for specifics countless times after joining her, but she'd always put his questions off, promising to tell him when, and only when, the time came.

Given how he'd come to his position, Myron had assumed she was just being cautious. He had no illusions about her opinion of his trustworthiness, and he did not take offense. Keeping mission-critical information hidden from a questionable ally was only logical. Now that he'd seen the location she'd chosen for the summoning, though, Myron was beginning to worry that Algonquin's reasons for keeping her spirit secret had nothing to do with security.

"Why are we doing this *here*?" he demanded, looking nervously around at the unnatural darkness of the Pit. "I told you when I joined, I'm not summoning any more death spirits." It had been his only stipulation. He'd seen where Novalli's deal with *that* devil had led, and he wanted no part of it. Not even to fulfill his dream of being Merlin. Fortunately, Algonquin was shaking her head.

"I'm well aware of the qualities of this place," she said, looking at the blackness as though she expected something to come charging out of it. "But as much as I'd prefer to do this somewhere that didn't reek of mortal fear and death, it must be here, because *here* is where it began."

She waved her water at the surrounding land, which Myron only now noticed wasn't flat like the rest of the city. It was sloping, the grid roads and destroyed yards of the crushed houses around them all tilting down at the same angle to form the bowl of a shallow, city-block-sized crater, which they were currently standing at the bottom of.

"This is where it started," Algonquin said, staring at the sloping land. "Six decades ago, this was the exact spot where the wave of my anger first crashed down. The echo of that rage mixed with the terror of those it killed to form the magic you feel now. The combination was so virulent and tenacious, I was forced to seal it off to prevent it from seeping back into my water. But sad as the loss of any land is, it's not *all* bad. The magic of the Pit may be vile, but it's thicker than anywhere else in the city, because this is where she was born."

A chill went through Myron's body. "She who?"

"My city," Algonquin said, tilting her head to stare up at the black underbelly of the Skyways above them. "Did you never wonder why I would conquer the very city that had abused me most? Why I chose to rebuild Detroit instead of washing it clean off the map?"

"Of course I wondered," Myron said, fighting to keep the excitement out of his voice. "*Everyone's* wondered. They've even got a name for it in the Spirit Affairs Office: 'the Paradox of the DFZ.' It's quite famous."

That was criminal understatement. The question of why Algonquin, who famously cared more for fish than people, would pour herself into rebuilding a human city from a flooded wasteland into one of the biggest, densest, richest cities in the world was the most hotly contested mystery of the post-magical era.

The leading theory was that she needed the DFZ to get a foot in the door for spirits on the international stage, but other than a handful of sweeping statements like the announcement she'd made after killing the Three Sisters, Algonquin had never bothered with politics. All she seemed to care about was growing the DFZ itself, reinvesting all the earnings from her multiple patents, technology companies, financial institutions, security contracts, and entertainment studios back into the city itself. The result was the fastest-growing metropolis in human history, and still, no one understood...

"Why?" he asked, looking her straight in his own reflected eyes. "Why the DFZ? Did you just want your own piece on the political board, or—"

Algonquin scoffed. "What you call politics is nothing but apes dancing in front of fires, marveling at the shadows they cast. But foolish and shortsighted as all human power structures are, your magic is real. The damage you do, the harm you cause, the monsters you create from your fear: *these* are humanity's powers, and they are what I built this city to stop."

"That makes no sense," Myron argued. "If humanity's evils are what you hate, then creating the Detroit Free Zone was the absolute worst thing you could have done. You made a place where vice runs rampant. Where drugs and guns are sold in vending machines, and murder is punished with a fine. The only reason this city isn't the most crime ridden in the world is because you also made nothing illegal. The only laws you've ever passed are anti-water pollution, fishing ordinances, and the ban on dragons. If you think we're all just ignorant dancing apes, why would you create a city that does nothing to restrain us?"

"Because you cannot be restrained," she said angrily, her watery voice sharp as cracked ice. "I've lived with your kind since you began. I've seen human nature in all its guises, and I can say without doubt that you are selfish, brutish creatures. You consume everything, including each other, in your relentless drive to rise to the top of your own sweaty heap."

"But we're not *all* like that," Myron argued.

"Aren't you?" she said coldly. "My city says otherwise."

"Because you made no laws!"

"If you were really good, you wouldn't need laws," she shot back. "That's my point. I've seen how you behave over generations. It would be easier to stop the sun from rising than to make humanity act in a responsible fashion, so I didn't try. Instead, I built you a place where you could be as awful, selfish, and self-destructive as you liked. No rules or restrictions, just desires and the freedom to pursue them. I gave you a blank slate, a Detroit *Free* Zone. You were the ones who turned it into this."

She lifted her hands up to the Skyways overhead. "The DFZ was *your* making, not mine. I built the elevated ramps because I needed conduits to channel magic into the proper forms for my Reclamation Land projects, but you were the ones who turned them into a division where the rich live literally on top of the poor. You're absolutely right when you say the DFZ is a terrible city, but I'm not to blame. I merely gave you the shovel and let you dig, and now that the hole is wide and deep, all I have to do is step back and let it bury you."

His reflection shot him a cruel smile as she finished, but Myron barely noticed. He'd thrown his lot in with Algonquin because that was the price of becoming the first Merlin, but whatever Emily thought, he wasn't a traitor. Sometimes you had to do the wrong thing to get the right end, up to and including working with a walking, talking natural disaster. It wasn't until this moment, though, that Myron realized the true depth of the contempt the Lady of the Lakes held for their kind, and the more she insulted him, the clearer her purpose in bringing him here became.

"That's it," he whispered at last, voice shaking. "The DFZ is ours, not yours. Humanity made it." He looked down at the silted ground in horrified wonder. "The city *is* the spirit."

Algonquin chuckled. "You *are* a clever human."

It wasn't a compliment, but Myron had no time to waste being insulted. Now that she'd put the pieces together for him, he felt like a fool for not realizing the truth sooner. The DFZ was Algonquin's Mortal Spirit. Not just the physical city, but the *idea* of it, the addictive promise of a city of absolute freedom that had been hammered down through countless movies, shows, novels, and video games over the past sixty years. The concept of the DFZ as a place where anything could happen and anyone could go to start a new life was so common, it was its own family of clichés, and *that was the entire point.* Algonquin hadn't built a city. She'd created a hook for people to hang their dreams on, a place to pin their hopes and ambitions and greed. The DFZ wasn't just a dot on the map. It was a concept, a collection of discrete ideas and hopes, fears and feelings. A Mortal Spirit, and he was standing right on top of it.

"Now you understand," Algonquin said, reaching out to pat Myron's graying hair with a watery tendril. "You were right, Myron. I had no need for a human city. What I needed was a vessel. A concept for you to cling to and fill with your own ideas, because that's how human magic works. You take something innocent, like a city, and you give it power by projecting your fears and desires on top of it. On a person-by-person level, it doesn't add up to much. But sell a dream to the world—combine the ambition of thousands, millions, *billions* of humans—and you end up with monsters no one can control, including yourselves." She tilted the reflection of his head. "Now do you understand why we were willing to die to stop the rising magic from bringing them to life?"

Myron had understood from the moment he'd first seen Marci Novalli's death spirit. All Algonquin's explanation had done, besides satisfy his curiosity, was add even more weight to his resolve and a new, broader target for his end game. "I understand you perfectly, madame," he said, stepping away from her touch. "These spirits are terrifying, and it is in all of our best interests to stop them." He moved to the edge of the circle. "Ready to begin when you are."

"Oh," Algonquin said, clearly surprised by his sudden and unequivocal agreement. "Well, glad to know there are humans who can grasp the larger picture."

"I have always had a clear vision of what must be done," Myron replied, flashing her his famous smile, the one he normally saved for photo shoots. But while his outside was perfectly collected, his mind was boiling with a terrified anger that could no longer be contained.

Sir Myron Rollins had always prided himself on being a man who got things done. He'd built his career doing what other, lesser mages claimed to be impossible. But while many did not agree with his methods, Myron had always found that no one complained after the battle was won. Today would be no different. Emily could call him a traitor all she liked, but when this was over, the world would know him as the Merlin who saved humanity from the spirits.

Starting with Algonquin herself.

Clutching Emily's head under his arm, Myron smiled one last time at the Lady of the Lakes and stepped into the circle. The moment he crossed the silver line, the loops of carefully arranged metal ribbon that had once been Emily Jackson's body lit up like phosphorus, filling even the inky dark of the Pit with blinding light. There was so much power, simply stepping into the circle should have burned out every mage in a ten-mile radius—including him—for months, possibly forever.

As always, though, Emily protected him. So long as he held on to the general's head, the spellwork Raven had carved inside it all those years ago shielded him as it had once shielded Emily's humanity from the relentless onslaught of spirit-level magic. But unlike his former partner, Myron was no mere pilot. He was a mage, the best alive, and his name now replaced Raven's at the spellwork's crux. With it, the blinding magic was his to control, to press and beat and mold like clay into the form he'd caught a glimpse of in the blood pool back in Reclamation land. The shape that, as he formed it, he realized he could now see mirrored beneath him.

It was a marvelous thing to witness a new spirit's birth. Normally, human eyes couldn't see magic the way spirits, dragons, or even magical animals could. With so much power in his hands, though, Myron didn't need to see. He could *feel* the DFZ spreading out below him like a bottomless pit.

Like most modern mages, Myron had spent years studying the Spirits of the Land. He'd even bound a few in an attempt to learn how their magic functioned. But while every spirit's structure was famously and frustratingly unique, the one characteristic they all shared was that they were measurable. The magic contained in the spirit of a lake or a mountain always mirrored their physical forms. Animal spirits were trickier since you were working with the combined volume of an animal population's magical potential rather than landmasses, but the general idea was the same. When it came to the magic of land and animal spirits, what you saw was what you got.

The spirit he stood on now was something else entirely.

It was unfathomably massive. How massive, he couldn't yet say, but the record-breaking mass of magic he'd crammed into Emily's circle barely registered beside it. Whatever was below him, it was far, *far* bigger than the city that had spawned it. Bigger than the Lady of the Great Lakes. Bigger than any spirit he'd encountered before. It was almost too big to comprehend, and to his amazement, it was already nearly full.

As he stood in the backwash of so much power, all Myron could think was that at least this solved the riddle of why the DFZ's ambient magic was always so much higher than the rest of the world's. It was sitting on *this*, a magical vein deeper and richer than all the spirits around it combined. He wasn't sure yet how much of that was the product of the Algonquin's magic-siphoning efforts in Reclamation Land and how much was the natural result of humans attaching their hopes to the city, but wherever its power had come from, the nascent spirit was on the cusp. It stirred as he watched, throwing off a mess of emotions every bit as wild, violent, and desperate as the city that had created it. One more drop, and it would wake completely.

Fortunately, a drop was what he had. Next to the thing below, the magic contained in Raven's Construct—the combined power of dozens of spirits, more magic than any human had ever gathered in one circle—was nothing, not even a percent, but it was enough. When Myron let the power go, it hit the sleeping spirit like a catalyst, spidering down through the seemingly bottomless magic like lightning. It was still going when an alarm began to sound from the phone in Myron's pocket.

A smile spread over his face. He didn't even have to bring up his AR to know what the alarm was for. It was the sensors at his New York lab, the ones he'd rigged to monitor the deep magic. Two weeks ago, that same alarm had tipped him off to Marci Novalli. This time, Myron knew it was ringing for *him*. Down below, the enormous magic was coalescing into a form. It was still chaotic, but within that chaos, structure was emerging, and structure meant rules. Rules Myron now set out to enforce as he took hold of Emily's spellwork and pushed his magic through it, closing the silver circle like a noose at the exact moment the newborn spirit breached the physical world for the first time.

Even though he'd worked out all the theory himself, seeing it in action was still miraculous. In the middle of his circle, magic was being forced into solid form before his eyes. It rippled and shifted several times before finally stabilizing into the shape of a person. An emaciated young woman wearing a long-sleeved black hoodie, black leggings, and sneakers.

Aside from her thinness, she looked shockingly normal. Even her clothes were remarkably nondescript, super generic, one-size-fits-all throwaways they sold in vending machines. She was the sort of person you saw everywhere in the DFZ, one of the millions of hungry, possibly homeless, definitely impoverished hopefuls who filled the Underground in droves. If he didn't know what she was, Myron could have walked past her on the street without so much as noticing, which he supposed was the point. In a city this big, anyone could disappear into the crowd. Looking unremarkable was a good defense in the DFZ, and defense was clearly what the spirit wanted given the fear rolling off her in waves as she looked around at the silver prison Myron had made.

What is this? Her voice was a panicked gasp in his mind. She pressed against the glowing wall cast by the spellwork next, beating on the barrier when it wouldn't let her through. *Let me go!*

"No," Myron said, gripping Emily's head, and the mastery it granted, firmly in his hands. "Allow me to explain what is happening. You are the spirit of the DFZ."

She spun around, looking at him in wonder through round eyes that glowed the same orange as the city streetlights. *That's my name!*

"It is," he said smugly. "And I know it. I am Sir Myron Rollins, and now, by your name and this circle, you are bound to me."

The spirit recoiled. *No,* she said, shaking her head. *I am free. I—*

"You are a dangerous spirit born of humanity's chaos, ambition, and greed," he said over her. "It is my duty as a mage to chain you for all of our protection. I will not be a cruel master, but I will not tolerate disobedience. Is this understood?"

No! she cried again, her thin lips curling in hate. *I have no master. I am the DFZ. I am freedom! I—*

Myron yanked on the magic running through the spellwork that bore his name, and a collar appeared around the spirit's throat. It was made from the same silver metal ribbon as the rest of the circle, but unlike the spellwork on the ground, these ribbons followed the movements of Myron's hand as he gripped down, squeezing the spirit in a binding as hard and unforgiving as steel.

"Is this understood?" he repeated as she fell to her knees.

The DFZ fought him frantically. She hissed and bared her teeth, scraping her bony fingers frantically at the noose around her neck.

Powerful as she was, though, she was also new. A baby, uncertain of her strength and terrified of the pain Myron was inflicting. It was terribly unfair, but ruthlessness was the only edge he had over a power so much greater than himself. If he was going to make this work, he had to be in control, so he ignored her pain and dug in deeper, binding the spirit until she was gasping at his feet. He'd almost cut her magic in half before she finally gave in, her head dropping in a limp nod as she finally acknowledged his control.

"Excellent," Myron said, easing up just a fraction. "Now, take me where I need to go."

The DFZ looked up from the ground in confusion. *Where you need to go?*

"The Merlin Gate."

When that failed to elicit an immediate reaction, he yanked the spirit to her knees. "I know you know where it is. Unlike Marci Novalli's premature horror, you were born of fully formed magic. You should know instinctively how to find the Heart of the World. Take me there now, or suffer again."

The ultimatum was a gamble. Myron knew better than to let his doubt show, but the truth was he'd only read mentions of the Heart of the World in stories. From what he could gather, it seemed to be some kind of Merlin headquarters, a safe haven built into the deep magic of the world. He knew it was real thanks to Algonquin, but the actual mechanics of getting there and entering the gate were complete guesswork. Marci Novalli's cat hadn't known anything, but he was hardly representative. His entire existence was a mistake, a premature Mortal Spirit born of death and the spillover from Algonquin's attempts to raise this one, but the DFZ was different. She'd been born properly, and since the Heart of the World was located in the spirit's side of things, and every Merlin had a Mortal Spirit by definition, it only made sense that she would be the key.

At least, that was Myron's hope. A hope that paid off when, after several seconds of confused staring followed by defiant glaring, the DFZ turned around and began to dig.

It was the strangest thing he'd ever seen. Hunched on the ground like a gremlin, the spirit attacked the silt-covered road with her bony fingers, flinging the dirt over her head and onto her back. But though she was moving an impressive amount of material, the hole beneath her never seemed to get any deeper. Instead, the DFZ herself began to change, her shape twisting beneath the piled, sludgy dirt of the Pit until she didn't even look human anymore. She looked like a rat. Not a normal rat, either, but one of the giant, magically awakened sewer rats that infested the pipes of old Detroit. The ones that ate large dogs and small children.

A few minutes later, it was no longer just a matter of looks. She *was* a rat. A huge, black, obviously unearthly one with beady eyes that flashed orange like water under a streetlight. It was absolutely terrifying, which, from the evil looks she kept shooting him, was undoubtedly the point. But no matter how much the DFZ changed shape, the collar around her throat never budged. So long as that was true, Myron was still in control, a fact he was tempted to remind her of when the spirit suddenly found whatever she'd been digging for.

She stopped at once, lifting up her paws to show Myron a wide, filthy disk. Between the dirt and the dark, it took him several seconds to realize it was a manhole cover. But while it made sense that there would still be sewers here—Grosse Point had been an affluent suburb before its destruction—the tunnel she'd unveiled didn't look like any sewer maintenance shaft Myron had ever seen. It didn't even have a ladder, just a round hole going straight down into blackness.

"Are you sure that's it?"

You told me to show you the way, the rat reminded him. *This is mine. If you're too chicken to jump, that's your problem.*

Myron glowered. Another time, he would have stopped everything and dealt with her rudeness right there. If things went the way he hoped, though, theirs would not be a long relationship, so he didn't bother. He just held out his hand and said, "After you."

With a final dirty look, the spirit scurried down the hole, her massive body sliding through the much smaller opening like a garden slug going down a straw. With a deep breath and a final look over his shoulder at the blinding wall of magic that hid Algonquin, Myron jumped after her. It wasn't until he started falling, though, that he realized he'd left his body behind. He could actually see it falling over at the edge of the shrinking hole with Emily's head still clutched in his hands. That was all Myron was able to catch before the DFZ's tail wrapped around him, dragging him down into the churning magical dark.

CHAPTER SEVEN

"It's you."

The Qilin's golden eyes flicked back to him questioningly, but Julius couldn't explain what he still couldn't believe himself. Even with the proof staring him in the face, the idea that Chelsie's disastrous affair in China hadn't been with some random noble son, but with the *Golden Emperor* himself seemed ludicrous. How had she managed to pull that off? How had they even met?

But crazy as the whole thing sounded, at least this explained why the Qilin had stopped to look at her back in the desert. At the time, Julius had written off the emperor's interest as caution. Chelsie was famous for being Bethesda's backstabber, after all. Now, though, he realized that was stupid. The Qilin was luck incarnate—he had nothing to fear from Bethesda's Shade. He'd been looking up at her in longing, the same longing that was plain on his face right now as he turned back to the unfinished painting. A painting that was obviously from the same expert hand as the picture Chelsie kept hidden in her room.

"It *was* you," Julius said with an excited grin. "You're her Chinese dragon!"

"Spoke of me, did she?" the emperor said, crossing his arms tight across his chest. "I'm surprised. One would think she'd tire of bragging about a six-hundred-year-old conquest."

The bite in his voice was enough to make Julius take a physical step back. "Whoa," he said putting up his hands. "I don't know what you think's going on, but she definitely wasn't bragging."

"Why shouldn't she brag?" he said bitterly. "I was her greatest conquest." He glanced over, clearly expecting Julius to agree. When it was obvious the younger dragon had no idea what he was talking about, though, the Qilin's angry scowl faded into confusion. "You really don't know what happened?"

"No," Julius said, shaking his head wildly. "You have to understand, no one tells me anything. Chelsie almost took my head off once just for mentioning China. That's not hyperbole, either. She literally had me pinned on the ground."

A smile ghosted over the emperor's lips. "That sounds like her."

"Then you know how stubborn she can be," Julius said desperately. "*Please*, I'm begging you, tell me what happened in China. Give me something to work with."

Give me a way to fix this.

The Qilin gave him a funny look. "I knew you were an odd sort of dragon," he said, turning back to the painting. "It's not a story I like to remember. I certainly don't come off looking like a glorious emperor. But the whole point of bringing you here was to make you understand why I have to conquer your clan, and you can't understand without knowing, so…"

He trailed off with a long sigh, staring at the picture he'd painted of Chelsie with an emotion Julius couldn't name.

"This was how I first saw her," he said at last, reaching up to brush a finger over the delicately painted flush of Chelsie's cheek. "I was walking in my garden, and she was just…there. Like a bolt of lightning. When I asked her what she was doing, she told me she'd been sent to China by Bethesda as a special envoy for the emperor's coronation. Needless to say, this was news to me. Old news at that since I'd been emperor for two months already at the time. When I told her she was too late and asked why she hadn't come to the palace to announce herself, she just shrugged and said the guards had turned her away."

"Wait," Julius said, confused. "So she didn't realize you were the emperor?" Because he had no idea how anyone with eyes could miss that.

The Qilin smiled. "In her defense, I wasn't dressed for court. I also wasn't expecting to meet an envoy from another clan in my private garden at the heart of the palace. To this day, I have no idea how she got in. My mother's security was very tight. There were wards, walls, guards, alarm spells, everything that could be had back then."

"Chelsie is the master of being places she shouldn't," Julius agreed. "But what was she doing in your garden if your coronation was over? What was she after?"

The emperor's expression grew sheepish. "I asked the same thing. Demanded, really. Naturally, I assumed she was there for me. The mate of the Qilin becomes his empress, and I've had to chase ambitious dragonesses out of stranger places than my garden. When I confronted her about it, though, it became clear that not only did she have no idea whom she was talking to, she didn't care. She claimed she'd only infiltrated my palace because she'd gotten bored with the city outside."

Julius arched an eyebrow. "And you believed that?"

"Honestly?" He smiled. "I did. I know how ridiculous that sounds, but she had a frankness to her that I'd never encountered. It certainly wasn't the normal awe of the Qilin. I was...charmed, I suppose. And a little insulted, because she seemed far more interested in the fish than she was in me. She'd never seen a koi before, apparently."

That mental image was enough to make Julius grin. He could absolutely see his blunt sister giving an emperor the cold shoulder. He also understood why someone like the Qilin might find that refreshing. "Is that what attracted you? Because Chelsie didn't treat you like a god?"

The emperor looked at him like he was crazy. "I was attracted because she was beautiful. Have you *seen* your sister?"

"Not in that way," Julius said, face turning red.

"She was the most beautiful dragon I'd ever seen," the Qilin went on. "And she was the daughter of the infamous Bethesda, whom even we'd heard rumors about. Anyone would be intrigued.

But that was just what caught my attention at the beginning. What held it was Chelsie herself. She was..." He trailed off, scowling in frustration. "I don't know the word in English. It's what animals are."

"Wild?" Julius suggested. "Scary?"

"Unworried," the Qilin said, his golden eyes bright. "The Golden Court is a place of tradition and status. It can be intimidating and cruel to outsiders, especially ones like her. Many of my dragons considered her an ignorant barbarian and treated her accordingly. But where anyone else would have taken offense, and rightly so, Chelsie didn't care. Quite the opposite. She used their disdain as an excuse to do whatever she wanted."

"My sister doesn't tolerate nonsense," Julius said, smiling at the absurdity of a court full of stuffy dragons trying to intimidate Chelsie. "She must have caused quite a stir."

"Like nothing else before or since," the Qilin said proudly. "My mother disapproved greatly, of course, but I wouldn't allow her to send Chelsie away."

"Because you already liked her?"

"Because I loved her." The smile slipped off the golden dragon's face as he looked back up at the painting. "From the first moment I saw her, I loved her. I know it's foolish, but I was young, and she was just so..."

"Beautiful?"

"Free," he said wistfully. "In a way I could never be. I understood that, but I still wanted my share. I wanted to forget with her. To laugh and not care, even if it was only for a little while." His jaw clenched. "I was a selfish fool."

That was the same thing Chelsie had said when she'd told Julius her extremely truncated half of this story, and now, as then, he heaved a frustrated sigh. "There's nothing wrong with wanting to be happy."

"Maybe not for you," he said. "But I was, *am* an emperor. I have a duty to my family, to my clans and my land. I knew that, and I still allowed myself to become infatuated with someone who was utterly unsuited to be empress." His lip curled in disgust. "I ignored my obligations to satisfy my desires. That is the definition of selfishness."

"It doesn't mean you were wrong," Julius said angrily. "And in what world is Chelsie unsuited to be empress? She's the most competent, hardest-working dragon in Heartstriker. But even if she wasn't amazing, which she *is*, that shouldn't have mattered if you loved her."

"My feelings were never in question," the emperor said. "I was willing to make her empress no matter what the others said. *She* was the one who did not care."

Julius flinched. He hadn't known it was possible for a voice to change so much in a single sentence, but by the time the Qilin finished, he sounded like a completely different dragon.

"I was a fool," he said again, the words quivering with rage. "I lived with your sister for a year in stupid, ignorant happiness. Over the months, my mother tried to warn me several times of your family's reputation, but I did not want to listen. I thought I was different, that the viper of Heartstriker would not bite me." He clenched his fists. "I was an *idiot*, a mouse transfixed by your treacherous snake of a sister, and I would have lost everything to her if my mother hadn't intervened."

This wasn't going to be good. "What happened?"

The Qilin looked down at the floor. "Reality," he said bitterly. "I thought I'd kept our affair a secret, but I was sloppy. By the time six months had passed, all of China knew what was going on. They pretended not to because I was emperor, but behind my back, the clans whispered that I was the Heartstriker's puppet. My mother told me what was going on and warned me to break it off before I did irreparable damage to our reputation, but I was too infatuated to listen. I thought Chelsie and I were greater than the rumors. That together, we could beat anything. She said so, too, but it was all a lie. She told me exactly what I wanted to hear, and then, one spring morning a year to the day after I found her in my garden, Chelsie vanished without a trace."

Julius blinked in surprise. "Vanished?"

The emperor nodded. "Naturally, I was upset. I thought something had happened, that she'd been hurt or killed. It didn't even occur to me that she would run away until my mother caught her."

"She ran away," Julius repeated, incredulous. "*Why?*"

"I don't know," he said, growling deep in his throat. "But she was on a boat to Russia when my mother's guards cornered her. She nearly killed one of them before they subdued her and dragged her back."

This story made less sense by the word. "Why did they drag her back?" Julius asked. "You going after her makes sense, but I thought the empress would have been happy to see Chelsie gone."

"She would have been," the Qilin agreed. "But I told you, I was *upset.*"

He said that the same way someone else would say "berserk," and a cold chill ran up Julius's spine. "What happens when you get upset?"

The golden dragon walked away, moving to the small, paint-splattered table beside the easel where all his art supplies lay neatly arranged. He fidgeted with them for a moment, rearranging the brushes and dropping the dirty ones into the tin cup of murky rinse water. Then, just as Julius was reaching the end of his patience, he answered.

"The Qilin is the heart of the empire," he said quietly, keeping his back to Julius. "When he is serene, good fortune favors everything his presence touches. When he is not, the opposite happens."

His shoulders hunched tighter under his golden robes with every word, but Julius wasn't paying attention. His mind was back in the desert this morning, to the strange pressure he'd felt building like a storm after Chelsie had vanished, ready to crush them all. "I see," he said at last, voice shaking. "Your luck goes bad."

"It goes far worse than that," the Qilin said, finally turning to face him. "My mother would have endured anything to pry me free of your sister, but not that. She has always been an empress first, and so long as I was being selfish, the empire needed Chelsie. She hated

190

every second of it, but she tolerated my indiscretion for the sake of harmony. When Chelsie ran away, I was…"

He trailed off, rubbing his hands over his face. "I was not myself," he finished at last. "I was out of control, a danger to my empire, and so my mother, ever the dutiful empress, bent all her resources to bringing Chelsie back to me by any means necessary. What we didn't yet know, though, was that Chelsie hadn't just been running. Bethesda's Shade had also reached out to her clan, calling in her mother to aid her escape and then, after she was caught, to beg on her behalf."

Julius had a very hard time believing that. No matter how bad the situation, he couldn't imagine Chelsie asking their *mother* for help. Ludicrous as it sounded, though, here again, Chelsie and the emperor's stories matched up. She'd told him herself that Bethesda had begged for her, and their mother had held a life debt over her head for it every day since. But even if this was all true, "What could Bethesda do?"

"Nothing," the emperor said angrily. "She *tried* a great deal, offered us wealth and power, lands, everything at your clan's disposal. But I didn't care about any of that. I just wanted Chelsie back, but she wouldn't even look at me. When I demanded to know why, the truth came out. She never loved me. She'd only seduced me for power, just as I'd accused her of conspiring to that first night in the garden. And it had almost worked. Before she ran, I'd been ready to name her my empress over my mother's objections, giving the Heartstrikers control over all of China."

That sounded more like Bethesda than Chelsie. It also made zero sense. "If she was seducing you for power, why would she run away just when you were about to give it to her?"

"Because she'd been found out," the Qilin said. "I was too besotted to see what she was doing, but my mother knew what Chelsie was up to. But while she was willing to turn a blind eye when it was just an affair, she'd never tolerate a Heartstriker as empress. None of my dragons would, and with the entire court aligning against her, it was just a matter of time before it all blew up. Chelsie knew that, so she did what any proper snake would do and bolted before she got trapped."

Again, that didn't sound like Chelsie. "Are you sure that's why she ran?"

"Why else would she do it?" he demanded. "I was her fool! Her pawn, just like everyone said. Even after she confessed everything to me, I was still ready to forgive her, but she threw my mercy in my face. She knew the game was up, but she also knew I didn't have the heart to execute her. She and Bethesda embraced their banishment and sailed home laughing, while we were the ones who suffered."

Julius dropped his eyes. The emperor's story was actually worse than he'd anticipated, *if* it was true. The Qilin clearly believed what he was saying, but nothing about his description fit the Chelsie that Julius knew. She'd admitted she wasn't proud of what she'd done in China, and six hundred years was a very long time, but no matter how much she might have changed, he simply couldn't imagine his sister betraying someone like that. Especially not someone she cared about as much as she still clearly did for the dragon who'd painted her picture. She definitely wouldn't laugh about it with *Bethesda*. Whatever had really happened, though, it was obvious the emperor felt he'd been betrayed, which begged the question…

"If you think she was using you, why are you here now?"

The Qilin heaved a long, defeated sigh. "Because I'm still her fool."

He turned away, putting his back to Julius again as he stared up at the painting. "The Heartstrikers were well named. Once their claws are in, you can never really dig them out. I should know. I've tried for six hundred years. I thought I was far enough away to manage it, that the years had finally buried what I never should have touched, but all it took was one glimpse, and I was seeking you out to ask after her. I even painted this ridiculous thing." He shook his head at the lovely portrait. "I'm eternally an idiot, it seems. But as much as I hate your sister for what she did, nothing has changed. I couldn't kill her then, and I can't leave her to die now."

Julius let out a relieved breath. "So you *did* come here to save her."

"Don't romanticize it," he growled. "Coming to your lands was even more selfish than falling for Chelsie's ruse in the first place. What sort of emperor uproots his subjects and marches them into enemy territory for the sake of a dragon that publicly betrayed him? I never should have come, but I couldn't see any other way. Heartstriker is doomed. Algonquin's on the warpath, and your clan's right on her doorstep. Even if the lake spirit let you live, another clan would come to finish the job. You're too wounded and too rich a prize to ignore. Sooner or later, someone was bound to reach out and take you, and as Bethesda's enforcer, Chelsie's head would be the first to roll. I couldn't let that happen, but I also couldn't betray my subjects by involving them in a clan war half a world away. I was caught, stuck between two impossibilities. The whole thing seemed hopeless until I realized there was a way for me to have both."

Julius nodded. "Your luck."

"Exactly," he said, turning back around. "My good fortune falls on all my subjects, no matter where in the world they are. If I conquered Heartstriker, then my luck would protect you just as it does all my other clans, and since you were already on the verge of collapse, coming here posed no risk to my dragons. Now do you understand why I couldn't take an alliance? You were right about it being the smarter move, but I don't care about fighting Algonquin or expanding my territory. All I want is to keep Chelsie from dying, and bringing Heartstriker into my luck is the only way I can do that without endangering those who depend on me. *That's* why I invaded your mountain, and it's why I can't leave it as anything other than your emperor. Now do you understand?"

He did. Julius understood the emperor's position perfectly now, and it made him want to bang his head against the wall. "I get what you're trying to do," he said when the urge had passed. "And I deeply admire the care you've taken not to hurt anyone in this, but *surely* it would be simpler to just, I don't know, *talk* to Chelsie instead of conquering her entire clan?"

The emperor arched a perfect eyebrow. "Do you not want my protection?"

"I do," Julius said quickly. "I'm not blind. I know how much trouble Heartstriker's in, but there has to be a better way to keep her safe than strong-arming all of us into your empire. I mean, that's ridiculous."

"It's necessary," the Qilin said firmly. "You've seen my luck in action. Once you're part of my empire, even Algonquin won't be able to touch you. The terms of surrender I've offered could not be more generous. Other than good fortune and protection, you won't even know you're in my empire. What more do you want?"

"Our freedom," Julius said stubbornly. "We might be down, but we're still dragons. We're not going to roll over and give up our sovereignty just because it solves a problem for you. Especially if it locks us under your dubious good fortune."

He jerked back. "There's nothing *dubious* about—"

"Everything about it is dubious!" Julius cried. "You talk about your luck like it's a sure thing, but from what you just told me about your behavior after Chelsie's disappearance and the way I've seen your court treat you, your 'unbeatable' good fortune isn't unbeatable at all. It depends on you not getting upset, on your *serenity*, and that's not good enough. I don't care how amazing your luck is, it's irresponsible for me to stake my clan's future on a power that's governed by something as capricious as an emperor's moods."

He must have hit the nail on the head with that one, because the Qilin dropped his eyes. "You're not seeing me at my best," he admitted, rubbing the back of his neck. "This whole mountain smells of Chelsie, and it puts me on edge. I'm normally much calmer."

"But your luck *does* depend on your feelings."

The Qilin said nothing, which was answer enough. "Well," Julius said with a sigh. "At least now I know why Lao was so insistent about not upsetting you."

"My cousin is overprotective," the emperor said dismissively. "But remaining calm is part of the responsibility of being Qilin. I've maintained my serenity and showered good fortune and prosperity on my clans for centuries. It will be no different once Heartstriker joins."

"Are you sure?" Julius asked. "We're the biggest clan in the world. Adding us will more than double the number of dragons you're protecting, not to mention we're on the other side of the planet. Can your luck even manage that?"

"Of course it can," he said proudly. "Thanks to my mother's sacrifice, I'm the strongest Qilin ever born. Even half a world away, my magic will protect all of you."

That sounded more inescapable than protective, but it was the first part of his statement that really caught Julius's attention. "Wait, your mother? I thought you got your power from your father."

"The luck magic passes from father to firstborn son," the emperor said. "I am the Qilin, as my father was before me, and his father was before him. But while the golden luck passes through the male line, it's always the dragoness who determines how strong her children will be."

"How?" Julius asked.

"By controlling their fire." The Qilin gave him a pitying look. "Not all clans follow the Heartstriker's shortsighted strategy of quantity over quality. By the time she'd defeated her rivals and won the right to become the Qilin's mate, my mother had already been hoarding her magic for a century in preparation. They were planning their mating flight when the drought struck, and all ambient magic vanished from the world."

"Why did that matter?" Julius asked, because the loss of magic certainly hadn't stopped *his* mother. Bethesda had popped out eggs like she was the Easter Dragon all through the drought, and she'd been young. Age was power for dragons, and the Empress Mother certainly had that. Add in a century of stored-up magic and the Qilin's mother should have been able to lay as many eggs as she wanted, but the emperor was shaking his head.

"If I were anyone else, it wouldn't have mattered," he said. "But the birth of a Qilin is different from other dragons. The preparation of the egg requires an enormous amount of magic, more than any single dragoness can hold on her own. Even with my father's luck to help her, with no ambient magic to lean on, my mother's chances of producing a Qilin egg strong enough to survive outside her body were nearly impossible."

That was unexpectedly bad luck for the clan of good fortune. "So what happened?"

"My mother did," the emperor said proudly. "She'd beaten a hundred other dragonesses for the right to be the mother of the next Qilin, and she refused to give up on her ambition. Even when the world grew so dull and magicless that lesser dragons were trapped in their human forms, she hoarded her magic patiently, cannibalizing her own fire to ensure that I wouldn't just be a Qilin, I'd be the *best*. She even convinced my father to hold on to his fading life for another century so he could die at the most auspicious time."

"Wait, *die?*" Julius said. "Why did he have to die?" What kind of mating flight did it take to make a Qilin?

"The old flame must die before the new can be born," the emperor said sagely. "Each Qilin's magic is built from the combined fires of all those who came before him. That's how the golden flame grows: leaping from father to son in an unbroken line that goes all the way back to the ancient clans of our lost homeland. As the latest to possess it, I would have been the strongest Qilin by default, but thanks to my mother's sacrifice, I am greater still. My luck is twice that of my father's, and my reach stretches not just across my empire, but all around the world. This is what my mother sacrificed to give me, and I thank her for it every day by ruling in serenity so that my good fortune may flow to everyone who depends on me. That is what it means to be Qilin."

He looked so proud of that, Julius didn't have the heart to tell him how horrible it sounded. To hear the emperor talk, you'd think he'd been given a great gift, but all Julius heard was the story of a dragon who'd been force-fed both his parents' fires for the sake of amplifying his power. A horrible, uncontrollable power, that required him to never get angry or upset.

At least now Julius understood why the Empress Mother looked the way she did. She wasn't withered because she was ancient. Her shriveled body was all that was left after she'd spent her fire super-charging her son. But while the Golden Empire's philosophy of putting all their eggs in one golden basket seemed to be working given how long they'd been around, Julius couldn't shake the feeling that entrusting your fortunes to a magical ruler who could never be unhappy was *not* a good idea. There were way too many ways this could all come crashing down on their heads, and the more Julius heard, the more desperate he became to find a way out.

"I'm not questioning the strength of your magic," he said, trying a different angle. "But I still don't think this conquest plan is going to accomplish what you want. Heartstriker is a big, stubborn clan. Even if you go completely hands off and let us rule ourselves, we're going to be a *lot* more trouble than you give us credit for. Why put yourself through that if Chelsie's the only one you really care about? If you'd just talk to her—"

"Absolutely not," the emperor said, glaring down at him. "Were you not listening? I must remain calm if the magic that protects my clan is to work. Talking to Chelsie isn't part of that."

"I get that," Julius said. "But that's no reason to drag us all into—"

"Your sister *betrayed* me!" he cried. "Just because I don't want her to die like a dog to Algonquin doesn't mean I'm willing to let her near me so she can do it again! Bringing Heartstriker into my empire lets me protect her without exposing myself to her treachery. It's the only way everyone stays safe. Why can't you see that?"

"Because I don't think you're right!" Julius said angrily. "You're making all these plans based on the assumption that Chelsie used you and then dumped you when things got too hot, but that's not the Chelsie I know."

The Qilin looked away. "Then she's deceived you, too."

"I don't think so," Julius said, stepping back into his line of view to make the golden dragon look at him. "I don't claim to know her as well as you did, but Chelsie's still my sister, and she's put her life on the line for me more times than I can count. That's not the sort of thing you can fake."

"Of course she saved you," he said dismissively. "You're her clan head."

"Not back then," Julius said. "I'm at the top now, but a month ago, I was the runt of J-clutch, the lowest of the low. Chelsie had no reason to even know my name, and yet she was always there. When I got myself in life-or-death trouble, she fought hard to get me out. She *always* comes to our rescue and never asks for anything in return. That's why I can't believe your story is as cut-and-dried as you say. I mean, you're claiming she worked with *Bethesda* to betray you, but the Chelsie I know hates our mother. The only way she'd ever ask for Bethesda's help was if she was absolutely back-to-the-wall desperate, which she must have been, because Bethesda's been holding whatever happened in China over her head for the last six hundred years."

"What are you talking about?" the Qilin sneered. "I might live on the other side of the world, but I'm not ignorant. I know Chelsie is Bethesda's Shade. They work together all the time."

"Not willingly!" Julius cried. "Chelsie only obeyed Bethesda because she was trapped in a life debt. They did a lot of awful things together, yes, but Chelsie was there as her slave, not her partner."

The emperor stared at him for a long time. "I never heard any of this," he said at last.

Julius shrugged. "Not many outside our clan have, but ask any of my siblings, and they'll tell you the same. Ask Fredrick. He's F-clutch, and you already know how Bethesda treated them. Now take the worst of those rumors and double them, and you might have something close to what my mother did to Chelsie. If you need more proof, I can show you the edict we signed to set Chelsie and F-clutch free when we formed the Council. Or you can just go out into the throne room. The Fang of the Heartstriker Chelsie threw down when she quit being Bethesda's Shade is still right where she dropped it. Go touch it yourself if you don't believe me."

"I did try, actually," the Qilin said, looking down at his hand as if it hurt him. "I knew it was hers from the scent, but..." He sighed. "This is very different from what I've always thought."

"I know," Julius said. "That's why I'm saying you shouldn't be so quick to jump to conclusions. I have no doubt that whatever Chelsie said to you back then was awful, but things in my family are rarely what they seem. You should know this. You loved her once. Would the Chelsie in that painting betray you?"

"I never thought so," he said. "But that's why it worked so well. Seduction for power isn't much use if your target doesn't believe you'd never sell them out."

"*Or*," Julius countered, "that could have been the *real* Chelsie, and the part where she betrayed you was the lie. You tell me which makes more sense. That she faked being in love with you for an entire year only to give up and confess everything the moment she got caught, or that she *always* loved you, but then something happened, and she had to lie."

"To what end?" the Qilin cried. "I offered to save her! What possible benefit could she have from throwing that back in my face?"

"I don't know," Julius admitted. "Which is why this doesn't make sense yet. But if you're right, and she really was playing you the whole time, then why did she run? You said your mother already suspected Chelsie, but could she actually have stopped you from marrying her if you'd really wanted to?"

The emperor shook his head. "She'd have fought me every step of the way. *Was* fighting me, actually, but she couldn't have stopped me if I'd been determined."

"There you go," Julius said, spreading his hands. "You're assuming she ran because she found out her jig was about to be up, but if she actually was the sort of dragon who'd seduce an emperor for power, then suspicion from your family would have only made her dig into you harder. Your opinion was the only one that actually mattered, so if you believed her, why would she care what anyone else said? Under those circumstances, running was actually the *worst* choice she could have made because it made her look guilty. So either Chelsie was both good enough to fool you for a year *and* bad enough to screw it up at the end, or she wasn't fooling you at all. She really was what she appeared, and something else happened to make her flee."

"But what could that be?" the Qilin demanded. "What would she be running from if not me?"

"I'm afraid only Chelsie knows that," Julius said. "But that story would definitely fit her better. My sister would never betray anyone, but she has a bad habit of running from her problems. Particularly the emotional ones, which definitely includes you. That's how I knew what you were telling me couldn't be the whole truth. You claimed Chelsie didn't care, but I know for a fact that she did. She still does."

The Qilin flinched. "That's not true."

"It is," Julius said stubbornly. "And I can prove it." He pointed at the painting between them. "She still has the watercolor you painted of her when she was asleep hanging on the door of her bedroom."

The emperor's golden eyes went wide. "She kept it?"

"Treasures it," Julius said with a smile. "She wouldn't tell me who painted it, but you don't keep paintings like that hidden in your room where you can stare at them from dragons you've betrayed."

For a moment, the Qilin stood in spellbound wonder. Then, like a door closing, the amazed expression vanished. "It's probably a trophy," he said bitterly. "My paintings are highly prized. Her hoarding one is not proof of lingering feelings."

"No," Julius said stubbornly. "I got *that* from her face. I saw the way she looked at your picture, and I'd have had to have been blind not to notice how much she still cared. She looked just as miserable as you do right now when I dragged her side of the China story out of her. That's what makes all of this so intolerable. Everything you've said since you got here has been based on the assumption that Chelsie betrayed you, but the sister I know? The one who treasures your painting in secret and threatens to bite the head off of anyone who so much as mentions China? That's not a dragon who's gotten away with something. That's a dragon who's been suffering for a long, long time, and if you really did love her once, you owe it to both of you to find out why."

The Qilin closed his eyes with a long sigh. "You make a good argument," he said at last. "But I can't accept what you're saying."

"Why not?"

"Because I can't," he said, turning his back to Julius. "You should go now."

"*No*," Julius said, darting around the painting so that he was standing in front of the emperor again. "If you'd just *talk* to my sister, I'm sure we could get to the bottom of—"

"This audience is over, Heartstriker," the emperor said firmly, pressing a tired hand over his eyes. "I've already made my decision. Our conquest of your clan will proceed as planned. I suggest you go back downstairs and make the most of your final day."

"But this is ridiculous!" Julius cried. "Don't you at least want to hear Chelsie's explanation? She's free of Bethesda now. If she was ever going to tell you the truth, this would be the—"

"Why do you think I'm telling you to *go*?" the Qilin cried, yanking his hand back down. It wasn't until his eyes came into view, though, that Julius realized how angry the emperor was.

"Do you know how badly I want you to be right?" he said, voice cracking. "I've clung to the fact that Chelsie betrayed me for centuries because it hurt less than knowing she just didn't care. Now here you come, saying they're both wrong. That she still loves me, and this could all be a misunderstanding, and I want to believe you so badly it hurts."

"Then do it," Julius said. "Chelsie's here in the mountain right now. We can go talk to her and resolve all of this."

"I can't," the Qilin said. "Don't you see? I—"

His words cut off as the mountain began to shake. All around them, the stacked paintings tumbled from their piles. Rather than simply falling on the ground, though, each one seemed to go out of its way to fall directly into the others, the wooden frames slamming into the canvases at the perfect angle to leave huge, ugly scratch marks all across the painted images. One large oil painting of a tree actually slid all the way across the floor to the easel holding the painting of Chelsie. It was barely moving by the time it got there, but just the tap of its corner against the easel's wooden leg was enough to tip the whole thing over.

Julius tried to catch it but overshot his grab, missing completely as the painting crashed down on the art table beside it, scattering the Qilin's neatly stacked brushes and splattering the cup of rinse water in every direction. A few drops actually flew straight into Julius's eyes, but most of the diluted paint water ended up on the Qilin's golden robes, leaving ugly gray-green splatters across the meticulously embroidered dragons that covered his chest.

It was all just coincidence. Pure bad luck. But by the time Julius had rubbed the paint out of his eyes, the Qilin's face was as pale as someone who'd just witnessed a murder.

"And now you see why," he said, his voice weak and shaking as he leaned down to rescue the fallen painting. "I've been down this path before. When I lost Chelsie the first time, I did unspeakable damage to my empire. Even if you're right, and this was all a misunderstanding, I can't risk putting my subjects through that ever again."

"But you also can't keep pushing it down," Julius argued. "I'm not saying it won't hurt, but if you haven't stopped loving her in six centuries, it's not going to happen. Putting all of Heartstriker under your luck might save Chelsie from Algonquin, but it solves nothing. All you're doing is kicking the can down the road. You'll have no real peace until you deal with this."

"I know," the emperor said. "But I can't right now." He covered his face with his hands again. "Just go."

"But—"

"*Go,*" he snarled as Lao burst through the doors.

"*Xian!*"

That must have been the emperor's name. Julius had never heard any of the Chinese dragons use it before, but Lao was clearly calling to his cousin as he charged into the room. He took one look at the Qilin's paint-splattered robe, and then he whirled on Julius. "*What did you do?*"

"Nothing," the emperor said, dropping his hands with a deep, calming breath. "It's nothing. The young Heartstriker was just leaving."

That was clearly meant to be Julius's out, but he couldn't take it. Not yet. Not like this.

"You can't keep pretending nothing's wrong forever," he told the emperor. "When you're ready to know the truth, come and find me. I'll take you to Chelsie, no questions asked."

Lao bared his teeth. "Do not speak that name!"

"If you can't talk about the problem, that's a problem," Julius said stubbornly. "If you really cared about him, you wouldn't be enabling this."

"That's *enough*," the emperor snarled, hands curling into fists as the mountain shook again. "You are *dismissed*, Heartstriker!"

That was a final warning if Julius had ever heard one. This time, though, he took it, hurrying out the door as fast as his feet would carry him.

Fredrick pounced on him the moment he got into the hall. "What happened?"

"Tell you later," Julius promised, grabbing his arm. "Right now, we need to go."

He started to run, but Fredrick didn't follow. No matter how hard Julius yanked on him, he remained frozen in the doorway, staring at the unveiled Qilin's face as though he'd never seen a dragon before. It wasn't until Lao starting marching toward them that the F finally snapped out of it, letting Julius pull him back into the hall seconds before Lao slammed the door in their faces.

"What was that about?" Julius yelled at his brother.

Fredrick raised a shaking hand to his face. "I—"

He cut off, his head snapping up. Julius jumped, too, hand going instinctively for his missing sword as he looked around to see what had alarmed his brother.

It wasn't a long search. At the end of the hall, one of the twin red dragons who served the Empress was standing at the door to Bethesda's treasury. Since they tended to come in pairs, Julius looked immediately for the other one. Sure enough, the second red dragon was behind them, blocking the doorway that led back to the throne room. This meant Julius and Fredrick were now trapped in the hallway between them. A trap that was rapidly closing now that the Qilin had kicked them out.

"Looks like the empress hasn't forgotten about killing us," Fredrick whispered as the red dragons began to move, stalking down the hallway toward their pincered prey in deadly, silent strides.

Julius had been thinking the same thing. "Is there another way out?"

"Not without going through them."

Fat chance of that. Fredrick might be old and bigger than expected, but Julius was still just a J. A fast one, perhaps, but definitely not Justin. He didn't even have his Fang thanks to Lao's requirement that he disarm.

He could actually see his sword from where they were standing, leaning against the wall right where he'd left it by the door to his mother's sitting room. It was barely twenty feet away, but it might as well have been with Ian in Siberia for all the chance Julius had of getting to it before the red dragons caught him. Unless he was hiding something under his fitted jacket, Fredrick didn't have a weapon either, which meant not only were they facing superior opponents in tight quarters, they were doing it completely unarmed. Julius was still processing how epically screwed that made them when a hand grabbed his shoulder.

It was a tribute to the insanity of his optimism that Julius's first thought was that Justin had somehow known he was in trouble and come back to do his knightly duty. The biggest J did have a sixth sense for violence, and it wouldn't be the most unlikely stunt Julius had seen his brother pull off. When he snapped his head back to look, though, it wasn't Justin who was standing behind him.

It was Chelsie.

Both red dragons froze. For several heartbeats, no one moved, and then one of the dragons said something in Chinese. Chelsie answered in the same language, speaking the unknown words in the low, terrifying voice she normally saved for siblings who'd particularly pissed her off. Even not knowing what was being said, the sound was enough to send chills up Julius's spine, and he wasn't the only one. Both of the approaching dragons were now backing off, putting up their hands in the universal gesture of surrender. When they'd shuffled all the way back to their respective ends of the hall, Chelsie's hold on Julius's shoulder turned into a shove.

"*Move.*"

"But my sword's still—"

"We'll get it later," she growled, leading the way into Bethesda's human bedroom, the one she used on the rare occasions she didn't feel like sleeping on a pile of gold. "The fearsome twosome learned not to try me in close quarters a long time ago, but they won't stay cowed for long. They're probably already getting help, which means we need to *go.*"

That explanation raised more questions than it answered, but Julius didn't have time to ask any of them. Chelsie had already shut the door, locking them inside their mother's bedchamber, which was apparently the only room the Qilin's kamikaze cleaning squad hadn't touched yet. Julius was still wondering why Chelsie had sealed them inside an apparent dead end when she herded them both into the sprawling maze that was Bethesda's walk-in closet. Once there, Chelsie went straight to the back, shoving aside a curtain of million-dollar dresses and hauling up the crimson carpet beneath them to reveal a wooden door the size of a porthole set flush into the stone beneath.

"Get in," she ordered, yanking the wooden door up to reveal a narrow hole going straight down.

Fredrick obeyed first, jumping down the dark chute feet first without hesitation. Julius wasn't quite as brave, sitting on the floor as he eased himself into the bolt-hole. "Where does this go?"

Chelsie looked nervously over her shoulder. "Somewhere safe."

"Good," Julius said. "Because we need to talk."

Chelsie didn't look happy with that announcement, but she didn't waste time arguing. She just shoved him down the escape and hopped in after him, catching her fall on the edge one-handed before reaching up with the other to close the secret door, plunging them all into the dark.

• • •

Fenghuang, Consort to the last Qilin, the Empress Mother, kept the look of relief off her face only through untold centuries of practice. "So he's chased the meddling Heartstriker out?"

The bowing red dragon—one of the twins, she'd never been able to tell them apart—nodded. "Yes, Empress. Lao is with him now."

"And the Heartstrikers?"

"Vanished through one of the secret passages."

That was vexing, but they would turn up again. Bethesda's children could always be counted on to pop up like weeds. Even so. "Search the lower levels," she ordered. "If you see a chance to kill him, take it, but don't do anything that might upset the Qilin further. This place is dangerous enough as it is. I don't want any more unnecessary stress placed on my son."

The red dragon nodded obediently and backed out of the enormous empty cave that had once been the Broodmare's gold wallow. When he'd closed the vault door behind him, the empress turned her attention back to her own unexpected problem. "You were wrong."

"I was nothing of the sort," Brohomir replied, his face irritatingly smug even through the terrible, grainy connection of the public AR terminal he'd insisted on calling her from. "I told you this would happen."

"You told me that if the Golden Emperor spoke to Julius Heartstriker, I would lose my position as empress," she said, scowling through the projected screen thrown up by her own, far superior,

personal phone. "But your whelp is long gone, and here I sit still."
She lifted her chin proudly. "You were *wrong*, seer, but I knew you
would be. I raised Xian to be dutiful above all else. We are nothing
like you barbarians."

"No one implied you were," Bob said, leaning against the wall
of the grubby public booth he'd crammed himself into. "But you're
thinking too short term. I'm afraid your precious golden treasure
has already fallen into the well-meaning clutches of my youngest
brother, and those are very hard to escape."

"Then I will kill him," the empress said.

"Such is the common refrain of Heartstriker Mountain," the
seer replied with a chuckle. "But Julius is harder to kill than he
looks. Even if you did succeed, I'm afraid it wouldn't do much good.
You lost your son years ago, Fenghuang. It's only the duty you value
so highly that's kept you from feeling it sooner."

"What do you know of duty?" the empress said haughtily. "You
are a traitor, a seer who sold out his mother and his clan."

"That I am," Brohomir said cheerfully. "Funny how you find
that so offensive now, yet you had no problem accepting my traitor-
ous ways when I was serving Heartstriker up to you on a platter. No
Amelia, no White Witch, no annoying siblings. Just my mother and
sister, hobbled and bound, as promised."

The empress sneered. "Hobbled and bound, indeed. Bethesda
was bound, but she was never the problem, was she? That honor
goes to her shameless daughter, and yet I arrived to find her still
running around loose." She leaned into the projected screen with a
scowl. "You told me you had the little whore in check."

"I'd thank you not to talk about my sister that way," Brohomir
said, his normally lilting voice sharp. "And I pulled off a *miracle*
with Chelsie. Even with your son's luck coming down on us like a
sledgehammer, she and the Qilin have yet to cross paths. It's coming, though, and soon, but you knew *that* was inevitable when you
came here."

"I had no choice," the Empress Mother said bitterly. "Xian had
been considering conquering Heartstriker for years. Algonquin's

foolish war was just the final straw. After that, there was no reasoning with him. Even I cannot defy the will of the Golden Emperor."

"But you manipulate it just fine."

"I used to," she said sadly, looking down at her withered hands. "He is my only son. My treasure, bought with everything I had. I made his luck greater than even his father's at its prime, a blessing that fell on all of us without fault, without fail. With one exception, he has always been a perfect emperor. A perfect son, respectful and obedient and utterly above reproach. The only thing that could ever break him was her." She clenched her bony fingers into fists. "I will not let her take him from me. You must have seen the mountain quake just now. You *know* what is at stake. She already ruined him once. I can't allow that to happen again. Not after all I sacrificed."

"That's the trouble with sacrifice," Brohomir said. "You paid for a Qilin, but you still hatched a dragon. You can't be shocked he has ambitions of his own."

The empress's lip curled in disgust. "Love is *not* an ambition."

"It is when you love a Heartstriker."

"I didn't call you so you could make jokes at my expense," she snapped. "You play the careless seer well, Brohomir, but you've worked too hard on your precious Heartstrikers for me to believe you're throwing them away now. I know this is all part of some greater plan in your twisted mind, but even your machinations cannot stand before the will of the Qilin. His luck moves the future of all our clans. It will smash your schemes to pieces if you presume to play games with the Golden Empire."

"A fair threat," the seer admitted. "Even I am powerless before the Golden Wrecking Ball."

"I'm glad you understand," the empress said, nodding. "But just because you are lower doesn't mean we can't still come to a mutually beneficial arrangement. Tell me how to save my son, and I will promise to spare your hateful relations."

"Such a benevolent offer," Bob replied, pressing a hand dramatically to his chest as he flopped against the booth's graffitied wall. "I think I might faint."

She gave him a cutting look, and the seer sat back up with a grin. "I'm afraid there's nothing I can do. I came to your aid six centuries ago when I wrote you that letter explaining how to corner my fleeing sister, but while this saved your empire from the worst ravages of a broken-hearted young Qilin, it fixed nothing. The damage was only put off, not prevented. Your son came to our mountain with pure intentions. He has not deceived you in the least. He really did plan to return home the moment he put Chelsie under his luck without seeing her at all. But while sterling duty guides his actions, his luck has always followed his emotions. From the moment he arrived, the Qilin's desperate, repressed longing to see the dragon he loves has been warping the future like taffy. It pulled Julius to him despite your best efforts, and now, as is his habit, the Nice Dragon of Heartstriker has made things infinitely more complicated. I've done all I can, but at this point I'm afraid there's not a single path of possibility remaining where your emperor and my sister do not meet, and where he does not learn the truth."

The empress closed her eyes with a shudder. "Then it is finished," she whispered, pressing a shaking hand to her eyes. "We are *all* finished."

"Not quite."

She lowered her fingers to see the seer leaning into the camera, his face filling the screen with a predatory grin the empress was not accustomed to seeing aimed at her. "Delightful as this has been, I didn't risk calling you just to rub your face in bad news. It's true there's no future left where your son remains only yours, but there's still a way to make sure he's not *hers*."

"Why would you betray your sister for me?"

"Because I'm not doing it for you," Brohomir said. "I'm doing it for *me*. The fact that you also benefit is merely a happy coincidence, but the *choice* still has to be yours."

The empress scoffed. "What choice? You said it was inevitable."

"It is," he assured her. "Nothing can stop the hammer now, but if you're quick, you can still choose where it lands. That's power, Empress. The only power you have left."

Fenghuang looked down at her red-lacquered nails, making a show of thinking it over, but only a show. In truth, her mind was already made up, because the seer was telling the truth. She'd fed Xian enough of her fire to make him the greatest Qilin ever born, and for twenty-one years, he had been. Then, just as he'd come of age and entered what should have been his full potential, the Heartstriker girl had ruined him.

Not immediately. The first year they were together, Xian's magic had been even more magnificent than she'd dreamed. His happiness brought more good fortune to their empire than his father's last two centuries combined. So much that even she had willingly turned a blind eye to the mud he was rolling in. A shortsighted, foolish mistake. Breeding always told, and when the Heartstriker girl showed her true colors at last, they had all suffered for it.

It had taken centuries to recover from the catastrophes the Qilin's misery brought down that year. Even after she'd patched things up, convincing her son that he had been betrayed, that it was all the Heartstriker's fault, his luck was never again what it should have been. No matter how many lovelier, better dragonesses she'd found for him, he'd always remained distant, and while his luck never truly faltered again after that first, horrible year, neither had it blossomed. He was simply diminished, her great work squandered. But then, just when the loss grew painful enough to make her actually consider summoning Chelsie back, the rumors arrived, and Fenghuang finally realized *why* the girl had run.

That was the final stroke. She had no proof, nothing but hearsay, but if any of it was true, then the Heartstriker truly had taken everything from them. Worst of all, she hadn't even done it on purpose. A calculated attack would have at least been something she could respect, but Bethesda's daughter had destroyed their clan out of foolish, selfish *ignorance*, which was as unforgivable as it was irreparable. Nothing could fix what the stupid girl had broken, so Fenghuang had done the only thing she could. She'd buried everything, walling off her son and her empire from the rest of the world. And for six hundred years, it had worked. Now, though, everything was unraveling.

From the moment they'd embarked on this cursed journey across the sea, this end had been inevitable, but like any proper dragon, Fenghuang could not accept defeat. So when the Seer of the Heartstrikers offered her a chance, *any* chance, to mitigate the damage, for all her hatred of his family and his smug green eyes, she found that she could not refuse.

"What must I do?"

The seer's smile grew sharp. "Exactly what I say."

Fenghuang had never hated anything as much as those words. But an empress did her duty even in defeat, so she swallowed her anger and nodded.

"Excellent," Bob said, reaching off camera to grab something waiting outside of the booth. "I have detailed instructions, multiple stipulations, and one ironclad rule you must never break, all of which I will explain in exhaustive detail. Before we go down that rabbit hole, though, there's someone you need to meet."

The Empress Mother had no idea whom he could be talking about. She wasn't even sure where Brohomir was, other than somewhere filthy. Certainly not the sort of place where any dragon worthy of her interest would be found. When he came back into view, though, there was indeed a dragoness with him.

She was a hatchling, a young one. How Brohomir had gotten a whelp that young into human form, she'd never know, but whatever he'd done to her, the child was obviously a Heartstriker. She looked like a mini-Bethesda with her thick, dark hair and high, haughty cheekbones, but her eyes were the wrong color. Even through the terrible camera, Fenghuang could see no green in them at all. Just gold. The pure, rich, glittering, metallic color she'd seen only twice in her life looking out at her from the little dragon's face.

And that was when Fenghuang knew to her bones that all was truly lost.

CHAPTER EIGHT

The Sea of Magic was roiling.

"What is going *on?*" Marci cried, clinging to the Empty Wind, the only thing in the entire place that wasn't violently shaking.

"It's the magic," Ghost said, his glowing eyes round as he stared up into the dark. "It's being forced apart. Something's coming through."

That didn't sound good, but before Marci could ask what, where, why, or how big, something new appeared at the edge of her vision.

She jumped with a yelp, whirling around so she could face… whatever it was. When she stopped, though, there was nothing. Just the churning magic, twisty and nauseating as always. She was about to write the whole thing off as nerves when it happened again.

There was no missing the change this time. She was looking right at the floor of the Sea of Magic when the ground rippled like water, the rough, uneven, seemingly stone surface smoothing and rounding before her eyes into what looked like a manhole cover. It couldn't be, of course, but that was what Marci saw: an iron manhole cover complete with air holes, tire scuffs, and the logo for the DFZ's private sewer contractors conglomerate.

"Do you see that?"

"I see it," Amelia said, squinting. "I don't understand it, but—"

An echoing *bang* cut off whatever she'd been about to say as the manhole cover shot off the ground like a bullet. It landed a few seconds later, crashing to the right of the pillar with a deafening clatter of thick iron hitting stone. The sound was still going when a man's hand reached out to grab the lip of the tunnel the blasted-open manhole had revealed, followed immediately by the man himself as Sir Myron Rollins hauled himself out of the ground and onto the floor of the Sea of Magic.

He collapsed immediately after, flopping over to heave on his back like a landed fish. The whole thing was so unexpected, so incredibly out of place, that Marci couldn't speak a word until Sir Myron rolled over to push himself up, and his eyes found hers.

"You!" he cried, eyes flying wide. "How are you—What are you doing here? You're *dead*. I *saw* your body. I—"

He stopped there, eyes going even wider as he finally spotted the Empty Wind standing behind her.

If things had been less dire, Marci would have relished watching Sir Myron Rollins have a mental breakdown over the abyss that was her spirit's true face. But as entertaining as it was to watch him break beneath the crippling truth of his ultimate insignificance, they didn't have time.

"Ghost," she said quietly. "Would you mind?"

He sighed and turned around, putting his back to Myron, who fell gasping back to the floor. "I suppose that explains how you're here," he said when he could speak again. "You sold your soul to a death god."

Since she'd made a deal with Ghost to escape her death and come to the Merlin Gate, that was technically accurate, but Marci didn't appreciate the way he said it. She was about to tell him as much when Myron sat up, moving his hand at the same time as if he were yanking on something.

When his fist stopped, she saw it was a string. A silver ribbon, specifically, covered in spellwork and wrapped multiple times around his hand. She was trying to read what the spells did when ribbon suddenly became a minor concern compared to what was at the end of it.

Something was climbing out of the manhole beside Myron. It looked vaguely human in the dark, but it moved like a rodent, skittering behind Myron like a rat running for cover. The combination reminded her of the megarats she and Julius had hunted in the DFZ back alleys when money really got tight, but despite the urban legends, Marci had never personally seen one bigger than a Doberman. By contrast, the thing cowering behind Myron now was the size of a car, with eyes that glowed like orange streetlights and the gleam of silver wrapped around its neck.

"That's a spirit, isn't it?" she said, her voice quiet and angry as she fixed the older mage with a deadly glare. "What did you do, Myron?"

"Nothing worse than you," he replied, clutching the silver line in his fist as he stood up. "Every Merlin needs a Mortal Spirit."

The creature on the chain hissed and scurried away, its teeth flashing like knives in the dark as it gnawed at its bindings. When the silver didn't give, it made a pitiful sound, and Marci's fists clenched. "That is not how this goes," she growled. "A Merlin works *with* her spirit. You have that thing chained up like a dog. What's it even a spirit of? Terror?"

"That is none of your concern," Myron said, looking down at her, which was rich given the circumstances.

"And you had the nerve to criticize Ghost."

"Judge me all you like," he replied haughtily. "But unlike you, I have no illusions about what I'm doing. You tried to make friends with oblivion, to reason with *death*, but I understand that these are forces that cannot be controlled. Mortal Spirits are not our allies. They're our shadows, the imprints left by humanity's lowest common denominator, and they'll be the end of everything if we do not strike first."

Marci stared at him in disbelief. "You sound like Algonquin."

"She would know, wouldn't she," he snapped. "Algonquin has always been our enemy, but that doesn't make her wrong. She understands better than any living thing that Mortal Spirits are monsters. *Our* monsters, made by our flaws, and like any other evil of humanity, they must be curtailed."

Marci crossed her arms over her chest. So that's what this was about. "I see Algonquin found someone willing to take the job I turned down. Let me guess: you're here to clamp down the magic and shut off the Mortal Spirits before they can rise, and in return, you get to be the first Merlin."

"Almost," he said, pulling the silver leash tight. "But I'm not just here to be the first Merlin. I also mean to be the last."

He turned on his heel and walked to the pillar, dragging his spirit behind him like a disobedient dog. When he reached the wooden door, he wrapped the silver lead tight around his palm, raising his fist to knock.

Just as when Marci had done it, the knock rang like a gong through the swirling magic. The door opened immediately, sending light flooding into the dark again as Shiro, Abe no Seimei's shikigami, the same bound guardian who'd shut the door in Marci's face, lowered his head in greeting just as he had for her.

"Welcome," he said, his mouth moving not quite in sync with the words as they filtered through the translation spell. "He who would be Merlin."

"Thank you," Myron said, smiling warmly as if he'd come here as a dinner guest and not someone bent on destroying everything. "I'm Sir Myron Rollins, Undersecretary of Magic for the United Nations, Chair of Tectonic Magic at Cambridge University, Master of Labyrinths, and Bound Mage of the DFZ."

Marci's eyebrows shot up. "Mage of the DFZ?" she cried. "Since when?"

"He means his spirit," Ghost whispered, nodding to the ratlike thing at the end of the silver ribbon, which was still pulling against Myron with all its might.

"No way," she said. "*That's* the DFZ? As in the place we live?" He nodded, and her eyes went wide. "A city can be a Mortal Spirit?!"

"Anything humans value can be a Mortal Spirit," Amelia said irritably, leaning forward on Marci's shoulder until she almost fell off. "Now hush. This is about to get good."

Marci didn't see how anything involving Myron becoming Merlin could ever be termed "good." But that must not have been what Amelia was talking about, because while Shiro was still smiling politely at Myron as he had for Marci, his inhumanly dark eyes were as hard as slate.

"You have indeed bound a Mortal Spirit," he said, glancing distastefully at the giant rat-thing pulling at the end of Myron's leash. "But her magic is not her own. She has been flooded with the blood of lesser spirits, and she reeks of Algonquin's water."

Marci didn't understand what he was talking about for that the first part, but now that he'd mentioned it, there *was* a strong smell of lake water coming off Myron's spirit, but not the usual kind. Even when it was flowing under the Skyways, Algonquin's water always smelled clean. The stench coming off this thing reminded Marci of the storm drain she, Julius, and Justin had climbed through what felt like forever ago. She was wondering if the spirit was sick when Myron stomped his foot.

"What does it matter where her magic came from?" he demanded. "She's a Mortal Spirit, and I am her bound master. That gives me the right to walk through this door."

"There you are wrong," Shiro said, looking more disgusted than ever. "You have no rights here, mage. As I told the young lady behind you, Merlins are champions of humanity. They cannot be beholden to foreign masters. You have bound a spirit in servitude, but as long as you yourself are the servant of the Lady of the Lakes, I will not allow you to enter this sacred place. You may try again when you have freed yourself from Algonquin's influence. Until then, you are unworthy to stand in the light of this gate."

And then he slammed the door in Myron's face.

Marci laughed out loud. "Serves you right," she said as Myron stumbled back. "I can't believe you agreed to work for Algonquin. You're such a traitor. How did General Jackson not shoot you, too?"

"Because I didn't give her the chance," Myron said, glaring over his shoulder at her with a look of pure hate. "Don't confuse us, Novalli. I am nothing like you. You're a PhD dropout who lucked into a spirit she never deserved. You've never known what you're doing because you did nothing to earn it. All you've ever had is dragons willing to use you and your own arrogant grasping, which apparently extends even after death. But I'm no dragon lackey, and I'm not Algonquin's servant, either. I am the Master of Labyrinths, the greatest living mage! Everything humanity knows about Merlins or Mortal Spirits comes from *my* research. *I* am the one who deserves to be here, and I will not be kept out."

The smile slipped off Marci's face. "Hold up," she said, putting up her hands. "Just what are you planning to—"

She never got a chance to finish. Myron wasn't listening, anyway. He just turned back to the door, tightening his grip on his spirit's lead as he ordered, "Break it down."

The spirit of the DFZ roared in defiance, a horrible amalgam of breaking cement and terrified human screaming. When it didn't stop, Myron pulled again, yanking the rat-monster forward until the silver cord choked it, cutting off its roar to a pathetic, defeated gasp.

After that, the spirit didn't fight again. It just cowered, looking more like a rat than ever as it obediently turned to the Merlin Gate and slammed its body into the door.

The crash went through the churning magic like a bomb blast, knocking Marci back even through the Empty Wind's protective gale. She was still getting her feet back under her when the spirit charged again, attacking the door with claws and teeth that sparked like the muzzle flashes from gunshots in dark alleys. And as it clawed and bit and clawed again, the thick wood of the Merlin Gate began to crack.

"*Stop!*" Marci shouted, stepping to the very edge of her spirit's protection. "This is stupid, Myron. You don't even know what you're doing."

"On the contrary, I know exactly what I'm doing," he said, raising his voice over the violent roar of his spirit. "You don't rise as high as I have by taking no for an answer."

"So you're just going to force your way in?" she cried. "Smash and grab the Heart of the World?"

"If that's what it takes." Myron said, glancing back over his shoulder. "I'm a mage, Miss Novalli. Audacity is the base line for entry."

Marci swore under her breath. She'd used that line so many times herself, she'd forgotten it was from one of his books. But while she absolutely agreed that a bit of recklessness was necessary to push modern magic to its full potential, this was insane. "Breaking something we know nothing about just so you can get what you want isn't audacity. It's selfish and stupid. What if you destroy something irreplaceable? It's not like we know how to make another one of these. And even if you do break in, it's not like Shiro's going to suddenly change his mind and give you your Merlin ticket."

"That's not his decision," Myron growled. "I've read enough to know a shikigami when I see one. He's a clockwork, magic shoved into a binding net of spellwork that mimics human intelligence. But mimicry is not being. He may have been left as a watchdog by the last generation, but he said it himself: Merlins are the champions of humanity. He can close the door and lock me out, but I have more right to be inside that pillar than he does."

"You don't know that," she said, exasperated. "You don't know any of this for sure. All you know is what you've scraped up from thousand-year-old texts and stories. You say you're the expert, but you have no more idea what's actually on the other side of that door than I do."

"Perhaps not," he said. "But use your eyes, Novalli. Do you think *this* occurred naturally?" He pointed up at the perfectly smooth pillar of stone rising like a skyscraper from the flat floor of the Sea of Magic. "Of course not. It was made by the Merlins. Made by *men*, not gods. And what man has made, man can break."

"Why would you want to break this?" Marci cried as his screaming spirit slammed into the door yet again, sending another *boom* through the black haze of magic that was now frantically swirling around them. "You've found the place that makes Merlins, and you're smashing in the door like a barbarian!"

As if to prove her right, the spirit of the DFZ chose that moment to slam its claws into the wood again, only this time, one of the boards cracked. It started as a hairline fracture then quickly widened into an inch-wide gap that sent the warm light from inside spilling into the dark.

"You see?" Marci said, dragging her hands through her short hair in frustration. "I know you want to be Merlin more than anything, Myron, but this is too far. You told me once that the Merlins were humanity's hope. The power that would finally put our species on equal footing with dragons and spirits. Now we're finally here, at the place where that happens, and you're *punching it down*. How can you risk something so vital to all of us for your personal ambition? Are you really that selfish?"

That last part was a desperate play, and for a moment, it seemed to work. Myron actually hesitated, lowering the hand that held his spirit's leash. But then, just when she thought that maybe she'd gotten through, he turned his back on her again.

"You understand nothing," he said, voice shaking with fury. "You think I don't know what I'm risking? I've dreamed of being Merlin since before you were born. I thought the Mortal Spirits were our salvation, our weapons. You were the one who showed me I was wrong."

"Me?" Marci said, but when Myron looked back again, it wasn't at her. He was staring at Ghost, and his eyes were full of fear.

"I thought I knew our enemies," he said. "But Algonquin and the dragons are nothing compared to the gods we made in our fear. Humans have always been experts at finding fates worse than death, and when I saw your monster and his army of ghosts walking through Reclamation Land, I knew that the only way to keep us from destroying ourselves was to stop the problem at its source."

Marci's jaw clenched. "You *have* been listening to Algonquin."

"I didn't need to," he said. "I already knew what had to be done. The only reason I played along with Algonquin was so I could get the Mortal Spirit she was building. Now that it's mine, I'm going to do what I've always done."

She looked pointedly at the cracked door. "Destroy things?"

Myron gave her a look of utter disgust. "Save humanity."

He yanked his spirit's leash again. When it cowered, he unclenched his right hand from the silver lead and reached out to place his palm over the glowing crack in the door. When it was pressed flat, he squeezed his fingers together, lining up the wide metal bands of his rings so that the intricate mazes engraved into their matte titanium surfaces matched up to form one continuous path. Marci didn't know enough about Myron's unique style of magic to say if the alignment was for show or if he actually needed the physical maze for his casting, but the moment the pattern came together, the labyrinth opened, and the dark magic swirling around them stopped spinning in circles and started pouring into him.

"*What is he doing?*" Amelia yelled over the roar. "I've never seen a human work magic that way."

"*No one else does,*" Marci yelled back, grabbing hold of Ghost as the Sea of Magic rushed past them into Myron. "Labyrinth casting is a Sir Myron Rollins original. I've read all three of his books on it, and I'm still not sure how it works, or how he's not burning himself out. I can't even touch the magic here."

"That's because you're dead," the dragon said, anchoring her tail around Marci's neck so she wouldn't get swept away. "He's not."

Marci scowled. "Then how is he here?" Because if Myron had gotten in without having to pay the piper, she was going to be *pissed.*

"Because he is not bound to death," the Empty Wind replied, his glowing eyes fixed on the rat cowering at Myron's feet. "I don't know how the DFZ brought him to this side, but she did it without killing him. I'm not sure where his body is, but so long as it breathes, he has protections you do not."

"Great," she muttered, glaring at the mage, who was happily pulling down fistfuls of magic that would have killed her, folding the power into complicated mazes that he laid down on the door in brightly glowing patterns of green and blue. She didn't know Labyrinth magic well enough to know what these particular mazes did, but it didn't take a genius to guess it wasn't going to be pretty. A blasting spell, a cutting charge, maybe something nastier.

Whatever it was, Myron had made it clear he wasn't pulling his punches, which meant she had to do something *fast*. His glowing maze already covered a third of the wood around the crack. At this rate, he'd have the whole door marked for destruction in minutes, along with Marci's hopes of ever being a Merlin. Or getting out of this alive.

"Screw this," she growled, turning to her spirit. "Ghost?"

The name wasn't out of her mouth before the wind surrounding them picked up. *I thought you'd never ask.*

She grinned at the eagerness of the voice in her head, but Amelia curled her body closer, wings twitching nervously. "Marci," she whispered. "I'm not sure sending him out is a good—"

A howl of wind drowned out whatever she'd been about to say. The protective magic surrounding them didn't budge, but Ghost himself was gone, his centurion's body blowing away like dust only to reappear directly beside Myron. The mage snatched his hand away from the door, turning to block himself instead, but Ghost wasn't going for him. He was reaching for the leashed spirit, snatching the black rat-thing up by the scruff of its neck and throwing it into the dark. But just as Marci thought they'd landed it, the DFZ twisted in midair, launching itself off of nothing to slam into the Empty Wind like a furious, sharp-toothed school bus.

"*Ghost!*"

He went down with a crash, his shadowy body crushed under the rat-shaped spirit, who was getting bigger as Marci watched. In the seconds they struggled, it had grown from bus sized to house sized, its orange eyes gleaming with wild fury. No matter how big or angry it got, though, Ghost was still a wind. When the monster tried to trap him, he simply blew away, racing through the dark to safety. The rat didn't give up, though. Ghost was infinitely faster, but the spirit of the DFZ was stuck on him as stubbornly as it had been on the door. No matter how deftly he dodged, it just kept coming, forcing him to run again and again, retreating farther and farther back into the dark.

"Why is he retreating?"

"That's what I was trying to warn you about," Amelia said quietly. "It doesn't look it, but Myron's DFZ is a *lot* bigger than your Empty Wind."

That couldn't be possible. "How is the spirit of a city bigger than the fear of being forgotten?"

"It isn't, but remember what the shikigami said: the DFZ was stuffed full of spirit magic. Ghost rose on his own. He has enough juice to be conscious and active, but he's nowhere near full, and you're not alive to feed him power anymore. That's a double whammy. Not only did he start in the hole, but he's still running on the magic that he came in with when you died. That's nowhere near enough to face a full-blown, fully juiced Mortal Spirit."

"Then I'll feed him magic!" Marci said desperately, looking around at the swirling dark. "There's plenty of it around."

"Too much of it. That's the problem, remember?"

How could she forget? The one time she'd touched the stuff without the Empty Wind's protection, she'd nearly lost her hand. Even so. "I have to do something!" She pointed at Myron, who was already back to working on his maze. "He's halfway done."

"Then don't help him by being stupid!" Amelia snapped. "I know you want to do something, but if you touch the raw magic out there without a physical body to help diffuse it, it'll burn right through you, and then Ghost will *really* be lost."

Marci clenched her jaw. Amelia was right. The spirit of the DFZ might not have looked like much at the beginning, but now that they were going head to head, it was obvious the Empty Wind was outmatched. If he hadn't been so fast, he'd have already been ripped to shreds, and while he retreated, Myron's maze on the door got bigger and bigger and bigger.

"Screw this," she growled, taking a step forward.

"*Marci!*" Amelia cried, digging her claws into her shoulder, but Marci wasn't listening. She didn't care if she burned out. That pompous idiot was *not* allowed to win. Not after they'd fought so hard to get here. So, before she could chicken out, Marci lunged forward, thrusting her hand through the protective swirl of winds Ghost was still maintaining.

Touching the raw magic felt like sticking her hand into a roaring furnace. The swirling chaos around them might have looked like ink-black water, but it burned like acid. Even braced for the worst, it still hurt more than she'd expected, but Marci didn't let go. She just took another step, grabbing as much of the raw pulsing magic as she could and shoving it through the spellwork that was still marked on the inside of her bracelets.

The chunky plastic held up better than she'd anticipated, probably because it wasn't actually plastic. Like all the rest of her, the colorful circles were only echoes, the residual magic of a life. For all that, though, her spellwork held up fine, as well it should. The founding theory of Thaumaturgy was that spellwork was a tool, a way for mages to keep the immensely complicated logic needed to cast spells straight in their heads. No chalk or marker could actually channel magic. Even the circle, the base of all casting, was just a physical line to serve as a mental barrier.

That was the theory, anyway. Of course, since nothing was physical in this place, casting this spell meant Marci had just accidentally proven the theoretical basis of the most popular casting method in the world. That should have been an enormous deal, but Marci didn't have time to think about the ramifications. She was too busy forcing the burning magic through the bracelet containing her trusty microwave spell and out into Myron's back.

As theory predicted, the spell worked perfectly. The moment she let it go, heat exploded from Marci's fist, shooting instantly across the distance to leave a blistering burn mark across Myron's back between his shoulder blades. He screamed in pain, dropping the maze he'd been carefully crafting as he reached instinctively for the wound. A blow that would have felt more like a victory if Marci hadn't been screaming, too.

She hadn't felt it during the rush of the attack, but now that the magic was gone, her whole arm was throbbing in pain. Even with no physical flesh to scorch, the burning magic had still blistered her skin to her elbow. Her entire right hand from the wrist down was a bloody, scorched mess, far worse than the second-degree burn she'd landed on Myron. But even knowing she'd come out the worse in that exchange didn't keep the defiant smirk off Marci's face when the older mage whirled around.

"Are you mad?" he yelled, stomping forward to face her. "What is it you hope to accomplish here? You've *lost*, Novalli. I have the bigger spirit, the ready magic, and the physical life needed to safely handle it. Even if we were on equal footing, I would still have the advantage because I'm the better mage. I'm more experienced, more educated, and my labyrinth casting is infinitely superior to your pedantic Thaumaturgy. I am better than you in every possible way. You have a zero percent chance of stopping me, and you'll only hurt yourself more if you try."

"If you wanted me to stop, you shouldn't have put my back against the wall," Marci growled, tucking her burned right arm to her side only to raise her left instead, pointing her uninjured fist at his face like a cannon. "I'll burn myself to a crisp before I let a cowardly, shortsighted, selfish man like you become Merlin!"

Myron rolled his eyes. "Is that what this is about?" he asked in a patronizing voice. "I never expected you to accept defeat gracefully, Novalli, but I didn't think you'd stoop to denying reality. Your part in this is over. The dead don't get to have a say in the affairs of the living. But I'm not a cruel man. Stand down, call off your spirit, and I'll give you another chance."

"A chance at what?" she demanded, holding her arm steady. "As you just so kindly reminded me, I'm already dead. This *is* my last chance."

"Mine, too," he said quietly, holding up his fist, which was still gripping the spirit's silver leash. "You're not the only one with your back to a wall. This is a mission I *cannot* fail. I don't want to kill what's left of you, but I will if I have to, and we both know I can, so be a good girl and *stand down.*"

Marci bared her teeth and clenched her fist, ignoring the pain as she yanked the burning magic into the bracelet containing her force choke this time. Unlike her microwave spell, which was capped specifically to prevent lethal damage, this one had no limit. With enough power, she could crush an armored truck, and power was no problem in this place.

"Marci, think about this," Amelia whispered as smoke began to rise from her curled fingers. "If he's talking to you, he's not breaking the door. Don't be hasty."

That would have been a good point if there'd been a reason to stall, but Marci saw none. No matter how much time she bought, nothing would change. Ghost just wasn't big enough to beat the DFZ, and even with the entire Sea of Magic at her fingertips, she'd burn out before she could give him what he needed to close the gap. She couldn't help him, couldn't beat the DFZ on her own, couldn't stop Myron's magic from blowing open the door.

The only win she had a chance at was beating Myron himself, but even that was slim, and stalling wouldn't make it better. Attacking was her only chance. If she didn't take it, what was the point of coming here at all? She'd left the safety of her death to become Merlin. Given up something precious, even if she couldn't remember what it was. If Myron won, all that was wasted. He'd already admitted he believed Algonquin's propaganda. She was the only thing stopping him from going in there and capping the flow of magic back down to what it had been right after the meteor hit.

If she backed down, if she let this happen, then all the Mortal Spirits would fall back asleep, taking humanity's magical future with them. Ghost, the Champion of the Forgotten Dead, would himself be forgotten. The whole *world* would be diminished, and it would be her fault. If she didn't fight, there would be no more Merlins. *She* would never be a Merlin, never know the truth of magic, never keep her promise to Ghost.

Never see Julius again.

That was the last straw. With a scream of pain and fury, Marci clenched her smoking hand tight. But just as she finished folding the roaring magic into a hammer that would bash the superior look off Myron's stupid face, his own hand flicked, and light blossomed from the ground.

Her eyes flicked down in surprise to see a maze of glowing lines rising from the stone under her feet. They rose faster than she could believe, working their way up, and then *into* her body. She could actually feel them forking like circuitry through her organs, and as they filled her, the nearly done spell in her hand began to unravel. She clutched it tighter, fighting to finish, but the glowing lines got there first, racing down her arm and into her clenched hand. Once there, they began to split, dividing and subdividing into thousands of tiny fractals that wiggled into the magic of the spell itself like tiny wedges, each one prying and twisting and pulling the magic apart until she couldn't hold on.

The spell exploded with a blinding flash. The backlash hit immediately after, slamming into her like the shockwave from a bomb blast. The only reason she wasn't blown to pieces was because Myron's labyrinth held her in place, the glowing, forking lines grounding her to the stone like roots. Dimly, she supposed she should be grateful he'd kept her alive—assuming a sentient ghost counted as alive—but it was hard to feel anything but fury as she blinked the glare out of her eyes to see Myron looking down on her in pity.

"I warned you," he said, curling his fingers. The glowing maze that ran from the ground into Marci's body obeyed the gesture, popping her up like a puppet before dropping her to her knees. Another flick of his hand shattered what was left of her bracelets and yanked her arms behind her, leaving Marci bound and kneeling on the ground in front of him.

"I can't claim this gives me no pleasure," he said as she struggled. "A lesson in the distance between your skill and mine has been long overdue. But whatever you might think of me right now, if you really have read my books, you know I'm not a murderer. That's why I'm giving you one more chance to stand down."

"Before you what?" she snarled. "Murder me?"

"Why can't you see that this isn't about you?" he snapped, pointing at the glowing labyrinth that had stitched her to the ground. "I just saved you from blowing yourself to pieces because you'd rather die killing me than lose your shot at being Merlin, but you have the nerve to call me selfish? Did it ever occur to you that I'm not doing this for me? That I might, given my decades as a public servant, be acting in the public good?"

"You're not the only one," Marci said desperately. "You're clearly drinking Algonquin's Kool-Aid, but did it ever occur to *you* that maybe she's not telling the truth? That maybe Mortal Spirits aren't the implacable world-destroying machines she's made them out to be? For pity's sake, Myron, you're chained to one. Did you even try to talk to her before you did that?"

His eyes narrowed. "That is none of your concern."

"But it is," she said desperately. "*All* of this is *our* concern, because this isn't human versus spirit, it's mortal working with mortal. I'm not a Merlin yet, but there's got to be a reason the bond between mage and Mortal Spirit is a job requirement. I won't know the truth until I step through that gate, but I'd bet my life we weren't stuck together so we could kill each other. Mortal Spirits aren't some alien force. They're us. Our spirits. We're meant to work together. That's why we're here. Not to fight. That's what Algonquin wants. She *wants* us to be afraid so that we'll cut the magic back down to the levels where she was the big fish, and she's keeping us terrified so we won't notice we're cutting off our magical inheritance in the process. That's her game, and you're playing right into it, which is why I'm trying to stop you."

He turned away in disgust. "You don't know anything about what I mean to do."

"Then tell me!" Marci cried desperately. "If I'm wrong, let me know! We were on the same team once. If we still are, say something, and we can work this out."

"Bold words from the mage who attacked me first," he said, leaning over so that he could look her in the eyes. "But I have no intention of wasting more of my very limited time arguing with someone who's already made up her mind. You can think whatever you like, but the only thing I care about, that I have *ever* cared about, is doing what is best for all. Next to that, everything else is meaningless, including you. I spared your life once because I am a civil man, but you've made it abundantly clear that your mind is set. I know now that you will not stop, and I have no more time for civilities."

He sighed bitterly, lifting his arm so his free hand was balanced in the air directly above her head. "Farewell, Miss Novalli."

His hand came down like an ax, and the magic binding Marci went with it. Each glowing line ripped through her like a metal wire, shredding the fragile magic of her naked soul. She was dimly aware of Amelia yelling and a flash of fire, but what she yelled and whom she burned were lost in the all-consuming horror of being torn apart. Even the pain from her burns couldn't break through the knowledge that she was dissolving, collapsing into a pile of little shreds that were themselves unraveling. But then, just when the consciousness that was Marci Novalli was beginning to disintegrate, a blast of the coldest wind she'd ever felt rose up from the ground. It cut through the swirling magic like a knife, snatching what was left of Marci out of Myron's glowing lines and into the dark.

• • •

After the recent turns in her life, Marci was getting pretty used to finding herself suddenly in the void.

Like so many times before, she was floating in the dark. Only this wasn't the quiet, still blackness she'd seen after her death, or even the churning dark of the Sea of Magic. This void was blowing, the freeing wind sweeping and tossing her like a leaf through an infinitely deep abyss. The uncontrollable movement terrified Marci more than anything else that happened since her death, so much that she began to worry that maybe she hadn't been snatched away after all. Maybe Myron really *had* gotten her, and this was what happened to souls who were torn apart. But just as she began to panic that this endless tumbling was her final destination, an icy wind blindsided her from below, stopping her cold.

"Don't be afraid," it whispered in Ghost's voice. "I've got you."

Thank goodness, Marci said, closing her eyes in relief. *I thought I was gone there for a*—She stopped, confused. *Why am I a disembodied voice?*

"Because I ate you," her spirit said, uncharacteristically sheepish.

You ate *me?* she cried, or thought she cried. It was hard to tell volume when your words were more impressions than sounds. *So that means I'm inside you?*

"Yes," Ghost said. "But not for the first time. This is where I brought you the time I saved you from Gregory."

Marci remembered. He'd snatched her out of the way of Gregory's fireball by yanking her into a black-and-white world. Her voice had been weird then, too, and again when he'd brought her into what he'd called "his world" of the dead during their attack on Reclamation Land. But weird as both of those times had been, they were definitely not like this.

Why did it change? The other times you brought me in, everything just went black and white. This is nothing but black. Way too much black.

"That's actually *your* change," the wind explained. "When you were alive, I brought you, body and soul, into my magic. That's why you could still see the physical world, because we were both inside my magic looking out. Now—"

No body, Marci finished for him, looking down at the empty darkness where her chest should have been. *Right.*

"I'm sorry."

You've got nothing to be sorry for. Myron had me dead to rights back there. You're the only reason I'm not gone *gone right now, so I'm not going to complain about a bit more dark.* She wiggled what would have been her hands. *At least my arms don't burn anymore. That's a bonus.*

"That was stupid," he said angrily. "I was protecting you."

But we were losing.

"Better that than losing you."

Marci shook what should have been her head. There was no point in explaining the stakes again. He already knew. As always, though, the one who seemed most afraid of her death was death himself. She'd always thought that was sweet. Now, though, looking around, Marci realized that his desperation to keep her with him might run deeper than she'd originally realized.

Not much here, is there?

The wind tilted, and she got the impression he was shrugging. "There's a reason I'm named 'Empty.'"

She looked down at the howling void. *I can see why you didn't want me to leave you alone. But what about the forgotten dead? Aren't they here, too?*

"They are," he said. "But I try not to bother them unless I absolutely must. It's my job to bring them peace, and they can be hard to find if they're not clamoring for my attention." The wind blew in a wide circle. "This place is so large, even the dead can't fill it."

Marci looked up in surprise, eyes going wide. *Wait,* she said. *I'm not just inside your magic this time, am I?* She looked around at the looming dark. *This is your vessel. The hollow our fear of being forgotten dug into the floor of the Sea of Magic that filled and became* you.

"If you say so," he said bitterly. "I've never had a name for this place. It's just where I woke up when the cries of the forgotten reached me, before I met you."

She nodded slowly, staring into the howling emptiness with new appreciation. The other times he'd pulled her in, there'd been too much in the way to see. Now, though, with no physical reality to obscure her view, Marci began to grasp for the first time just how *big* her spirit actually was.

Spirits were large by definition, but she'd always thought about them as being on the same scale as Algonquin: huge, but still understandable. The Great Lakes were enormous, but you could still look down on them from an airplane and think "that's a lake."

Ghost was different. She'd known he had the potential to be bigger than Algonquin ever since Amelia had explained the concept of Mortal Spirits, but it wasn't until this moment that Marci understood just how *much* bigger. If Algonquin's vessel was big enough to hold the Great Lakes, Ghost's would have encompassed the entire United States of America.

The cavernous space was so enormous, so vast, there was no possible way to see all of it at once. The only reason Marci knew it even *had* an end was because she could feel the edges through Ghost's magic. The longer she thought about that, the more she understood why Amelia, Raven, and even Algonquin sometimes called Mortal Spirits "gods." There was simply no other word for something so large.

Well, she said at last. *At least I don't feel so bad now about never being able to fill you up.* Now that she knew the truth, Marci was surprised her magic had made a difference at all. Even Amelia's fire wouldn't be a drop in a bucket this big.

"It's because I was close to the edge already when you found me," he said dismissively. "A little goes a long way when you're talking about hitting a hard line."

Just don't ask me to fill the rest, she said, awed. *I don't know if there's enough magic in the world to fill a space like this. It's incredible.*

"I'm glad you like it," he said quietly. "I don't."

Why not?

The wind grew colder. "It's too big. Big and cold and…"

Lonely?

"The dead are always alone," he said. "Alone in their deaths, and then alone here. The only company they have is when I rescue them from their collapsing graves, and then they are terrified of my face." The wind holding her began to quiver. "Everyone is terrified of me. Of this place. Everyone, except you."

Never me, Marci promised. *I'll never be afraid of you, Ghost.*

"I know," he said as his wind squeezed her tighter. "Why do you think I try so hard to save you? I know your work is important, but you're all I have. If I hadn't been so fast, Myron would have ripped you apart."

But he didn't, she said firmly. *Thanks to you. But you of anyone should know how hard I am to kill. The two of us together? Unstoppable.*

"Not that unstoppable. Myron and his rat stomped us."

Stomped us down, she said. *Not out. But while the DFZ might have more magic than you right now, and Myron's clearly got the casting edge on me, they don't have what we have. They don't have this.* She ran a mental hand over the bond that connected them. *That's our strength, and it's how we're going to beat them.*

The wind sighed. "I know I chose you for your determination, but I think you've finally pushed too far. Myron did enormous damage to you. I barely caught your soul before he shredded it, and the only reason your magic is still together is because I'm keeping it that way by holding you in the one place I have total control. If you go out into the chaos of the Sea of Magic again, even with my winds to protect you, you'll be extremely vulnerable. A ghost."

Then we'll match, Marci said. *I'm not giving up on this. You know what could happen if Myron blasts his way into the Heart of the World, assuming he hasn't done so already.* She wasn't sure how long she'd spent flipping through the dark, but Myron's maze had to be nearly complete. *I know it's dangerous, but we have to do this, Ghost. If we don't become a Merlin together, you're toast and I'm dead. For real, this time. Even if I could go back to my death, you wouldn't be there to pull me out when it finally collapsed, would you?*

"No," he said gravely. "Without Mortal Spirits, no one would come to save you."

Exactly, she said. *That's why we can't stop. This is more than just our lives. I don't even know enough to describe the full breadth of what's at stake here, but we've already run the 'personal safety or Merlin' scenario, and we both know what I chose.*

"We do," he said, his voice resigned. "All right, what are we doing?"

Trying another angle, Marci said, peering out toward where she could feel the edges of his dark. *I need you to take me to the DFZ's vessel.*

The wind went still.

I know you can do it, she said before he could argue. *The two of you were born right on top of each other. Right in Algonquin's shadow. I'm betting that means you know where her vessel is. I want you to take me there.*

"I do know where she is," the Empty Wind admitted. "And you're right, she is close, but…"

But?

"She's not like me," he said at last. "Not like I am now, anyway. You remember how I was in the beginning? How lost and angry and eager to control you?"

How could I forget? Marci said, rolling her eyes, or where her eyes should have been. *You tried to make me your pet human. But you had good reason for feeling that way. You'd just woken up with no help and your domain screaming at you to fix things. Of course you were angry and confused.*

"So is she," Ghost said. "Only she's much bigger and has far more reason to be enraged. She is not a kind city, Marci."

I know that, she said. *But she's my city. I didn't run to the DFZ just to get away from Bixby. I'd always wanted to live there, because it was the place where anything was possible. That's the dream of the DFZ. It's the city where anyone can start over, and anything can happen. Myron can't put a chain on that. No matter how mad she gets, if she's still the DFZ I know, I'm betting I can talk to her.*

"I'm sure you can," he said. "I just don't know if she'll listen."

That's a chance we'll have to take.

The Empty Wind heaved a long sigh, and then he started moving, whisking her through the dark at what must have been ludicrous speed. "I just hope you know what you're doing."

I don't, she confessed. *I can't. We're in brand-new territory here. There is no knowing. We'll just have to give it a shot.*

That was a terrifying truth, but in a way, Marci was used to it. From the moment she'd bound Ghost, everything had been new and strange and unknown. She'd been making things up as she went for months now, but that was the price of being at the cutting edge. She just hoped being on this one didn't cut her to bits. But there was no turning back now. Ghost was already slowing down, his wind buffeting her gently as they reached the edge of the dark.

Like everything else in this place, the Empty Wind ended at a cliff. It rose from his depths like a wall. Unlike the hole at the top of Marci's death, though, there was no upside-down pool of liquid dark or barrier of any kind. It was just a stone lip, the place where the floor of the Sea of Magic fell off into the chasm that was humanity's fear of being forgotten, and over it, pouring down into the abyss below like a thousand-mile-high waterfall, was the swirling magic.

Wow, Marci said, staring in awe as her spirit lifted her over the silent spectacle of a black sea pouring into an even blacker chasm. *Is that the magic filling you up?*

"Trying to," he whispered as he pulled her into the space above his vessel at a much slower speed. "It's been flowing like that for a long time, but I am a very big hole to fill."

So I see, she said, tearing her eyes off the waterfall of magic to look at what was up top instead. Or try to. They were definitely flying over the floor of the Sea of Magic, but there wasn't actually much to see here. The chaotic swirls and nauseating waves that had made her eyes cross earlier were now so small she could barely see them. She was trying to figure out if this was because the magic had changed, or if she had, when Ghost explained.

"The magic is thin here," he said, sweeping them low over the stony floor. "The Sea of Magic is still filling. That leads to uneven spots, especially in places where many Mortal Spirit chasms need to be filled. The magic pours into us faster than it can be replaced, creating localized shallows."

Is that why we're going so slow?

"No," he said, setting them down on the sea floor. "We're slow because we're here."

Marci jumped. Now that she was down, she could feel the stone beneath her feet, which meant she *had* feet again. A quick inventory revealed she had hands, too, along with the rest of her body. She still couldn't see anything in the dark, but it was an enormous relief just to feel her physical parts, or at least the illusion of them. She was turning to ask Ghost if this was due to their leaving his domain or if he'd done something to put her back together, but the question died before it could form in her mind when she looked down and saw where they'd landed.

They were on the edge of another chasm with magic pouring over the edge just like Ghost's, except this one wasn't empty or dark.

It was vast and shining, a Grand Canyon of glittering light below them that stretched down and out as far as she could see.

What am I looking at? she whispered, kneeling at the edge of the sea floor.

"What you asked me to show you," the wind whispered nervously in her ear. "The city."

Marci's eyes went wide. It was so bright after the emptiness of Ghost's void, she hadn't realized until he named it that all that glittering shine below them was a *city*. An impossibly huge, double-layered city that stretched out in all directions.

With the exception of the sea floor they were standing on, every angle inside the canyon below them was filled. It was like staring into a mirror box. Look to the side, and it was all superscrapers rising to infinity. Look down, and there were infinite warrens of stairs, underpasses, and sewer pipes descending to the vanishing point in a neon-lit tangle. And if she looked straight ahead, it was just city. Miles and miles and *miles* of buildings and overpasses and advertisements and cars racing from elevated Skyways down to the grid streets below. But for all its impossibilities, every view was familiar, because this wasn't just any city. It was *her* city, the one she'd come to think of as home, despite only living there for a few weeks.

It's the DFZ.

"It's the ideal of the DFZ," Ghost said.

It would have to be. In addition to existing in a crack in the floor of the Sea of Magic rather than the shore of Lake St. Clair, the city in front of them was orders of magnitude larger than the actual DFZ. It was also architecturally impossible, not that that mattered here. The laws of physics only applied to the physical world. This was the realm of spirits, of magic and ideas, and *this* was humanity's dream of the new Detroit: an endless metropolis where anything could and did happen. She was staring into the vessel of the Mortal Spirit of the DFZ. Not the rat it chose to represent itself. That was no more her than Ghost's cat. This was the real DFZ, the heart of the human dream of the city itself, and now that she was here, Marci knew what she had to do.

I'm going in.

"I can't go with you," the Empty Wind warned. "That's her domain, the place where all magic is hers. I can't—"

I know, Marci said, smiling him. *Don't worry. This was the plan, remember? I'll be fine, I'm just going to talk. Wait here. I'll be back before you know it.*

It was clear from his shaking that Ghost was *not* fine with this, but he didn't fight her again. He just swirled tighter around her, his icy hand gripping the bond of magic that flowed between them with all his strength.

"I'll pull you out if things get bad."

If things went bad, there wouldn't be much left to pull out. She was walking into the lion's den. She was just a soul, the leftover magic of a human life. Once she dropped into the DFZ's domain, she'd be at the city's mercy just like all the other magic in there. But she knew her spirit well enough to know Ghost wasn't holding on for her. He needed their connection, so she let him cling, giving the magical link between them a final reassuring squeeze before stepping off the edge.

The change was instantaneous.

The moment her foot left the ground, everything—the dark, the swirling magic, her Empty Wind—vanished in a flash, instantly replaced by bright sun cut up into thousands of reflections from the superscrapers overhead. She wasn't falling, wasn't floating, wasn't anything strange at all. She'd simply stepped from being a soul on the edge of a magical crevice to being a normal person again, standing in the middle of a crowded square somewhere uptown on the Skyways under the blinding midday sun.

Ghost?

The word was soft in her head, which suddenly felt very small. Small and empty. Their connection was still there in her hands, but her spirit's voice was gone from her mind and her ears. Just as she'd been in her death, Marci was alone in her head again, but not anywhere else.

Just like in the real DFZ, there were people everywhere. They crowded in around her, tourists and office workers, street cart vendors and kids cutting school. Normal people, the sort she'd seen every day, laughing and talking and going about their lives. That was what made the crowd so odd, because these people didn't have lives. They were shadows, aspects of the spirit that ruled this place. The spirit who had to know she was here.

Sucking the city air deep into her lungs—which were also whole and normal again, just as they'd been in her death—Marci turned in a circle, scanning the crowd for a sign. Something that would out this for what it was: an illusion, an ideal, a home for a spirit.

But the more she looked, the more real the city felt. Down here on the ground, she couldn't even see the weird infinite skyline anymore. The people looked and sounded like any other crowd on a sunny afternoon on the Skyways, and the smells coming from the street carts were delicious and nostalgic, exactly as she remembered. If she didn't know better, she could almost have believed she was really—

"Home."

Marci jumped a foot in the air. The voice sounded like it was right behind her. When she whirled around, though, Marci saw she was actually across the street, looking at her through the unknowing crowd.

When she'd first seen it crouched behind Myron in the dark, the spirit of the DFZ had looked like a giant, evil sewer rat. When he'd sicced it on Ghost, it had just looked like a monster. Now, though, the thing staring at her looked almost human. A very sickly and tragic human with a hunched back and a black cloak made from trash bags. Its bowed head was covered in a deep cowl from which huge eyes shone out like street lights in a dark alley. For all this, though, the thing staring at Marci still looked far more human than the monster that Myron had ordered to attack, and that gave Marci hope.

Hello, she said, hiding her wince at still being a disembodied voice behind what she hoped was a friendly smile. *I don't believe we've been properly introduced. I'm Marci—*

"I know who you are," the spirit murmured, her voice soft this time, like the white noise of a crowd. "I saw it all when you jumped in. You're a mage of the DFZ. One of my own." She smiled then, her orange eyes gleaming. "Welcome home."

Thank you, Marci said nervously. *But I'm afraid there's been a mistake. It's true I lived in the DFZ, but I'm not yours. I belong to the Empty Wind.*

"Not anymore," the DFZ said. "You came to me. You live here." She pointed at the street under their feet. "That makes you mine. Someone *must* come home. A city can't be empty."

But you're not empty. All these people, the buildings—

"They're not mine," the spirit snarled. "*He* put them here."

The raw disgust and hatred in her voice went through Marci like shrapnel. Given that Ghost read her mind all the time, she really shouldn't have been surprised, but it was impossible not to flinch at the sudden rush of bitter, toxic anger flooding through her thoughts. The only good part was that at least she didn't have to wonder whom the spirit was talking about. The moment she spoke, Myron's face appeared on every floating billboard and projected sign in the city, leering down at them like a hateful god.

"He chained me," the DFZ snarled up at the pictures. "They did it together. The lake has always been my enemy, but I never thought a mage would turn. I am their city, their freedom." She reached into her trash bags, scraping her clawlike fingers over the silver ribbon wrapped around her throat. "How could he chain me!?"

What he did was monstrous, Marci agreed. *That's why I'm here. I can help you.*

"I know," the spirit said, darting through the crowd like a rat until she was standing right in front of her. "That's why I let you in. You're not a coward like he is." She smiled at Marci. "You walked with death, but you were not afraid. Now you can walk with me." Her smile grew sinister. "I'm going to make you mine."

No, Marci said firmly. *I'm flattered, but I already have a spirit.*

"But I'm better," the DFZ argued. "I'm the best city in the world! Everyone wants me, including you. You lived here. That makes you mine, and if you're mine, you can break this." She pointed at the silver noose around her neck. "This is good business for both of us.

238

Free me, and I'll give you what he wants. We'll tear down the door he's obsessed with and make you Merlin instead. Then *we* will have power, and he will have *nothing*."

Again, the spirit's anger sliced through Marci like a rusty knife, but far more worrisome than the feeling itself was what it signified. She'd been with Ghost long enough to know what that sort of raw emotion meant. The spirit of the DFZ might be full to bursting, but she was still just as new and lost as Ghost had been when she'd found him. Unlike the Empty Wind, though, the DFZ had had no one to help her work through it, not even cats. She'd been born to Myron and his chains. No wonder she was so unstable. What she needed was a real Merlin, someone who could be her partner through all of this. But while Marci couldn't be that for her, it didn't mean she couldn't help.

I don't have to be yours to give you freedom, she said, looking the spirit in her glowing orange eyes. *I'm sure he didn't tell you this, but Myron had no right to chain you in the first place. Mortal Spirits are supposed to choose the human who suits them best, not the other way around, and it doesn't happen through chains. I don't know what he did to bind you so thoroughly, but if you'll let me get close, I might be able to break it, and then you'll be free to do whatever you want. You can go home, go back to your city and find a mage who won't abuse you, and you don't have to break anything.*

That was more hope than fact. Marci had no idea if she could actually crack whatever insanity Myron had pulled off to subjugate a spirit this enormous. But as he'd put it himself: anything man built, man, or woman in this case, could break. She just had to convince the DFZ to let her get close enough to try. But it looked as though Marci's play was working even better than she'd intended. She'd barely made the offer before the DFZ lurched forward and grabbed her hands.

"Yes!" the spirit cried, her voice as roaring and chaotic as a rioting crowd. "Do it! Free me, and I will make them both pay for what they've done."

The hatred in her voice at the end was a new and terrible thing. It wasn't as sharp as the anger, but it was bigger and stronger. It rose through the city like a haze, dimming the lights and turning the crowd that was still walking around them into a mob. The sudden roar of their angry voices was so terrifying that even Marci—who'd died herself as a direct result of the Lady of the Lake's actions, and who'd suggested this idea in the first place—hesitated.

"What are you waiting for?" the DFZ demanded, clutching her silver noose with both hands. "Free me!"

I will, Marci promised, though she made no move to get closer. It wasn't that she begrudged the spirit her anger. So far as she could tell, the poor thing had been bred in blood and chained the moment she woke up. Algonquin and Myron both had treated her like a tool, a crowbar to pry apart the Merlin Gate for the sole purpose of eliminating the DFZ and every other Mortal Spirit like her. She deserved to be angry. Marci was, too, but unlike the city, she hadn't been born today. She knew that lashing out in fury, no matter how righteous, always came with consequences.

I'm not forgiving Myron or Algonquin anything, she said cautiously. *You have every right to want their heads on a platter for what they did, but you're a very large spirit. If you rage, you could destroy a lot more than just your enemies.*

"So what?" she cried. "I am the DFZ! Whatever I destroy, I can rebuild. Everything can always be rebuilt."

Not people, Marci said. *Places and things can be restored, spirits can be reborn, but mortals just die. Look at me.* She placed her hands against her chest. *I'm dead. The fact that I am here talking to you right now is entirely due to a miracle named the Empty Wind. If I ever get back to the land of the living, it will be because I've had miracles on top of miracles, but not everyone gets so lucky. The rest of your city, your people, they don't have what I have. If you lash out at Algonquin, it will be well deserved, but there's nothing in it for you if you destroy your own domain in the process.*

"If you won't help me, you are useless," the spirit snarled, getting closer. "I don't have to let you be here, you know. You're already dead. I can finish the job."

I'm well aware, Marci said angrily. *You think I don't know what I risked by coming here? My spirit is worried out of his mind. But I did it because I can't let Myron and Algonquin win. That makes us allies, and I never said I wouldn't help you. I'm just trying to make sure you understand what's at stake. Algonquin already flooded Detroit once.*

"You think I don't know?" the DFZ cried. "I was the one who was drowning! But things are different now. You talk like I'm walking into a trap by attacking, but Algonquin's the one who should be afraid. Of the two of us, I am the larger spirit, which means I'm not her city. She's *my* lake, and the only thing keeping me from putting her in her place for good is this." The DFZ yanked the silver rope taut against her neck. "We both want the same thing. Free me from this binding, and I will strike Algonquin down so hard, she will never rise again."

That was a very tempting offer. There was no question that unleashing a young, angry, and uncontrolled Mortal Spirit into the world was a very bad idea. At the same time, though, the DFZ was exactly the type of spirit Marci had been fighting for this entire time. She was a Mortal Spirit, human magic. Her rage wasn't just the madness of a caged animal. It was humanity's anger at Algonquin, the spirit who'd drowned them by the millions and taken their city for herself.

Unlike the humans who'd created her, though, the DFZ was big enough to push back. If Marci freed her, not only would she keep Myron out of the Merlin Gate, she might get Algonquin out of the DFZ as well. Permanently. Surely that was worth taking a risk.

Wasn't it?

She bit her lip, trying desperately to think through everything logically, but it was impossible. Everything was too powerful, too volatile to be certain. In the end, it came down to the spirit in front of her. The spirit of the city whom she'd come to think of as hers, who'd been unfairly abused, bullied, and imprisoned. The spirit who, if Marci didn't do something, would be used to kill all others, including Ghost. There was also the selfish but still terrifying fact that, if Marci didn't get the DFZ's help, she was likely never getting out of this city again.

Next to all that, a spirit's righteous anger was a risk Marci decided she was willing to take. If the DFZ really was bigger than

Algonquin, freeing her could prove to be the first real blow human-ity had ever struck back against the lake. Even if it backfired, the fallout couldn't be worse than leaving her to Myron and letting his fear hand Algonquin her victory. That was logic enough for her, so Marci reached out, touching the spirit for the first time as her fingers closed around the silver noose at her neck.

When Marci touched the metal, several things became imme-diately apparent, starting with just how big a hornet's nest she'd shoved her hand into.

Whatever magic had gone into making the bindings that held the DFZ, it was way more than just Myron's. The silver labyrinth the metal ribbon had been bent into was definitely his work, but the rest of it—the thousands of layers of overlapping spellwork that covered both sides of the thin-hammered metal, the incredibly sophisticated logic controlling the flow of the DFZ's magic power—contained multiple magical signatures. It was incredibly sophisti-cated, the work of hundreds of hands, including what felt like a spirit's touch, and not Algonquin's. Which spirit, she had no idea, but one thing was certain: this was not Myron's spell, and that was where Marci found her way in.

Proud as she was of her spellbreaking, the binding on the DFZ was far too complicated for her to crack on her own. The good part of that, though, was that Myron was in the same boat. He'd bril-liantly manipulated the spellworked silver ribbon into the labyrinth that bound the city, but no amount of aftermarket tweaking could change the fact that this binding wasn't the spell's original purpose. Myron's commands were all layered on, not baked in, which meant that if Marci could locate the bits he'd changed, she could switch them back and revoke his control.

With that in mind, Marci got to work, hunching over the DFZ as she started meticulously picking her way through Myron's maze. It was tedious, delicate work, but not nearly as bad as it could have been. Though she hated the man with all her heart, Marci couldn't deny that Myron's spellwork was elegant. Even though he'd done some obvious jury-rigging to force the spellwork into a new function, the modifications he'd made were still masterpieces of elegance and simplicity. It was painful to pry such perfection apart, but anger kept her going, and soon enough, Marci found herself at the crux that held it all together.

The silver ribbon wasn't just looped around the spirit's neck. Once the trash bags came off, Marci saw the binding covered the DFZ's entire body like mummy wraps, only they didn't wrap around her in circles. Instead, the ribbon had been folded into a prison that was half origami box, half Gordian knot, which the spirit had grown into like a gourd growing into a mold.

As brilliant as that structure was, though, it had a clear weak point. A single piece of metal—not a ribbon, but a bar that ran like a horse's bit across the base of the spirit's throat. Even here, where nothing was physical, it looked old and battered, but one set of markings was new. Myron's name, scratched deep into the metal's scarred surface. The place where everything came together.

The moment she touched the letters, the entire spell unfolded like a flower. For a dizzying moment, she was touching the spirit directly, reaching right into her living magic until Marci could actually see Myron through the DFZ's eyes. Or at least the orange eyes of the rodent version of her that was still cowering beside him.

Time inside the spirit vessels must have been different just as it had been inside her death. Marci felt like she'd been in here for hours, but when she spotted through the spirit's eyes, he was still drawing his maze on the Merlin Gate's wooden door. He must have felt Marci's hand on his spellwork, though, because the moment she saw him, he stopped, yanking his hands off the almost-finished spellwork.

"No," he said, turning on his spirit with a horrified look. "It can't be. You *can't* be doing this!"

Marci grinned, placing her hands on either side of the spellwork that surrounded his name. *Wanna bet?*

She didn't realize he could hear her voice in his mind same as his spirit's until she felt his panic flooding down the thread that connected him to the DFZ. By that point, though, Marci was in too deep to care. She squeezed with everything she had, crushing the spellwork he'd modified to hold the spirit captive. It was a brute-force solution to an incredibly elegant puzzle, and it never would have worked save for one factor: the DFZ was on her side.

The city was pushing along with Marci, biting and clawing and fighting with all her might against the binding Marci was ripping apart. Alone, neither was enough. Together, though, their combined force was more than any spellwork could hold, and Myron's was no exception. Seconds after they began, the silver binding snapped like thread, and the DFZ poured out with a scream, leaving Marci alone in a city that suddenly was no longer there.

With nothing left to hold her up, she plummeted through the dark, but not Ghost's dark this time. She'd been kicked out of a different spirit, which meant she was now falling through the swirling dark chaos of the Sea of Magic itself. Falling *alone*, with no protection and nothing to grab on to.

The moment she realized what was happening, Marci began to panic. Without the Empty Wind to shield her, the raw magic that had burned her arms was now burning everything, eating through what little was left of her soul at a terrifying pace. She couldn't see anything but swirling, oily dark, couldn't even scream for help. Whenever she opened her mouth, burning magic rushed in. But then, just when Marci was sure she'd finally reached the end of her train of miracles, a wall of wind slammed into her, knocking her to the ground she'd only just realized was there.

"*Marci!*"

She'd never been so happy to hear a voice in her life. Ghost must have broken a record to get to her, because he seemed as frantic as she was when he snatched her up off the stone, pushing her magic back together as fast as he could.

"Are you okay? Do you hurt?"

She hurt everywhere, but she was too excited to care. "We did it!" she cried, laughing in delight at the sound of her voice speaking out loud again. "I broke the binding. I set her free!"

"I know," the Empty Wind said. "I felt her leave. She's on her way to the other side, and she's *mad.*" He shuddered. "I wouldn't want to be Algonquin right now."

The way he said that made Marci shudder, too. "Did I just kick something I shouldn't have?"

"Probably," he said. "But we ran out of good options a while ago. All we can do is work now with what we have. But I have to get you back to the Merlin Gate."

"Why?" she asked, suddenly terrified. "Did Myron break it? Is it ruined?"

It was impossible to tell with his empty face, but Marci would have sworn her spirit was smiling. "No, it opened."

He pointed down, and Marci turned to see that she hadn't been lost in the dark Sea of Magic after all. Or, at least, not as lost as she'd thought. They weren't off in some forgotten corner of the magical plane. They were right beside the pillar of the Merlin Gate, barely twenty feet away from where Myron had been working. The only reason she hadn't been able to see that before was because the swirling chaos had blocked her vision.

Now that she was back inside Ghost's calming winds, though, she could see everything again. Including Amelia, who was curled in a little ball on the ground, surrounded by a bubble of fire. A bubble that popped as soon as she spotted Marci.

"*Never do that again!*" the dragon cried, launching herself at them like a fiery arrow. She slammed into Marci like one, too, knocking her back down on the ground.

"Sorry," Marci grunted.

"Don't 'sorry' me!" Amelia snapped, her voice shriller than Marci had ever heard it. "Being alone here is the most terrifying thing I've ever been through, and I know terrifying! I was part of Bethesda's learning clutch, remember? You're just lucky I'm awesome enough to protect myself, but look what it did to my fire." She spread her wings, which were indeed burning much less brightly than they had been before. "It's not like I can get more of this stuff!"

"I'm sorry," Marci said again, pushing herself up. "I didn't plan for this to happen. If it makes you feel better, it was terrifying for me, too, but I think it worked."

"Oh, it worked, all right," Amelia said, scrambling onto Marci's shoulder. "Look."

She nodded at the Merlin Gate, and Marci's eyes went wide. Just as she'd seen through the DFZ, Myron's incomplete maze of a spell was still glowing on the wooden door. That didn't seem to matter, though, because just as the Empty Wind had said, the door was now standing open on its own, shedding its golden light into the dark like an invitation. Unlike every other time it had opened, though, there was no smug shikigami standing in the way. Just the open doorway and a clear shot into whatever lay beyond, and on his knees in front of it was Myron.

If it wasn't for his trademark suit, Marci wouldn't have recognized him. He'd come in like a conqueror, throwing spells around and treating the Sea of Magic as if it were just another UN war zone. Now, though, his hunched body was even more transparent than Marci's, and it was getting fainter by the second as he curled into a ball. A position Marci understood all too well, because she'd just been there herself.

"He's being eaten by the magic."

"Of course he is," Ghost said coldly. "Without his spirit to shield him, he's nothing here."

"He's nothing anywhere," Amelia said, turning up her nose. "Let him dissolve. He deserves it after the mess he made."

The Empty Wind nodded and started walking toward the open door, but Marci didn't follow. When he looked back to see why, she sighed. "We can't just leave him like this."

"Of course we can," Amelia said. "Just don't do anything. Easy-peasy."

"I agree with the dragon," her spirit said. "He deserves no compassion."

"I know," Marci said tiredly. "He's a terrible man who's done terrible things, but…" She trailed off with a long breath. "He's still human, and he's not *all* bad. He gave me several chances to retreat earlier, if you'll recall. And anyway, I can't let him just die in front of me."

They both looked at her like she was crazy, but Marci was already walking over to Myron, pushing right out to the edge of the wind in the trust that Ghost would follow. Which he did, albeit grudgingly.

"This is a mistake."

"This is a *tragedy*," Amelia said. "Think about what you're doing, Marci. Leaving someone to suffer the consequences of their actions isn't cruel. It's natural selection at work. You're only encouraging more bad behavior if you spare him."

"Probably," Marci admitted. "But I'd rather deal with that than knowing I walked off and left another mage to die. Besides, it's not like he can do anything. I mean, look at him."

The UN mage was little more than a shadow of himself. His body was even more transparent than Marci's, and he wasn't moving at all. He was just kneeling there on the ground, waiting for death to come. It was a truly pathetic sight, and angry as she was with Myron, Marci couldn't stand to see him end like this. If nothing else, she couldn't let him die before she gloated her victory over him, so she took one more step forward, forcing Ghost's protective winds to expand until they covered the older mage as well.

The moment the Empty Wind swept away the burning magic, Myron collapsed, clutching what was left of his transparent body with a sob. The heartbreaking sound cemented Marci's belief that she'd done the right thing, but Amelia rolled her eyes.

"Fantastic," she said, crossing her forelegs with a huff. "Now we have this to deal with on top of everything else." She shot Marci a dirty look. "Julius has been a terrible influence on you."

Marci didn't agree with the terrible part, but the rest was true. She certainly hadn't shown Bixby or his men mercy, but a lot had happened in her life since then, and Marci was no longer so quick to kill. Besides, while he definitely didn't deserve anything after what he'd done, letting *the* Sir Myron Rollins die when she could easily save him just felt like a waste. As she'd just seen from the

DFZ's binding spellwork, he was still a brilliant mage. The world needed those, even if they were jerks. Of course, now that she'd saved Sir Myron, Marci had to figure out what to do with him.

She was turning to ask Ghost if there was a way to just kick him back to his body in the physical world when Myron suddenly rolled over, collapsing on his back to stare up at Marci with a look of absolute incomprehension.

"You saved me."

"I did," she said, pausing expectantly for the flood of gratitude that usually followed such statements. But not this time.

"Why?" he demanded, sitting up in a rush. "Why would you do that?"

"I'm starting to wonder," Marci grumbled.

"You know, a little groveling wouldn't hurt," Amelia said, hopping off Marci's shoulder to land on Myron's head, which she immediately started pushing down toward his lap. "Bow, idiot. You owe her your life."

Myron waved the little dragon away furiously. An inconsequential gesture, since his transparent hand went right through her. "Why would I be grateful to Novalli? She just freed a Mortal Spirit!"

"That you raised and bound," Marci said angrily. "Seriously, what were you thinking?"

"What are *you* thinking?" he yelled back. "I had to bind her. Do you not have eyes? She's a monster!"

"My eyes work just fine," Marci said, rising to her feet. "But the only monster I see is you, Myron."

"That's because you don't understand," he said, scraping his hands desperately through his graying hair. "You've ruined everything. Without the binding, she'll run rampant!"

"Yeah, well, whose fault is that?" Amelia asked. "You guys were the ones who got her all riled up."

"I had everything under control."

"No, you didn't," Marci said, exasperated. "You tried to put a leash on something a billion times your size! Of *course* it went wrong."

"Only because of you," he snapped. "The collar was never meant to be permanent. I just needed to keep control long enough to become a Merlin. If you hadn't meddled, I'd be one right now, and this whole spirit problem would be *fixed*."

Ghost's wind grew terrifyingly cold. "You should have let him die," he growled.

"Not too late," Amelia said cheerfully.

Marci was secretly starting to agree. But as infuriating as Myron was, her decision was made.

"Done is done," she said, glaring down at him. "For better or worse, your life is saved. Go home, Myron. We don't need you here."

The haughty look fell off the mage's face, leaving him with an almost sheepish expression. "I don't know how," he admitted, looking down at his hands in his lap. "The spirit brought me here by her own path. I don't...I don't know how to get back to my body on my own."

Another time, Marci would have laughed herself sick at the irony of the world's greatest expert on deep magic getting lost in it. Right now, though, it was just one more annoyance.

"Then you'd better stop complaining," she snapped. "Because I'm out of time to waste on you." She turned on her heel, putting her back to him as she walked toward the open door. "Suck it up or get left behind, but I'm going to finish what I started."

Myron started to say something, but Marci wasn't listening anymore. All this talk about Julius and death and things being ruined forever had only reminded her of how much was at stake. She didn't care what it took or what she had to do—she *would* become a Merlin, she *would* fix this, and she *would* get home. She was going to make this right for everyone, and then, when it was over and she finally got back to Julius, she was never letting him go again.

With that certainty burning in her like dragon fire, Marci marched across the stone to the wide-open Merlin Gate, stepping over the threshold without hesitation out of the dark and into the streaming light.

• • •

At the same time, back in the DFZ, in the sealed-off cavern beneath the Financial District locals called the Pit, Algonquin clutched her water.

She didn't even need to look at Myron's still-unconscious body lying face down in the circle to know things weren't going well on the other side. Her magic was there, too. She'd felt it just like everyone else. Something had broken in the Sea of Magic, something huge. Myron, however, had not woken up. He was alive, his chest rising and falling beneath the Phoenix's head, but that didn't mean much. Whatever was going on, he clearly hadn't made the jump to Merlin. His spirit, though, was sweeping through the magic like a battering ram, which meant they were now in a worst-case scenario.

"Lady Algonquin!"

The human voice was more fearful than usual, so Algonquin forced her water into a passable semblance of a mortal face and turned to deal with the problem, which turned out to be one of her commanders. Which one, she couldn't say. All mortals looked the same to her, and they died so quickly there was no point in learning their names. Fortunately, she paid her troops enough not to care about such things, and the armored woman didn't even hesitate before she gave her report.

"Lady," she said, saluting. "The mages are reporting that Sir Myron is no longer in control of his binding. The circle itself is holding for now, but no one knows how long that will last. The mage commander is requesting your permission to move the binding circle away from the city center to avoid infrastructure damage and civilian casualties."

That was a sensible request. Mortals were easily replaced, but Skyways were expensive. Moving the silver circle made from the Phoenix's innards would make it infinitely more difficult for Myron to find his body again, but if he'd failed to become Merlin as it appeared, then he was as good as dead anyway. Algonquin was through with him in any case, but as she opened her mouth to give the order to fall back to the wastes beyond Reclamation Land, the ground began to shake.

Algonquin bolted, abandoning her watery body under the Pit entirely as she rushed back to check on her lakes, but her fish were calm. This was no earthquake. Whatever was shaking, it only seemed to be affecting the city. It was still going when she returned to the Pit, animating her water there once again in a terrified rush.

"Evacuate the Skyways."

Her commander's head snapped up. "Lady?"

"You heard me," she snarled, flowing over the ground to the unmanned circle that still contained Myron's sleeping body. "I want everyone out. Empty the city."

There was no backtalk this time. The commander didn't even salute. She just started running for the trucks, yelling into her comm that they were now in Evac One, and this was not a drill. Algonquin shut her out after that, focusing all her water on the magic she could now feel rising from the ground beneath her like a fist.

This will confuse your history, the Leviathan whispered, his deep, alien voice sliding through her water like oil. *They will call you merciful.*

"What do I care how the humans remember me?" Algonquin said, expanding her water to surround the silver circle. "I'm not doing this to save them. I'm evacuating the city because a city without people is nothing but a shell." And given the size of the magic bearing down on them, she was going to need every advantage she could find.

You can't win, you know, the Leviathan said, creeping closer through the dark. *I warned you at the beginning that this was a losing battle. The humans are too many, and their fears are too strong. They will destroy everything you love. Only I can stop them. Only I can save you.* His tentacles rose to wrap lovingly around her. *Rest, Algonquin. Let me fight for you.*

"Not yet," she growled, shoving him away as she called her water, raising Lake St. Clair to burst through the protective walls she'd built to stop the contamination and flood the Pit once more. "I'm not beaten yet."

You will be, he whispered, his tentacles brushing her once more before sliding away. *But I am patient. I will wait for you, and when the time is right, you'll be mine.*

"Good," she said, pulling more water in. "Because until that happens, you're still *mine*. Now keep your promise and help me hold this down."

The monster chuckled. *As you command, my Lady of the Lakes.*

His whispering voice was mocking, but Algonquin had nothing left to put him in his place. Everything she had, all the water she could safely pull without stranding her beloved fish, was focused on pushing down the magic that was rapidly building toward critical inside the unmanned circle.

"Not yet," she whispered, bearing down with all her strength. "You haven't won yet."

The trapped Mortal Spirit howled, an earsplitting cry of rage and vengeance that shattered every piece of glass on the armored convoy that was still peeling out of the Pit. Algonquin answered in kind with rage of her own, making the whole Pit tremble as she crushed it under a ten-foot wave of violent, rushing water.

And far, far away, farther than even spirits could comprehend, the Leviathan bided its time.

CHAPTER NINE

When he'd jumped down the bolthole in Bethesda's closet, Julius had fully expected to end up in a panic room. Powerful as his mother's paranoia was, though, even she couldn't control physical space. The cramped quarters that came from living inside a mountain peak simply didn't allow for a private bunker. As a result, Bethesda's emergency exit dumped Julius, Fredrick, and Chelsie into Bob's room one floor below.

Through the ceiling. Of a dragon-sized cave.

Naturally, Chelsie and Fredrick took the twenty-foot fall just fine, landing on their feet as dragons should. Julius's descent wasn't nearly so graceful. He didn't quite plummet like a rock, but it was close. Thankfully, there was plenty of junk around to break his fall.

He landed in a pile of old magazines, dusty Post-It notes, and at least a dozen boxes containing T-shirts for the New Mexico Carrier Pigeon Appreciation Society. He was struggling to get his feet under him when Chelsie grabbed his arm.

"We have to keep moving," she said, yanking him up. "I don't think they'll chase us, but that doesn't mean I want to be here if they do."

She finished with a sharp shove toward the door, but now that he was back was on them, Julius planted his feet stubbornly on the stone. "We need to talk."

"What is it with you and talking?" Chelsie snapped, turning to Fredrick. "Grab him and let's go."

Fredrick clenched his jaw and moved toward Julius, but not to grab him. Instead, he took up position at Julius's side, turning to face Chelsie with his arms crossed stubbornly over his chest.

"Seriously?" Chelsie said.

"Yes," Fredrick growled back, his not-quite-green eyes gleaming in the dark. "Julius is right. You have a lot to explain."

"We don't have time for this."

"Then we'll make time," Julius said. "Because this is important." He stared pleadingly at his sister. "What are you doing, Chelsie?"

"What I always do," she snapped. "Saving your tail feathers."

"Not that," he said angrily. "I meant what are you doing down *here?* Why aren't you upstairs right now talking to the Qilin?"

"Because that's a terrible idea."

"Why?" Julius demanded.

Chelsie's reply was a silent death glare before turning away. She was walking to the exit when Julius said, "I know what happened in China."

"I know," she said, yanking Bob's door open. "I've been stalking you, remember? How do you think I got there in time to save you?"

Julius hadn't actually thought about that. He was so used to her just appearing behind him, he hadn't realized what that meant. "So then you heard the Qilin say—"

"I heard enough," Chelsie growled, sticking her head into the hall. "It's clear. Let's go."

"We're not going anywhere until we settle this," Julius said stubbornly. "He still loves you, Chelsie."

She stepped back from the door with a long, bitter sigh. "You don't know anything."

"I know you were in love with the Qilin," he said. "I know he was your Chinese dragon, the one who painted the picture in your bedroom. I also know that he's doing all of this for *you.* Stopping Algonquin was never anything but an excuse, because even though he thinks you betrayed him, he couldn't bear to let you die. All he wants is for you to be safe, and I don't understand why you keep running away."

"You wouldn't," she muttered, glaring at him over her shoulder. "Drop it, Julius."

"*No*," he snarled, clenching his fists. "Can't you see? You're our way out of this mess! Whatever happened in the past, it's obvious you both still care for each other. That's why you've been doing this stupid dance. But if you'd stop running for five minutes and *talk* to each other, this whole invasion could be over."

He stopped there, waiting for an answer, but none came. The whole time he'd been talking, Chelsie had been pulling into herself, folding her arms over her chest and hunching her shoulders until they were up to her ears. Even her eyes were down, locked pointedly on the floor as she muttered, "I can't."

"Why not?" Julius demanded.

"I don't owe you an explanation."

"No," Fredrick said. "But you do owe me one."

Julius looked at the F in surprise. He wasn't sure what Fredrick was referring to, but Chelsie must have known, because her face went from angry to spooked. "Stay out of this, Fredrick," she warned, voice shaking. "This isn't your business."

"This is all of our business," Fredrick growled, taking another step forward. "*Mother.*"

The room went silent. Even Julius was stunned speechless, his brain racing as he looked back and forth between Fredrick—eldest of the six-hundred-year-old F-clutch who'd been kept in the mountain and treated like a dirty secret since birth, despite Bethesda's frenzy to boost her ranks—and Chelsie, who'd returned from China also six hundred years ago after running away from her lover with no explanation. Returned with *Bethesda,* who'd supposedly laid F-clutch within days of returning despite not being pregnant when she'd set sail *and* not flying a mating flight in China...

Julius slapped his hands over his mouth. That was it. *That* was the secret. "You're F-clutch's mom!"

The words exploded out of him, but no one was listening. While he'd been putting the pieces together, Fredrick and Chelsie seemed to have forgotten he existed.

"Who told you?" she said at last.

"No one," Fredrick said with a sneer. "We're not stupid. Bethesda might have frightened everyone else into not asking questions, but we were the ones who were told that our birth was the reason we'd been sealed and trapped in servitude. Naturally, we investigated, and once we started digging, the truth became obvious pretty quickly. The only thing we didn't know was which member of the Golden Emperor's court was our father."

"Why does that matter?" Julius asked, genuinely confused. "None of us knows who our dads are. I certainly don't know mine."

"It doesn't matter to you because you're Bethesda's actual son," Fredrick said bitterly. "She cared enough about your clutch not to want to share, but we were different. Despite claiming to be our mother, Bethesda never treated us like she did the rest of you. We were servants to her, not dragons. She didn't even bother trying to manipulate us."

"That's a good thing," Chelsie said.

"Is it?" Fredrick snapped, glaring at her. "Why do you think we searched so hard for our father? Given how you left China, we knew he wouldn't be happy, but however unwanted we might have been, no dragon would tolerate his children living as slaves in another's house. He would free us out of pride, if nothing else. For centuries, that was our hope. Even after the others gave up, I kept searching, but I never found him. Now, at last, I understand why. I was looking too low. When I saw the emperor's unveiled face, I *knew*."

Julius frowned. "How did you know?"

Instead of answering, Fredrick reached up to brush his fingers across his face. Dragon magic bit down as he moved, and when it faded, Fredrick's eyes were no longer Heartstriker green. They weren't even the wrong color green they'd been all morning. They were gold. The perfect, warm, buttery, metallic color of golden coins.

The moment she saw them, Chelsie recoiled. "How?"

"How do you think?" Fredrick said angrily. "We were Amelia's guinea pigs, remember? She was just trying to show up Svena by breaking Bethesda's green-eyed curse, but the moment she saw my eyes, she started laughing. I pleaded with her to tell me what the gold meant. I *begged*, but she refused. Brohomir wouldn't say anything, either. No one would." He lifted his fists, his body shaking with rage. "*Why didn't you tell us?*"

Chelsie shook her head. "I couldn't take that risk."

"What risk?" Fredrick cried. "He's an emperor! And he *loved* you! I always assumed you ran away because our father was dangerous, but the dragon I met with Julius today isn't like that at all. His mother is, but even she has to obey the Golden Emperor. Everyone does. He could have saved us! Why did you run from him?"

"Because he *was* dangerous!"

This whole time, Chelsie had been clinging to calm, but the more Fredrick, the more her *son* accused her, the more she cracked.

"Do you think I wanted this for you?" she yelled. "Stuck with me under Bethesda's boot? If there was any other way, I would have killed to get it, but there *wasn't*. I didn't keep this from you because I wanted to. I couldn't tell anyone the truth, because keeping you secret was the only way I could keep you safe."

"Safe from what?" Julius asked.

Chelsie shot him a lethal-caliber version of the *stay out of this* glare, but Julius refused to be put off. Everyone had stayed out of this problem for far too long. It was going to be painful, but if they were ever to have a shot at actually fixing this mess, he couldn't spare the wound.

"Fredrick's right," he said firmly. "The Qilin's not a vengeful dragon. If he'd known he had children, I'm certain he would have come for them, and for you. He might have been upset about being lied to, but he wouldn't have been violent."

"Xian is never violent," Chelsie said, her voice faltering when she spoke the emperor's name. "It wasn't him I worried about. It was his magic. I heard him tell you how Qilin's luck works, but do you know *why* he has that power?"

"He inherited it from his father," Julius said.

"Exactly," Chelsie said. "The Golden Emperor's magic is unique among dragons. When a seer dies, their power is reborn into whatever dragon of the appropriate sex happens to hatch first after their death. With the right timing, any dragon clan can have a seer, but Qilin's power is different. It was cultivated. Xian told me that his clan has always had a tradition of fortune magic, but the power wasn't reliable. To solve this problem, his ancestors bred their lines together, consolidating their clan's magic into one perfect dragon, the first Qilin."

Julius had his own thoughts about the "perfection" of the Qilin's magic, but Chelsie wasn't finished.

"That perfection wasn't natural," she went on. "Like an ornate garden, it had to be carefully maintained. To make sure all the magic transfers from one generation to another, each Qilin fathers only one child, and only after an elaborate ceremony with a mate specifically chosen for her ability to complete the magical endurance run that is carrying a Qilin egg to term. Even then, the empress doesn't actually lay the egg until the old Qilin dies to ensure that every bit of his fire is passed on." She sighed. "I'm sure you can see where this is going."

Julius nodded, glancing at Fredrick, who was the oldest of a clutch of twenty and, despite his golden eyes, most *definitely* not a Qilin. "You laid too many eggs."

"That's the least of what I did," Chelsie said angrily. "When I got pregnant, I broke the line. Even with the Golden Emperor's luck, it takes an insane amount of preparation to arrange the auspicious circumstances necessary to create a new Qilin. Each emperor only gets one shot at passing on his flame, and I took it."

"How can you say that?" Julius asked. "You're acting like this is all your fault, but it takes two dragons to make a clutch, and it's *his* line. I know you said you were young and stupid, but—"

"Not *that* young and stupid," Chelsie snapped. "I was your age when I went to China, but I knew where eggs came from. Dragonesses aren't even supposed to be fertile until they clear a hundred. Even then it takes a mating flight, which is why Xian and I stayed in our human forms at all times. It should have been *impossible* for me to get pregnant, but apparently I'm Bethesda's daughter in more ways than one, because it happened anyway."

"That still doesn't mean it's your fault," Julius said gently. "Making the impossible happen is what the Qilin does." And considering how happy he seemed to have been with Chelsie, his luck would have been running hot indeed. "Did he want children?"

It was hard to see in the dark, but Julius would have sworn his sister blushed.

"He told me once that he did," she said quietly. "We both knew it was impossible. Maintaining the Qilin's fire and passing it on to the next generation is the Golden Emperor's most sacred duty, and Xian has *always* done his duty. But knowing something can't happen doesn't stop you from wanting it."

Her lips curved in the hint of a smile. "I thought it was sweet. When I told him I wanted children too, though, he freaked out. He told me never to say that, to never give him hope. At the time, I thought it was a lot of trouble for nothing, but that was before I understood just how little control Xian had over his luck. If he wants something—even subconsciously, even if he *knows* it's a bad idea—the Qilin's magic works to make it happen. So when he said he wanted a family..."

"He got one," Julius finished with a sigh.

Chelsie nodded, lowering her head to stare shamefaced at the floor. "I should have realized it sooner. I should *never* have encouraged him, but I didn't understand. I thought so long as we were together, we could take on anything, but we couldn't. Because of our selfishness, the Qilin's line is broken forever. Even if Xian finds a perfect mate with perfect bloodlines and perfect control, there will *never* be another golden dragon."

"That's terrible for them, I'm sure," Fredrick growled. "But what does that have to do with us? The damage was already done. Why did we have to suffer for it?"

"Because the damage isn't over," Chelsie said, her head shooting up. "Don't you get it? The Qilin *does not control* his luck. That's how I got pregnant even though it should have been impossible. Because Xian secretly wanted a family, so his magic gave it to him. Now, what do you think that magic is going to do when the Qilin realizes that he's failed his most sacred duty?"

Julius bit his lip. "It's going to lash out."

"Exactly," Chelsie said. "The Qilin's luck exists to make him happy. That includes removing any causes of *unhappiness*. Xian was raised his whole life to believe he's the custodian of a priceless gift. When he realizes that's gone, it won't matter that killing you won't actually change a thing. So long as you and your siblings are the living incarnation of his failure, his luck will seek to remove you, and the only reason—the *only* reason—it hasn't done so already is because *he doesn't know*."

The whole time she was talking, Julius's stomach had been sinking lower and lower. "That's why you ran," he said softly. "Why he thinks you betrayed him. You lied."

"Of course I lied," Chelsie said. "The moment I discovered I was pregnant, I ran as hard as I could, but you can't get away from a luck dragon. Every escape I tried failed catastrophically. When they finally cornered me and dragged me back to the palace, I knew it was all over if the truth came out, so I did the only thing left that I could do: I lied my feathers off. I let him think the absolute worst of me, made sure he never wanted to see me again, and it worked. It *hurt*, but it worked. When he banished me, the only ones who knew the truth were Bethesda, Bob, and me. We've kept the secret ever since."

Julius sighed. All of that made sense, he supposed, except, "Why did you tell *Bethesda*?"

"Because I had no one else," Chelsie said with a helpless shrug. "Don't forget, this was six centuries ago. I wasn't Bethesda's Shade back then. I was just a young dragon with no connections thousands of miles from home. If the Empress Mother decided to kill me, there was nothing I could do to stop her. But as terrible as she was, Bethesda was still the head of a major clan. Even in China, that was power, and I was alone and pregnant with eggs I couldn't protect by myself."

"So you just gave us to her?" Fredrick snarled. "Sold us into slavery to Bethesda?"

"I kept you safe," Chelsie snapped.

"*Safe?*" he roared. "We've spent our entire lives locked in a mountain!"

"Exactly!" she yelled back. "I didn't sacrifice to save your lives so you could be reckless with them! Why do you think I locked you up?"

Fredrick froze, shocked into silence, and Chelsie clenched her fists. "I'm happy to let you hate Bethesda," she said, more calmly now. "She deserves it, but not for this. I was the one who asked her to seal you in the mountain. I didn't want to, but I felt I had no choice."

"Why?" Fredrick whispered.

Chelsie sighed. "Because Xian's not stupid. I'd done my best to make him hate me, but if you were out there in the world being normal Heartstrikers, it'd only be a matter of time before he looked at the dates and started to wonder. Once that happened, his luck would inevitably drag everything out into the open. I couldn't take that risk. I *had* to keep you secret, no matter the cost, but I swear on my fire, Fredrick, I did everything I could to make it easier on you. I served Bethesda like a dog to keep you all alive. Maybe not happy, maybe not free, but *alive.*"

Fredrick looked down with a curse. Julius couldn't say anything, though at least now he understood how Bethesda had gotten such complete control over Chelsie. She'd had her children by the throat. But that was over now. Chelsie and F-clutch were free, and he saw no reason to let any of this continue.

"Is there anything else?" he asked. "Any other secrets about China we should know?"

"Nope," Chelsie said, giving him a sour look. "Congratulations, Julius. You've finally ferreted out my entire sordid history."

"So what do we do about it?" he asked, ignoring her sarcasm. "How do we fix this?"

"We *don't*," she growled. "Weren't you listening? The only way to keep the Qilin from going nuclear on us is to make sure he never learns the truth."

"But that's ridiculous," Julius argued. "No one keeps a secret forever."

Chelsie set her jaw stubbornly. "I've kept this one for six centuries."

"By keeping your children locked in a mountain!" he cried. "But there's no putting this dragon back in the bag. The Qilin is *here*, and if we don't find a safe way to deal with this, being conquered is going to be the least of our problems."

"And whose fault is that?" she said, baring her teeth. "If you weren't constantly prying into other dragons' business, none of this would have happened!"

"If Julius hadn't pried, we'd still be slaves," Fredrick said coldly. "But he didn't bring the Qilin here. The Golden Emperor came to save *you* from Algonquin, so unless you want to lay the death of the Three Sisters at Julius's feet, you can't blame this situation on him. Quite the opposite. If not for Julius's efforts, all of us would have still been enslaved to Bethesda when the Qilin arrived, and you *know* she would have sold us out in a heartbeat. You'd have been delivered to Qilin on a silver platter the moment he landed, and how long would your secret have lasted then?" He placed his hand on Julius's shoulder. "It's because of your brother that you have a chance to keep this secret at all. You should be thanking him, as I do, not trying to pin blame."

Julius looked down, face burning. He hadn't expected Fredrick to say all that. But while Chelsie looked chastised, she didn't look defeated. "I don't think you appreciate just how bad this is about to get. When the Qilin finds out—"

"How will he?" Fredrick asked. "He's already seen me. I was there in his room with Julius for an entire conversation, and he never suspected a thing. Amelia showed me how to cast the illusion that makes my eyes look green before she died. All I have to do is put that back on, and no one will be the wiser."

"That won't work much longer," Chelsie warned. "It doesn't matter how much magic you paint over it, the more you draw the Qilin's interest, the better his luck works against you. If he suspects anything, whatever you're using to hide the truth from him is going to break at the worst time, and then everything will come out."

"So I'll find another way," Fredrick said angrily. "I can keep a secret, Chelsie. I've kept yours for years. Why are you treating me like I'm incompetent now?"

"I've never thought you were incompetent," Chelsie said quickly. "But even with the illusion, have you looked in a mirror? For the love of fire, Fredrick, you look just like him."

It was true. Julius hadn't realized it until she pointed it out, but Fredrick really did look just like the Qilin. He had the same thin mouth and sharp nose, the same straight eyebrows. Add in the golden eyes and he was the spitting image of his father. Even after he returned the illusion, popping the magic back into his eyes, Julius couldn't unsee it, and that worried him. *Everything* about this did.

Keeping secrets from the Qilin while he was on the other side of the world was one thing, but trying to do it when he was right on top of them felt like a losing game no matter how well they played. Even if Julius put his head down and surrendered Heartstriker tomorrow without a fight, they'd still be part of the Golden Empire. The whole point was to wrap Heartstriker in the Qilin's luck, and once that happened, it wouldn't matter if the Qilin went home to China or to the moon. Chelsie's secret was *bound* to come out, and the more Julius thought about that, the more this whole thing felt like a fool's errand.

"Maybe we should try something else."

"There is nothing else," Chelsie snapped. "How many ways do I have to explain this before you understand? The Qilin can't learn that he has children. *Ever.* And the only way that happens is if those of us who *do* know keep our mouths shut."

She looked pleadingly at Julius. "I've learned the hard way not to underestimate your ability to think outside the box, but there *is* no box this time. No matter how clever you get, there's no win-win solution to a binary problem. If the Qilin finds out we're the death of his line, we die. End of story."

"But what if it's not?" he said desperately. "You're *assuming* the Qilin will be terminally upset when he finds out his line is broken."

"I assume nothing," she growled. "It's *fact.* I know him."

"You *knew* him," Julius corrected gently. "But the last time the two of you talked was six hundred years ago. That's a *long* time, even for dragons. I, on the other hand, just spent half an hour listening to him talk about you. I'd never claim to know Xian as well as you do. I didn't even know that was his name until a few minutes ago. But none of that changes the fact that the dragon I met up there dragged his entire clan across the ocean against their will and his own better judgment to save *you*, the one he believes betrayed him the most. Any normal dragon would have broken out the popcorn and enjoyed Heartstriker's fall, but not him. He knows coming here makes him look like an idiot. He *feels* like an idiot, but he put you ahead of his pride because he loves you and he wants you to be safe, even if it's not with him. *Those* are the facts I've observed, and they're why I think you're selling him short in this. I have no doubt that he will be *very* upset when he learns the two of you accidentally destroyed his magical line, but you're forgetting that the primary goal of the Qilin's luck is to make him *happy*, and for Xian, happiness is you."

He finished with a hopeful smile, but Chelsie had already closed her eyes. "Stop it, Julius."

"Stop what?" he asked. "Trying to see his side?"

"Stop getting my hopes up," she said, her green eyes popping back open with a resentful glare. "Maybe you don't realize what you're doing, but I do. You're not 'seeing his side' or 'stating facts.' You're spinning the truth into wild shapes with your ridiculous optimism just like you *always* do. You've gotten away with it up till now because you had a seer in your corner, but Bob's not here anymore. This isn't some misunderstanding you can nice your way out of. This is my life. *His* life." She pointed at Fredrick. "I didn't do Bethesda's dirty work for six centuries to let you play dice with the children I gave everything to protect!"

"I'm not playing dice," Julius said, truly insulted. "And I'm not spinning the truth into anything. I really do think you've got this all wrong because you're making assumptions based on old information."

"Better than speculating wildly off a thirty-minute conversation!"

Julius's jaw clenched, and his sister looked away with a huff of smoke. "Look," she said, gently now. "I understand you want to fix the problem. You *always* try to fix things. Normally, I like that about you, but there's no fixing this. Xian's held on to me this long because he's a romantic, but there's nothing stopping him from finding another dragoness and being happy. He can let go of the past anytime he wants, but even if he lives in perfect happiness for the next ten thousand years, he can never fix what we broke. Nothing can. That's the cold, hard truth, and no amount of talking is going to change that."

"I'm not claiming it will," Julius said. "I'm just saying maybe that doesn't matter as much as you think. All your doom and gloom is based on the assumption that Qilin will be so upset when he learns the truth, his luck will wipe you all out before he realizes what he's done. But that claim doesn't match his actions. If the Qilin *really* valued his line and his duty above everything else, then he would have stayed safe in China and let Algonquin eat us, but he didn't. He came here, bending all of his luck and power and resources to the point of conquering our clan against the will of his own people, so he could protect you."

He held out his hands to Chelsie. "If actions speak louder than words, then his are screaming from the rooftops that *you* are what's really important to him. That's why I can't believe you when you say we can't fix this. Because if you're really as vital as his behavior shows you to be, then there's no way his luck—the same luck that got you pregnant despite *physical impossibility* because he wanted a family with you—would let you die."

Chelsie dropped her eyes. He could still feel her anger radiating through the room like a physical force, but something he'd said must have gotten through, because she didn't keep arguing. Fredrick, on the other hand, was watching Julius with intense excitement. "You have a plan, don't you?"

"I do," Julius said with a deep breath. "A simple one. We tell him the truth."

"I *knew* it," Chelsie snarled, head snapping back up to glare at him. "You can't leave well enough alone, can you?"

"No," he said firmly. "Because leaving this alone will only make it worse. The truth is going to come out one way or another, but if we tell him ourselves instead of letting him discover it on his own, we have a much better chance of controlling the impact."

Fredrick nodded. "We can break it to him gently. Soften the blow."

"I don't think this blow can be softened," Julius said sadly. "If Chelsie's right, and the Qilin's line is truly lost forever, that's a huge loss no matter how we spin it. But it's not *all* bad." He smiled at his sister. "You did say he always wanted children. Now he's got twenty. That gives him something to hold on to and protect."

"Or a list of targets," Chelsie grumbled.

Julius slumped. "Why are you always so negative?"

"Because someone has to be," she snapped. "Everything you're saying sounds good in theory, but if you tell him the truth, and you're wrong, then we're *dead*. Sorry if that makes me a killjoy, but the potentially horrible demise of everyone I love puts a bit of a damper on my enthusiasm for experimentation."

"It *is* a risk," Julius admitted. "But no more of one than trying to keep this secret. We're up against the wall either way, so why not go for the solution that would actually make things better? All we get in return for successfully keeping the secret is the chance to go through all of this again. But if we tell the Qilin the truth, and he gets past it, then everything changes. I think that's worth the risk."

"Easy for you to say. *You're* not risking anything." She jerked her head at Fredrick. "Ask him. It's his life you're gambling."

That was a fair point, but when Julius turned to look at his brother—*nephew*, he realized belatedly—Fredrick looked more resolute than ever. "I believe in Julius."

Chelsie gaped at him. "You told me last week you thought he was delusional!"

"I did," Fredrick said. "But that was last week. Since then, I've seen him do the impossible. He overthrew Bethesda. He set us free.

He set *you* free. He's changed our clan with nothing but his will and his words. If he says the Qilin's luck won't kill us, I believe him."

"You ready to bet your life on that?"

"Yes," Fredrick said without missing a beat. "Because according to you, my only other option is to stay a secret forever. I think I speak for my entire clutch when I say that I'd rather gamble on Julius than live out the rest of our lives as Bethesda's shame."

Chelsie gritted her teeth. Fredrick glared right back at her, daring her to argue again. When she didn't, Julius took his chance.

"We have to try, Chelsie," he said gently. "And not just because we can't keep this secret anymore. Even if it will hurt him, telling Xian the truth is the right thing to do." He smiled at Fredrick. "They're his children, too. He deserves to know them."

Fredrick smiled back at him, but Chelsie just turned away, reaching up to dig the heels of her palms into her eyes. "How do you always do this?" she muttered. "How do you *always* convince me to go along with things I *know* are suicidally stupid?"

"Because you're secretly an optimist," Julius said confidently. "Does this mean you're on board?"

She dropped her arms with a sigh. "What do I have to do?"

"Nothing much," Julius assured her. "Just talk to him."

"'Nothing much,' he says," Chelsie grumbled, giving him a sideways glare. "You know, for a dragon who claims not to be greedy, you sure do have a habit of asking for the moon."

Julius could only shrug at that, and she rolled her eyes. "Fine," she groaned. "Fine, fine, *fine.* You win. I'll talk to him. But not right now."

Julius—who'd already started walking to the door to go back upstairs—whirled around. "Why not?"

"Because this is a delicate operation, and he's already caused two quakes today," Chelsie said in a practical voice. "This is going to be hard enough without him being upset before we even start. Also, I'd like some rest. I haven't slept for more than four hours at a time since we overthrew Bethesda, and I'd rather not walk into a conversation with the dragon I've spent the last six hundred years avoiding when I'm too tired to string together a proper sentence."

Considering she had no problem stringing together arguments against them, that sounded like an excuse to Julius, but he didn't call her on it. He'd already pushed Chelsie a lot today. It'd do no good to push her over the edge just when he'd gotten her to agree with him. Unfortunately, they didn't exactly have the luxury of time. Between the Golden Empire's takeover of the mountain and everything that had come after, the twenty-four-hour reprieve he'd won was almost gone.

"Don't worry," Chelsie said before he could mention it. "I've been stalking you, remember? I know the schedule. I promise I'll talk to Xian well before tomorrow's surrender."

Julius breathed a sigh of relief. "Thanks."

She shrugged. "I don't want Heartstriker to be part of the Golden Empire any more than you do. Sordid history notwithstanding, I *like* Xian, and I wouldn't wish Bethesda on my worst enemy."

That sounded more like the sister he knew. "Thank you, Chelsie."

"Don't thank me," she said with a wince. "This whole thing is my fault. If I'd had an ounce of sense when I was your age, none of this would have happened."

She said that flippantly, but the moment it was out of her mouth, Julius felt Fredrick stiffen. "I'm glad it did," the F said quietly. "Or my siblings and I wouldn't have been born."

"At least some good came out of it," Chelsie said, walking toward the door. "I'm going downstairs to sleep. Call me if you hear anything from Bob, and keep an eye on—"

"Do you regret us?"

The question came out of nowhere, making Chelsie freeze. Julius didn't dare move, either. There didn't even seem to be a safe place to put his eyes as Fredrick stepped forward, his normally blank face so full of emotion, Julius hardly recognized him.

"You've always said what happened in China was a mistake," he said, voice shaking. "We knew Bethesda didn't want us, but I thought that you…"

He trailed off, the words crumbling, and Chelsie sighed. "You were always the sharpest one, Fredrick," she said as she turned back around. "So I won't insult you by lying. The day I found out I was pregnant was the worst day of my life. I thought I'd ruined everything: my future, Xian's future, a hundred thousand years of carefully cultivated magic. Everything. That's why I ran to Bethesda. I didn't just need a bigger dragon to hide behind. I needed a fix for what I'd broken, and horrible as she is, my mother's the greatest expert on dragon eggs alive. I thought if she could teach me how to change the eggs before I laid them, I could still salvage the situation. But new dragon fire catches hot and fast, and even with Bethesda's help, I was decades too young to control it. I couldn't even condense your fires into fewer eggs, much less the single male egg needed for a Qilin. I couldn't do *anything*."

"I see," Fredrick said, his eyes sinking to the floor. "So you didn't want us."

"That's not what I said," Chelsie said sternly. "I was in a panic trying to fix what I'd broken. When I realized I couldn't, I decided then and there to spend the rest of my life making sure you suffered as little as possible for my stupidity. I swore to keep you secret so the Qilin's curse could never touch you. I would have saved you from Bethesda, too, if I could, but it was already too late on that score. The moment she learned the truth, you became the rope she wrapped around my neck. There's no force in the world that could've stopped her from abusing that, but I did everything I could to lessen your suffering. I know the last six hundred years have been miserable, but I've kept every single one of you alive. I didn't get to choose how you began, but you're still my son, and I love you."

A strange expression came over her face as she said that, and Julius realized with a start that that was probably the first time Chelsie had ever spoken the truth out loud.

"My son," she whispered, reaching up to cup Fredrick's face. "My oldest, cleverest son. I hate the events that brought you into this world, but I've loved every single one of you from the moment you hatched, and I..."

Her voice cracked after that, but Fredrick didn't say a word. He just stepped forward, wrapping his arms around his mother. Chelsie held out for a few more seconds, and then, like a dam breaking, she threw her arms around him as well, her whole body shaking.

"I'm sorry," she sobbed. "I'm so sorry for what I did to you, Fredrick. All of you. Your suffering was all my fault, and I'm sorry. I'm so, so *sorry*."

"It wasn't your fault," Fredrick said, hugging her hard. "You were the one who protected us. When the rest of the clan treated us worse than the human servants, you cared for us and taught us and kept us together. Even before we suspected the truth, you were always our mother."

That last part set Chelsie sobbing all over again, and Julius decided it was time for him to go. This was a private family drama, but it wasn't his anymore, and he didn't want to intrude. But while that was a perfectly polite excuse, the truth was that he didn't want to deal with painful, irrational jealousy that came from seeing Fredrick hugging a mother who honestly and wholeheartedly loved him. He might not envy the F any other part of his life, but Julius would have traded mothers with him in a heartbeat.

He was still brooding over that as he stepped into the dark hallway outside Bob's room. But as he leaned against the wall to wait, his phone buzzed in his pocket. For an irrational moment, he hoped it was Bob. This was the sort of dramatic timing the seer lived for, and even if the source couldn't be trusted anymore, Julius would gladly welcome any hint at the future.

When he pulled the phone out of his pocket, though, the ID that popped up wasn't the Unknown Caller. It was the one that never failed to make his heart sink, and Julius couldn't even look at it now without feeling like the target of some special brand of universal irony as he raised the phone to his ear.

"Hello, Mother."

The greeting came out even sourer than usual. But while he was sure Bethesda noticed, she gave no sign that she cared. "Where have you been?"

"With the Qilin," he answered, which was true enough. "I met his mother first, but then—"

"Never mind that," she said impatiently. "Get to the main hangar as fast as you can. I'm already on my way down."

"Why?" he said, alarmed. "What's wrong?"

"Everything," she said with a mirthless laugh. "But at this particular moment, it's Ian. He's coming home."

"Now?" Julius said, checking the time. "But it's only six. The surrender's not until nine a.m. tomorrow. Didn't you send him the message to stall?"

"Oh, I sent it," she growled. "But it seems there's been a change in plans. Considering how badly the rest of the sky is falling, though, there's a chance this might actually work in our favor."

Julius didn't see how that was possible, but he knew better than to ask over the phone. His mother would tell him when she was ready, which would probably be as soon as Ian arrived with whatever undoubtedly bad news he was bearing. "I'll be right there."

"Hurry," she snapped. "Main hangar. Five minutes. *Don't* be late."

"I won't," he promised. "And Mother…"

"*What?*"

Julius sighed. "Nothing. I'm on my way."

She hung up before he could finish, leaving him standing alone in the empty hallway, talking to no one.

• • •

The main hangar was one of Heartstriker Mountain's many side buildings. Located just off the runway Bethesda had built to keep her remote desert citadel connected to the rest of the world, it was big enough to house both of the clan's private jets. But since Ian had taken the newer plane to Siberia, and Conrad had made off with the backup last night, the giant metal building was empty when Julius walked in except for Bethesda herself.

"Took you long enough," she snapped, tapping her alligator-skin stilettos in a nervous rapid fire against the cement. "Did you crawl down here?"

Considering he'd made it all the way from Bob's cave at the top of the mountain out to the hangar, a total journey of a mile and a half, in six minutes flat, Julius didn't dignify that with a response. "Where's Ian?"

Bethesda nodded through the open door at the brightly lit runway. "About to land."

The words weren't out of her mouth when Julius heard the low rumble of a jet coming in fast. That was all the warning they got before a plane broke through the low clouds like a rocket. It touched down a few moments later, skidding onto the runway faster than any vehicle should ever hit the ground. If it had been a traditional jet, that would have been the end, but Bethesda spared no expense with her private planes, and the custom AI pilot managed to save the landing by spinning the jet out into the soft dirt at the end of the runway. Proper dragon that he was, Ian had the rear door open before the almost-crashed plane finished moving, jumping the ten feet from the hatch to the ground as easily as a normal person would step off a curb.

"Do you mind?" Bethesda yelled over still-spinning engines. "That's my custom suborbital Gulfstream you just put in the dirt!"

Ian shot her a murderous look. Everything about him looked murderous, actually, which was even more alarming than the botched landing. If the normally collected and calculating Ian looked this upset, things were a whole new level of bad. Even Bethesda picked up on it, stepping back to give her seething son space as he stalked down the pavement toward the hangar, motioning for them to follow him inside. Nervously, Julius did, ducking under the rolling door along with his mother before Ian slammed it down.

Bethesda eyed the jangling metal warily. "I take it things didn't go well."

"They didn't go at all," Ian growled. "Svena sealed herself inside her mothers' ice fortress before I got there. I couldn't even find the door."

"So why did you come *back*?" Bethesda asked angrily. "Svena was always a long shot, but I thought I made it clear in my message that you being in Siberia was the only thing keeping the Golden Emperor from—"

"I am well aware of our situation," he snapped. "I didn't come back because I wanted to. I came back because I didn't have anywhere else to run."

Julius and his mother exchanged confused looks, and Ian rolled his eyes in disgust. "Does *no one* watch the news?" He had his phone out before they could answer, waving his hand over the screen to bring up a series of photos in the public AR, which he proceeded to shove in their faces. But though Julius's field of vision was now crammed with floating pictures, he still didn't understand what he was supposed to be looking at.

"That's just the DFZ," he said, flicking through multiple pictures of cars crammed like sardines onto the Skyways. "Traffic looks worse than usual, but I don't see what that has to do with—"

"That's not traffic," Ian said. "It's an evacuation. Algonquin ordered the entire city out."

"What?" Julius grabbed his brother's phone, flipping through the pictures with new horror. "*Why?*"

"No one knows," Ian said, snatching his phone back. "But it's got every mage in the world in a panic."

Bethesda arched a perfectly groomed eyebrow. "Human or dragon?"

"Both," Ian said, his new brown eyes grim. "Svena's still refusing to talk to me, but Katya says she's moved their entire clan, including my children, into the Three Sisters' old sleeping chamber beneath the ice. I've never been down there myself, but it's supposed to be one of the most heavily warded locations in the world. It's also the place Svena hates most, so if she's down there voluntarily, she's legitimately scared of something, and she's not alone. I keep multiple human mages on call for my various businesses. We're talking two dozen mages on three continents, and every single one of them has called me in a tizzy about some kind of mana surge building under the DFZ."

"Mana surge?" Julius frowned. "Are you sure? I haven't felt anything."

"Of course you haven't," Ian said, disgusted. "You're a dragon. Unless you've been studying magic all your life like Svena, the only magic from this plane that we can feel is the local ambient kind. This is much deeper, down in the primal magic, and it's *big*. Ten minutes after Algonquin's evacuation started, the United Nations issued an international casting ban, which includes magically augmented flight decks. Thankfully, I'd already decided to come back at that point, and the ban didn't cover planes that were in the air. I'm just glad I took the suborbital jet. If I'd been in the old supersonic, I'd still be over the Atlantic."

"So you just ran home?" Bethesda said angrily. "Without my eggs?"

"Yes," he snarled. "Because if this is as bad as it looks, *my* children are safer under Svena's wards. We should find a way to follow suit."

"How?" Julius asked. "You're talking about magic big enough to make Algonquin panic, but without Amelia or Svena, we're helpless. We have no wards, no shelter. Even our staff mages didn't show up for work. What are we supposed to do, hide in the panic bunker?"

"I don't think the panic bunker's going to be deep enough," Ian said gravely. "That's why I decided to come home. With me back, the Heartstriker Council is complete again, which means we can go ahead and surrender to the Golden Emperor tonight."

Julius stared at him in horror. "Surrender?" he got out at last. "You're the one who said you didn't crawl your way to the top of two clans just to lose both!"

"I know," Ian snapped. "I still feel that way, but the situation's changed, and at this point, the Golden Emperor's our best shot at surviving it. I read the surrender document you and Bethesda sent over, and while I agree it's suspiciously generous, we don't have time to be picky. Unlike us, the Qilin has mages, not to mention his luck. If we join his empire, we'll get both. And let's be honest, unless a miracle happened, we were going to surrender tomorrow morning anyway. We might as well do it now and get our protection from whatever this thing is in the bargain."

"But you don't even know what it is!"

"I know it's more than we can handle," Ian said, glaring at him. "I fought for this clan just as hard as you did, Julius, but it's time to face facts. We're in over our heads. There's no point in standing firm if the ground's washing out from under us. The Golden Emperor has offered us extraordinarily generous terms of surrender. I say we take them and use his luck to the hilt to keep ourselves alive. When this current disaster is over, we can rebuild and rebel at our leisure."

"That's what I said!" Bethesda cried. "*Finally*, another dragon who understands reason. Julius has been gone all afternoon, running after some crazy idea he thinks will save us."

"It's not crazy," Julius growled. "I know why the Qilin is here now. I know what he wants, and I think I know how to help him get it, *without* conquering our clan."

Bethesda rolled her eyes at that, but Julius kept his locked on Ian. "If there's a way we can get through this without joining the Golden Empire, we need to try, because rebelling against the Qilin will not end well for anyone. Just give me until tomorrow morning."

"We don't have until tomorrow," Ian snapped. "This disaster is happening *now*. I'm sure you think you've got the answer to everything, but do you realize how stupid it would be if we missed our shot at safety by a few hours because you were trying to have your gold and spend it, too?"

"But that's exactly what we might get," Julius argued. "If I can pull this off, the Qilin will be our ally, not our emperor. We can keep our clan *and* enjoy the shelter of his luck. Just give me an hour. I'll go wake up Chelsie right now and—"

"Chelsie?" Bethesda said sharply. "*She's* your plan?"

"Yes," Julius said. "She's—"

"Forget it," the Heartstriker snarled, turning to Ian. "Don't listen to him. Whatever his plan is, it'll never work. I don't know what delusion he's under, but Chelsie would die before she'd do anything with the Qilin."

"But she's already agreed to talk to him," Julius said frantically. "All I have to do is convince him to talk to her, too, and this whole thing could be—"

"Don't listen to him, Ian," Bethesda warned. "I can't explain the details since *someone* made me swear not to, but trust me when I say that Chelsie and the Golden Emperor will *never* make peace. Normally, I'd be content to let Julius learn that lesson the hard way, but if things are truly as bad as you say, then upsetting the Qilin is the absolute last thing we want to do. We should be keeping Chelsie as far away from him as possible, not smashing them together."

"But that's what got us into this mess in the first place," Julius said. "This may be our only chance to keep our clan intact, and we might just fix six hundred years of broken relations with the second-largest dragon clan on the planet in the process. We *have* to take it."

"The only thing we have to do is stay alive," Bethesda snarled. "I will not be told what to do by a whelp who's never even—"

"*Enough,*" Ian roared, shocking them both into silence. When the echo faded from the hangar, he turned to Julius. "Can you fix the problem tonight?"

Julius nodded determinedly, and Bethesda threw back her head with a hiss. "This is suicide. You're toying with a nuclear weapon. If Julius's stupid plan upsets the Golden Emperor, he could *cause* the disaster, not stop it."

"I know," Ian said.

"You came home to prevent this," she went on. "This entire thing was your idea!"

"I *know*!" he yelled. "But that was before I knew Julius had a plan."

Bethesda took a step back. "You're trusting him over me?" she said, eyes wide. "Who do you think built this clan?!"

"As of right now?" Ian jerked his head at Julius. "He did, and so did I. This isn't your show anymore, Bethesda. It's ours. I was prepared to bow if that was what was necessary to save Heartstriker, but if Julius thinks he can do it without giving up what we've fought for, I'm willing to let him try. At this point, I've seen him do the impossible too many times not to."

Julius broke into a grin, but the smile slipped off his face just as fast when Ian turned back to him. "You have until midnight," he growled. "If the Qilin hasn't agreed to shelter us as allies by then, my vote goes with Bethesda to surrender."

"I'll do my best," he promised.

"You'll have to do better than that," Ian said darkly. "Because if you screw this up for us, I will eat you myself, Fang or no Fang."

Julius swallowed. He'd thought he was used to death threats, but Ian looked like he really meant that one. When it was clear Julius understood he was serious, Ian leaned down to grab the hangar door.

"I'm going to change my clothes," he announced, throwing up the rolling steel. "And then I'm going to find someone to help me get my plane out of the dirt. Call me the moment you have something concrete."

Julius nodded again, but his brother was already gone, leaving him alone with Bethesda, who looked as if she was going to be sick.

"I don't know how you do it," she said, shooting him a poisonous look. "*Every* time I think you couldn't possibly ruin us more, you find a way."

"I'm not ruining us," he said angrily. "I'm—"

"I don't care," she said, pulling out her phone. "You do whatever you want. I'm going to check informants to see if I can pinpoint when we're all going to die. If you need me, I'll be in the bunker.

The deep one. Maybe when you're done destroying everything, I can come out and be queen of the mutants who remain."

From anyone one else, Julius would have called that a joke, but Bethesda looked absolutely serious as she stalked out of the hangar as fast as she could without actually running. A few seconds later, Julius followed suit, except he *did* run, sprinting as fast as he could down the brightly lit runway back toward the mountain.

CHAPTER TEN

Marci considered herself pretty well traveled when it came to the metaphysical. She'd been through portals and to the dead plane of the dragons. She'd been trapped in Algonquin's Reclamation Land and inside a spirit. She'd *died*, fought her way out, and then journeyed across the Sea of Magic. At this point in her life-slash-death, being able to keep on trucking despite industrial levels of weirdness was a point of pride, but no matter how jaded the insanity that was her life since she'd met Julius had left her, it was impossible not to stop and stare at what was waiting on the other side of the Merlin Gate.

From the outside, the wooden door had looked deceptively simple. As simple as anything leading into a giant stone pillar rising from the floor of the Sea of Magic could be, anyway. But the moment she stepped over the threshold, everything changed. There was no more dark, no more swirls of nauseating magic. Even the grave-like cold of Ghost's wind vanished, giving way to a warm, tropical breeze blowing down from what could only be described as paradise.

She was standing in a circular courtyard paved with rough-hewn interlocking white stones at the foot of a verdant mountain. At the paving's edge, tropical plants grew in wild abundance, creating undergrowth so thick, a cat couldn't have squeezed through. But while the jungle surrounding it was a wall, the courtyard itself was clear and open to the blue sky, and standing at the center was Shiro, the conjured servant of the ancient Merlins who'd turned her away before.

Seeing how she'd let herself in, Marci fully expected him to tell her to get right back out, but the shikigami made no move to oust her. He didn't even say anything when Ghost, Amelia, and finally Myron came through the door—which looked like a massive iron gate on this side—after her. Only when the iron slab swung closed again did the shikigami finally make his move, stepping forward and bending at the waist in front of Marci in a deep, formal bow.

"Welcome, Merlin," he said respectfully. "To the Heart of the World."

"Merlin?" Marci took a step back. "You mean I did it? I'm *finally* a real Merlin? Like officially?"

"You can be nothing else," Shiro said as he straightened up. "The Heart of the World was created by and for the Merlin Circle. Its door opens only to those deemed worthy, and it opened for you. That makes you a Merlin by every possible measure. As I am a servant bound to the Heart of the World by order of the Last Merlin, Abe no Seimei, it is now my duty to welcome you and your guests."

"If it's your job to welcome us," Ghost said skeptically, crossing his arms over his transparent, shadowy chest, "why did you turn us away before?"

"That was my duty as well," Shiro said. "I only welcome the worthy, which is a title your mistress had not yet earned when she first knocked."

"But has now," Amelia said, tapping her claws thoughtfully. "I wonder what did it." She looked at Marci. "Did you pass a test or something?"

Marci shrugged and looked at Shiro, who shook his head. "I'm not privy to its logic, so I can't say what exactly you did that caused the door to open, but the Heart of the World does not make mistakes. If you are here now, it's because something you did between our last meeting and this one was enough to earn the Heart's trust, and that's proof enough for me."

Marci bit her lip. There was a lot to unpack in that statement. She was trying to decide where to start when Myron beat her to it.

"Where are we?" he demanded, looking up at the forested mountain. "All my research said that the Heart of the World was a spell, not a place."

"It is a spell," the shikigami said, "to make a place."

"So it's an illusion?" Marci said, tapping her foot on the paving stones, which certainly felt real.

"I think it's more like a model," Amelia said excitedly. "I've always wondered how the great mages overcame humanity's inherent magical handicaps. I mean, you live in a dual-natured reality, but your perception is confined to the physical world while you're alive, and stuck in your deaths after that. Even if you *do* claw your way out to the actual Sea of Magic, you still need a spirit to ferry you around and point stuff out since you can't see squat. That's a crippling limitation, especially when you're talking about the *really* big scale magic Merlins were famous for. But if your secret base is actually a constructed reality—a place that takes all the stuff you can't normally see and translates it into something you can interact with—that would explain a lot."

"Of course," Marci said, staring up at the mountain, which she could now see wasn't craggy or rocky at all, but perfectly regular. A flawless cone, which was nothing but a bunch of circles stacked on top of each other.

She dropped to one knee, brushing her hands over the courtyard's paving stones, which she now saw weren't rough at all. They were carved, their stone faces engraved with so many tiny, interlocking lines of spellwork, they felt like sandpaper.

"It's all a spell," she said, awestruck. "This whole place was built by people."

"Of course," Myron said, dropping down beside her. "Humans can't see or navigate the Sea of Magic, so they built an artificial physical space inside it. A safe haven."

"Or a lens," Marci said, looking up at the blue dome of the cloudless sky. "We're still inside the Sea of Magic, it just makes sense now. That must be what this place does. It translates all that chaos into something we can interact with."

"You are both correct," Shiro said. "The Sea of Magic is as huge and unfathomable to mortals as the actual sea it was named for. Such confusion prevented magical advancement, so the mages who came before my master, the ancient Merlins, built this place to act as an interface. It is a tool that provides both shelter from the chaos of the Sea of Magic and light that renders that chaos of magic into a form humans can understand and use."

"But that's incredible!" Marci cried, shooting back to her feet. "You didn't just draw a circle in the Sea of Magic, you made an entire world!" She looked up at the green mountain. "We're standing in what has to be the biggest superstructure of magical logic ever built. One made without any of the modern tools like computer simulations or spell-checking software. That's like discovering a new Great Pyramid built inside of Atlantis!"

"I don't know what either of those are," Shiro said apologetically. "But I'm happy you understand the importance and power of this place."

"The power of this place was never in question," Myron said, scowling. "What I want to know is what's all this power *for*? Novalli's right. This is the biggest spell I've ever seen by several orders of magnitude. But I've worked for the United Nations long enough to know that humans don't build things on this scale unless it gives them a serious strategic advantage."

Marci snorted. "How is that even a question? We're talking about a tool that lets humans see and interact with magic like the spirits do. That's a *huge* strategic advantage."

"It is," Myron agreed. "*If* that was all it did. But look."

He marched over to the edge of the clearing and grabbed one of the thick bushes, pulling it down to show Marci the flat green leaf.

"Holy…" Marci grabbed the waxy leaf from his hands, staring down at the delicate veins that ran through it, but not in the usual branching pattern.

"This is spellwork," she said, running her fingers over the looping ridges of the ancient symbols growing inside the leaf where its chloroplasts should have been. The other leaves were the same, as was the branch they grew from. "It's *all* spellwork," she whispered, reaching out to touch the spirals of symbols that formed the patterns in the bark. "Every inch of it."

"And you know what that means," Myron said, letting the tree go. "You never finished your PhD, but even undergrads should know that interlocked spellwork is exponentially co-functional. If all of this is inside the same circle, and I see no reason not to believe that the Heart of the World is one circle, then all of this—the stones in this courtyard and the leaves in the forest and anything else we find—are parts of the same whole. It's like—"

"Programs running in the same operating system," Marci finished, nodding.

"Don't put your dated Comp Sci analogies in my mouth," Myron said disdainfully. "I was going to say 'organs functioning in a body.' We're doing magic, not writing point-of-sale software for minimum wage. I know you Thaumaturges have a hard time telling the two apart, but while Shamanistic magic has its drawbacks, at least they understand that magic is an organic force. We're playing god with the stuff of life itself. Not writing logic chains for mindless computational systems."

Marci rolled her eyes. "Says the man who wrote a book called *The Logic of Magic*."

"Yes," he said proudly. "And since you claim to have read all my work, you'll remember I said that the logic of magic functions like the logic of every other natural system: a chaotic mess governed by a few universal rules, one of which is that all spellwork inside the same circle works together. *That point made*, take a moment and think about just how much spellwork we're talking about."

He stepped back to look up at the densely forested mountain rising above them. "Not counting anything else we might find, but if all of those trees are spellworked like this one, that right there is more magical notation than all the modern spellwork libraries combined. Considering the amount of logic we saw crammed onto one leaf, we might be looking at millions of spells, perhaps *billions*, all working together. If that's true, then the next question has to be: working toward what end?"

Marci frowned. "Aren't they making this?" She tapped her foot on the stone. "You know, supporting the Heart of the World?"

"As amazing as the Heart of the World unquestionably is, it's not that complicated," Myron said confidently. "I could probably create something similar given enough time and the space on the trees that immediately surround us. Even if you doubled those requirements, though, the spellwork required to make a separate reality, even one as complicated as this, still wouldn't be anywhere near enough to fill all the trees and rocks and other presumably spellworked landscaping that blankets this island. And it's not even confined to the *ground*. Look up."

He pointed up at the sky, and Marci gasped. Now that he'd pointed it out, she could plainly see that what had initially looked like a clear blue sky wasn't actually clear at all, or a sky. It was a dome, a blue shell covered with hundreds of thousands of millions of tiny symbols like pixels on an old-style LED screen.

From all the way down here, they blended together into a flat blue expanse, but if she squinted, Marci could see the symbols were arranged into spellwork, just like everything else. Not just single lines, either. The sky was a grid, a hatch of symbols arranged in a spellwork pattern that could be read not just from side to side, but up and down and maybe even diagonally as well. The complexity behind such a design was enough to make her head spin, but it was also one Marci had seen before.

"It's like the inside of my Kosmolabe."

Myron gaped at her. "*You* have a Kosmolabe?"

"Had," she said. "But you're right. As incredible as this place is, there's way too much spellwork here just to keep the magic out and support a translation interface. It has to do something else."

Probably a lot of something elses, including choosing to admit her as a Merlin. But even that kind of seemingly intelligent decision fit within the parameters of the logic that governed wards. Just as she could make a shield that blocked bullets or trapped spirits,

the ancient Merlins could surely write a spell that kept out everyone except for the humans who met their requirements. It would
take a ton of spellwork—abstract wards always did—but there was
definitely enough here to do it. More than enough, which was the
problem. *Nothing* took this much spellwork.

Marci's stomach began to sink. If she followed Myron's logic
and assumed the rest of the forest was jam packed like the tree and
the stones under their feet, then there was enough spellwork here
to hold all the world's magic through twice over. And given why
Myron and Algonquin had wanted to get in here, Marci had the
awful feeling that was the entire point.

"You claimed this place was built to be a tool," she said, turning
back to Shiro, who'd never stopped watching her. "Something that
wouldn't just let humans see the magic here, but use and control it
as well."

"Correct," the shikigami replied.

Marci nodded, crossing her arms over her chest. "So what were
they using it to do?"

The shikigami smiled wide. "To answer that question is my
purpose," he said, walking toward her. "But to do so, we must go
higher."

Before she could ask what that meant, Shiro reached the edge
of the courtyard, where the trees met the stones. Then he lifted his
hand, and the thick line of trees Marci and Myron had been examining peeled back like a curtain.

"Come, Merlin," he said as he walked into the now-open forest.
"I will take you to the Heart of the World."

"I thought we were already there," Marci muttered, hurrying
after him into the tunnel of trees. Myron followed right behind her,
then Ghost and finally Amelia, flapping her way after them out of
the sunny courtyard and up the path turned cool green by the dark,
leafy canopy of spellwork overhead.

Given the height of the mountain, Marci was braced for a long
climb. Apparently, though, constructed magical islands didn't follow normal rules of distance. After less than a minute of following a

footpath uphill between the trees, Shiro pushed aside another wall of undergrowth to reveal a landscape of smooth stone and open sky. Blinking against the suddenly blinding light, Marci followed, stepping out of the forest into the bright, open, and strangely windless world of the perfectly flat plateau that was the mountain's top.

After the blatant artificiality of everything else here, that really shouldn't have surprised her, but it was just so odd. Beneath the blanket of forest, the mountain itself was perfectly conical, except for its peak. That was as flat and smooth as a factory floor, as though a passing giant had lopped the mountain's point off with a razor. The only deviation from the flatness was at the peak's center, where an elegantly gnarled pine tree grew from the stone beside what appeared to be a well. Aside from that, the only thing to see up here was the ocean.

"Wow," Marci whispered, staring in wonder at the wild, strikingly blue water. "It really is a *Sea* of Magic."

"It is," Ghost agreed quietly, his glowing eyes round in the void of his face. "Though I've never seen it from this height before." His voice softened. "It's beautiful."

It was more than that. The beautiful, clear, jewel-blue ocean stretching out around them was nothing like the nauseating black chaos Marci knew as the Sea of Magic, which was the entire point. This was the lens of the Heart of the World at work, transforming the confusing mess of the Sea of Magic into a form her brain could understand: a clear, shallow sea.

From the top of the mountain—which Marci could now see was indeed a perfect cone with no beach at all, just the vividly green jungle running right up to the waves like a wall—she could look straight down to the ocean floor. A long way down, too, because the base of the Heart of the World didn't slope out gradually like a natural island. It went straight down like a peg, the stone column they'd seen from outside. And if *that* was there, then all the thousands of holes and cracks pitting what should have been the ocean's sandy floor suddenly made a lot more sense.

"Look at all the spirit vessels," she said, getting right to the edge of the mountain's flat top.

The land beneath the vibrant blue water was so riddled with gouges, there was barely room for rock between the cracks. Some of the holes were so deep, the water was still pouring in, forming giant whirlpools as the sea was sucked down into the seemingly bottomless pits. From where she was standing, she could only look down into a handful, but the whirlpools were everywhere, dotting the choppy sea like freckles all the way to the horizon.

"Terrifying, isn't it?"

Marci jumped, whipping around to see Shiro standing right beside her. "I would have said beautiful," she said when she'd recovered. "Is this what you wanted to show me?"

"Part of it," he said, staring solemnly at the endless sea. "This was what the Heart of the World was meant for. From up here, things are compressed, allowing us to safely and easily observe the Sea of Magic in its entirety."

Compression would explain why the cracks looked so small. Or, at least, not the size of mountains and lakes.

"Those are the Mortal Spirits, aren't they?" she said, pointing at the whirlpools. "The ones that haven't filled up yet."

"Correct," Shiro said, his expression darkening. "Even more than observing, this place was created to protect. With so many spirits rising, we needed a watchtower, somewhere we could see the monsters coming, and prepare to strike back."

"Monsters, huh?" Marci shook her head. "Have to say, though, I didn't expect that from you guys. I thought forming partnerships with the Mortal Spirits was the Merlins' whole shtick."

"It was," Shiro said. "Until we got overwhelmed."

He turned away from the cliff, motioning for her to follow. Curious and frustrated, Marci did so, dogging his heels across the flat stone to the center, where Amelia, Ghost, and Myron were already waiting in the shade of the gnarled pine beside the stone well. Or, at least, she'd assumed it was a well. As they got closer, though, Marci realized that was wrong. The waist-high circle of stone wasn't a well.

It was a seal.

It was all one piece: a huge, circular disk of white stone three feet tall and ten feet across, laid on its side under the tree at the exact center of the circular mountain-top. Like everything else here, its surface was covered in spellwork, but unlike the leaf or the stones from the clearing below, which had merely been parts of a larger whole, this spellwork was contained within its own circle. The edge of the seal had been gouged to form a hard line, creating a clear border between the rest of the mountain top and the spellwork inside.

As always, she couldn't read a word of it, and not just because it was in a language she didn't know. The spellwork on the leaves had been fairly normal looking, but the organization of the spell on the seal was something Marci had never encountered before.

Instead of spiraling around the circle as Thaumaturgical spells did, or even forming a grid pattern like the spellwork in the sky, these lines—each of which was smaller than the fine print on a legal document—wove in, out, and around each like threads. The result was a fractal knot that filled the surface of the circular seal without leaving so much as a centimeter of the white stone blank. It was absolutely magnificent, the sort of marvel that could spawn an entire new school of anthropological magic, which was why it was so tragic that the tightly woven spellwork was damaged.

At the top of the circle, the beautifully interwoven lines of spellwork were broken by a hairline crack. Along the break, beads of water welled up like blood from a paper cut, eventually joining together into a tiny rivulet that trickled down the side of the seal, across the mountain's flat top, and eventually off the edge. It was such a tiny thing, a little leak from a little crack, but when Marci touched her finger to it, the water burned just as the magic outside had.

"Guess Algonquin wasn't being metaphorical when she said the Merlins sealed the magic," she said, flicking the burning water off her fingers. "This is it, isn't it? This is the *literal* seal on magic. She was right."

"Of course she was right," Myron said angrily. "Do you think I'd have gone along with her if I believed otherwise?"

Marci glowered at him. "I think you would have gone along with anything that bought you a shot at being Merlin. But don't try to pretend you knew all of this. I remember you saying back in the diner that you didn't even know what Merlins did."

"I didn't, specifically," he said with a dirty look. "But we've always known that humans are the only species with the ability to alter the magical landscape. Nothing else can do that, and considering that the total magic of the world has historically trended *up*, not down, it only made sense that its unprecedented total disappearance had to be caused by man."

"Don't feed me that," Marci snapped, pointing at the seal. "There is no way you knew this was here for certain until now."

"I never said I was certain," he snapped back. "I said I *believed*. I *theorized* the drought was caused by humans. I *suspected* the ancient Merlins had some kind of control over the tectonic magical flows. A hypothesis that was further correlated by Algonquin's desperation to get her own Merlin inside before one could rise naturally. I had no *proof* of anything, but when the opportunity arose, I was confident enough in my theories to bet my life on getting in here. And I was *right*."

He placed his hand on the cracked seal. "This is the smoking gun. The magical drought, the long sleep of the spirits, the loss of our knowledge—it all started here. Magic didn't vanish because of some natural disaster or dip. It was *us*."

Marci stared at him in horrified disbelief. "*Why?*"

"Because they had no other choice."

The reply came from Shiro, and Marci turned on him in disgust. Because if there was any line her recent life had taught her to hate, it was that one.

"'They had no other choice,'" she repeated through clenched teeth. "Do you know the damage their *choice* did to us? The scope of what we lost? Before it reappeared sixty years ago, people didn't even think magic was real. Everything we'd built, the knowledge of how to do stuff like this." She waved her hand at the beautiful spellwork of the seal's surface. "It was all *gone*. Everything we know about magic now, we've had to reinvent from scratch!"

"But you did it," the shikigami said. "Because *you* were not gone. Humanity survived the death of magic, but did you ever stop to wonder how? Why it was that, in a world of dragons and spirits and monsters, humanity rose to become masters of the Earth? It's not because you are so great or so special. It's because the Last Merlins sacrificed to give you a safe haven."

"By eliminating everything else!" Marci cried. "You put every spirit in the world to sleep!"

Shiro sneered at her. "Why do you think we did it? You have no idea what things were like back then. How it felt to see Death riding through the sky, or to look out on a battlefield and witness War laughing as he collected heads from both sides. These were not metaphors to us, not stories. They were *real*, and they were terrifying. The Mortal Spirits of our time were gods in truth. They did whatever they pleased, and the more they did, the more people believed in them, and the more powerful they became. It was a vicious cycle, and the only way to keep it from grinding the whole world to dust was to stop the wheel entirely."

"So the Merlins sealed off the magic," Myron said, nodding. "No magic, no spirits. Makes sense."

"No, it doesn't," Marci said angrily. "They took magic from *all* of us! Talk about throwing the baby out with the bathwater."

"You think my master and his fellow Merlins made this choice lightly?" Shiro said angrily. "They were mages, too. Just like you, they'd dedicated their lives to magic, but it wasn't enough. No matter how many times we slew the Mortal Spirits, they would always rise again. For all our efforts, we could never gain ground, because our enemy was fear itself, and fear is an intrinsic part of humanity. Finally, desperate and overwhelmed, Abe no Seimei did the only thing left that he could: he sealed away that which he loved most for the good of all."

Just hearing that made Marci want to cry. "You can't possibly call that a victory."

"No one did," Shiro said, shaking his head. "Humanity was defeated that day, and yet, thanks to my master, you survived. Survived and thrived, because, unlike spirits, humans are more than magic. In the thousand years since the seal was created, I have watched you grow to the world's greatest power. Even dragons tremble before your weapons now, and it is all thanks to the Merlins' sacrifice."

He smiled at her. "That is what I was left here to say. Before he was forced out by the failing magic, my master, Abe no Seimei, the Last Merlin, bound me to the Heart of the World so that I would be able to tell future generations the truth of what happened. Part of it was that he hoped to be forgiven. Mostly, though, he wanted you to understand why the seal he sacrificed so much to create must never be undone."

Marci understood that much. She didn't *agree*, but she understood the logic of cutting off one's nose to spite one's face. What she didn't understand was *how*.

"Okay," she said slowly, rubbing her temples. "I get why he wouldn't want his work undone, but how did he do it? Even if it's not actually a sea in the literal sense, we're still talking about building a wall big enough to block *all* the world's magic. How is that even possible?"

"It isn't," Shiro admitted. "Magic is a natural system. We could no more stop it than we could stop the rain from falling or the wind from blowing. But my master's genius was in realizing we didn't need to keep it out. We just needed to keep it *in*."

Marci's eyes went wide. "Of course," she said, looking down at the mountain under her feet. The perfectly circular mountain topped with a perfectly circular seal.

Now that he'd pointed it out, Marci could have kicked herself for not realizing what was going on earlier. The whole point of circles was to hold magic. The bigger the circle, the more you could hold. Add in efficient spellwork, and you expanded that capacity by a power of ten, and if there was anything this place had in abundance, it was spellwork.

"This whole place is a circle," she said, shaking her head. "You didn't stop the magic. You sucked it up and sealed it *in*. That's why the Heart of the World stayed up when every other spell stopped working. You were sitting on all the magic." She looked down at the stone under her feet. "This whole mountain is a holding tank!"

"This mountain is only the tip," Shiro said. "There's also the column below it, which goes down quite a ways. It was originally built to lift the Heart of the World above the Sea of Magic so we could see, but when he realized what he needed to do, my master redesigned this entire place to act as a funnel."

He pointed at the spellworked sky. "Like the water it resembles, magic is constantly cycling. It flows from the sea into the physical world, where it is used up and dispersed into small pieces that eventually drift back to this side, where they fall into the sea again like rain. To break this cycle, we built a net to catch the incoming magic before it could reenter the system, funneling it into the mountain instead. Once stored, it was removed from the cycle, and without rain—"

"The sea dried up," Marci finished, staring out at the blue water. "Just like a real drought."

"And it's *all* in here?" Myron said, kneeling to rap his knuckles on the mountain's smooth top. "All the magic of the old world?"

The shikigami nodded. "All the magic that was in the sea of our time plus all the new magic that's fallen since."

Myron's head shot up. "Wait, *new* magic? You're sure it's new?"

"It has to be new," Shiro said. "My master and his circle used the seal to suck the Sea of Magic dry before they were forced out. The net in the sky was only there to catch the magic left on the physical side as it filtered back in. My master, Seimei, estimated it would take a couple of years for all the ambient magic to filter back through, but the seal has continued collecting small amounts of magic all the time I've been here. Since all known magic was already accounted for, I can only assume it is new."

Myron and Marci exchanged an excited look. "Do you know what that means?" he asked.

Marci grinned. "That the Murthy Theory of Magical Genesis is true? *Oh* yeah. But we knew it had to be since total magical levels trend up over time, and how can that happen unless new magic is entering the system? The only thing we didn't know was where it came from."

"But we still don't know," Myron said, brows furrowed. "Where *does* the new magic come from?"

"Other planes, most likely," Amelia popped in. "Planes aren't closed systems. There are lots of ways magic can enter, though I couldn't say for sure which one is happening here without doing a few centuries of observation. Right now, though, I'm way more concerned about the fact that we're sitting on top of a thousand years' worth of compressed magic." She turned to Shiro. "Just how long was Abe no Seimei planning to let this go on?"

The shikigami began to fidget. "As I said before, it was an emergency decision. Gods of death and fear were threatening every living thing. There simply wasn't time to—"

"So there was no plan."

"Just because he acted quickly didn't mean he didn't plan!" Shiro said angrily. "My master built the seal to catch and compress magic safely for thousands of years. That should have been more than enough time for humanity to grow and learn. His plan was to buy safety for future generations in the hope that one day they would have the wisdom to solve the problems he could not, and it would all still be working just fine if that *rock* hadn't cracked it!"

"Rock?" Myron repeated. "What rock?"

"I think he means the meteor," Marci said. "You know, the one that brought magic back."

"A meteor did *not* bring back magic," Myron said authoritatively. "It was just a bit of space debris hitting the ground in Canada, nothing magical about it. It was just a coincidence the panicked media jumped on as an explanation for what was inexplicable at the time."

As ever, Myron said this as though it were the one and only truth, which struck Marci as crazy. While it was true the meteor theory had never been proven, it was still a widely accepted explanation for what had happened that night. Before she could start arguing with Myron, though, Shiro beat her to it.

"But it *was* the meteor."

"Impossible," Myron said. "I hold the Chair for Tectonic Magic at Cambridge University. I've spent my entire life studying the deep magic, and I can tell you definitively that physical disasters such as earthquakes and meteor strikes have negligible impact. We weren't monitoring the deep flows back then, obviously, but I can *guarantee* there is no way a chunk of iron pyrite falling from space caused enough impact on this side to break anything, much less an ancient seal inside the fortress of the Merlins."

"That would be true," Shiro said, "if it was a normal meteor."

Marci blinked. "It wasn't?"

"No," he said. "It had its own magic—"

"It did not," Myron snapped. "That meteorite has been tested thousands of times. I've handled it myself, and I can tell you first-hand that it's no more magical than any rock."

"Maybe not by the time you got it," Shiro said gruffly. "But I was here when it happened. I felt that meteor hit the seal just as I felt the jolt of alien magic inside it that caused the shift in pressure that made the crack."

Myron's eyes were wide by the time he finished. Marci's weren't any better. It sounded like the plot of a bad movie, but hearing someone as in the know as Shiro talk seriously about *alien magic* was absolutely terrifying. Especially if that magic was no longer contained inside the meteor it had arrived in. That was like getting to the alien queen's egg-laying chamber only to see that all the eggs had already hatched, and Marci had watched enough movies to know how *that* scenario ended.

"So where did it go?"

"I don't know," Shiro said, shoulders slumping. "I lost it in the chaos after the seal cracked. Since you haven't had any problems,

I presume it integrated safely with the rest of the world's magic. The important thing, though, is that whatever fell from the sky that night did in fact crack the seal, and magic's been leaking out ever since."

"Wait," Marci said, looking down at the tiny crack oozing magic like a paper cut. "You're telling me this little trickle caused all of *that?*"

She pointed at the wild blue sea surrounding them on all sides, and Shiro nodded. "I told you, this place is compressed. It's meant to convey the idea of the sea, not the accurate scale."

"Seems like a pretty important difference," Marci said, leaning down to get a better look at the tiny leak that was the apparent source of the rebirth of magic. "That said, though, I think this was a blessing in disguise. The crack let magic into the world gradually, giving us time to learn and adapt. I mean, can you imagine if the whole thing had gone at once? It would have been terrible."

"I *have* imagined," Shiro said angrily. "That's what I'm trying to tell you. This isn't a stable situation. The crack you see there is twice the size it was at the beginning. It's been getting bigger every year, letting out more and more magic."

Marci didn't like where this was going. "So you're saying it's going to, what? Keep widening? Break all the way?"

"Have you seen a seal break under pressure?" Shiro asked grimly. "It's not going to slowly open. It's going to burst, and soon. A few months if we're lucky, weeks if we're not, though even *that* might be a stretch if the magic keeps jerking around like this."

Marci frowned. "Jerking around?"

"The Sea of Magic is unsettled," Ghost explained, glancing over his shoulder at the choppy blue waves. "I told you it was rougher than usual. Probably because a Spirit of the Land sacrificed her fellows to artificially inflate the spirit of a city."

That last part was accompanied by a murderous glare at Myron, who sighed. "In my defense, it seemed necessary at the time," he said, rubbing his hands over his face. "And I didn't know we were dealing with a crack."

"Well, that's just peachy," Marci growled. "Algonquin gets to screw us all over again." She turned back to Shiro. "So what can we do?"

"There's only one thing *to* do," the shikigami said. "You have to repair the damage."

"Me?" she squeaked, looking down at the masterpiece of ancient spellwork in front of her. "Fix *that*? Did you miss the part where I can't even read it?"

"But it can only be you," Shiro said firmly. "The seal is Merlin magic, and you're the Merlin. You are the only one who can change the spellwork of this place. Even I'm just a talking part of the scenery."

"But I don't even know how it's structured," Marci protested. "And there's the part where modifying a spell while it's still in action is horrifically dangerous. If I make one mistake, I could blow this whole place. And even if I do miraculously get everything right the first try, won't repairing the seal make magic go away again?"

"It will," Shiro said, looking relieved. "That's why I was so determined not to allow anyone who might be compromised to enter the Heart of the World. A human under the control of dragons or spirits might be tempted to shift the balance of power back toward their masters, but a true Merlin serves humanity alone, and humanity is best served when there is no magic at all."

He smiled at her as he finished, holding out his hands in invitation, but Marci just stared back in horror. "No."

The smile fell off the shikigami's calm face. "I do not understand."

"What's there not to understand? N-O. *No.* I'm not taking magic from the entire world again."

"But you are the Merlin," he said. "It's your job to do what serves humanity best."

"And I'm telling you that plunging us back into the magical drought isn't the way to do that," Marci said firmly. "You don't make humanity stronger by making everyone else weak. That's not power. That's just shooting everyone in the foot because you happen to be better at limping than the other guys. Also, we just got our magic *back.* I didn't even know this place existed until today. There's a lifetime of learning just in the spellwork in front of me. I'm not giving that up."

"But you must," Shiro said angrily. "It's the duty of the Merlin to abandon selfish desires and do what is good for *all.*"

"Who are you to say sealing the magic does that? It's not like you guys took a vote."

"There was no time!" he cried. "Weren't you listening? The gods had won! Faces of Death were riding through the sky! We had to seal the magic or die."

"I understand that," Marci said. "But that's not how things are *now.*"

"Not *yet*," Shiro said, pointing at the whirlpools dotting the sea around them. "The holes humanity dug have only gotten deeper as the population has grown. If you don't repair the damage, if the seal breaks, the resulting flood of magic will fill those chasms, causing hundreds, perhaps *thousands* of Mortal Spirits to rise all at once. That's a greater disaster than anything we faced, and the only way to prevent it is to act *now*, while we still can."

Marci looked away with a curse. Of all places, she'd never thought she'd hear Algonquin's argument repeated here. This was supposed to be the place where Mortal Spirits were celebrated and accepted as part of humanity's magic. The Heart of the World had opened its door to her only after she'd freed the DFZ, for pity's sake. It wasn't that she didn't understand what Shiro was saying, but the world had changed a lot in the last thousand years, and as much as Marci revered Abe no Seimei as one of history's best mages, he was dead. It was her turn now, and Marci wasn't convinced things were bad enough yet to blindly repeat the nuclear options of the past.

"What about a compromise?" she said, turning to Myron. "When she was trying to recruit me, Algonquin said she wanted to get a Merlin in here so they could cap the magic back down to the level it was immediately following the meteor. I disagreed at the time because I didn't trust her and I didn't want to rob Mortal Spirits like

Ghost of their chance to be alive, but I don't actually mind the idea of a limit. Could we do something like that? Modify the seal to only let out a certain amount of magic?"

"Absolutely not," Shiro said.

"I wasn't asking you," Marci said, keeping her eyes on Myron. "I'm asking him. You're always going on about how you're the expert, Sir Myron, so go ahead. Advise me."

Myron scowled, but Marci had never met a know-it-all who could resist giving advice. Sure enough, after half a minute of pouting and sneering, he answered.

"I suppose it's possible. The seal's already leaking, so we wouldn't have to change the underlying spellwork. We'd just need to layer something on top of it that could relieve the pressure enough to let the magic out without pushing the crack wider."

"Like a spillway on a dam," Marci said, nodding. "Gotcha."

"I don't believe you do," Myron said coldly. "Since you asked for my advice, you should know that I agree with the shikigami. Algonquin got me the spirit I needed to come here, but I didn't become a Merlin because I wanted to follow her plan. I came here to save humanity from monsters like her by shutting the magic off for good."

Marci took a step back. "What? But you were the one who told me about Merlins in the first place! You said they were our weapons, our chance to meet the spirits on an equal field."

"That's what I believed," he said. "Until I met you."

Her eyes went wide, but Myron wasn't done.

"I know you think I sold out," he said bitterly. "That I betrayed my team and all of humanity when I went to work for Algonquin, but what you don't understand is that I was just doing what needed to be done. What I have *always* done. My entire life has been dedicated to doing what is best for humanity as a species. That's why I joined the UN and stayed there for decades. Despite receiving countless offers for far better-paying positions, I chose to remain where I could do the most good, pushing our understanding of magic and advancing humanity's ability to stand up to the monsters that were so much stronger than us. For years, I thought the Merlins were the key to that victory. They were the mages of legend, the weapons that would finally elevate us to the level of spirits and dragons. That was my hope, but then you came along."

His dark eyes narrowed. "You showed me the truth, Marci Novalli. Through you, I saw that Mortal Spirits weren't our shining swords. They were our monsters. Our deaths. Even bound, your Empty Wind was always greater than you, *always* stronger."

"But that's a good thing," Marci argued. "Ghost is my partner. His strength is my strength."

"Is it?" Myron asked. "Do you really think your Empty Wind couldn't kill you in an instant if you angered him? Or the dragons? Do you think you've ever been anything to them but a tool?"

"Hey!" Amelia said. "Don't bring us into this."

"Why not? You're part of the problem." He turned back to Marci. "You stand there and criticize Abe no Seimei for taking away magic, but now that I understand what he was up against, I think he was a hero. The thousand years of peace he bought us with his drought were the greatest in our race's history. We were the unquestioned masters of the world. Even dragons were forced to pretend to be human to survive. When magic returned, though, we went right back down to the bottom, and that's where we've stayed. Emily and I were trying to change that when we sought you out, but now I know we were doomed from the start. No matter what we invent or how clever we get, humanity just can't win so long as magic is in play. Even if we learn to deal with the dragons and Algonquin, we would still be doomed, because of things like *him.*"

He pointed at Ghost, and Marci clenched her jaw. "I get it. You've never liked my spirit, but—"

"This isn't about *your* spirit," he snapped. "It's about *all* spirits, Mortal ones in particular. You heard Shiro's story about how the ancient Merlins were overrun, but I don't think even he understands just how bad these new ones will be."

"But—"

"The world's population when magic vanished was roughly three hundred million people," he said over her. "Today, there are nine billion. That's a thirty-fold increase, and that's not even taking into account the global spread of ideas caused by mass communication. You saw how huge the DFZ was, and she's not even naturally occurring. Algonquin created her specifically so that she'd have a Mortal Spirit small enough to fill before the others did. The *real* Mortal Spirits, the ones who're a natural result of humanity's collected fears, are bigger than we can comprehend."

"You think I don't know that?" she said, jerking her head at the Empty Wind. "I'm bound to one. I know how big he is, but just because something *can* kill us doesn't mean it *will.* Ghost helped you, if you'll recall."

"But will the next one?" Myron said. "We're talking about a plague of gods unleashed on an unsuspecting world. You're asking me to believe that all of them can be controlled like your Empty Wind, but you didn't have full control over him at the beginning, did you? You told me yourself that you had to bind him multiple times, and that was with the handicap of him barely being awake. We won't get that break with the rest of them, and I'm not willing to gamble humanity's future on the hope that all these spirits of death and anger will miraculously turn out to be reasonable."

Marci rolled her eyes. "That's not—"

"I don't care," he snapped, placing his hand on the broken seal. "You want my advice? This crack should be repaired as quickly as possible, not enshrined. Even without Mortal Spirits, the return of magic has already caused irreparable harm and loss of life to people all over the world, particularly in Detroit. Sealing it away again is the only responsible course of action. To do otherwise is to doom us all."

Shiro nodded as he finished, looking wistfully at Myron as if he were seriously regretting not letting him attempt to enter the Heart of the World first. The rejection stung, but Marci couldn't blame the shikigami for it. She couldn't make herself be mad at Myron, either, because pompous as he was, he wasn't wrong. Mortal Spirits *were* a threat. What Myron was saying now was the same thing Amelia had said before the fight with Vann Jeger: that if Marci didn't control her spirit, he'd end up controlling her.

It had almost happened, too. If she'd been less bold in the moments after he'd first remembered his name as the Empty Wind, he would have taken over. Their entire relationship had been a delicate exercise in trust building, and as happy as she was with the end result, Marci had no illusions that it was the sort of process that could be easily reproduced. Even if she could come up with a process, every Mortal Spirit was different, as was every mage. Every pair had to forge its own unique connection, build their own bridge of trust. That was hard enough between two normal people, but when the price of failure was a god rampaging out of control, Myron's argument made a lot of sense.

And yet…

"I understand what you're saying," Marci said slowly. "There's no question that sealing off the magic again would save lives, but you're missing the part where human lives aren't the only things at stake here. This isn't just *our* planet, Myron. It's home to spirits and magical creatures of all kinds, many of whom were living here long before we came down from the trees. If we bring back the drought, we might save humanity, but we'll hurt everything else."

Myron sneered. "If you're asking me to feel sorry for the dragons who have to stay in their human forms—"

"I'm not just talking about dragons," Marci said. "I'm talking about magical animals, the chimeras and tank badgers and unicorns and all the other magical species that have reemerged since magic returned. If I seal magic away again, I'll send them back into hibernation, possibly forever. And what about the spirits? They're not all like Algonquin. There are millions of land and animal spirits all over the world that live peacefully with their human neighbors. Many of them even help us. Are they monsters? Do they deserve to die?"

"Of course not," he said. "But we do what we must to survive."

"Do we?" she asked. "Are we really surviving?"

"You're alive, aren't you?"

Marci lifted her chin. "Am I?"

He sighed. "Bad example. But your death was—"

"My *death* is why I can talk about this!" Marci cried. "Magic isn't just power, Myron. It's our *soul*, and I'm not speaking poetically. When my body died, *this* is what was left."

She held up her hands, which were still transparent in the Heart of the World's brilliant sunlight. "We're magic, too. Maybe not as much as spirits, but it's still a part of us. Obviously, humanity physically survived the drought, but just because our race kept multiplying doesn't mean the loss of magic didn't hurt us terribly. When I died, my magic was what lived on inside my death. I would have been stuck in there until it collapsed if Ghost hadn't come to save me."

Marci put her hand on the Empty Wind's shoulder. "You're always going on about how 'he is death,' but what you're forgetting is *that's not a bad thing*. All humans die, and it's spirits like Ghost—the Mortal Spirits of *death*—who care for our souls afterward. If you take that away, if you put those spirits to sleep, what happens to us? Where do we go?" She turned back to Shiro. "What happened to the people who died during the drought?"

"What do you think?" he said stoically. "They died."

"But what happened *after*?" Marci pressed. "If there's no magic, then what happens to the magical part of us? To the soul? Does it just die?"

"All things die."

"Answer the question," she growled, stepping closer. "What happened to their souls?"

Shiro dropped his eyes. "Nothing," he said at last. "They didn't go anywhere, because they weren't there to begin with."

"Stop," Myron said, putting a hand to his forehead. "Just stop. This is insanity. Are you really telling me that humans born during the drought didn't have *souls*?"

"They had something," the shikigami said quickly. "Humans need a certain amount of magic to live, and my master was very careful to leave a small buffer. He couldn't leave much since it takes very little for the smallest spirits to rise, but the entire outer ring of spellwork you see there on the seal is dedicated to making sure the seal never sucks in that final percent of magic necessary to let humans keep their magical half while they are alive."

"What about after?" Marci asked.

Shiro winced. "There, I'm afraid things had to change. It takes only a tiny bit of magic to let humanity live, but death is far more demanding. Keeping souls together on this side requires more magic than we could allow, so we were forced to let them disperse."

"Disperse?" she repeated, her voice shaking. "As in poof? No more? You're just gone?"

"It was very peaceful," Shiro said quickly. "Much more so than the torments some Mortal Spirits would—"

"That's beside the point!" Marci cried. "You took away the afterlife from hundreds of generations! Your master *stole* that from them!"

"Yes!" he yelled back at her. "To save the living! I keep telling you, this isn't a solution we came to lightly. My master had to make a hard choice, and he chose to do whatever he could to keep humanity going."

"I understand that," Marci said. "My problem isn't that Abe no Seimei had to make a tough call in a bad situation. It's that you're asking me to do it *again*, and I won't. Not if there's even the slightest chance of a better way."

Shiro dropped his eyes after that. When Marci turned back to Myron, though, the older mage was just standing there staring at the seal.

"I didn't know," he said at last. "I had no idea there was an afterlife until..."

His voice wavered at the end, and Marci sighed. She'd grown up reading his books, but she'd despised the real-life Sir Myron Rollins almost from the moment she'd met him. He was a bombastic, pompous, cocky jerk who made terrible choices, but despite all that, he really did seem to care deeply about saving lives. That wasn't actually surprising for someone who'd spent his entire life working for the United Nations, but it was a new discovery for Marci, and for the first time since her rosy image of Sir Myron Rollins had been crushed by the real thing, she felt a flash of her old admiration.

"We're not going to let that happen again," she said, reaching out to touch his arm. "The Mortal Spirits, the gods of death, they were created by us so our souls would have someone to help them. The Empty Wind is full of people who've found peace, and those are just the forgotten. There are other faces of death, other ends. They might not all be pleasant, but any afterlife has to be better than just dissipating into nothing."

"Does it?" Myron asked, dropping his hands with a sigh. "That's what I always thought would happen to me. I thought I would die and that would be it. I'm not sure how to feel knowing there's more to it."

"It's kind of a shock," she agreed. "But however we feel about it, we don't have the right to take eternity from the people who do care."

"Perhaps," he said tiredly. "But I'm not just mourning a thousand years of lost souls. I'm also grieving for the death of our last acceptable solution. I thought if I stopped the magic, everything would go back to how it was before. Now you're telling me there's an afterlife, and if we stop the magic, we're taking that away, too. If we *don't* halt the magic, though, we still face Armageddon. The Mortal Spirit problem doesn't go away just because a few of them have side jobs shepherding our souls. We're going to be facing even bigger versions of the terrors the ancient Merlins couldn't handle. Are we supposed to just accept that as the price for not killing our own afterlife?"

"I don't know," Marci said honestly. "Every choice has consequences. The trick is to pick the one with the fallout you can live with. Or die with, as the case may be."

"There'll be a lot of that if you let the Mortal Spirits rise."

Marci gave him a scathing look. "You know, for someone who's dedicated his life to defending humanity, you sure have a low opinion of us."

"It's not an opinion," Myron said angrily. "It's fact. My work for the UN took me to countless disaster sites, everything from spirit tantrums to dragon attacks to magical terrorism. It was all horrible, but do you know which disasters were invariably the worst? The most cruel?" He leaned in closer. "The human ones. Genocide, child soldiers, school bombings, human trafficking—I've seen it all. Magic was the weapon of choice in the situations I was called to work on, but it didn't really make a difference. Cruelty is cruelty, and humans excel at it. That's why I wanted the Mortal Spirits so badly. I thought they were our better angels, and if I could just get my hands on one, I could solve so many problems. Right so many wrongs."

He heaved a long sigh. "Imagine my disappointment when I realized they were an accurate reflection. That's when I decided to end it, even if it meant teaming up with Algonquin. I'd finally realized you were right, Novalli. Mortal Spirits *are* us, and that's what terrifies me."

"But it shouldn't," she said. "Yes, people can be terrible, but so many more are decent. That matters for Mortal Spirits especially, because they're not the work of a single person. Those huge chasms are dug by our collective feelings, and if at least some of the diggers are good people, then every spirit has a positive side, even the terrifying ones. Look at the Empty Wind. He's always been terrifying, but he's still one of the best things that's ever happened to me. That might sound like a contradiction, but so is everything else about being human, which is all they are. Human, just like us. So when the bad ones come, and they *will*, we'll handle them just like we handle bad people. We'll oppose them with good ones."

Myron stared at her like she was crazy. "What are you talking about?"

"Merlins," Marci said with a grin. "I'm talking about Merlins. An army of them. Abe no Seimei sealed the magic because he got overwhelmed by the worst parts of us, the murder and war spirits and so forth. But the world has come a long way in the last thousand years. Modern humanity is more educated, more enlightened, kinder, more civil, and less violent than it's ever been. When our

Mortal Spirits rise, I have no doubt there will still be monsters of fear and violence, but we've never been more prepared to combat them as a society than we are right now."

Myron sighed. "I keep forgetting how young and optimistic you are."

"So what?" she said. "Those are good things."

He sneered. "Optimism won't beat a god."

"But the Spirit of Optimism might," Shiro said thoughtfully. "Has humanity really advanced that much?"

"I think it has," Marci said. "Universal literacy, modern medicine and agriculture, the spread of democracy, equality for women—these things bring a lot to the table. We've still got our problems, as Myron pointed out, but we're trying to fight them. That's why organizations like the UN exist: to foster peace and improve people's lives. Even when we fail at that, I'd still rather be alive right now than at any other time in history. That has to count for something."

"It does," the shikigami said, tapping his chin. "How would you build an army of Merlins?"

"Why are you asking?" Marci asked coyly. "Have you decided to come over to my side?"

"There are no sides," he said primly. "I care only for what is effective. In my master's time, that was the seal, and even he admitted that was a defeat. If the situation has changed such that we no longer need such heavy-handed measures, I am delighted to switch course. *If* it's true."

"Oh, it's true," Myron said. "I just don't know if it's enough." He glared at Marci. "Our enemies are gods. Even if we can stabilize the crack to prevent a full breakdown, they'll still be here sooner than we like. How do you propose we handle that? It's not like we can just recruit Merlins and have them ready."

"Why not?" Marci asked, glancing at Shiro. "What would you say the chances are for your average mage to become a Merlin?"

The shikigami looked offended. "Such things cannot be measured in chance."

"On a large enough scale, *anything* can be measured in chance," she said. "Just give me your best guess."

He sighed. "To be clear, I don't believe Merlins can be accounted in this way, but if I *had* to give a number, I'd say that perhaps one in a million mages is skilled, disciplined, and lucky enough to find an appropriate Mortal Spirit, forge a bond, and make it all the way through the gate."

"Fantastic," Marci said, doing the math. "So if the current world population is nine billion people, and the chances of being born a mage are roughly one in ten, that gives us approximately nine hundred million mages alive right now. If we apply your one-in-a-million guess to that number, we get nine hundred potential Merlins."

That actually didn't sound like much for a global organization, but Shiro's eyes went wide. "Nine *hundred?*"

"How many did you have before?"

"Never more than a few dozen," he said, his voice awed. "Nine hundred Merlins would be incredible."

Marci grinned. "What did I tell you? It's a brand-new ballgame. I'm not saying it'll be easy, but we are absolutely not out of this fight. I know we can make it, because no matter what Myron says, humanity's not all fear and death and war, and neither are our spirits."

Myron shook his head at that, but Shiro was staring at her with new eyes. "Now I understand why the Heart of the World let you in," he said. "You are a champion of humanity indeed, Marci Novalli."

"She's going to get humanity killed," Myron said angrily, glaring at her. "You've won over the shikigami, but I still say we should repair the seal."

"Are you crazy?" Marci cried. "Even if you don't care about the spirits or the magical animals or everything else we'll be ruining, did you miss the part where blocking off the magic will destroy our afterlife?"

"Better than destroying our living life!" he shouted back. "At least fading into nothing would be peaceful. You're talking about raising armies of Merlins so we can recruit gods to fight against other gods. Even if you can pull that off, which, for the record, I don't think you can, the results will be catastrophic. Even if you win every conflict, can you conceive of the damage a fight between spirits of that size could do? How many innocent lives would be lost? It's unthinkable. It's *irresponsible.*"

"It's still better than screwing over every magical entity on the planet," she said, glaring at him. "Trading our eternity for a little more safety right now is *not* a good bargain."

"It is if you like being alive," Myron growled. "Safety and security are not to be scoffed at. Not everyone has your cozy relationship with death."

"Why are you so convinced we can't make this work? Of all mages, I didn't expect defeatism from the great Sir Myron Rollins."

"Because you haven't had to deal with as many disasters as I have!" he yelled.

"Well, maybe that's the problem," Marci said. "You've had your face shoved into the gutter of humanity for so long, you've forgotten the great things we're capable of."

Myron looked away in disgust. "Why are you even trying to convince me, anyway?" he said bitterly. "You're the Merlin. I'm only here on your charity. Pretending you care about my opinion is an insult to us both."

"That's not true," she said, walking around the seal so that he had to face her. "This is a decision that affects everyone, especially you. You're one of the greatest living mages who also happens to be tied to the only other Mortal Spirit in existence right now. She might not be chained to you anymore, but the link between mage and Mortal Spirit is forever. Until one of you dies, that makes you the closest thing to the next Merlin we've got."

Myron's lip curled in a sneer. "Don't act like that makes you happy."

"It doesn't," Marci snapped. "You're a cynical jerk who wants to wipe out all magic because he's afraid. But you're also a mage who wants to save humanity, just like I do. That's not a lot of common ground to work with, but we have to use it, because no matter what we decide to do in the end, something has to be done about this seal before it snaps, and I can't do it on my own."

That was the bald truth. Marci was rightfully proud of her spellwork, but even in her greatest moments of hubris, she'd never claim to be as good as Sir Myron Rollins. He'd literally written the books on ancient casting languages and complex spellwork system modification, both of which were vital if they were going to have a prayer of transforming the cracked seal into something stable.

"I'm not asking you to agree with everything I say," she said gently. "I just want you to take a chance. You came here ready to give up your magic in order to save mankind. That's not something a mage would do if he weren't serious about his convictions. We disagree a lot, but in this at least, you and I are the same. We both want to fix things, so let's do it, but let's do it together."

She held out her hand to him as she finished, and Myron gave her frankly skeptical look.

"Really?"

"Really," she said sincerely. "We've got too many enemies to keep fighting each other. Now are you with me or what?"

She flashed him her best smile, the one she used to close deals, but Myron just smacked her offered hand away.

"Come *on!*" she cried. "I saved you!"

"Which entitles you to nothing," he said, crossing his arms tight over his chest. "A shikigami of the Last Merlin flat-out told you that the Mortal Spirits are going to overrun us, and you're planning to ignore him. Not because of facts, but because you *feel* different. Because you *believe* in the power of human goodness. That might make a nice inspirational poster, but it is lunacy to bet the lives of every man, woman, and child on such shoddy logic, and I refuse to ride at your side while you tilt at windmills." He kicked the broken seal with the toe of his fancy shoe. "You want to destroy the world? Do it yourself."

Marci was imagining dropping that stone seal on his head. "Why are you so stubborn? It's like you want to give up your magic!"

"What I *want* is to ensure the survival of the human race," he snarled. "You're the one who cares about magic more than people."

"But people *are* magic!" she yelled. "This isn't humans versus spirits. It's *all* of us finding a way to live together without killing each other!"

"Tell that to Algonquin," Myron said. "She's certainly made up her mind. And since you were right about me still being bound to the DFZ, I might as well tell you that she's already back in her city, and it is not a happy homecoming. She and Algonquin are determined to tear each other apart, which means the chaos I warned you about is already happening. You could stop it if you cared to. I'd gladly help you repair the seal and shut all this down for good, but that's not what you want. You want to fight. You want to have it all, even if it means people die. I can't allow that, so unless you change your mind, we have nothing further to discuss."

He turned away after that. Marci turned her back on him as well, grinding her teeth as she fought the urge to throw him off the mountain. Julius made this turning-enemies-into-allies stuff look so easy when he did it, but Myron must have been more stubborn than a dragon, because she was getting nowhere. She just didn't understand how such a smart man could be so cynical and shortsighted. If he weren't the only other mage here, Marci would have written him off completely. She didn't need this nonsense.

Unfortunately, she *did* need his help. Even if Amelia could translate the words, the crazy spellwork on the seal was way outside Marci's area of expertise. If nothing else, she needed another pair of hands to maintain the circle that would hold the magic steady while she made changes. Myron might not be able to change the spellwork here, but he could still move magic, and unlike her, he could actually read what the spell did. That was kind of important when you were trying to modify a spell where a single mistake could send a thousand years of magic cascading down on an unsuspecting world.

There was nothing for it. She needed him, and since appealing to Sir Myron's reason and better nature was clearly a waste of time,

Marci decided to try a different approach. "How about we make a deal?"

Myron glanced suspiciously over his shoulder.

"I get that you don't want anything to do with this," she went on. "But the seal still has to be stabilized. I can't do that on my own, so how about you help me figure out a way to jury-rig this thing into letting out magic at a safe, sustainable rate, and in return, I will build you an emergency shut-off."

"You mean like a kill switch?" he said, turning back around.

"*Exactly* like a kill switch," she said. "I'll even let you design it so you can be certain it works. This way, I can do my thing, and if you're right about it destroying humanity, you've got something you can hit to shut things down anytime you want."

For a moment, Myron looked as if he was actually giving the idea serious consideration, and then he scowled.

"I see your trick," he said bitterly. "You're letting me build a kill switch because you know I won't be able to use it. Even if you made me a big red button right on top, I wouldn't be able to push it, because only Merlins can manipulate spellwork in the Heart of the World, and I'm not a Merlin."

"Of course there's a trick," Marci said with a smile. "I'm offering you a deal, not a surrender. Why would I let you build a kill switch if I knew you were just going to mash it the first moment you could? No, no." She wagged her finger. "Here's my part of the deal. I will let you make a kill switch, *but* you're going to have to become a Merlin yourself if you want to push it."

Myron stared at her, uncomprehending. "A Merlin?"

Marci, Ghost growled in her mind. *What are you doing? You can't make him a Merlin. He wants to destroy us.*

"But that's just it," she whispered back, keeping her eyes on Myron. "I can't 'make' him a Merlin. The Heart of the World decides that, not me, and that's why this is going to work. Think about when the gate let me in. It didn't open because I was a hotshot mage with a Mortal Spirit. I was only let in after I freed the DFZ, because that was when I'd proved I understood that Merlins are champions for *all* of humanity. Spirits and ghosts included, not just the physical people alive right now. That's why I can build Myron a kill switch, because if he can understand that truth to the point where the Heart of the World opens to him, then he'll no longer be the sort of man who wants to push it."

That didn't stop the other Merlins, the Empty Wind argued. *They were the ones who made the seal in the first place.*

"And considered it their greatest defeat," she said, raising her voice so that Myron could hear too. "I know it's a gamble, but it's a safe one, because I'm *right*. If Myron can become a Merlin on his own merit, then I won't have to say a word. He'll understand for himself just how foolish and cowardly he's being, or he won't be a Merlin at all."

The older mage sneered. "And if I refuse?"

"You won't," Marci said confidently. "Refusing would mean you've given up on becoming a Merlin entirely, and I don't believe that for a second. You might have lost your shot at being the first, but this is still something you've wanted all your life. There's no way you're giving it up now. Not when you're so close."

That, at last, seemed to get through. "I'll *never* give up," he said firmly. "I deserve to be a Merlin."

"Great," Marci said. "If you can dump that sense of entitlement, you might just make it. In the meanwhile, how about translating this seal? Because I have no idea where to start."

Myron heaved a long-suffering sigh. Then, slowly, he leaned down over the seal. "For the record," he said. "I'm only doing this because I'm terrified of what you'd do in ignorance without me. The moment the crack is stabilized, though, you're taking me back to the physical world. I need to get my body back so I can find another spirit and come back here as a Merlin to do what you could not."

"Fair enough," she said. "But before you get your hopes up too high, you're not getting another spirit. First, the DFZ is the only Mortal Spirit in the world aside from Ghost right now, and second, did you miss the part where you two were bound for life?"

Myron shook his head. "I can't use her. She hates me."

"Tough," Marci said. "She's your responsibility. You raised her. You pissed her off. Now you have to clean up your mess. Or do you not believe a Merlin should be responsible for his mistakes?"

When Myron flinched, Marci knew she had him. "Just give it a chance. The DFZ is famous for being a place where people start over. Talk to her. Apologize for being a jerk. Treat her like a city instead of a monster, and I bet you'll be surprised."

He rubbed his hands over his face. "If she sees me again, she's going to kill me."

"Then you'd better make sure she has a good reason not to," Marci said, joining him by the seal. "Either way, you've already said yes, so let's get to work. I want to get this thing stable pronto so I can get back to the real world, too. I left a lot of irons in the fire when I died. The faster I get back to deal with those, the happier I'll be. And speaking of…"

She glanced at Shiro. "How *do* I travel back and forth from here to the real world? Do I click my heels together or spin widdershins or what?"

"What are you talking about?" the shikigami asked, genuinely confused. "This *is* the real world."

"I meant I want to go back to being alive," Marci clarified. "Since I was bound to a death spirit, I had to die to get over here. Now that I'm officially a Merlin, though, I'd like to remedy that. You know, get a new body, return to the physical world, all that good stuff. History's full of famous Merlins, so I know it has to be possible. How do I do it?"

"That depends," Shiro said. "Does your spirit have an aspect of rebirth?"

Marci looked at Ghost, who shook his head.

The shikigami shrugged. "Then I'm afraid there is no way back."

She froze. For a long heartbeat, Marci just stood there like a statue. Then she exploded into motion, grabbing the shikigami's shoulders with both hands as she shrieked, "*What?*"

CHAPTER ELEVEN

Finding Chelsie was never an easy task. Even when you thought you knew where she was, she had a bad habit of vanishing whenever your back was turned. This was why, even though he'd just left her in Bob's room, the first thing Julius did when he reached the mountain was pull out his phone to message Fredrick.

And was immediately rewarded. He'd barely hit send before Fredrick messaged back that he and Chelsie had retreated down the mountain to her room in the basement. Thanking him profusely for saving him a long and pointless climb, Julius started down the stairs, using his years of experience in hiding from his family to avoid all the emperor's dragons and servants as he made his way down to Chelsie's lair in the mountain's roots.

Fredrick was waiting when he got there, camped out on the narrow couch in Chelsie's cramped library where Marci had slept the one night she'd spent here. He rose to his feet when Julius walked in, his false-green eyes worried. "What's wrong?"

Julius didn't have time to explain Ian's ultimatum, so he got right to the point. "Where's Chelsie?"

"Asleep," the F replied, tilting his head toward the closed bedroom door. "And before you ask, I wouldn't suggest waking her."

"But this is an *emergency*."

"So is this," he said, crossing his arms over his chest. "Chelsie's a bad sleeper on her good days. Exhausted as she is right now, she'll take your head off before she realizes what's going on."

314

Julius scowled. Fredrick was always so dry, it was impossible to tell if he was being serious or not. Given that Chelsie herself had warned Julius multiple times never to wake her up, though, he was leaning toward *not*. He was trying to come up with a plan that would let him get to Chelsie while still keeping his head on his shoulders when Fredrick threw something at him.

Julius caught it by instinct. "What's this?" he asked, examining the object in his hand, which looked and felt like a small brick that had been shrink-wrapped in white plastic.

"Emergency rations," the F replied apologetically. "I know it's not ideal, but the Golden Emperor's servants have taken over all the kitchens. After what happened with the Empress Mother, I don't trust them not to try and poison us, so I dug into Chelsie's stash."

He wasn't surprised at all to hear Chelsie had a stash of emergency rations. She probably had ten years' worth of everything a dragon could need squirreled away down here. Given the dust in the plastic's wrinkles, the ration in his hands was probably older than him. Unappetizing as that was, though, now that the subject of food had been broached, his stomach was pointedly reminding him that he hadn't eaten since breakfast, and freeze-dried food was a lot better than nothing.

"Thank you," he said, ripping the plastic open.

Fredrick smiled. "I believe that's my line. It seems I owe you another debt. Thanks to you, my clutch has a history for the first time in our lives. After six centuries of being Bethesda's shame, we have a lineage with a mother and a father we can be proud of."

"That wasn't me," Julius said, biting a chunk off of the tasteless, rock-hard ration. "You'd already figured out all the dots. I just happened to be there when they connected."

"But you were the one who convinced Chelsie to own them," Fredrick countered. "You got her to talk, which is more than I could ever do. You'd already freed us from being servants, but with this, you've freed us from Heartstriker as well, and for that we can't thank you enough."

He said this with absolute sincerity, but Julius was staring at him in horror. "Wait," he said at last, swallowing the hard lump of ration. "What do you mean 'freed us from Heartstriker?' You're not leaving, are you?"

"Why would we stay?" Fredrick asked, his not-quite-green eyes staring straight into Julius's. "We were servants in this mountain for six centuries. To most Heartstrikers, that's what we'll always be. We were already dreading the fight for our rightful position as an upper-alphabet clutch, especially since we suspected we weren't actually Bethesda's children, but now we don't have to worry about any of that. Thanks to you, we're no longer the lowest clutch in Heartstriker, but the first clutch of the Golden Emperor."

"We still don't know how he's going to take that."

"It doesn't matter how he takes it. It's the truth. Even if he's furious, unless the Qilin is ready to disavow us—and I think you'll agree the dragon we met this morning is far too honorable for that—he has no choice but to welcome us as his children." Fredrick broke into an excited grin. "Don't you see? In one stroke, we've gone from servants in our own home to royalty. The children of an emperor! Do you know how much that will mean to my brothers and sisters? How much it means to me?"

Julius did *now*. The truth had come out so quickly earlier, he hadn't stopped to think about what these revelations would mean to the dragons of F-clutch. He hadn't even considered the idea that they would leave, which was ridiculous in hindsight. Who'd want to stay and fight for recognition in the clan that had always treated them like trash when they could have a new start as the children of an emperor? Assuming the backlash of the Qilin's luck didn't kill them all, Julius could easily see Xian being over the moon to discover he had children. Once he got over his shock, he'd probably welcome all of them with open arms, and to his shame, Julius wasn't sure how he felt about that.

He *should* have been delighted. Ever since he'd learned the truth of their situation, he'd been fighting to free F-clutch, and what better future could he wish for them than one full of love and stability? At the same time, though, Julius had been really been looking forward to having at least one faction of Heartstrikers who didn't view him only as a tool. He was also afraid of losing Chelsie, because if the Fs left, she would too, and why not? With the exception of Julius, their entire family hated and feared her. Without her children, she had no reason to stay, and selfish as it was, that made Julius incredibly sad. All of it did. Even if the cause was happy this time, he was so *sick* of losing the ones he cared about.

He was still trying to work through that tangled knot of emotion when his phone went off in his pocket. *Loudly*, which was strange since he distinctly remembered muting it. Once the ringtone made it past the first three notes, though, he understood why. His phone was playing the Imperial March from *Star Wars*, which was the ringtone he'd assigned to the Unknown Caller.

Bob's number.

Julius threw his half-eaten ration on the ground, grabbing the phone from his pocket as fast as he could. When the AR display popped up, though, he saw that it wasn't actually a phone call. Bob had sent him a picture. A selfie, to be precise, and a bad one. His face was hardly in the shot at all. Instead, the focus was on the landscape behind him, which was one Julius realized with a jolt that he recognized. Bob was standing in the dirt lot under the Chance Street Skyway, just a couple blocks away from Julius and Marci's old house in the DFZ. He was racking his brain over why Bob would send him a picture like this when the phone was snatched out of his hand.

There'd been no sound of a door opening, no footsteps on the stone floor, but given whose rooms they were in, Julius wasn't surprised at all when he looked up to see Chelsie standing next to him with his phone clutched in her hands and a killer's terrifying snarl on her face.

"Found you," she growled.

"Chelsie, *wait*," Julius said. "Let's not jump to—"

But when had she ever listened? His phone clattered to the ground, flung from Chelsie's hands as she lashed out at the empty space between them. Dragon magic followed the movement like a razor, slicing the air open like a claw through blubber before she dove into the gap, disappearing right in front of his eyes.

"*No!*"

Julius lunged after her, but all his reaching hands caught was empty air as the rip snapped shut again. When it was obvious she was really gone, he whirled on Fredrick. "What was *that?*"

"She teleported," the F said grimly.

Julius had figured out that much already. "But how? She doesn't have her Fang." She hadn't been carrying a weapon at all. Julius didn't even think she'd been wearing shoes.

"She doesn't need the Fang anymore," Fredrick said proudly. "In case you couldn't tell from all the wards she put on this place, my mother's not a bad mage, and she used that Fang for six hundred years. That's more than enough time for any reasonably clever dragon to reverse-engineer a spell."

Julius still couldn't believe it. "You mean Chelsie's been able to teleport on her own this *entire time?*"

"How else do you think she manages to be everywhere at once?" Fredrick said with a shrug.

That would explain a few things. "So she can teleport at will to anyone in the family?"

"No, that part *was* the sword," Fredrick said. "As a relic of the Quetzalcoatl, the Defender's Fang is directly connected to Heartstriker's clan magic, and all of us through it. On her own, Chelsie can only cut to places she knows, and she can't transport others. Without a blade, the holes she cuts are only big enough for her, and only if she's fast."

"But she *could* teleport to the DFZ?"

"Easily," Fredrick said. "But don't worry. Sword or no sword, she won't lose to Bob."

"That's not what I'm worried about," Julius said, reaching down to grab his phone off the floor.

The seer's picture was still on the screen. Julius flicked it away, pulling up his news feed instead. Sure enough, the ongoing evacuation of the DFZ was the top story on every network, followed by warnings about the unprecedented elevation of ambient magic levels.

"This is bad," he muttered, turning the screen so Fredrick could see. "I don't know what or why, but something terrible is about to happen, and Bob just lured Chelsie right into the middle of it."

Fredrick's face went pale. "When did this happen?"

"Just a few hours ago," Julius said. "I only found out because Ian came home, but the whole world's going nuts about it. That's why this is all so suspicious. Bob's been avoiding Chelsie since I freed her. Now he pops up just in time to lure her into the heart of the biggest magical upheaval since the night it first returned? There's no *way* that's coincidence."

"Nothing with seers is coincidence," Fredrick agreed. "But what's he trying to do?"

"I don't know," Julius said angrily. "But I'm pissed he used me to do it." He scowled at the terrifying headlines calling for people all over North America to seek shelter. "We have to stop him. This is too dangerous. I don't care if he can see the future. If he plays chicken with whatever Algonquin's doing, he's going to get someone killed."

"He already got someone killed," Fredrick reminded him.

"That's why I need to go," Julius said, whirling toward the door. "I already lost Amelia to this. I'm not losing anyone else."

He was halfway down the hall before Fredrick grabbed his sleeve. "Maybe that's why you shouldn't."

"*What?*"

"The Black Reach said the best way to foil Bob's plans was not to do what he asked," Fredrick explained. "He may not be directly giving you orders, but Bob sent that picture to *your* phone, not Chelsie's. He has all of her numbers, even the secret ones. He could have easily sent that picture to her directly. The fact that he didn't means he must have wanted *both* of you to know that he was in the DFZ."

Julius stared at him in confusion. "How do you know what the Black Reach told me?"

"The door was very thin," Fredrick said with a shrug.

"You *eavesdropped* on me?"

"How am I supposed to serve you if I don't know what's going on?" Fredrick snapped. "Of course I listened. Better than you did, apparently, because I remember that the last thing the Black Reach said was 'See you in Detroit.' He knew Bob would lure you there, which tells me that you *shouldn't go.*"

That was a good point. Still. "I can't let Chelsie go into that alone," Julius said. "The DFZ's more dangerous than ever, and she's too angry to make good decisions. She needs our help, and if Bob really is headed down some kind of dark path, then so does he. We can't just sit here and do nothing!"

"I'm not saying we should," Fredrick said. "But you should have more faith in Chelsie's ability to take care of herself. Brohomir is older and a seer, but he's never been a fighter, *and* he stole her egg. Chelsie is Heartstriker's most deadly dragon, and I've never seen her as angry about anything as she's been over this. If Bob gets in her way, she'll gut him like a fish, and why would he risk that?"

"Why would he do *any* of this?"

"To lure *you!*" Fredrick yelled, grabbing Julius by the shoulders. "Haven't you been listening? You're his focus. Whatever power play Bob's making, you are undoubtedly at the heart of it, which is exactly why you need to stay away from this. He's not luring Chelsie. He's using her to lure *you,* and if you believe the Black Reach, then the only way to stop this is not to go."

That argument made a tremendous amount of sense, but Julius couldn't follow it. The image of Amelia's ashes piled on her divan was burned into his brain, and she was the one Bob had loved most. If he was willing to kill the sister who'd been a mother to him for his plots, what would he do to Chelsie? He'd known everything, and he'd been perfectly fine with leaving Chelsie and her children in slavery for six hundred years. Surely he wouldn't stop at killing her now if that was what it took, and as good as Chelsie was, no one could beat a seer.

"I have to go."

Fredrick bared his teeth. "Why?"

"Because I'm not losing anyone else!" Julius cried, yanking out of his grip. "It doesn't matter who wins. If Chelsie fights Bob, we lose." And he was so *sick* of losing. He had no idea what choice was right, what he should do. It was all just plots inside of plots, spiraling down forever. Bob was obviously pulling his strings, but Julius was too angry to fight it. He was sick of death, sick of tragedy. If Bob was counting on him to try and save Chelsie, then Julius was going to play right into his hands. He'd lost too much to do anything else.

"We're going to the DFZ."

Fredrick growled deep in his throat, but Julius didn't give him a chance. "My mind's made up," he said as he marched out of Chelsie's bunker. "I know this is a seer plot, I know I'm falling for it, and I don't care. I won't sit here and play the long game while my family kills each other."

"But what are you going to do?" Fredrick asked, running after him. "Chelsie can teleport. We can't. Even if Ian's brought the sub-orbital jet back, flying to the DFZ will take—"

"I know," Julius said, picking up speed as he ran down the Fs' hall and into the stone tunnel that led to the stairs. "But I'm not going to fly."

"Then where *are* you going?"

Julius flashed his nephew a grim smile over his shoulder. "To see if I can't get lucky."

Fredrick's face paled, but if he had more to say, Julius didn't hear it. He was already bounding up the spiral service stairs toward the top of the mountain.

● ● ●

Though knowingly walking into a seer's trap might suggest otherwise, Julius wasn't stupid. He knew exactly how big a bullet he'd dodged when Chelsie had saved him and Fredrick in the hallway. So, since it wasn't likely the Empress Mother had changed her mind about killing him in the last hour, Julius decided to try the diplomatic approach: grabbing one of the emperor's human servants off the stairwell and calmly but firmly refusing to let the man go until he called Lao.

"You have a lot of nerve," the emperor's cousin growled over the phone when Julius identified himself. "Can you even comprehend how much trouble you've caused?"

"Nothing like what's going to happen if you don't let me talk to him."

He didn't even realize how terrible that sounded until Lao snarled, "Is that a threat?"

"No, it's an emergency," Julius said quickly, scrubbing a hand through his hair. "Look, I've got some information he's going to want to know, but it's not the sort of thing I can explain over the phone, and I can't go up there with the empress trying to kill me. I just need you to let me talk to him for five minutes without dying."

The blue dragon sighed, and then there was a click as he put Julius on hold. Thirty seconds later, Lao's voice snapped back into his ear. "Come up."

"What about the empress?" Julius asked nervously. "Can you send us an escort to make sure we don't get beheaded on the way or—"

"You don't have to worry about the Empress Mother," Lao said, his voice hurried. "Just get up here. The Qilin will see you in the throne room."

He hung up after that, leaving Julius staring at the terrified servant's phone in confusion. "What was that about?"

"A trap would be my guess," Fredrick said, looking up the open stairwell. "But at this point, what isn't?"

"No way to know except to try," Julius said, putting a hand on the place where his sword should have been before remembering he'd left it upstairs. One more reason to go back. "Let's go see how far we can get."

Fredrick scowled, but he followed Julius up to the very top, where the spiral servant stair discreetly ended behind the elevator at the end of the now-empty Hall of Heads. When the hidden doorway slid open, though, two red dragons were waiting on the other side.

Julius froze, eyes going wide in surprise and fear. Fredrick was far more sensible. He grabbed the door, yanking Julius back into the stairwell as he slammed it shut on their enemies. He was about to lock it when one of the red dragons ripped the sliding door off its track and threw it aside. Julius was preparing to jump down the stairwell's open center to get away when Lao pushed his way to the front.

"It's all right," the blue dragon said quickly, scowling at his fellow imperial dragons. "The clans of Mongolia obey the emperor."

The two red dragons nodded, though they still looked like they were waiting for a reason to rip Julius and Fredrick apart as Lao ushered the Heartstrikers back into the hallway.

"Come," he said, walking toward the throne room at a speed mortals would have called a run. "The emperor is not accustomed to being kept waiting."

Julius didn't have to be told twice. He sprinted after Lao, blowing past the two red dragons with Fredrick right behind him, reaching Lao's side just as he threw open the throne room doors to reveal the Qilin sitting alone on the white-jade half of the two-seated golden dragon throne.

The moment he saw the emperor, Julius knew it was bad. Even with his veil down again, the angry hunch of the emperor's shoulders said volumes. He actually looked even more upset than he had when he'd told Julius to leave, clutching the engraved arms of his throne as he waited impatiently for Julius and Fredrick to take their places.

"Thank you for seeing us again so quickly," Julius said.

"Lao said it was an emergency," the Qilin said, his deep voice clipped and sharp. "Though I should warn you, this is not a good time. My mother has gone missing, and I am anxious to find her."

Julius blinked. "Missing? Are you sure?"

"*Yes*, I'm sure," the Qilin snarled. "You think I don't know where my empress is?"

Considering that was the entire problem, obviously not, but Julius didn't have to say a word. The Qilin just growled and moved on, leaning hard on one arm of his throne as he tried to explain. "I don't keep tabs on her specifically, but my mother has always been the one tied closest to my luck. Whenever I wanted her, she would appear, even before I knew I desired her company. This time, though, she hasn't."

"I'm sure she's fine," Julius said. "I just saw her here an hour ago." And really, how far could the old dragon hobble in an hour? "But this is urgent. I—"

"You don't understand," the emperor snapped. "My mother *needs* me. She sacrificed nearly all of her fire to give me life, and what little she has left relies on my luck to remain stable. If we were safe at home, it wouldn't be an issue, but in enemy territory, as I am now—"

The mountain rumbled, and the emperor stopped, his chest rising as he took a deep breath.

"Again, not a good time," he said when the shaking finally stopped. "Unless you're here to tell me where my mother is, it's probably better if you deal with your emergency on your own."

"I'm afraid we can't," Julius said, taking a deep breath of his own. Here went nothing. "We need your help."

The Qilin laughed. A deep, mirthless sound. "You can't be serious."

Julius stared hard into the golden veil so the emperor could see just how serious he was. "Chelsie's in trouble."

The emperor slumped back in his throne. "Of course she is," he growled, pressing his hand hard against his veiled forehead. "What else would she be? But you already know how to solve this problem. Surrender, embrace my rule, and—"

"I would at this point if I thought it'd do any good," Julius said. "But this is no longer something we can solve with broad strokes. My sister's gone to the DFZ, and I'm afraid—"

"The DFZ?" The emperor's head shot up. "But terrible things are happening there."

"I know," Julius said, frustrated. "Why do you think I'm here?"

"Why did you let her *go*?" the Qilin snapped back.

"I don't *let* Chelsie go anywhere," Julius reminded him. "She's free to do what she wants now, and she never listened to me even when she wasn't. Anyway, she's not there because she likes it. She was lured by Bob."

The emperor tilted his head in confusion. "Bob?"

"He means Brohomir, Great Seer of the Heartstrikers," Fredrick explained quickly. "Bob is his family name."

The golden dragon seemed baffled. "Why would one of the three seers want to be called—" He shook his head. "You know, never mind. It's not important. Why is Chelsie chasing your seer?"

Julius bit his lip. That was as good an opening as he was ever likely to get to tell the Qilin that Chelsie was chasing down the last remaining egg of the clutch she'd made with him, but the timing couldn't be more wrong. The Qilin was already extremely upset, and while the truth would certainly get him moving, telling him the real reason Chelsie had run all those centuries ago now might be the straw that broke the dragon's back. It certainly didn't play to Julius's plan to break things gently, so he settled for a half-truth instead.

"Bob stole something very precious to her," he said, keeping his voice earnest and even. "He knows she'll stop at nothing to get it back, and he used that to get her to chase him into the DFZ. Why or for what purpose, I don't know, but the DFZ is the last place any dragon should be right now."

"I don't disagree," the Golden Emperor said. "But what you're saying makes no sense. Brohomir is the Great Seer of the *Heartstrikers*. Why would he work against you?"

"Again, I don't know," Julius said honestly. "There's a good chance this is all part of his master plan for our clan, but that's actually what scares me the most. He might be our seer, but I've seen Bob in action enough now to know that his idea of acceptable sacrifices doesn't match mine. He's already killed one of my sisters for his plots. I'm worried Chelsie is next."

Saying those words out loud felt like betrayal. No one was more aware of just how much he owed to Bob than Julius was. The changes he'd made in his family, the battles he'd won, the fact that he was still alive to keep pushing—it was all thanks to his brother. That constant support had earned the seer Julius's blind faith in a lot of things, but when Bob had asked him not to free Chelsie, Julius had finally seen the line that divided them. That had *always* divided them. The same line Bob himself had warned him about every time he'd reminded Julius that he wasn't nice.

"When I overthrew my mother, I swore I'd never let anyone in my family be thrown away ever again. That applies to Bob, too. Even if this is all part of a plot to make a better future, what's the point if we have to throw away our family to get there? Even if I'm wrong about Bob, Chelsie's mad enough to kill him right now, and I can't let that happen. I don't want *anyone* to die, especially not to another Heartstriker, so please. *Please.*"

He clasped his hands in front of him. "You already came all this way for Chelsie's sake. Help me save her now. Lend me your luck, your magic, your fastest jet—*anything*. Just help me do *something* before it's too late."

He was begging by the time he finished, pleading so shamelessly, any proper dragon would have been appalled. But Julius had never been a proper dragon, and he'd never had much use for pride. If it would have gotten him to the DFZ faster, he would have crawled on his belly. He was about to try it when the Emperor heaved a long sigh, reaching up to remove the golden veil from his face so he could look Julius eye to golden eye. "I can't."

"Why not?" Julius demanded.

"Because it's not my problem," the Qilin said calmly, rising from his throne. "If you want to surrender, then we can—"

"How is this not your problem?" Julius cried over him. "Chelsie's the entire reason you came here! How can you abandon her?"

"*Because I swore I wouldn't do this again!*"

The emperor's shout was still echoing when the mountain began to shake again. Unlike before, though, this was no tremor. The throne room rocked under Julius's feet, splitting open the patched cracks left in the floor from the battle with Estella. Cracks spread through the ceiling as well, setting the empty chains that had once held the Quetzalcoatl's skull swinging wildly. One actually snapped, crashing to the floor directly behind Julius. If he hadn't been so quick on his feet, the giant metal chain would have landed on top of him. He was on the watch for more projectiles when the shaking stopped as suddenly as it had begun, and he looked up to see the Qilin hunched over on his throne with his head clutched in his hands.

He was so still, he looked even more like a statue than the golden dragon he was sitting on. He didn't even seem to be breathing when the emperor suddenly slumped over the arm of his throne, his whole body shaking.

"You should leave," he panted, his perfect face pale and beaded with sweat. "I'm not...I am not calm right now."

"That's okay," Julius said. "I'm not calm, either."

"So I've noticed," the emperor said. "But when you get upset, you don't do *this*." He waved his hand angrily at the broken floor, but Julius just kept shaking his head.

"I don't care if you wreck the throne room. I just want your help."

"How do you not understand yet?" the emperor cried, shooting to his feet. "I *want* to help you. If I were anyone else, we would already be on the way, but I'm *not*. I'm the Qilin, the good fortune that upholds the Golden Empire and the *bad* fortune that will destroy it if I fail in my duty. I learned that the hard way because of your sister once before. I will not put my empire through it a second time."

"Then why are you here?" Julius demanded. "Why are you bothering us at all if you won't help Chelsie when she needs it?"

"Because I can't!" Xian shouted, his golden eyes flashing with a terrible light. "I came here because I thought that I'd found a way to cheat the system. I thought if I conquered Heartstriker and put Chelsie under my luck, I could keep her safe without having to…without being weak. But obviously I can't." His eyes flicked to the damaged floor again, and he sank back down to his throne in defeat. "I should never have come."

"But you *did*," Julius growled, glaring at him. "You came here. You conquered our clan. You put this pressure on us. You did all of that because you didn't want Chelsie to die. Now she's in real trouble, and you're going to turn your back on her because you're afraid?"

The emperor's jaw clenched. "Yes."

"I don't believe you."

"You should," the Qilin growled, glaring down with a rage Julius had never seen. "I've made no secret of the love I have for your sister, but an emperor's life does not belong to him alone. The last time I was selfish, my empire paid the price. Now you're telling me to do it again, and you have the nerve to question my sincerity when I tell you no?"

"Yes," Julius said. "Because I don't think you're saying it to be a good emperor." His eyes narrowed. "I think you're scared."

"Of *course* I'm scared!" the Qilin cried. "You've seen what I can do!"

As if on cue, a large chunk of the damaged ceiling chose that moment to fall, crashing to the ground directly between them. Julius jumped out of the way with room to spare, but when he looked up again, the emperor was hunched over his throne, defeated.

"You see?" he said miserably, looking down at the rubble. "It's always like this. Even when I'm calm, I'm afraid, because I know the moment I get upset, I'll destroy everything. When your sister left me, we had earthquakes every day for a year. All of Nanjing burned down. *Twice.* My maternal aunt, Lao's mother, died of a heart attack after she mentioned Chelsie's name in my presence. Dragons don't even *get* heart attacks, but I gave her one. I caused it all, disaster after disaster, misery after misery, on and on and *on.*"

He buried his face in his hands. "I can't risk that again. You're right when you say I love your sister, but that's the problem. Love brought me lower than anything else before or since, and when the Qilin goes down, he takes everything else with him. That's the truth of being the Golden Emperor, and it's why I can't help you now. Because no matter how much I love her, I can't fix this problem, and I have no right to drag my empire through the mud with me again."

He said that like it was the end. Like there was nothing more that could ever be said, but Julius shook his head. "You're wrong."

The emperor looked up. "What?"

"You're wrong," Julius repeated sadly. "Everyone calls you a luck dragon, but the more I learn about you, the more I realize you're actually the opposite. You're not lucky. You're cursed, in a lot of ways. Your whole empire is built around capitalizing on your magical good fortune, but that fortune's only good when you're happy, and *no one's* happy all the time. You go on and on about how it's your responsibility to stay serene and bring good fortune to your people while overlooking the fact that it is utterly *ir*responsible to bet the fate of twenty dragon clans, hundreds of millions of humans, all the land in China, and now *Heartstriker* on the happiness of one dragon. Especially since you don't even seem to be getting your fair share of the deal."

"That's absurd," the Qilin said dismissively.

"Is it?" Julius crossed his arms stubbornly over his chest. "When was the last time you were actually happy?"

The emperor's jaw tightened. "I endeavor always to maintain the serenity—"

Julius held up his hand. "I didn't say serenity. I asked about happiness. When was the last time you actually enjoyed being *you?*"

"I can't remember," the Qilin said irritably. "But that's not the point."

"It's the *entire* point!" Julius cried. "You've been telling me since you got here about how it's your responsibility to bring good fortune. That your all-powerful luck would rain down blessings and protection on us if we'd only agree to join you. But that's not what I've observed. From what *I've* seen so far of how your empire runs, it's mostly about avoiding the consequences of your *un*happiness."

He pointed over his shoulder at the closed throne room doors, where Lao was presumably still waiting on the other side. "Your cousin, your mother, the ones that you should trust most, they all treat you like you're a living nuclear weapon, and they're *right*. You're a disaster waiting to happen, because no one's life, not even the Golden Emperor's, is devoid of suffering. Being alive means being unhappy at points, and yet the entire Golden Empire is based on the idea that you're somehow exempt from that. You've built your entire civilization on a fallacy! The very concept of an eternally serene Golden Emperor sets an impossible standard, and you've bought into it. You tell yourself you're just being responsible, just staying calm, but the reality is that you've become so afraid of your own magic, you'd rather let the love of your life go into danger alone than risk making yourself upset."

His words echoed off the cracked walls, but the Qilin said nothing. Julius wasn't even sure if the emperor was listening anymore. He just sat there on his throne with his head down and his fists clenched, and the longer Julius watched him, the more his heart went out to the Qilin.

"I know how tempting it is to give up your own happiness for others," he said gently. "*Believe me*, I know, but that kind of thing only goes so far. It might seem good and noble, but there's a point where self-sacrifice becomes a liability, not a gift, and I think you passed that a long time ago. You've spent so much of yourself trying to be a good emperor, it's left you with nothing of your own. No happiness. No hope. No love. Since you arrived, I've heard the story of how you're the most powerful Qilin ever born over and over, but what's the point of all that power if you can't use it to save the one you love?"

"Because it isn't *my* power," the Qilin said, looking up at last. "I have responsibilities. Dragons who depend on—"

"You have dragons who are perfectly capable of taking care of themselves," Julius said. "They're *dragons*! Every other clan in the world survives without the Qilin's luck. It's perfectly possible to live a long, fulfilling life without the blessing of a magical emperor, so maybe it's time you stopped worrying so much about your dragons and started worrying about *you*. What do *you* want? What makes *you* happy? And before you dismiss that as selfish, I think there's a lot of evidence that a happy Qilin would do his empire a lot more good than one that's merely calm. If nothing else, whatever damage you cause now by going to save Chelsie will be minuscule compared to the fallout of knowing you could have saved her but were too afraid to try."

The Qilin closed his eyes with a sigh. "What you say makes sense," he admitted. "But I don't know if that's because you're actually right, or because I want to believe you so badly, I'm willing to twist logic."

"Why can't it be both?" Julius asked. "Not to sound like a stereotypical Heartstriker, but what's the good of being emperor if you can't do what you want now and again?"

Pale as he still was, Xian actually smiled a tiny bit at that. "I lied to you before," he said. "When you asked about the last time I was happy. I do remember. It was when I was with your sister. With Chelsie." His smile widened. "She also wasn't afraid to argue with me."

Julius smiled back. "Heartstrikers aren't known for being meek."

"No, you're not," the emperor agreed. "But that's what I liked about her. She wasn't afraid of upsetting me, wasn't afraid of anything. I used to think that was reckless. Now, I wish I'd been reckless, too. How much of this could have been avoided if I'd acted differently?"

"We'll never know," Julius said. "But it's not too late. Before Bob lured her out, I'd convinced her to meet you."

The emperor's eyes went wide. "You did?"

"You're not the only one who's been bottling things up for centuries," Julius said smugly. "She wanted to talk, or at least make a start, but then Bob called and everything went wrong. She teleported to the DFZ, and—"

"She can teleport?" the Qilin said, amazed.

"It was news to me, too," Julius assured him. "But that's not important. What matters is that Chelsie's alone with Bob *right now* in the middle of whatever mess is going on in the DFZ. If you want to get a chance to talk to her, then we need to get there, too. Before things get worse."

The Qilin lowered his eyes. He was clearly on the edge, but Julius could almost see the centuries of fear hanging from his neck like millstones, all the years of hard lessons that had made him a prisoner of his uncontrollable luck. If things had been less dire, he would have stepped back and left the emperor to figure it out on his own. There was no time, though, so Julius decided to give it one final push.

"If you weren't a luck dragon, would you go to her?"

"Of course," the emperor said without hesitation. "But—"

"Then do it," Julius said, holding out his hand. "Your luck is supposed to make you happy, right? Make it earn its keep. Come with me. Use that luck to find and save Chelsie. Let it do something good for a change before we miss our chance forever."

That must have been the final straw. Like a dam breaking, the Qilin let out a long sigh, and the tension that had been hanging over the room since the first earthquake melted away. "All right," he whispered, stepping down from his throne to take Julius's hand. "All right."

"Thank you," Julius said, gripping the Qilin's elegant fingers.

"Don't thank me yet," Xian said nervously, pulling back his hand to take off his heavy outer robe in favor of the lighter and more mobile, though still very golden, inner one. "I just hope she doesn't run again as soon as she sees me."

"She won't," Julius promised, secretly hoping that was true. "So any thoughts on how we can get to the DFZ in a hurry?"

The Qilin froze. "I thought you had a plan."

"Getting your help *was* the plan," Julius said with a shrug. "You're the walking miracle."

The emperor muttered something under his breath in Chinese. "You *do* know I don't control my luck?"

"But the things you want still tend to happen," Julius reminded him. "And you want to save Chelsie, right?"

"More than anything," the emperor said grimly. "Including, apparently, the safety of my clans."

"And that's why it'll work," Julius said quickly, before Xian could start talking himself back down into guilt. "If you want it, it will happen. All we have to do is wait and—"

A loud crash cut him off. Seconds later, a green dragon, one of the watchers who'd been perched on top of the mountain since the Golden Emperor's arrival, came hurtling down past the open balcony with a jut of broken rock from the mountain's peak still clutched in his claws. He righted himself quickly, but not before his snaking body crashed into the half-moon jut of stone that formed the balcony's landing, snapping it clean off.

The *crack* echoed through the desert. Outside, the dragon grabbed the broken edge of the balcony and yanked himself back up, babbling what were clearly apologies and explanations in Chinese to his emperor. Xian dismissed the whole thing with a wave of his hand, sending the embarrassed dragon scrambling back up the mountain to his post.

"Did he slip?" Julius asked when he was gone.

"Ping doesn't slip," the emperor said. "The rock he was perching on broke beneath him." And from his pained expression, Xian knew why. "We'll repair the damage, of course. I just don't understand why it happened. I'm actually calmer now than I've felt all day. I don't know why my luck is still intent on breaking your mountain."

"I don't think that's it," Julius said, breaking into a smile. "Look."

He pointed at the balcony's cracked edge. The falling dragon's impact had broken the jutting slab neatly in two. But even a clean break puts pressure on the remaining stone. Though it hadn't been hit directly, the surviving half of the broken balcony was still riddled with cracks, some of which were already crumbling. The biggest crack by far was right in the middle, a massive split that was getting wider by the second, and lying across it like a bridge over a canyon was Chelsie's sword.

If Julius had had any lingering doubts this was the Qilin's luck at work, what happened next would have buried them. The moment the emperor turned to look, the rock beneath Chelsie's discarded Fang gave way, the cracked stone crumbling dramatically from both sides to drop the sword into the desert below. It had just started to fall when Fredrick darted forward, sprinting across the throne room just in time to snatch the sword to safety.

He jumped back the moment he had it, leaping off the damaged balcony seconds before the rest of it collapsed, the broken stones clattering down the mountain. Cringing at the near miss, Fredrick palmed Chelsie's sword and backed away. He'd just gotten both feet back on the solid ground of the throne room floor when he looked back to see everyone staring at him.

"What?" he said defensively, clutching his mother's unsheathed sword to his chest. "It's an irreplaceable heirloom. I didn't want it to fall."

"Forget falling," Julius said with a grin. "Fredrick, you're holding a Fang of the Heartstriker!"

"So?" he said. "I've held it for Chelsie several times when she was injured."

Julius stared at him in confusion. "You mean it never bit you?"

"No," Fredrick said, looking nervously at the weapon in his hands. "Should it have?"

"Apparently not," Julius said happily, turning back to the emperor. "I know how we're getting to the DFZ."

Fredrick's face grew horrified as he realized what Julius meant. "No."

"Fredrick—"

"*No,*" he said again, throwing the sword to the floor at his feet. "Absolutely not. I am *not* a Fang of the Heartstriker. I refuse."

"But it's already done," Julius pointed out. "The Quetzalcoatl's Fangs bite every hand except the one meant to hold them. If Chelsie's Fang hasn't bitten you, that means her sword's already accepted you."

"Well, it can find someone else," Fredrick growled, carefully avoiding eye contact with the Qilin, who was watching the whole thing with rapt interest. "I thought I'd made it clear I want nothing more to do with this family."

"But it's your family, too," Julius said. "Like it or not, Heartstriker blood runs in your veins, and that sword was made to protect it." He pointed at Chelsie's Fang. "That's the Defender's Fang, the blade that guards the clan. Bethesda made Chelsie use it in all the wrong ways for centuries. Even so, it never bit her hand, because no matter what horrors our mother made her do, Chelsie's goal was always to protect us. That must be why it's never bitten you either, because deep down, you and Chelsie are the same."

"But I'm not like her," Fredrick said frantically. "She's the deadliest dragon in the clan. I don't even know how to hold a sword properly. Until you unsealed us, I was forbidden from touching a weapon unless I was carrying it for someone else."

"That doesn't matter," Julius said. "As I learned from my own sword, Fangs don't care about your experience. They care about your intent. Your character, not your skills, and in that, you're Chelsie's logical successor. Just like her, you've always done whatever it took to keep your family safe, even when the only way you could do that was by helping me. You're both protectors, and the Fang respects that, because it never belonged to Bethesda. It's a product of the Quetzalcoatl's magic, just like mine. That's why she could never give Fangs out to her favorites, because they weren't hers to give. The swords choose the hand that holds them, and that one's chosen you."

"But I can't use it!" Fredrick cried. "I...I might have tried once, and nothing happened."

"Because it was still serving Chelsie," Julius said confidently, nodding at the weapon on the floor. "Try it again. I bet you'll be surprised."

Fredrick blew out an angry plume of smoke. But though he clearly wanted nothing more to do with anything Heartstriker, his eyes kept going back to his mother's sword.

"What does it do?" the Qilin asked curiously, crouching down to peer at the bone-colored sword that curved like a tooth. "I'd heard

Bethesda's Shade had a special weapon, but I never found out what it did."

"Normal sword stuff, mostly," Julius said with a shrug. "But it can also teleport the wielder plus anyone they touch to any Heartstriker in the clan, no matter where they are."

"Then why aren't we using it?" the emperor said, shooting back to his feet. "That's our answer."

"Because if I accept it, I'll be tied to this clan forever," Fredrick growled. "And I don't want that."

"But you're *already* tied to us," Julius said gently. "I know Heartstriker hasn't been kind to you, and you have every right to hate us, but this is more than just our way to Chelsie. I think that you getting this sword is a stroke of good fortune for everyone. Wielding a Fang of the Heartstriker automatically makes you one of the most influential dragons in our clan. It gives you a vote on the Fang's seat of the Council, and when I step down in five years, you'll have my vote to replace me, and probably all the other Fangs' as well. If you take them, that would make you, an F, one of the three members of the Heartstriker Council."

"That won't happen," Fredrick said.

"It absolutely will," Julius said, smiling wider. "Think of it, Fredrick. You'd be a clan head! I know that doesn't make up for the last six hundred years, but as part of the Council, you'll have the power to change everything. You can help make a clan where what happened to you and your siblings can never, *ever* happen again. At the very least, that Fang gives you the power to help Chelsie, who never hesitated to help you."

Fredrick growled low in his throat. "For a dragon who claims not to like debts, you certainly know how to leverage them," he said bitterly. But angry as he clearly was, he still reached down, wrapping his hand around the Fang's hilt.

Julius didn't bother hiding his relieved breath as the F picked it up. "Thank you."

"I didn't do it for you," Fredrick growled, hefting the sword distastefully. "I owe you our freedom, but even that debt doesn't go this far. I thought nothing did, but apparently I meant it when I said I'd do anything for Chelsie." He shook his head again before turning back to Julius. "You'd better grab your own sword."

Julius nodded and ran to the door to what had been his mother's rooms, startling several servants as he raced down the hallway, grabbed his Fang, which was still right where he'd left it leaning against the wall by the sitting room door, and raced back. By the time he got back to the throne room, Fredrick was looking grimmer than ever.

"I hope your luck is running hot," the F said as he held out his arm to the emperor.

"I'm still not sure what just happened," the Qilin replied, shooting a questioning glance at Julius, who motioned for him to grab onto Fredrick. "But my luck appears to be going fine, so far as I can tell."

"Good," Fredrick said, waiting for Julius to latch on as well before he raised the sword over their heads. "Because I've never done this before."

The emperor's golden eyes went wide, but whatever he was about to say was lost in the sharp bite of dragon magic—Fredrick's, not Chelsie's—as the Fang came down, slicing cleanly through the air in front of them. That was all Julius had time to see before Fredrick dragged them through the hole, following Chelsie's scent into an empty city on the edge of bursting.

CHAPTER TWELVE

"*What do you mean I can't go back?*"

"I am sorry," Shiro said. "But I do not control these things. As Merlin, the Heart of the World is yours to use and command. In this place, you are aware and stable, possibly for a very long time. But while you are safe in this sanctuary, traversing the Sea of Magic and the barrier that divides it from the physical world has always been the sole realm of the spirits. That is the practical side of why a partnership between human and Mortal Spirit is required of every Merlin. They control the roads."

"I know that," Marci snapped. "How do you think I got here? But if Ghost can fly me around, why can't he fly me back out?"

"Because he is what he is," the shikigami said helplessly. "Ask him yourself."

Ghost flinched in her mind at that suggestion, but Marci was too panicked to read the warning. She'd already let the shikigami go and whirled to face her spirit, her body shaking in fury. "Why?" she demanded. "Why didn't you tell me I couldn't go back?"

"I'm sorry," he whispered, his voice shaking. "I needed you, and I thought...I didn't realize I was the only way."

"But you brought those other ghosts back," she argued. "Why not me?"

"Because they were different," he said, looking at her at last. "I shepherd the forgotten, Marci, and that's not you, nor should you want it to be. You've seen my true face. You know what I am. I'm the only one who remembers the souls I care for, and I can only bring them across the barrier in service of their final regrets. That's why you had to die to come here, because this is the realm of the dead, but our original problem remains. I am the Spirit of the Forgotten Dead. Unless you are both dead *and* forgotten, you are not part of my domain, and since our domains are how spirits straddle both worlds, that means I can't take you back, no matter how much I might wish to."

Marci closed her eyes with a curse. She wanted to scream at him that he was wrong. That he'd *promised* her she could go back. She couldn't even form the words, though, because they weren't true. Ghost had only promised to get her to the Merlin Gate. He'd never said anything about going back. She was the one who'd jumped to that conclusion.

She'd *assumed* Merlins could go back because she'd assumed they had to be alive to do their job. Given what Shiro had just said, though, it was apparently perfectly possible to be both dead and a Merlin, because that's what she was. Dead. Really dead. Really, *really,* doornail dead. Never-going-home dead. Never—

A sob ripped through her, sending Marci to the ground. A second gut-wrenching sob landed right on its heels, and then another and another until she was curled into a ball on the stone floor. It felt terminally unfair that this was happening when she didn't have actual tears to cry or guts to wrench, but she couldn't seem to stop.

I'm so sorry, the Empty Wind whispered in her mind, his voice desperate. *I never meant for this to happen. I should have—*

"It's not your fault," she said weakly. "I was dead either way. If anything, I'm grateful. You're the reason I'm here and not still stuck in my death. It was stupid to get my hopes up. I should have been smarter, known better. I just always thought..."

She'd thought she could go home.

From the moment she'd first woken up in the dark, that had been her prize, her reward for all this suffering. She would become a Merlin, use her fantastic powers to fix whatever was wrong, and then pop back to life so she could go home to Julius. That was the hope that had given her the strength to keep going, and now it was gone. She was a Merlin with more power than she'd ever imagined, and it didn't make a lick of difference. Even if everything worked out and she kept the magic, beat Algonquin, and forged a world where humans and spirits could live happily ever after, there was no happy ending for her. Whatever good she did, she was still just as dead as she'd been when she'd bled out in Julius's arms, and selfish as it was, that *sucked*. She wasn't ready to die. There was so much left she'd wanted to do, wanted to say. She hadn't even gotten to tell Julius goodbye.

That was the final straw. With that one thought, all of Marci's ability to keep it together fell apart, and so did she. She was painfully aware that everyone was watching her, but she couldn't stop sobbing.

It was just so unfair. Hard work and sacrifice were supposed to be rewarded. The good guys were supposed to *win*, not end like this. Not with nothing. But just as she was sinking to the lowest circle of despair, Amelia flapped down to land on the ground beside her head.

"That's enough of that," she said, folding her wings tight against her small, snaking body.

Marci turned away. "If this is about bootstraps, Amelia, I don't want to hear it."

"As if I'd sink to something so trite," the dragon said with a huff. "You're free to have all the emotional breakdowns you want, but before you wallow too deeply, you really should take the time to explore your options."

"Options?" Marci sat up, wiping her red eyes as she glared down at the little dragon. "What *options* do I have? I'm dead, and my spirit can't take me back."

"It's true the Empty Wind can't take you back because returning souls is outside of his jurisdiction," she said. "But Ghost isn't the only one here with you, is he?"

After having her hopes crushed so epically, getting them up again felt like lunacy, but Marci couldn't help it. "You can take me back?"

Amelia's grin grew painfully smug. "Who do you think you're talking to? Do you really think *I* would die without a solid exit strategy?"

Marci clutched her aching chest. "Don't do this to me, Amelia," she said angrily. "Can you bring me back to life or not?"

The dragon shrugged. "When you're playing with stakes this high, nothing's a hundred percent, but I wouldn't have gotten on this roller coaster with you if I didn't think we both had a good chance of getting off again. Bob and I—"

"Bob?" Marci said, eyes wide. "What does he have to do with this?"

"Everything," Amelia said. "Whose plan do you think this was? If all I wanted was to get a look at the magical half of this plane, I could have hitched a ride inside any old human death, but I didn't. We chose you specifically, because Bob foresaw that you and you alone could get me *here*. To the place where it all comes together."

She turned to gaze hungrily out at the wild Sea of Magic, but Marci didn't understand. "How did Bob foresee me? I'm not even a dragon. And what do you want with the Heart of the World? This is Merlin land. You can't do anything here."

"You don't have to be a dragon to get swept up in a seer's plot," Amelia said smugly. "And Bob's had his eye on you for a long time. Who do you think posted the advertisement you answered the first night you got to the DFZ? It certainly wasn't the little old lady being possessed by an angry newborn Mortal Spirit so he could feed her body to his legion of stray cats. Bob put it up because he'd foreseen that you would take the job, bind Ghost, and eventually team up with Julius."

"You're kidding," Marci said. "I mean, that's just ridiculous."

"It is not," Amelia said. "Giant chains of coincidence are how seers work, and my brother is a brilliant one. The moment he foresaw that a Mortal Spirit would rise early, Bob started maneuvering to make sure we had someone in position to catch him. Someone who would value the things *we* needed her to value, and who would take the risks *we* needed her to take." The dragon smiled at her. "You."

Marci still couldn't believe it. Ghost looked equally shocked, though the others didn't seem surprised at all.

"I *knew* you worked for dragons," Shiro grumbled.

"Not on purpose!" Marci cried, staring at Amelia in horror. "So none of it was real?"

"It was *all* real," Amelia said. "Bob pointed you at the pins, but you were the one who knocked them down. You fought all the fights and made all the hard decisions that got you to where you are, which is why my brother picked you out of all the other potential mages. He knew you had the ambition and the guts to get where we needed you to be. I did, too. That's why I gambled my life on you. Because of all the humans who had the potential to walk through that gate and become the first Merlin, *you* were the only one who'd choose not to shut the magic off again."

"Why did you even care?" Myron said, glowering. "Dragons make their own magic. You would have survived another drought just fine."

"Surviving isn't the same as thriving," Amelia snapped, giving him a dirty look before turning back to Marci. "You've been to our original plane. You know our race's tragedy better than any mortal and, sadly, most dragons. What you don't know, though, is what we were before. Before we fled to this plane, the average lifespan of a dragon was thirteen thousand years. Thirteen thousand! Can you name a dragon even half that old today?"

"No," Marci said. "But dragons don't normally make their ages public, so that doesn't mean—"

"It does in this case," Amelia said. "The reason you can't name one is because they *no longer exist.* Estella and Svena are revered as ancient dragons, but by the old standard, they're not even middle aged. If you look at our history, it's easy to blame our lowered life expectancy on clan infighting. Bethesda certainly wasn't the only dragon who killed her father for power. But dragons have *always* tried to kill their parents. The difference is that they've been uncommonly successful over the last ten thousand years. This isn't because modern dragons are cleverer, stronger, or more ruthless than previous generations. It's because old dragons like the Quetzalcoatl, who should have been unbeatably powerful, were weakened by living *here*."

She dug her little claws into the stone. "This isn't our world. We came here as refugees, and though we conquered, we never fully adapted. That's no big deal for young dragons who're still small enough to be supported entirely by their own flames, but once we achieve a certain size, fire alone won't cut it. Like every other magical creature, including humans, we need native magic to buoy us up and keep us stable. We were able to limp along before the drought, because even though we couldn't actually use the magic of this plane, we could still lean on it."

"But then it vanished," Marci said.

Amelia nodded. "We had nothing after that. Most dragons couldn't even change into their true shape during the drought, and the ones that could manage couldn't maintain it for more than a few minutes at a time. But even the trick of staying in our far less magically intensive human forms only really worked for the young and small. The truly large dragons, the ones who'd fled here from our original plane, they had to either go to sleep or find alternate sources of supplemental magic, like my grandfather and his Aztec blood sacrifices. Those who could left this plane entirely in search of greener pastures, but it was always just a crutch. Even the richest power of a foreign plane is no substitute for the magic of your home."

Marci frowned, thinking her words through. As Bethesda's daughter, Amelia had been born right before the drought hit, well after the dragons fled to this plane. But though she couldn't have lived through their loss, she still sounded as if she were speaking from personal experience, and suddenly, Marci realized why.

"That's why you were always on other planes, wasn't it? You weren't running from Bethesda. You got too big to stay."

"Don't write my mother off totally," Amelia said. "Avoiding her was a *huge* part of why I didn't come home, but I was also nearing the edge of what this world could handle."

She fluffed her smoldering feathers proudly. "You remember my impressive wingspan back on the beach? I might have mentioned this before, but thanks to the time dilation between planes, I'm a *lot* older than I should be. How much older is impossible to say since no one's ever managed to make a reliable inter-planar calendar, but my best guess is I'm actually around four thousand, give or take a century."

"That's impossible," Myron said. "That would make you the oldest dragon on Earth."

"Now that the Three Sisters are dead, I am," Amelia said matter-of-factly. "I'm older than Svena or Estella, and well big enough to have major problems with my magic. During the drought, I couldn't be on this plane for more than a few days before I started feeling dangerously drained. Now that the magic's back, I can manage a month, but it's still unpleasant. This isn't just a matter of my comfort, though. When the Merlins sealed the magic a thousand years ago, there were over a dozen ancient dragons remaining. By the time the seal broke, only the Three Sisters remained, and that was only because they'd slept through the whole thing. That's a *lot* of world-class dragons dropping dead in a relatively short period of time, and while none of them died as a direct result of the loss of magic, it's no coincidence that they were all defeated by lesser dragons who should never have had a chance of beating them, including my charming mother. That weakness is why I'm here, because unless someone does something, *that's* the future of my species."

Myron snorted. "Dying to your children?"

"Dying to a lot of things we shouldn't," Amelia said. "And while I know you don't have a problem with that, this is far more serious than a few old dragons dying before their time. It's the loss of our elders, the only dragons with the power and experience to keep the young idiots in line. Why do you think the clans have been so volatile since we got here? It's not just because there was a land grab the moment we arrived. It's because, by traditional dragon standards, we're all children. We're an entire race of young, hot-blooded fools, and when one of us *does* survive long enough to learn some sense, there's not enough magic around to sustain us, which causes us to reach for power we shouldn't in order to survive."

That didn't sound good. "What kind of power?" Marci asked.

Amelia shrugged. "Anything we can find. Blood sacrifice was a popular choice. Even during the drought, there was power in blood, but it wasn't exactly an efficient exchange. Even with an empire offering him sacrifices, the Quetzalcoatl still lost to Bethesda, and only part of that was due to her backstabbing the hell out of him. Personally, I've never cared for blood, so I made up the difference by Planeswalking to places that had magic in abundance. It worked well enough, but it was always a temporary fix, and it's not like Planeswalking's a common skill. Even Svena's never mastered it, and she's one of the greatest dragon mages in modern history, though if you ever tell her I said that, I'll have to kill you. The point is, even if I could teach everyone how to Planeswalk, dimension-hopping in search of food is no way for most dragons to live. We're stupidly territorial. We need land. We need a *home*. And since we're all already here, I've decided it's time to properly move into this one."

"How are you going to do that?" Myron said, trying and failing to hide his obvious curiosity behind a wall of academic disdain. "Dragons operate on a fundamentally different magical system. You can't just 'move into' our plane."

"But we already have," Amelia said, looking up at Marci. "Do you remember how nice your death was? How big and spacious and well furnished? Whose memories built that for you?"

"Julius's," Marci said. "But—"

"Exactly," Amelia snapped. "Julius, a *dragon*. By everything we know about magic, his memories shouldn't have done squat because, as Captain Curmudgeon here just reminded us, dragons aren't part of this world's magical mojo. Or, at least, we weren't ten thousand years ago. But that separation must be starting to blur, because as you and I both saw, Julius's memories mattered. And if a dragon's memories can help build a human death, what else can we do? The question is no longer 'is integration possible?' It's how *much* integration has already occurred, and how much further can we take it?"

By the time she finished, Marci's mind was racing. "It's absolutely possible," she said excitedly. "Magic is a natural system, and natural systems change and evolve when pushed."

"Not this much," Myron said, glaring at both of them. "This whole theory is ridiculous. Dragons have only been here for ten thousand years. That's nothing on an evolutionary time scale, especially given how slowly the dragon population turns over. There can't possibly have been any meaningful change in such a small period of time."

"But we've already seen it," Marci argued. "Amelia and I were both inside the death Julius shaped for me with his memories. How would that be possible if this isn't happening?"

"Are you sure it was him?" Myron countered. "It's no secret you were infatuated with your dragon master. Do you have any proof that it was his memories doing this and not your own wishful thinking?"

"Yes," she snapped. "Because I was *dead*, and as my *death spirit* has informed me, human deaths are holes dug into the floor of the Sea of Magic by the memories of the *living*. None of my old friends from Nevada even knew I was in the DFZ, much less knew what kind of house I lived in. Julius is the only one those memories could have come from. Plus, the whole reason I was trapped there to begin with was because I was too remembered for the Spirit of the Forgotten Dead to find me. Where were those memories coming from if not from dragons?"

"They were from dragons," Ghost confirmed. "Memories are memories no matter which head contains them. A mage who is remembered by a dragon cannot be said to be forgotten."

"And thus we see how the wires get crossed," Amelia said. "Even during the drought, dragons were part of every human culture. We filled your stories and your legends, decorated your art, and fought your heroes. Even today, you make endless video games and books and movies about us. It's dragons all the way down with you guys! And as we've firmly established, nothing moves magic like humans."

"Wait," Marci said, staring at her in wonder. "Are you saying that humans integrated your magic into ours *for* you?"

Amelia nodded rapidly. "That's exactly what I'm saying. We don't need to wait for physical evolution to naturalize us because humans have it covered. Our magical bed has already been made, so to speak, and the only reason we're not in it already is because we're still lacking a connection between our fires in the physical world and this one."

Marci's eyes went wide. "You need a spirit."

"Actually, we already have one," Amelia said, pointing a curved talon at the blue sea. "Remember what I just said about dragons being a huge part of cultures all over the world? That's a *lot* of human attention, and when a lot of humans pay a lot of attention to something, what happens?"

"You get a Mortal Spirit," Marci said immediately.

"Bingo," Amelia replied, staring at the swirling waters of the Sea of Magic with hungry eyes. "Somewhere out there, beneath one of those whirlpools, there's a giant hole created by humanity's collective idea of 'Dragons.' When that hole fills up, the magic inside will become the Spirit of Dragons, or at least humanity's idea of one. Left on its own, that wouldn't mean anything for us real dragons except trouble. Who wants a god made out of someone else's stereotypes meddling in your affairs? But if an *actual* dragon got to that hole first and exerted some good old draconic influence over the magic building up inside, you'd end up with a very different sort of spirit."

"What kind of influence?" Marci asked nervously. "Are you going to try and become its Merlin or something?"

"No way," Amelia scoffed. "Merlins are a strictly human gig. I'm a dragon." She showed her sharp teeth in a predatory smile. "I'm going to conquer it."

Everyone stared at her in horror.

"*What?*" Marci cried at last.

"You can't conquer a Mortal Spirit!" Myron said at the same time. "They're enormous, pure magic on a geologic scale. You're the size of a cat."

Amelia snorted. "As my brother would say, 'Judge me by my size, do you?' I might be little now, but I'm magic, too. Everything is on this side. That's one of the greatest things about this plane: parts is parts. Just as mages can suck down magic from anything to use in their spellwork, *I* can set fire to any magic I come in contact with. That's why I gave Marci the dragon's share of my fire. Since this isn't our world, there's no afterlife here for dragons. Once our fire's gone, that's it. We're ash. But when Marci died with my fire inside her magic, she smuggled me across the border, and then she brought me here, to the only place on this plane where I could possibly make this work." She grinned up at the spellworked sky. "The sanctuary of the Merlins."

"I *never* should have let you in," Shiro growled. "Dragons are always trouble."

"But why did you want to come *here*?" Marci asked. "The Sea of Magic I get, but only Merlins can manipulate the Heart of the World. What good is that to you?"

"None at all," Amelia said. "*If* I was here for the spellwork, which I'm not. I'm here for this." She pointed up at the blue sky. "Calm, light, not getting burned alive—that's what I'm after. Don't forget, the Sea of Magic was every bit as dark and terrible and dangerous for me as it was for you. It's all well and good to know there's a hole out there in the shape of a dragon waiting for me to claim it, but if I had to bumble around in the dark looking for it, the Sea of Magic would chew me up before I got close. From up here, though, I can look for my spirit's vessel without having to worry about getting ripped apart. That's critical, because once I find our spirit, I'm going to need all the fire I've got left to claim it, because that sucker's going to be huge. We're talking about all of humanity's collective idea of dragons gathered in one place. Do you know how many stories there are about us? We're practically a genre."

"I'm sure it's very big," Marci said. "But isn't that a problem? Even if you can spread your fire, how are you going to take over something that size?"

"By getting in early," Amelia said, her gleaming eyes more serious than Marci had ever seen. "The return of magic is a once-in-eternity opportunity, Marci. That's why I was willing to risk everything for this. Somewhere out there is an enormous vessel for a dragon spirit, and this is the only moment in history that it will ever be half full. If I can get in there at the right moment and spread my fire through the magic before it develops a consciousness of its own, I won't have to take over anything. I'll just be the mind that's already there when the new spirit wakes up. Once that happens, we'll blend together, and its magic should naturally become mine. *That's* what I'm here for. That's the trick. Other than the nature of the force that carves their vessels, there's no actual difference between a lake spirit and a Mortal one. They're both just craters in the floor of the Sea of Magic that fill up and get a personality. Dragons can't dig out a spirit because this isn't our world, but if I can take over the one that humans dug for us and fill it with real dragon fire, the end result should be a spirit of dragons by *dragons,* just like every other animal spirit on this planet. And once we've got *that*—"

"You'll be a native species," Marci finished excitedly.

"Better," Amelia said with a grin. "We'll be rooted here. *All* of us. They all might burn individually, but every dragon's fire sparked from the same original source: the magic of our home plane. The power that birthed us still burns in every dragon. It's a thin connection, but if my theory is correct, that shared inheritance means that if I take over that spirit, it won't just be me and my fire. It'll be *all* of us. I'll become the tie that binds dragonkind to the magic of this plane. We'll no longer be stunted and limited to whatever power we can scrape together or cook up on our own. We'll be home again, dragons of *this* plane, and it'll all be thanks to me." She took a deep breath, amber eyes gleaming. "I'll be their *god.*"

Marci sighed. So that's what this was about. "I knew all that 'saving the species' stuff was too altruistic for you."

"I'd hardly be a dragon if there wasn't something in it for me," Amelia said unapologetically. "And it's not as though I'm being underhanded. I'm the one who had the idea and who took the ultimate risk—it's only fair that I should reap the rewards. Besides, it really is good for everyone. The whole world benefits when dragons become invested in our mutual long-term future, not to mention live long enough to grow out of our rampant megalomania stage."

"*Do* you grow out of that?" Myron asked sarcastically.

"We mellow with age," Amelia replied with a sniff. "Just look at me. My play to become the god of dragons was all wrapped up in the greater good. I'm practically a saint."

Marci had to laugh at that. "At least now we know you weren't kidding when you said you had bigger ambitions than Heartstriker."

"Please," Amelia said, disgusted. "I never wanted Bethesda's job, and I think Bob owes Julius an apology for saddling him with that dumpster fire of a clan. This is *way* better. If I can pull this off, not only will I be the god who solved the deepest existential crisis of our species, I'll be a spirit, which means I'll be *truly* immortal. Even if someone does manage to kill me, I'll just respawn in my domain. The only downside is that I could technically be bound by a mage, but I've never had a problem managing humans, so I'm sure it'll be fine. Certainly worth the risk to lock in this much power *and* put my entire species in my debt." She winked at Marci. "That's what *I* call a win-win."

Marci rolled her eyes. Amelia looked disgustingly pleased with herself, but while she didn't like that the dragon had kept her in the dark about her true intentions, she didn't actually have a problem with Amelia's plan. It felt a little questionable to take over the Spirit of Dragons before it could wake up, but considering there wouldn't even *be* a spirit of dragons without actual dragons, it could be argued that it was their spirit already. In any case, dragons needed a way to integrate, because after ten thousand years, they were definitely here to stay. The sooner they got properly merged into the native magic, the more peaceful and better off everything would be.

If it worked.

"Not that I doubt your brilliance, Amelia," Marci said, "but how are you actually going to pull this off? I got you into the Heart of the World, but there's still a lot of whirlpools out there, and even if you can find the right vessel, how are you getting inside? This place is a model, not the real thing. You can't just dive in."

"Actually, that's exactly what I plan to do," Amelia said. "Remember, this model is not to scale. Considering how big the Sea of Magic is, that's a critical advantage. I might fly for years without finding anything outside, but in here, everything's all nicely squished together." She smiled at the sea. "I bet if I fly out into that wild blue yonder, I'll find my vessel. After that, it's just a matter of winging it."

"Winging it," Marci repeated bleakly. "*That's* your plan?"

The dragon shrugged. "It's been my M.O. since I got here. Worked so far. Remember, no dragon has ever been to this side of the plane, and Bob can't see what happens on this side."

"You mean you've been making it up this whole time?" she cried. "What's the point of following a seer's advice if you're just going to fly blind?"

"Plenty," Amelia said, giving her stern look. "Bob picks horses, not races. He chose you not because of any specific event, but because your personality and choices gave you the best chance of success over the long term. The rest was up to us. This whole thing has been one giant long shot from your death all the way to here, but we pulled it off. Now we just have to keep that up. That said, this final part is the hairiest bit, which is why I've taken the precaution of enlisting some outside help."

Shiro's head snapped up in alarm. "What kind of outside help?"

"The very best," Amelia said, glancing up at the twisted pine tree. "I'm actually surprised he hasn't already outed himself. He normally can't resist a dramatic entrance."

Marci didn't see anything in the branches, but Shiro still looked utterly appalled.

"Where do you think you are, dragon?" he cried, reaching down to snatch Amelia up. "You are a guest in the Heart of the World! The sacred fortress of the Merlins! You have no authority to bring in others. The fact that a snake like you was permitted entrance is itself a miracle. You can't expect such a thing to—"

He stopped, eyes going wide, though Marci had no idea why. Nothing on the mountaintop had changed that she could see. When she asked the shikigami what was wrong, though, all he said was, "There's a bird here."

Confused, Marci looked up again to see he was right. There *was* a bird in the tree above their heads. An absolutely massive black raven with a very familiar gleam in his intelligent eyes. "My ears were burning," he croaked, hopping down to perch on the edge of the cracked seal. "Did I miss anything?"

"Hello, Raven," Amelia said as she wormed out of Shiro's slack fingers to join him. "Right on time."

"I should be. I've been checking this place every few minutes since I heard you'd died. Though I must say, Amelia love, you look worse every time I see you. And the company you keep..." He turned sideways to examine Myron with a black eye. "*Dreadful.*"

Amelia lifted her lip in disgust. "*I* didn't invite him. He's a stowaway on Marci's better nature. One of the bad habits she picked up from my baby brother."

"Really?" Raven said, turning gravely to Marci. "You must be more discerning, Madame Merlin. Betrayal is usually a repeated behavior."

"I don't have to defend myself to you," Myron said, lifting his chin. "I did what I felt was necessary to preserve the future of mankind."

"I know," the spirit said tiredly. "It's one of humanity's worst traits. Good intentions justify all kinds of terrible behavior."

Myron was opening his mouth to argue when Shiro cut him off. "How are you here?" the shikigami demanded, his normally calm demeanor abandoned as he made a grab for Raven. "You're an animal spirit! How did you get into this place?"

"Well, firstly, you can't keep ravens out of anything," Raven said, dodging easily. "And second, I'm only partially an animal spirit these days. I started out that way, but I've been improving myself over the years."

"What do you mean, 'improving yourself'?" Marci asked.

"Nothing too drastic," Raven assured her. "But as I'm sure you've picked up, humans have been my hobby for a *very* long time. I've been helping your kind since you first discovered language. With such a long run, it wasn't hard to insert myself into your stories and mythologies, start building my legacy. Every culture in the world has tales of clever ravens and crows, which I might have also coopted."

Amelia snorted. "You stole Crow's stories?"

"Crow is a curmudgeon who wasn't taking advantage of humanity's incredible abilities," Raven said, utterly unapologetic. "And most people can't tell us apart anyway, so I helped myself to his share."

Marci stared at him in wonder. "You *weren't* exaggerating the first time we met. You really are Raven from the stories. Not just the Spirit of Ravens, but Raven the Trickster God. You used our myths and legends about you to make yourself a Mortal Spirit!"

Raven puffed out his chest. "*Finally*, someone's figured it out. It's about time I got credit for my brilliance." He poked his beak at Amelia. "Where do you think she got the idea of taking over the dragon spirit? She cribbed it from me."

Marci was opening her mouth to ask him about that when Myron grabbed her shoulder and physically pushed past her. "You were a Mortal Spirit?" he yelled at Raven. "This *whole time?*"

"Slow on the uptake, aren't you?" Raven said coldly. "But before you achieve critical hypocrisy by calling me a traitor, I'm not a true Mortal Spirit. My original vessel has always been the one carved out for me by my ravens all over the world. All I did was craft myself an expansion using the human tales of my actions as the mythological Raven. The result was a sort of hybrid blend of the two, but though it's a lot of work playing two roles, I've always enjoyed a challenge. And before you bring it up, there's still not quite enough magic yet to bring my Mortal Spirit side up to snuff, so I couldn't have solved our Merlin problem any faster than Marci here did. Not that you were any help in that regard. In fact, *you* are a big part of why I'm here."

Myron's brow furrowed, but Raven had already turned back to Shiro. "You're one of old Seimei's shikigami, aren't you?"

"Yes," Shiro said, his voice suspicious. "What of it?"

"Nothing," Raven said. "Just appreciating a master's work. I make servants, too, though I stick to physical constructs, not intelligent magic like yourself. Still, I have a deep appreciation for the art. Tell me, are you bound directly into this place, or were you just locked up like a message in a bottle for the next person who happened to stumble through the door?"

That struck Marci as a reasonable question, but Shiro looked terminally insulted. "My master would never be so irresponsible as to leave his shikigami with no anchor," he said haughtily. "Of course I am properly bound to the structure that governs the Heart of the World."

"Excellent," Raven said, turning back to Marci. "That means he has to do what you say. As the current and only Merlin, you are the undisputed master of the Heart of the World, which, as Shiro has just admitted, includes him. So, Madame Merlin, would you be so kind as to order your shikigami to bring up a scrying circle on the DFZ?"

Blinking in surprise, Marci turned to Shiro. "You have to do what I say? Why didn't you tell me that?"

"I did," he said sourly. "I told you I was bound to the Heart of the World *and* I told you you were its master. I simply assumed you would put two and two together."

"Of course," Marci said, rolling her eyes. "Do as Raven says."

Shiro set his jaw. "You should not listen to him. He's an unbound spirit and a trickster god, and he is *not* supposed to be here."

"Well, I'm giving him permission to be here," Marci snapped. "And a scrying circle is a good idea. If I'm going to be Merlin, I need to be informed, so fire it up."

With a final scowl, the shikigami turned and walked across the flat top of the mountain to a clear spot near the outer edge. When he reached it, he pulled the folding fan out of his sash and waved it in a circle in front of him. It wasn't until a corresponding completely spellworked circle lit up on the stone below, though, that Marci realized what had just happened.

"*Holy*—"

She rushed over, dropping to her knees at the edge of the glowing circle to get a closer look, but she wasn't mistaken. There were no markings on the ground, no carved circle or premade spellwork for him to activate. Shiro had just waved his fan, and the whole thing—the circle, the spellwork, the variables, all of it—had appeared out of thin air.

"How did you do that?" she cried, jaw hanging open. "You just freecast a scrying circle!"

That was a sentence she'd never thought she'd say. Freecasting, or casting spells without written spellwork, was one of the core elements of Shamanistic magic. It worked okay for small spells if you didn't care about safety or quality standards, but doing anything complicated was out of the question, which definitely included scrying spells. Particularly a fancy one like this. The circle at Shiro's feet was now a clear window looking straight down through the mountain into an aerial shot of the DFZ. There was no haze or distortion, and it *moved*, the picture swirling around as the shikigami steered with the top of his folded fan.

"You have *got* to teach me how to do that."

"Of course," he said, his voice resigned. "I was bound here to inform and protect. But I still do not understand why we are doing this."

Looking down, Marci didn't either. "I don't get it," she said, staring at the city. "It's just the DFZ."

"Exactly," Raven said, hopping over to perch on Ghost's shoulder, which the bigger spirit didn't seem to mind at all. "It's *just* the DFZ. No cars. No people. Nothing."

He was right. The longer Marci looked, the creepier the picture became. There were no automated taxis, no delivery drones, not even people on the sidewalks. In a city that had barely paused when the Three Sisters had been shot out of the sky above it, the emptiness was just plain wrong, but when Marci glanced at Raven to ask why, the answer found her.

"*GET OUT!*"

The words came from the ground itself. They echoed through the city in a roar of rage, breaking windows and cracking the supports of the abandoned Skyways. That would have been terrifying enough, but what made it a thousand times worse was the fact that Marci recognized the voice.

"Is that—"

"Yes," Raven said. "It's the spirit of the DFZ. The one boy genius there used my spellwork to bind and fill because he couldn't stand the idea of someone else becoming Merlin."

"No," Myron said, jerking his head at Marci. "I couldn't stand the idea of *her* becoming Merlin. An opinion I still maintain since her plan to deal with the upcoming magical apocalypse is to hurry it up."

"Congratulations, then. You beat her to it," Raven croaked, bobbing his head down at the city. "Thanks to you, we've got a fully formed and fully enraged Mortal Spirit on the loose. The only reason she's not burning a swath right now is because Algonquin is holding her down, but that won't last much longer, which is why I'm here."

Amelia's head whipped toward him. "I thought you were here because I asked."

"I'm always here for you, my darling snake," Raven said. "But this is slightly more pressing than old favors." He turned back to Marci after that. Then, to her surprise, he lowered his head, bowing down before her until his beak touched the stone.

"I've come on behalf of all spirits to beg the Merlin's help," he said quietly. "In her fear, Algonquin used the spirits of the land who were afraid of change to fill the DFZ to the brim. This has left a newborn Mortal Spirit filled with the land's old anger. Needless to say, it's a volatile and dangerous situation that's only been made worse by Algonquin's order to evacuate the DFZ."

"How does evacuating make things worse?" Marci asked. "I'm amazed Algonquin cared enough to get people out."

"She didn't do it to save the humans," Raven said. "The DFZ is the spirit of the city. As such, her instinct is to protect her population, because people are the soul of a city. Without them, though, the DFZ is empty in more ways than the obvious. She has no anchor, nothing but the rage and fear of the spirits Algonquin stuffed her full of, and with no Merlin to help her calm down, she's rapidly spiraling out of control. Algonquin's managed to keep her in check thanks to Myron's plagiarism of the spellwork I created for Emily, but the DFZ is a Mortal Spirit. She's orders of magnitude bigger than the Lady of the Lakes. Even my brilliance can't handle that sort of power difference. If we don't do something soon, she's going to break free, and when she does, she'll destroy Algonquin, and probably her own city as well."

"Saving the DFZ is obvious," Marci agreed. "But why do you care if she destroys Algonquin? I thought the two of you hated each other."

"That doesn't matter right now," Raven said. "Whatever happens, we cannot allow Algonquin to believe she's lost." He turned to Shiro again. "Show us the lake."

The shikigami didn't move a muscle. Only after Marci motioned for him to go ahead did he finally flick his fan, turning the scrying circle's magical window to show the lake below Algonquin's white tower, and the shadow floating above it.

"Wow," Marci whispered, eyes wide.

She knew what she was looking at, of course. Algonquin's Leviathan was almost as famous as the Lady of the Lakes herself, and Marci had gotten her own up-close-and-personal introduction to him when she'd been Algonquin's prisoner. But the monster floating in the air above Lake St. Clair was multiple times bigger than the one they'd fought in Reclamation Land. Even with his tentacles stuck down in the lake water, which was lower than Marci had ever seen it, the crest of his rounded, beetle-like back was taller than the Skyway's superscrapers.

"Wow, he got an upgrade."

"No, he didn't," Raven said, his normally joking voice grim. "He's just not bothering to hide his true nature anymore, which is our sign that this situation's gone critical."

Marci looked sideways at him. "The Mortal Spirit of a city has gone psycho, and the *Leviathan's* your line for critical?"

"Yes," he said, his talons tightening on the Empty Wind's shoulder. "Do you remember what we discussed on the jet before you died? When you asked me about the Nameless Ends?"

"You mean what we *didn't* discuss?" Marci said, crossing her arms. "Because I distinctly remember you saying it was too dangerous for mortals to know."

"I said it was too dangerous for *normal* mortals," Raven corrected. "But I did promise to tell you if you became a Merlin, which you have."

Marci smiled. Finally, a perk to being the Merlin. "So what are they?"

"Whoa," Amelia said, pointing at Myron, who'd gone suspiciously silent. "Should you really be outing this in front of the freeloader? He's not exactly trustworthy."

"He's a traitor," Raven agreed. "But that might actually work in our favor. If this plays out how I think it's going to, Myron's position as Algonquin's inside man might be our only chance of getting out of this alive."

Myron looked visibly relieved by that, but Marci was starting to get frustrated. "So what's going on?" she demanded. "Why's the Leviathan getting so big? What's Algonquin doing?"

Raven sighed. "What she feels she has to."

He hopped off Ghost's shoulder, flapping down to land on the cracked seal. "Algonquin didn't always hate humans," he said, tapping his talons on the spellworked stone. "This changed that. When the Merlins cut off all magic and plunged the world into drought, Mortal Spirits weren't the only ones who vanished. We all did."

This was not new information, but the way he said it was. Marci had never heard one of the really old spirits sound anything other than demanding or cocky or angry, but this was different. This time, Raven sounded afraid.

"Do you know what that was like for us?" he whispered. "We are the immortal spirits, as old and immutable as the land itself. Our changes happen on geologic timelines: mountains eroding into plains, or tiny proto-birds evolving into ravens. That was our reality, the world we'd always known. Then, all of a sudden, it wasn't. Magic, the very stuff of our existence, dried up like a river in summer, and without it, we—the deathless—died."

"That's a little dramatic," Marci said. "I mean, you came back."

"We didn't know that then," Raven said bitterly. "The Merlins made their decision without consulting us. They knew what would happen to us, but they decided we were an acceptable sacrifice for humanity's safety. There's not a spirit in the world who took that well, but Algonquin took it personally."

"But I'm not going to take the magic away again," Marci said quickly. "The Last Merlins made a tough call with a lot of negative externalities, but the situation now is different. I'm not going to repeat—"

"I know," Raven said. "Why do you think I'm so delighted you beat Myron to the punch? But while we know you're not like your predecessors, Algonquin *doesn't*. I got in here because I'm clever and adaptable, but Algonquin's a true spirit of the land, stubborn as a rock. She has no access to the Heart of the World and no idea what's happening on our end. All she sees is what's in front of her, which right now consists of Myron's comatose body and an unbound Mortal Spirit running amok. She thinks her bid to get a Merlin failed, and now Myron's stuck on this side while his spirit goes haywire, which means it's up to her to put the DFZ down again before it destroys her lakes."

Marci bit her lip. "I see why you came. Algonquin and the Leviathan are bad enough on their own, but if they start beating the spirit of the DFZ into submission, the whole city could be destroyed. It'll be the night of the flood all over again."

"Actually, that's the *good* part," Raven said. "We want her to fight the DFZ, because fighting means she hasn't given up hope yet that she can salvage the situation. The real danger comes when she gets desperate."

"How much more desperate can she get?"

"Plenty," he said. "Remember what I just said about the night the magic vanished? We thought it was the end of the world. We'd never even contemplated death, and then suddenly everyone we knew was dropping like flies. We had no idea how to stop what was happening or if the magic that sustained us would ever come back. That sort of fear drives even the wisest spirits to do desperate, stupid things, and Algonquin was no exception. She thought the end of the world was upon her, so she did the only thing she could. She cried out for help, offered everything she had if this would only stop, and unfortunately for us, something answered."

"What?" Marci asked breathlessly.

Raven opened his beak to answer, but Amelia beat him to it.

"A Nameless End."

Marci whirled to face the little dragon. "You knew about this?"

"'Course I knew," Amelia said with a shrug. "Raven and I have been in cahoots for a long time. Plus, I'm the Planeswalker. This is kind of my area."

"How so?" Marci asked. "Are Nameless Ends something from the planes? What are they?"

"Good questions," Amelia said. "I have answers for both, but to understand them, we need to do a little Planeswalking 101." The small dragon sat back on her haunches, making herself comfortable on the spellworked seal like she was about to tell a story.

"There are uncountable millions of planes in our collective multiverse," she began. "Some are enormous, like this one. Others are much, much smaller, but they're all self-contained with their own magic, physics, and rules. Most of the time, these rules overlap with only a few minor differences. The rules of physics in particular appear to be universal. Alike or unalike, though, every plane is its own specific *thing*. A little universe all its own separated from everything else by a planar barrier, which is what I, as a Planeswalker, have to cut through whenever I want to walk between them."

"I know that much," Marci said impatiently. "You're describing the principle behind all portal magic. Even we've figured that out."

"Ah," Amelia said, lifting her talon. "But what you modern mages haven't rediscovered yet is that you can't just cut the hole anywhere, because not all planes touch in all places. Imagine the multiverse as a room full of balloons. There are places where the balloons touch and places where the curves form gaps. Obviously, it's not quite that simple since we're working in multiple dimensions, but the basic idea of all Planeswalking is that you want to make your portal where you know your plane is touching the one you want to travel to. That's why artifacts like the Kosmolabe are so incredibly cool. They show you where planes touch."

"And where to cut through," Marci said, nodding. "But what does this have to do with Nameless Ends?"

"I'm getting to that," the dragon said. "Go back to that room full of balloons. Just as there are places where the surfaces touch, there are places where they don't. Those bits of emptiness, the spaces between the curves of the planar barriers, are where the Nameless Ends reside. They're what we in the business call 'extra-planar beings,' entities bigger and broader than anything we can imagine. They're so huge and old and alien, no one I've spoken to on any plane knows where they came from, but they do all seem to be unique. They've all got their own goals and ways of doing things. Despite their diversity, though, all Nameless Ends perform the same function within the planar ecosystem: decomposition."

"Decomposition," Marci repeated slowly. "You mean they eat dead planes?"

"Dead, collapsing, on the brink." Amelia shrugged. "You name it, they take care of it in their own way, and there are a *lot*. I've never heard an exact number I believed, but the common saying is that there are as many Nameless Ends as there are ways for things *to* end. Each one's got its own flavor: violent explosions, infinite expansion to point of collapse, the heat death of the universe, classic annihilation—you get the idea. But even though they can be wildly different, every Nameless End is called such because it represents a way the world can, and *will*, end, which is why it's cause for alarm that Algonquin has one."

Marci clapped a hand over her mouth. "The Leviathan," she said. "*That's* why no one knew where it came from, because it's not from our world at all. It's a Nameless End!" When Raven nodded, she leaned forward eagerly. "Do you know what kind of end it is?"

"Nope," he said. "And seeing how there's no way *to* know until it starts actually ending things, I don't want to. I just want it gone."

Marci was about to ask how to do that when Myron spoke over her.

"If the Leviathan is what you claim, why aren't we already dead?" he asked. "That monster's been at her side since the night magic returned. Possibly earlier, if your story about Algonquin calling for help is true. That's a long time for something called a 'Nameless End' to hang around and not end things, especially given the way Algonquin treats it. She acts like it's her pet, which is not how I'd expect a spirit to treat a supposed end of everything. For that matter, why would she call out to a monster like that in the first place? Whatever she's guilty of, no one can doubt Algonquin's dedication to her lakes. Presumably, a Nameless End would destroy those as well. Why would she risk that?"

He had a point there. "How did she even get a Nameless End?" Marci asked. "If he's an extraplanar being, wouldn't him being here inside our plane end the world?"

"It would," Amelia said. "*If* he were really inside. Thankfully, he's not. At least not yet." She pointed down at the shadow of the Leviathan staining the scrying circle. "I'm sure you've noticed how he always seems to be made of shadows. That's because what we know as the Leviathan in this world is just a projection. A broadcast of a bit of his magic into our plane from the outside. If he were *actually* here, our world would already be toast, and we wouldn't be having this conversation. But the trick with Nameless Ends is that they only 'clean up' planes that are already breaking apart. Before that point, the planar barrier keeps them out, like how a healthy cell wall keeps out viruses. This is a strong, stable plane. Normally, a Nameless End wouldn't be able to slide so much as a tentacle through our barrier. With enough force, though, anything's possible, and I'm afraid we had a breach."

She tapped her claws on the crack in the stone seal, and Marci cursed. "The meteor. *That's* what was inside it, the alien magic Shiro was talking about. It was the Leviathan."

"It was," Raven confirmed. "Algonquin called out to it when the magic vanished. What she promised, I don't know, but a thousand years later, the Leviathan came to collect, striking our planet hard enough to crack the Merlins' seal and wake the spirits again."

"That must be why none of the space agencies saw the meteor coming," Marci said. "It didn't come from space. It came from outside our *plane*."

"It also explains the mystery of how a physical space rock was capable of cracking the Merlins' spell," Myron admitted, despite clearly not wanting to. "It wasn't a rock at all."

"It was a piece of a Nameless End," Raven finished. "Called here by Algonquin, and now we're all in hot water."

"But why now?" Myron pressed. "If it was in the meteor—"

"It was," Raven said.

"Then why didn't it kill us all sixty years ago?" the mage finished. "And why did it only send a piece? If this thing's so huge, why didn't it blast its way in?"

"Because it *can't*," Amelia said. "I just told you, Nameless Ends only devour collapsed planes, and our plane isn't in collapse. The only reason it was able to get anything through the planar barrier at all was because someone let it in. Probably Algonquin, given the whole 'crying out in desperation' story. Or maybe it just waited until it found a gap. Those do occur naturally sometimes. Either way, this plane is healthy enough that it was only able to get a tiny sliver of itself inside. If it wants to bring in the rest, someone on the inside has to help. Someone powerful, with enough magical weight to drag the rest of that thing's body through the planar wall. Someone like Algonquin."

"That's why it woke her up," Raven said, "and why it's served her ever since. The Leviathan needs Algonquin to pull it the rest of the way inside so it can destroy our world."

"But why would she do that?" Marci asked. "Destroying the world would mean destroying her lakes as well. Even Algonquin's not *that* crazy."

"Not yet," Raven said. "But that's only because she still hopes to turn things around. So long as there's no Merlin to break this seal, she still has a chance of clamping the magical flow down to a level that stops the rise of the Mortal Spirits while leaving the rest of us intact. That's her entire end goal. In her mind, the full return of magic is the end of the world. If that happens, she *will* be that crazy, and we'll all be toast."

Marci blew out a long breath. "I see what you mean. But if our survival depends on keeping Algonquin's hopes up, we've got a problem, because she's already lost. I'm the Merlin, not Myron."

"You could repair the seal," Myron suggested. "That would stop her."

"I'm not going to screw over all of humanity, the Mortal Spirits, *and* Amelia's shot at integrating dragons into our plane because Algonquin's holding a gun to our heads," Marci said angrily. "That's extortion. We'll just have to find another way to beat it."

"I don't think you *can* beat a Nameless End," Raven said. "But that's fine, because if we play our cards right, we won't have to."

Amelia chuckled. "The trickster at work."

"I have a reputation to live up to," Raven said, winking at her before turning back to Marci and, surprisingly, Myron. "Here's my plan. As of right now, Algonquin has no idea what's happened in the Heart of the World. She still thinks that *you're* dead"—he nodded at Marci—"and that *you* screwed up." He nodded at Myron. "She doesn't know yet that anyone's become a Merlin, and so long as she stays ignorant, we have a shot at fixing this."

"How is she not going to know?" Marci asked, pointing at the empty city on the other side of the scrying circle. "She's about to be in an all-out war with the spirit of the DFZ. I don't care what evacuation orders she gave—you can't empty a city of nine million in a few hours. There are still people down there, and I'm the Merlin. Dealing with rampaging spirits is my job. I have to do something.

What, exactly, I have no idea, but the moment I do it, I'm pretty sure Algonquin's going to know I'm not dead."

"Not if she doesn't see you," Raven said. "It's a big city, and she's a huge spirit, but you're human sized. If we sneak you in, you can deal with the DFZ. Bind her, drain her, knock her out, whatever. Just get her back under control. Once she's locked down, Myron can come in and claim the credit."

"Excuse me?" Myron said.

"Why him?" Marci said at the same time.

"Because he's the one Algonquin sent," Raven explained patiently. "Remember, Algonquin's a spirit of the land. She's heard stories and seen the pillar, but she's never actually been inside the Heart of the World. If the DFZ goes quiet and then Myron walks out cocky as ever with a good story about how he temporarily lost control of his spirit, but everything's good now, Algonquin has no reason not to believe him. That's a totally plausible story to her, and even better, it's the one she wants to hear. She *wants* to believe that she's won, that she's successfully hacked the system. Once we've got her buying that, all Myron has to do is promise to knock the magic levels back down as ordered, but only if she boots the Leviathan first."

Myron looked horrified. "You want me to *scam* Algonquin?"

"You already scammed her," Raven said. "You can't fool me. I've worked with you for decades. I know you came in here intending to shut the magic off completely, and I'm equally certain you didn't tell Algonquin that while you were ripping Emily to pieces. You've already played her. Now we're just taking things a step further."

"Misleading Algonquin about my true intentions is a far cry from pretending to be Merlin to her face," Myron said, his eyes wide and fearful. "How am I supposed to explain my knowledge of the Leviathan?"

Raven shrugged. "Just say I told you. She already thinks the worst of me. What's a bit more?"

"Especially since it's the truth," Marci said. "But there's a critical flaw in your plan. If we're going to have any chance of making

Algonquin believe Myron's her Merlin, he's going to have to show up with his Mortal Spirit, and I just don't see that happening right now."

Myron whirled on her. "You just told me not ten minutes ago that you wanted me to rebind the DFZ legitimately!" he cried. "That was your *entire requirement* for building a failsafe into the seal. Now you're saying I can't do it? Make up your mind!"

"It *is* made up!" Marci yelled back. "You can do it, just not like this."

She threw out her hands at the scrying circle, where the city was groaning like a chained animal. "When I was talking before, I assumed we'd be waiting until she calmed down and then go in slowly, building trust back from the ground up, but this situation is lunacy. She's beating against Algonquin with everything she has. If you go down there now, assuming we can even find a way to get you down there, seeing how we're both ghosts, I'm pretty sure she's going to eat you."

"Then you'd better figure out a way to change her mind," Raven said. "Because Algonquin's already losing her control over the situation. Even with the Leviathan helping pump in water to hold her down, it's only a matter of time before the DFZ breaks free. When that happens, it'll be all-out war between Algonquin and the world's only full Mortal Spirit, and considering the size difference, I think we all know how that's going to end."

"Don't write Algonquin off so easily," Ghost warned. "She may be much smaller, but she's experienced, determined, and desperate. The DFZ is maddened, young, and lacking a human anchor. If she throws her power around without thought or a mage to feed power into her, she will very quickly run out, and then Algonquin will have the upper hand."

"You can't kill a Mortal Spirit," Marci reminded him.

"But you can destroy her domain," Ghost replied, looking down at the familiar buildings. "The DFZ is the soul of a city. Algonquin can't remove that from people's minds, but she can easily destroy

Detroit again. It won't kill the DFZ's spirit, but a setback like that will probably keep her from rising again for decades."

"And meanwhile, the entire city will be destroyed," Marci said grimly. "*Again.*"

She scowled down at the scrying circle for a long moment, and then her head shot up. "Is there a reason we couldn't just fake the whole thing? What if Ghost pretended to be Myron's Mortal Spirit. Would that work?"

The blast of cold in her mind made the Empty Wind's opinion of that plan very clear, but Raven's answer was the one that made her slump.

"No," he said. "Even if the Empty Wind could pull off his part, Algonquin would never believe it, because Myron doesn't look like a Merlin."

"Merlins look different?" she asked, staring down at her body, which, other than the ghostly transparency, looked normal enough to her. "How?"

"Lots of ways," Raven assured her. "Humans generally can't tell because you don't see things like we do, but there's not a spirit born who can't tell a Merlin on sight. No. If we're going to sell Myron as Merlin, then he's going to have to actually *be* a Merlin, and since the DFZ is one of only two Mortal Spirits in existence right now, he'd better brush up on his groveling."

Marci didn't think any amount of groveling would make up for what Myron had done, but the other thing Raven said gave her an idea. "What about you?" she asked, looking the bird up and down. "You said you're half Mortal Spirit."

"And the last one in the world Algonquin would trust," Raven said, shaking his head. "If Myron showed up with me as his Mortal Spirit, Algonquin wouldn't believe a word he said, which defeats the entire purpose. We need her to believe she's won. It's the only way she'll feel confident enough to give up her trump card."

"Assuming she hasn't decided to destroy everything already," Myron said bitterly. "She has a very low opinion of the world."

"I don't think that's it," Marci said thoughtfully. "Don't get me wrong. I'm sure Algonquin hates all of our guts individually and by name, but no one who's fought as hard, long, and creatively as she has is going to give up before the bitter end. So long as there's even the faintest hope of turning this around, I don't think she'll sell out to the Leviathan. That buys us time."

"Let's just hope it's enough," Raven said, folding his wings tight against his body. "Right, let's do this. First things first, we need to get the two of you back to the physical side of things. Myron will be easy. We just have to find where Algonquin's stashed his carcass and take it back. Your return, Marci, will be slightly more involved, but I'm pretty sure I've covered all the angles, so if you're ready…"

He trailed off, but Marci was just staring at him, too afraid to speak. "I—" She stopped, swallowing against the terrible tightness in her chest. "You're saying you can take me back? As in bring me back to life?"

"Absolutely," he said, giving her a wink. "Why do you think Amelia begged for my help? Ravens *are* famous for bringing back the souls of the dead."

After having her hopes dashed so hard, Marci couldn't bring herself to believe it. And yet…"*Really?*"

"Really," he promised. "I actually made up that part of my legend myself. It seemed like it would be useful, and it has been. I'm glad it stuck."

"So you can take me back," Marci said again. "Actually back to life?"

"Yes," he said, turning to Amelia. "Is she always this suspicious?"

"She's been through a lot recently," the dragon said. "And you *are* a trickster."

"Not about this sort of thing," Raven snapped. "I'm not cruel." He turned back to Marci. "Yes, Miss Novalli, I am sincerely offering to bring you back to the world of the living. That said, since I'm not your bound spirit or even a true Mortal one, I should warn you the journey will be—"

"I don't care," Marci said immediately. "So long as I don't wake up as a zombie, I don't care what you do. Just, *please,* take me back."

"I already offered, but your begging is noted," he said happily. "Now, let's get this—"

"*Wait!*" Amelia cried, jumping off the seal to dig her claws into Marci's arm. "You can't go yet!"

"Why not?" Marci cried, staring at her friend in betrayal. "You brought him here to do this."

"Yeah, but not yet. Remember how I said this was all part of Bob's plan? Well, he warned me about this. No one is allowed to leave the Heart of the World until we get the signal."

Marci couldn't believe this. "What signal?"

"I don't know," Amelia admitted. "But he said I'd know it when I saw it."

"That's it?" she cried. "*That's* our reassurance? You'll 'know it when you see it?'"

"That's all I need," Amelia said firmly, letting go of Marci's arm. "I trust Brohomir with my life *and* my death. If he says something is important, I listen, especially since this was the only specific information he gave me about this entire trip. He said that if I got to the Heart of the World, I shouldn't let anyone leave until I got his signal, and that I'd know it when I saw it."

"And you believed that?" Raven said skeptically.

Amelia gave him a burning look. "Why do you think I haven't flown off to find the vessel for the Spirit of Dragons yet?"

Raven sighed. "Good enough for me," he said, settling down on the seal. "Looks like we wait."

"You can't be serious," Myron said. "What happened to 'we have to move now' and 'let's hope there's still time?'"

"Oh, that's all still there," the bird spirit said. "But when a dragon seer says you should do something, it's generally a good idea to follow instructions. They see the future, you know."

"But how long can we wait?" Marci asked, glancing at the scrying circle. "The DFZ will break out at any moment."

"I don't know," Amelia said. "But it'll be worth it. You've seen Bob in action. You know what he can do. Trust him."

Marci covered her face with her hands. She was so close, *so close* to going home, and now this. As much as she hated it, though, Amelia was right. She *had* seen Bob in action, and while she didn't always like where his plans led, she'd yet to see the seer be wrong. If he said there would be a signal, then there would be a signal. The only question left was would it come in time for their plans, or his?

There was no way to know. With so many power players pushing their own agendas, picking out what was actually right felt like trying to catch a single snowflake in a storm, though it did give her renewed sympathy for Julius's position. He had to deal with stuff like this all the time. If he'd been here, Marci was sure he'd already have a brilliant compromise that pleased everyone. But Julius wasn't here, and if she ever wanted to see him again—ever wanted to be *alive* again—she was going to have to make a decision.

"Okay," she said, letting out a long breath. "We'll wait."

Are you sure? Ghost whispered.

"No," she said. "But while I'm certain Bob would have no problem discarding us all as pawns in his game, he wouldn't do that to Amelia. If he says she needs to wait, then that's how she's getting out of this alive, and since that's what I want, too, we're playing along."

And if we get played?

Marci laughed. "Little late for that. According to Amelia, Bob's hand's been in my life since before we met. But other than the dying part, I like where he's taken me, so I'm going to stay on the ride. If nothing else, it's nice to have someone on our side who knows what he's doing."

"I'm not so sure about that," Myron said, giving Amelia a dirty look. "Isn't Bob the crazy one who nearly ran you over with his car at the diner outside Heartstriker Mountain?"

"He's not so bad," Marci said with a shrug. "And he's never wrong." She sat down on the ground beside the scrying circle. "We'll wait for his signal."

"You won't be sorry," Amelia promised, hopping into her lap. "My brother put a lot of work into this. Trust me. It's going to be awesome."

Myron rolled his eyes at that. Raven didn't look particularly happy, either, and Shiro seemed ready to throw them back out into the dark. For all the mixed reactions, though, they must have respected Marci's authority as Merlin at last, because no one challenged her further, not even Myron. They all just stood there in silence, watching the empty shell of the evacuated DFZ through the scrying circle as the spirit's groaning grew worse and worse and worse.

CHAPTER THIRTEEN

Chelsie appeared in the empty darkness of Julius's old house, the only place she was certain no one would be. Sure enough, it was deserted. There weren't even signs of squatters, despite the fact that the entire front wall was still hanging open from where Conrad had cut it in half.

That was to be expected, though. Even if they didn't know what they were looking at, humans instinctively avoided dragon lairs. Not that Julius had made much of a lair here, but it must have been enough, because Chelsie couldn't so much as smell a human.

Her eldest brother was another matter.

After chasing his shadow for so long, Bob's scent hit her like a punch. He was *here*, and he was close. So close, she didn't even have to search. She just followed her nose, following his scent out of the house and through the dark of the rumbling DFZ Underground like the predator she was.

Not surprisingly, the scent led her straight to the empty lot from the picture: a flat, desolate stretch of mud wedged between the road and the river. The steep drop to the water was lined with rocks to prevent erosion, and the stretch of mud above it still bore the marks of a sunken foundation where some idiot developer had learned the hard way not to build on a flood plain. Beyond the shore, the Detroit River ran wide and silent, its night-black water glittering in the colored lights from the Skyway promenade that jutted out above the water like a cement boardwalk. Other than that, the only light came from the single orange streetlight that marked the end of the road, and beneath it, leaning against the battered wooden pole like a juvenile delinquent, was the dragon she'd come to find.

"You're early," Bob said, looking up from the glowing screen of his ancient brick of a phone. "Did I lay the trail too well?"

He smiled at her like he always did, but Chelsie wasn't playing. "Give it back."

"'Give it back?'" he repeated, eyebrows shooting up in faux astonishment. "That's it? No trademark Chelsie 'Hello, brother,' or 'Why did you do it, Bob?'"

"You taught me long ago that asking you for explanations was useless," she snarled. "But things are different now. I'm free, which means I don't have to care about you or your plans anymore. I'm just here for what's mine." She thrust out her hand. "Give me my egg, Brohomir, or we'll see how good your knowledge of the future really is."

Bob heaved a long sigh. "There you go," he said, pushing off the pole. "Straight to threats. No attempt at reasoning or to discover my motivation." He shook his head with a *tsk*. "We really need to work on your conflict-resolution skills."

"There's nothing to resolve," Chelsie said, looking around the lot for some sign of what she'd come for, but there was nothing. No bags or boxes, nothing that could contain a dragon egg. Bob wasn't carrying anything, either. Not even his Magician's Fang, not that he ever wore it. Still, his lack of a weapon or anything that could serve as a hostage made Chelsie nervous. She'd known this was a trap from the moment Julius had gotten the call. Everything was with Bob. But traps could be broken, and thanks to Julius, she was off the seer's script. She just had to stay on target, and speaking of targets...

"Last chance," she growled, looking him in the eyes again. "I'm prepared to do whatever I have to, but this doesn't need to end in violence. Just tell me where my egg is, and we can both go our separate ways."

"I didn't go through all the trouble of getting you out here just so we could *leave*," Bob said, exasperated. "Don't you want to know *why* I stole your Precious? Because I'll tell you. I'm dying to, actually.

Do you know how hard it's been to keep all of this brilliance to myself? It's killing me. So go ahead. Ask, and I'll tell you everything."

He finished with his most charming smile, but Chelsie had seen this ploy go down too many times to fall for it herself. Bob might have fooled the rest of the clan into thinking he was an unpredictable mad genius, but Chelsie had watched him just as she'd watched every other Heartstriker. His motives were inscrutable to anyone who didn't also know the future, but his habits were as ingrained as any other old dragon's, and the only time he ever offered to explain himself was when he was stalling.

Whatever plot he'd called her out here for must not be ready yet, she realized. That meant if Chelsie was going to get her egg and escape before the trap closed, she needed to do it *now*. So she did, pushing off the dirt with her bare feet as she lunged at his throat.

As expected of a seer, Bob dodged her first strike, but no amount of precognition could save him from the second, which landed her balled fist right in his stomach. As he gasped in pain, Chelsie seized the chance to step in and wrap her arm around his throat, pinning him in a choke hold against her chest.

"That was…uncalled…for," Bob choked out, gasping for breath as he grabbed at her arm. "Can't we…talk about it?"

Chelsie's answer was to squeeze tighter. She was trying to make him pass out when Bob somehow managed to hook his foot behind hers. She was repositioning when he kicked up hard, yanking her off balance just long enough to break free.

He scrambled away into the dark, getting as much distance as possible before whirling around to watch her with a wary expression Chelsie had never seen on her eldest brother's face before.

"For the record, I did not expect that." He swallowed against his bruised throat before flashing her a weak smile. "Brava. You're faster than I anticipated."

"That's *your* fault," Chelsie said, circling. "Bethesda's Shade couldn't afford to let anyone know the full extent of her abilities, even you. And who made me that?"

Bob sighed. "You can't blame everything on me, you know."

"Why not?" she growled. "Everything *is* your fault. You're the all-knowing seer. You saw my disaster coming—all of it, from the very beginning—and you did *nothing.*"

"I did a great deal more than nothing," he said, insulted. "Do you have any idea how hard I've worked to bring us to this point? How delicately and painstakingly I've planned every little detail leading up to—"

"*You did this to me!*" she screamed at him. "I owned my mistakes in China, but everything I've suffered since is *your* fault. You were Bethesda's seer. One word from you was all it would have taken to free me and my children, but you said nothing." She bared her teeth. "*Nothing!* For six hundred years!"

"What could I have said?" Bob asked, his voice tired. "I needed you, Chelsie. Bethesda was useful, but you were the glue that kept everything together. Fear of *you* is what united Heartstriker, or at least kept us from flinging ourselves apart. You were the one who enabled us to become the largest clan in the world. Larger than even the Golden Empire. Large enough to get us here." He pointed at the ground between them. "To *this* moment. This future. Everything I've done leads right here, right now, and the only way I did it was you."

"Save it," Chelsie snapped, edging closer. "I don't care if this was the only way to avoid the end of the world. You used me. You used my *children.* But all that stops today. You want to talk about the future? These are the only words you need: it's over, Brohomir. You will never use me or my children *ever* again, and if you don't give me back my egg right now, you're not leaving this place alive."

"Let's not be hasty," he said, putting up his hands. "You have every right to be upset. I know certain actions of mine look callous out of context, but there's a good reason for that. I'd be happy to explain it to you if you'd just stop being such a *Chelsie* for a minute and just—"

She teleported behind him. The move got her so close, she actually felt the tips of his long hair before Bob leaped out of the way, dancing nimbly across the mud. But not far enough.

The moment he slowed, Chelsie teleported again, burning through her magic to reappear right on top of him. She wasn't even aiming for a hit this time. She was just recklessly charging forward, pushing with everything she had until she was moving too fast to see, too fast to plan.

It was a terrifying way to fight. Chelsie was normally a careful hunter, the sort who always had a plan. When your enemy was a seer, though, no plan was good enough. Brohomir had already foreseen every possible iteration of every clever idea she could come up with, so Chelsie didn't bother. She just attacked, going after her oldest brother with nothing but her bare hands, her killer's instinct, six centuries of pent-up rage, and a roar that echoed to the Skyways as they both went down in the mud.

And below them, unnoticed in the fray, the ground continued to tremble.

• • •

The moment he stepped through the portal, Julius knew something was deeply wrong. The DFZ had always felt more powerful than other places, but the pea-soup-thick magic he'd grown accustomed to while living here was now more like a boiling pot. He could actually feel it rumbling under his feet when Fredrick's cut dumped them out into the empty dirt lot from Bob's selfie, and under any other circumstances, that would have had his full attention. Now, though, the trembling pressure was relegated to the background, just another crisis to add to the list as he, Fredrick, and the Qilin looked up to find themselves in the middle of an assassination in progress.

As promised, the Defender's Fang had dumped them practically on top of Chelsie, which was how Julius had a perfect view of his deadliest sister's back as she launched herself at Bob. The seer dodged, of course—this was Bob, after all—but Chelsie didn't even slow down. She just turned and attacked again, slamming her foot into the dirt to use as a pivot as she spun to grab the seer's shoulder.

For a terrifying moment, Julius saw Bob's eyes widen in surprise before Chelsie yanked him backward. She brought her unbraced leg up at the same time, slamming her knee into the small of the seer's back for a kick that sent him flying into the dilapidated garage across the street like a cannonball, shattering the one remaining unbroken window and collapsing what was left of the roof.

Even for a dragon, that was a serious hit. Julius was already moving to go help his brother when Bob kicked his way out of the debris and rolled back to his feet. He took a second to shake the dust out of his long hair, and then stepped to the left just in time to avoid Chelsie as she teleported behind where he'd just been.

But while the quick move let him dodge her first punch, nothing could save him from the second. Julius hadn't even seen her arm going up. Her hand was just suddenly there, slamming into Bob's side as she took him down to the ground with her on top.

Chelsie shifted position the second they hit, turning in a flash so she ended up crouching above Bob's chest with her knees on his arms and both hands free to go for the seer's exposed throat. Julius was desperately grabbing his Fang to stop her before she clenched down for the kill when a calm, deep voice beat him to it.

"Chelsie."

The name sailed through the dark like a warm breeze. Wherever it passed, the world stopped to listen, though none so much as Chelsie herself.

Julius had never seen anything go as utterly still as his sister did in that moment. For five long heartbeats, she was frozen. Didn't twitch. Didn't flinch. Didn't even breathe. Then, with painful slowness, she turned her head, tearing her eyes away from her pinned prey to stare in horror at the golden dragon standing on the street behind her.

"Xian."

The whisper was a terrified curse. If anyone had said *his* name that way, Julius would have been haunted, but the Qilin didn't look upset. He looked relieved, his golden eyes almost hopeful as he watched her watch him. They were both still just staring at each other when Julius caught the scent of Bob's blood.

377

With a nervous glance at his sister, Julius darted across the street and into the destroyed garage. He wasn't sure how he was going to get his brother out from under Chelsie, but the Qilin's effect must have been even stronger than he realized. His sister didn't so much as twitch when Julius crept up beside her and grabbed Bob under the arms to ease him out of her hold.

It was still hairy. Chelsie was basically sitting on top of him, but Bob was twisty in more ways than one. With Julius's help, he managed to wiggle out from under Chelsie's weight, scooting several feet back into the relative safety of the collapsed garage door.

"Thank you, Julius," Bob said, falling onto his back with a relieved sigh.

Julius was too angry to answer, so he just focused on removing the six-inch shard of twisted metal from Bob's shoulder. There was an equally large shard of glass buried in his leg, probably from his crash through the garage door. The scariest wound by far, though, was the one Chelsie had left on his throat: two perfect handprints of bruised skin that wrapped around the column of his neck like a collar.

"Bob," he said at last, voice shaking. "What were you *thinking*?"

"I know," the seer said, looking down in dismay at the blood seeping through his red velvet coat. "I thought if I wore red, it wouldn't stain as badly, but—"

"Who cares about your coat?" Julius hissed, glancing nervously back at Chelsie, who was still spellbound by the Qilin. "She almost killed you."

"I'm not *that* soft," Bob said, his voice insulted. "Though I admit things did go worse than anticipated."

"You stole her egg and taunted her into coming after you!" Julius cried. "*How did you think it was going to go?*"

"Don't blame me," Bob said. "This is your fault. I *told* you not to set her free. If she'd still had her Fang, this would have been an entirely different fight. She's used that sword for hundreds of years. Fighting her with it would have been like following a script. Barehanded conflict wasn't nearly as predictable, as you can see."

He nodded at his bloody leg, but Julius had had enough.

"You should be grateful you're alive to complain," he snarled, growing more furious by the second. "This was the stupidest thing I've ever seen you do. You nearly got us all killed! You *did* kill Amelia, and you almost killed yourself just now by—"

Bob slapped a hand over Julius's mouth, cutting him off. He pressed another finger to his own lips next, flicking his green eyes pointedly at their sister. Julius had been so caught up with Bob, he hadn't even noticed Chelsie getting to her feet. She was on them now, though, her whole body poised to run as she eyed the Qilin. But while everything about her reminded Julius of a violent cornered animal, the Golden Emperor was still staring at her as if she were the most wondrous thing he'd ever seen.

"You..." he said at last. "You look well."

Chelsie's jaw tightened. "You never were much of a liar."

"But *you* were," he said, stepping closer. "Julius told me the truth, Chelsie. You *did* lie the day I banished you, but not about what I thought. You lied at the end, when you said it was all a ploy. Your brother claims he doesn't know why, but I've decided I don't care. I'm sick of living in the shadow of things that happened six centuries ago. I want to be alive now. I want to be happy again. I want..."

He trailed off, holding his breath like he was waiting for something to break. "I want you," he finished at last. "Only you. Always." He put out his hand. "Please give me a chance."

Julius stared at the emperor in shock. That was not how he'd expected this to go. He'd thought the Qilin would demand answers, but it seemed he'd underestimated his own words earlier. Apparently, Xian really did just want to be happy again. Chelsie, though, looked more afraid than ever.

"I can't."

The emperor flinched. "Will you tell me why?"

"No," she said sharply, crossing her arms tight across her chest. "I know how tempting Julius's sweet talk can be. He got to me, too, but our past isn't something we can just write off. It's easy to say you don't care when you don't know, but—"

"Then tell me," Xian said, taking another step closer. "I'm not afraid, Chelsie. Whatever happened, we'll work through it. I know we can, because we've already tried the alternative, and it was awful. I have no illusion that this will be easy, but if I'm going to be miserable, I'd rather be miserable with you. Just tell me what happened."

"I can't," Chelsie said, her voice starting to shake. "And you don't want me to. You've got this idea that things can be okay again, but even if I told you everything, it wouldn't make a difference. We can *never* go back to how we were before, because I'm not..." Her words trailed off as she curled her bloody hands into fists. "I'm not the girl from your paintings anymore."

"So what?" the Qilin said angrily, taking another step. "You think I'm the same? It's been six hundred years. Of course we've changed." Another step. "I want to know who you are *now*, Chelsie. I want to talk to you again, see you again. I miss you. You can throw that back in my face if you want, but I'm done pretending that I don't love you. That I don't still think about you every single day. That's why I'm not afraid, because there's *nothing* you can say, no secret you can tell me that could hurt me more than all the years I spent thinking you didn't care."

"You don't know that."

"Try me," he growled, closing the final distance. "Tell me the truth, Chelsie, and we'll work from there, but don't write me off before we even start. You owe me that much." He smiled down at her. "And you never used to be a quitter."

Chelsie cringed at that, but she didn't back down. She was actually leaning toward the emperor now, her hands fisted hard at her sides as if she was struggling to keep them from reaching out for his. But then, just as she seemed to be losing the fight, a new voice cut through the dark.

"An emperor shouldn't be so quick to promise pardon before he knows the crime."

The Qilin's head whipped around like a shot. Chelsie jumped, too, turning to look at something across the road. Fredrick and Bob were already looking, which meant Julius was the last one to turn and see the Empress Mother stepping out of a dark car hidden behind the Skyway support by the river.

"Mother," the emperor said, clearly as surprised by this as the rest of them. "What are you doing…"

His words trailed off. The Empress Mother was carrying something in her arms. As she stepped into the light of the lone street lamp, Julius saw it was a child. A little girl, barely more than a toddler, with a head full of straight, fine, ink-black hair. She was dressed haphazardly in striped leggings and a purple sweatshirt with a pigeon embroidered on the front, but while the clothes were human, the child was obviously not. Julius had never seen a dragon that young in human form before, but there was nothing else the little girl could be, and she smelled of his clan. It wasn't until the child raised her eyes, though—giant, beautiful eyes that flashed like golden coins in the orange glare of the streetlight—that he finally understood.

"No," Chelsie whispered, her face pale as ashes when she whirled on Bob. "*What did you do?*"

"Seems to me that question should be turned around," the Empress Mother said, thumping across the dirt with her cane in one gnarled hand and the little girl clutched tight against her hip with the other. "What did *you* do, daughter of the Heartstriker?"

Chelsie cringed, eyes flicking nervously to Xian, but he wasn't looking at her anymore. He was staring at the baby dragon like he'd never seen one before.

"Who is that?"

"I see the shock of her betrayal has blinded you, my emperor," the Empress Mother said sadly. "Allow me to make her crime clearer."

She swept her gold-handled cane at Fredrick, who was also staring at the child in speechless wonder. Magic followed. Not much, not even enough to label a spell, but with Fredrick's illusion already on the edge, a flick was all it took to shatter his false green eyes completely. He cursed as the magic snapped, which only made things worse, because it made the Qilin look, and there was no hiding the truth after that.

"You, too?" he whispered, staring into the mirror image of his own golden eyes before finally turning back to Chelsie. "What is this?"

There was no accusation in his voice, no anger. He just sounded lost. Lost and terrified and clearly counting on Chelsie to say something that would explain what he was seeing, but Chelsie couldn't even look at him. A fact that did not escape the empress as she moved in for the kill.

"I warned you," she said, clutching the little girl so tight she squirmed. "I *told* you the Heartstriker was using us. Now, at last, we see how." She bared her teeth. "Like mother, like daughter."

The emperor held up his hand, silencing her, but his eyes never left Chelsie. "What is she talking about?"

Chelsie took a shuddering breath. Again, though, she couldn't seem to find the words, and again, the empress took her chance.

"She was pregnant," the old dragoness said. "That's why she ran, and it's why she wouldn't accept your forgiveness just now. Even she knows there can be no pardon for this crime. She *stole* your children, my emperor. She lied to you and secreted them away to Bethesda's mountain in the Americas, where they lived as Bethesda's Shame." She pointed her cane at Fredrick. "Your son works as Julius Heartstriker's servant. Your *eldest* son."

"No," the Qilin said, taking a step back. "That can't be true."

"It is true," the empress said firmly. "Look on him, great emperor, and see for yourself. See with your own eyes what she has taken from us."

She pointed her cane at Fredrick until, at last, the Qilin dragged his eyes away from Chelsie and turned to face him. Fredrick stared right back, his golden eyes locked on his father's. Face to face like this, golden eye to eye, it was impossible not to notice how alike they looked. You'd have to be blind not to see the family resemblance, but the emperor seemed determined to try as he turned to face Chelsie once again.

"Is it true?"

She lowered her head and said nothing, which only made him angrier.

"*Is he your son,* Chelsie?"

Everyone was looking at her now, but despite the naked fear on her downturned face, her voice was clear when she said, "He is."

"But he can't be," the Qilin said desperately. "I'm still alive. There's only ever one Qilin." He lurched forward, grabbing Chelsie's shoulders in his hands. "Tell me you're lying! Tell me he's not—"

"*I can't!*" Chelsie yelled at him, her head coming up at last. "I can't lie anymore, Xian. Fredrick is my son, the first of my clutch." She took a deep breath. "And yours."

The whole world fell silent. There were no cars on the Skyways, no people on the street or noises from the city. Even the river behind went still as it waited for the Golden Emperor to realize what this meant.

"No," he said softly, releasing Chelsie's shoulders as he stumbled away. "*No.*"

"Yes," the Empress Mother said, turning to glare at Chelsie with pure, naked hate. "Our line is destroyed. The work of generations, a hundred thousand years of magic, *gone.* You are now the last Golden Emperor." She bared her yellowed teeth. "And it's all her fault."

That was going too far, but Julius didn't get a chance to come to his sister's defense. The Qilin was already falling to his knees on the broken street, and as he landed, a tsunami of dragon magic rose to meet him. It was the same pressure Julius had felt before at the mountain, but exponentially bigger, and growing by the second. Then, just when he was sure it couldn't get any worse, the spiking pressure snapped, and it did.

From the moment the Qilin arrived at the mountain, Julius had been warned over and over of what could happen if the emperor got upset. He'd thought he'd understood the danger. He even thought he'd experienced it for himself. It wasn't until now, when it was far too late, that Julius finally realized he'd had no idea at all. There was nothing—no magic, dragon or otherwise, no single force he'd ever felt—that could have prepared him for the tidal wave of misfortune that crashed into them as the Qilin's magic crashed.

It wasn't just that the ground shook—it was *how* it shook, twisting and moving exactly as needed to hit each tiny weakness in the Skyway supports' earthquake-ready joints. Even then, the supports didn't merely break. They crumbled like rotten wood, falling away from their steel cores in huge chunks that crashed to the ground like boulders ahead of a landslide.

With nothing left to support them, the Skyway bridges began to buckle next, the giant slabs that supported the buildings, sidewalks, and roads of the DFZ's famous upper tier cracking like plates before sliding into the city below. They would have slid right down onto Julius's head, but while he was transfixed by the collapse going on above him, other dragons had better instincts. By the time Julius realized he should probably run, Chelsie was already screaming.

"*Go!*"

She crashed into him like a train, knocking him out of the way seconds before a garbage-truck-sized chunk of Skyway landed where he'd been standing. And that was just the first. Whole buildings were collapsing now as the Skyways gave out beneath them. This time, though, Julius didn't stay to watch. He was already running, feet barely touching the ground as he raced across the empty lot toward the safety of the river, diving headfirst into the swift water beyond the stony bank.

The cold of the November water nearly shocked him numb. For a terrifying moment, he was tumbling blind in the dark current, and then his feet found the muddy ground. He pushed up, breaking the surface with a gasp. When he turned to see what had happened to the others, though, all he saw was dust.

The empty lot was gone, crushed completely beneath a block-sized chunk of the upper city. For several heart-stopping seconds, Julius was sure everyone else had been crushed as well, and then he saw Fredrick burst out of the water several feet downstream. Chelsie was right beside him and already swimming for the bank. Bob, however, was nowhere to be seen.

Now that he thought about it, Julius realized he hadn't seen the seer since the Empress Mother had appeared. Whether he'd sneaked off while everyone was distracted or fled during the crash, though, Julius didn't know and didn't have time to find out. Bob could look out for himself. Right now, Julius was far more concerned about the Qilin.

Given that he'd been directly below the Skyway when it fell, he should have been crushed with everything else. That would have been the logical outcome, but logic didn't seem to touch the Qilin any more than dirt did. For all the chaos all around him, the Golden Emperor was perfectly safe beneath a slab of roadway that, miraculously, had landed sideways, plunging into the dirt at the perfect angle to create a thick shelter of cement and asphalt above his head. His mother was there as well, smiling at the Heartstrikers' misfortune with the golden-eyed girl in her arms. A smile that only grew wider when Chelsie pulled herself out of the river.

"You *hag!*" she snarled, lunging at the empress. "*Give me my daughter!*"

The scream was still leaving her throat when a car-sized boulder that had been hanging from the ledge above them by a thread of steel rebar suddenly broke free. Chelsie dodged being crushed, just barely, but the force of the falling rock's impact knocked her right back into the river.

"You deserved that," the Empress Mother said when Chelsie came back up with a gasp. "All of you." She turned her red glare on Fredrick, who was helping Julius to the bank. "Your horrible family has destroyed everything I sacrificed for centuries to build. Thanks to you, the line of the Qilin is broken, and this world is forever diminished." She lifted her chin haughtily. "You deserve everything you get."

Chelsie bared her dripping teeth, but Julius grabbed her shoulder. "Why are you doing this?"

"*Because she took my child!*" his sister roared.

"Not you," he said quietly, grabbing the rocky bank so he could face the Empress Mother without being pushed downstream. "Why are *you* doing this?"

He pointed at the Qilin, who was still doubled over on the ground at her feet. "That's your son who's suffering. He told me how much he respected you, what a good mother you'd been to him. Just hearing him talk about you was enough to make me jealous, which is why I can't understand what you're thinking now." He looked around at the destruction. "What kind of mother does this to her child?"

"A fine question, coming from a Heartstriker," she snarled back. "But I do not do this as a mother. I do this as an empress."

She stabbed her cane into the dirt and reached down to place a gnarled hand on the Qilin's back. "My son is the heart of our power. I raised him to be incorruptible, to always put duty first, as I did. And in almost every way, he was perfect, but he had a secret weakness. By the time I realized what it was, your sister had already ruined him."

"Ruined him how?" Julius demanded. "Love made him *happy*. That's when his luck is greatest, isn't it?"

"Why do you think I tolerated it for so long?" she growled. "Do you know how relieved I was when Bethesda took her away? I thought here, at last, was my chance to get my son back, to pry her hooked claws out of him. But I did not yet understand the extent of her crimes. When I heard the Heartstriker had laid a new clutch within a year of the last, all became clear."

Chelsie went still. "You knew?"

The empress sneered. "I'm not stupid. Even the Broodmare can't manage two clutches in two years, not to mention she hadn't been pregnant when she'd left China. By the time I heard, though, your ill-gotten spawn were already a year hatched. Even if my worst fears were true, everything was already lost, so I buried my worries and pressed on. I had an emperor to console and lands to manage, and there was no proof. I didn't think of you again until the seer called me."

"Seer?" A cold lump formed in Julius's throat. "What seer?"

The old dragoness gave him a pitying look. "Which do you think?"

There was no question. Even if Julius had been willing to delude himself into thinking she was talking about the Black Reach, the little girl in the empress's arms made it impossible. There was only one egg that child could have hatched from, and Bob had taken it. Right before the Golden Emperor had landed on their heads.

"Why?" he said, his voice cracking. "Why did he betray us?"

The empress shrugged. "I didn't bother to ask. All I cared about, all I have *ever* cared about, is my empire. Really, though, Brohomir's treason just confirmed what I'd always known in my heart: that your sister is a grasping snake who cares nothing for others. She already broke my son once with her selfishness, and that's before we knew the depths of her sin." She looked away with a sneer. "It's only fitting she die for it here."

Julius couldn't believe what he was hearing. "You think Chelsie *wanted* this?"

"I don't care about what she wanted," the empress snapped. "I care about what she did. She broke my son and destroyed my clan!"

"If that's what you think, why are you finishing the job?" he yelled back, pointing at the Qilin. "Maybe he is the last Golden Emperor, but your son was fine until you got here. *You* did this to him. *Why?*"

"Because he was already broken!" she roared, red eyes flashing. "No matter what I did, no matter how I tried, he *never* got over her! He should have been the strongest Qilin ever born. Fortune should have rained on us from the heavens, and yet we have no more than we got under his father. No new conquests, no new lands, *nothing*. For six centuries, the Golden Empire has been stagnant, and then he suddenly announces his intention to conquer Heartstriker?"

She shook her head. "I knew. Even before the seer removed all doubt, I *knew* the end was upon us. I knew that he would break, so I took it upon myself to make sure it happened in a place where it would only hurt our enemies."

By the time she finished, Julius could only stare in horrified awe. "That's why," he whispered, looking up at the evening sky through the jagged circle of the broken pavement. "I thought you were just being callous, but now I understand. You broke the news to him in the worst way *on purpose*. You used him as a *weapon*."

The Empress Mother said nothing, but she didn't have to. The evidence was all around them. They were temporarily safe since there was nothing directly over their heads left to fall, but the Qilin's bad luck was still raging through the city. Julius could actually feel the dragon magic like hungry, malevolent teeth on his skin. It had no target, no purpose. It was just fury blindly lashing out, and everywhere it struck, disaster followed.

All over the city, more Skyways were crumbling, filling the air with the sound of cracking stone. Helicopters fell out of the sky as he watched, their engines just stopping as the emperor's bad luck crashed into them. With every second that ticked by, the noise of crashes and collapse and disaster grew louder and louder and louder, until the whole city was consumed. Already, the adjacent Skyways down the river were starting to tilt as everything that could go wrong did. If this went on much longer, the whole DFZ would collapse, and as much as Julius hated Algonquin, he couldn't let that happen. Not the city where he'd met Marci, and not to Xian.

"I know that look," Chelsie said quietly, moving closer to him in the water. "You've got a plan."

Julius nodded, glancing at Fredrick, who was grimly holding onto the bank beside them. "Can you get us up there?"

He looked pointedly at the triangular shelter beneath the fallen road where the Empress Mother was standing above the collapsed Qilin with the baby dragon in her arms, and Fredrick scowled.

"I can try," he whispered back, glancing down at his Fang. "But this thing only works on Heartstrikers, so I'm not sure—"

"It'll work," Chelsie said confidently. "She's your sister, Fredrick. That makes her one of us."

He didn't look convinced. "But—"

"If you're going to try, do it now," Julius said, glancing nervously down at the water. "Because I don't think this is going to be a safe zone much longer."

It hadn't seemed important during all the other disasters, but since they'd been in it, the river had dropped several feet. Julius wasn't sure if that was due to the Qilin or because of the other magical weirdness going on in the DFZ, but it was getting worse by the second. Just in the time he'd been talking to the Empress Mother, the water by the bank had sunk from his chest to below his waist, and he couldn't imagine it was due to anything good.

"Go," he whispered, grabbing on to Fredrick. "Now."

With a final nervous look, Fredrick obeyed, slicing his Fang through the water under their feet. Since he'd done it right beneath them, they didn't even have to step through this time. They simply fell from one place to another, dropping out—along with several gallons of icy river water—onto the pristine, still-untouched dirt directly behind the Golden Emperor, and directly in front of his mother. Her red eyes were still widening in surprise when Chelsie lunged forward, arms shooting out to snatch her daughter away from the old dragoness.

It happened so quickly, the Empress Mother had no chance to dodge. Or at least, that was what Julius assumed when she failed to move. As Chelsie's arms extended, though, he realized that he was wrong. The Empress Mother hadn't failed to dodge. She hadn't needed to, because the moment Chelsie reached out, a car had slipped off the collapsed road above them, and was now plummeting straight down toward her head.

If Chelsie had been alone, that would have been the end. It took more than a car to kill a dragon even in human form, but it would definitely have knocked her out. Probably worse with the Qilin's terrible luck making everything go so catastrophically wrong. For once, though, Chelsie *wasn't* alone. Fredrick was right behind her, and he yanked her out of the way at the last second, spinning them both to the side as the car plummeted past. Unfortunately, this put the two of them directly in the path of the truck that fell immediately after, crushing both dragons into the mud.

"*No!*" Julius screamed, rushing forward. He was trying desperately to push the truck over when it moved on its own, quivering and then launching out of the way entirely as Chelsie tossed it aside. She was muddy and bloody but alive. So was Fredrick, though he looked decidedly more shaken. The Empress Mother just looked smug, smiling at the two of them with the insufferable confidence of someone who knows they've won.

"Care to try again?" she said, beckoning them closer to her safe position beside the silent, kneeling Qilin. "Charge me all you like. The end will always be the same for the emperor's enemies."

"How are we his enemies?" Julius said angrily. "You're the one who did this!"

"I did nothing but tell him the truth," she said, glaring at him. "I am his mother and his empress. It is my duty to tell him what he needs to know when he needs to know it. Xian understands and respects that. The duty he owes me has been drilled into him since birth. I could spit in his face, and his magic still wouldn't allow me to be harmed, but you're another matter entirely."

Her red eyes flicked to Chelsie. "You are the source of his suffering, and your children are living proof of his greatest failure. Now that he knows, his luck will correct the problem, and none of you will leave this city alive."

Chelsie's face was ashen by the time she finished, and for once in his life, Julius knew exactly why. What the empress described was exactly what Chelsie had been afraid of all this time. But while everyone else seemed convinced this was the only end, Julius refused to give up.

"He won't kill them."

The Empress Mother snorted and looked pointedly at the truck that had nearly crushed Chelsie and Fredrick. "Don't be delusional."

"You're the one who's delusional," Julius growled. "You might not care about your son, but I know you need your emperor. You want to talk about ruining him? How do you think he's going to react when he snaps out of this and realizes you let his luck kill Chelsie and his son?"

"Nothing worse than what's already happened," the empress said with a shrug. "But you misunderstand what's happening here, whelp. I'm not doing this. He is. Look."

She bent over, reaching down to brush the Qilin's long, dark hair aside. When she lifted the curtain, though, the emperor's face was a stranger's. His beautiful features were completely slack, as though he were asleep, but his golden eyes were wide open and terrifyingly blank.

"And now you know the truth," she said, letting the emperor's hair fall back into place. "The Qilin's magic has never been controllable, and my son is the strongest yet. He can rein it in to a point, but when he encounters something that goes too far, breaks too sharply, the luck takes over. Once that happens, he's as good as gone, and he won't come back until his magic has eliminated everything that makes him unhappy."

"You mean eliminated everything *period*," Julius said, voice shaking.

The empress shrugged. "It's not a precision tool, but one suffers the bad to enjoy the good, and who knows?" She flashed Julius a cruel smile. "Maybe when your hateful sister finally dies, he'll get over her at last."

"Or he could break entirely."

"She saw to that already," the empress growled, turning to glare hatefully at Chelsie's bloody face. "But no matter what comes of this, I won't let the Heartstrikers win. By breaking him here, I've snatched a measure of success from our clan's greatest disaster. My son may never be the same, but at least he'll have destroyed you, this city, and all of Algonquin's lands in the process. When this is over, the world will be a better, safer place for our empire, which, if Xian were aware, he would agree is the only thing that matters." She laid a proud hand on the emperor's motionless shoulder. "I raised him well."

"No, he came out well *despite* you," Chelsie snarled, her eyes locked on the little girl clutched in the crook of the empress's arm. "What about our daughter? Will you sacrifice her, too?"

"Of course not," the empress said. "You ruined the line of the Golden Empire forever. We are owed recompense, and Brohomir has informed me that this little urchin is the next seer. A fortune teller who reeks of Bethesda is no replacement for a Qilin, of course, but in times of trial, one must take what one can get."

Chelsie growled low in her throat. Julius felt the same way. He had no idea what game Bob was playing here, but he'd never felt more betrayed in his life. Working with the Empress Mother was bad enough, but to give her his *niece*—their niece, because as Chelsie's daughter, she was Julius's niece as well—it was unforgivable. He was as bad as Bethesda, throwing away his family like pawns for his end game, and now, as always, Julius had had *enough*.

"She doesn't belong to you," he snarled, taking a menacing step forward. "She's a Heartstriker. One of us. She's not *recompense*."

"I won't let you have anything," Chelsie said at the same time, reaching down to snatch a broken length of steel rebar off the ground. "My children, Xian, they're *mine*. I won't let you touch them!"

"Then you should have thought about that before you carelessly destroyed what was *mine*," the empress snarled back, moving closer to the emperor. "But what's done is done. Everything is already broken beyond repair. All I can do now is try to make something out of the ashes."

"Or save it before it becomes ashes."

Julius and Chelsie both jumped. The growling voice had come from behind them, but it was so angry, Julius didn't even recognize it as Fredrick's until he stepped forward, sword in hand.

"You did this to us," he growled, the words so low and bloody that even the empress stepped back. "You are a terrible empress and a worse mother, but awful as you are, it doesn't have to end this way. The Qilin's line is broken, but we're still here. Our two clans, the biggest in the world, are united by blood now. We have a seer and a Qilin who's still alive. I don't care what Brohomir told you—we can still change our future if we work together." He narrowed his golden eyes at her. "Grandmother."

"You have no right to call me by that name!" she roared, crouching over her son. "You're an embarrassment! Your mother and the Broodmare who bore her were both grasping, selfish harlots, and you're just more of the same. The only blood of yours I'm interested in is when it's spilled on the ground."

She spat at his feet as she finished, and Fredrick growled menacingly, but it was too late. The empress had already reached down to grab the Qilin's motionless shoulders, clutching him like a rock in the sea as she cried, "Save me, Xian!"

As always, the Qilin didn't move, but when his mother cried his name, the rampaging magic jerked. For a terrifying second, Julius could feel it rising up like a viper readying to strike. Then, just like before, the magic snapped, and the whole world shook.

Julius covered his head instinctively, but it wasn't the Skyways he had to worry about this time. Those had already fallen, and no amount of bad luck could lift them up again. But though the ground was shaking, the roar in the air wasn't coming from collapsing buildings or breaking cement. It was coming from the river.

The water had been sinking since they'd first dived into it to avoid the falling Skyways. When Julius looked back now, though, the entire half-mile-wide Detroit River had shrunk to the size of a stream, leaving acres of mud, debris, and flopping fish exposed to the air. Julius had no idea what had caused the dry-up, but the Qilin's magic must have reversed it, because the missing water was now rushing back down the empty riverbed straight toward them in a wave of violent, muddy water twenty feet tall.

It was *wide*, too. That was the noise Julius had heard. The wave wasn't just coming down the river. It was crashing through the riverside Underground like a bulldozer, picking up everything in its path—fallen debris, dumpsters, even whole cars—and sweeping it downstream, straight toward them.

"Chelsie," Julius gasped, grabbing his sister. "We need to—"

He never got to finish. He barely had time to brace before the building-sized wave was on top of them, crashing over the collapsed bit of Skyway that protected the Qilin and his mother to slam down on Chelsie and Fredrick, but not Julius. By a stroke of luck, he was still standing where he'd been when he'd moved closer to the Empress Mother, which meant he was in the lee of the collapsed hunk of Skyway. The water didn't even touch him thanks to the perfect angle of the fallen road overhead. It just poured down like a waterfall behind him, hiding Chelsie and Fredrick as they were washed away.

"*No!*" he cried, lurching forward before he came to his senses. The wave was still crashing. If he walked into it, he'd just be washed off, too. The only reason he hadn't been swept away already was because he'd happened to be standing in the exact right place. Because of *luck*, and the moment he realized that, Julius knew what he had to do.

Ripping himself away from the still-falling wall of water that had eaten his sister and Fredrick, Julius made a break for the kneeling emperor. He moved so fast, he actually made it to Xian's side before the empress grabbed him.

"Stay away, Heartstriker," she warned, her red eyes glowing like coals. "I don't know why his luck spared you, but it's over. There's nothing more you can do."

"There's always something I can do," Julius growled back, getting on his knees in the dirt beside the Qilin. "And it starts with talking to him."

"To what end?" the empress said, moving so that she was physically between Julius and her son. "He's gone. There's no one left to hear you."

"He heard you say his name just now."

"That's different," she snapped. "I'm his mother. You're no one."

"Then you won't mind if I try," he said, reaching around her. But when he started to pull back the curtain of black hair that hid the Qilin's face, the Empress Mother grabbed his wrist.

"Stop."

Julius looked up at her, staring her right in the eyes. "No."

"Arrogant whelp," she snarled, digging her nails into his skin. "You think I won't kill you?"

"Actually?" He shrugged. "I do."

The empress sneered, but Julius wasn't finished. "You said it yourself: the Qilin's luck isn't a precision tool. It's an instinct lashing out at cues, as it did for you just now when you cried for help. But unlike you and Chelsie and everyone else here, the Qilin doesn't care about me. At least, not on the deep, personal level he feels for the rest of you. I'm just another Heartstriker, one who's done him no harm, and that makes me invisible."

"And you think that will save you from me?" she growled.

"No, I think that really was luck," Julius said. "*Actual* luck, as in I was standing in the right place at the right time. The reason I think *you* won't kill me is simple: you haven't already."

"Then I will remedy that," the empress hissed, letting go of his arm to wrap her hand around his throat. But even when her sharp nails bit into the soft flesh behind his windpipe, Julius didn't flinch or fight. He just knelt there and took it, staring defiantly up at the empress until she was the one who looked afraid.

"What's wrong with you?" she cried. "Defend yourself!"

"I *am* defending myself," Julius said, letting his arms fall slack at his side. "The Qilin's luck isn't as uncontrollable as you claim. You're trying to manipulate it right now. If I attack you, I make myself your enemy and get punished accordingly. But if I do nothing, I won't be a threat, and his luck won't care. You do, though, which is why I'm *sure* you won't kill me, because if you could, I'd already be dead."

The wrinkled hand on his throat began to shake. "That's a dangerous assumption."

"Not really," he said. "I mean, I'm taunting you, and you still haven't done it. I think I know why, too." He smiled. "You said that Bob was the one who sold us out, and I'm the one dragon Bob can't kill."

The moment he saw her face go pale, Julius knew he was right. He still had no idea what game Bob was playing. For all he knew, the seer really had sold them all out. But if the Black Reach's visit this morning had proved anything, it was that Bob's investment in Julius was long term, and while his hatred of being a pawn was still very much there, Julius wasn't above using it when the need was great.

And right now, the need was *very* great. Two families were on the line, including the little dragoness, who was still in her grandmother's arms, watching the flood with a child's fearless interest. She deserved better than to be traded between clans like a war prize. They *all* deserved better than this, so Julius held firm, trusting in his brother's manipulations, if not his intentions, until, at last, the empress let him go.

"It seems you're more of a dragon than you appear," she said bitterly. "But knowing the rules of the game doesn't make you safe. Brohomir warned me that if *I* killed you, Xian would die, but he never said anything about you falling victim to bad luck."

"But I'm not going to have bad luck," Julius said confidently. "Because I'm not going to hurt you, and I'm not going to hurt him." He nodded at the motionless Qilin. "I'm going to do what you should have done. I'm going to help your son stop this, and there's nothing you can do about it."

"I don't have to do anything!" the empress cried. "Don't you understand? You've *lost*! Just because I can't stop you from talking to Xian doesn't mean he'll listen. I raised him to be an emperor before all else, and now, thanks to your sister, he's failed his greatest responsibility. The ancient line of the Qilin is *dead*, and there's nothing you can say that will bring it back."

"You're right," Julius admitted, turning back to the Qilin. "I can't change the past, but I don't have to, because that's not where we live. We're alive right now, and if there's one thing being Bob's tool has taught me, it's that *now* can always be changed for the better."

The Empress Mother looked baffled by that, but Julius had already put her out of his mind. He also banished the sick feeling of worry for Chelsie and Fredrick, whom he hadn't seen since they'd been swept away in the flood that was still raging behind him. He let go of everything, focusing only on the dragon in front of him as he got down on his stomach in the cold mud so he could look at the Qilin face to blank face.

"Your Majesty?"

Nothing.

"Emperor?"

Nothing again.

"Xian?"

It was probably wishful thinking, but Julius would have sworn he saw the emperor's golden eyes flicker at his name. It wasn't enough to go on, but Julius took it anyway.

"Do you remember what I told you in the throne room?" he said softly. "Chelsie told you the truth today, and while you are the very last Qilin, I don't think that's necessarily a bad thing. You've been held prisoner by a power you can't control for your entire life, holding everything in and making yourself miserable for centuries in the name of duty. But if misery is the price of the Qilin's good fortune, then it's not good fortune at all. It's a *curse*. I wouldn't wish your luck on my worst enemy, and I don't think *you* would, either."

He smiled. "Look at it that way, and this whole thing becomes a blessing in disguise. You haven't lost an irreplaceable gift. You've spared your son from having to suffer as you have, and that's more good fortune than your luck has ever brought you."

He paused there, holding his breath, but the emperor's face was still as blank as ever, and Julius sighed.

"Chelsie told me you always wanted children," he said, trying a different approach. "Well, now you have twenty. Twenty-one, counting the baby. You've got Chelsie, too. She never wanted to cut you off. The only reason she lied was because she was afraid of *this*."

He waved his hand at the destruction around them.

"But it doesn't have to be this way. You can't control your luck, but you *can* control how you react to things, and this isn't the catastrophe your mother claims. Yes, the Qilin line is broken, but you're still emperor. You've still got your dragons and your lands, but now you have a family, too. *Your* family, who needs *you*. You already lost Chelsie once because of this. How much more are you going to let being Qilin take from you?"

As he said that last part, Julius felt the ground shift under his hand. When he looked down, he saw that the Qilin's fingers had dug deep into the soft dirt. He didn't know if that was because of him or not, but it was the first movement he'd made since he'd gone down. Julius was scrambling to think how best to build on that when Fredrick burst out of the water with a gasp.

The giant wave had passed while he'd been talking to the Empress Mother, but the flood was still raging. Julius was high and dry thanks to the lee of the fallen Skyway and the little hill the emperor had chosen to collapse on, but the rest of the lot, the street, and the buildings on the other side were consumed beneath several feet of violently churning brown water.

It flowed so fast, the water dragged Fredrick right back off his feet. He fought his way up again a second later, grabbing a chunk of the collapsed Skyway to keep his head above water as he looked around frantically. It wasn't until he dove back into the flood, though, that Julius realized Chelsie hadn't come up yet.

An icy stab of dread went through him, and he turned back to the emperor. "Please, Xian," he begged. "Don't let them use you like this! You're not a weapon. You're a dragon. An emperor! Who cares what your mother wants? You can still have everything *you* want: Chelsie, your son, your children, your empire. You can have it *all*, but you have to come back right now and save it before—"

A splash interrupted him. When Julius looked over his shoulder, though, it was just Fredrick coming up for air. He looked panicked now, tossing his sword up onto the broken hunk of Skyway before diving back down. When he'd vanished under the swirling water, Julius turned back to the Qilin, grabbing the emperor's head and forcing him to look.

"Your son is going to die," he said, voice shaking. "He's going to drown down there searching for Chelsie. She might be gone already. That's a much bigger tragedy than losing the Qilin. You said you just wanted to be happy. Well your happiness is down there under that water, and if you want to save her, save *them*, you need to snap out of this and go *help your son!*"

He was shouting by the end, clutching Xian's blank face between his shaking hands. And nothing happened. The emperor didn't blink, didn't flinch, didn't do anything. Then, just as Julius let go and jumped to his feet to go help Fredrick himself, a tiny voice whispered, "My son?"

Julius whirled back around. The emperor was still exactly as he'd left him, his eyes blank as a doll's, but there was a strain in his muscles that hadn't been there before. A tightness that quickly became violent shaking as he forced himself to move.

"My son," he breathed, prying his curled hands out of the ground. "I have a son."

"*Yes,*" Julius said, dropping back down to his knees so he could help the emperor. "You have ten sons and eleven daughters, one of whom is apparently the next seer. You can't let her go through that alone! She needs you. They all do, but Fredrick needs you *now*, so come back. You said you'd be our emperor, but what emperor leaves his subjects when they need him most? If you really cared about your duty, you'd come back and do it. Come help us. *Right now.*"

He stopped there, holding his breath, but the dragon didn't move. Behind them, the water splashed as Fredrick came up for air and went back down, but Xian didn't even flinch. Then, just when Julius was on the edge of giving up, the emperor blew out a long line of smoke.

What happened after that came in painfully slow bursts. Julius didn't know what was actually going on, but from the outside it looked like the Qilin was trying to force his body through a wall of cold, heavy clay. He came back in bits and pieces, his muscles straining and giving up then straining again until, all at once, the magic released him, letting go as fast as it had taken hold to drop him in the mud beside Julius.

"*Xian!*" Julius offered him his hand at once. The Qilin grabbed it, lifting his face—which, of course, was completely free of mud—to look around in confusion.

"What happened?"

There was no nice way to put it, but Julius tried anyway. "You did," he said. "But that's over now. It's time to make things right, starting with Chelsie."

The emperor's already pale face went even paler, and he shot to his feet. "Where is she?"

Julius pointed at the flooding water, and the Qilin started pulling off his golden robe to dive in. Before he'd gotten his arm out of the sleeve, though, Fredrick broke the surface again, and this time, Chelsie was with him.

"*Julius!*" he yelled, his normally calm voice frantic. "*Help me!*"

Julius was there before he could finish, charging into the water to help his brother haul Chelsie's dead weight into the shelter of the broken skyway. When the emperor moved in to help as well, though, Fredrick turned on him with a snarl. "*Don't touch my mother!*"

"It's okay, Fredrick," Julius said, putting up his hands. "He's himself again."

The Qilin nodded rapidly, but Fredrick wasn't paying attention. He was leaning down to do CPR on Chelsie, breathing into her mouth five quick times before sitting up to press his locked hands into her chest for the compressions. He repeated the cycle twice, alternating between forcing air into her lungs and pushing it back out through her chest. Then, just as he was about to start the third round of breaths, Chelsie's body convulsed.

She rolled over with a gasp, coughing out lungfuls of muddy water as Fredrick slapped her on the back. She was still struggling to breathe when a voice called the emperor's name.

"Xian?"

Everyone looked up to see the Empress Mother standing in the farthest recess of the fallen skyway, her silk slippers pressed together on the last remaining dry patch of land.

"Come," she said calmly. "Let's go."

The Qilin looked at her like she was insane. "I'm not going anywhere."

"You can't possibly want to stay with *her*," the empress said, sneering at Chelsie, who managed to glare back even while choking. "Whose fault do you think this is?"

"Mine," Xian said firmly, rising to his feet. "And yours."

He looked around at the destruction as if he was seeing it for the first time, which, to be fair, he probably was. "I did this," he whispered, voice shaking. "But you helped push me to it." His jaw clenched as he turned back to his mother. "You used me."

"I did," she said, lifting her chin. "You are the Qilin. You exist to be used for the good of our Golden Empire. A weapon against the enemies who would—"

"Enemies?" he cried, flinging out his arm toward Fredrick. "Is my *son* the enemy? Is *she?*" He shifted to point at the little dragon the Empress Mother was still clutching in her arms. "How long have you known I had children?"

The empress's jaw tightened beneath the sag of her wrinkled skin, and the Qilin began to growl. "How long, Mother?"

She sighed. "I suspected the truth shortly after hearing Bethesda had clutched two years in a row, but I knew nothing for certain until today. That is the *truth*, Xian, but it wouldn't have mattered if I'd known from the beginning. I still wouldn't have told you, because I knew you'd do *this.*"

She waved her hand at the flooded lot dotted with collapsed roads. "To allow such a disaster would have been a disgrace to my name and yours. But it had to be done eventually, so I chose to let it happen here. This way, it is Algonquin who suffers, not our subjects. I should think you'd be glad of my foresight."

"I am glad," Xian said quietly. "Glad it wasn't worse. Glad I didn't—" He cut off with a wince, and then he turned away, putting his back to her. "Go home."

The empress's red eyes went wide. "I will not be dismissed like a—"

"So long as I am emperor, you will be whatever I say," he growled. "Go *home*, Empress. And leave the child."

Her arms tightened on the little girl. Before she could say anything else, though, Chelsie blew a puff of fire into her hands to warm them.

The moment the magic flashed, the girl's head popped up like a cork. She started to scramble, biting the empress with her baby fangs when the old dragoness wouldn't let go. The empress dropped the whelp with a pained cry, and the little girl skittered across the ground before launching herself straight at Chelsie, latching on to her torso with all four limbs like a baby monkey.

From the look on her face, Chelsie was as surprised by this as everyone else. Julius, though, could only grin.

"I bet it's your fire," he said, smiling down at the little dragon, who seemed to be trying to burrow her way into Chelsie's ribcage. "You did feed it to her every day for six hundred years. It makes sense she'd recognize it now."

"I think you're right," Chelsie whispered, putting a hesitant arm around the little dragon. The shyness only lasted a second before she crumpled, wrapping herself around the little dragon with a sob. "I've got you," she whispered, pressing kiss after kiss against the child's fine black hair. "It's okay. You're safe now."

In classic whelp fashion, the little dragon immediately tried to bite her. She actually landed one, sinking her teeth into her mother's arm. It looked painful, but Chelsie didn't seem to mind at all. She just laughed, prying the little dragon's jaw off her arm with an indulgent smile while Julius stared in shock.

He didn't think he'd ever seen his sister smile like that. He'd *definitely* never heard her laugh, but she must have been too exhausted to hold back, because she was doing both in earnest now, the relief making her look centuries younger as she beamed down at the daughter she'd never thought would hatch.

"A proper dragoness," she said, bopping the whelp on the nose and then snatching her finger back before the little dragon could bite it off. "At least I can see Bob hasn't been starving you."

The baby dragon chuffed, and Chelsie laughed again, but the happy look fell off her face when she looked up to see Xian watching the interaction with an expression that could have been wonder or terror.

"I have a daughter," he whispered.

"Actually, you have several," Chelsie said, lowering her eyes. "I thought this one was a dud, but apparently, Bob found a way to hatch her." She heaved a long sigh. "I suppose I owe him for that."

Considering what Bob had put them through, Julius didn't think she owed him anything. He was about to say as much when Xian dropped to his knees in front of Chelsie.

"I'm sorry."

"Don't be," she said, shifting uncomfortably. "It's my fault. I was the one who ran."

"Because you were afraid of me," he said angrily. "I should never have made you fear. You were everything to me, and I let you go. I believed the lies, even when I should have known better. I left you alone with Bethesda, left you to suffer." He clenched his hands. "I'm *sorry*, Chelsie. I've done you so much wrong, and I can't—I'm just—" He cut off with a frustrated scowl that quickly turned into a regretful one. "I'm so sorry."

"Don't make this all your fault," she snapped, meeting his eyes at last. "I was the one who panicked and lied. I should have trusted you more. I should have told you."

"You did what was needed to protect yourself and them," Xian insisted. "Someone had to protect them from..."

He didn't finish, but his haunted eyes said the rest, and Chelsie sighed.

"Maybe I did," she admitted. "But that doesn't mean it was right. So much of this could have been avoided if I hadn't tried to do everything myself. Even if my intentions were in the right place, I had no right. After all"—she smiled at him—"they're your children, too."

Julius had said the exact same thing, but he never could have gotten the look of pure joy that spread over the Qilin's face when she said it. "They are, aren't they?" he said, his golden eyes going from Fredrick to the little dragon and finally back to her. "We have *children*."

"If you can call six-hundred-year-old dragons children," Chelsie said, her dark brows furrowing. "I'm not even sure where most of them are right—"

She didn't get to finish, because that was the moment when the Qilin swept down, throwing his arms around Chelsie and the little dragon on her lap. By some serendipitous stroke, he managed to snag Fredrick as well, dragging the tall dragon down with him as he pulled them all into a tight embrace.

"It's not lost," he said in a voice that was neither controlled nor serene but vibrant with relief and happiness. "I have you. We have a family."

No one could say anything after that. Xian was squeezing them too tight for words, but other than the little dragoness, who was wiggling fiercely, no one seemed to want to escape. They were all just... happy, which Julius took as his cue to turn around before he got all maudlin about missing another warm family moment, which he was absolutely *not* going to do. They deserved their happiness, and he wished them nothing else. He just needed to look away for a while.

Thankfully, there was plenty to look at. The flood was receding now, the muddy river trickling peaceably back to its banks. He poked around the rubble for a bit in the vague hope of finding some trace of where Bob had vanished to, but the water had washed the seer's scent clean away.

He was contemplating going to check on the Empress Mother's car next. She'd made herself scarce once the baby had jumped ship, but Julius still wanted to make sure she'd really left and wasn't waiting in the shadows to get revenge or anything stupid like that. He was about to walk over and check when someone tapped him on the shoulder.

It felt like Fredrick, but when Julius turned around, he found himself face to face with the Golden Emperor. It didn't seem possible, but the Qilin looked even more astonishingly perfect now with his muddy robes and wild hair than he had when he'd landed in the desert. It was the smile that did it, Julius decided. He'd never seen anyone look as perfectly happy as Xian did right now, which made it even odder when the elegant dragon dropped to his knees.

"Julius Heartstriker," he said solemnly, bending down to press his forehead to the dirt at Julius's feet. "You have saved me and my family from my mother's treachery. On behalf of the Golden Empire and all the dragons who benefit from my fortune, thank you." His voice began to tremble, and he bowed lower still. "Thank you from the bottom of my heart."

Julius cringed in horror. He hated when anyone bowed to him, but this went beyond anything he could have imagined. The only thing that saved it for him was the thank you. *That,* he would treasure for the rest of his life, but the rest of this experience made him want to sink into the ground.

He was trying to figure out how to make the Qilin stop when the emperor raised his head on his own. And as his eyes met Julius's, the full power of the thankful Qilin's magic landed on him like a golden mountain, knocking everything else away.

CHAPTER FOURTEEN

If Marci had had a life left to lose, the last thirty minutes would have taken twenty years off it.

Not five minutes after she'd agreed to wait for Bob's signal, the DFZ had started shaking like gelatin. The collapses came next. It started by the river, but within minutes, every Skyway in the city was either cracked or falling. It was the worst disaster since the original flooding of Detroit, and stuck here in the Heart of the World, she couldn't do a thing about it.

"I don't know how much more of this I can take."

"Bob will come through," Amelia assured her. "Just wait."

"If we wait much longer, there'll be nothing left to save," Myron said, clenching his fists. "We have to stop this."

"But what do we stop?" Marci asked, pointing at the collapsing city. "Is this the DFZ's doing or Algonquin's?"

"I don't think it's either, actually," Raven said, head tilting quizzically. "I've never felt magic like this before."

"Neither have I," Amelia said. "But there's definitely a dragon involved. A big one." She leaned out over the moving image, peering curiously down through the scrying circle into the destruction. "I wonder who it is?"

"The dragon's the least of our worries," Ghost said, pointing at the city's northern edge. "Look."

Marci swore under her breath. Below the Leviathan's shadow, Lake St. Clair was dropping at an alarming rate. So was the Detroit River, the muddy water retreating, like something upriver was sucking it in. The riverbed south of Fighting Island dried up as she watched, leaving a flat swath of barren mud and gasping fish all the way to Lake Erie, which was also drying up. All the water was, and the longer Marci watched, the more afraid she became.

"I think we're out of time."

"Not yet," Amelia said. "Bob will come through."

"I'm sure he will," Marci said. "For *you*. But we've got to do something *now*. Look at this!" She pointed at the city, where buildings were collapsing and helicopters were falling out of the sky like dead bugs. "This has gone way past 'wait and see.' Whatever that dragon's doing, it's kicked off a full-blown disaster, and if we don't do something to stop it, Algonquin will."

As though it'd been waiting for its cue, the retreating water chose that moment to break, surging back down the riverbed in a wave as tall as the Skyways. It crashed through the city, tearing telephone poles out of the ground and picking up trucks like dead leaves. The water hit the crowded bridges next, knocking buses sideways against the guardrails and ripping people unlucky enough to have their windows down out of their cars and into the churning river below.

"That's it," Marci growled.

"Marci, *no*," Amelia pleaded, digging her claws into her arm. "Trust me!"

"I do," she said, staring down at her friend. "I absolutely believe you when you say Bob's got a plan. I just can't wait for it anymore. There's more at stake here than buildings and people's lives. Our plan relies on getting the DFZ on our side. That was always a long shot, but it'll be *legitimately impossible* if we let her domain be destroyed."

"She has a point," Raven said.

"I never said she didn't," Amelia snapped, looking back at Marci. "You're absolutely right, but that doesn't change the fact that if we move too early, we're not going to win." She clasped her claws together. "*Please*, Marci, I'm begging you. Give Bob more time, and I swear on what's left of my fire, he will come through."

Marci clenched her jaw, glaring down at the collapsing city as Algonquin's wave finished washing through it. She was still trying to make a decision when Shiro's voice spoke behind her. "I don't know if we have the luxury of more time."

She looked up in surprise. The last she'd seen him, the shikigami had been to her left, controlling the scrying circle. He must have walked away while they'd been watching the destruction, though, because he was now back at the center of the circular mountain top, standing over the seal with a pale, worried look.

"Merlin."

Marci was at his side in an instant. Myron joined her a split second later, his eyes widening in alarm as he reached down to touch the crack in its surface. The damage that had once been a hairline fracture, but was now big enough to slide his fingernail into.

"How did this happen?"

"I already told you," Shiro said. "It's the volatility." He looked pointedly out at the Sea of Magic, which now looked like footage of the Florida coast during a hurricane. "Algonquin and the DFZ are two *very* large spirits. When they fight, the whole sea churns. If we don't calm it down, *quickly*, it'll no longer be a question of how to fix the seal. The whole thing is going to break."

And send a thousand years of magic flooding back into the world all at once. "So how do we stop it?" she asked, turning to Myron.

"I don't know if we can," he said nervously, leaning over the stone to study the marks split by the crack. "Patching the Merlins' seal was always going to be the spellwork equivalent of putting duct tape over a crack in the Hoover Dam. Now we've got Algonquin and the DFZ taking a hammer to the other side as well." He shook his head. "Frankly, I'm amazed the crack's only widened this much."

"You have to calm them down," Shiro said desperately. "Even before it was damaged, the seal was not made to withstand this sort of abuse. If your plan to return the magic slowly is to survive, this war between gods cannot continue."

"It can't continue if *any* of us wish to survive," Raven croaked from where he was still perched on the edge of the scrying circle. "The DFZ's domain is getting hammered. If she goes down, our best chance to trick Algonquin into getting rid of her Nameless End goes with her."

"And if she breaks out, the Sea of Magic will grow even more violent," Myron said, turning back to Marci. "We can't wait anymore. The seal is at its structural limit. Also, with all the water Algonquin's throwing around, my physical body, which I left in the Pit, is probably in serious danger. I'm not tied to a death spirit like you. If I drown, I just die, and Raven's plan comes to nothing. The longer we wait, the smaller our chance of success becomes. Seer or not, you have to go *now.*"

"If she does that, it won't work!" Amelia said angrily. "This isn't a question of chance. Bob's already seen the future. He knows what's going to happen, and the only way we land the future we want is by following his instructions and waiting for the signal." She put a claw on Marci's hand. "He'll come through," she whispered. "Wait."

Marci let out a long breath. She knew Amelia was right. Going against a seer's advice was monumentally stupid, and yet...

She turned and walked back the scrying circle, looking down at what was left of her city. The wave that had washed through the Underground was receding now, but the damage it had caused was immense, and that was her fault. She was the one who'd cut Myron's leash and sent the DFZ back, the one who'd decided not to stop the magic again. Those were *her* decisions, and while she still believed she'd done the right thing, the costs were greater than she could have imagined. Everywhere she looked there was chaos and destruction, and the longer they waited, the worse it would get.

The logical choice was to do as Amelia said and wait for Bob's cue, but when the stakes were this high, did she have the right to make it? To stand here and wait for the right moment while others suffered for her decisions?

No.

Marci closed her eyes. The voice in her head was cold comfort, literally. But while Ghost's opinions could be sharp, they were usually spot on, so she sucked it up and asked, "Why?"

No one has the right to make others pay for their choices, her spirit said, stepping up beside her. *But that's the price of making decisions that matter.*

Marci didn't understand. "But—"

You are Merlin now, he said. *No matter what you decide, there will be consequences. Someone is going to get hurt, and it will be your fault. That's the burden of leadership, but I wouldn't have chosen you if I didn't think you could carry it.*

He looked over his shoulder at Amelia, who was still watching Marci like a tiny red hawk. *The dragon and I both chose you because we trusted you to make the right decisions when the time came. Not the safe ones or the easy ones, but the choices that will actually get us to where we need to be. That's the burden we place on you, but you don't have to carry it alone. We are with you, whatever you decide.*

He held out his ghostly hand as he finished. After a moment, Marci took it, sliding her shaking fingers into his still, freezing ones. It felt wrong and reckless to accept so much trust. She'd been punching above her weight class since the night she'd blown up her childhood house. Even now, standing as a Merlin in the Heart of the World, she was making it all up as she went. She had no idea what she was doing, how she was going to pull it all off without disaster, and yet, despite everything, she was the Merlin. Even if Bob had pulled the strings that got her in front of it, the Merlin Gate had opened for her. That had to count for something.

"Audacity is the baseline for entry," she whispered, clutching her spirit's hand as she turned back to Amelia. "We'll wait."

The dragon slumped in relief, but she was the only one. Everyone else looked deeply concerned, including Marci herself. But then, just as she opened her mouth to tell them—and remind herself—of all the times Bob had pulled off the impossible, something incredible happened.

Later, looking back, Marci was never able to say exactly what it was. There'd been no jolt, no flash of light or swell of magic. It was just a feeling. An odd giddiness that spread through her mind like golden sunshine.

If it'd been only her, Marci might have written it off as the relief of finally making a decision, but Amelia had clearly felt it, too. The moment the happiness had blossomed in Marci's mind, the little dragon had jumped, leaping so high, she nearly fell into the scrying circle.

"Did you feel that?!"

Marci nodded, eyes wide.

"I felt it, too," Ghost said, his deep voice rich with wonder. "It was beautiful. What was it?"

"Dragon magic of some sort," Amelia said, her eyes round. "Insanely strong, too. Almost primal. I've never felt anything like it."

"Is that good or bad?" Marci asked.

"I don't know," Amelia said with a sharp-toothed grin. "But I bet it's our signal."

Myron scoffed. "I didn't feel anything."

"Neither did I," Raven said, his croaking voice deeply disappointed. "Can you describe it?"

"No," Marci said, grinning as wide as Amelia. That only made Raven more upset, but she couldn't stop. The beautiful golden feeling was getting bigger by the second, filling her to bursting with happiness and an insane confidence that whatever she tried, no matter how risky, it would work. Today was her lucky day. It was all going to work!

After a terrifying half hour of waiting, the sudden joy was like a starter pistol. Amelia was already racing for the mountain's edge, flapping her little wings frantically as she shot off the cliff, over the green forest, and out toward the tumultuous blue sea.

The smile fell off Marci's face. Even the supernatural giddiness wasn't enough to stop the flood of panic as she realized what Amelia was doing.

"Wait!" she cried, running after her friend.

"No more of that," Amelia called back, flapping faster. "I've waited centuries for this. I'm not waiting another second. Somewhere out there is the spirit of dragons, and I'm going to find it!"

"But you don't even know where it is!" Marci shouted, skidding to a halt at the cliff's edge. "There are thousands of spirits out there. At least wait until I can help you find—"

"I told you," the dragon yelled, her voice fading as she flew farther and farther away. "No more waiting. This was my signal as much as yours. I don't know what's going to happen, but Bob told me it was the only way, and he's never let me down."

She looked back over her shoulder, her eyes flashing with excitement. "I've got this, Marci! Go with Raven. He'll take you back so you can actually do all that Merlin stuff we went through all this nonsense for." She turned back, folding her wings close against her body as she prepared to dive. "Just stick to the plan, and I'll see you on the other side."

"But how are you even going to get there?" Marci yelled. "*Amelia!*"

But it was too late. The little dragon was already falling like an arrow, her serpentine body vanishing with barely a splash into the intense, endless blue of the Heart of the World's interpretation of the Sea of Magic. Marci was still staring at the place where she'd gone under when a heavy weight landed on her shoulder.

"There, there," Raven said, clutching her gently with his talons. "She told you she was going to take over a Mortal Spirit, and she can hardly do that from up here."

"I didn't know she was going to dive into the water!" Marci said frantically. "She could barely keep herself together in the Sea of Magic without Ghost. How's she going to find the right vessel before the magic grinds her to paste? She doesn't even know where she's going!"

"That's her yoke to bear," Raven said with a wink. "But you're not the only one who's good at playing things by ear. I've known Amelia since she was younger than you are. She's as twisty and conniving as the next dragon, but she never jumps unless she knows she's going to land on her feet. She'll be fine. You need to worry about yourself."

He ducked his head, leaning over to stare straight into her eyes with his black, beady ones. "It's time to keep your promise, Merlin."

With a shaky breath, Marci nodded. She turned away from the cliff where Amelia had vanished and walked back toward the others, who were still standing beside the cracked seal. "Myron," she said firmly, "keep an eye on that crack. Block it with your own magic if you have to, but do *not* let it break."

"I'll do what I can," he said. "It'll be about as useful as putting my finger in the dike, but I'll try. Just don't take too long. And good luck." He glanced nervously at the wild sea. "You'll need it."

In the strangest way, Marci felt like she already had it, because scared as she was, she'd never felt luckier in her life. She wasn't sure if that was from knowing she was safe in Bob's matrix or what, but the moment Myron said it, Marci knew from the top of her head to the tip of her toes that he was right. This was her lucky break, and she was going to need every bit of it.

"Ready?" she asked Ghost.

Rather than answer, her spirit jumped at her, turning back into a fluffy white cat just before he landed in her arms. When he was safely curled in a freezing ball against her chest, Marci turned back to Raven with a determined look.

"Take us back."

It was impossible to tell, thanks to the beak, but she would have sworn the bird spirit grinned at her as he spread his wings. When he flapped them, his talons dug painfully into her shoulder, yanking her soul out of the Heart of the World and into the dark beyond.

• • •

Back in the DFZ, everything was going wrong.

Algonquin knelt at the bottom of the lake she'd made in the Pit. The lake that was *supposed* to hold the monster down, but was now

413

draining away. She didn't even know how it had happened. The water was hers, pulled from all her bodies through rivers and lakes and storm drains, from the very bottom of herself. This entire section of the DFZ should have been under her absolute control. Hers to command, just like the beds of the lakes that gave her her name. And yet, somehow, it wasn't.

Water had slipped. Magic had failed. Leftover spellwork from her mages had interacted poorly. The crazed spirit below had gotten a few lucky hits. Alone, none of it would have mattered. Together, though, it had been too much, and she'd been forced to let the water—*her* water, her life, the essence of what she was—go. Now it was all flooding uselessly through her city in a wave of failure, and she didn't know if she had the strength to pull it in a second time.

I told you it was lost.

"It's not lost," Algonquin said bitterly, looking back at the shadow that was always behind her. "It's just bad luck."

Bad luck like this doesn't happen by accident, the Leviathan said. *You saw the reports of the Chinese dragons' arrival in New Mexico. You knew the Qilin was close. I warned you to be careful.*

"I've been careful!" she cried. "I've killed every dragon that dared enter my city, but I can't do anything about worms on the other side of the world. What would you have me do, flood China?" She rippled with rage. "I can't exterminate their entire species by myself!"

I can.

"Yes," she said, her voice quiet. "Yes, you can. But not yet."

Why not?

"Because I'm not ready," she snapped, turning back to the circle. "I'm not defeated yet!"

Black tentacles came out of the dark to curl around her. *There, there,* he whispered. *You've fought so hard, but there's no point in lying to yourself. You always knew it would come to this. That's why you called to me. No one can say you haven't gone above and beyond, but one spirit cannot stand against the world.* The tentacles snaked through her water, wrapping through her like coils. *Let me finish your work. Let me in, and I will devour all your enemies.*

The words were cool darkness in her mind, welcoming as sleep, but Algonquin had already slept enough for an immortal lifetime. "No," she said stubbornly, shoving his touch away. "Not yet." Her water clenched. "I'm not beaten yet."

But you will be, the Leviathan promised, his huge head lifting above her in the dark. *It's already coming. Listen to the wings.*

She couldn't miss them. There was no way to see the sky from down in the Pit, but this bird wasn't in the sky. He was in the world that belonged only to them, a huge black specter flying through the Sea of Magic with prey in his claws. Raven, the traitor, was bringing someone back from the other side. Who or for what purpose, Algonquin didn't know, but if he could do that...

Then the end is even closer than you thought, the Leviathan finished, shaking his head. *There's no stopping this, Algonquin. Every second, the trickle of magic pouring back into the world widens, and your dream of turning back the clock grows fainter and fainter, if it was ever possible at all.*

His tentacles flicked over the circle Myron had made out of Raven's construct. The one she was currently using to keep the monster they'd built at bay. *Your would-be Merlin is lost, your city is in ruins thanks to the dragon's cursed luck, and you have already given everything you have. You are finished. Now's the time to give up. Let me help you. Let me save you while you still have something to save.*

Algonquin clenched her water tight. But before she could tell him she would *never* go down, not so long as she had a drop left in her, the circle of spellwork she'd been keeping closed through sheer brute force finally burst open, sending what was left of her water flying into the dark as the spirit she'd been desperately holding back exploded into the world.

"ALGOOOOOONQUUUUUUIN!"

The name was a hateful cacophony, an ugly combination of car horns and gunshots and every other terrible sound the hideous city could make. The Lady of the Lakes roared back, slamming the thing trying to crawl out of the broken circle back down under a wave of pounding water, river silt, and raw determination.

"Not yet!" she screamed, hammering it again and again. *"I'm not dead yet!"*

She wasn't even sure whom she was screaming at: the city trying to claw its way through her, or the shadow waiting like a vulture behind her. Either way, the words were true. Even like this, even now, she was still Algonquin, Lady of the Lakes. The only spirit who'd ever stood up to humanity and survived. Her fury had already drowned Detroit once. If the DFZ pushed her now, she'd gladly do it again, and this time, the city would never be rebuilt.

"I'm not dead yet," she whispered, the words bitter as old runoff as she looked up at the dark. "The pact still stands! I gave you your name, Leviathan! I called you here. I let you in. Until I die, you are *mine*, and I order you to help me!"

A sigh rattled through the giant shadow, and then black tentacles began landing around her like falling bombs, crushing the screaming Mortal Spirit back down into the black, fetid mud.

"And keep her there this time," Algonquin snapped, sinking back into the flood. "I'm going to get more water."

I'll do what I can, but it won't be long. Until you let me in, I'm only a shadow, and shadows can't fight gods.

She knew that, but a shadow was what she had, so a shadow was what she would use. It wasn't as though she had a choice now, anyway, so Algonquin left him to it, rushing off through the flooded landscape to ready her lakes for war.

And behind her, hidden by the dark, the Leviathan held on just long enough. The moment he'd honored the letter of the deal that had bought him a name and a crack in this plane, he faded into the dark, releasing the screaming spirit of the DFZ into the ruins that had been her city.

• • •

Marci was still in the dark when Raven let her go.

"Wait," she cried, grabbing his talons before he could escape. "You can't leave me here!"

"Why not?" he croaked, curious. Or, at least, he *sounded* curious. She couldn't tell for sure since she couldn't see anything but black.

"You said you'd take me back to the world of the living," she said angrily. "This is just back where I started."

She'd know this particular dark anywhere. It was the same empty blackness she'd seen right after she'd died, before she'd figured out how to open her eyes. Or maybe someone had taught her? Marci couldn't remember, and she didn't have time to worry about it now. Even Ghost wasn't with her anymore, which was cause enough for panic.

"This is no time for tricks, Raven," she said, trying not to sound scared. "Take me back to my body *now*."

"Silly child," the spirit replied, his mocking voice soft as a feather in her ear. "Where do you think you are?"

His talons vanished from her hand as he finished, and the darkness became heavy in a way Marci had never felt before. Heavy and cold and solid, like a cement blanket pressing down on top of her. She was still trying to figure out what had happened when she realized she couldn't breathe.

Terror shot through her. Marci began to panic in earnest after that, fighting and clawing and kicking at the black weight that was holding her down. Dirt, she realized as her fingers dug in. She was buried under *dirt*. Buried alive.

"*Marci!*"

Ghost's shout was a real sound in her ears, not a sensation in her head. It was also muffled, coming from somewhere above her. When she tried to yell back, though, all she got was a mouth full of soil. In the end, she had to settle for digging, pawing frantically at the dirt with her hands until, at last, she broke through, plunging her arm up out of the shallow grave someone had built over her body.

The moment her hand punched free, deathly cold swallowed it. A second later, Ghost yanked her up, plucking her body out of the dirt and into the too-bright light of the world. The *real* world, filled with real air that she sucked deep into her lungs before collapsing

417

back to the torn-up ground, coughing and spitting the dirt out of her mouth as she fought to catch her breath.

"Are you okay?" Ghost asked, slapping his hand down hard on her back to help clear her lungs.

Marci coughed again, raising a shaking hand to brush the dirt off her face. "I'm alive," she said, her voice hoarse from disuse. "I'm *alive*."

It felt too good to be true, and since things that were too good to be true usually were, Marci began frantically checking her body. Other than being filthy and numb with cold, though, she was fine.

Her limbs were all there, whole and unbroken. Her head was good, and her lungs were working great now that she'd coughed out all the dirt. Even the hole General Jackson had shot through her chest was healed, though you'd never know it from her T-shirt, which still had a giant bloody hole in the front. Below the filthy fabric, though, her skin, muscles, organs, and bones all felt perfectly fine. *Too* fine.

"How is this possible?" she asked shakily, pressing her dirty hands to her face. "I didn't even rot."

"You can thank *me* for that."

Marci whirled around to see Raven directly behind her, perched on top of what looked like the blackened remains of a gigantic bonfire. The fine ash and charred bits didn't smell like fire, though. They didn't smell like anything. After all the weirdness of her recent life, that seemed like a minor detail. At least until Marci realized where they were.

"You've got to be kidding me," she said, leaning into Ghost as she looked up at the picturesque valley surrounded by forest and crowned with a mountain that she knew way too well. "You brought me to *Reclamation Land?*"

"Technically, you never left," Raven said. "This is where you died, if you'll recall."

It wasn't something Marci could forget. Now that she knew where she was, though, the giant burn pile Raven was sitting on had a new, far more sinister edge.

"Is that...?"

"Yes," Raven said, shaking the fine ash off his feathers. "This is all the remains of the dragons Algonquin bled for power in her first attempt to raise the DFZ. There wasn't enough magic left in them for another try after you and the Empty Wind wrecked things, so Algonquin just abandoned them here when she moved on to Myron's plan. But I'm a thriftier bird. I hate seeing anything go to waste, especially something as rare and valuable as a dragon corpse. So, since I had an inside tip that you and your kitten might not actually be out of the game, I decided to put them to use."

He pointed his beak at a shallow ditch that someone had dug from the base of the ash pile to Marci's grave. Fittingly, it was lined with chicken-scratch spellwork, though Marci supposed it was technically Raven-scratch. She couldn't read it either way, but she didn't really need to. The bloodstained channel that ran from the pile of dead dragons to her *grave* made it pretty obvious what had happened here.

"Ugh," Marci said, putting a hand over her mouth. "You used *dragon blood* to bring me back to life?!"

"No," Raven said. "I brought you back to life with my own fantastic powers. The dragon blood was just to make sure your physical vessel was back in working order when the time came to return you to it." He puffed out his chest. "Pretty neat trick, if I do say so myself, and quite fitting. Everyone's always accusing you of being a dragon's pawn, so it's only fair that you actually get to enjoy a bit of their power for once."

Marci supposed that made sense, but she was too busy dry heaving to appreciate his cleverness. "I can't believe you used *blood magic* on me."

"That's a fine thank-you for a miracle," Raven said, turning up his beak. "And for the record, it's only blood magic if all parties involved are human. If I'd been a mortal mage like you, *then* it would be necromancy, but seeing as I'm a spirit using dragons he didn't even kill, it's all aboveboard."

Technically, but..."You used *corpses!*"

"I'm a *scavenger!*" Raven cried. "I'm not going to leave perfectly good power lying on the ground when I can use it, and I didn't hear you griping over the details when I was *bringing you back to life!*"

"Okay, okay," Marci said, reaching up to brush the dirt out of her short hair. "I don't mean to complain. It's just...I personally knew at least one of those dragons, and the idea that you healed me using the magic left in dead bodies is really freaking creepy."

"Says the woman who just crawled out of her own grave and keeps an aspect of death as a pet."

Marci winced. "Touché," she said, looking down again at the smooth skin of her healed stomach through the hole in her shirt. "And, um, thank you."

"You're welcome," Raven said, hopping into the air. "Now, if you'll excuse me, we both have pressing business to attend to. I have to collect an old friend, and you, I believe, have a city to save."

"Right," Marci said, getting her head back in the game. Now that the initial shock was fading, it was finally starting to sink in that she was alive again. *Actually* alive, breathing and everything. She had a body, a real one, with no hole in her stomach. Which reminded her...

"Wait!" she cried at Raven as he flew into the sky. "So am I a hundred percent human again?"

"What else would you be?" he cawed, circling over her head. "You're as human as you ever were, and on a related note, you should probably try to avoid dying again. I was able to bring you back this time due to an *extremely* fortunate series of events. We won't be so lucky again, so you might want to think twice before you jump in front of any more bullets."

Marci had no intention of *ever* going through anything like this again. In fact, when this was over, she was going to corner Shiro and make him teach her everything the ancient Merlins had known about life extension, because she'd heard stories of mages living for centuries, and she wanted in on that. She had a dragon to keep up with, after all. A dragon she was going to find as soon as things stopped being on fire.

"Come on," she said, reaching out for Ghost to help her up. "We've got a lot to do and no time to do it. First, though, we need to get back into the city. I say we break into one of the Algonquin Corp garages, steal a car, and—"

"We can do a lot better than that," the Empty Wind said, grabbing her hands and lifting her, not to her feet, but into his arms. Before Marci could ask what he was doing, a freezing wind whipped up from the ground, lifting them both smoothly into the air. It was just like when he'd flown her through the Sea of Magic, but much shakier and way scarier now that Marci could actually see the ground shrinking under her feet.

"Whoa," she said, wrapping herself around his body like a koala clinging to a tree. "Since when can you fly on this side?"

"Since you became Merlin," Ghost replied, his deep voice rich with pride. "Our bond has always been strong. Now that you've seen my true face, though, we are unbreakable, and you have a physical body again in a place that's brimming with magic. Both of these give me leverage to do things I never could before. Not on this side, anyway."

Now that he'd mentioned it, Marci knew exactly what he meant. The air was tense with magic, but not the usual sort. The wild, heavy Reclamation Land magic that normally dominated here was completely overpowered by a sharp power that smelled of grease and wet asphalt. It was the same magic she'd felt in the endless city where she'd confronted the DFZ. What really caught Marci's attention, though, was the way the magic clung to her skin, seeping into her body like water that then flowed in a torrent straight down her connection to Ghost.

"Are you *drinking* magic through me?" she cried. "Without my permission?"

"We're connected," he said innocently as they picked up speed. "And I needed power. I haven't gotten anything new to eat since before you died."

That was true. But still. "I am *not* your sponge," she growled, though it was hard to be mad at him for taking what he needed, and it wasn't as though Marci had to worry about him getting the upper hand on her anymore. After what they'd been through, she trusted the Empty Wind with her life and death, and she could get used to traveling like this.

Ghost was flying them through the air the same way he'd moved through the Sea of Magic. Other than the occasional wobble and the ground whooshing past below, there was no sensation of movement, which was crazy seeing how they'd already cleared the forest at the edge of Algonquin's Reclamation Land. By the time they were over the tumbledown old neighborhood where Marci had first settled into her hoarded cat house, she was a hundred percent on board with this new and improved mode of transportation.

"This is awesome!" she cried, turning around to get a better look at the rapidly approaching city. "You're better than a helicopter!"

"I *am* a wind," he reminded her, but his voice sounded nervous. "Careful. We're close now."

Marci nodded, looking down to check her bracelets, which were thankfully still on her wrists. A quick search also turned up a miraculously unbroken piece of casting chalk in her pocket. Given how wet everything looked, her markers would have been more useful, but though Marci had gotten her body back, her bag seemed to be a total loss.

It was probably in the hands of some sellout Algonquin corp mage, along with her Kosmolabe, the loss of which upset her even more than her two-hundred-dollar marker set. Still, after her miraculous rise from the dead, complaining about losing a Kosmolabe was like criticizing the color scheme of your winning lottery ticket, so Marci shoved her disappointment to the back burner. She was looking up to ask Ghost about their next step when a blast of magic shot up from the ground below.

For a terrifying second, the impact sent them reeling. Even after Ghost regained control, wild power was whipping through the air around them in waves, forcing him to weave and dodge to avoid being socked again. After several sickening drops, he gave up and went for cover, setting Marci down on the pointed roof of one of the superscrapers that hadn't started leaning yet.

"What was that?" she cried, clinging to the building.

The Empty Wind hovered, his glowing eyes worried in the void of his face. "Not sure, but I think Algonquin just lost control of the situation."

He hadn't even finished speaking when a second wave of magic even bigger than the first ripped through the city like a cannon blast. Just like before, the magic was a physical presence, a moving wall of power that shattered windows and set Marci's ears ringing. This time, though, there was a voice inside the blast. A screaming wail of rage and loss that rose from the city itself.

"*ALGOOOOOONQUUUUUUIN!*"

"Oh boy," Marci whispered, tightening her grip on the roof. "That can't be good."

"At least she's not mad at us," Ghost whispered back, crouching down beside her. "A common enemy works in our favor."

"Not if she runs us over on her way to battle." Marci peeked over the building's edge to get a better look at the city below. "We have to calm her down, convince her that blindly lashing out at Algonquin will hurt more than it helps. Shouldn't be too hard. Her city's already broken all to—"

The building groaned beneath them, and it wasn't alone. All throughout the DFZ, the ground was swelling. It rose up like a building wave, sending the broken Skyways and toppled buildings sliding in all directions for a terrifying heartbeat before they suddenly jerked back together, the cement foundations and support beams twisting together like wires as the ground opened up below them, gaping up at the night like an enormous mouth.

"SLAVE MAKER."

The roar came from the city's foundation, echoing from the sewers and the storm drains and the forgotten warrens of the Undercity in a cacophony of bending metal and breaking glass. Even with so much noise and distortion, though, Marci recognized the voice. It was the same one she'd heard after Ghost ate her in the Sea of Magic. The voice of the city itself, rumbling like an earthquake.

"*DIE!*"

At the word *die*, a volley of debris shot out of the city's gaping maw. Cars, buses, chunks of buildings, entire intersections broken off during the chaos were sent flying over Marci and Ghost's heads and into the water of Lake St. Clair. Each missile landed with a tremendous splash, sending water flying hundreds of feet into the air. But this was just the start, an opening ruse to cause confusion. Before the water finished falling, the DFZ roared again, and the superscraper Marci and Ghost were clinging to began to lurch violently. A second later, the whole thing tipped sideways as the gigantic building tore itself out of the ground and launched like a missile straight at Algonquin's Tower.

That was the last thing Marci saw before she was flung off the side and sent spinning into the empty air beyond.

• • •

"Come on," Julius said, tugging at his sister's arm. "We need to *go*."

He never thought he'd have to say that to Chelsie, but between the Qilin's unexpected thanks and the incredible rush of magic that had come after, everyone had just sort of...stopped.

Not that Julius could blame them. After years of anxiety, worry, and misfortune, the power of the Qilin's luck going full bore was like a drug. Everything felt right, perfect, as though nothing could ever be wrong in the world again.

But even the happy haze of good fortune couldn't hide the fact that the ground was shaking worse than ever. Scarier still, the magic was moving with it, trembling like a wire about to snap. The absolute worst part, though, was that Julius would have sworn he could smell Marci on it.

That was impossible, of course. The magical craziness going on here was new, and Marci was dead. It was probably just confusion caused by the fact that her scent and the DFZ's magic were so closely linked in Julius's mind. Unfortunately, knowing it was an illusion didn't make it go away. Every time he breathed in, there she was, faint but unmistakable.

Each breath left a little crack in the wall he'd built to keep the pain of her death from washing him under. It had already worn down the happiness of the Qilin's good fortune, leaving him scrambling to get his family moving before he broke down again. But just when he'd finally managed to get the dragons to their feet, a horrible screech sent them all right back down.

It sounded like an entire steel factory going through a shredder, but angrier. The sort of fury you felt to your bones, even when it wasn't yours. Julius was still trying to get his body to unclench when the unnatural scream hit him again. This time, though, the rage formed a word.

"*ALGOOOOOONQUUUUUUIN!*"

It came from everywhere and nowhere, vibrating from the cracked pavement and the toppled buildings and the broken edges of the collapsed Skyway overhead. It came from the water and the dirt, from the air itself. Even the Qilin was knocked out of his thankful, serene haze, looking around in alarm for the source of the sound. "What was that?"

Before Julius could say he didn't know, the voice blasted them again.

"SLAVE MAKER."

"That's our signal to go," Chelsie growled, tucking her daughter against her side as she turned to her son. "Fredrick."

The F was way ahead of her. But as he lifted his Fang to cut them all back to Heartstriker Mountain, a third scream exploded through the air.

"*DIE!*"

The word went off like a bomb. The whole city lurched, throwing them all sideways, along with what was left of the tilted Skyway ramp. If the miracle of the Qilin's luck hadn't still been flowing through them, the ramp that had been their shelter against the flood would have landed on their heads. But as impossible as it seemed, the broken slab of Skyway didn't fall. It actually lifted *up*, hurtling into the dark sky as though it had been plucked out of the ground by some giant, invisible hand.

It wasn't the only one. Through the hole in the broken Skyways, Julius could see the air was full of flying objects. Vans, cars, hunks of cement, dumpsters—whatever wasn't nailed down was hurtling over the city to bombard Lake St. Clair.

Or, at least, that was what Julius assumed. From where they were on the river's southern bend with all of downtown between them and Algonquin's lake, he couldn't see a thing. A few seconds later, though, he realized he didn't need to. The explosion of water when the attack landed was so big, he could see it over the tops of the superscrapers. And that—watching the white water shoot up so high it cleared the skyline—was how he saw the two figures standing on top of one of the Financial District's tallest buildings.

They were so far away, a human wouldn't have seen them as more than specks in the night. Now that he was unsealed, though, Julius's eyes were back to their usual dragon sharpness, which meant he could clearly make out the woman standing nonchalantly on the superscraper's peak.

A young woman with short dark hair, standing beside a tall man wearing a Roman centurion's helmet.

"Julius?"

Chelsie's voice was sharp in his ear, but Julius barely heard it. He was too busy rubbing his eyes, grinding his palms into them until he saw spots. When he looked again, though, the woman was still there. She'd actually turned toward him now, her face tilted down to look at the city below. The beloved face he'd know anywhere, but never dreamed he'd see again.

Marci.

"*Julius!*" Chelsie yelled, grabbing his shoulder. "What are you—"

He tore out of her grasp, throwing his Fang away to ditch the extra weight as he charged forward. He ran so fast, his feet barely touched the ground, and then they didn't touch at all. He didn't even realize he'd changed shape until he was in the air, flying through the broken Skyways faster than he'd known he could go.

But still not fast enough.

Like the world had gone crazy in slow motion, he saw the building Marci was standing on rise up just as the skyway had done earlier, as though it were being picked up by an invisible hand. A hand that then tossed the entire hundred-floor building like a spear straight at Algonquin's tower, and sent Marci flying off in the other direction.

She sailed through the empty air, helicoptering her arms as she tried desperately to slow her fall, and Julius's heart clenched in the terrible realization that he wasn't going to make it. No matter how fast he flew, there was no way he could get to her in time before she hit the ground. He was desperately trying anyway when the Qilin's magic rang through him like a golden bell.

When the emperor had thanked him, his luck had been a hammer, a blunt, overwhelming presence that had no aim except to bring happiness. This was different. This time the luck was as sharp as his own claws, eager to slice the world to ribbons to give Julius what he wanted. What he desired most.

Marci, Julius thought frantically. *Marci. Marci. Marci.*

He was still repeating her name when a violent wave of magic—the same magic that had tossed the buildings around—shot up from below. Julius folded his wings instinctively, letting the explosive force slam into him.

In any reasonable universe, that should have smashed him flat. But the Qilin's golden luck was singing in him now, twisting his body in just the right way that the magic threw him instead, launching him faster than he could ever have gone on his own. Faster than Marci could fall. Fast enough that, when she hurtled through the broken hole in the Skyways toward the ground beneath, Julius was already there, his wings spread to catch them both as she slammed into him.

CHAPTER FIFTEEN

Marci was falling through the night sky.

It had happened so quickly. One second she was clinging to the building, watching the city come alive. The next she'd been flung into the chaos, her body spinning wildly. Then she'd started to drop, plummeting toward the ground faster and faster and faster. And then, just as the words *terminal velocity* were repeating like a chant in her mind, she crashed into a yielding mass of soft, royal-blue feathers.

"*Marci!*"

The familiar voice was frantic in her ears. Bigger and deeper than she remembered, but no less recognizable as she looked around in shock to see she was clinging to a dragon's back. A blue-feathered dragon with wide wings and beautiful, frantic green eyes.

"Julius."

The name slipped out of her, which was a miracle in itself, because the rest of Marci seemed to be shutting down. After every-thing that had happened—of which falling off a superscraper had been just another turn in the road—to have him suddenly *there*, right here under her fingers…It was too much. She'd fought her way back to life for a lot of reasons, including saving the world, but her deepest, most selfish desire had always been to get back to him. To her dragon.

And he was *right here.*

There was no playing it cool after that. Marci grabbed Julius with all her strength, hugging him so hard she almost spoiled their landing as he set them down on the broken street. The moment he touched down, Julius grabbed her back, coiling his long body around hers like a snake as he hugged her with everything he had.

"It's really you," he whispered, squeezing her tight. "You're alive." He pressed his broad forehead against hers with the happiest gleam in his green eyes she'd ever seen. "Marci, *you're alive!*"

Marci nodded against him, too happy to speak. Too happy to think. Too happy to do anything except cling to him for dear life, which was fitting since he had, in fact, just saved hers.

I would have caught you, Ghost grumbled.

"Don't ruin this for me," Marci hissed, shooting a warning look at her spirit over Julius's wings. When she turned back to her dragon, though, his giddy happiness was quickly giving way to confusion.

"I can't believe it," he said, pulling back a fraction to look her up and down. "I'm so happy, but how…How is this possible?"

Marci bit her lip. "It's kind of complicated."

"Complicated?" He stared at her in disbelief. "Marci, you *died*. I saw it. Chelsie *buried* you."

That would explain the dirt she'd had to dig through. But as much as Julius deserved an explanation, there simply wasn't time.

"I promise there's a perfectly reasonable story behind this," she said, doing her best to keep her voice calm. "But I can't get into it now. Algonquin's trying to destroy the DFZ. If I don't stop her, the two of them will bring this whole city down."

As if to prove her point, an echoing crash sounded in the distance, followed by an equally enormous splash. When Marci tried to turn to see what new bit of the city had just gone into the drink, though, Julius grabbed her shoulders with his forefeet.

"Why do you have to stop her?" he asked, sheathing his curved talons before they could touch her. "You just came back from the dead! I'm not going to let you die again fighting Algonquin. I've already got a way out. Just come with me and—"

"No," she said firmly, staring straight into his green eyes. "I can't run from this, Julius. This mess is partially my fault. I'm the one who cut the spirit of the DFZ loose."

Now he looked even more confused. "Since when does *the DFZ* have a spirit?"

"Since about six hours ago," she said with a helpless smile. "Again, no time to explain, but the short version is that if I don't fix this, we're all going to be in a lot of trouble on a *lot* of different levels."

That was a ridiculous cop-out even by Marci's standards. To her surprise, though, Julius didn't launch into a barrage of questions. He just sighed and reluctantly uncoiled his body from hers. "What do we have to do?"

She blinked in surprise. "We?"

"Yes, *we*," he said, incredulous. "I just got you back from the dead. That's a *miracle*, Marci. I don't care if you're marching straight down Algonquin's throat. I'm not leaving your side. Whatever you have to do, we're doing it together, so hop on and tell me where we're going."

He lay down on the ground after that, lowering his wings so she could climb into the space between them, but Marci could only gape. "You want me to *ride* you?"

"It's the fastest way to get around, and it lets me stay by you," he said stubbornly. "And I *did* promise you a flight."

That he had. "It's going to be nuts," she warned as she climbed onto the ridge of his feathered back.

"All the more reason to stay close," he said, swiveling his head to look at her with an intense expression. "I lost you once, and it was the worst experience of my life. I am *never* losing you again."

He sounded so serious, Marci almost cried again. It was a ridiculous way to react, but she couldn't help it, because he was always like this. No matter what happened, Julius had *always* stayed by her side. He'd always helped her, always had her back. Even now, when he had no idea what they were up against and the whole city was coming apart, he didn't hesitate. He was right there with her, ready to jump into the fire feet first, and as she had since the very beginning, Marci loved him for it.

"Thank you," she whispered, her voice thick.

He pressed his head against her shoulder, breathing her in deep, and then he jumped them into the air, forcing Marci to hold on tight as his wings pumped on either side, lifting them into the cloudy night with astonishing speed. Or not so astonishing. For all his claims that he was a mediocre dragon, Julius had always been fast, and now was no exception. Even Ghost had to scramble to keep up as they shot through the gaping holes in the collapsed Skyways and back into the shaking city.

Or what was left of it.

"What the..."

All her life, the DFZ had been the city of the future. A famously huge, neon-lit, double-layered wonder of human magic, commerce, and ingenuity in all its forms. Now, though, it looked like an active war zone.

Every bit of construction was damaged. Buildings were cratered or collapsing or on fire, filling the sky with plumes of black smoke. Most of the elevated Skyway bridges were down, and those that hadn't collapsed outright were cracked and sagging. Without their support, the city's famous superscrapers were leaning like poles in quicksand, but the damage wasn't limited to the upper city.

Down in what had been the Underground, fires were raging as gas lines snapped and electrical boxes exploded. Other blocks were still flooded, the streets washed under several feet of dirty water. But as horrible as all of this was to see, what made everything a thousand times worse was the fact that the destruction was *moving*.

The city wasn't just broken. It was undulating, the buildings and roads twitching and shifting and curling in on themselves like cornered animals. Across the smoking skyline, out in the middle of the shallow green waters of Lake St. Clair, Algonquin's white tower was in ruins. Since she'd been falling at the time, Marci hadn't seen what had happened, but the uprooted superscraper must have struck true, because the entire top of the Lady of the Lakes' famous stronghold had been knocked clean off.

From Julius's back, Marci could actually see the tower's elegantly swirled peak—and all the speared dragon head trophies that'd been stacked on top of it—lodged in the dirt several hundred feet inland on the lake's Canadian side. But crazy as it was to see Algonquin's Tower, the icon of the city, decapitated, that was nothing compared to the spirit beside it.

Marci had seen Algonquin many times now, and in many guises, but never like this. This was no Lady of the Lakes, no personification or humanizing element. This was Algonquin as she must have appeared that very first night magic came back: a skyscraper-sized spout of furiously spinning water.

The only thing bigger was the shadow of the Leviathan behind her. At first, Marci thought he was just hovering, but then she saw his tentacles down in the lake, sweeping water into Algonquin as her swirling pillar rose higher and higher, bigger and bigger, until, without warning, she burst, collapsing on the writhing city in a crushing, skyscraper-sized wave.

"*Julius!*"

He was moving before she'd even opened her mouth. Wings pounding, he flew them to a safe height moments before the tsunami of lake water crashed into the buildings. The city screamed when it hit, an inhuman cry of pain and rage Marci felt to her bones. Even Ghost trembled, his fear shooting up their connection like a spear of ice.

We have to stop this! he cried in her mind. *At this rate, Algonquin will drown the city before we even make contact.*

"I know!" Marci yelled back, leaning recklessly off Julius's back to scan the city below. "We have to figure out a way to talk to her, convince her to stop fighting."

She's not going to stop fighting while Algonquin's trying to destroy her.

"Then we'd better get to her before Algonquin throws another wave," Marci said desperately. "She can't keep this up. The DFZ's the bigger spirit, but she doesn't have Myron feeding her magic anymore, and she's burning through it fast. Look."

She pointed down at the buildings, which were all waving frantically like water plants in a storm. "I don't know how much power it takes to make cement move like a snake, but I'm guessing a lot.

With the seal still in place and no Merlin to pump extra magic into her, the DFZ's bound to be out of gas soon. Once that happens, Algonquin can pound her into grit at her leisure."

So what do we do?

"Stick to the plan," Marci ordered. "We find the DFZ, defuse the situation, bring in Myron, and move on with Raven's ploy while there's still some city left to save."

Or we could let them fight, the Empty Wind suggested, his glowing eyes eager. *The DFZ has no Merlin, but as of right now, she's still bigger than Algonquin. If we fought with her, we wouldn't have to depend on Raven's ruse. We could defeat Algonquin the old-fashioned way, smashing her power and draining her magic before she has a chance to call out to her Leviathan.*

"Or we could drive her right into his slimy tentacles," Marci pointed out. "We can't take that risk. For all we know, her watery finger is already on the trigger." She looked down at the flooded city, her face grim. "We stay the course."

If you say so, the Empty Wind said bitterly, moving directly in front of Julius, who gave no sign he saw anything. *I'll go search for her, but be careful, Merlin. Algonquin's back is to the wall, and the dragon's not as fast as I am.*

"That's why you're the one doing the looking," she said with a smile. "I'll be fine. Just be fast."

Ghost's sigh whispered through her head one last time, and then he was gone, vanishing into the rumbling night.

"So I only heard half of that conversation," Julius said nervously, darting behind a huge building to hide them from Algonquin's water spout, which was already rising again. "But I take it we're staying up here while Ghost goes to look for...what again?"

"The spirit of the DFZ, soul of the city."

"Right," he said, landing on the side of the superscraper with his claws like a lizard on a tree. "And how do we find something like that?"

"Honestly, I have no idea," Marci admitted. "But I'm hoping Ghost will—"

An earsplitting *boom* cut her off. It was so close, Marci's first thought was that something had hit them. The fact that they were still in one piece proved that wasn't the case, thankfully, but reality wasn't much better.

Unsatisfied with merely flooding her enemy, Algonquin was now catapulting water directly into the city, flinging truck-sized shots of water at high speed directly into the DFZ skyline. One of these shots, the boom they'd heard, had scored a direct hit on the building they were hiding behind. As a result, the entire superscraper was now falling like a toppled tree, and Julius and Marci were on the wrong side.

"*Go!*" she screamed.

Julius pushed them off the side, wings pounding as he struggled to get clear, but even he wasn't fast enough. The falling building was simply too big, and the space for acceleration too short as the skyscraper fell over on top of them with a groan of bending steel and breaking concrete. But then, just when the falling side of the building was close enough that Marci could see her terrified face in the cracked glass windows, it stopped.

For a breathless second, the building hung suspended in the air, and then it rolled to the left like it was rolling away down a hill. Marci was still trying to understand how that had happened when the broken building finally rolled far enough out of the way to reveal the enormous golden dragon floating serenely on the other side.

After that, she couldn't do anything but stare. The dragon wasn't the biggest she'd seen—that honor still went to Dragon Sees the Beginning—but he was hands down the most spectacular. The scales that covered his long, snaking body were pure gold, each one glinting like treasure in the light from the fires below. His shining eyes were golden, too, and he had no wings at all. If not for the white smoke curling like incense from his mouth, Marci would have sworn he was a giant floating statue.

Even when he began snaking through the air toward them, the movement looked too perfect to be real. She was wondering if he was some kind of conjured illusion when a slightly smaller—but still terrifyingly large—dragon with matte-black-dyed feathers and familiar green eyes appeared in the air beside him.

"What do you think you're doing?" the new dragon snarled in Chelsie's voice, glaring murder at Julius, who was nearly hyperventilating from his race to get out from under the no-longer-falling building.

"You're supposed to fly *away* from danger, idiot, not straight into..." She trailed off as her green eyes spotted Marci clinging to Julius's back, and then the black dragon heaved a long, smoke-filled sigh. "Well, that explains a lot."

"Who is she?" the golden dragon asked in a voice so beautiful, Marci almost fell off.

"His significant mortal."

The golden dragon looked confused. "I thought she was dead."

"So did I," Chelsie said. "But I should know better by now than to assume anything with these two." She flashed Marci a wall of teeth that was probably meant to be a smile. "Welcome back."

Marci nodded slowly, but scary as the teeth were, she was far more interested in the tiny dragon she could now see clinging to Chelsie's neck, its little golden eyes wide with excitement. "What is *that?*"

As usual, everyone except Julius ignored her. "It's her daughter," he whispered. "And the golden dragon is the Qilin Xian, also known as the Golden Emperor."

"You mean the dragon who rules China?" When he nodded, Marci gasped. "What's *he* doing here?"

"I'll have to tell you later," Julius said with a tired smile. "You aren't the only one who's had a lot going on."

Clearly. Before she could say anything else, though, Julius turned to the golden dragon and lowered his head. "Thank you for saving us."

"That wasn't me," the emperor said. "It was my son."

He pointed down with a perfectly curved claw, and Marci and Julius both looked to see a *third* dragon hovering below them.

He was just as big as the Golden Emperor, but like Chelsie and Julius, he had wings and feathers. Glossy, true-black ones that set off

435

his self-satisfied golden eyes beautifully as he shook the bits of building from his claws, which he'd clearly dug into the building before he'd pushed it away. But even that wasn't the most impressive part. What *really* made Marci gasp were the bone-white sheaths covering each curving talon, augments she'd learned to recognize as the telltale sign of a transformed Fang of the Heartstriker.

"Who is *that?*"

"It's Fredrick," Julius said, eyes wide in amazement. "He's *huge.*"

The Qilin smiled proudly. "He is my eldest son."

"*Fredrick's* your son?" Marci said incredulously. "The stuffy butler dragon?" When the Qilin nodded, she turned back to Julius in bafflement. "You've gotta tell me what happened while I was gone."

"As soon as we get time," Julius promised, glancing nervously toward the lake. "Right now, we have bigger problems."

That was putting it mildly. Despite hurling what had to be an entire Great Lake's worth of water at the city, Algonquin's torrent was bigger than ever. She was now as tall as the Leviathan behind her, and she showed no sign of stopping.

Neither did the city. Down below, the flooded DFZ was rumbling like a drum. On the heavily built-up lakefront, the few buildings that hadn't been flattened were shifting, curling over like fingers into a fist before crashing into the water below. One by one, the Lakefront developments punched into Algonquin's water, forming a stone barricade against any new waves.

It was the same in the Underground. Old buildings, parked cars, even collapsed pieces of the Skyways rolled into position, stacking themselves like bricks to form a makeshift wall across the places where the lower city was open to the water.

Once the barriers were in place, the pounding magic in the air tightened like a pulled knot, closing so fast it made Marci gasp. Even the dragons winced, ducking for cover instinctively as the city roared and launched a new volley into the air.

This one was even bigger. The first attack had thrown a building into Algonquin's Tower. This time, whole blocks went into the air, hurtling over the barriers at Algonquin herself. The buildings slammed into her water, breaking her apart and sending sprays of water flying so high into the air, they came down on the Canadian shore like rain. When she tried to re-form, the city hit her again, screaming with a triumphant wail of twisting metal as it continued to hurl buses, buildings, even whole hunks of overpass into the lake.

"That's it," Chelsie said as a car hurtled past her. "Time to go. Fredrick, take Julius and his mortal first. Xian and I can dodge until you—"

"I'm staying," Julius said.

"*Are you crazy?*" Chelsie yelled, ducking the bus that flew by next. "I don't know what's going on here, but it looks like the city's gone to war with Algonquin!"

"Actually, that's *exactly* what's happening," Marci said. "The DFZ—"

"This isn't something we want to be in the middle of," Chelsie said over her, swooping down to grab her brother. "Come on."

"*No,*" Julius said stubbornly, dodging her. "I'm not leaving until I've helped her!"

There was only one person he could be talking about. Sure enough, all the dragons looked at Marci. But while the urge to cringe under the eyes of so many giant, magical predators was pretty intense, Marci was no longer just a mortal. She was a Merlin, and while she wasn't as versed in the history of that title as Myron, she was pretty sure Merlins didn't cower.

"I have to stop this," she said, proud that her voice only shook a little. "Everything you see is happening because Algonquin is fighting the Mortal Spirit of the DFZ, and it's going to get a lot worse. But despite what's going on, the DFZ isn't actually a violent spirit. If I can just get to her, I'm pretty sure I can talk her down."

Chelsie looked unconvinced. "And you need Julius for this because...?"

"Because I'm not leaving her," Julius growled. "*Ever.*"

His sister blew out a frustrated huff of smoke. "What is it with you? Why do you never *run* from danger like a sensible dragon?"

Julius clenched his jaw. "Because I—"

"That was rhetorical," she snapped, turning around to face Algonquin's pillar of water, which was now nearly to the sky. "You want to stay? Fine, but let's not be stupid about it. You go with your human. I'll head down there and find a way to keep the waterspout distracted. Fredrick, you get the emperor and your sister back to the mountain."

Julius blinked at her. "What?"

"That's *my* question," Fredrick growled, flying up to join them. "What do you think you're doing?"

"Nothing I want to," Chelsie growled back. "But Julius isn't going to leave his mortal, and since I owe him pretty much everything at this point, that means I don't get to leave her, either."

"I never said you had to stay!" Julius cried.

"I'm not leaving you to fight alone," Fredrick said at the same time. "You're good, Chelsie, but even you can't beat Algonquin."

"If a single dragon could beat Algonquin, we would have fixed this problem years ago," she said. "But I'm not going to fight her. I'm just going to buy Julius time so his mortal can do whatever she's here to do and we can *leave.*"

"For the last time," Julius growled. "You don't have to—"

"Then I'm going with you," Fredrick said, ignoring him. "I also owe Julius, and I'm not letting you do this alone."

"Neither am I," the Qilin said, moving closer to Chelsie. "I didn't go through all of this to leave your side now. Besides, if you want your distraction to last longer than sixty seconds, you're going to need my help."

"Luck *would* help," Chelsie admitted, though she didn't look pleased. "But we do this my way. No heroics, nice and clean."

"NO!" Julius yelled, shoving his way between the other dragons. "Do none of you have ears? I said no! N-O. *No.* You are *not* fighting Algonquin."

"Now who doesn't have ears?" Chelsie snapped. "We're not fighting her. We're occupying her attention."

"Same difference," Julius snapped back, his breaths coming fast and panicked. "I won't let you do this."

"That's not your choice to make," Fredrick said calmly, glaring at Julius in a way that did not fit the subservient F Marci remembered at all. "This debt is ours to pay. If you want to stay with your mortal, we'll keep the lake spirit off you as long as we can. At the very least, she'll be shooting at us instead of the city."

"That would be *really* useful, actually," Marci put in. "It'll be a lot easier to talk the DFZ down if she's not being actively punched in the face by Algonquin."

"So she should punch my family instead?" Julius cried.

Chelsie sneered in disgust. "Like we'd let her get so close." She started flying toward the lake. "Decision's already been made, Julius. Take it and go, because we won't be able to get you much."

With a bob of his head, the Qilin took off after her, snaking through the night like a golden ribbon.

"Looks like that settles it," Fredrick said, smiling at Julius as he turned to follow the others. "Good luck, sir."

"*Wait!*" Julius yelled. "This isn't how it's supposed to..."

But the three dragons were already gone, shooting through the night toward Algonquin.

"Go," Julius finished, head sagging.

Marci bit her lip. "I'm sorry. I didn't mean for—"

"It's okay," he said quickly. "Not your fault. It's just..." He blew out an angry huff of smoke. "Dragons are very stubborn."

Marci was tempted to tell him to look in the mirror on that one, but there wasn't time. She wasn't entirely sure about the dynamics of the dragon debts at play here, but if Chelsie, Fredrick, and the Qilin were determined to use this as an excuse to pay Julius back, she wasn't going to waste it. Especially since Ghost was tugging on their connection.

Found anything? she thought at him.

There was a long pause, and then an image slipped into her mind. A dark, man-made cavern filled with water and debris and the lingering reek of death.

"Gotcha," Marci said, looking down at Julius. "She's in the Pit."

He shuddered, his feathered body shaking under hers. "Of course she'd be there. Why would we ever go somewhere nice?"

He heaved another smoky sigh and cast one last look at the dragons flying toward Algonquin. Then, like he'd come to a decision, he dove down, flying toward the cluster of miraculously still-standing Financial District superscrapers and the polluted Pit that was hidden beneath them.

• • •

This trip to the Pit was very different from the last time Julius had been here.

It was still terrible, of course. Even the boiling magic that swelled up to cover the city wasn't enough to overpower the deathly, oily feel of the DFZ Underground's most polluted magical wasteland. Instead, the two mixed, forming a noxious amalgam that reeked of old decay, motor oil, and fetid lake water. In fairness, though, that last one was probably more physical than magical thanks to the five-foot-deep layer of dirty floodwater that currently covered the Pit's silted floor.

"Lovely," Marci said, holding her nose as Julius flew them in. "And here I thought this place couldn't get any worse."

"At least it's not as dark as before," he said, looking up at the Skyway ceiling, which, like all the other overpasses in the city, was now laced with cracks letting in light from above. Mostly the orange glow of the fires that were springing up all over town, despite Algonquin's flood, but light was still good.

"We have to end this," Marci muttered, her fingers clenching on his feathers. "At this rate, there'll be nothing left to save."

"No argument here," Julius said. "But what are we looking for?"

She sighed against him. "No idea. The last time I saw her, the DFZ couldn't make up her mind between smallish human and giant rat, but since spirits are just sentient magic, that doesn't mean much. She could be anything, but I have a feeling we'll know her when we see her."

Julius hoped so, because right now, he couldn't see much of anything. The last time he'd been here, the Pit had looked like a flattened, abandoned suburb buried like a body under the thickest part of Algonquin's elevated city, which made sense since that was exactly what it was. As the first victim of Algonquin's flood, the Pit—or Grosse Point as it was known in those days—had never really recovered.

While the rest of Detroit had been either rebuilt or built over, this place had been sealed up like a tomb, covered with Skyways and locked in the dark like a dirty secret. Nothing had been improved or changed. Even the silt from the first flood was still here, lying like a blanket over the broken streets and the foundations of the houses crushed by Algonquin's wave, making it looked like the suburb was at the bottom of a dark and unpleasant sea.

The illusion was only made stronger by the new layer of water that covered everything. But while there were streams of water falling from the broken Skyways overhead, Julius didn't think this flooding was from the wave earlier, or even from the river's flood before that. He couldn't say why, exactly, but he felt certain that this water was from before that, the fallout of some earlier disaster.

It smelled old, he decided. Old and very strongly of lake. He was trying to figure out if that was important or not when Marci yelled out.

"There!" she cried, pointing.

Once he saw it, Julius had no idea how he'd missed it. Even in the Pit's strangely thick darkness, it should have been impossible to miss the giant pile of trash rising from the lowest point of the Pit's bowl-like landscape.

Pile was the wrong word, he decided as they got closer. This was a tower, a leaning column twenty feet in diameter made from busted cars, washing machines, bricks, drywall, outdated computer parts—all sorts of nonsense.

The sideways-tilting stack went all the way from the Pit's flooded floor to the ceiling of the broken Skyways thirty feet overhead, connecting the ground to the city like a giant root. Not being a mage, Julius had no idea what that meant, but the structure *definitely* hadn't been here before.

"Is that our target?"

"Nothing else it could be," Marci said excitedly, pointing at the rusted hood of one of the cars at the bottom of the pile. "Set down there. Ghost's already headed inside to check it out."

Even for a death spirit, going inside a giant pillar of mysterious trash that might be the heart of an enraged spirit sounded like a *really* bad idea. Julius didn't even want to get near it. Now that they were closer, he could actually feel the thing pulsing with the same magic he'd felt roaring through the city. But this was the whole reason they were here, so he sucked it up and landed where Marci had pointed, setting down on the edge of the car's bumper like a bird landing on a windowsill.

An extremely *disgusting* windowsill.

"Ugh," he said, lifting his feet. "It's all slimy. Like that time we walked through the storm drain."

"It *does* feel slimy," Marci said, hopping off his back to touch the car for herself. "Weird. I wonder if that's from the flooding or something else?"

Given how creepy this place was, Julius's money was on *something else.* He'd felt more of Algonquin's magic than any dragon should at this point, but while her lake water was cold and clammy and unpleasant in the extreme, it had never felt polluted. This stuff felt like the filthy magic of the Pit turned physical, and the more Julius thought about that, the less he liked this whole situation.

"I don't think this is a good place for the spirit of the DFZ to be."

"Me neither," Marci agreed, walking across the car hood to stand in front of the wall of debris that formed the pillar. "I've noticed that Mortal Spirits seem to be highly influenced by emotions in their magic. Remember back in Reclamation Land when Ghost got all huge and scary? It was because he was channeling the anger of everyone Algonquin had killed. I wonder if the same thing is happening to the DFZ? I mean, she was already pissed at Algonquin, but this is the place where the wave first crashed down. Not a good memory."

"Definitely not," Julius said, covering his nose with his wing. "The magic smells awful."

"Really?" Marci turned around with an excited smile. "You have to let me study how you smell magic sometime!"

The demand was so like her, it made his heart clench. It still didn't feel real that Marci was back, alive and smiling and asking to study him. It really was a miracle, and perversely, that bothered him. As happy as he was, she was too important for him to just accept all of this on faith. The whole idea of mortality was that no one came back from death, and while he was used to Marci doing the impossible, it never came without a cost, which begged the question, what had Marci paid? What had she suffered or promised or given up to return, and how could he help her? He was working up the courage to ask when she went still.

"What?" he asked, instantly alarmed. "What's wrong?"

"Nothing," she said, scowling. "Ghost was just in the middle of telling me something, and then he stopped."

"Do you think something happened?"

She shook her head. "I don't know. He didn't sound alarmed, but it's not like him to just drop out in the middle of a conversa—"

Marci cut off with a gasp. From deep inside the slimy column of trash she'd been poking, two arms had shot out. They were long and slender, like a thin woman's, but they grabbed Marci like a steel trap, wrapping around her neck and waist before snatching her backward into the trash.

"*Marci!*"

Julius threw himself after her, crashing into the wall of random objects, but he wasn't fast enough to snatch her back. The last thing he saw was her eyes wide with surprise as the trash ate her, opening like a mouth before snapping shut again in his face.

"*No!*" he roared, clawing at the wall. No, no, *no*.

He'd lost her. He'd had her and he'd lost her again. He'd lost—

Julius roared, shaking the Pit to the Skyways as he slammed his full weight into the slimy wall of random debris. The tower shook like a tree, sending bits of trash splashing into the water around him. He was about to hit it again when a croaking voice called out.

"I wouldn't do that."

Julius's head snapped up. Even with his excellent night vision, though, it took several seconds to spot the enormous black bird perched in a shadowy nook beneath the broken Skyway ramps, much as the magic eaters had the last time Julius had been here. That wasn't a pleasant connection, and Julius growled low in his throat as the giant bird spread his wings and hopped off, coasting down through the dark to land on the broken antenna of the car the dragon was standing on.

"Hello again, Julius Heartstriker," Raven said. "You remember me, I'm sure."

"How could I forget?" Julius replied, baring his teeth. "Your human killed Marci."

"Now, now, let's not bring poor Emily into this," the spirit said. "You already took your chunk out of her, and you should be delighted to see me."

"Why?" he growled, because he couldn't think of a single reason.

Raven turned his head to peer at him with one bright black eye. "Because I'm the one who brought your beloved Marci back from the dead."

Julius's growling grew louder. "Why should I believe a famous trickster?"

"Because I'm also famous for bringing souls back from the dead," Raven croaked cheerfully. "Look it up sometime, but not right now. We have to go after our Merlin."

Julius lifted his head. "Merlin?" he said, smiling despite himself. "Marci's a Merlin?"

"The greatest one we have," Raven assured him. "Also the *only* one we have, which is why we're in a hurry. I carried Marci's soul back to her body as part of a rather brilliant plan, the details of which I don't have time to go into and, quite frankly, you lack the expertise to understand. Marci's actually still on track to hold up her end, but I'm worried because things have gone a little strange."

"Strange how?" Julius demanded. "And what is Marci supposed to be doing in there?"

Raven looked pained. "The answer to both is the DFZ. Again, I don't have time for a proper explanation, but the quick-and-dirty version is the city's gone mad with power. Marci's supposed to be talking her down, but only after she starts to run out of power. That should have happened several minutes ago, but as I'm sure you've noticed, her fight against Algonquin hasn't exactly washed out." He chuckled. "That's a pun."

Julius growled, and the spirit quickly moved on.

"Anyway, since the DFZ's still going strong, I can only conclude she's found another way to keep her magic flowing, and I don't like that. She and Algonquin are holding toe to toe right now, but if the battle starts to turn and Algonquin gets desperate, things will get very bad very quickly."

"Wait, Algonquin?" Julius sputtered. "You're worried about Algonquin?"

"I'm worried about a lot of things," Raven said. "Including a certain human girl who's almost guaranteed to be in over her head right now. I can help you go in there after her, but you have to do exactly as I say."

To get Marci back? "Anything."

The spirit chuckled. "That's what I thought." He hopped off the antenna to land on the bend of Julius's wing, glaring at the wall of trash. "The creature in that pile has taken something precious from both of us. Neither of us is enough on our own, and I'm not sure if we'll be enough together, either. But if my hunch is correct, we won't be too much longer."

Julius had no idea what any of that meant, and he didn't care. He just wanted to get to Marci. "Just tell me what to do."

The spirit's black eyes glittered. "Burn it down."

Julius blinked. "What?"

"You breathe fire, don't you?" Raven said, bobbing his head at the slimy trash. "Use it. Burn it down."

"But Marci's inside!" he cried. "I can't just—"

"If she was close enough to get hurt by your flames, we wouldn't be having this conversation," the spirit said. "Like I told you, things have gone a bit *strange*. But that can work to our advantage, too. Just give it a try."

Breathing fire was the last thing Julius wanted to do. He'd never been good at it, and he couldn't get over the idea that Marci was on the other side of that wall. If he went too hot, he might cook her before he knew it. But fear of losing Marci again made a dragon do crazy things, so he breathed in deep, reaching down into the fire that burned inside him until his skin heated and his throat tingled.

Not including his attack on General Jackson, which he barely remembered and thus didn't count, Julius hadn't breathed fire in a very long time. As a result, his first try came out both too fast and too wide. His second attempt was much better, a blast of flame that turned from orange to yellow to white as he pushed harder and harder.

He melted the wall Marci had vanished through in seconds, then the car waiting behind that. Next came a large stretch of drywall that he turned into a blackened hunk, then a washing machine and a dumpster, but still there was more. The column of trash was only twenty feet across, and yet the more he burned, the more there was. Soon enough, he'd made a tunnel of slag he could walk inside, folding his wings tight against his body to avoid the glowing edges of the hole he'd cut.

He was now far deeper into the pillar than it was wide, but there was no end in sight. Every time he tried to stop, though, the Raven on his shoulder cawed for him to keep going, keep pushing.

He was in serious danger of overheating when the spirit suddenly flew up to perch on top of his head, his black eyes shining in the light of Julius's flames as he leaned toward them to whisper, "Ready?"

The word went through him like a knife. He could actually feel it traveling down his fire, and then, deep inside, deep down in the parts Julius didn't touch easily or often, something clenched. It was like teeth had bitten down on the source of his flames, but not to yank them out. Instead, a strange breath breathed him hotter, filling his fire with new color and heat as a familiar female voice spoke through the flames.

Ready.

The word was still dancing when Julius's fire leaped out of his mouth. Literally jumped, the flames moving with a life of their own as they twisted and roared together into the shape of a dragon. An enormous red one with wide, flaming wings and sharp, sharp teeth that ripped into the endless wall of trash like flaming swords, but didn't harm it. This flame didn't touch the physical world Julius had been slowly burning his way through. It burned the slimy magic itself, cutting through the muck like a blowtorch through paper until the pillar of trash was completely consumed, and in the ashes, a new world appeared.

Julius stumbled back in surprise, coughing as the smoke filled his lungs. They were standing in the Pit. Not the current flooded one, but the Pit as he remembered it from their fight with Bixby.

A few seconds later, Julius realized that wasn't quite it either. This Pit was far bigger than what he remembered, a huge open cavern that smelled like a grave. Strange as that was, though, Julius couldn't spare it more than a glance. His instinctual focus was pinned on the new dragon in front of him.

The one that had come out of his fire.

"Who are you?" he whispered.

The dragon looked over her shoulder, her red flames flickering like laughter. *Don't you recognize me, Baby J?*

Julius jumped. Like before, the words had come from inside him, but not from his mind. This was deeper, down in the roots of his fire. Weird as that was, though, what *really* knocked Julius for a loop was the part where she was right. He *did* recognize that voice. It was one he knew well, but never thought he'd hear again.

"Amelia?"

In the flesh, the fiery dragon said with a grin. *Or not, as the case may be. But I see how all this awesomeness might be a little intimidating. Give me a second.*

She spread her wings, and the fire that was her body shifted, the flames swirling into something far more compact. By the time they settled again, Amelia's human form stood in front of him exactly as he remembered her from the first time they'd met, right down to the red dress and the flask on her hip.

"There," she said in a physical voice this time, looking at Julius with eyes that gleamed like the fire she'd just been. "*Man*, it's good to be back."

She flashed him a cheeky smile, but Julius just stood there sputtering.

"How?" he got out at last. "You were—"

"Dead?" She laughed. "Only temporarily."

"But Svena saw Bob kill you," Julius said angrily. "I collected your ashes."

"You did?" she said, her voice touched. "That was sweet of you, kiddo, but you should have known there was no need. This is me we're talking about! I take 'what doesn't kill you makes you stronger' to a whole new level."

"Modest as always, I see," Raven said, flapping over to land on her shoulder. "But I have to say, you're looking much better."

"I *feel* much better," Amelia said, looking down at her body. "Julius gave me one hell of a light." She flashed him a grateful smile. "Thanks for that, by the way. You wouldn't believe what I've been through today."

Julius didn't believe any of this. "So Bob *didn't* kill you?"

"Oh no, he killed me good," Amelia said. "But only because I asked him to."

He stared at her in horror. "*Why would you do that?*"

"Because he was the only one who could," she said, lifting her chin proudly. "In case you haven't noticed, I'm a hard target. But it was all part of our plan. He killed me so I could hitch a ride on Marci's death to the spirit world and become *this*." She threw out her hands in a grand gesture as her voice echoed again through Julius's fire.

Say hello to the Spirit of Dragons, your new god!

Julius stumbled backward. Even the joy at discovering his sister wasn't actually dead and Bob might not actually be the murderer he'd feared couldn't gain traction next to the incredible strangeness of feeling another dragon in his fire. "I don't think I'm ready for this."

"No one's ready for this," Amelia assured him, smiling her cockiest smile yet. "I *told* you I had bigger ambitions than Heartstriker. But I'll have to fill you in on the details later. Right now, we've got bigger fish to fry."

She turned as she finished, pointing through the dark of this new Pit at the structure that marked its center. In the same place the pillar of trash had been back in the real world, a silver casting circle glittered on the silted ground. Inside it, silver ribbons of spellwork crisscrossed like the net across a dream catcher, pinning down an older man Julius recognized immediately as Sir Myron Rollins, the UN's undersecretary of magic. What he was doing there, Julius didn't know, but though his eyes were closed, his hands were moving, clenching and unclenching around the dark, irregular object he held clutched to his chest. A head, Julius realized in horror. Emily Jackson's head.

"Why is *that* here?"

"Because she's the key," Raven said, his croaking voice suddenly huge and terrifying. "So *that's* how she was doing it."

"Doing what?" he asked.

Both spirits ignored him.

"That would explain a lot," Amelia agreed, looking around. "The only question now is where's the owner of this house of cards?"

"That's not the only question," Julius snapped, his voice frantic as he realized there was no one else waiting in the dark.

"Where's Marci?!"

• • •

Marci was getting pretty darn sick of being snatched into the dark.

The hands that had dragged her into the pile of debris let go almost immediately, leaving her to fall backwards through trash that felt increasingly like the world of spirits she'd just left. What little light there was in the Pit had vanished in the first inch, leaving her struggling in a crowded dark that reeked of fetid water, grime, and magic.

So much magic. More than she'd ever felt floating freely on this side. It was so strong, it burned her skin, making her hiss even as she reached out frantically with her mental hands, grabbing as much of the ambient power as she could to use as a barrier. And a megaphone.

"Ghost!" she cried, letting the power amplify her call. When there was no reply, she tried again.

"*GHOST!*"

Again, there was no answer, and Marci clenched the magic with a curse. She'd *known* something was wrong when he'd stopped talking. But when she went to grab another handful of magic to try blasting her way out of whatever this was, something struck her from behind, shoving her out of the dark and into a blinding sea of lights.

Marci fell on the ground with a grunt, blinking rapidly as she struggled to adjust her eyes. When she could more or less see again, she raised her head and found herself in a familiar place.

It was the DFZ. Not the ruined one, but also not the one she remembered. Instead, she was standing in the crowded square from the endless city she'd found inside the DFZ's vessel in the Sea of Magic, and the DFZ herself was right in front of her.

"Welcome back."

Marci shoved herself to her feet, glaring at the hooded figure of the girl who appeared to be the city's self-image when she wasn't being a rat. "Where's my spirit?"

The DFZ's glowing orange eyes twinkled cruelly in reply, and then she flicked her hand to drop something small, white, and limp at Marci's feet. Something that looked terrifyingly like a dead cat.

"Ghost!"

She scooped her limp spirit into her arms. "*What did you do to him?*"

"Only what was inevitable," the city replied casually. "He was weak. I was strong. He set himself against me. I struck him down. Cause and effect."

"But he *wasn't* against you!" Marci shouted. "Neither of us is. We're here to *help* you!"

"Do I look like I need your help?" the DFZ said, looking up at the endless expanse of superscrapers that rose above their heads. "Where do you think you are?"

Now that she'd said it, Marci realized with a start that she didn't know. It *looked* like they were back in the DFZ's domain at the bottom of the Sea of Magic, but that was impossible, because they weren't *in* the Sea of Magic. This was the physical world, not the land of spirits, and yet it felt all wrong. The magic here wasn't the normal soft, ambient power she was used to. It wasn't even the heavy magic of Reclamation Land, or the boiling magic she'd felt when Ghost had flown her through the city. Whatever was going on here, it was new, and it was getting stronger by the second.

"What did you do?"

"What I had to," the DFZ snarled. "Algonquin tried to smother me, to hold me back, but she's no longer the biggest spirit around. *I* am. I have all the power now, and I will destroy her for what she has done to me."

"You're destroying yourself," Marci said angrily. "Look outside! Your city is in ruins."

"Because of Algonquin."

"Because of *you!*" she cried. "You're the one throwing buildings! Algonquin gets more water every time it rains, but you can't grow new superscrapers."

"Of course I can," the DFZ said. "Detroit always rebuilds."

You can't rebuild lost lives.

Marci jumped, snapping her head down to the cat in her arms. He still looked terrifyingly faint, but his ghostly blue eyes were open and glaring at the spirit in front of them with righteous fury.

Can you not hear them? he growled. *Algonquin evacuated your city to weaken you, to rob you of your heart, but she did a sloppy job. The poor, the forgotten, those who couldn't leave, they're all still here. Your people, the blood of your streets, they're here, and you're killing them.*

The DFZ sneered. "They're just mortals."

WE are mortal! Ghost roared, his mouth opening in a silent hiss. *We are the souls of humanity's care, of its hopes and fears! We are them, they are us, and you are sacrificing both to Algonquin!*

"I'm standing up to Algonquin!" the DFZ roared back, her orange eyes painfully bright. "I'm the only one of us with the guts to fight her and her monster! I don't care if it takes every building I have. I *will* destroy her lakes. I will kill her as she tried to kill me!"

The spirit's anger vibrated through the magic, and Marci shuddered. She had no idea where the DFZ was getting all this power, but for once, the amount of magic was less important than the source.

As a Thaumaturge, Marci had been taught that magic was magic. No matter where it came from, once it went through spellwork, it was all the same. The more time she spent with spirits, though, the more Marci realized this wasn't the case with them.

Spirits weren't spells. They were magic itself. Their vessels gave them shape, but the *type* of magic that filled that space determined the spirit's mindset, or lack thereof.

She'd seen it happen at least twice with Ghost: once when they were fighting Vann Jeger and once in Reclamation Land. Both times, he'd been consumed by the rage of the Forgotten Dead, and both times, she'd had to pull him back. Now, Marci suspected the same thing was happening to the DFZ.

This wasn't just righteous anger at Algonquin for hurting her. This was blind rage, self-destructive madness. The DFZ was willing to destroy her own city, her very self, to strike back at the Lady of the Lakes. Most telling, though, was that this kind of nihilism didn't match the city Marci knew at all.

The DFZ was a city of hope and ambition, a place where fortunes were made. People came here to make a new start, not break themselves for revenge. The anger in the air, the rage that shook the girl in front of her—it wasn't the magic of the DFZ she knew, but it *was* the magic of spirits angry enough to give their lives for Algonquin.

It's more than that, Ghost said, his nose twitching. *She's drenched in old death. Old rage and revenge are all over her like oil.*

That sounded familiar. "It's the Pit," Marci said, snapping her fingers. "She's pulling in magic from the Pit."

"Why shouldn't I?" the DFZ cried, her voice taking on a terrifying, desperate edge. "That's where I was born. Algonquin has always drowned me. From the very beginning, she's held me under, made me suffer. But now it's *her* turn." The spirit lifted her face to the illusion city's false sky. "I will bury her lakes and destroy her water! I will make her *pay!*"

The word came out in a scream, and the thrumming magic tightened like a fist. The resulting pressure crumpled the buildings and flattened the faceless crowds of her domain. It cracked the ground and shook the air and set Marci's head ringing. Even Ghost looked pained, his ears pressed flat against his skull.

The only one who didn't seem to feel it was the DFZ. She laughed at the cracking pressure, clenching her hands into fists to match. "I will kill her!" she cried joyfully. "I will make her suffer! I—"

There was more, but Marci had already shut the mad voice out, focusing instead on the magic around them, and how to stop it.

We have to cut her off, Ghost said in her head, his freezing claws digging into her flesh. *She's not just full. She's overflowing. I don't know where it's all coming from, but no Mortal Spirit can control this much magic without a Merlin.*

"She's got a Merlin."

Not one she wants.

"But he's the one we've got," Marci said, mind racing. "And actually, I think that's why this is happening."

She turned back to the DFZ, who was still ranting at the sky. It was a horrifying sight, but Marci forced herself to push past the fear and really *look* at her, noting all the details of the spirit's black hoodie and plain clothes, the sort that came from the cheap clothing vending machines that were so popular all over the DFZ. Her streetlight-orange eyes and short, spiky, rat-brown hair. With the LED around her wrists, neck, and ankles shining like neon against the dark of her outfit, she really did look just like the stereotype of the DFZ street rat, and yet—

"*There!*" Marci threw out her hand, pointing at the flash of silver that trailed from the spirit's left pinky. It was so thin, so fine, it was barely visible against all the other chaos, but it was there, falling from her hand to the sidewalk below, where it vanished into the cement like a fishing line into water.

"Gotcha," she whispered, hugging her cat tight as she shoved up off the ground and ran across the false square toward the stairwell that, in this version of the DFZ at least, still led to the Underground.

Where are we going?

"To where it started," she panted, racing down the stairs. She was taking them two at a time when the spirit in her arms transformed, leaving her hugging not a cat, but an angry solider with a shadow for a face and eyes that burned with blue-white determination.

"Then let's go," he growled, whisking them both off the stairwell and into the shadows of the sprawling Underground as fast as the wind could blow.

CHAPTER SIXTEEN

"We have to find Marci," Julius said frantically. "I don't know what this place is—"

"I do," Raven said, hopping around the strange silver circle where Myron was tied down like a spider's dinner. "This is the DFZ's domain. *Both* halves of it, overlapped. She's pulled in so much magic, she's torn the barrier, and now the physical world and the Sea of Magic are blending."

"That doesn't sound good."

"It's a disaster," Raven agreed. "But it's an unsustainable one."

"And we're standing on the weak point," Amelia finished, kneeling beside the strange silver ribbon. "Pull out the pin, and the whole thing blows."

"Still not reassuring," Julius said, lifting into the air. "If this place is going to blow, I'm going to find Marci."

Amelia grabbed his tail. "Relax," she said, yanking him back to the ground. "Marci's a Merlin now. That makes her the biggest girl around. She'll come to us. We just need to make sure we're ready when—"

The rest of what she said was drowned out by a sudden roaring wind. It swept through the cavern of the Pit in a freezing gale, blowing the silt into a dust storm. Then, fast as it had arrived, the wind vanished, leaving…

"*Marci!*"

Just like before, she appeared out of nowhere, standing straight and determined in the center of the cloud of falling dust. She was shaking the debris out of her hair when Julius pounced on her.

"Are you okay?" he cried. "Where did you go? What happened?"

"I'm fine," Marci said, staring at him in confusion. "But how did *you* get here?" She turned to the Empty Wind, whom Julius only now realized was standing right behind her. "Did you bring him?"

"Not I," the spirit said out loud.

Marci frowned. "Then how—"

"It was me," Amelia said, walking over with a cocky grin. "Well, team effort, really. Julius provided the fire, and I did the rest."

"*Amelia!*" Marci cried, delighted. "You did it! You're alive!"

"I'm way more than that," the dragoness said with a wink. "But we'll talk about that later. Right now, we need to deal with *him.*"

She turned to point at Myron, and Marci's face grew grim.

"I thought so," she said as she walked over to the silver circle. "I knew the DFZ had to be getting all her magic from somewhere, and the only thing that feeds magic to spirits is a mage. For her, that means Myron."

"But how?" Julius asked, hurrying after her. "He's unconscious."

"This is just his empty body," Marci explained. "His soul is still back in the Sea of Magic."

That sounded a lot worse than unconscious. "Can you fix him?"

"That's the plan," she said, getting down on her knees beside the silver circle. "First, though, I have to get him out of..." She faded off, leaning over to peer at the spellworked metal ribbon. "Um, what is this?"

"My spellwork," Raven said angrily, flying over to perch on her shoulder. "Myron and Algonquin had nothing that could chain a Mortal Spirit, so they stole my creation."

He nodded at the head in Myron's hands, but it must have taken Marci a few seconds to realize what she was looking at, because Julius could see the moment her curious confusion turned to horror.

"*Holy*—" She jumped back, eyes wide in horror. "Is that...?"

"It is," the raven spirit said, his voice dark and angry. "It's bad enough that Algonquin and Myron altered my Emily to be a vessel, but then Myron was reckless enough to follow the DFZ to the Sea of Magic while leaving his physical body hardwired to her magic.

Now the overgrown city's taking advantage of that to suck magic through that idiot's empty body like a straw to continue her war with Algonquin, which would actually be pretty brilliant if it weren't so horrifically destructive."

"And dangerous," the Empty Wind added, looking out at the dark. "The magic of this place is deeply polluted. Taken directly, with no Merlin to help mitigate it…"

"It's driving her nuts," Marci finished, her face pale. "So how do we unplug him?"

"Very carefully," Amelia said. "The DFZ's already pulled in enough magic to overwhelm the barrier that divides this plane, blending her physical domain with her vessel in the Sea of Magic. I didn't even think that was possible, but apparently anything's game if you use enough force. Unfortunately, this means we're basically standing inside a magical pressure cooker."

Julius might not have known much about magic, but he'd seen enough Internet fail videos to know what happened when a pressure cooker went wrong. "You're saying this place could explode."

"Only if we're not careful," his oldest sister said. "Or unlucky."

There, at least, Julius had an edge. It wasn't as overwhelming now, but the golden music of the Qilin's good fortune was still humming in his bones. If there was ever a time he could count on not being unlucky, it was now. "Let me help."

"I was just about to ask," Marci said, flashing him a warm smile as she motioned for him to come closer. "I need to borrow your magic."

"Why *his* magic?" Raven asked as Julius sat down beside her.

"Because he's a dragon," she said, reaching up to bury her hand in the soft feathers of Julius's neck. "Amelia might have connected them to our plane, but no amount of spirit representation can ever make them truly native. So long as they have fire, they're always going to be on a different wavelength from everything else, and different is what I need."

She turned back to the silver circle. "There's so much power running through this right now, I can't even touch it without cooking myself. But if I can get some dragon magic in there, the disconnect might disrupt the flow long enough to yank Myron out."

"Use a foreign element to jolt the system," Amelia said. "Clever. But does Julius have enough juice for that? I might have made him use up a lot of fire getting in here."

"I don't think I'll need too much," Marci said. "Source seems to play a much bigger role in spirit magic than it does for normal spells, and dragons have always been part of the DFZ. Also, Algonquin *hates* them. That makes dragons a DFZ ally by default, and given how much anger she's wallowing in, I think some friendly magic would go a long way right now."

"And no one's friendlier than Julius," Amelia said with a grin.

"Technically, personality's not an issue here, but it can't hurt," Marci agreed. "I just need something to make her hesitate long enough to let us break the chain without getting fried."

"I don't like all this talk of frying and cooking," Julius said nervously. "Can't we just *talk* to her? We're all on the same team against Algonquin."

"You can talk to her all you like once we knock her out of her cackling madness phase," Marci assured him. "That's actually what I'm counting on. Like I said, she's not bad. She's just drunk on power."

"I think you mean high on revenge," Ghost said, his eyes glowing brighter as he watched the dark above them. "Be careful. She's—"

He never got to finish. There was no sound, no warning—the Empty Wind just doubled over, his glowing eyes wide in shock at the slender hand that had been stuck through his ribs. It vanished a second later, and his warrior's body crumbled like sand to reveal the figure standing behind him. A figure that appeared to be a human girl in very plain clothes but smelled like madness and death.

"*Ghost!*" Marci threw out her arms just in time for a white cat to fall into them, his transparent body panting and smaller than Julius had seen it in a long, long time.

"Are you insane?" she cried at the newcomer, shooting to her feet as she clutched Ghost to her chest. "I'm trying to *help you*, and it'd be a lot easier if you *stopped hurting my cat!*"

"You're the one hurting people," the DFZ replied, her strangely glowing orange eyes flicking to the mage bound in silver ribbons. "Step away from him."

"No," Marci said stubbornly. "You're using him."

"He used me first!"

"That doesn't make it right!"

"That's how I *win!*" the DFZ screamed, throwing her hand out like a spear.

Magic seized at the same time, forming a wave so dense, Julius could actually see the outline of it shimmering in the air. He got an even closer look a second later when he jumped in front of it, taking the full blast before it could slam into Marci.

In sober reflection, it was a smart move. As his family's favorite punching bag, Julius knew how to take a hit. He knew how to brace his magic and use it like a shield, just as he had against the giant lamprey in the DFZ storm drain what felt like forever ago.

But clever as all that was, Julius hadn't actually considered any of it. He'd just jumped, because whatever happened, it couldn't hurt more than losing Marci again. The fact that everything else lined up was just happy coincidence. More good luck.

Or, at least, that was what he'd thought before he realized just how *big* the spirit's magic was.

The attack crashed into him like a cruise ship running aground. It was stronger than his mother's fire, stronger than anything Julius had ever been hit with before. It hadn't even finished washing over him before he felt himself start to dissolve. But then, just as he realized he was probably going to die, something in his fire twisted, and a dragon appeared in front of him.

She'd already done it once before, so Julius wasn't too shocked to see Amelia suddenly flicker into existence. What *was* shocking was the fact that there was no fire this time. She was simply there, grabbing the hardened lump of pure, angry magic the DFZ had thrown and tossing it away.

It landed like a bomb in the dark several blocks over, exploding in a blast wave that sent everyone except Amelia and the DFZ to the ground. Even Raven was knocked to the dirt, flapping and cawing, but Amelia didn't so much as flinch. She just stood there and took it, watching the DFZ with a sly smile as she lowered her smoking hand.

"What did you do?" the city demanded, looking nervous for the first time. "This is my domain. How did you do that?"

"Easy," Amelia said casually. "I'm bigger."

The DFZ narrowed her orange eyes. "You lie."

"Try me," the dragon taunted, blowing out a line of smoke. "You might be all 'roided up on stolen power right now, but that doesn't change the fact that your domain is nothing compared to mine. I am Amelia the Planeswalker, the Spirit of Dragons, and *that*"—she pointed at Julius—"is my vessel. I'm no longer a dragon who has fire. I *am* dragon fire, and I've burned better cities than yours."

She grinned as she finished, showing the DFZ all of her sharp white teeth. It was pure predator, the essence of what it meant to be a dragon. Even Julius cringed away, and she wasn't even facing him. But though she couldn't hide her flinch, the spirit of the DFZ didn't falter, and she did not back down.

"This is my world," she said, clenching her fists. "My one chance to destroy the tyrant that has always held me down. You will not stop me!"

"She's not trying to," Marci said, pushing herself up from the ground.

"Oh yes I am," Amelia snapped, keeping her fire-colored eyes on the city spirit. "I'm sick of this nonsense. I'll keep her busy. You cut the cord."

"*No,*" Marci said angrily, glaring at Amelia's back. "You are *not* helping." She turned to Julius. "Tell her."

"Don't you dare sic Julius on me," Amelia said, but to his surprise and despite her obvious anger, she did step back. A concession that did not escape the DFZ.

"The Spirit of Dragons takes orders from a human?"

"I don't take orders from anyone," Amelia said flippantly. "But unlike you, I'm smart enough to listen to sense when I hear it. Marci's never done anything but try to help spirits like us. She's the one who freed you to go crazy, in case you forgot. If you had the brain of the rat you're always pretending to be, you'd listen to—"

She cut off when the ground heaved. Julius's first thought was that it was the DFZ again, but she looked as surprised as they were.

"What was that?" Marci asked, clutching the ground.

"Algonquin," the DFZ growled, her face contorting in hatred. "She's landing another wave." The city shook again, and this time, it *was* the DFZ. "I will kill her for this! I will—"

"*Julius!*"

His name was the only warning he got. He was still staring at the DFZ's tantrum when Marci grabbed his left hind foot, and he felt the belovedly familiar—but still extremely uncomfortable—sensation of Marci yanking his magic out of him.

She grabbed the silver circle surrounding Myron next. As she connected them, Julius felt the full scale of the DFZ's magic for the first time. How huge she was, and how *angry*. It was only for a fraction of a second, but in that fraction, he was connected to the magic of the world like never before.

To his amazement, it really *was* a sea. A vast, violent ocean of power rocking in a storm, and he was part of it. They all were. Deeply. Intrinsically. How had he never realized this before?

Because it wasn't true before, Amelia whispered through his fire. *Bob and I did this, and we'll do a lot more. Just wait and see.*

The last thing Julius wanted was to wait. Before he could demand an answer, though, the incredible connection vanished in a blinding flash as the surging power finally overwhelmed Marci's interruption, causing a backlash that knocked them both into the air.

As always, Julius missed landing on his feet. He managed to scramble back to them in record time, though, following his nose frantically to Marci, who was groaning on her back a few feet away. "Are you all right?!"

"I'm fantastic," she croaked, reaching up to wipe away the trickle of blood running down from her nose. "Haven't been backlashed that hard in a long time, but look." She tilted her head back toward the spirit. "It *worked*."

Sure enough, the DFZ was frozen when he turned around, her mouth hanging open as the roaring magic drained out of the air. "No," she whispered, desperately grabbing at the emptying space in front of her. "No, no, *no!*" She turned on Marci. "*How could you do this to me?*"

"Actually, she was just the interruption," Raven's voice croaked from the dark. "I'm the one who took your power."

The spirit whirled around only to freeze again. Raven was sitting inside the silver circle, which was still shining as bright as ever, though it was no longer shining *out*. All the light was focused inward now, shining in a laser pinpoint on the piece of metal where Raven was perched, the only bit of the circle that wasn't gleaming silver.

It was steel. An old, battered chunk of debris on which someone had carved a name. Which name, Julius couldn't tell. The letters had all been clawed out, and above them, squeezed in along the metal's edge, Raven's name had been written in shaky talon marks.

"You stole it," the DFZ whispered.

"I can't steal what was never yours to begin with," Raven said as the silver light converged on his name. "Emily the Phoenix is my creation. She belongs to *me*. Not to you, not to Myron, and never to Algonquin."

The light flared as he finished, and all the silver ribbons began to flail like whips. They whistled through the air at Raven's call, unraveling from the spiraling circles and folds they'd been so carefully arranged into, including the net of bindings that held Myron's body down.

He was thrust from the circle like a dead fish, thrown facedown on the dirt beyond. The silver ribbons plucked Emily's sleeping head from his hands as he fell, sucking it back into the coiled silver cocoon that was now forming at the center of the circle. Raven jumped in next, folding his wings and diving into the swirling spellwork with a loud caw. That was all Julius saw before the spinning ball of silver vanished with a flash, leaving nothing but the smell of ozone and burnt feathers.

"What just happened?"

"Raven took back his construct and left," Marci said, holding up her arms so he could pull her to her feet. "We should, too. I'm not sure what happens to magical pressure cookers when you pull the plug, but it's probably not—"

The ground split, opening a huge crack that ran across the floor of the Pit and all the way up one of the support beams to the skyway above.

"—good," she finished, staring wide eyed at the destruction before turning to scramble back onto Julius's back. "Time to bail."

"Bail to where?" he asked frantically, helping her up. He grabbed Ghost next. The poor spirit cat was hobbling now, his glowing eyes dim as Julius placed him in Marci's arms. "And how? I'm still not entirely sure how I got here."

"We go out the same way we got in," Amelia said, suddenly appearing beside them. "We burn through. First, though…"

She turned and scooped Myron's body up under her arm like a sack of flour. "Can't leave without our prize."

"What about her?" Julius asked, looking over his shoulder at the DFZ, who was still sobbing on the ground.

"Nothing we can do," Marci said. "This is her domain. We can't take her out of it any more than we could take her out of herself. But she's an immortal spirit. She'll be pissed, but she'll recover. We, on the other hand…"

"Right," Julius said, looking around at the quaking Pit. "So do I need to find an edge or a wall or—"

"Just use your fire," Amelia said, tossing Myron onto his back behind Marci. "I'll do the rest."

Julius's throat was still raw from his fire earlier, but he did as she asked, breathing a gout of flame into the empty space in front of them. Amelia waited beside him, watching his fire go from red to orange to bright white. Then, just when Julius was starting to overheat, she reached out and grabbed his flame.

He nearly choked. She wasn't just grabbing the fire in front of him. She'd grabbed *him*, her fist clenching around the fire that burned at the heart of his magic.

Julius was still trying to wrap his brain around that when Amelia lashed out, slicing the flames through the dark like claws. It was just like what had happened when they'd cut their way in through the trash, only this time it wasn't the air in front of them that ripped. It was everything else.

Like a spark to tinder, the false DFZ was consumed by flames. Everything burned, surrounding them in an inferno. It should have been terrifying, but Julius wasn't afraid at all. The heat was actually comforting, because it was his. This was *his* fire, his magic amplified through Amelia, and when it faded, they were back in the real world, standing in the flooded Pit at the base of the DFZ's column of trash.

Which was collapsing.

"*Move!*"

Amelia's shout was still ringing in his ear when Julius rolled to the left, skidding through the shallow water just in time as the whole pillar came crashing down on top of itself.

It fell like a demolished building, the stacked cars and dumpsters and washing machines sliding apart like knocked-over wooden blocks before crashing into the water below. When everything finally clattered to a stop, all that was left was a pile of trash rising like an island from the floor of the flooded Pit, and kneeling on top of it with her head buried in her shaking hands was the DFZ.

"It's over," she sobbed, her voice raspy and pitiful. "You've broken everything. She'll kill me now."

"No, she won't," Marci said firmly, sliding off Julius's back. "We won't let her."

"What can you do?" the DFZ said bitterly, lifting her head, which didn't even look human anymore. "You can't fight Algonquin. No one can. That's why I did this. I had to protect myself." She fisted her hands, which now looked more like rat claws. "*Why did you stop me?*"

The question was screamed at Marci, but it was Julius who answered.

"Because you were killing yourself."

"This is none of your business," the spirit snarled, glaring at him with beady eyes. He'd been watching her the entire time, but even Julius couldn't say for sure when the human-looking DFZ had changed into a rat. That's what she was now, though. A giant, angry, wounded rat, cowering in the trash.

"What do *you* know?" the rat cried. "You're a dragon. You can fly away any time you want! But I'm chained to Algonquin forever, and she will *never* let me be." The spirit bared her yellow teeth. "You have no right to tell me what to do!"

"I'm not trying to tell you what to do," Julius said calmly. "But the DFZ was my home. What Algonquin does hurts all of us, but so does what you do to yourself."

The rat glowered. "What do you care?"

"I care because I know what it's like to be under someone's boot," he replied. "I know how it feels to be at your enemy's mercy, how it feels being helpless. All this anger and rage isn't hurting Algonquin, but it's ripping you to bits. You're just doing her job for her, but it doesn't have to be like that."

He looked over at Marci, who was hovering beside him. "Marci's the best mage I've ever met. She and Ghost have stood against Algonquin before. They'll help you do it now. So will I, because Algonquin's my enemy, too. There are dragons out there *right now* risking their lives against Algonquin and her Leviathan to buy us time to help you." He smiled at her. "You don't have to fight alone."

His plea was a long shot. He still didn't fully understand the situation or Marci's plan for fixing it, but while Julius wasn't a mage or a spirit, he understood despair very well. He knew what it felt like to be trapped and stomped on, but where he'd had Marci and Justin and Chelsie and even Bob, the DFZ had no one. She was a city of millions, but she thought she was fighting alone, and as one of those millions, Julius couldn't let that be.

"We're your allies," he said firmly. "You can't stand against Algonquin, but Algonquin can't stand against the world. She's the one who's alone, not you. We *want* to help you. You're our city, our home, and we'll fight to defend you if you'll just let us."

The rat stared at him for a long time after that. "I remember you," she whispered at last. "You lived in the house under the underpasses, and you cleared rats from the sewers. You had a business here. A life, even though you're just a little dragon."

Her round eyes dropped. "I'm touched you want to fight for me, but you're wrong. Even with your help, we're no match for Algonquin. All the magic I gathered is gone. Without it, I'm no longer bigger than she is." She looked up at the flooded Pit with a shudder. "When the next wave comes, she'll drown us all."

"Then we'll just have to make sure it doesn't come," Marci said, marching up the pile of trash. "That's what I've been trying to tell you. Raven has a plan."

"Raven?" The rat cringed. "Raven hates me."

"Raven doesn't hate anyone," Marci said. "I don't even think he hates Algonquin. He's just mad because you took his construct and ran amok. But he was the one who came to the Heart of the World to help me, and who brought me back to this world so I could help *you*. It's all part of his plan to stop Algonquin's threat for good, and that starts with you letting Myron back into his body."

"*What?*" The DFZ cried, skittering backward. "NO! He's the one who chained me!"

"He did," Marci said. "And he was an idiot. Just like you, though, he only did those stupid, self-destructive things because he was afraid. He thought the rising spirits were going to destroy humanity, and he made some very bad choices because of that. If you give him another shot, though, I think you'll find he's had a change of heart. At the very least, you need to release your hold on his body so he can come back from the Heart of the World."

The rat looked surprised. "He got in?"

"I let him in," Marci said. "So he wouldn't die. Now he's trapped there until you let him out."

"I don't want anything to do with him," the spirit grumbled. "Why can't Raven do it? He brought you back."

"Because I was *dead*," Marci reminded her. "Myron's not. At least not yet."

She glanced back at Julius, who was still carrying Myron's unconscious body on his back. "However it came to be, you're his Mortal Spirit. The two of you are intrinsically linked, connected across the two halves of this world. Just as you were the only one who could get him into the Sea of Magic, only you can get him out." She smiled. "If nothing else, it'll give you a chance to yell at him."

That argument seemed to appeal to the DFZ more than any other, but when Julius walked up the pile of trash to carefully lay the unconscious mage in front of her, the spirit looked nervous. "I'm not sure how to—"

"Just reach out to him," Ghost said. He was still a cat in Marci's arms, but his eyes were open and bright again, looking at the DFZ with the exasperated patience of an old hand talking down an excitable, foolish novice.

"Reach out, and he'll grab back," he said. "Humans are quick learners, and Myron's probably ready to come home."

The DFZ didn't look convinced, but she leaned down, nudging Myron's body with her pointy nose. For several seconds, nothing happened, and then Myron's body convulsed, his eyes shooting open as he gasped for breath.

"Myron?" Marci said, waving her hand in front of his wide eyes as he lay panting on the trash. "You back?"

Myron's answer was to scramble to his feet, waving his arms frantically as if he were under attack. "*We have to stop!*"

Marci jerked back. "Stop what?"

"Everything," he said, his eyes haunted as he scrubbed his shaking hands through his graying hair. "The seal, Novalli. I tried to hold it, but Algonquin's attacks, whatever the DFZ did to blend her domains, *you!*" He stabbed his finger at Amelia. "You plunged all the dragon fire in the world into the Sea of Magic at one time! What were you *thinking?!*"

"Easy," Amelia said, putting up her hands. "What's wrong?"

"Everything!" he cried, whirling back to Marci. "The seal is breaking. I kept it together as best I could, but with all of you down here swinging magic around like bats, there was nothing I could do. If we don't calm everything down right now, the seal's going to break wide open."

"It's okay," Marci said. "We'll just—"

"It is *not* okay!" he shouted. "That's what I'm trying to tell you! When you left me up there holding the dam together with my bare hands, you didn't tell me you were going to shake the tank! That crack is as wide as my arm! It's—"

"*Myron,*" she snapped. "We *get* it. Things are FUBAR. But we can still fix them, because *your* spirit"—she looked pointedly at the rat behind him—"has already taken her chill pill, so why don't you chill, too?"

"You're still not understanding," the mage said through gritted teeth, glancing nervously over his shoulder at the DFZ, who watched him back warily. "I'm very grateful to the DFZ for deescalating, but the damage is already done. The only reason a thousand years of magic isn't falling on our heads right now is because I rigged up the world's most ridiculously temporary barrier, and it's not going to hold much longer. This is bigger than the DFZ. What you did here has sent tidal waves all through the Sea of Magic. If we can't reverse them, the whole mountain's going to crack."

"What mountain?" Julius asked, thoroughly confused.

"He means the Heart of the World," Marci explained. "It's the place where the ancient Merlins put all the magic they sealed off during the drought."

"Wait," he said, horrified. "*Merlins* caused the drought?"

"It's a long story," she said. "What matters is that all that magic didn't just go away. It's built up behind a seal."

"And the seal's cracking," Julius said, nodding. "I got that part."

"The crack is the least of our worries," Myron said angrily. "A *crack* can be managed, which is exactly what I was doing when you reckless idiots started rocking the boat. We're on the edge of catastrophic failure. Once my barrier fails—and it *will*—we're looking at a total shattering, and not just of the seal. The whole mountain could blow, releasing a thousand years of magic back into the world in a single blast."

"Oh," Marci said, pursing her lips. "That's worse than I thought."

"So how do we stop it?" Julius asked.

"I told you," Myron snapped. "We have to calm the Sea of Magic down. I mean press it *flat*. If we can do that, there's a chance Marci and I may be able to build some kind of housing around the seal before it reaches critical mass."

"That's a lot of 'chances' and 'mays,'" Amelia pointed out. "But you're forgetting a critical factor in all of this: *us*." She turned to Julius. "Who did you say was keeping Algonquin busy?"

"Chelsie and Fredrick," he answered at once. "And the Qilin."

Amelia's eyebrows shot up. "No way! The Golden Emperor's in on this?" When he nodded, she whistled. "That explains a lot. I can't believe Bob wrangled the Qilin into his deck. I knew that kid had talent!"

Julius stared at her. "You can't think this is all Bob's doing."

"Who else's doing would it be?" she asked. "How do you think I got here? Or you? Why do *you* think you were in the DFZ at the exact right moment to see Marci come back and get involved in this merry venture? Luck?"

Normally, Julius would say no, but with the Qilin..."Maybe?"

Amelia snorted out a ring of smoke. "You need to trust your brother," she scolded. "We're all pieces on his board, even me. I'm cool with that, though, because Bob always *wins*. That's his superpower. He takes an impossible situation, and he makes it his. And speaking of impossible situations, I'm going to go lend my dear little sister and her golden boyfriend my godly assistance. That should buy you"—she turned her glare on Myron—"enough time to do your part of this job."

"Weren't you listening?" Myron cried. "There *is* no more job! Raven's plan is a wash. The seal is far more—"

"Raven's plan is all we have," Amelia snarled at him. "That seal is nothing compared to what will happen if Algonquin goes to her End, get me?"

Julius didn't at all, but whatever she'd said was enough to make Myron go pale. He was still opening and closing his mouth when the pile of trash beneath them began to shake.

"It's not me," the DFZ said when everyone looked at her. "I'm not—"

She didn't get to finish, because at that moment, one of the flattened cars flew up off the ground like it had been launched, sailing into the dark to land with a distant *splash*. The water was still falling when Raven flew out of the hole where the car had been, and behind him was...Julius wasn't sure, actually.

It looked like a modern art statue made from spare bits of metal bound together with silver ribbon. Aside from having the right number of arms and legs, though, the only part of it that actually looked human was its head, which was that of a stern, middle-aged, dark-skinned woman, her brows furrowed in grim determination as she maneuvered her scrap body out of the muck.

"Sorry for the delay," Raven said cheerfully. "I had to fix my favorite toy soldier."

"Are you sure you succeeded?" Amelia said, looking the amalgam up and down. "She looks like a bunch of trash tied together."

"I'm a scavenger," Raven said defensively. "I made do with what I had. But that's the lovely thing about my Phoenix: she may not look pretty, but she always rises from her ashes."

"Sorry for being out of service," General Jackson said, her voice creaking and rusty but unmistakably human. "I'm obviously not field ready yet, but Raven's been filling me in, and when we heard you were planning to go fight Algonquin, we had to come out ahead of schedule."

"Got jealous, did you?" Amelia asked, wiggling her eyebrows. "You're welcome to come with."

"You're not going at all," Raven said firmly.

"*What?*"

"He's not saying you can't fight her," Emily explained patiently. "But Raven's plan requires Algonquin to think she's won, which will be difficult if there's a brand-new hybrid Spirit of Dragons blasting fire at her."

Amelia's face fell. "I suppose if you put it *that* way."

"There's no other way to put it," the general said, turning to Myron. "Have you convinced the DFZ to do her part yet?"

"Not yet," he said. "I was just about to…that is…" He trailed off, looking at her in helpless bewilderment. "Are you not mad at me, Emily?"

"Mad at you?" she asked, crossing her makeshift arms over her makeshift chest. "You abused your position, sided with the enemy, ripped my body apart, and used it to launch yourself to power. Now I'm stuck in this rusted-out hodgepodge made from whatever bits Raven could scavenge out of the Pit. I'm *furious* at you, Myron, but we don't have time for that now. We're on a mission here, people."

"What mission are we on?" Julius said, utterly lost yet again as he turned back to Marci. "How many people did you bring with you back from the dead?"

"It was pretty busy," Marci said. "But I'm glad you asked about the mission."

She turned to face the DFZ, who'd been quietly trying to slink off into the dark. "Julius was right when he said you weren't alone. We're all here to fight against Algonquin, but what you don't know yet is that Algonquin *does* have an ally. A terrible one."

"Not so free with that information, if you please," Raven said quickly, flapping his wings. "Remember what I said about this being a *very big secret* for *Merlins only?*"

Marci rolled her eyes. "It's a little late for that. If Julius is putting his neck out for this, he deserves to know why, and the DFZ *needs* to know. She's kind of integral to this whole thing."

"Why me?" the DFZ squeaked, glaring at Myron. "I'm only here because he and Algonquin yanked me up."

"Exactly my point," Marci said, turning back to her. "You're not a natural Mortal Spirit. You were engineered by Algonquin specifically so she could get her hands on the first Merlin and gain control of the magic. She's *terrified* of you and Ghost and all the other Mortal Spirits because you're bigger than her, and she hates humans because we cut off her magic and sent her to sleep. To be fair, those are both valid. Mortal Spirits *are* dangerous, and the ancient mages *did* screw her over. But rather than deal with that herself, Algonquin brought in outside help."

"What do you mean 'outside help?'" Julius asked nervously. "What's outside for a spirit?"

"She's talking about the Leviathan," the DFZ said, her voice shaking. "I *knew* he wasn't a spirit."

"He's not anything we know," Marci said. "He's not part of this world at all. He's an extra-planar being called a Nameless End, and though he answered Algonquin's cry, he's not here to help. He's here to take advantage of her."

"It didn't help that she made herself an easy target," Raven said bitterly. "Algonquin's so obsessed with the wrongs that have been done to her that she'd rather destroy the world than accept them." He looked pointedly at the DFZ. "I imagine you can sympathize with that."

The DFZ dug her claws in stubbornly. "I was just trying to protect myself."

"So is she," Raven said. "In her own fashion. But that's actually good for us. So long as Algonquin has hope, she'll keep fighting, and as destructive as that is, it's preferable to the alternative."

Julius winced. "What's worse than fighting Algonquin?"

"What happens when she gives up," Marci said quietly.

"Nameless Ends survive by eating planes," Amelia said. "Normally, this happens after the plane collapses, but it seems the

Leviathan convinced Algonquin to let him in early, and the only reason he hasn't eaten everything already is because he's here on a probationary basis."

"What does that mean?" Julius asked.

"Nameless Ends are *extra*-planar powers," Amelia explained. "As in outside. Since our plane is healthy, that means he can't cross the planar barrier unless someone with power on the *inside*—like, say, a giant lake spirit—gives him an in. It's kind of like what I did for dragons when I became their spirit. We could live here, but we weren't actually part of the native magic until I blended my fire with the magic in the vessel I took over to become a spirit. Now we have an anchor, a magical connection. If the Leviathan wants to come all the way inside, he's going to need the same. That's why he's playing Algonquin. If he can get her to surrender her magic to him, that's his way in. Algonquin hasn't given in to him yet because she's still hoping to salvage the situation, but if she loses that hope—"

"She'll let the monster run rampant," the DFZ growled, lip curling to show her pointed teeth. "Prideful lake."

"So how do we stop her?" Julius asked, looking at Raven. "Everyone keeps saying you have a plan."

"A very clever one," Raven assured him. "We—"

"We trick her into thinking she's won," Marci said excitedly. "If she thinks she's got control of the magic, she'll have no reason to keep the Leviathan around. In order to convince her of that, though, we need to prove she's got control of the Heart of the World, which means sending *her* spirit/Merlin pair in to break the news."

Julius wasn't quite sure what that meant, but the DFZ jumped like Marci had taken a swing at her. "No."

"It's only—"

"*No!*" the spirit screeched, her beady eyes staring at Myron in fear and rage. "He chained me! Bound me! I am *not* accepting him as my mage."

"Assuming the Merlin Gate would let him in even if you did," Amelia said with a snort. "What?" she added at Marci's angry glare. "Someone had to say it."

"Amelia," Marci said through clenched teeth. "You're *not* helping."

"But she is right," Myron said, turning to face the DFZ, who took another step back. "I'm sorry."

"Little late for that," the rat hissed. "You let me be born into chains."

"I did you great wrong," he agreed. "You and many others, but I was only trying to do what I thought was best for everyone. I was…"

He trailed off with a sigh. "I was afraid," he said at last. "In my work for the UN, I saw human cruelty in all its terrible forms. I spent my whole life believing that Mortal Spirits would be our salvation. That they were the good and righteous forces in us that would finally elevate humanity to an equal playing field with dragons and spirits. That was my dream, but after the Empty Wind, after I saw Algonquin's pool of blood, I felt like a fool. Then, later, when Algonquin told me the real reason the magic had vanished was because the Merlins had bound it to banish the monsters that were humanity's uncontrollable gods, it fit my own experiences too well for me to disbelieve her. That was when I decided to seal the magic away again forever. That's why I used you. I wanted to save humanity from itself."

The DFZ glowered at him. "But?"

"There is no but," Myron said. "Humanity is foolish, selfish, fearful, and violent, and our spirits reflect that. If I've learned anything from all of this, it's that you truly are *Mortal* Spirits. You are *us*, and I am sorrier for that than anything."

Marci put her hand over her face. "Myron," she groaned. "This isn't useful."

"It's not meant to be," he said angrily. "I'm telling her the truth. I watched everything that happened here from the Heart of the World. I saw the DFZ's rage, and I know it wasn't only from the spirits Algonquin used to fill her. My anger was in there, too. I was also ready to destroy myself and all of human magic if it meant defeating Algonquin and everything like her. I *still* think it would be a worthy sacrifice to give my life to make a safer world for future generations.

That's why I joined the UN, why I've done *everything* that I've done. The only difference now is that I no longer see Mortal Spirits as an enemy to be defeated."

He looked at Marci. "You were right, Novalli. They *are* us, and that's better reason than any to lock the magic away again forever. It's the only way to make sure they don't suffer as we do. If you think about it, all Mortal Spirits are is magic that we've dragged down to our level. The only reason I'm here doing this instead of dragging you back to the Heart of the World to banish all spirits forever is because that *doesn't work*. We can't stop the magic. It just keeps flowing no matter what we do. Even if we could make another seal, it would just be this problem all over again in another thousand years."

"That's what *I* said," Marci grumbled.

"And I'm admitting you were right," Myron snapped. "I don't like it, but anyone who can't change his mind in the face of evidence is an irrational fool, and for all my other flaws, I've never been one of those."

Marci stared at him in wonder, but before she could follow up, the DFZ beat her to it.

"So what are you going to do?" the spirit asked warily. "Just because you've given up trying to block the magic doesn't mean the rest is forgiven. Good intentions don't excuse what you did to me. Why shouldn't I cut you loose?"

"Because we need each other," Myron said sternly. "I thought cutting off the magic was the silver-bullet solution to all our problems, which was why I was willing to do such terrible things to get it. I'm sorry for that, and I don't expect you to forgive me, but that doesn't mean I've quit. I'm still in this for the future of humanity, only now, instead of a single simple solution, we have to do things the hard way. We have to change, fight humanity's inclination toward cruelty and violence spirit by spirit, mage by mage. That's not a task I can accomplish in my lifetime. I'm not confident it can be accomplished at all. But we will *absolutely* fail if Algonquin gives the Leviathan what he wants."

He held out his hand. "I'm not asking for your forgiveness. All I want is for you to help me stop this disaster. Let me be your Merlin long enough to fool Algonquin, and I promise, I will set you free immediately after."

"Set her free?" Ghost said, incredulous. "There is no setting free. The Merlin bond is for life."

"Then I'll end mine," Myron said without missing a beat. "I've staked my life on far less. If I have to die to help humanity avoid this disaster, I'll count it cheaply bought, but I will not stand by and do nothing." He thrust his hand at the DFZ. "Let me be your Merlin, and I swear, I will not live to see you regret it."

That was a terrifying way to put it, but to Julius's amazement, the DFZ was smiling. She shifted next, her rat-shape collapsing into her human body, who was staring at Myron with a new gleam in her orange eyes.

"You're crazy," she said. "And a pompous jerk. But I've always been a city of people who don't take no for an answer. Dreamers, too." She tilted her head at him. "Being Merlin was always your dream, wasn't it?"

"My greatest ambition."

The DFZ grinned, and then she grabbed Myron's hand. "I accept," she said, squeezing his fingers until he winced. "If only to see how you'll try to cheat your way out of death."

"That's *her* department," Myron said, tilting his head at Marci, though his attempts to play it cool did nothing to hide his obvious relief. "Shall we go try the door again? With less breaking, this time?"

The spirit's answer was to jerk him forward, and then the two of them vanished down an open manhole that *definitely* hadn't been there a second ago. It vanished a second later, leaving Myron's body lying facedown on the piled trash, empty again.

"That can't be healthy," Amelia said.

"Myron's never been one to let physical limitations get in his way," General Jackson replied, walking over to flip Myron onto his side so he could breathe more easily. "Do you think he'll survive?"

"You mean, 'Will he make it through the Merlin Gate?'" Marci shrugged. "I don't know. I'm still not sure what logic governs the gate's decision, but I'd say he's got a much better chance this time around. Other than having a Mortal Spirit, the only real requirement for being a Merlin is 'be a champion of humanity.' You don't have to be a nice person or even a good one. You just have to be willing to protect humankind. All of it, including our spirits. I think Myron's got that now. We'll just have to hope the Heart of the World feels the same."

"Oh, goody," Raven said with a sigh. "Our survival depends on a vetting program written by the same humans who thought cutting off the magic was a great idea."

"It's *your* plan," Marci reminded him. "And speaking of, we'd better get into some kind of position, because if this is going to work, it'll work fast."

"So what happens next?" Julius asked as Marci climbed onto his back.

Raven fluffed his feathers. "For us? Hiding. This whole thing depends on making Algonquin believe Myron has the Heart of the World under his sole control, and there's no chance of that if she spies Little-Miss-Miracle-Merlin-Back-From-The-Dead running around." He poked his beak at Marci. "I say we all get somewhere high and dry and watch the show."

"What about my family?" Julius said worriedly. "They're still fighting Algonquin, or at least they were."

"Then you'd better tell them to stop," Raven croaked. "The calmer she is when Myron talks to her, the better. We want her cocky and confident, not in a dragon-induced rage."

That was a good point, but Julius still hesitated. He needed to warn Chelsie, but that meant leaving Marci behind, and he didn't think he'd ever be able to do that again. If he didn't go, though, he'd leave his family in trouble, which he absolutely couldn't do, especially since they'd flown into that trouble for him. He was warring back and forth between these two priorities when Amelia's hand landed on his wing.

"Go," she said gently. "I'll keep an eye on Marci. You go get our sister out of danger. Bob didn't reunite her with her lost love just so she could get herself killed."

Julius's heart clenched. "You really think that's what Bob was doing?"

Amelia flashed him a smile. "I was never privy to that part of the plan since it happened after my death, so I can't say for sure, but it fits his style. He might run you over a few times to get there, but Bob's endgame is always worth playing. Trust me, he's a good kid."

Julius didn't see how anyone who let their sister and her children suffer for six hundred years just to line up a coincidence qualified as a "good kid," but Amelia's words were still like water in the desert. All this time, through all the evidence to the contrary, he'd wanted so hard for Bob to be exactly what she said. He didn't know if he'd ever be able to accept someone who thought it was okay to run over you so long as he made it up to you later, but just knowing Bob had killed Amelia at her behest in the pursuit of greater power was a *lot* better than what he'd thought for the last twenty-four hours.

It wasn't perfect, but Julius was so tired of losing people, he was more than ready to take it. Especially since, if he could just keep Chelsie safe now, he wouldn't actually have lost anyone at all.

"I'll go get her," he said, steeling his nerves.

"Atta boy," Amelia said, helping Marci down off his back again. "Round 'em up and get to a safe distance. We'll take it from here."

Julius nodded, but his attention was already back on Marci. "Be safe."

"I'll be fine," she promised. "I'm a Merlin now, and I'm with Amelia and Raven and everyone else. What could happen?"

"You were with a lot of powerful people the first time you died, too," Julius said. "Including me, and I...I can't take that again, Marci. I'm sure you can't, either, but I just..."

He leaned down, resting his head against hers. "*Please* be safe."

She smiled warmly at him, rising up on her tiptoes to press a kiss against the short feathers of his nose. "I will," she whispered. "Now go save your sister."

He pulled away reluctantly, but as he was spreading his wings to take off, Raven flew in front of him. "One more thing," the spirit said quickly. "Don't breathe any fire."

Julius hadn't been planning to, but that didn't make the warning less alarming. "Why not?"

"Because Myron wasn't wrong. I don't even need to go back to the Heart of the World to know the seal protecting us from a thousand years of magic under high pressure is hanging by a thread. This wouldn't normally be a problem for you since dragons make their own magic, but now that you've got a spirit of your own, you're in the drink with the rest of us, and that has consequences."

He flapped in Julius's face. "This is a team effort now, so don't breathe any fire, don't let anyone else breathe any fire, and whatever you do, do *not* let the Qilin drop another one of his giant luck bombs. Good or bad, they're horribly disruptive, and I don't know if we can take one now that Amelia's sunk all of you into the Sea of Magic."

"I'll do what I can," Julius said nervously. "But I don't know how I'm going to stop—"

"Don't think," the bird said, giving him a push with his claws. "Just do. Now *shoo*. We don't have much time left."

Feeling more nervous than ever, Julius cast one final worried look at Marci and took off, flying as quietly as he could out of the Pit, through the holes in the broken Skyway, and into the smoke of the burning city.

CHAPTER SEVENTEEN

Algonquin's millennia-old hatred of dragons was getting a lot of new ammunition.

She rode high over her lake, looking down from on high at the smoking city she'd built. The city that *should* be washed off the map again. But though the DFZ was heavily damaged, it had not yet fallen because of the three dragons in front of her. Two black, one gold.

And they wouldn't die.

She turned her waterspout with a hiss, sucking in new water from the part of her body that the mortals of this time called Lake Erie. The waves rose at her command, shooting up like spears at the dragons above. She hammered down on them at the same time, launching an enormous wave from the top of the spout she'd formed beside her broken tower.

The attack was bi-directional and nearly a mile wide. It should have been unavoidable, and yet somehow, *again*, it missed. The dragons moved as though they knew in advance where every drop of water would be, dancing through her waves like eels through a fishing net. As they had *every single one* of her waves since they'd appeared.

And yet you keep sending them.

Algonquin's water hitched as her attention slid to the shadow behind her. *You really think you can win like this?* the monster said, his sneering voice slipping over her like the oil that had covered her shores when she'd first risen. *That's the Qilin. The dragons' living luck. You can't just beat him down.*

480

"I don't have to," she snarled back. "Dodging doesn't equal winning. All I have to do is make a wave big enough that luck can't save him."

That would work, the Leviathan agreed. *If you could. But you can't, can you?* The shadow's head turned toward the smoking city. *You've already spent more water tonight than you did destroying Detroit the first time. Do you even have enough to finish this?*

As if to prove his point, the dragons chose that moment to dive, streaking their fire across the falling water left by her attacks, evaporating it instantly. The golden one's flame was biggest, but it was the female who burned hottest, atomizing Algonquin's lake all the way down to the sandy floor.

"I will feed her head to my fish," Algonquin whispered, yanking in yet more water from her lake to replace what the dragons had burned off. "I'll turn their bodies to river mud. I'll—"

It's too late for that.

One of the Leviathan's tentacles snaked out in front of her, dipping into the churning water of Lake St. Clair. But though he'd chosen what should have been the deepest point, the appendage barely sank past its blunt tip before hitting the sandy bottom.

You're at your limit, Algonquin. Your water is dangerously low. Your fish are dying. You cannot keep fighting.

"I will," she snarled, pulling in water from every one of her bodies. "I've killed hundreds of dragons. *Thousands.* These are nothing."

They are the step too far, the shadow whispered. *You're not infinite, but I am.* The black tentacles rose up, bashing one of the dragons sideways before swinging out to curl around her swirling water. *Let me in. Let me finish what you've started, and I will—*

"*No!*" Algonquin roared, throwing another wave at the dragons to keep them busy while she turned to deal with the threat behind her. "I am not dead yet. Until I decide otherwise, you are bound to *me,* Leviathan. You serve me, obey me, listen to me. That is our deal, and if you don't stop undermining it, I will revoke your—"

She stopped, her water going still. Deep below them, the Sea of Magic was ringing like a gong. It was hard to hear over the storm, but the vibration was unmistakable. A human soul had passed through the gate.

A second soul? the Leviathan said angrily. *Impossible. Where did it come from?*

"There is no second soul," Algonquin said, her water spinning faster. "It has to be a second try."

I thought there were no second chances.

So had she, but the only constant about humanity was change, and she knew so little about the Heart of the World. The first time the Merlin Gate rang through the Sea of Magic today, she'd thought victory was in her grasp. But then the DFZ had erupted, and everything had gone wrong. From there, she'd had no choice but to assume Myron had failed, leaving his Mortal Spirit to run mad.

But unlike the traitor, Raven, she'd never actually been to the Merlin Gate herself, much less seen inside it. What if there was something she didn't know? An angle she hadn't anticipated? What if Myron wasn't dead?

What if it's a trap?

"How could it be a trap?" she asked, sinking back to her waters to avoid the dragons as they came round again. "The only human soul in the Sea of Magic is the one I put there. It *has* to be him."

Then let him come to you, the Leviathan warned. *Your water is dangerously low. If you stop paying attention, the dragons will burn what is left of it out from under you, and then neither of us will have anything to work with.*

"If I'm right, that won't matter," Algonquin said excitedly. "I'll be reborn with the next rain, but this might never happen again."

The shadow rumbled, but she wasn't listening anymore. She wasn't fighting, either. She was diving, flitting between the pools of water that covered her ruined city until she reached the dark, stagnant lake covering what remained of the Pit.

The moment she rose, Algonquin knew something had changed. The DFZ's raging magic was calm now, almost orderly. The quiet sent her hopes soaring. In her experience, gods didn't stop rampaging until they'd destroyed everything or were defeated.

Since her lakes weren't filled with buildings yet, that left only one option, and Algonquin found him standing on an island of trash at the Pit's very center.

He didn't look well. Algonquin had seen mortals at all stages of death, but Sir Myron Rollins looked as if he'd been through the entire spectrum today. Even so, he was standing, and kneeling at his side was the humanoid reflection of the DFZ.

Algonquin began to tremble, but excited as she was, she was too old to take anything at face value. She would have to test him, to make sure this really was the miracle it seemed. To that end, she rose from the black water in front of them, shifting her face into a reflection of Myron's own.

"Did you do it?"

"I did," he said, his voice weak but confident as he reached out to touch the city's bowed head. "I apologize for the trouble the DFZ caused you. We had a bit of a false start, but I turned it around. My second attempt at the Merlin Gate was a success." He lifted his chin haughtily. "You're now in the presence of the First Merlin, Master of the Heart of the World."

Algonquin frowned, her mask shifting into the mage's own skeptical look. He was lying—she could feel it in his pulse. Mortals always lied, though, especially the egotistical ones. The question was: was he lying about the one thing that actually mattered?

"Did you cap the seal?"

"I did," he said firmly. "I can't do anything about the magic that's already leaked out, but the flow of new power has been staunched. In a few weeks, everything that was spilled tonight will filter out, and the world will be left high and dry once again."

"How dry?" Algonquin demanded. "Did you honor our agreement?"

Myron looked insulted. "Of course I did. I hate Mortal Spirits as much as you do. I capped the magic back to what it was the night you woke, exactly as requested. And I am Merlin, exactly as *I* requested, which means our bargain is at an end, Lady of the Lakes." He smiled. "We won."

Algonquin wasn't listening. She was too busy checking every inch of her domain, sinking down into the deep, cold waters that ran through her vessel at the bottom of the Sea of Magic. But even though she was there, she couldn't tell for sure if he was speaking the truth. Everything was still too turbulent. Too riled up. There'd be no way to know for certain until the magic calmed down, and yet...

She returned to her water in the Pit, flowing up onto the island so she could stare directly down into the mage. Into what made him human. But there was no lie here. The shifts and marks she'd seen in every Merlin since mortals had first started calling themselves such were plain on his soul.

Her water began to tremble. Whatever else he might be, Sir Myron Rollins was unquestionably a Merlin now. *Her* Merlin. Her agent, her tool, the weapon she'd given everything to make, saying it was done.

"I won," she whispered, the reflected mask dissolving as her water rippled in excitement. "I *won*."

"*We* won," Myron corrected, leaning on the cowed city spirit beside him, who had yet to make a sound. "Tonight was a victory for the entire world. You are free from the tyranny of our mad spirits, and humanity is safe from itself. I get the Heart of the World as my own personal laboratory, and you get to stop worrying about the DFZ."

He was right. Now that the spirit of the DFZ had done its job, she could finally scrub its filthy city from her shores. She could scrub *all* the cities and boats and humanity that polluted her waters. First, though, she would take tonight's leftover magic and finish what she'd started when she'd killed the Three Sisters.

There was more than enough power left to melt Heartstriker Mountain and all the other clan strongholds to their foundations, especially since the Golden Emperor had already served himself up to her on a platter. Once she'd destroyed their safe havens and gutted their clan leadership, it was only a matter of taking the time to hunt down and exterminate the snakes that remained, and now that the Mortal Spirits were no longer a threat, Algonquin had all the time in the world. An eternity of safety lay stretched out before her, a return to the time before mortals and their gods. A chance to go home again.

And it was *hers*.

Not yet.

Algonquin turned around. Her mind had been racing so fast, she hadn't felt the Leviathan's approach, but that didn't matter. He was where he always was: right behind her.

"What basis do you have for saying that?"

Common sense, he replied, his tentacles spreading out to surround the island where Myron stood. *Your mage is a known traitor who went to a place you cannot see. Now he's come back to tell you he's done the impossible, which also happens to be exactly what you wanted. You are a fool to believe him so quickly, especially since he has yet to produce any proof.*

"I felt him enter the Heart of the World," Algonquin said. "That is proof."

Proof he served his own interests, the monster whispered, his many eyes skeptical. *But his service to you has yet to be verified. Can you not feel the magic?*

She couldn't feel anything else. But the Sea of Magic had been churning like an ocean in a hurricane even before Myron woke the DFZ, and large systems took time to calm down.

"It will drain," she said confidently. "Because if it doesn't, I will kill the mage and destroy his spirit's city. For good this time." She glanced back at Myron. "But you *are* telling me the truth?"

"I've never told you anything else," Myron said. "It's you who's been lying."

He lifted his chin, looking over her water at the dark shadow behind her. "I learned things in the Heart of the World, Algonquin. For example, I now know what your Leviathan really is, and I will not tolerate it."

"My actions are not yours to tolerate," she said coldly. "I am the Lady of the Lakes. You're just a man."

"I am much more than that," Myron said. "I am the Merlin, champion of humanity. I'm also the one with my hand on the spigot you're so desperate to control."

She went still. "Is that a threat?"

"Absolutely," he said, looking at her head on. "Personal ambitions aside, I went along with your plan to banish the Mortal Spirits because I wished to make this world safe for humanity, not so you could gamble all our futures to a darker god. I know the Leviathan is here at your request, and that he's the one who cracked the Merlins' seal in the first place. But however he got here, a Nameless End has no place on a healthy plane. Send him away, or I will undo everything I just did."

Waves went out in rings across the flooded Pit as Algonquin's rage began to rise. "You think to threaten *me*? I am the land you stand on, fool. I will not be dictated to by a dying insect!"

Myron's smile grew infuriating. "If that were true, you never would have agreed to work with me in the first place. Looks like you *do* need us dying insects. You should embrace that, because I've won you more today than he's ever delivered." He nodded at the Leviathan. "His victory is your defeat. He's a Nameless End, a force that eats failed planes. There's nothing in this for him if you succeed. The only way he gets what he wants is if you fail. I, on the other hand, have as much of a stake in this world as you do. I *want* you to win because we share a future. That makes me infinitely more trustworthy than him."

Algonquin scowled. That was true.

No it's not, the Leviathan hissed, moving until his huge shadow was right on top of her. *We had a deal, Algonquin.*

"We did," she said, looking up at him. "But that's why he's right. Our deal was that you would serve me until I failed. Only then, only if I couldn't make it, would I let you in to finish the job. I always knew you'd only agree to such an offer if you thought I couldn't win, but I did. I've *won*, Leviathan." She looked up into his shadows. "I don't need you anymore."

You will always need me, he boomed, his echoing voice vibrating through every bit of her water. *You called me here. You gave me a name. I am your end, Algonquin. I will not be sent away empty when the deal is not yet done.*

"It *is* done!" she cried, rising up in front of him. "The magic is cut off! In a day, the sea will calm, and this current glut will vanish. In a year, the ambient magic will be back down to what it was that very first night. With so little magic, the Mortal Spirits can't threaten us, no matter how many humans there are. The world belongs to the land again, as it was always meant to. I am victorious, Leviathan, and your failure to accept that is proof that what the Merlin says is true."

Is it, now? The enormous shadow began to spread, filling the dark recesses of the Pit with tentacles that spread and multiplied, shooting across the flooded ground and up the remaining Skyway supports like spilled ink spreading across a picture. *Poor Algonquin, you've grown so gullible. So desperate. You used to be the wisest spirit, but now any charlatan mage can charm you. All he has to do is say what you want to hear, and you eat it up.*

"And you are wasting my time," Algonquin said, drawing in her water until she stood taller than him. "You were a good failsafe, but winners don't need those, do they? I don't regret our deal. It's only because of you that I was able to be victorious today, but it's over. We both gambled, and I won."

She lifted her water to point at the smoke-filled sky. "Go, Leviathan. Leave to find new prey, because there's no more hunting for you here."

Algonquin had been waiting a long time to say those words. Six decades, to be precise. They felt every bit as good as she'd imagined, but there was a problem, because Leviathan wasn't leaving. He didn't even seem to be listening. He was just hovering there in the dark, making the flooded Pit churn as his tentacles spread in every direction.

She couldn't tell if he was searching for something specific or grasping at straws, but either way, Algonquin was losing her patience. But then, just as she opened her mouth to banish him for good, the Leviathan's tentacles snapped back, snatching something small, surprised, and mortal down from the cracked Skyways and dropping it in the trash at Algonquin's feet.

• • •

Marci was biting her nails again, ripping each one down to the quick.

"Don't do that," Amelia snapped, reaching from her perch at the edge of the broken bridge to smack Marci's hand away. "You just got that body back. Stop ruining it."

"Sorry," Marci said, peering down through the crack at Myron, who was holding out impressively in the face of Algonquin and the eldritch horror behind her. "I just hate waiting. Can you hear what they're saying?"

"A little," the dragon spirit said. "Myron's lying like a champ. Didn't know he had it in him."

"Myron Rollins is a man of many talents," Emily said from where she was lying on her back, staring up at the smoky night sky while Raven continued working on her piecemeal body. "It's why we put up with him."

"I just hope he picks up the pace," Raven said around the piece of metal in his beak that he was shoving into General Jackson's chest cavity. "I know a good con takes time, but if he drags this out much longer, Algonquin's going to notice that the magic's getting *more* potent, not less."

Marci had no idea why she hadn't noticed already. Myron hadn't been kidding about the crack getting wider. Now that she was sitting still, she could actually feel the ambient magic levels rising like the tide coming in.

"And we're *sure* the seal's not broken already, right? I mean, no one's watching it, so—"

It's not broken, Ghost said.

She looked skeptically at the transparent cat in her lap. "How do you know?"

Because we're still sitting around talking, he said between licks of his wounds. *This is more magic than we're used to, but it's not even close to dangerous yet. When the seal actually breaks, that'll change. Trust me. We won't be able to miss it.*

"I suppose that's reassuring," Marci said, biting her nails again. "Is Julius almost back?"

"He's coming in fast," Amelia said, breaking into a grin. "This is *so* cool. Now that the magic's jacked up, I can actually feel each individual dragon's fire." Her grin turned into a smirk. "I can't wait to sneak up behind Chelsie for once."

Given Amelia's total lack of stealth, Marci didn't see that happening anytime soon. Before she could say as much to Amelia, though, the water beneath the Leviathan began to churn.

"What's that?"

Everyone moved to the Skyway's crumbling edge. "I think they're tentacles," General Jackson said. "He's sending them out."

"Ugh," Marci said, disgusted. "I hate those slimy things."

"How many does he have?" Amelia asked at the same time.

"As far as I can tell, as many as he needs," the general replied grimly. "Number, length, and size all seem to be as variable as the rest of him, but what else can you expect from a creature who's not really here?"

Marci shivered. "He felt real enough to me."

"Me, too," Emily said, her frown deepening. "I wonder what he's trying to—"

She cut off with a curse, jumping back as one of the black tentacles suddenly surged upward, smashing through the crack in the Skyways they'd been using as a peep hole. Marci jumped back, too, yanking Ghost with her as she scrambled backward down what was left of the elevated street.

And right into the second tentacle.

She yelped as cold slime touched her back. But just as she braced her feet to start running full tilt in the opposite direction, the tip of the tentacle whipped down to wrap around her chest.

Found you.

She choked in fear. Even Ghost jumped at the cold, liquid voice that whispered through them both. He dug his freezing claws into her arms to get away, but for once, even he wasn't fast enough. The Leviathan yanked them both backward, snatching them through the crack in the Skyways and then down, down, down through the dark before unraveling suddenly, dropping Marci and her spirit in the trash at Myron's feet.

The impact knocked the breath out of her. Marci was still trying to get it back when a cold voice said, "What is this?"

The question came from high above. Then Algonquin's watery voice was enhanced by a bathtub's worth of *actual* water as the spirit lurched down to grab her by the throat.

"*What is this?*"

Marci grabbed frantically at the whip of water that was wrapped around her neck, but though it was choking her, it was just water, and her fingers went right through it.

"Answer me, Leviathan!" the lake roared, thrusting Marci into the air as she spun around. "What trick is this?"

A low rumble went through the land like thunder, and the Leviathan leaned closer. "The Merlin."

He spoke aloud this time. That was, if you could say a voice that was more pressure than sound was speaking "aloud."

"You've been played, Algonquin," he went on, bringing up his tentacles to poke at Marci's kicking legs. "Look at her. See what she is. She is Merlin, too." The rumbling morphed into deep laugher. "Myron Rollins betrayed you. He didn't try two times. There were *two Merlins.*"

"How?" Algonquin demanded. "How did you know?"

"Because I knew better than to believe a mortal who'd bound death could be defeated by it," he said simply. "Because I knew Raven had to be poking around your pile of dragon corpses for a reason. Mostly, though, I knew because I saw her flying around earlier."

The tentacle came up again to pat Marci wetly on the head. "Next time you decide to fake your death, little creature, you might want to exercise a bit more discretion."

Marci closed her eyes with a wince. Stupid, stupid, stupid. When she opened them again, though, she realized that blowing her cover might be the least of tonight's fatal mistakes. The whole point of this farce had been to raise Algonquin's hopes to the point where she felt safe enough to dismiss her Nameless End. Now, wrapped up in Algonquin's water, Marci had a front-row seat as all those hopes crumbled.

"No," the water whispered, the clear flow turning cloudy. "*No!*"

Her scream echoed through the Pit, and the water wrapped around Marci's neck clenched tight. If she'd been alone, it would have cut her head off, but Marci was never alone now. She was a Merlin, and the moment Algonquin moved, Ghost moved back, his grave-cold magic exploding out to blast the water away, dropping both of them into the trash beside Myron.

The older mage helped her up at once, yanking her to her feet as the Empty Wind stepped protectively in front of them. The DFZ scrambled forward as well, hissing at Algonquin like an animal guarding its territory, but the lake spirit made no move to attack again.

She wasn't even a towering pillar of water anymore. All that had fallen away, leaving just the soaked and wavering reflection of the old Native American woman that was Algonquin's public face kneeling on the surface of the Pit's black water.

"It was a lie," she whispered. "It was all a *lie.*"

"Only parts of it," Marci said quickly, coughing. "We didn't cap the magic, but the seal is still in place. You don't have to give in to him, Algonquin. He's a monster from outside. He's not part of this world. We are. We can help you."

"No, you can't," the spirit said as her human form began to melt. "You're not part of my world, because my world is gone. I tried to save it, but Raven was right. Our paradise is gone, and it's *never* coming back."

With every sorrowful word, she collapsed further. "There's nothing to look forward to. Just gods and humans and dragons and monsters walking all over us, crushing the land forever. We have no escape, not even death. Nothing—"

"*Algonquin!*"

The name was an earsplitting war cry as Raven swooped down, but not the Raven Marci knew. That spirit was just a big black bird. This one was a god in truth, a giant Raven the size of an elephant with clever eyes that flashed like lightning as he landed on the water.

"Algonquin, listen," he said, his croaking voice booming. "Nothing is lost unless you give it up. The Nameless End is your enemy, not us. Send him away, and we will help you rebuild." He ducked closer, his eyes desperate. "Come back to us, old friend."

Algonquin lifted what was left of her head to give him a glare so hateful, it didn't fit on her human face. "I was never your friend, and I have *nothing* to go back to."

She sank as she finished, the final remains of her human disguise vanishing into the black water without a sound. The Leviathan disappeared at the same time, his giant body melding into the shadows as though he'd never been anything but one of them. When they were both gone, the water covering the floor of the Pit began to drop.

"What's happening?" Marci asked.

Raven shook his huge head in dismay. "Nothing good."

The words weren't out of his beak before Marci felt the truth for herself. It wasn't the water that was receding. It was Algonquin. The lake spirit was collapsing into herself, her waters pulling back into her lake like the tide going out. And as the water drained, the pressure began to build.

"Not good," Raven said, spreading his enormous wings to fly back up to the Skyways. "Not good, not good, not—"

A horrible sound cut him off. Marci covered her ears, but that didn't help at all, because the violent roar wasn't a physical noise. It was magic. Algonquin's magic was roaring like Niagara Falls as she pulled everything—every drop, every wave, every bit of magic in every lake—into the center of Lake St. Clair. Through the new cracks in the Pit's protective walls, Marci could actually see the water rolling itself into a giant ball as Algonquin pressed herself tighter and tighter, and still the pressure rose.

And then, just when it felt the tension would keep building forever, something big cracked.

• • •

Under normal circumstances, Julius would have struggled to keep up with the larger dragons flying around him. Tonight, though, they were struggling to keep up with him.

"Slow down!" Chelsie yelled over the wind. "I know you're in a hurry, but it's all for nothing if you tear a wing."

"Something's gone wrong!" he shouted back. "We have to get to Marci!"

"I'd be more worried about ourselves," Fredrick said, flying up beside him. "Look down."

Julius didn't have to look. He could *feel* Algonquin's magic sucking in as she curled herself into what he could only assume was the spirit equivalent of the fetal position. Either that, or she was building up for an all-out final attack. Whatever it was, it wasn't good, and he had to get everyone he cared about far away from it as fast as possible. Especially his sister, who was doing all of this with her *child* clinging to her back.

"I still can't believe you brought a *baby* into this!" he shouted at her.

"What else was I supposed to do?" Chelsie shouted back. "I couldn't leave her alone! She's a hatchling, and Bob's still down there somewhere. As is the Empress Mother."

"And taking her into a fight with Algonquin is better?"

"Absolutely," his sister said. "She's a dragon. Going into battle with your mother used to be a rite of passage. If Amelia were still alive, she could tell you all kinds of stories about the ridiculous things Bethesda made them do."

"Actually," Julius said, smiling for the first time since this started, "I meant to tell you, Amelia is—"

He cut off with a choke, eyes bulging. Behind him, the others gasped as well. Even the Qilin faltered, his golden body jerking.

A second later, Julius realized it wasn't just them. The whole *world* was jerking. The air, the ground, the buildings—everything he could see was hitching and splintering like the epicenter of a magnitude-nine earthquake. Terrifying as that was, though, what nearly dropped Julius out of the sky was what was happening on the *inside*, deep in the core of his fire.

There was no pain, no injury he could identify. Just an unyielding pressure accompanied by the absolute knowledge that something had gone horribly, fatally wrong.

"*Julius!*"

He forced his head up to see Chelsie hovering beside him, her green eyes pained. "What was that?"

"I don't know," he said, forcing the words out.

"It's magic," the Qilin said, his normally calm voice on the edge of panic. "Everything is in uproar. What is happening?"

"I don't know," Julius said again, forcing his wings to keep flapping. "But Marci will. We have to get to her."

Chelsie scowled. "I don't know if that's—"

But he was already gone, putting on a burst of speed before folding his wings to dive down past the now-dry lakebed and through the broken walls that were supposed to protect Algonquin's water from the Pit. The others followed a second later, matching his speed as they raced through the no-longer-flooded Underground cavern following Marci's scent...and then nearly ran over Marci herself, who was flying up with Ghost to meet them.

Julius was too relieved to speak. He didn't even mind her freezing spirit as he landed hard to grab her in his wings. "Are you okay?"

"Right now? I'm fine," she said quickly. "Long term, not so much."

"What happened?" Chelsie demanded, checking her dive with her wings.

"The stupidest thing possible," said an irritated voice above them.

Chelsie's head shot up, and then her eyes went wide as the giant red dragon with feathers made of actual fire swooped down to grin at her.

"What?" Amelia said. "No hello?"

"*What are you doing here?*" Chelsie yelled at her. "You're *dead!*"

"So people keep telling me," Amelia said with chuckle. "But I'll have to explain later. Algonquin's hissy fit just broke the Merlins' seal, which means we're about to get one thousand years of pent-up magic in the face unless we move."

"Move to where?" Julius said frantically. "That doesn't sound like something you can dodge."

He was looking at Amelia, but it was Marci who answered. "Got it covered," she said, scrambling up onto Julius's back. "Head for our house."

Julius blinked. "Our house? You mean the one here in the city?"

She nodded rapidly. "Remember all the wards I put up? I know it feels like forever, but we've only *actually* been gone for a week and a half, which is well inside the upkeep window. If the building's still standing, all my protections should still be on it, but we gotta move fast. Ghost estimates we've only got a couple of minutes before the wave hits us."

"Less than that," the Empty Wind said, giving Julius a freezing push. "Stop talking and *go.*"

Julius didn't wait to be told twice. He took off like a rocket, keeping his wings tight to make sure Marci stayed on as he wove his way through the now bone-dry Pit. "What about the others? Myron and the rest?"

"Already ahead of us," Marci yelled over the wind. "I told them where to go before I went looking for you."

Any other time, hearing that would have made his heart skip. This time, though, Julius couldn't do anything except fly, racing through the collapsed Underground on memory and instinct until he reached the spiral of onramps that hid the house Ian had rented them.

Please be there, he prayed as he dove into the tunnel that led through the spiral of cracked overpasses. *Please don't be destroyed. Please. Please.*

He burst out into the open again, spreading his wings to check his speed before he slammed them into the opposite wall. It all happened so fast, he didn't see anything at first but a blur of light and dirt. Once he was sure he wasn't going to crash, he looked up and saw what he'd been hoping to see.

"It's still here," he said, staring in wonder at their miraculously uncrushed three-story house. "It's still intact!"

"Except for the wall Conrad chopped in half when Estella came for me," Amelia said, flying in right behind them. "Marci, help me fix it. Best ward in the world's no good if you've got a big honking hole in the front."

Marci nodded and hopped down, sliding off Julius to run after Amelia. Chelsie, Fredrick, and the Qilin were swooping in now as well. Raven was already here, and a *lot* bigger. He barely fit inside the slashed-up porch where he and Emily were frantically fitting the front door and parts of the wall that Conrad had cut in half back together.

"Should we be doing this, sir?"

Julius looked over his shoulder to see Fredrick standing behind him. And above him, since the F was easily five times Julius's size in this form.

"What else would we be doing?"

"Going back to Heartstriker Mountain, for a start," Fredrick said, lifting his claws, which were still encased in his Fang. "Bethesda's still there. Probably in her panic room. It'll take a few trips, but I can cut us all back to her, and a bunker under a mountain seems much safer than—"

"*NO!*" Amelia yelled, appearing above them in a flash of red fire to smack Fredrick's claws back to the ground. "No teleporting!"

"Don't yell at him!" Chelsie snapped, getting physically between Fredrick and her sister. "It was a good idea."

"Maybe under normal circumstances," Amelia said. "But there's nothing normal about this! Just because the ambient magic isn't literally crushing us to death yet doesn't mean it's not going haywire. Do you have any idea what would happen if we opened a portal of any sort under these—" She froze, eyes going huge. "I have to warn Svena."

"If you know not to do it, I'm sure the White Witch does, too," Chelsie said, dropping her dragon form with a puff of smoke, which left her standing naked on the stairs with a baby dragon the size of a Doberman clutched in her arms. "If this is as safe as we're going to get, we stay. Everyone inside."

The other dragons changed, too, running after her into the house, except for Amelia, who stayed to help Marci, Myron, and Raven with the front porch. Julius should have followed suit. He might be small, but his dragon was still too big to fit through the newly repaired front door. Unlike Amelia, though, he couldn't conjure up clothing at will, and there was no emergency in the world that could get him to be naked in front of so many, especially not at his own house.

So while everyone else was busy out front, Julius hopped into the air again to wing his way around to the back of the house. He landed on the roof, sliding the window to his bedroom open with one claw before changing shape and diving inside. The second he was in, he grabbed the first clothes he saw and started shoving himself into them. He was still pulling a shirt over his head when Chelsie burst in.

He had no idea how she'd managed it ahead of him, but she was wearing one of Marci's college T-shirts and cut-off jean shorts. She didn't even ask permission before she walked over to Julius's dresser and started tossing clothes to Fredrick and the Qilin, who were right behind her. As for her daughter, she was still in dragon form and climbing the walls like a lizard, poking her claws through the drywall to keep herself up, and thoroughly enjoying the chaos.

"I'll fix the damage," Chelsie said before Julius could say a word. "Just get downstairs."

Julius nodded and ran out the door, taking the steps three at a time down to the living room. He'd just hopped the banister on the last landing when everyone—Marci, Ghost, Myron, Amelia, Raven, Emily, even the DFZ, who was back to her giant rat—rushed in through the hastily repaired front door. Amelia came in last, slamming the freshly nailed and spellwork-covered wooden door closed behind her just in time.

Through the windows, Julius could see the faux cavern outside getting brighter and brighter. Then, when it was almost too bright to look at, the light broke apart. Just fell into pieces until it looked like snow. A soft, thick, glowing blizzard of pale light in all colors, only it wasn't cold, and it wasn't falling from the sky. It was rising from the ground, and it was beautiful.

"That's it?" he said, walking to the window. "That's what we're afraid of?"

"Yes," Amelia said, her face grim. "Don't let the pretty light show fool you. That's pure magic of a grade this side of the world has never seen."

"It looks like the barrier between the Sea of Magic and the physical world absorbed most of the impact," Marci added as she joined Julius by the window. "That's better than I'd hoped, but there's still way more magic out there than the physical world has ever experienced." She bit her lip. "We are going to see some *weird* stuff coming out of this."

"We'll have a rash of new mages for certain," Myron said, glowering at the beautiful glow from the window by the fireplace. "Everyone who was on the edge is going to get shoved right over, and it's not going to be pleasant."

"Animals, too," Marci said. "Remember all the crazy mana beasts that popped up around the meteor crater? Take that and spread it all over the world. Detroit's probably going to get the worst of it since the DFZ thinned the barrier here, but I don't think anywhere is safe."

"How long will it last?" Julius asked, transfixed by the glowing particles rising from the ground like fireflies.

Amelia shrugged. "Who knows? Even I've never seen a magical surge of this magnitude."

"I'd guess two weeks, tops," Marci said. "They weren't this big, but we've had magical disasters before. In those cases, the majority of the fallout—"

"Generally settled within forty-eight hours," Myron finished. "But you're assuming this follows the same fallout pattern as events that happened on this side of the divide. This magic is coming from the Sea of Magic itself, and we don't have any data for that."

Marci scowled thoughtfully, and then she turned and headed for the stairs. "We need to get a better look. I've got an observation circle in my lab upstairs."

"Do you have a phone?" General Jackson asked, chasing after her. "The UN office in New York will have accurate readings for sure."

"*If* the phone networks are up," Myron said grimly as they all went up the stairs. "It's a miracle this building still has power."

That was a good point. Now that he thought about it, all of this—the intact house, the power, the wards—struck Julius as suspiciously convenient. Another time, he would have stewed about the implications of that. Right now, though, he couldn't do anything except stand there and watch Marci walk up the stairs with everyone else. Walk away from him.

He was still watching when a hand landed on his shoulder, and he turned to see Chelsie waiting beside him with her daughter, who was now back in human form as well and wearing one of the T-shirts Justin had left behind like a dress.

"There's a lot going on," she said quietly, her green eyes flicking pointedly at the bend in the stairs where Marci had just disappeared. "She's just busy right now. It doesn't mean she doesn't care."

"I know," Julius said, taking a shaking breath. "She's a Merlin now. She's doing what she needs to do, and I'm happy for her."

He didn't sound happy. For once, though, Chelsie didn't call him on the lie. She just squeezed his shoulder and set off toward the kitchen. "I'm going to raid your freezer. There's no telling how long this will last or how long we'll have power. Better to stock up now. Want to help?"

Julius tried for a moment. He *really* did. He even managed to walk all the way to the kitchen door. In the end, though, he just couldn't. This entire night, through everything that had happened, he'd been holding it together on sheer adrenaline. Now that things were suddenly calm, there was simply nothing left.

"I'm sorry," he said, his body shaking. "I...that is..."

"It's fine," Chelsie said, looking over her shoulder. "Go to your room and do whatever you have to do to get yourself together, because we're going to need you."

Technically, she had no business telling him what to do, but Chelsie's words weren't a command. They were an escape, and Julius leaped on it, whirling around and going up the stairs to his room as fast as he could without actually running away. He was turning to lock the door behind him when someone else grabbed the opposite handle.

Julius froze, confused. Then confusion turned to joy when Marci pushed her way in.

"Hey," she said.

"Hey," he replied lamely, running a hand through his hair. "I thought you guys were talking big-time magic stuff."

"We were," she said, stepping into his room. "But then I thought, you know, this is going to be going on for a while, and I didn't want to sit there being a third wheel while they called every mage at the UN, so I told them I was tired."

He frowned at her. "Are you tired?"

"I *was* dead for four days," she reminded him, closing his door so she could lean against it. "So yeah, I'm pretty tired. But I don't want to sleep in *my* room."

She flipped the lock on the door behind her with a *click*, and suddenly, Julius understood what was going on.

"Oh," he said as his heart began to hammer. "That is, I mean..."

He had no idea what he meant. Fortunately, it didn't seem to matter. Marci had already closed the distance, reaching up to wrap her arms around his neck as she pulled him down for a kiss.

Julius jumped when their lips met. Practically leaped out of his skin. She'd clearly anticipated that, though, because Marci's grip on his neck just clenched tighter, keeping her locked against him as she started walking them both backward toward his bed.

It was at this point that Julius's brain started to fail him, which was a serious problem, because he'd never needed to think more. This was all happening *way* too fast. Marci had just come back from the dead. They were in the middle of a magical apocalypse. He needed a chance to decompress and process it all. He needed to *talk* to her about all the things he hadn't gotten a chance to say before she'd died: how much he needed her, that he loved her, that he'd never missed anyone as much as he'd missed her. Everything he'd spent the last week desperately repeating to her memory was still there, eating at him.

He needed to get that out, but he couldn't bring himself to push Marci away. She was just so *close*. So here and alive and kissing him and...and...

His thoughts were still stuttering when they reached the bed. The moment the back of his legs brushed the mattress, Julius's knees gave way, and they both dropped down together. It wasn't until Marci's hands left his shoulders and slid down his chest to grab the hem of his shirt, though, that Julius finally realized if he was going to say anything, it had to be now.

"Wait," he gasped, grabbing her hands as he sat up. "Stop for a second."

The hurt that flashed over Marci's face sent him into a panic. "It's not like that," he said as fast as he could. "I want this, but—"

"Good," she said, leaning back in with a smile. "I want this, too."

He grabbed her arms. "Marci," he said, voice shaking. "You were *dead.*"

"Why do you think I'm in a hurry?" she asked irritably, struggling against his hold. "I already lost everything once. I'm not wasting any more time."

"Neither am I," he promised. "But I can't let this go any further without...without saying..."

Marci went very still. "Without saying what?"

Julius clenched his hands. Here it went. "I love you."

She took a deep, satisfied breath. "You love me," she repeated, savoring each word.

"Not a little, either," he added. "A lot. And this isn't just something I only realized after you died. I've loved you for a long time, but I never said anything because I didn't want to hurt our friendship and because it would make so many problems for you."

She stared at him like he was crazy. "Why would you loving me be a *problem*?"

"How can you ask that?" he cried. "I've caused nothing but problems for you! Gregory tried to *kill* you—"

"And I kicked his butt."

"—and things are only going to get worse now that I'm a clan head. I've nearly died three times in the four days you were dead. I can't ask you to be part of that. It was my fault you died *this* time."

"You're not asking me," she said angrily, yanking her arms out of his grip at last. "*I'm* choosing. You think you're the only one with a crazy life? I'm a Merlin now. You've already seen how scary that can get, and you weren't even there for the stuff on the other side. Is that going to scare you off loving me?"

"No," he said immediately.

"*Exactly*," Marci said. "So stop expecting me to be different." She crossed her arms over her chest. "I am *well* acquainted with the dangers of being your girlfriend, Julius Heartstriker. I've seen it all, and none of it has changed my mind. So if it's all the same to you, I'd like to sample the *benefits* of our relationship for once before I die again."

Julius went pale. "That isn't funny."

"It wasn't meant to be," she said firmly. "I'm only saying it so you'll understand I'm going into this with eyes wide open. I know what you are, and I know what that means, and it doesn't change a thing. You've always been the one I wanted. There's nothing you can say at this point that's going to change my mind, so while I know you mean well, kindly *cut it out*. I love you. I want this. End of story."

That was pretty clear, but Julius couldn't help it. "You love me?"

"Duh," she said as her cheeks turned red. "In case kissing you in the hotel wasn't a big enough hint, I've had a crush on you pretty much forever."

He was grinning like a happy idiot by the time she finished, and Marci rolled her eyes. "So is there anything else embarrassing you want me to admit, or can we go ahead and do this? Because I'm not sure how much of a breather we'll get in this crisis, and I'd rather not miss what might be our only chance to—"

Julius pulled her back against him. She responded in kind, frantically kissing him back as she pushed off the floor with her foot to send them both tumbling backward into the bed.

The moment they landed, Julius knew they'd crossed the point of no return. Marci was on top of him now, her scent and warmth all over him as she helped him take off her shirt. His went next, and when she settled back down on top of him, pressing skin to warm skin, he thought he was going to die.

Surprisingly, not of anxiety. The few times he'd let himself imagine this scenario, he'd always been slightly terrified. Now that it was actually happening, though, the fact that he was a virgin who had no idea what he was doing suddenly felt like a minor concern next to the absolute wonder that was having Marci so close to him. It was completely overwhelming. Too good to be true. The sort of good fortune that shouldn't be questioned. But then, just as he was getting the hang of things, Marci froze.

"What?" he asked, terrified he'd done something wrong, but she wasn't looking at him. She was looking at his window.

"There's a bird out there."

Julius sat up in alarm. Sure enough, a pigeon was sitting on his windowsill. A perfectly normal-looking city pigeon wearing a little flower hat that someone had tied to her feathered head at a jaunty angle.

She pecked the glass when she saw Julius looking, her throat fluttering as she cooed questioningly. She was still cooing when Julius reached up and grabbed the string for the blinds.

"Wait!" Marci cried as the blinds crashed down. "Wasn't that Bob's—"

"Yes."

"Then why did you—"

"Because I don't care," Julius said, burying his face in her neck. "Whatever it is, whatever he has to tell me, it can wait."

"But what if it's important?"

"Doesn't matter," he said stubbornly, pushing up just enough to stare down at her. "I am *done* putting other things ahead of us, Marci. The last time I chose Heartstriker over you, you died. That's not a lesson I'm going to forget. Bob can take care of himself for a few hours, but I am *never* taking you for granted again."

He was holding her too tight by the time he finished. When he tried to let go, though, she wouldn't let him. She kissed him instead, dragging her lips over his until they were both lost again, cocooned in a warm world where, for once, they were the most important things.

• • •

High above the dry bed of Lake St. Clair, on the last remaining steel support beam of what had been the elevated boardwalk for the elegant—and currently collapsed—lakeside hotels, a dragon sat cross-legged beneath the protective bubble created by his enormous fang-shaped sword, eating a chicken sandwich and watching the magic rise from the ground like a heavy snowfall in reverse.

It was a little cramped—even the Magician's Fang of the Heartstriker was hard pressed to ward off this much disaster—but Brohomir was quite content. After all, it wasn't every day you got a front-row seat for the end of the world.

He'd just finished his sandwich and was reaching into the paper bag for another when a pigeon wearing a pretty hat fluttered down to land on his leg.

Alone.

"I take it that's a 'no,' then?" Bob said, lowering his sandwich sadly.

The pigeon bobbed its head, hopping onto his knee to peck at the sandwich he'd just set down.

"I suspected he wouldn't come," the seer said, opening the bread so she could eat it more easily. "But there was a small chance, and I'd much hoped I'd get a chance to talk to him properly before..."

"Before the end."

Bob looked up just in time to see the Black Reach drop out of the sky. Not as a dragon—things weren't *that* far gone yet—but his human form was bad enough.

"Do you mind?" Bob asked irritably. "Not that I object to a good cryptic drop—which was nicely done, I admit—but there's not enough room up here for two."

"I won't be long," the Black Reach assured him, helping himself to a sandwich from the paper bag beside Bob's bloodstained leg. "That looks serious."

"Things are always serious with my sister," Bob said with a laugh that quickly turned into a wince as the movement irritated the bruises on his chest. "Even with her Fang, that fight would have been a gamble. Without it..." He grimaced. "Let's just say I'm happy to still be in possession of all my organs."

"Couldn't have been that bad if you're able to joke about it," the Black Reach said as he unwrapped his stolen sandwich from its paper. "And I noticed your tool arrived right on time to save you."

Bob smiled serenely. "Punctuality is one of Julius's many virtues."

"So I've seen," the oldest seer said, giving him a piercing look. "That's the trouble. I've seen *everything*, and I *still* don't understand. This meeting, for example." His eyes flicked to the pigeon, who was still happily pecking at her sandwich in Bob's lap. "You have everything you need now. What are you waiting for?"

"If you truly saw everything, you wouldn't be asking me that," Brohomir replied, reaching down to stroke the pigeon's folded wings with his finger.

The Black Reach crushed the sandwich in his fists, and Bob sighed. "Really, did you just come up here to waste food or—"

"Why?" he growled, throwing the sandwich aside as he knelt down in front of the younger seer, getting right in his face. "I've been watching you every step of the way, waiting for you to reveal yourself. To surprise me. But *every single step* has done nothing but bring us closer to the inevitable."

"That's the problem with inevitable things," Brohomir said. "They always—"

"*WHY?*" the Black Reach roared at him, pointing at the pulsing ball of water floating above the dry bed of Lake St. Clair. "Your plans have done nothing but make things worse! You have irritated and agitated and destroyed, and for *what?* The future is still what it always has been. All your work, your cryptic secrets, it's all been for *nothing!*"

"Ah," Bob said, lifting a finger. "That's where you're wrong."

"Tell me," the older seer demanded, grabbing him by the collar. "Tell me how these things add up to anything but disaster."

"I can't," Bob said, hanging limp in his grasp. "You said it yourself. The end is inevitable."

The Black Reach bared his teeth. "Then why do you seem to be doing everything in your power to make it come *faster?*"

"Because I need it to," Bob said, growing serious at last. "I *need* this chaos, because *this*"—he nodded at Algonquin's ball—"was always doomed to happen. I've spent my entire life looking down these paths. I've lived through every way this night ends, and the only way we live on to see tomorrow is if I make sure every disaster from here out happens on *my* terms."

The Black Reach let him go with a long sigh. "There's the fault in your logic," he said tiredly. "There is no tomorrow for you, Brohomir. Thanks to your actions, there might not be a tomorrow for any of us."

"You won't let that happen," Bob said confidently. "You're Dragon Sees Eternity, the guardian of the future. If there's no more future for dragons, you're out of a job."

The Black Reach reached up to rub his eyes. "I'll try," he said. "But has it ever occurred to you that I'm a construct, not a god?"

"Oh, that's occurred to me many, *many* times," Bob promised. "But don't worry. I wrote in a part for you, too. It's a bit of a grand one, but I promised my darling a show, and I never disappoint a lady."

He leaned down to press a kiss to his pigeon's head, and the Black Reach's lip curled in disgust. "That's no lady," he growled. "That's a—"

"Ah, ah, ah," Bob said. "Not another word. I will tolerate no maligning of my consort."

"Your consort?" The Black Reach snorted. "You're *her* consort, and she's *using* you."

"It would only be using if I weren't aware," Bob said, leaning back against his Fang. "But I know exactly what's going on, because it was all my idea. Not that it's any of your business, but I asked *her*, so if you have any ideas of me being an innocent victim, you can toss them. I went into this with eyes wide open."

"Then you should have seen more," the Black Reach said coldly, turning to face the ball of compressed water and the enormous shadow that covered it like a cloud. "Last chance, Brohomir."

The Seer of the Heartstrikers smiled as he stood up, yanking his sword out of the support beam and resting the giant blade on his shoulder. He snagged his bag of sandwiches next. Then, with a polite bob of his head, he stepped backward, dropping off the jutting beam like a stone.

He landed nimbly as a cat a good thirty feet below, hitting the sandy dirt of the dry lake bed without leaving so much as a footprint.

"See you soon," he called up to the Black Reach, waving at him with his sword before returning the blade to his shoulder and strolling into the Underground, using his Magician's Fang like a machete as he hacked a path through the thick strands of toxic, glowing magic waving like wheat in front of him.

"One more time," the eldest seer muttered back, reaching down to grip the strap of the battered messenger bag he'd been carrying since he'd left Heartstriker Mountain. The one that—now that Brohomir had refused his final chance to lift himself from the rails—held their last hope for the future.

With a grim shake of his head, the Black Reach sat down in the spot Brohomir had vacated, settling in to watch as the glowing magic began to swirl around Algonquin's darkening ball of compressed water like stars around a black hole.

EPILOGUE

There'd been a time, once, when Algonquin hadn't believed in losing. After all, when you lived forever, you could never truly be defeated. There were only setbacks, temporary interruptions that would eventually erode, leaving her free once again to do what needed to be done.

But not today.

She crouched at the very bottom of her domain, curled in a ball in the sand with her water drawn in as close as it would go. Above her, the Sea of Magic raged like a typhoon. If she'd been willing to rise, she could have seen it filling the vessels of the Mortal Spirits, but she wasn't willing. She'd seen too much tragedy already, including hers. It was all gone: her chances, her hopes, her future. It had all been stolen, and no matter how long she waited, how long she persisted, how hard she fought, it was never coming back.

But it can.

She lifted her water to see a familiar shape in the darkness where no one else should ever be.

But this is where I live, too, the Leviathan replied softly, reaching up with his tentacles to smooth her shaking waves. *You invited me here. I answered your call, Algonquin. I came to your aid when no one else would, and we made a bargain. For sixty years now, I've acted as your second, supporting all your efforts to win back your world from the out-of-control forces of human magic. Not because I thought you would succeed, or because I wished you harm, but because in order for me to truly help you, I needed you to be like this.*

"What?" she snarled. "Defeated? Hopeless?"

Empty, he replied, his voice echoing. *Living things are always full. You're all so packed with rage and hope and plots and expectations and dreams that there's no room for anything else. It is only when you realize that all is lost, when you give up, that you are free to reach beyond yourself. Only in emptiness can you find the victory you were too small to realize on your own.*

"There is no victory anymore," she said, sinking lower. "The Mortal Spirits are filling, and when they rise, we will be crushed. Even if humanity died tonight, the trenches they carved in the magic are too deep to fade. Don't you see?" Her water began to cloud. "I will *never* be free."

Then let go, he whispered. *I promised to help you fight until the end. Until all hope was lost, and now it is. It's time to let go of yesterday's war and start winning the next one.*

"But I can't!" she cried. "They're too big, too strong! I can't beat—"

I can.

The Nameless End moved closer, his tentacles creeping across the floor of her vessel until she was surrounded.

I am greater than all of your enemies combined, he whispered, sliding into her waters. *Let me devour you, and I will destroy everything that has ever stood in your way. The spirits, the humans, the dragons—everything that causes you pain. I will eat them all. All I need is your life. Give me your undying spirit, your vessel to be my foothold, and I will wipe everything clean. I will scour the filth that has hurt you from this world, and when I am finished, your plane will be born anew. A blank slate, a pure land from which new spirits will rise. Clean ones. Free souls without shackles, without pasts or pain. That is what I offer, Algonquin. You can have your paradise back again, and all it will cost is you.*

It was a tempting picture, but..."What good is paradise if I won't live to see it?"

That is for you to decide, he said, raising the smooth black shell of his face to the storming magic above. *Though a better question might be, what good is your life now? What are you really giving up? A failure. A loss. That's all I'm taking, and in return, I will give you what is now impossible: a second chance. A better life for all the spirits of the land who come after you.*

"But what about the spirits now?" she asked. "My life is one thing, but what of the trees and the animals and the mountains? We are the land. If we go, what is left?"

There can be no new beginnings without an End, he said quietly. *It's time to make a choice. Either you accept this failure forever, until the end of time, or you give yourself to me and let me start everything over. I will devour without prejudice or mercy, starting with you. When I am finished, your world will indeed end, but I promise I won't let it collapse. When I am done scraping it clean, I will leave your plane with just enough magic to start over. Maybe this time you'll get it right.*

Algonquin curled back into a ball. His words were nothing new. This had always been their agreement, but she'd never thought her price would actually come due. She'd been so sure she could fix this, so certain she could overcome as she always had. This time, though, Algonquin saw no way out.

Even on her longest timeline, the Mortal Spirits were there, raging across the landscape that was her body. She and her fellow spirits would suffer at the mad gods' whims from now until forever. There was no escape, no hope, no reprieve. All she could see of the future was a living hell. Next to that, was death really so bad?

Death is peace, the Leviathan promised, his tentacles closing over her like a net. *Aren't you tired?*

She was exhausted. Exhausted and sick. Sick of humanity. Sick of fighting. Sick of getting her hopes up only to lose again and again. Sick of it all.

Then let it go, he whispered as his darkness curled in tighter. *I'll take care of everything. All you have to do is let me in.*

She turned away, looking down into herself at her water, at all she would lose.

You mean have already lost, the Leviathan corrected patiently. *It's over, Algonquin. Let me in.*

She had nothing left to say. He was right. No matter how hard she fought, she couldn't win as herself. Not anymore.

So, with a sigh, the Lady of the Lakes gave up. She relaxed her clutched water, letting it flood her vessel and over the Leviathan, whose black tentacles were already sinking in to drink her down. As his shadows spread to every part, his black tendrils working through her like roots, the immortal Algonquin, the land herself, began to die.

And in the physical world, in the night sky above a smoking city lit up like a fairy circle with new magic, the Leviathan's shadow began to become real.

THANK YOU FOR READING!

Thank you for reading *A Dragon of a Different Color*! If you enjoyed the story, or even if you didn't, I hope you'll consider leaving a review. Reviews, good and bad, are vital to any author's career, and I would be extremely thankful and appreciative if you'd consider writing one for me.

Want to know when my next novel is available? Visit www.rachelaaron. net and sign up for my New Release Mailing List! List members get first looks and bonus content, including the list-exclusive Heartstrikers short story, *Mother of the Year*. The list is free, and I promise I will never spam you! You can also follow me on Twitter @Rachel_Aaron or like my Facebook page, facebook.com/RachelAaronAuthor, for up-to-date information on all of my new books.

I'm already hard at work on the fifth and final Heartstriker novel, which I hope to have out early next year. If that's too long to wait, you can always check out one of my other already completed series. Simply click over to the "Want More Books by Rachel?" page in your eReader's table of contents or visit www.rachelaaron.net to see a full list of all my books complete with their beautiful covers, links to reviews, and free sample chapters!

Thank you again for reading, and I hope you'll be back soon!

Yours sincerely,
Rachel Aaron

WANT MORE BOOKS BY RACHEL AARON? CHECK OUT THESE COMPLETED SERIES!

THE LEGEND OF ELI MONPRESS

The Spirit Thief
The Spirit Rebellion
The Spirit Eater
The Legend of Eli Monpress (omnibus edition of the first three books)
The Spirit War
Spirit's End

"Fast and fun, *The Spirit Thief* introduces a fascinating new world and a complex magical system based on cooperation with the spirits who reside in all living objects. Aaron's characters are fully fleshed and possess complex personalities, motivations, and backstories that are only gradually revealed. Fans of Scott Lynch's *Lies of Locke Lamora* (2006) will be thrilled with Eli Monpress. Highly recommended for all fantasy readers." - **Booklist, Starred Review**

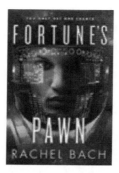

PARADOX
(written as Rachel Bach)

Fortune's Pawn
Honor's Knight
Heaven's Queen

"*Firefly*-esque in its concept of a rogue-ish spaceship family... The narrative never quite goes where you expect it to, in a good way...Devi is a badass with a heart." - **Locus Magazine**

"If you liked *Star Wars*, if you like our books, and if you are waiting for *Guardians of the Galaxy* to hit the theaters, this is your book." - **Ilona Andrews**

"I JUST LOVED IT! Perfect light sci-fi. If you like space stuff that isn't that complicated but highly entertaining, I give two thumbs up!" - **Felicia Day**

To find out more about Rachel and read samples of all her books, visit www.rachelaaron.net!

ABOUT THE AUTHOR

Rachel Aaron is the author of twelve novels as well as the bestselling nonfiction writing book, *2k to 10k: Writing Faster, Writing Better, and Writing More of What You Love,* which has helped thousands of authors double their daily word counts. When she's not holed up in her writing cave, Rachel lives a nerdy, bookish life in Athens, GA, with her perpetual motion son, long suffering husband, and obese wiener dog. To learn more about me, my work, or to find a complete list of my interviews and podcasts, please visit my author page at rachelaaron.net!

As always, this book would not have been nearly as good without my amazing beta readers. Thank you so, so much to Michele Fry, Jodie Martin, Christina Vlinder, Kevin Swearingen, Judith Smith, Rob Aaron, Hisham El-far, and the ever amazing Laligin. Y'all are the BEST!

Made in the USA
Columbia, SC
18 September 2020